INVISIBLE WARRIOR

– WITH –

FULL DISCLOSURE

INVISIBLE WARRIOR

– WITH –

FULL DISCLOSURE

NONFICTION

BY

T. RANDALL

PENTAGON'S HAMMER Series, Book IV:

INVISIBLE WARRIOR – FULL DISCLOSURE
Copyright © 2019 by T. Randall. All Rights Reserved.
Graphics Design Copyright © 2019 by T. Randall. All Rights Reserved.
First addition © 2019 – Publisher: PREMIER TECHNOLOGIES, INC.

ISBN:
Soft Copy: 9780989738057
ePub Copy: 9780989738064
Hard Copy: 9780989738088

DISTRIBUTOR:
Book Distribution for Independent Publishers:
Ingram Spark Book Company
    One Ingram Blvd.
    La Vergne, TN 37086
http://www.ingrambook.com/default.aspx

Print-on-demand Hard & Soft copy:
    Lightning Source Inc.
    1246 Heil Quaker Blvd.
    La Vergne, TN 37086
    http://www1.lightningsource.com/

Printed in the United States of America
Primary sales outlet, Amazon Books.com
First Printing May, 2019
10 9 8 7 6 5 4 3 2 1

DISCLAIMER

This book is based on real events, places, and times, though the names of the participants, and their identities have been changed to preserve their privacies. *INVISIBLE WARRIOR* is both fiction, and nonfiction in nature, using fictitious names for the principle cast, and real names where authorized. Locations, and events are based on actual events, and experiences during a career filled with challenges, and rich with action. Much of my career was spent overseas in the vastness of the Pacific, Asia, Indonesia, Indochina, and Europe.

Although after thirty years working as a government contractor, and at times had access to highly sensitive information inherit to the Intelligence community, it is not my intention to disclose any sensitive or classified materials to the public, or to the enemies of the free world.

Notwithstanding being an autobiography, I have intricate knowledge of organizational, and governmental structures, and their workings in the arenas of Intelligence, defense, and science, and technologies as described, and exemplified in this, and previous books written in the form of novels. The initial sections of the book are written from my true point of view with all subsequent sections written, and illustrated from Alex Bauer's perspective, a perspective carried throughout this book, in the form of narrative nonfiction. The change in personalities became necessary to reach into the recesses of my mind on how I perceive the world between my early years of existence, and the present. The transformation, though dramatic, took place when I was unexpectedly torn from the reality of life, and thrown into the realm of mystique, stealth, and secrecy.

Alex Bauer is not singled out as an only invisible warrior. There were many others during the various phases of the AUTODIN system, the highly-classified precursor to the modern-day Internet, each equal in personal dedication to serve the nation. Regardless of individuals coming together from every possible way of life, the collective goal was universal: to protect the United States government, and citizens from atomic annihilation. Where over the following decades most of the invisible warriors have retired, or have passed on, the system, though transformed numerous times from the original blueprint into a modern-day autonomous self-serving engine, is very much alive, alerting the country about ill-intended adversaries and intrusions to the world's best protected nation.

FOREWORD

INVISIBLE WARRIOR is a comprehensive narrative nonfiction based on the vulnerability of the United States defense system. Due to the complexity of my life, and career, this story expands in volume size over the average novels, and many chapters were necessary in its development. Making up the chapters within the sphere of this writing were dozens of characters, and organizations from the national defense sector to military organizations dependent on each other, in the case of an all-out attack.

My principle reason is to create public awareness of an ever-increasing threat on the nation's safety, and the wellbeing of the American citizens. Despite warfare having been with mankind since the dawn of the ages, with the development of modern weapons, and communication technologies it seems that fighting has increased exponentially, making warfare evermore probable to remain with mankind through mass killings, and slaughter inflicted by warmongers, rogue nations, extremists, and radicals.

The book is about individuals that held important, and critical positions in government, military, commercial contracting, and support functions necessary for the design, engineering, deployment, operations, and management of its functions so that the citizens of the United States could prosper in a safe, and protected environment. An army of invisible warriors is diligently at work supporting the multitude of critical projects, and programs necessary to protect the wealth, and prosperity of a free nation.

The primary concept of this book is in writing my autobiography. It deviates from the norm in that it is written from several perspectives, mine, and my career colleagues, as well as the principle character of Alex Bauer, and his Castle crew. The transformation was necessary to produce a meaningful product written from perspectives journeyed through a lifelong career. In real life, along with my dependents, coworkers, and support personnel, due to the critical nature of their work, have never attained public credit, and recognition. In this book, at least, we will have the opportunity to obtain proper credit, and deserving gratitude bestowed through the dedication of the reader.

My Mission

Develop the series of novels was based on missions that absorbed much of my adult life. Educate the general population on why the country needs a strong defense system which can only be achieved through maintaining the nation's leadership in technology, continued advances in sciences, and knowledge to develop products desired by an insatiable world population.

The system

The AUTODIN system, highly controversial at times for infringing on the individual's constitutional rights, was solely designed for the protection of these rights. But to achieve, and preserve these rights, with crime, and disorder increasing, not only in the U.S., but across the globe, it is integral that the system is maintained. AUTODIN is not the only system highly classified in nature. Many government information systems operate within a similar environment. The U.S. citizen was given an equal chance, though unclassified, when the AUTODIN system was released in August, 1991, in the form of the modern Internet. Whether it was the right thing to do so, I'll let the gained popularity speak for itself.

Storyline
The preceding trilogy, summarized in *PENTAGON'S HAMMER,* was based on my career experience, and work environment. While many of the plots, and actions were illustrated as real events, the storylines were suggested possibilities that could, in today's unstable political climate, explode at a moment's notice, or take place in the near future. In contrast, events as described in this book, *INVISIBLE WARRIOR*, and *FULL DISCLOSURE,* are based on realistic scenarios possibly triggered by world powers, and rogue nations such as China, Russia, North Korea, Iran, Pakistan, and more. It would not take much to elevate a diplomatic dispute into a major conflict, which would be fought with unconventional weapons of mass destruction in the form of chemical, biological, and nuclear weapons. To cite recent events, North Korea, Iran, and Pakistan are real life examples.

For those readers not familiar with the term Full Disclosure, I'll explain it to you. I may sound biased against conspiratorial mongering, and rightly so. Life is difficult enough just coping with everyday challenges, and problems with meeting obligations, and responsibilities. Therefore, I pose the question, "Who gives them the right to confuse, and interrupt everyone else's lives?"

"It is people themselves who demand it."

Many people thrive on the unknown, the mysterious, and the enigmatic. It is us that need the unexplained to maintain individual sanity in a world full of uncertainties. It is mankind longing for the impenetrable. Without it the world would be a dull place. Perhaps yes, perhaps no. It all depends on how busy, and realistically-minded the individual is. At least making up stories provides for interesting reading, and listening material. One only has to visit bookstores, and libraries to get the idea of how much material there is to serve the diversity of readers.

Through all of the prevailing confusion, my principle intentions with this book, no matter what the consequences, is to "set the record straight" for the majority of readers. It is up to the individual to pass personal judgement. Life will go on as it always has because some people question the unexplained while others shrug it off as nonsense. It all depends on one's perception to an experience. Some are in tune with their genetic inherited body, and mind; others are not. The point to remember is that mankind needs, and provides both, the aware, and the unaware. It is what divides us into leaders, and followers.

All chapters within this book are one hundred percent factual in describing my life, and career. Some of the dialogue with career associates, and family members may slightly vary due to the passage of time, but the context remains as accurate as recollected. There are three exceptions, in Volume Three, Part One: *"FULL DISCLOSURE, "* the last three chapters, "The Pentagon, National Security, and Central Intelligence" were written in transitional fiction to maintain continuity with upcoming work. With nothing but favorable feedback from readers on character development, storyline, and suspense action, the author has decided to maintain the character values as a guarantee to his valued reading audience.

AUTHOR DEDICATION

The INVISIBLE WARRIOR, section of the book is my autobiography. Rather than explaining my rationale for writing in pseudo-narrative, the following verses state my reasoning.

I was born a Nobody…

I realized my dreams…

I achieved my goals…

I will die a Nobody…

But the legend of Alex Bauer lives on.

Anno Domini – 2019

T. Randall

AUTHOR BACKGROUND

As a preamble for you reading this book, I feel obligated to explain my reasons for writing it in first place. Due to the insistence from my daughters that I write my autobiography, primarily to reveal my life, and where I came from, since we never talked about it because of the nature of my work, and lifestyle, it was meant to be a nonfiction work. However, shortly into the initial chapters I was compelled to change direction primarily based on the declaration of the previous page. With all the knowledge, and opportunities my career presented, I felt it my duty to share what was considered reality, but sensitive material, nevertheless, unknown to the general public. Over the past several decades, so much confusion for unexplained behavior, and strange conduct by this nation's leadership has been displayed, and propagated that the record had to be set straight. I made it my mission to explain the stated behavior to the reader without compromising the parameters of national security.

My principle reason was to acknowledge an army of scientists, architects, engineers, designers, technicians, and support personnel instrumental in achieving the goal set in 1962 by President John Fitzgerald Kennedy, in creating a survivable communication system for the protection of the United States citizens, as well as in safeguarding the country's acquired wealth. For those who were not born then, what led to JFKs inception was the 1962 standoff with the Cuban Missile crisis that brought us to the brink of an all-out nuclear war. With both, Nikita Khrushchev and John F. Kennedy's fingers on launch triggers, the following thirteen days of standoff proved to be the most critical in U.S. history.

The result, after four years of manufacturing work in hardware, software, and system development was a secure network, connecting the Pentagon with the White House, DOD organizations, other government offices, U.S. Embassies, military Command and Control, and Intel communities in the case of an all-out nuclear attack by our adversary, which was then the Soviet Union, and other potentially hostile nations.

In response to JFK's directives, three levels of classified systems were built, and deployed worldwide wherever there was a U.S. presence, and allied assets to protect. Where the complex system was initially a five-year program, it turned into a 30-year career event, and more for many of its participants. Numerous upgrades rapidly followed based on technological advancements, such as satellite integration in the 70s, moving land-based trunk lines into the skies, technological upgrades to the ever-growing internal computer demands in speed, and memory capacity, external data storage devices, and increasing transmission speed, with the plan for eventual autonomous self-governing implementation by its visionary creators.

The 80s brought on more changes due to corporate demands to integrate large businesses into the well-established global communications grid. First, national laboratories were tied into the system which was quickly followed by major universities such as MIT, SRI Stanford, Cal Labs, and leading computer manufacturers such as IBM, UNIVAC, CDC, NCR, RCA, GE, DEC, Honeywell, Sperry Rand, Westinghouse, and Bell Labs, with Philco Ford holding the primary contract award. To achieve a seamless public transition, the highly classified top-secret network accesses needed to be declassified to a proprietary-level use, while still maintaining network, data, information, and access integrities. This challenge was accomplished through rigorous background investigations by the FBI, and other processing authorities such as DISCO[1], Military, and Intelligence agencies.

The next integration challenge came with the early 90s. By this time, the system had run flawlessly without one single security breach or hacking intrusion for thirty years. What elevated the system to an unexpected, unpredicted performance level to a public shift were several elements falling into place, namely: IBM produced the PC; Microsoft developed Windows, 2000 server platform, and business applications; Intel creating the microchip; and DARPA releasing the TCP/IP network protocol tying it all together.

What followed took the "NET" by storm. Public demand for cheap computers, challenging games, and designer software put such a great demand on the network, now declassified for public use, that it grew like uncontrollable, distributed spiderwebs, first in the U.S., and rapidly followed by Europe, Japan, Russia, and elsewhere, impossible to ever be stopped, or shut down. Unfortunately, JFK did not witness the monumental growth of his vision, today's Internet, but his goal has been achieved to a much greater extent than ever envisioned.

While public users were presented with the world's most sophisticated information system to enjoy, and benefit from, an army of hackers, spammers, and criminal elements were quick to make use of it with illicit intentions. Regardless, we, the visionaries, designers, and engineers, had never envisioned the potential benefit for private, public, and industries that has elevated humankind to an unimaginable level in information sharing, communication speed, and education, affecting every lifestyle from using the Internet.

Furthermore, some autobiographies can be quite bland, and boring unless the subject personage is of importance, such as a prominent leader or perhaps a ruthless dictator. As such, I took the liberty to illustrate my life, and career through the eyes of the main character in my previously written novel series, Alex Bauer. In addition, I present many important events that occurred, and affected my real life as well, embracing capable individuals that became part in my career. Aside from the cast of principle characters, and work teams postulated in this book, I encountered thousands of individuals having had personal interactions with, within my thirty-year career, representing many organizations, agencies, and corporations working for, and within the parameters of the Department of Defense and military Intelligence. Every one of these individuals was important to the cause of protecting the nation from foreign attackers constantly putting pressure on the western world.

Regardless of the many efforts initiated to protect the nation, lasting peace, while a possibility, will never become a reality unless world leaders change their ambitious, egotistical, and self-serving mindsets. There is always someone, or faction, ambitious enough with a desire to take down the Giant, in this case the United States of America.

---

[1] DISCO – The Defense Industrial Security Clearance Office is a component of the Defense Security Service (DSS) that maintains historical, and current investigative records on all DSS-issued (mostly government, and civilian contracting) personnel, and facility clearances.

AUTHOR DECLARATION

It must be understood that Volume One, in this book, *INVISIBLE WARRIOR,* was not an endeavor by only one single person. To make the defense system work, an army the size of multiple brigades was necessary to design, develop, built, and deploy it to the world, with follow-on obligations to maintain all functions by another multitude brigades, hired and commissioned to manage the system for the duration of its functional lifespan.

The system, designed, and developed in conjunction with DARPA, DCA (currently DISA), and numerous other public, and private entities was built, delivered, and managed for the DOD by one or another government contractor, with segments subcontracted out to a multitude of smaller corporations, applying specific skillsets as required. Once all system elements were delivered as a whole, they were tested by an independent government monitoring agency prior to operational release. For deficiencies identified, and corrections necessary, a primary contractor was retained for a specific time, after which the system was turned over to one or more military organizations to be managed. Where a typical lifespan of a government and military system is designed for a duration of ten years, many lifespans were extended beyond the original lifetime by ten, twenty, thirty years, or more years (i.e., the Nuclear Defense System), directed by the nation's budget limitations, economic conditions, political settings, and global state of affairs.

While every sector deserves acknowledgement, the principle software architects, and specialists warrant special consideration for developing, and maintaining the world's most sophisticated software designs for its time.

Regardless of accrued costs and expenses, a national defense system is necessary to initiate, and maintain readiness to protect citizen's wellbeing, and the nation's safety. It is these conditions that drive and dictate cost, and readiness by government and military forces with a runaway technology in a world of uncertainty by an otherwise peace-loving, humanitarian, and democratic people of the western world. The struggle may all be in vain for the survival of mankind, but, in the end, humankind is created to enjoy the beauty of life to its fullest extent, hoping for a prolonged, and healthy existence in a relatively unstable environment created by a species driven by ambition and inspiration, destined to expand into the universe.

One should only hope that the future will provide a more manageable, and organized environment for all, striving for a better, and safer existence. Whether globalization is a good thing or not, it is our eventual destiny, nevertheless. It takes a dedicated, and well-educated authority panel, sanctioned by all nations, to fight inhumane behavior initiated by terrorism, repression, and totalitarianism, to assure, and maintain the livelihood of each and every one of us. It is awareness, understanding, and compassion that elevates us above the animal kingdom, and should be valued, and preserved at all costs.

This book, as well as my previous three novels, was written to establish a trusting relationship between myself, the authorities, and my readers. Regardless of my intentions, many readers, especially the ones aspiring to conspiracies, paranormal, and supernaturally-inclined behaviors, refuse to accept the truth. They are the invincible who think that they know it all when, in fact, the only thing that matters in the cosmos are facts proven through science, not through fantasy, spirituality, or dreams, no matter how vivid, and believable a vision may be.

The second volume, *FULL DISCLOSURE*, is specifically written for the general public, and the logically, levelheaded individual to set the confusing, and mystifying accounts of Aliens, and UFO phenomena straight. *FULL DISCLOSURE*, the world's most anticipated announcement, expected by the public to be released directly by the government, will never take place. Volume Two, in this book will present the reasons.

The third Volume, *REALITY TODAY,* are mostly my own impressions and opinions after many years of research and studies into the worlds of science, human behavior, and ancient history, among others. Though biased to my own personal intellect, alternatives are not ruled out. It is up to the reader to investigate and formulate their own conclusions. I am only one brain pitted against eight billion presently living on earth.

ACKNOWLEDGEMENT

This attribute is for my family to let them know for how much I appreciate all of them. I could not express the patience each has displaying during my lengthy absences from family fun, and obligations. To justify my cause in the pursuit of a childhood dream, in hind-sight, I had no right to ever get married, and have children while hopping from country to country pursuing a full-time dedication to my job, and my country. No sane person would knowingly have put up with me, but in my defense, events overtook my rationale, resulting in a marriage to a beautiful woman, who managed to raise three girls in her image into responsible adults, bringing joy into our lives.

Also, my gratitude to my families across the oceans for keeping in touch with me, notwithstanding my many job-related, at times, lengthy disappearances without me sending back reports on my whereabouts and well-being.

My friends, and coworkers deserve as much reverence for treating me with respect, and gratitude equal to their own. I appreciate all of their efforts, and support, extended no matter what the situation—we all knew what I am inferring to—The Invisible Warriors.

Right from the start of my career contracting with DCA/DOD, I gained a new self-awareness after adapting to Alex Bauer. For the remainder of my life I plan to maintain this awareness by retaining recognition, and notoriety, as deserving of my alter ego, since it rewarded me with adventure, exploration, and a lifetime of fulfilling rewards. Since my acquired notoriety would quickly fade, reverting back to my birth identity, after retiring from contracting work, life would have reverted back to becoming nameless again. To preserve my acquired status, I continue to write as Alex Bauer within the volumes of my fiction work, which not even my eventual death will erase. After all, while human life is limited, fiction prevails into eternity.

In the name of national security, this book is dedicated to an army of Invisible Warriors, who, much like myself, devote an important part of their lives to a career instrumental for a critical cause. To share my recognition, I would have liked to list the names of core elements working on the AUTODIN, and other highly classified programs, with many more assigned from every military sector, civil services, government organizations, Intel agencies, and commercial contractors, but would require their permissions to do so.

Many at this time are still alive, while some have passed away, or enjoy retirement, but their efforts are not in vain. Their legacy will stand tall for many years, and ages to come, in a human, and technological evolution destined for a passage from Earth, eventually causing us to migrate through the cosmos, and on to the vast spaces of the universe, where we "Invisible Warriors" will leave our mark for eternity.

There is one important person that deserves special acknowledgement, not only for dedicating his career, but devoting his entire life to our cause. His name, as all of you will recognize is Robert Lawrence Krantz Sr., within the defense community also known as Mystery-man. "Why Mystery-man," one could ask. Because not many, outside of his immediate career family, knew much of him other than his name. In contrast, I had a special connection with the man dating back to the closing of WWII. We were interdepending in each other in planning, testing, and evaluating new technologies not only for AUTODIN, but other classified systems he took part in. I dearly miss him, and so does his family. I was granted permission from his family to attribute the next section to his accomplishments.

ROBERT LAWRENCE KRANTZ SR.

SPECIAL DEDICATION

Computer Systems Analyst
Robert L. Krantz Sr., of Unison, Virginia, born April 16, 1921, in New York City, NY, passed away peacefully on January 26, 2013 at the Warren County Hospital in Front Royal, Virginia from a lengthy illness.

He was the only child of Frederick L. Krantz and Marietta Reirden Krantz. He spent his childhood living between New York City and Old Greenwich, CT. He graduated from Greenwich High School with the class of 1939. He later received his BS in Business Administration, from the University of Maryland.

He was a member of the General Motors Parade of Progress until WWII began. At that time, at age 20, he enlisted in the Army Air Core, and served as an Army pilot and instructor. He married Edna Ann Winters, from Providence, R.I., in Coffeyville, Kansas, while in the second phase of his flight training. At the end of the war he left the military for a short period and then joined the Army in 1948.

During his long Army career his family joined him, in Japan, Korean War, Germany, and several stateside assignments. He took only one assignment without his family, and that was to France. It was during his long Army career that he began his lifelong work with computers in the early 1960's. At that time a computer was the size of a tractor trailer, as he called it. He never could have imagined that they would shrink to the size of a chip, held in one's hand. He helped design the first computer for the Army Signal Corp, as the Army Intel it was known back then. Retiring from the Army in 1964, after serving from 1942, he remained in the Army Reserve until retirement.

His next career was with the Department of Defense, Army Strategic Communications Command as a Computer Systems Analyst working with DCA's AUTODIN system development. As program liaison to DOD, installed defense communication systems throughout the world during the Cold War. His vast knowledge in defense communication systems allowed him to be a mentor to thousands of others working in the defense industry. He, and most of his peers, spent much time overseas in the company of the military, embassy staff, and other more covert arenas. It was for people like him that the nation today is a safer place to live than it was during the Cold War.

Following his permanent return to Washington, DC, he continued to work with the Overseas AUTODIN system working on the 73 AUTODIN Enhancement Project, developing the A&E Design Criteria for the relocations of the Alaska ASC to Taegu Korea, and Nha Trang, RVN to Augsburg, Germany.

With the drawdown in Southeast Asia, he developed plans for the re-homing and removal of the three ASCs in that area, after which he worked with a task force charged with developing the specifications for the Memory/Memory Control Upgrade of 1978, and the 78/79 AUTODIN Upgrade Project. During the late 70's, he conducted many consolidation studies and analyzed plans for installation of Army AMME'S in CONUS and Overseas.

The AUTODIN Processor Replacement Project, which advanced the Overseas ASCs to keep them operational until the mid-90's, was the first large project which was solely under the control of DCA. Mr. Krantz had been deeply involved in that project from its origin, having participated in the development of the Statement of Work, Request for Procurement, Proposal Evaluation, and the review and critique of contractor deliverables. He continued to work with this project until retirement at age 73.

While at DCA, Mr. Krantz received eight outstanding performance awards, one Sustained Superior Performance award, three high quality performance awards, and the Director's Meritorious Civilian Service Award.

He enjoyed his retirement to the fullest living on his farm in Unison, with his wife of 70 years, Edna Krantz, his herd of Registered Black Angus, and keeping his farm equipment operational. He stayed active and involved with the Loudoun County Library Foundation, The Loudoun County Hospital Sale (in charge of electronics), Election Polls, reading, writing his autobiography, and spending many hours each day on his computers keeping informed and in touch with his many friends around the world. He was a member of the Returned Services League of Australia, and a member of the American Angus Association.

He was a man who had a "Joie de vivre" and exuded that to all around him. He worked, and traveled the world, clocking millions of miles and making lasting friendships. A voracious reader with an inquisitive mind, he enjoyed a glass (or two) of wine and good conversation with family and friends. He was known for his huge smile, and his laugh, and never met a stranger.

TABLE OF CONTENTS

VOLUME ONE

INVISIBLE WARRIOR

POSTWAR GERMANY

How do I begin to describe my persona, or rather, the dual personas of the author of this book, and action man Alex Bauer, chosen to defend this nation against radical Islam, and other potential threats? Where one was born into postwar Germany, the other, Alex Bauer, did not emerge until adulthood, seeking out an adventurous future, but instead was provided with endless challenges extended by the nation's largest Intelligence organization, the Department of Defense. To reach this point in my life, and to understand what created the foundation for my very being, I must start with the beginning.

I can remember certain snapshots of life's splendors while securely cuddled under a blanket resting within the security of the baby stroller my mom put out in the backyard to catch the day's waning sunrays while hanging up washed linen on the drying line. My brain, still in its infant state, was not yet capable of assimilating the big picture, the immediate environment, until several years later during my first school years. For now, I was content with watching the most prominent face in my life occasionally checking in on my wellbeing while my eyes kept staring at the blue of the afternoon sky. Then something wondrous happened. A small creature darted in and out of my vision every so often, too quick for my brain to comprehend. What I watched was a bird picking cherries off the tree. Many months would to pass before my brain registered the similarity of the incidence when introduced to my first picture book. There are many more snapshots like this, all absorbed, and recorded in my brain.

When I entered first grade, I was overwhelmed by the many kids crammed into the classroom I had to share my days with. Already then, I sensed that there were certain differences between me, and the other kids. Since I had been brought up in a very sheltered environment, primarily by my mom protecting her child from the aftermath of WWII, the results clearly reflected on my personality. Undernourished, withdrawn, and introverted when on, and off school ground, I was bullied almost daily, if not by the class's principle bully, then by other kids trying to get their licks in on a timid young boy. It was not an ideal environment for any child to grow up in. Winding up with an occasional black eye, bruised rib, or blue toe with the nail falling off some days later, I was fearful many days while walking the mile to school, not knowing what the day had in store for me. Well, one endless year went by after another, only broken up by the annual, and too short, school break, mostly spent at my grandma's farm.

It was there where I blossomed over the six weeks of summer break by forgetting the world of obedience, and discipline. For most of the year my days were occupied with learning, and homework, but here it was nothing but playtime. My days were filled with adventures, whether it be fishing in a creek, boating along the Danube River banks—which, by the way, bordered the farm's property line—or accompanying my uncle, and Grandpa on their frequent hunting trips. It was a time to explore the wildlife, plentiful along the wooded riverbanks, and to receive much of my early education on worldly things. It was also a time that formulated desires for a life of adventure in the times ahead.

While I had siblings, one sister, and one brother, I spent much of the time alone. Then one day at age seven, we children were split up; my siblings were sent to Austria to live with one of Dad's brothers, and family, and I sent to another of Dad's brothers, and family as a result of the early death of my mom, a casualty of the war. I silently watched while Dad grieved for years. He was heartbroken.

I was too young then to realize the great loss of a personal death other than watching Dad fall apart emotionally as well as physically. But as the saying goes, time heals all wounds. Dad showed up two years later at Grandma's place to take me back home to his household. Right away I realized how empty the home had become with only me, and Dad living in the house. My siblings would remain with my Austrian relatives through the remainder of grade school. He did not have the time, and dedication to care for all of us. With him working fulltime, and me finishing up what remained of my grade school years—after which I thought the misery of going to school back home would turn around—somehow, I managed to keep afloat. But it did not last. Our bond was broken one day with the appearance of a stepmother. Dad had remarried for the reason of having the family back together again, but things would never be in harmony as they had been with my deceased mom.

Life with a new woman in the house became unbearable at times, especially for me. For reasons I would never understand, Dad turned against me. I became the whipping boy for my stepmother until she bore her own children over the following years. Already in my early teens, I became even more withdrawn. Well, grade school finally came to an end, but not without leaving lasting deep psychological scars. I came to dislike the culture I grew up in because everybody bore down on me in an environment where I had to endure disciplinary acts wanting to escape it all. But destiny, as unpredictable it is, kept a hold on the independent future I so desperately sought.

Not all was misery. Since Dad was a mechanical engineer, on a relatively harmonious day, I learned quite a bit from him. From him, I picked up the basics of analytical thinking, troubleshooting approach, and problem solving. The best way to learn any of it was through demonstrating by example. It avoided learning through books, and shop manuals. One day Dad came home with a bicycle frame, and a couple of pedals, and wheels somebody had ditched at the junkyard. He spent some money on wheel bearings, and other minor parts to get started. Then we put the rest of the bike together, aligned the handlebar, and wheels, and tested it.

I was the proud owner of my first bike. It took me around the neighborhood, and to nearby stores, though not without mishaps. First, there were no brakes. Drum brakes were not available, and the handbrake was not usable. It lacked innertubes for the wheels. Rubber products had been used up by the war, and manufacturing had not yet geared up. The resultant bike ride consisted of shudders to the spine, and blurry vision accompanied by many spills from the lack of brakes. The bike received an upgrade the following year after innertubes became available. But it got me places for several years.

Years later, after landing my first job, again with instructions, and help from Dad, I would learn how to strip, and rebuild my first motorcycle.

Following grade school, at age twelve, due to my dad's insistence, I spent some time on the farm, "to get in shape." I even entered the agricultural school in a nearby city to get educated in farming, and raising livestock. What I inherited from the ordeal were heaps of hard labor, and complete social separation, but this resulted in the physical strength I had been lacking. I could have never believed the dedication, and labor the small farmer puts into making a meager sustenance. It was up before daybreak tending to livestock, milking cows, and taking care of barn, and property, spending a minimum of eight hours in the fields. Depending on the season, the days might be occupied with sowing, weeding, watering, mowing grass for fodder, and plowing fields for eventual harvesting the fruits of the earth. Life was difficult. The ten-minute lunch break in between morning, and afternoon shifts, which wore away the limited energy I had, refueled me only with a cold bowl of milk accompanied by a slice of bread in the morning, and the day ending with the only warm meal, hearty, but limited by selection. After tending to animals, and the stable at days end, I then dragged my weary body to bed, totally exhausted, only to repeat the pattern the next day, then the next, and another, and so on, year in, and year out.

At the end of the second year my dad came to visit. Surprisingly, he presented choices. There were only two. "You can stay here, and become a farmer," he offered, "or you can come back home again, and find a job."

Neither choice was very appealing, but I made up my mind without much consideration. I chose the latter. I was not cut out to be a farmer, and preferred to live with my dad, hoping things would work out with my stepmother. The reason was clear to me. While farming, by its very nature, may contribute to personal health, and longevity from intense physical activity, the rewards back then were very limited. From a recreational perspective, there were none. From the incentive point of view, there were even less, and the same for intellectual rewards. With nothing but work, there was not much time or energy left for the farmer to enjoy life. Situations today are quite different, but not everywhere. I have learned the hardship farmers have, cutting out a meager living in poor countries. In industrialized places, with the aid of mechanization, and automation much of the physical labor has shifted to machinery, but this came with a new burden: higher prices on goods, and services being passed on to consumers. Regardless of its effects, it is called progress, nevertheless.

At the end of my time on the farm, my personal reward was a second-hand bicycle presented from the matron of the farm before bidding me goodbye. Since my dad arrived on his bicycle after a strenuous, twenty-hour ride, at least now, he had company on the way back. Unlike today, the bike was built solidly, and heavy, but came without a shifter. The ride back home from dawn to way into dusk turned out enjoyably. Aside from the bike, and learning the rudimentary of farming, I had acquired one more benefit. I had gotten in shape, as Dad had wanted. Our talks on the way home were mostly huffs, puffs, in between grunts while straining uphill, followed by cheers of the downhill rush. Riding in file, conversation was limited because of traffic rushing past on the open roads. We made it home in one piece without mishap, and much like after a day's work on the farm, I was exhausted.

Showing off my only possession in the world to my buddies back home, I was proud of my "new" bike. My old bike, to my dad's objection, went to the junkyard. Being the proud owner of new transport meant I was ready for the world. In the following years during summer break, this bike took me to places I used to only dream about.

Where many of my school buddies would spend summer lounging at the lakeshores of the Bodensee (bottomless lake), I adventured across the borders into foreign lands, and languages. Over the span of several summers, I made it to Italy, Spain, France, Austria, and Switzerland, sometimes seeking campgrounds, and other times spending the nights at a hostel. Aside from absorbing nature's splendors—the Alps left in the distance, the slowly passing terrain on both sides of the way to the next destination—I was able to visit places like Rome, Pisa, Venice, Milan, Florence, Monaco, Nice, Marseille, Barcelona, and Gibraltar, as well as enjoying pristine beaches all along the Mediterranean Sea.

My most memorable place of it all was Venice. Even though I had just entered puberty at age thirteen, I could sense a romantic energy prevalent throughout the city amid the narrow passage ways, canals, gondolas, San Marcos Plaza, and Lido Island with its clean, but popular beaches. In the evenings, while leisurely strolling alongside the canals, aside from getting hit by an occasional whiff of sewage odor, the attraction was overwhelming. After several more visits there, to this day I can still feel a great sense of romantic notions when thinking of the place. Since then, while waste removal still presents a problem throughout Venice, attempts have been made, though gradually, to treat, and process waste with modern day techniques to attract more pampered, and demanding travelers.

Despite the pleasures of enjoying my travels, it was not always fun. To get to places, I had to overcome the barrier of mountains blocking easy passage. Mostly headed southward toward the Mediterranean Sea, my annual destination, I had one of three choices, and challenges to overcome. They were Brenner Pass through Austria, Saint Goddard Pass through Switzerland, or Saint Bernard Pass through France, in addition to several minor foothill passes along the way. Getting across the passes was backbreaking, and laborious. With only one gear on the bike, loaded down with a backpack, and tent strapped onto the carrier, my weight on the pedals was not always enough to move the bike along. The only option was to walk, and push uphill on foot for close to four hours until I reached the top, the border crossing. But a reward was waiting after reaching the peak. The downhill ride, with the wind pressing against my face, and body, was pure pleasure for the next twenty minutes into the valley. From there on it would be another eight hours of laborious peddling until I reached the next target destination to bed down for the night.

Though strenuous for most part, the six weeks of travel always paid off. After only a few days the results became clearly visible on muscle tone, physical endurance, and mental disposition. All problems accumulated throughout the year melted away, waning by the day. At the end of the journey, my body was as hard as could be with a mind to match the year's challenges ahead until the next summer.

A change came at age twelve with Dad having an announcement one day after returning from his work. "Son," he said, with the sternness I had grown used to, "I've got a job for you." I had been preparing for college, but the announcement was not an unwelcome revelation. Dad was an established mechanical engineer, and had been on the design, and development team for the Hindenburg airship among other renowned engineering achievements, such as the very first hydrofoil-powered ship. It became apparent that he wanted me to follow his career line. Although I was startled at first because of the trust he extended, it only took minutes for me to decide on accepting, as though I had a choice.

Learning the location for the job, I readily accepted. The workplace was located some twenty miles from home nearby an ancient city. Lindau, a walled city built into Lake Constance near the Austrian border, is a jewel among German cities. Built by the Romans two thousand years before as their last outpost expanding to the north, it has served the local population well. Its walls are still standing today, its buildings reflect a Roman architecture of the same age, streets bedecked by cobblestone, it's isolation from the mainland by two bridges, and ships, and townspeople are protected from the natural elements by a harbor guarded by two landmarks, a lighthouse on one side, and the symbol of the city on the other, a huge monument signifying the city's heritage, a challenging lion for anyone not welcome from across the lake. The city, confined by walls, maintained by a steady population of fifteen thousand, had been stable since it was built, and is solely dependent on small merchants to serve the citizens, and tourism. No other industry was home to the place.

To get from home to my workplace involved commuting almost two hours each way beginning with a lengthy walk to the station. A train ride, followed by another lengthy bus ride, got me to my final destination. In spite of the time wasted in transit, it did not take long for me to embrace my new environment. I was introduced to my training coaches, met new faces my age, and was exposed to the wonders of modern-day industrial technology. I had earned a scholarship with one of Germany's aircraft companies. The reason I was hired on so early, at age twelve, was due to the country's post war situation. I was recruited during the first wave of a new industrial workforce for the purpose of rebuilding German's industry, followed by managing it once we were trained, and proficient with handling the foreign labor the industry was forced to employ.

With the loss of seventy five percent of the capable male population during the war, Germany was caught up without a labor force. The women who had worked in the industries, primarily weapons and munitions manufacturing, while their sons and husbands were fighting on several battle fronts, could not support the industrial plans the Allies had in mind for rebuilding the collapsed nation. As a result, the borders were opened, offers were extended, inviting labor forces from Italy, Spain, Yugoslavia, Greece, and other surrounding countries. Much like in the present day E.U., available prospects arrived by the thousands. The only difference between then, and now was that the arrivals were invited, and extended a five-year green card with possible citizenship as long as the demand for labor was there, whereas today the onslaught of unskilled labor forces fleeing their countries has been a great burden for E.U. nations to carry.

It was this diverse labor force that made up postwar German industry, and population expansion. There was only one catch to it all. None of the immigrants were trained for the jobs, let alone how to manage others. It was this situation I acquired when entering the Industrial Academy of Southern Germany. Organized, and run much like any academy, our morning hours were spent in classrooms, with industrial training for the remainder of the day, much like an apprenticeship covering all forms of industrial machinery, materials shaping and processing, metals fabrication, and whatever skills it took to create an industry left in shambles by the war. The success became obvious in only a short time. There was, however, still the question of managing the rapidly-growing demand throughout the various industry sectors, namely automotive, transportation, power, and every other part of infrastructure necessary to build a successful nation.

My future was promising, and I was destined for success. But to achieve it, I spent four years of daily intense education at the academy, followed by many laborious hours at the industrial complex, emerging fully exhausted at the end of an arduous day to commute another two hours back to my home town. What made the experience somewhat endurable was that we were paid a stipend of 50 DM, a small, but welcomed monthly earning. Unfortunately for me, my earnings were mostly absorbed by train and bus fares. At the end of the month, I had a few bills left to buy, and enjoy one bunch of bananas, which had just come on the German marketplace, and which I thought was the marvel of fruits, and a cone of ice cream on Sundays, and that was it. The few measly Deutsch Mark remaining I saved up for nine months to be able to purchase my first pair of pants, a jacket, and a shirt with matching tie, in the fashion of the world popular singers' attire back then, such as Elvis Presley. The singer, popular in the United States, found new notoriety overseas after he entered the U.S. Army, and shipped off to Germany for his tour of duty. He became everybody's idol, including mine.

I should point out that the four years at the academy was not only demanding work, and rigorous learning. While limited on recreational activities, there were times for fun, and games as well. Aside from scholastic achievements, I also participated in intercollegiate soccer, sculling (single, dual, and four teams), fencing (skilled in foil, and dagger), and sailing at the shores of one of Europe's large freshwater bodies, Lake Constance. Most enjoyable was the spectacular view into the world known as the Bavarian Alps locally, the Austrian Alps to the east, and the Swiss Alps to the south, across the lake. It did not take many years of a prospering Germany to draw a society of affluent travelers seeking to enjoy the southern shores of the lake, which became the northern European's vacation paradise to enjoy swimming, diving, boating, and fishing pleasures the expanse of water offered.

Growing into early adulthood surrounded by likeminded friends, I enjoyed my time while in back of my mind a germinating seed was growing, to explore more of what the world had to offer. Television was already an established entertainment vehicle in America, but it was not yet available in Germany. With a limited budget, though my stipend grew to 100 DM over four years in meager advancements, my only options available were frequent visits to the local library, or an occasional American-made Western film, which I totally enjoyed. I became an avid reader. It was here where my future was ultimately forged into becoming an adventurer. My environment, as promising, and rewarding as it would have been, was not good enough anymore. Though mostly dormant, and subconscious at the time, my aspirations were set much higher.

As a result of my reading everything I could get my hands on, one day sparked my interests. I should mention that because of Adolph Hitler's burning of literary works, not much German cultural reading was available in schools, and libraries.

Schools were prohibited to teach about the world wars, and there was a scarcity of materials available as well. There was, however, ample material on hand from other countries, especially those authored by British, and Americans. It was these that changed my life. At first, I came across a set of adventure novel series written by James Fennimore Cooper, a prolific, and popular American writer of the early 19th century, translated into German language by Karl May. Cooper was best known for adventure novels set in the American Old West, spurring my spirits.

Months later, I took on a series of novels written by British novelist Perl S. Buck, the daughter of missionary parents to China, Indonesia, and other oriental places, who further inspired my dreams, though distant, and unreachable at the time. As I was highly intrigued by writings from her Asian travels, it added fuel to my future planning. Only a dream then, it took more years of labor before destiny would allow me to fulfill my aspirations.

The relationship with my dad, for the most part, was tolerable. Though there were times of tension, and disagreement, life at home was endurable as long as I played by his rules, which was not always the case. As every youngster can attest to, there is a feeling of injustice usually accompanying the end-result in a disagreement, with the youngster succumbing to the parent's ultimate decision. One such example became a major dispute between me, and Dad. It was over the first automobile I had purchased without his prior approval. The thought of asking him never occurred to me. I will cite the dialogue exchange that followed. The vehicle in question was a BMW 1928 classic, which I purchased in the spring of 1956. I had just turned sixteen, and obtained my driver's license.

My first choice was the newly manufactured Beetle, the most popular car at that time. Unfortunately, because of its popularity, there was a nine-month waiting period for a delivery. Aside from that, I couldn't afford its purchase cost. My second choice was a dated vehicle, pre-war, which was cheapest at the time. I suspected that someday these vehicles would be appreciated once more, but classic cars had not made their appearance yet. To find an affordable vehicle, I canvassed the German countryside on weekends. As luck had it, the car I found turned out to be a vintage model, red in color, sporting a black top, and trimmings, large, and shiny headlights: a first-built model 1928 BMW coupe. The current owner, a farmer, remembered one stored by his father, but forgotten under a haystack in the barn. After digging it out from beneath the hay, I bought it on the spot for the mere cost of 400 Deutsch Marks, equivalent to $100.

Right after Dad came home from work, he spotted the vehicle sitting in the driveway. As I recall, the dialogue was heated, and went like this:

"Whose piece of junk is sitting in the driveway?"

"It's mine, and it's not junk. It's in mint condition."

"I don't care. Get rid of it."

"But why?"

"What will the neighbors think when they wake up?" Life was lived for the neighbors. It was a common result caused by the war, where everybody, mostly woman, and children, was dependent on each other.

"I don't care. I want the car."

"Get rid of it or I'll have the police lock you up."

"That's not fair. I just bought it."

"As long as you live in my house, you do what I tell you."
"Then I'll move."
"You stay until I say so."
"For how long?"
"Until you are twenty-one."
The decision was made. I was trapped for five more years. One week later, I was given one last ultimatum to get rid of the vehicle. Unhappy, and beaten, I returned my precious classic to the farmer. He was just as unhappy about having to face the "piece of junk" again, as he called it. I told him to hang on to it for a few more years, because I'd be back again. Unfortunately for the BMW, and for me, the opportunity never came. To keep in harmony with Dad, I had purchased a scooter instead. Though it looked more like a toy, it pleased him while it got me around cheaply.

Living for your neighbors, was the prevalent mentality back then, not only for my dad, but with others as well for keeping law, and order. Dad lived, and abided by this law until the end of his days. Even to this day, many elderly Germans still live in the fear set forth by Hitler's propaganda chief, Heinrich Himmler. It became a cultural condition not easily broken.

That's the story of my first purchase, the controversial BMW. It was one of the reasons adding to the cause for me turning my back on Germany, its people, and its culture. But that was still years ahead.

Another sore point in my early life was a stamp collection I lost to my younger stepsister. The collection included an extensive set of postage stamps I had gathered since childhood. Many came from an uncle, and relatives living in Switzerland. As director of the Swiss commodity exchange in Zurich, my uncle received mail from around the globe. Knowing my passion for collecting stamps, every so often he would send me a package containing the precious cargo. For this reason, I acquired a complete set of stamps featuring Hitler in full-colored uniform, in every possible portrait variance, slightly aging with time, popular during the initial years of his reign. The printed stamps were considered ordinary postage during the war years, but became valuable with collector's decades after the war. I don't miss the acquired value of the stamps. What I do miss was the hard-earned, collectible commodity from a past time of tyranny within a lingering, livid memory.

Four busy years later, after graduating from the academy with diploma in hand, I was set to conquer the world. Still being a minor in age, in order to leave home, I had to get permission from Dad, the ultimate decision-making power. When I approached him on the subject of leaving, naturally he refused. "You'll stay until you are twenty-one." That was it. I had not expected an absolute refusal. My dreams of moving on were shattered. In his mind, after my mom gave birth, and he raised me, in return, as was common in Germany, I was to pay my dues. There was no alternative, or way out. I was trapped living at home for several more years. It took weeks of mulling over the rejection to come to my senses, and see it his way. My life would be on hold until age twenty-one, at that age an eternity.

"What are my options?" I asked.

Dad, as usual, was ready with an answer. "You can work at my place. I already prepped management, who agreed to hire you." What I did not know at the time was

Dad's influence with executive management at the manufacturing plant. Germany, in pre-war times, had five aircraft manufacturing firms: Messerschmitt, Heinkel, Junkers, Focke-Wulf, and Dornier[2]. After the war, there was only one still in existence. It was the firm Dad worked at, and that I entered. Though prohibited at the time by the Yalta Summit Agreement,[3] a joint Allied resolution on German's future banning them from building aircraft, or other war-related machinery, the company had geared up by producing weaving machines for linen, and cloth production. While it was a lucrative business for its time, supplying weaving products worldwide, the firm's executive management could not abstain from building further aircraft. After lengthy deliberations with NATO Allied command, the company was eventually granted the first postwar craft assigned to the drawing board.

It was here where I started my job. Being member of the design, and development team, I partook in the production of the first postwar aircraft. The design, a reconnaissance craft, proved to be successful, with numerous foreign countries placing purchase orders for military use. With the end of the developing phase, the challenges I sought also came to an end. I had no desire to revert my job back to weaving production, and secretly prepared for an exit strategy, but it was not as simple as I had expected. Moving away from home, regardless of age or status, taking on a job, or relocating out of one's birth town required a local police clearance, picture ID, or passport. Obtaining any of those was a lengthy process of waiting until a personal background investigation was completed, and a certificate granted. Without one, due to national travel and employment restriction laws, it was impossible to find work in another town, or city. So, my patience was tested for several months.

The day finally came with the notification to pick up my approved documents. The next challenge was to get a job release certificate from my employer. Dad would surely be notified, but I lucked out. Unaware of my planning, he was stunned when I confronted him with the news. "I am leaving home."

"You can't do this. Not possible. I forbid it," was his response. "I'll have you put in jail."

Regardless of his refusal I stood firm, my plans set. "I already quit my job." It was another bombshell to him. In spite of his anger that followed, I felt sorry for my dad, watching the resultant emotional changes he underwent. Arguing was never an option with him, as was prevalent throughout German culture. A father's decision was the law. It had to be upheld by any son or daughter. After demonstrating my insistence over the following days, we finally came to an agreement. I did not have to further explain my decision to leave home. He was well aware that my life had turned into sheer misery after he remarried. My stepmother had it in for me. For years, where my

---

[2] Dornier Flugzeugwerke (Manufacturing) was a German aircraft manufacturer founded in Friedrichshafen in 1914 by Claude Dornier. Over the course of its long lifespan, the company produced many designs for both the civil, and military markets.

[3] The Yalta Conference, sometimes called the Crimea Conference, and codenamed the Argonaut Conference, held from February 4 to 11, 1945, was the World War II meeting of the heads of government of the United States, the United Kingdom, and the Soviet Union, represented by President Franklin D. Roosevelt, Prime Minister Winston Churchill, and Premier Joseph Stalin, respectively, for the purpose of discussing Europe's post-war reorganization. The conference convened in the Livadia Palace near Yalta in Crimea.

friends would be out playing, I would be forced to take care of the house, including her two daughters. She forced me into a slave-like position with household chores awaiting me from morning to late at night when not at school.

For this reason, Dad allowed me to temporarily visit Zurich, home of my deceased mom, under the supervision of her brother, the executive director for the Swiss Commodity Stock Exchange, who I would be living with. Expecting an independent life free from controlling adults, I readily agreed just to get away from home, and especially my stepmother. The day finally arrived when I stepped off the platform onto the train, ready to depart with Dad waving goodbye. It was the first time I saw him with tears in his eyes. Waving back, surprised but pleased, I surmised, "There are emotions in everybody." The train slowly pulled away from the station, accelerating rapidly towards my destination.

The train ride turned out pleasantly. The four hours, restricted within the coach compartment, went by quickly while I enjoyed the mountainous landscape amid lush green pastures spreading across the prolific habitat of the Swiss countryside. What the future held in store was uncertain. I did not dwell on it. My mind was open to any opportunity. It gave me time to think about the past, what could have been, and what should have been if my mother were still alive, in which case I may not have been sitting on the train. Thinking of her, and the short few years under her loving care brought on a certain sadness, but switching my thoughts to the present, and the reason impelling me to leave home brought me back to reality. I felt no guilt, and harbored no anger to either one. What did stay with me were two pieces of advice from Dad I would live by in the years ahead that essentially drove my ambition, and formulated my career. One set up the foundation for my future: "One must create one's own destiny." Most of us are not fortunate enough to either inherit wealth, or have the means for paving the way into one's future. The second rule I heard a number of times during childhood, ranking equal in importance, was his insistence: "Don't come crying to me unless you have the answer."

It may sound cruel to a child, but it certainly left its mark. Having heard the rulings throughout my growing up, they left Dad's permanent fingerprint on my brain.

SWITZERLAND

I will not dwell on the year that followed in Switzerland, but let me assure you it was filled with pleasure, and excitement. A city ranking amid the world's best in culture, industry, commerce, and trade, Zurich was built on an independent heritage dating back to Wilhelm Tell, and its founders. Why the city was built in the first place was the result of constant battles between the adjacent nations of Germany, Italy, and France during the medieval ages in late 15th century.

What made Zurich unique was its isolation from the rest of the world. But that was then, and on into the 20th century. Now, it is a thriving metropolis for business, and travel, much like any international city. Most renowned is its fame for secure banking, commodity trade, and weapons specialties. Yes, many of the world's precision weapons, and munitions are designed, and manufactured there. Ask any armament trader, and he will confirm it.

It did not take much with my credentials to find a job. I landed at one of the precision manufacturing places, which provided me with the means to support my prolific lifestyle, reserved for evening, and nightly hours spent at one of the city's thriving nightlife spots, the Niederdorf. One could find every conceivable activity from simple bars serving any drink fashionable at the time to more secluded, and private happenings taking place behind closed doors. As far as my participation was concerned, my recollection for the year could best be described as hazy, probably because it was the first time, I was free of the bondage my dad had held over me for seventeen years. While I was allowed out on weekends while living at home, my activities had been limited to a strict cultural abidance of: "What will the neighbors say?"

In contrast, now, living in America, where many of my neighbors live in an independent "Do whatever pleases you" manner, I still live by the standards of my inherited values, but I am not complaining. My standards are that of extending respect for "thy family, and neighbor, treasure nature, and its splendor," and enjoying the beauty of life every waking hour no matter what the political, and economic conditions may be.

The mistake I made that lost me the independent life I had gained was from the prodding of Dad to come home for the end of the year holidays. I agreed, though reluctantly, and made the journey home only to find out that, because I was still a minor, Dad had confiscated my passport, and visa to Switzerland since he still held ultimate responsibility over my life. The reason for his actions was that I broke my promise to live with my Swiss relatives. I had rented a small, but clean room from an aging lady, who welcomed the additional earnings received from my rent.

Facing a restricted life at home again for the next three years, I endured it with a "grin, and bear it" attitude. It turned out to be tolerable since I had come to an agreement for him to be more accepting due to my current age, as well as my being a seasoned traveler with foreign working experience to boot.

My former employer offered me my old job back, and everybody was happy. Dad was happy I was able to pay rent for staying at his home; the employer was happy because they reaped the rewards of their investment on me. My former friends were happy they had their school buddy back. As for me, I tolerated my return to my former life in a disciplined establishment with a reserved reluctance, but made the best of it. I met a girl that I liked, had a deserving income, and did much traveling weekends, and vacation times, but one thought always stayed with me: seek out foreign lands. But, to achieve that, I had to wait three more years to earn the right as an adult.

The day finally arrived. I celebrated my 21st birthday with friends, and colleagues, a most joyful event in my life. To the disappointment of family, friends, and girlfriend, it marked the most important milestone to my existence. I made the announcement, "I am off to see the world." But the world still had to wait for my arrival. I was short of funds. While I received an earning appropriate for my job skills, it was an apprentice's pay, again with only a few Marks left after paying for commuting, and rent to Dad. On the positive side, my present job held a promising career with rapid advancements into management, and eventual directorship, but it would also absorb my life in its entirety. It was something I was educated, and trained for, but it was not the life I had dreamed of for so many years. I had to completely sever myself from the present environment, which I eventually did.

The only difference on the railway platform this time was that, instead of Dad bidding me goodbye, it was my girlfriend in tears. I promised, "I'll be back to visit soon." By then everyone knew of my plans, and ambitions, conquer the world. My immediate destination was Munich, where I spent one year earning enough to sustain a living, but not enough to save up for the voyage.

"A voyage where?" I had not the slightest inkling as to its ultimate aim, that of immigrating to America. While it was still a dream, it was not an option. The requirements for anyone to enter the U.S., aside from a passport, was by having a personal sponsor. My next stop was a visit to the immigration, and naturalization office. Conveniently, there was one in Munich. Six weeks later I held the green, bright, and shiny document to the world in my hands. I felt euphoric. Investigating further, to my displeasure, only Canada, and Africa were my options as an immigrant. Since Canada was too far away without the money for the voyage, I applied to Johannesburg, South Africa for acceptance. It was a place where it was feasible to reach with the meager savings, I had acquired working in Munich, and sharing an apartment with a friend.

With this immediate goal in mind, I considered it only a temporary step. I set out to purchase a vehicle, a used, but spacious sedan I converted to a sleeper by modifying its front seats to collapse. It would allow sufficient room to stretch my body for a night's sleep after a planned-out daily journey headed south. Yes, I planned to drive the eight thousand miles to my destination. I had the route, and cost already planned, with direction, fuel stops, nightly intervals, and total driving time calculated to the day, providing nothing came along, such as breakdowns, interruptions, and delays which, by the way, I had no provisions for. I was forced to wing it all the way. The day finally came when I quit my job, packed my belongings into the trunk of the vehicle, and headed southwest on the lengthy trip. What made the time enjoyable was my best friend decided to accompany me for the journey. His goal was to reach his older brother, who had migrated to Africa years earlier.

The morning arrived when we headed off into an uncertain future in anticipation of hopefully reaching our destination without any unforeseen mishaps. Finally, on the road of my dreams, for the first time I felt like a true adventurer. The first leg would take us into France, followed by stops along the way in Spain, Gibraltar, crossing the Mediterranean Sea into Algeria, then on through Niger, Nigeria, Chad, the Republic of Congo, Zambia, and Botswana, with final destination Johannesburg, South Africa.

All went well traveling along the Riviera coastlines for the first several days until we reached Gibraltar. It was here where we decided to rest a couple of hours to enjoy the sandy shores, and blue swells of sea waves, too enticing to ignore. But fate was not in our favor. After spending time on the beach, and in the water, it was time for lunch. Having calculated out our budget to last the trip, we usually skipped breakfast, and stopped for lunch, and dinner with whatever we could scrape together from marketplaces along the way. Today, even lunch was denied us. As soon as we approached the vehicle, "Dammit," my buddy raged, "we've been robbed." Taking stock, we saw that we had been ransacked of all of our belongings. Gone were our clothes, shoes, suitcases, money, and passports. We were stranded.

What does one do after realizing such misfortune? One panics, if only briefly. Rational thinking quickly takes hold over the unfortunate situation. What could one do when stranded, penniless, and unfamiliar with the Spanish language? Seek out the local embassy.

We lucked out. There was a German consulate in town. After submitting a theft report, we were issued temporary travel papers for the return trip, and handed some money, just enough, with our promise to repay after getting back to where we originated from. My dreams were shattered. It was the end of my becoming an adventurer. Disgruntled, disillusioned, and starved, three days later we arrived back at the German border crossing.

We did not return to Munich since I had quit my job, and gave up the apartment there. I had a better idea. I needed to be close to the Allied bases in order to get me into either Canada or the United States. With that in mind, my buddy, and I landed in Manheim, a city surrounded by American military bases.

BACK IN GERMANY

While the city by the Rhine River was an unplanned change in direction, it was still a new start. Finding work did not present a problem since industrial jobs in the area were plentiful. My problem was getting close to English-speaking servicemen. I found American soldiers everywhere I could, but it was not easy to make acquaintance. Many did not speak German, some only a few broken-up sentences, and hardly any could converse in my language. One morning I took the bull by its horns, and paid a visit to the largest military base, Coleman Barracks – USAREUR[4].

"HALT," the sign proclaimed. While a barrack was indicated, referring to a small army base, I found it to be a busy air field, adjacent to Rhein-Main International Airport. After asking the gate guard, who spoke the local language fairly well, for a job, I was directed to the management building. I lucked out once more when the desk administrator handed me a job application to fill out. I must have qualified for it since I received a call from the office a few days later stating, "You are hired. Report to the base tomorrow."

My heart skipped a few beats as I readily accepted the position assigned. I could not have done better to get in amid the Allied forces for the goals I had set out years ago. Reporting for duty the next day, I was embraced by likeminded employees at the airfield, all working for the German Civil Service. Until that day I had not even been aware that there was such a service in the country. It suited me well. For once, I did not have to think, and the job was easy. It was a breeze, literally, driving an aircraft refueling tanker across the fields after acquiring the appropriate Class A commercial license. In addition, weeks later after receiving more training, I was able to shuttle arriving aircraft from the passenger port to the dedicated tie-down place assigned to the arriving craft. Military pilots, due to their mission requirements, were considered the world's best pilots, but did not necessarily have the patience to maintain the craft. That was a task for people like me.

Almost from the first day, I began pestering American soldiers with my plight of finding a sponsor. While I captured many an ear, nobody was willing to commit to the responsibility. After all, a soldier was on overseas assignment detached from home with only one thing on his mind: having fun while in Germany, and they did. Local bars, and clubs were full of military patrons. For the establishments they were the best customers because they had the money to spend which, consequently, attracted many young girls, in turn benefiting both customer, and hostess. I learned that many of the girls held similar aspirations to me, wanting to find a sponsor.

I always wondered where the notion originated for wanting to leave one's birthplace. It might have been the post-war conditions driving the desire, having lost most of one's family, or another personal reason. From what I read in newspapers, every ocean liner that left Hamburg, and Bremer Haven was filled with refugees headed for the North American continent. The driving factor for me was the adventure novels I used to read. Part of it came from Fennimore Cooper books, illustrating the vast lands across the Atlantic with everybody being a successful rancher owning large stretches of land, aside from a nation having a prospering industry, and healthy

---

[4] U.S. Army, Europe command.

economy. But that was then, in the 60s. Many things have changed since in the once proud, and world-renowned nation. One can only hope that stability, and prosperity will return, and become part of the American nation again in the near future. I personally would like to see that day while I'm still alive.

Having nothing but fun on the job, the days on base went by quick. Work for me began at 7:00 am, and lasted until six with a one-hour lunch break. Exposed to mostly American-speaking soldiers arriving, and departing on the base, I quickly learned rudimentary phrases in the language. While many were commands spoken or called out in simple sentences, there was much joking, and humor during periodic breaks, especially during the winter months when employees, and hosts alike sought out the warmth of an indoor stove or fireplace. The base could get pretty cold with ever-present winds whipping across the airfield. Aside from learning the basics of English, there were two things new to me I immediately embraced. The first day on the job, one of my coworkers on the crew took me to a nearby kiosk for lunch. Since I was not familiar with the offerings in food, he pointed at the menu, and suggested, "Try this. You'll like it."

Being the adventurer that I was, not only in visiting foreign lands, but also in sampling new cuisine, and other novelties. "Hamburger, please," I said, placing my order. Unwrapping the contents when they were handed over through the window, I was surprised by a packet of rounded buns stacked with meat, and lettuce, topped off by slices of tomato, and cucumbers. It tasted much as it looked, juicy, and scrumptious. Much like American kids, I took to the hamburger from then on. Having reached a certain popularity among the GIs, the next tasty surprise came one Saturday evening when I was invited to a party. I only had to take one bite of the slice of pizza served before I was sold on the miracles of fast food, again for much of my life.

Almost one year had gone by at the busy airbase, and I still had not made a connection for a sponsor. What I did make, though, was many friends. There was one particular establishment in the area popular with the GIs. Since the owner, and many of the patrons spoke some sort of English, the club predominantly catered to foreign soldiers. It was a busy place on weekends. It was also a place that attracted fights. As was the case with the young, confrontations were almost always over one thing, girls. As if there were not enough young women to go around with most of the capable male population lost to the war. Most fights were short lived. But some turned more violent, especially after a few bottles of beer, with a local patron defending his girlfriend from an inebriated, aggressive soldier. At times, one only had to throw a glance at a good-looking girl, and the fight was on, usually ending with one, both, or several more drunks getting involved, and hurt to a point where an ambulance was called. Having all of the right male qualities myself, I can speak from my own personal encounters. I too had my share of fisted bouts.

On one such evening I had the good fortune of helping out one soldier I though was a decent fellow. He was very appreciative for my coming to his aid. From that day on, to his dismay at times, I kept pestering him for a sponsor. Several more months had elapsed when one evening, out of the blue, he walked up, announcing, "Your wish has been granted." I was dumbfounded. I did not know whether to hug or to kiss him. That's how euphoric I was. We shook hands instead to seal the bond. I would be grateful, and indebted to him forever. He later told me that he was getting sick and tired of being pestered, and one day had called home. It turned out that his aunt was willing to provide sponsorship. That was all I had to hear to confirm his promise to be the truth. Weeks later I received a personal invitation, a letter, and confirmation from Anna, also a German immigrant.

"Now what?"

Again, I was confronted by a challenge. But this time it would involve the very dreams I had harbored since childhood. As I was still penniless, without a passport, unfamiliar with how to go about getting the paperwork started, Anna came to my aid. She sent the required documents via the American embassy to be filled out, and notarized. It seemed to be a straight forward task but turned out to be lengthy.

As before, I had to go through the same process of getting not only a local police clearance, and an employer release, but it also involved the German FBI, since I was permanently leaving the country. The background investigation, though my life had been straight forward without criminal incidents, still took its time because of government bureaucracy. Three months later all documents were submitted, processed, and approved. I was the proud holder of a new passport, an immigration document, and a ticket for a sea voyage on the oceanic ship *Berlin*, scheduled to leave the Bremen docks two weeks later.

Bidding my newly acquired friends goodbye was not so easy, especially the girls I had met. There were promises to keep in touch with possible visits or reunification in the near future, but all turned out to be empty promises. I had no plans for coming back, and my friends had no desire to leave their glorious homeland. My immediate destination was a last visit to Dad. After a lengthy eight-hour train ride home, he appeared heartbroken after I made the announcement, "I am leaving for America."

"But why?" he wanted to know. "You have such a great career future here. You're going to leave it all behind?"

"Dad," I tried to persuade him, "it's my dream. It's what I always wanted." We debated back, and forth for two days, him trying to change my mind with me holding steadfast to my dreams. My brother, and sister, who were living at home with Dad once more, were equally shocked when they heard of my plans. In spite of the promise of visits, back in the 60s it meant goodbyes forever. I should mention that, on the contrary, destiny was kind to me. Because of my successes, and effort, there would be many later visits.

The day for departure arrived with Dad seeing me off early morning at the train station. Waiting to board, I could see the sadness in his eyes. Similar to the day my mom had died, he seemed on the brink of tears. After I hugged him with promises of return, he handed me a bon voyage package. I boarded the train with a huge sigh of relief, and headed straight into the future, the United States of America, the destiny I was born with. I had only one day of layover at Bremen before boarding the ship, and the first leg of my lifelong journey began.

In retrospect, all my peers that I left behind landed executive positions with firms large, and new, flourishing into early retirement after enjoying a life of prosperity, and leisure. "But—what about him? What happened to him?" It was a question posed to my dad by many of my former colleagues after they heard that I had turned my back on what could have been a very successful career.

"Left the country," was his usual reply. When prodded further, he was only too willing to share the successes I had found in my new land, the "land of milk, and honey." A land of unlimited opportunities, America. The label "United States" was not used, and had little meaning in foreign countries. It was Americans setting the trends, and creating technological advancements.

VOYAGE TO AMERICA

Spending my growing up years amid poverty, with a shortage on everything, and being completely undernourished, was an arduous journey to get to this point in my life. If I had been a vain person, I would have been ashamed of showing my emaciated body on public beaches. I weighted a mere 110 pounds at 6' tall, and age twenty-three. After settling in on the ocean liner that left the dock well past noon, taking in the initial breeze blowing in from the British channel, I found that the dinner call was not far off. Famished as usual, especially during the past nine months of living on a pauper's budget, I needed to save up 800 DM[5] for the voyage, and had a mere savings of $50 in my pocket to get by for the initial weeks once on land again. The first on-ship meal was a memorable affair I had not experienced before. As I stepped up to the dedicated table identified by place cards seating twelve, and after exchanging hellos with everybody, dinner was served by a team of waiters. I cannot recall the specifics of the evening's fare, but I assure you that it was a feast fit for royalty. Service, and attention were nonstop for the following two hours from appetizers to soup, and salad followed by several selections of side dishes added to the main course, and finished up with a dessert of choice.

The voyage was expected to last ten days. The route taken after leaving the English Channel headed north past London with the Thames River to the left, with the Netherlands, Denmark, and Norway gradually passing to the right of the stern. I expected each day to be like the previous day, but that was a mistaken assumption. The first day at sea we passengers were instructed in safety procedures in case of fire, and other catastrophes. Part of it was inspecting the ship for evacuation exits, ending with a visit to the captain's bridge. Lunch followed and, in case you missed it, each deck had rows of buffet tables lined against the hallways stacked with snacks, fruits, and drinks in addition to the scheduled meals. When I asked a passing waiter about meal times, I was told the kitchen was open from 6:00 a.m. for breakfast through dinner past the midnight hours. Having been starved for much of my early life, it seemed inconceivable to me to be able to eat whenever, and whatever was served, all-inclusive with the voyage's fare, and so I ate with the slightest hunger pangs, uncertain if this food-laden paradise would last.

In keeping up my health, and my weight down, I spent many hours swimming at the indoor pool. It became obvious that after the first day, as soon as we reached the open seas, less, and less people showed up for lunch, and dinner. It did not take much to figure out, and confirm that people were getting seasick. By the third day, I was the only one left eating at the breakfast table. For lunch, two or three trickled in to make their appearances. When it was time for dinner, I was either alone or joined by a couple more diners.

"What is this?" I asked the waiter in bewilderment, watching him dish out servings for every dinner place setting.

"We serve the food regardless of who shows up," I was told. I could not help but wonder, "What happens to the leftovers?"

---

[5] 800 DM in the 60s was equivalent to $200 at a 4:1 exchange rate.

"Gets dumped overboard," was his response. Again, I could not find words for such wastefulness, and wondered what life would be like in the Promised Land. If I could have had psychic abilities, I would have seen many more surprises waiting along my journey.

After such a revelation, I cast the short phrase at the daily waiters taking the order, "What's for dinner?" I did not care what was served. It all was plentiful, and tasted delicious. After the third day, my daily routine was set. Up for breakfast, one-hour swim, strolling the decks, late morning buffet snack, catching the sea breeze up front while swaying with the waves, late lunch, afternoon swim, deck time to enjoy the vast expanse of the ocean, dinner followed with one or two bottles of beer at the bar, late night buffet snack, ending the day's culinary journey with a night of sound sleep until early morning. Entertainment as is offered on today's ocean cruises were not available on the *Berlin* since it was configured as a refugee ship. Drinks were served, nevertheless. Coming from Germany, and practically raised on beer, I had not yet developed a taste for wine or other alcoholic drinks.

Exactly as forecast, by dawn ten days later, to the relief of the sick, the world-famous Statue of Liberty grew from the horizon the closer as we came. The splendorous view appeared straight ahead of the ship's bow. When it was announced, every able body rushed to the front, craning over the rails for a closer look; otherwise the ship may have capsized if it had appeared windward or leeward. We had arrived. I had arrived at the beginning of the fulfillment of my dreams.

ARRIVING IN AMERICA

Docking was not announced until the next afternoon. It did not matter. I enjoyed every minute spent on deck, my watchful eyes darting between Liberty, Ellis, and Staten Islands, and the Manhattan skyline in the distance. I absorbed it all including the ozone given off by the sea, the blue skies above, and the busy ferry traffic in, and out of the harbor. The sight was so impressive it would stay with me for life, and draw me back to the city in the years to come. Stepping from the gangplank onto the docks brought back reality, and the reason I took the voyage. After ten days aboard the ship, the first few steps back on solid ground felt strange. I felt like an old sea hand still swaying to the imaginary motion of waves. With over one thousand passengers dislodging from the ship it took a while to locate my sponsors, who had promised to pick me up at the docks. I had landed in America on 12 May, 1961.

"You must be Anna," I joyfully announced, approaching a pleasant-looking woman in her fifties craning above the sea of arrivals, and carrying a welcoming smile on her face. I recognized her from the photo she had sent. Her husband was not far off, rather a reserved person, keeping an eye on her. I was glad for the reception. As one can attest about a first foreign journey, they have their challenges. Collecting my suitcase, we left the dock, loaded up the car, and off we went to our final destination, Philadelphia, my new home. Anna offered the passenger seat up front which I happily accepted. My first view was the lengthy Lincoln Tunnel taking us a hundred some feet below the water surface onto the mainland. The rest of the way I enjoyed the scene accompanied by lively conversations.

Anna, an immigrant herself like Rudy her husband, was only too eager to get firsthand news on the progress of their distant homeland. I illustrated as much as I could with information I had. Two hours later we arrived at their home. Stepping through the entrance, right away I noticed signs of their German heritage, with a cuckoo clock ticking from the mantel, and other European-style ornaments hanging from walls, all neatly arranged. The place, a typical two-level suburban style home including basement, attic, and fenced backyard, would be my home for the next two years, as required by immigration policy. Regardless of my success in finding work or not, my sponsors were responsible for my wellbeing.

After being served a hearty German meal I was ready for bed, and promptly fell asleep. It was not until 7:00 a.m. the next morning when I heard Anna's voice calling from below. "Time for breakfast." Unsure what to expect or what steps to take next— shower, dress, or eat—I went downstairs to the kitchen to find out what was customary. Breakfast was already dished out so I took the chair reserved for my presence. Following a short prayer, which I recognized being Catholic, my faith as well, I was instructed on the house rules, and regulations.

"Lodging, and boarding will cost you fifty dollars."

"Months?" I asked to verify.

"Yes, a month. For it I'll serve breakfast, and dinner. Lunch is at your expense."

The arrangement was acceptable once I had a job to pay for it. I realized that there were questions I should have addressed before I departed from home, but she assured me that I could pay off any dues after earning money. The next demand was not so clear.

"You will take two showers a day."

When I looked at her somewhat dumbfounded, she insisted, "No exception."

I felt that I had to explain my hesitation to her ruling. Coming from Europe, Germany was no exception to the shortcomings of hygiene as it was practiced in America. A not so clean body was as much a shortcoming as medical, dental, and grooming practices. In spite of Germany's long-standing leadership in science, and medicine, once considered pioneering in those respective fields, in actuality, personal hygiene had suffered. My time growing up in Germany, not having a standard to gauge customs against other than my visits to Italy, and France, which had similar practices, or the lack of, made taking a daily shower seem extremely wasteful. My daily cleaning routine growing up was either a quick body cleansing at the kitchen sink, sharing the same washcloth, and toothbrush with other family members, or waiting until Saturday when the bathtub heater was fired up for the weekly bath. In contrast to American living, most of the homes had no shower facility.

Any visitor to Europe in the last century, especially after riding a bus, train, or other public transportation, getting a frequent whiff of stale body odor, I am not proud to say would agree. Growing up in such an environment did not necessarily create an offensive awareness. Personal sensory receptors tend to adjust to the environment. Visiting home in Germany on several following occasions, especially during summer when local high schools were closed, I found myself headed for the lake many mornings with soap in hand, and towel draped across my shoulder to wash, and cleans off the previous day's natural body residues. On such visits I was keenly aware, but also sympathetic of the hygienic shortcomings of not having a shower stall in every home. I am certain that conditions have changed since.

After accepting Anna's house rules, the first day I went off on my job hunt. This would set my daily trend for the weeks ahead, with breakfast, a walk to the bus stop, a trip downtown to one of numerous industrial parks, knock on office doors, inquire about a job opening, get rejected each time, eat a hotdog for lunch at one of many mobile stands, continue the job search through the afternoon, return home empty handed, only to have this repeated the next day and, in the process, watch my meager savings dwindle. Though I was very optimistic, and expected to land a job within days, reality would prove otherwise. Unbeknownst to me, the economy had gone into recession during the Kennedy election year, setting off numerous union worker strikes in Philadelphia, and other East Coast industrial parks, as was explained to me by Anna.

My break came six weeks later. After knocking on metal gates all day, a worker dressed in overalls, face, and hands streaked with grease, opened the gate, demanding, "What do you want?"

"I am looking for work," I replied.

He must have detected my German accent, and responded, "Ach so." His face turned into a grin. "Ein Landsman. Komm doch mal herein." (Ah yes. Fellow Countryman. Come on in.)

I was overjoyed to hear him speak my language. "You speak German."

"I should," he said. "I am from there. Let's meet the boss."

"How so?" I was still puzzled at the unexpected invitation as I was led to an upstairs office at the far end of the manufacturing complex. Striding along the interior, I immediately recognized the environment. It was a spacious place packed with metal processing machinery each manned by a worker. The reason the place appeared so huge was because the machines in use required enormous space. It was a typical industrial building reaching from one street to the next in length, spaciously wide in similar dimension, and tall to allow space for fabricated structures, filled with the hollow sounds of hammering, shaping, and bending as metal was processed, and fabricated. There were clusters of machines I identified as lathing, honing, and shaping ones. In addition, there were boring mills for cutting, dicing, slicing, and shaping all kinds of metals. I was impressed at the sheer size of the machinery. As he strode along the hall, my lead said something puzzling that aroused my curiosity. "Everybody here speaks German."

We arrived at an office door identified by a "Visitor" sign. On entering, I was introduced to the general manager whose formidable persona, and smile would remain with me for the next five years. He listened attentively to my brief working history, which I followed up by handing him a copy of my diploma. After a quick glance at the document, he said, "How soon can you start?"

"Tomorrow," I said with a grateful grin. I had a difficult time suppressing the euphoria I felt.

"How about Monday? Seven o'clock."

I realized that the weekend was coming up. "I will be here," I assured him, and hurriedly left. I wanted to share my good fortune with Anna.

Though I did not know it at the time, I learned in the days that followed that he had been searching for a qualified operator for one specific machine nobody at the factory was willing to operate, the boring mill. Among industrial processing machines, the Cincinnati Milling Machine was considered the killer of all machines. It took a special breed of worker to operate. Nobody lasts very long without damaging eyesight, cuts on hands, or having their skin sliced from flying metal shavings. In spite of it all, I had committed myself to the monster.

I began work the following Monday. Filled with expectations, I showed up on time, falling in line by the entrance to punch the time clock. Working hours were from 7:00 AM to 5:00 p.m. with thirty minutes for a lunch break. The foreman who hired me, a German trained Meister[6] by trade, led me to my dedicated workplace. Approaching the monster machine, I momentarily hesitated. "Guess we'll have to train you on the machine," the Meister suggested, looking around the hall for a willing subject, but nobody stepped forward.

"Not necessary," I replied, to his astonishment. "It's my specialty." It was challenges such as these I needed to get up in the morning to face the day. Drudging through the day on mundane things would have been a waste of my time. I could detect some doubts in the face of the Meister since they had not been able to find anyone that could have operated the machine. It had been sitting there for close to two years in pristine condition.

To my surprise a contraption was already mounted, awaiting processing. The metallic piece, securely strapped onto the operations platform which was about four

---

[6] Meister, translated Master, was the German equivalent of the Plant Manager.

feet off the ground, was huge in itself. I was about to ask what it was when the Meister volunteered, "Nosecone."

"Nosecone for what?" I said.

"Mercury space capsule." I did not need more explanation. It being the early 60s, space exploration had just begun, and was at its height in demands on the industry. Every major industrial complex in the nation was jogging for position in the government-sponsored space endeavor. NEMCO[7] was no exception. I had found my new home. Familiar with most of the boring mill's controls, and mechanisms, I took my time to inspect the job at hand. While the piece was securely mounted onto the highly-polished steel platform, right away I faced a serious challenge. The shape, size, and composition of the piece was cast in tungsten, which, aside from diamonds, is the hardest material on earth. It was this composition presenting the challenge. The shaping tools necessary for processing the material had only recently been produced from a combination of alloy containing carbon, tungsten, and diamond fragments, molten, and heat-treated to sustain the required hardness for shaping special metals. Luckily, the proper tools were available, waiting for me at the tool shed. I was set to tackle the monster machine.

I suspected that wagers may have been placed about finding a victim willing to operate the boring mill. I felt dwarfed as I took a step towards the control panel to reach for the 'Start' button. I went to work. As soon as the tool took its first bite into the hardened metal alloy, neighboring workers, hearing the cutting sound, quit what they were doing, and gradually crept up to watch. The sound from the diamond-studded tool cutting into tungsten was eerie. The monster, sitting idle for years, had come alive. There was even applause, and cheering as the crowd gathered closer. I was dumbfounded at turning into an instant celebrity. It did not take long before the president of the plant, alerted by the sound, showed up, trailed by his office staff.

"Mike Milestone," he introduced himself. "Welcome to my place." I stopped the machine to shake his extended hand.

I was speechless, but managed to mutter, "Thank you for giving me a job." What was even more enthralling was that the owner personally stopped to speak with a common worker. It had gone quiet. Glancing around the place, I noticed that my coworkers had stopped working as well. I also detected certain envy among the gathered.

Mr. Milestone, as I addressed him properly, went on asking personal questions about my home place, training, and what had brought me here. Much of his questions were interpreted by the plant manager, the Meister.

"Adventure," I said, hoping he would understand.

"Well," he gestured at the machine with a grin on the face, "looks like you found it."

"Sure did," I said before he walked off, with the crowd slowly dispersing.

"Looks like you made a friend," the Meister said. "It's not every day the boss comes down here."

"Why me?" I asked.

---

[7] National Engineering, and Manufacturing Company, at the time was a sup-contractor to GE, the place that gave me a head start in America.

"You made his day," he explained. "Welcome aboard."

I have to mention something of importance here. In the German industrial, and business environment, a distinct hierarchy from the executive board through management levels, and down to the general worker was strictly observed. It was very much a caste system. The structure was much different in America. Here, it was more of a causal relationship, especially in more recent years, as practiced in places like Silicon Valley.

In the old country, one strictly observed the establishment protocol. For the worker, one was only allowed to interact with the next level up, his or her immediate supervisor, and the supervisor with his manager, and so on up the hierarchy. Having the president of the company, in the years to follow, not only stopping by my workplace on his weekly visits, but actually caring for my wellbeing, was something unfamiliar to me. I was sure that during his first few visits I stammered quite a bit, and mostly listened. It took nine months before I was confident enough to converse fluently, though accented, with just about anybody.

The plant Meister came by daily to check on my progress, with the president making his weekly stop to chat, mostly on Friday. He always had a ready joke on hand to share with me. Whether I completely understood the meaning, or not did not matter. It was the gesture, and courtesy he extended through his sheer presence. I would also learn his heritage. He was a Jew with a family ancestry of long persecution not only by German Nazis, but Bolsheviks, as many Ashkenazi[8] Jews endured. What impressed me most was that he did not hold a grudge against the Germans. Whereas I carried the stigma of being German open for ridicule at many a time, he seemed to have made peace with the past, and his ancestry's persecutors.

I still marvel to this day when thinking back on how humble, and grateful the man was. Mike Milestone: not only an industrial tycoon, but a true humanitarian hero.

Nosecone processing, while slicing into the metal cut after cut, was a lengthy process subjected to tool breaks, and machine mishaps. I could hear by the sound the tool made when to back off on the tool's pressure sensors. In spite of their tempered hardness, tools had to be replaced frequently so they could be sharpened. Several days later, I completed my first job. The capsule was ready for the next Mercury launch into orbit. A new piece had already been delivered, awaiting my attention, and so, in time, my position was assured as one cog in the machination wheel of the American space industry.

While there were other processing orders stacking up in my "in-bin," such as fabricating the first communication satellites, the Explorer series, among many other parts to shape, and support the nation's industrial endeavors, my mind wandered while the machine kept tearing into metal. After setting the machine's cutting parameters, I could switch the task to automatic, and dedicate my time to learning the local language. To accomplish this, I would take a copy of the previous day's Gazette my sponsor would set aside, reading column after column with a dictionary alongside. Complementing my learning progress, I soon acquired friends, and became proficient while on outings exploring nearby clubs, and other entertainment attractions. One such

---

[8] Ashkenazi Jews are Jews of Eastern European origin, mostly Russian, Polish, and Ukraine in heritage, constituting more than 80 percent of all worlds Jews.

place, I recall, was Club Gigi, the city's first topless bar, which everybody seemed to flock to. Though I was not much impressed by nude entertainment, I checked out its novelty nevertheless. Closer to my taste in entertainment, I joined a popular gathering place in town, the German social club.

What interested me more was my future, and where I was headed. While immensely grateful to my employer for giving me the opportunity, it seemed I had reached my pinnacle. With the growing demand in the country's industrial sectors, I would have been set for life. It was a sound means with a steady income, compensated by periodic pay increases for any worker, but it was not what I set out for. My ambitions were much higher. To achieve them I considered having a serious talk with my employer on his next weekly visit. But destiny beat me to it.

"Draft notice?" I yelled out, staring at the paper handed me by my sponsor. The notice was a printed card notifying me of the date on the mandatory promise I had made upon entering as an immigrant six month earlier. I had completely forgotten about the pledge. My initial reaction was panic. In no way was I prepared to be drafted into the Army. I could have accepted entering the Air Force or Navy, but it was too late for that. Once the draft notice was issued, it was a binding contract with the Army. I had made it a personal pledge that if I was forced to join a service, it would be the Air Force. Based on the pledge, I had a personal notion to become a fighter pilot, but never pursued it. Since the U.S. educational system did not honor a foreign college degree at the time, it would have meant four more years of college I was not prepared for. I was dumbfounded. What, and where one was educated should be honored in any country, but it was not the case here, not at the time. It would take many more years before a policy change would take effect to allow foreign education to become valid.

"There's got to be a way out," was my first thought. When I had entered the country, I was told about the possibility of getting drafted. My hope was that I would be passed over since my name fell towards the end of the alphabet-oriented draft procedure. Drafting was linked to a potential soldier's name, with the odds in favor of the early letters, but luck was not on my side.

"Now what?" My only option was to report to the local draft board the following month.

The next day, still shocked but informed of the recruiting policies, I marched into the Meister's office, and handed him the draft notice, expecting the worst. It became obvious by the change in his face that he had never expected such a disruption to the established, productive harmony between the firm, and their prized employee. After he placed a call to the company president, his face took on a less sinister bearing. "He'll talk with you tomorrow," I was told.

Sure enough— "Report to the office," the PA speaker said the following morning. The next hour would prove to be the most intimate I had ever faced with a superior. To start with, Mr. Milestone put me completely at ease, stating, "Don't worry about the draft. I've got the Local 123 in my back pocket."

In the following hour, to my great relief, he proceeded to reveal more secrets of his prominence. As it turned out, his brother was the local teamster boss of the Philadelphia transportation union. There was more, but I shall leave that to history. More important was the fact that I was assured freedom from being drafted. "You've got my guarantee," he promised me with a knowing grin on his face. Sure enough, two weeks later I received a deferment notice. "Due to mitigating circumstances, you are excused from reporting to the draft board."

I was euphoric, and celebrated with my buddies the same evening with several rounds of beer. The real reason for the release from the draft, I learned the following day, came with conditions attached. It came in the form of Mr. Milestone's visiting my workplace, stating, "I hear you received the deferment notice."

"Sure did," I said. "I don't know how to thank you."

"Your continued work here is enough thanks. But," he paused, seemingly gathering his thoughts. Slightly surprised, I momentarily stopped the monster machine to pay strict attention to what he had to say. A "But" was never to be ignored. Right away I sensed a feeling of unavoidable commitment which was not in my plans.

"You will have to remain in my employment for the next five years."

And there it was, the unexpected compromise, the ultimatum. What option did I have but to agree? I took a few seconds to evaluate the commitment, then shook his extended hand. "Agreed." For the time being, for better or for worse, at least I had paid him lip service. What the future had in store for me I would handle when confronted.

Brought up as a righteous person by my father, with honesty, and integrity foremost to answer life's challenges, I did not regret my promise, but took to considering alternatives to my current job obligation. What I really wanted was a meaningful career outside of an industrial environment. Again, fortune was on my side. At just about the same time, I became aware of a newly developed, highly innovative technology on the horizon, that of the computer. I had always been intrigued by electricity, and its atomic mysteries.

Having learned the English language proficiently enough in reading and writing by reading beyond the daily news, I checked further into the technology. Unfortunately, there was only sparse information available. One had to enroll in college to acquire specifics on the discipline of computer science. It did not take much deliberation to convince myself to take the necessary steps. Shortly after, I enrolled in a new institution created for technology education, annexed to Drexel University. It would be a commitment of four years, demanding much of my time. To make the schedule fit with my job, I signed up for evening classes in addition to fulltime Saturday.

Though I was honoring my promise to Mike Milestone, and the five-year commitment, because of the anticipated schedule conflict of working many hours overtime, such as past 5:00 p.m. and Saturday classes, I disclosed my ambitions to him, expecting pushback. To my surprise he congratulated me on my decision. "Just remember," he said, holding me to my promise, "your soul is mine for five years."

I realized then that even he, my employer, aside from showing nothing but kindness, had a selfish side. It did not matter. My time was numbered, not so much by the hours or days, but definitely by the years. "A few more years of hardship," I calculated. "I can handle it."

Arriving in the States in May of 1961, after being hired on at NEMCO, it was obvious why the toughest materials were needed for nosecones. Everything else would burn up on reentry. I would receive the raw cones just delivered from the foundry, machine the necessary facing for a tight fit to the reentry body, finish windows, and other openings to fit together without causing air leaks, and hurry it out of production to the next scheduled rocket launch. The pressure for an on-time delivery was always present, and because of it, I worked late many a night, as well as on Sundays.

In between processing nosecones, the next project I was handed was to build a set of satellites. It was a military project involving eight communication satellites. At that time their function, and purpose were unknown to me. I had to assume that management had more information on military activities than I did, but perhaps not. Secrecy exercised back then by the government was not much different from now. Many projects initiated by the government were classified, including some space launches. It was not until years later that I figured out the connection between the project I handled, and the Explorer series of satellites launched into orbit in 1962. The numbers matched, as well as the materials, and the configuration of the units.

Working prolific overtime was the reason why I could afford to pay cash for my first adult transportation after saving up nine months of earned wages. Relying on local trolley commute to get me to, and from work until then, I remember the joy I felt in taking possession of my first automobile in my new country at the cost of $2,400. I was the proud owner of the largest, and most sophisticated car on the marketplace I could afford, a brand-new Pontiac Bonneville convertible, a cream colored, chrome encircled vehicle of my dreams. It had every conceivable built-in convenience, including an automatic retractable top, antenna, and unidirectional seats. I was truly amazed at what the American automobile industry had to offer. The purchase, after my immigration, was the second most important element of my dreams-come-true. I was on my best way, destined for success, ready to take the next major step into the future.

Unfortunately, the vehicle did not last long. Within two years, it was destroyed. First, the vehicle was hit one night by some drunken driver while it was parked alongside the street in front of my place. Second, only days later I got T-boned on the passenger side, quickly followed by another distracted driver hitting the back of the car. To make things even worse, cold weather had broken in, accompanied with rain, during which time the convertible top was sliced open by some unknown, vindictive person. The interior leather seats, and dashboard cracked apart from rain, and sleet. Only two years old, my pride and joy became an eyesore to me, and the neighborhood. Making it even worse, due to my lack of collision insurance, none of the accidents had been fixed from people driving without an insurance. To make things worse, it seemed that I only carried liability insurance. Whether collision insurance was not available back then, or it was an oversight on my behalf, it didn't matter. I made the unhappy decision to have it junked. My replacement vehicle was another Pontiac Bonneville, but with a hard-top hoping it would last.

PHILADELPHIA

1966 exemplified the end of my educational training. It was a time when I gained a new identity, that of Alex Bauer. It was also the time my life took on an unexpected turn of events. In only a short time, after paying tribute to learning new computer, and communication subjects, my aspiration took on solid roots.

More than three years had passed of my dedicating all my time to reeducation for a potentially rewarding future when one day my software instructor asked me into his office after classes. It being close to midnight with my senses not at their sharpest. Curious about what he had to say, suspecting a pep talk on my grades or another related topic, I followed. To my surprise, it would become a revelation that ultimately would change my life, if I would make the right decision. But I am getting ahead of myself.

On entering his office, he gestured for me to take a seat across his desk. Sitting quietly, not knowing what to expect, I watched as he reached for a pad, and started to scribble something on the paper. I patiently waited for him to finish, and to speak. Anxious minutes went by before he finally looked up, handing me the pad. Holding a serious expression on his face, pencil in hand, he pointed at what appeared an organizational flowchart, saying, "This is where I want you."

Staring at the plot, unable to understand his thought process, I asked, "What's that?"

"This," he revealed in a most mystical voice, "is the structure of the Department of Defense."

I was completely at a loss. Having been in the country for close to five years, working on government projects such as space exploration, and communication satellites among others, getting educated in computer technology, I was completely taken by surprise. Not only had I never heard of a "department of defense," the notion that there might be a secret organization was beyond my comprehension. During my entire life, whether in Germany or the United States, the topic of clandestine acts, and secrecy had never come up. My ignorance must have been painted on my face.

"Okay," he said, waiting for my failure to respond. "Let me explain." Holding the pad so I could follow at the various blocks drawn on the paper, he explained, "This here," pointing at the top graph, "is the office of the Secretary of Defense. Next," indicating a series of blocks in the next level down, "the Joint Chiefs of Staff, representing the various armed services."

With him guiding me through the maze of office symbols, completely lost by now, I took his word for it while gazing at the successive levels of blocks indicating the various departments reporting upwards, illustrating segments of a military command hierarchy, space command, ground surveillance, and Intel agencies, aside from even more secretive operations such as the CIA, and the NSA. While I had heard of the Central Intelligence Agency during the failed Cuban invasion, to me it was only another political strategy at the time played out by the nation's only covert organization. Being never the wiser, I did not have the slightest inkling about the many Intelligence services laid out on the flowchart. The box my instructor had indicated was labeled, "Defense Communication Agency."

Aside from a confused stare at him, the only question I had was, "Why there?"

"It's what you are being trained for."

There was no point in delving deeper into the secrets of the nation. Checking my watch for the time, I saw it was already past midnight. He must have noticed my suppressed yawn, and offered, "Think about it, and let me know before the end of the semester."

I had heard enough for one night, and hurried home to my apartment, trying to catch some needed sleep without giving it more thought. The topic never came up again for the next six months until he confronted me just after I'd finished finals. "Have you thought about the offer?" he asked.

I had hoped he would have forgotten by now. What had transpired within the previous three months were a series of job interviews with some of the major computer manufacturers with names such as IBM, RCA, DEC, NCR, CDC, UNIVAC, General Electric, Burroughs, Westinghouse, and Honeywell. I could proudly claim that I had passed every one of the logical, mathematical, and psychological examinations, and tests presented by the various companies. But with the company that I thought the most prestigious, and desirable, and that I wished would hire me, IBM, I had flunked the exams, denying any chance for employment.

Once more I had been speechless. "How come?" I asked, questioning my failure for not passing. On further examination, the answer dawned on me the following day. While the school trained us students in advanced electronics, and computer theory, the exams provided by IBM were still geared for electrical systems employing electricians, by then outdated by years. "It's their loss," was my concluding thought, knowing that there would be opportunities with the other companies. Evaluating the various job offers over the following weeks, there were several choices I considered to satisfy my career ambitions. The first was an offer from UNIVAC with plans to send me to Germany as a regional system engineer; others were offers to various locations near, and far, located mostly in lager cities.

After the finals, my instructor confronted me once more. This time, I could not brush him off; he insisted. Reminding me of the efforts he had spent educating me— the earlier employment opportunity, the DOD—he insisted I hear him out. What else could I do? I owed him that much. Sitting in the school's cafeteria, he went into the details, and insisted, "You'll never get an opportunity like it again."

Without getting too detailed, the following was his monologue, and my brief responses.

"There is a government directive in place for foreigners like you."

"Like me? Why?"

"Ever hear of Operation Paperclip?[9]"

"Not to my knowledge," I stalled, tying to recall anything close to it.

---

[9] Operation Paperclip was the United States Office of Strategic Services (OSS), predecessor to the CIA, program in which more than 1,500 Germans, primarily scientists but also engineers, and technicians, were brought to the United States from Nazi Germany for government employment starting in 1945. One purpose of Operation Paperclip was to deny German scientific expertise, and knowledge to the Soviet Union, and the United Kingdom, as well as to inhibit post-war Germany from redeveloping its military research capabilities. Another was to hire, and place the German scientific pool, once granted highly classified access, to innovative laboratories such as Alamogordo, and Sandia to develop the atom bomb. The operation was in effect until 1973 when it was eventually terminated.

"It's an organization," he explained. "Created by the Allies at the end of World War Two to allow German scientist immigrants into the country. It permitted the government to bypass foreign immigration policies." I listened patiently, but was unclear of what he was implying. He kept on talking. "You fall into a similar category."

"Explain please."

"I wished that I could hire you directly into the DCA, but with you being foreign born, the best I can do is place you with a contractor."

There it was again, secret domain, and all that, I quietly thought. Then the light in my brain suddenly snapped on, and I questioned him, "You a recruiter?"

"That I am," was his somewhat humble response, followed with, "and an instructor."

With all of the cards dealt openly, he appeared free to talk, and talk he did. "There is a newly-created corporation, Ford Aerospace, who will offer you assignments to various countries in Europe, and in Asia."

It was the word Asia that immediately perked my interests. Since I already knew most of Soviet-free Europe, the most logical, and desirable choice would be with that company, if the offer was sincere. It would fulfill another wish of my dreams, that of the adventurer.

"But there is one hurdle to overcome," he went on.

Too good to be true, was my responding thought, as I waited quietly for him to continue.

"The job requires a top-secret clearance."

"What's that?" I said, baffled once more. The talks with him were full of mystery, getting more confusing with each session. "It's probably best I get a job with one of the other companies offers," which I had informed him of earlier.

"Not necessarily," he quickly replied, pacifying me. "There are ways for getting around."

"Well." I submitted myself into his hands. Aside from not giving me a chance to reject it, the opportunity to travel into foreign lands was too great, so I asked, "What do you need from me?" I practically watched the heavy burden he had carried for the past six months fall from his shoulders, uncertain of my acceptance.

"You've got the qualities they are looking for."

"Despite the complications?"

"As I said before," he indicated with a sincerity I had to believe, "you've got inside help."

So, the dice for my future had been cast. "I accept the offer."

The next step was to inform my current employer, Mike Milestone, of quitting my job. Not knowing his response, especially after he'd given me the chance to start a life in America, I approached him with mixed feelings, stating, "Remember your promise five years ago?"

"I've been expecting it," he said, accompanied by a sad sigh. "Where are you going?"

"DCA," I said, equally saddened.

"Defense Communication Agency?" he said, highly surprised. "It's my favorite customer." Although I had suspected a direct connection between NEMCO, and the government for some time, he had never divulged his association. I realized then how critical national defense really was. Every aspect of it was held in secrecy between partnerships, and individuals for that matter. I then told him of my decision for a career change. Though reluctant, he understood. "I knew you were only temporary," he admitted. "You are way too ambitious for working in the factory. As a matter of fact, I was going to offer you a position in management. Interested?"

"I would have accepted three months ago, but I'm already committed. We'll be working for the same cause."

"I understand," he said, bidding me goodbye. "Come back anytime if things don't work out."

"I will," I said, realizing this departure would be final.

I was free to go. I was free to face a world with challenges of undefined proportions. What I did not tell him were my inner feelings about the industrial environment, which I'd harbored ever since arriving here. I am talking about the cultural, as well as professional, attitude people held within the heavy industrial environment. Whereas in Europe, in general, potential employees were specifically trained over four years to perform a future job with pride, respect, and gratitude, here it was just another job open to anyone willing to work. Aside from the German speaking recruits, most of the new people working for me on the various projects came right off the streets without any training. It was what it was, an opportunity for the moment to make some earnings without long-term commitments, which, in turn, reflected on personal attitudes and performance. What was lacking was pride in doing the work, no matter how trivial the job may have been.

"Have a great future," were Mr. Milestone's words when we shook hands, parting forever. I still called him Mister Milestone rather than Mike, as he'd offered on past occasions. It was the training, and discipline just indicated above. I never looked back other than an occasional reminiscent thought as I sit here by the laptop writing my life's story.

"I am free," was the euphoric thought on my mind the following week while driving to accept my new job. It was a forty-minute drive from Philadelphia, the city where I lived, to the place of my new employment. But that would change as soon as I was able to locate a suitable, and affordable apartment. I knew it would only be a short-term lease until I was assigned somewhere overseas.

When I started work at NEMCO, my earning was at an hourly pay of $1.80, at the time minimum wage. Now, five years later, my pay had increased to $3. The new job at Philco-Ford would start at $3.20, minimum wage at this time. Recollecting the past five years of job advancement, and responsibilities, I believed Mr. Milestone got a great bargain when he hired me. It made me feel better. Though I'd been taken advantage due to my ignorance at the economy scale, I was still grateful for him taking a chance on me.

To begin with, I had been in the country for five years. There was one more missing element I had anxiously been waiting for. Though it should not present an obstacle since, unlike some of my German friends who got into legal troubles during the immigration period, and as a result were expelled from the U.S., I had kept my record clean. The day finally arrived where I was to be sworn in as a citizen of the United States. By now, I had already bought my second vehicle, taking the drive downtown to city hall early in the morning. Upon arriving, I was surprised to see the hall packed with immigrants waiting for the ceremony. Although everybody present would become a citizen, I could see in the faces that tensions were running high. The judge finally arrived at the scheduled time to proceed with the glorious act of granting permanent citizenship. Applause, and copious handshaking followed. There was nobody by my side to share my feeling of euphoria other than my affirmative nod accompanied by a broad smile. "I did it."

Commuter traffic outside of the city back then was nonexistent. Facing an unknown environment, I purposely let my mind roam freely. "What is my aim?" I thought, amid the hum of the engine purring beneath the hood of the car. I could not answer the question. I did not know what the future held in store for me. In contrast, I was keenly aware of what I had accomplished to date. The past was the only time I could freely let my mind wander. As a prerequisite, I never took the time to plan out the future. It was too much of an open door to explore, no matter what opportunity or inopportunity was waiting. For the most part, my mind was geared to wrestle with daily challenges. I never complained or turned the job down. These were the challenges I needed to face the day, otherwise I probably would have thrown in the towel long ago, and become a drifter.

I could not fathom a rudimentary desk job. Much like a scientist, and inventor, I needed the creativity to move forward. I was facing new challenges with every project I was handed. Today was special. I began a new journey in the land of unrestrained opportunities.

"What do I want out of life?" I thought, driving on. It was a question easily answered. "I came to America to explore, and to conquer." Well, it wasn't quite that easy. I had put in a lot of hours filled with concerns, worries, and apprehension for doing my best. As Dad had taught me, complaining, and messing up were not options.

CAREER TRANSITION

It was the end of 1966, with education, studies, and learning, part of the past. It was a time for changes, as dramatically as they would turn out. From here on, it would only be a matter of time until the beginning of a new phase in my life's journey. Fervent, and filled with expectations, I would soon learn that my dreams were put on hold for two more years while awaiting the clearance process, and the background investigation (BI) if it was approved. While I was optimistically looking ahead, there were mixed reactions from coworkers, and friends, with comments such as, "You'll never get cleared," to "wishful thinking," and, "better find another job." Receiving mostly negative input I never wavered from the original path. There were, however, two major issues that surfaced that I had to solve while my BI was in process. One was getting naturalized, and the other was committing to the contractor involved with the program I was being processed through.

The first issue presented no obstacle. It was only a matter of submitting the necessary documents, birth certificate, legal papers, and relinquishing my German passport to get naturalized. The rest was awaiting due process to take place with a final pledge of an allegiance ceremony. The entire process took six weeks after which I proudly announced to my peers, "I am now an American citizen."

I felt that celebrations in the company of friends were in order. Sadly, I had to leave my former work buddies behind, but embraced the opportunity for making new friends. Along with the career change came a new set of interests, and activities. The mentality, and mindset between blue-, and white-collar workers became clearly visible, and reflected in my attitude, aptitude, and interests. I became aware of being elevated into a new level in society, that of high tech. Regretful for the buddies I had left behind, I felt that I had come closer to my level of intellect.

The second issue proved to be more of a challenge, but was eventually solved through internal DCA[10] processing I shall expound on. Regardless of whether I would be granted the Top Secret clearance or not, I was offered an entry position with Ford Aerospace, the primary contractor holding the AUTODIN program award. To understand the political ramifications in association with my case, being foreign born, in accordance with congressional laws, I would never be permitted to be directly hired into any of the numerous Intelligence agencies. There were ten such agencies at the time. When I was informed, my heart sank to its lowest. It could mean the end of my dreams. All the training, the education, and sacrifices I made during the past four years to get into the rapidly growing computer industry was slipping from my hands. I was faced with the choice of returning to my old job or taking an offer from one of the competing computer manufacturers, which by the way were barely keeping above water with the economic recession prevailing at the time. It would take more years for

---

[10] DCA – Defense Communication Agency was one of the DOD's Intelligence agencies. In contrast to the Defense Intelligence Agency (DIA), DOD's analytical body, DCA, built the global Intel infrastructure, connecting the Pentagon with U.S. Military Command, and Control centers, U.S. Embassies, the White House, NATO, CIA, and NSA utilizing Oceanic sub-surface comm cables (Trunk Lines), later replaced, and integrated into the sky-based Satellite network.

JFK's promise of space exploration to take hold, in return benefiting the economy, and manufacturing industry.

In the process of making the selection, destiny came through, but this time in my favor. I received a call from the Ford Aerospace program director for an interview. I was only too eager to comply, and showed up at their strategic headquarters the following morning. As I drove the forty minutes from my apartment, in a residential area located near the city's renowned Thomas Jefferson University Hospital, to my destination in Willow Grove, my mind was churning with questions about how to handle the interview. From a technical perspective I would win hands down because of my credits in computer science, and extreme interest in the technology. Ford Aerospace, aside from managing a government program of epic proportions for its time, required all employees working on the program to be top secret cleared.

On arrival, a temporary ID badge was waiting at the reception desk, which I clipped to the lapel of my suit. Wearing a business suit for white collar workers in the sixties was mandatory no matter what the job was. An escort led the way along the corridors. I was surprised at being received in the executive's office.

"Come on in," I was greeted by a seemingly seasoned, command-experienced director. "We finally get to meet." I had not expected this type of greeting. It was as if he already knew me. "Coffee?" he offered. I readily accepted. Drinking coffee served at break stations, and offices seemed to be the norm here, not only in the mornings, but throughout the day. It was a new experience, but a welcoming one as well. I took to the aroma, and flavor like everybody in the industry. *Must be a government practice,* I surmised. Right away I sensed the change from my previous job environment. Here, everybody acted extremely professional, which was not the case at the numerous manufacturing environments I had left behind. I felt at home from the first moment on.

"Should I know you?" I replied, startled at his informal introduction. I already knew his name since the nameplate was prominently displayed above the office entrance: "Robert "Bob" W. – Director."

"Let me fill you in." He ushered me into his office in a friendly manner. Not having to address my personal concerns, with him taking the lead, was okay by me. "You'll report directly to me," he stated. Again, I was floored. "I understand there is a problem with your clearance," he added.

"So, everybody says," I muttered self-consciously, shrinking deeper into the chair.

"Let's not worry about it for the moment. I'll keep tracking the progress with DISCO. Nothing you can do about it. I've got a job for you regardless of how the clearance turns out."

I was dumbfounded once more. It seemed that I had been pushed ahead without having to lift a finger. He acted as if I was already hired. Awed, and overcome with wonder I had absolutely no objection to any of it, and completely submitted myself into his hands. "Ex-B-52 commander, SAC," he proudly proclaimed when I asked about the many bomber pictures framed along the office walls. It was all brand new to me, the friendly attitude, his volunteering what must have been a challenging but rewarding career, the director position presently held on a program I had absolutely no inkling about. So, patiently I waited for what appeared to be my future, being laid out with a company I knew nothing about, but I promised myself I would get informed, and up to speed.

"Guam," he said, explaining the combat pictures. "Pacific Theater. Call me Bob."

"B-52s?" I asked. It was another thing I was ignorant of. "Never heard of it." I realized that I had entered a zone only privy to the military. It was a zone, in due time, I would become intimately involved. But that was still years ahead. "For now," Bob W. said without hesitation, "you'll be an instructor until your clearance comes through."

"What subject am I teaching?" There was no end to the unfolding marvel.

"Basic electronics, and computer theory. Mainframes."

There it was in plain facts, my entrance into the wonders of electronics, circuits boards, and computers. I felt euphoric leaving his office. "Monday morning," he said with a hearty handshake. "Office hours are eight to five, one-hour lunch break. Hope to see you."

"I'll be there," I promised without reservations. "Thank you." That was it. I was hired without having to sell myself. It was the second break I had had in the new world. With my spirits at a peak, it seemed I was moving in the right direction. Destiny was on my side. I had several days to prepare for the job. But prepare what? The only thing I could bring to the table was my scholastic knowledge, and my verbal skills which, by the way, had improved over the last five years. But when it came to my inherited German accent, I had not been able to shake it, though I had not put much effort into doing so. I learned from experience that when it came to accents, and slang the credo was, "You either loved it or hated it." Whether openly or concealed, people will let you know up front. It's either "Love your accent," or prevailing silence. In the end, it did not matter. People match up based on chemistry.

WILLOW GROVE, PA

Anxious to learn about the job, and project, I arrived at the work place ahead of time. My wrist watch indicated 8:00 am. It was the first time in my life I did not have to punch in on the time clock. Dressed impeccably in suit and tie, I was ready to tackle the world. While waiting for management to arrive, seated in the lobby, I took the time to check my current space. "So," I muttered into the quiet. "This' how white color workers live. What a contrast," I thought, slightly euphoric at the very thought, interrupted only by an occasional swishing sound from the entrance doors, whenever someone entered the building. Minutes later, I recognized the face on approach through the door glass. It was Bob W. Stately, assertive, prominence figure deserving his position, he headed directly in my direction when he spotted me, "Got here early, did you," he said, beaming at me.

"Work used to start at 7:00 am," I said.

"Ah, yes. Manufacturing. Office hours here start at 9:00 am. It's when the students arrive. Follow me." I promptly followed his lengthy strides to his office. "Have a seat," he directed. "Want coffee?"

"No thanks. Already had my cup."

"One thing you'll learn here," he indicated with a grin at the percolator, "how to drink coffee. But first things first." He paused, apparently with something on the mind. "I have good news and bad news for you."

I could feel my heart leap a few beats at the unexpected turn of events. *Maybe the job was too good to be true,* went through my mind while quietly waiting for him to tell. "The bad news is you won't be teaching."

"Ever?"

"Only temporary. Let me explain." After a brief moment he continued, "I was informed by DISCO that you need a Secret clearance first. It's government requirements. Without it, you won't be able to be an instructor. Here is the situation. You need Secret before you can touch the equipment. You need Top Secret to be involved with the software. You have neither. But rest assure, I have plenty of other jobs for you."

I saw the career, I so desperately wanted, slip away. "How long will it take?"

"To get Secret? Nine months."

I was devastated. My mind was already in the Far Eastern regions with its mysteries waiting for me to explore. My face must have reflected the desperation when he said, "Only nine months. It'll go by fast. Trust me. Besides, I need you for a more important job."

Now that was something I didn't mind, but what could be more important than exploring the world?

"I'll assign another engineer to you. You both will be working from downtown, our manufacturing facility. It's night shift, but only for a month."

Well, I quietly thought, *it's not too bad,* but said, "What's the project?"

He then explained what it entailed. Apparently, the company, Philco Ford, had just recently installed computer systems in certain school districts in Philadelphia. It's a pilot project for the educational system never implemented before. What it entailed was computerizing education, the entire process from curriculums to reports, tests, and final exams. The program had already been in operation for several months, but proved problematic right from the onset. The program, project GROW, stood for the City's major high school districts, Germantown, Roosevelt, Overbrook, and Wannamaker schools. "The problem is," Bob W. explained. "Grades averages have fallen from the 40s to the 30s ever since."

"You mean student grades?"

"Yes. Student grades."

"Nobody is passing exams?" I was stunned. Not so much at the new system, as to the grade averages prior he just mentioned. "What's going on?" It took a minimum score of 70 to pass tests. But 40s?

"It's what we need to find out," he said. "Not only scores, but the system gets broke all the time. It's up to you guys to find out what the real problem is."

I met up with the other engineer the same evening at the designated location, the first school location. The night custodian led us to the various classrooms, delineating our workplace for the evening, to be repeated the following nights with the other schools. From here on, it became our nightly routine to fix problems the students caused during the daytime. Right away the problem became obvious. "What do you think," I said, expressing my concerns.

"Sabotage?"

"I think so too." It'd turned out that some students purposely damaged keyboards, monitors, and printers. The following week, we reported our findings to HQs management who, in turn, directed us to keep fixing the damages. We followed our nightly routine until called into the office some weeks later.

"This is what we need to do," Bob W. informed us. "The two of you will monitor classroom activities for the next few weeks to get to the source of the problem."

"You mean," I said, somewhat surprised. "Sit in with the students?"

"We installed one-way mirrors between classrooms and offices. You'll cover each class, but only to observe. I don't want any of you to get involved. That's up for me and school administration. You report to me only. Is that understood?"

"Understood." We left to face the boredom of classes for the following morning. As we already had expected, the students, high school graders, were separated into three distinct groups. There were the diligent students trying to get educated, not only with the computers, but the subjects taught as well with tasks ranging from arithmetic to biology, language, science, and more. They came in with the passing scores. What brought the average down were the other two groups with one specifically leading. Their strategy, we observed, was to interrupt everybody else from completing the self-paced curriculums, with some shorting out power supplies, manipulated in the back of monitors using knives, while others used pencils to hammer down on the keys until they snapped off. Where their strategy called for pacing through the course as quickly as possible time allowed with the rest of the sessions spent goofing off by playing all sorts of games and personal tricks, with ensuing secondary resultant damages to the equipment.

We reported our results to HQs, who in turn informed principle school administrations. What made the whole thing pathetic, none of the teachers complained during the entire time. They just sat through each class reading paperbacks. I would learn later that they had been instructed to distance themselves from reprimanding and disciplining students. It was a critical time, sensitive to racial conflicts the country was facing. Unfortunately, the issues could not be resolved. At the end, four years later, the computer systems were removed from teaching with only one lesson learned: self-paced computer learning was ahead of its times. It would take another twenty years before the next attempt was made, but this time it met with success.

Four weeks had passed since we started the project when Bob W. recalled and terminated our project GROW support. It was decided that routine computer technicians could handle repairs rather than using us higher paid engineers. "I've got another job for you guys," he happily announced the next morning. As it'd turned out, we joined a team getting ready to deliver a new cluster of computers around the country. Performing final test and analyses on a newly manufactured computer system, the PDP-8, built by Digital Equipment Corporation (DEC), first generation Mini-computers, was destined for the country's eight major cities from New York to Chicago and other East Coast regions, on to San Francisco and Los Angeles. What it entailed was computerizing the nation's postal system to automatically read mailing addresses, sorted by size and destination, to be routed and delivered to their final destination.

Since it was another pioneering project, again, we faced challenges, but this time only from mechanical failures. It seemed, while computers functioned as designed, frequent mechanical failure plagued the system. Once the mechanical issues were solved, as it'd turned out, the system would prove highly successful. After multiple technological integrations and improvements, the system is still in operation to this day, but greatly improved in reading speed and accuracy.

The day finally arrived when I was called into Bob W.'s office once more. I arrived at the work place as promised. At the admin office, I was handed paperwork to fill out, documents to sign, and report to the reception station to have my photograph taken for the picture ID. Two hours later I was set, and ready for work. "Trailer 12," I was directed. Stepping outside, I headed straight for the trailer park located across the sizable parking lot. At the far end was a cluster of trailers arranged much like a tactical command center, interconnected with wiring, cabling, and antennas, but here it housed a dozen temporary classrooms set up to process, and educate hundreds of newly-recruited technicians, and apprentice prospects into a program nobody knew anything about. Stepping up to the desk holding piles of neatly arranged books in a room filled with lively chatting students, I wrote my name on the blackboard.

"I'm your designated instructor for the next three months," I declared. It was the timeframe allocated for a crash course in basic electronics, and computer theory to be forced into the heads of the students. It would not be sufficient time to learn about computers, communication equipment, software, circuitry, and programming, but it was the time allocated for one of the most pressing, and time sensitive government programs conceived after the creation of the atom bomb. Being one of a dozen instructors, in hindsight, I can attest that we did our share in fulfilling contract obligations that were delivered in time, and on budget. When it came to government expectations, the allocated timeframe, and bottom line were the two most important factors to success. It was the contractor score card for winning successive project awards.

From here on out, instructing the student body proceeded at the scheduled pace, rapidly. With the backlog of newly hired there was no time to individually evaluate everyone's aptitude, and skills beforehand. I made the decision during their allocated semester. What was important was to get each student qualified, and certified for the field. By this time, already four years into manufacturing hardware, building computer equipment, and developing the operating system, the push was on for upcoming system deployments to overseas locations.

All I will state about the two-year teaching period was that it was hectic, and demanding to have the student body rotating in, and out every three months. To compensate for theoretical teaching at the classroom, it was just as important to get hands-on training on the equipment. This was what I mainly provided. Working the nightshift for the most part, my students, and I had the complex, a replica site of mainframes, switching gears, and associated storage, and peripheral equipment to ourselves. I did my share in cranking out newly-instructed students assigned to the various positions, and locations overseas in Europe, and Asia, as well as Hawaii, Guam, and all of the Pacific Rim nations, and islands. In complement, there was a parallel program implemented for processing the students as well. It was for the CONUS[11] arena. The program called for fifteen secret strategic locations dispersed around the globe, but it also called for an equal complement within our own borders between the Atlantic, and Pacific coasts, ranging from the Arctic Circle up north to the Mexican border to the south.

Aside from remote monitoring outposts in Australia, Diego Garcia, Turkey, and more obscure places, it assured global surveillance coverage for U.S. military, and Intelligence, an important aspect for the country's national defense posture, and security awareness. Unfortunately, national defense, to be effective, comes with a high taxpayer price tag, causing unavoidable controversy among the citizens in today's educated societies. Where a strong military presence used to be sufficient as a deterrent, today, it is not enough to keep terrorist attackers at bay. From all indications, the modern terrorist, some with a mentality for self-destruction, seems to welcome the opportunity for personal sacrifice to the ravages of war. For the sake of Islam, one can only hope that the Almighty will appreciate the many sacrifices on His behalf.

Up to this state in my life, authoring, and assessing past historical accounts was pretty much an individual choice driven by two ambitious goals, satisfying my adventurous spirit, and enjoying eventual successes in my career, and personal life. I considered both desires to be of equal importance since they were interdependent for my ambitious notions, as well as my personal quest in gaining a wholesome knowledge on the world, its people, and the intrinsically colorful diversities in customs, and cultures. There was nothing extraordinary with my persona, habit, and lifestyle. I am one of eight billion individuals fitted into today's society populated by every conceivable color, creed, belief, and desire to strive for success, or at least a better life.

---

[11] CONUS – Military abbreviation for "Continental U.S." meaning "American Continent."

Fame and fortune did not play a role in the goals I had set. Like many, I took life day by day as it was presented, driven mostly by my newly-acquired career change. I considered it a career for gaining new skills, and knowledge. What I did not expect was the personal recognition that came with it. It was this recognition that would eventually transform my future identity. But I am jumping ahead of myself again. First, I will explain the basic reasons for the transformation.

Teaching a new technology, as computer science and communication theory was, proved to be fun, sharing my acquired knowledge with my students. Most took to it with the enthusiasm I had experienced when I was taught in college, but with one difference. I taught it for a specific purpose and application, an opportunity providing the creation of a future career for anyone inclined to follow. It was not just for a job one could acquire. It was for a program unknown to the general public, and in many cases, not well known to the government and military, which had not been indoctrinated. It was for a highly secure program conceived by John F. Kennedy, and his secretary of defense elect, Robert S. McNamara administrations, AUTODIN. [12]

Whereas Western Union, the primary contractor for CONUS, was already well into building AUTODIN centers across the country, deployment to overseas locations was still pending facility construction completion managed by overseas construction firms within each foreign country. The first Philco-Ford (to become Ford Aerospace) built system was scheduled for deployment the following spring to a secluded, joint U.S. and Royal Air Force-operated AFB in England. The next location on the schedule was Germany, followed with Italy, with a dozen more sites located in Asia, and other continents.

With world politics constantly changing, long-term projects involving other nations needed to be fluid for the deployment. Over time, some countries were added to the list while others were relocated or removed. One example was the war escalation

---

[12] AUTODIN was the program acronym for Automatic Digital Network, at the time, aside from nuclear weapons development, deemed the highest classified program designed, and conceived by DARPA, and the U.S. Department of Defense. The reasons for such high classification was to protect national assets against adversary powers with ill intended purposes for the wellbeing of the citizens of the United States of America. Conceived in 1962 by then president JFK, and Secretary of Defense Robert S. McNamara, it was designed as a survivable communications grid in case of an all-out nuclear attack by the Soviet Union. To assure its intentioned design, dozens of communications, and command centers were built in strategic locations around the globe, and within CONUS.

Robert S. McNamara, after graduating from the University of California, Berkeley, in 1937, earned a graduate degree at the Harvard Business School, and later joined the Harvard faculty. Disqualified from combat duty during World War II by poor vision, he developed logistical systems for bomber raids, and statistical systems for monitoring troops, and supplies.

After the war, McNamara was one of the "Whiz Kids" hired to revitalize the Ford Motor Company. His plans, including the implementation of strict cost-accounting methods, and the development of both compact, and luxury models, met with success, and McNamara rose rapidly in the corporate ranks. In 1960, he became the first person outside the Ford family to assume presidency of the company.

After just one month as Ford's president, however, McNamara resigned to join the John F. Kennedy administration as Secretary of Defense. In his new post he successfully gained control of Pentagon operations, and the military bureaucracy, encouraged the modernization of the Armed Forces, restructured budget procedures, and cut costs by refusing to spend money on what he believed were unnecessary or obsolete weapons systems. McNamara was also at the center of a drive to alter U.S. military strategy from the "massive retaliation" of the Eisenhower years to a "flexible response," emphasizing counterinsurgency techniques, and second-strike nuclear-missile capability.

in Vietnam which took priority with two AUTODIN installations ahead of the schedule. These were the locations immediately following the acceptance testing at Croughton AFB, England. The Department of Defense, U.S. military, and Intel organizations were extremely anxious for the test results. It was to be the first ever email generated by mankind. A success it was. The first test message (email) was a "Hello" message sent from England to the Pentagon in April 1967. It was the beginning of a new era in communication that would eventually explode into a spider-like web over the entire globe. But the commercial world was not ready for that. It would take another twenty-five years to achieve that after four major elements came together. In the early 90s the world was ready after Intel manufactured the microchip, IBM built the first commercial PC, Microsoft developed Windows 95, and DARPA provided the TCP/IP network protocol.

Back in the classroom, I was teaching the fundamental elements describing design, development, manufacturing, testing, the number of people involved in manufacturing, installation, and built led by scientists, engineers, technicians, operations, support, management, and the very purpose of AUTODIN.

"What's AUTODIN?" was always the first question fired at me at the start of each new class.

"How many of you have been cleared for a need-to-know?" I would ask. All hands went up. It was enough assurance to proceed. After all, it was not my responsibility to lead the students through the gateway to national defense secrets. It was DISCO's, the respective military services', and Intel's responsibilities.

"Okay then," I would reply. "Since we know now the program you were drafted for, or selected by choice, let's go on with the material. Please refrain from interrupting with questions. Ours is a fast-paced curriculum, and we have a lot of ground to cover. I assure you that I will answer each, and every question you may have at the end of the sessions."

In its fundamental principles, the program blueprint was conceived in 1962 by the DOD, designed, and developed by DARPA's engineering pool in Reston, VA, over the next four years, manufactured at Ford's Manufacturing Plant 55, Philadelphia, PA, with preliminary testing conducted at the PPM (Pilot Production Model), Willow Grove, PA, in conjunction with the Army's signal school at Ft. Monmouth, NJ, principle test facility to ready the system for world deployment.

The original "Survivable Communication System," and extended AUTODIN systems located at the various stateside, and overseas locations were under the management, and operational control of DCA (Defense Communication Agency). It provided the DOD with a worldwide, highly efficient, computer-controlled system to meet the ever-increasing demand for faster, and more accurate communications. In 1972, the Defense Special Security Communications System (DSSCS) was integrated into AUTODIN to provide communications support for the Intelligence community of the DOD. After the DSSCS integration, the National Security Agency, in conjunction with NATO, commissioned and operated the European site at Augsburg, Germany.

In its operational principles, each site was a store, and forward message switching center providing critical, immediate, time-sensitive information, as well as routine messages, to other communication centers, DOD, and its subscribers, overseas embassies, military bases, Intel centers, and CIA outposts around the globe.

In between the fundamental, and operational principle a new era was born, the staging for the age of information technology, the high-tech industry. There was much to teach from basic binary to the sophistication of the OSI stack, from digital designs to software applications, from hardware, and network protocols to systems language, from circuit boards to operating panels, from computer management to Comm, Comsec, and Crypto technologies, from shift supervisor to site manager, from logistics support to customer liaison, and, most important of all, for contracting personal to effectively interact, and coexist with the customer, in this case the government, and military services.

It had taken an army of engineers, technicians, ops personnel, logistics, and management to implement the program with an initial budget slated, and appropriated at $50 million. That would eventually escalate to a final price tag in excess of $125 million over thirty years when the program was released to the public. At the time, it may have sounded like a lot of money, but in the end, it proved to be worth it, considering the impact the Internet had on the world not only from a survivable perspective, but for social implication as well.

AUTODIN, as the program was originally labeled, underwent numerous identity iterations, technological upgrades, and functional enhancements before being turned over to the public as it is known today, the Internet, a scalable network that has taken on its own life. Whether the invention was a good thing or not, time will be the judge. For now, it is an invaluable tool benefiting mankind in a fast-paced, public demand-driven world. But, as is the case with many innovations, it serves both factions in a world of behavior, and conduct, the good, and the bad, the benevolent, and malevolent, the criminal, and hacker.

Those were the essential functions for the instructor to instill onto the students who would be selectively assigned according to their skills to their respective positions, and site locations. As far as my teaching experience went, there were no dropouts. Although individual challenges were pervasive, all-encompassing, and energy absorbing to say the least, each student was trained to become one individual part in the complex of an information system the world had never before seen.

TRANSITION PERIOD

The 60s was also a time when the whole nation underwent changes—traumatic changes. They were changes such as the civil rights, women's liberation movements, fights for equality, civil protests against many issues, and the dismantling of the establishment. I, as well as many others had a difficult time adapting, and adopting. It was also the time when my transformation was taking place from the author to that of the "Invisible Warrior." It was not a sudden change. It was a change that came on gradually over a period of several months, affecting my personal identity, as well as my behavior, and lifestyle. Being absorbed into a highly classified system, for better or for worse, reflected on a person's identity.

Where previously, an individual may have been free-spirited, free thinking, and independent, now that same individual had to live by strictly-enforced rules. Every action, decision, and choice became a judgment call, consciously at first, but eventually turning into subconscious action. It was a call where national security became the most important aspect in one's life. It affected not only the time while on the job; it dictated the individual's social activity, friendship circle, discussion topics, and personal judgment calls. In short, each action became a topical subject that could compromise the acquired career position. In a way, if one wanted to maintain a sound status within the Intel-affiliated organization, the constraints helped develop a strong, and disciplined character. Every decision became the basis for the following ruling: Abstinence from gambling, drinking, and sexual inclination, three major factors for compromising not only the project, but its community members as well. The results became clearly noticeable. People thought first before they spoke or acted. It only took a slip of the tongue for the individual to be immediately escorted from the secured premises, and banned from the program forever. The chances of getting another job within the Intel community became impossible. I personally experienced inadvertent compromises on several occasions where one minute an employee would be working alongside, and the next minute he was escorted out without being seen, or heard of again. Big Brother was always watching and listening. An occasion like this always left a lasting impression not easily forgotten.

The question then becomes, is it all worth it—the restriction, the dedication, the devotion, or is the impact on personal life too great to handle?

The answer was irrevocably the same: "There better be a God." The resultant choices, regardless of personal sacrifices, were always the same. Nobody ever quit.

It was the time the Invisible Warrior fully emerged.

DEFENSE PROJECTS

Beginning with 1966, after its four-year design, and developing phase, I was assigned to become a team member with the AUTODIN program. With the program's development phase at an end, the next, and immediate stage was training, and deployment to specific overseas locations. Assigned locations at the time were based on trouble spots in which the U.S. military was involved. With the Cold War escalating after the Cuban missile crisis, the U.S. government-staged medium range, nuclear-tipped missiles to Europe, England, Germany, and Italy became our eastern defense perimeter. It was here where survivable communication became most important. These were the sites where first ASC[13] were deployed.

Because of the political tensions prevalent across the globe involving the Soviet Union, Cuba, and Vietnam, the world watched unrestrained space launches initiated in the 60s by JFK, without having knowledge of AUTODIN, and its classified nature. That was how tightly security was enforced. Any compromise would have had dire consequences for the individual. However, there were occasional internal security breaches, though they were not through intentional or malicious behavior. It was mostly through a slight mistake carried by an inadvertent slip of the tongue, revealing a classified word, or program parameter. Despite being a miniscule, and innocent act by the individual, the information could have easily been picked up by an adversary Intelligence agency to the disadvantage of U.S. Intel status on foreign policies.

To get the idea, I will cite one example of a security breach. During the installation process at the NATO Intel site in 1972, near Augsburg, Germany, just prior to taking procession of the facility, during a final security sweep on the building more than seventy listening bugs, Russian in nature, were found implanted into walls, and ceilings during the construction of the building. The resultant dilemma was clear: should the incident be made public, or should it be suppressed? If revealed, the implications could escalate, and even become hostile with accusations thrown at each other, endangering an already tense political climate. It was these conditions pressing on national Intelligence issues instigated from both sides.

All in all, thirty AUTODIN communication centers were built in three construction styles: underground to protect against foreign Intelligence intrusions, partially underground with management floor above ground, and tactical centers above ground in conflict, and war zones, with each serving its special purposes. Structure type one, underground, was a heavily-fortified, and shielded strategic center providing maximum protection against EMP strike, nuclear attack, and intelligent leaks from within COMM activities, and classified information processing.

———————————————

[13] ASC is the acronym for Automatic Switching Center, the label designated for one complete AUTODIN system deployment. Each site entailed a number of departments ranging from the computer section to comm, comsec, tech-control, crypto, UPS, logistics, and management facilities. Many of the technologies, classified as they were, were housed below ground, but management, and support functions were generally located above ground for ease of access for visiting dignitaries, which were frequent.

Structure type two, partially underground, was similar in construction, and protection, but only to COMM, and COMSEC sections, while operations, and command personnel were situated above ground for convenience of access.

Structure type three, above ground, was protected against Intelligence leaks, spying, and compromises, but not against EMP pulsing. The reason was tactical orientation for a quick abandonment of the site in case of an enemy overrun, and takeover in a war zone. A typical example was the 1975 U.S. battle defeat by North Vietnam where highly classified materials had to be quickly destroyed from computer, and communication equipment, hardware, software, memory, and storage devices, an incineration process by strategically placed thermal bombs. No worthwhile information, and data were left to the North Vietnamese takeover other than the vacated facility with melted-down computer, and COMM equipment.

Security was tight from the onset of system deployment. It increased even more during actual operations. To gain access to an operational facility, without exception, everybody was subjected to strict security scrutiny. A top secret clearance was required, processed by the respective organization. If the site was operated, and managed by the Department of the Navy, it was Naval Intel handling the process. The same departmentalized process was followed by the Air Force, Army, Marine, and NATO Intelligence. Where the isolation may have improved security with responsibilities placed on the respective services, it was a duplicated effort, nevertheless. Aside from the cost factor, due to the uncooperative nature between different organizations, at times this hindered personal background investigations, and individual surveillance. Cost, and effort set aside, the result was a security barrier that was never breached in the lifespan of AUTODIN.

IDENTITY TRANSITION

The following year, 1967, more than one year had passed since I was hired on with the AUTODIN program. Students came, and went. The first lot had already been dispatched, and had taken up positions at the European, and Asian theaters while I still remained at the training center. I became more envious of my colleagues as the months went by. "Take care," I would bid the departing people goodbye when another crew left for overseas. "Wish I was going." Tensions ran high amid the students ready to face the world. I could see anticipation painted across dozens of faces getting ready for departure. "See you there" and "hope to see you soon" some responded on the way out. I always felt despondent when one class finished up, and left. Though it was only a temporary feeling until I became part of a new student body arriving for the next training class.

I felt the chill of another winter on approach. Being November, it had turned cold. I would face another winter in Willow Grove. What used to be a quiet residential town at the outskirts of Philadelphia, had turned into a busy place with town's people wondering about the sudden influx of young, and energized male arriving weekly taking over every available apartment and room for rent. Then just as mysteriously, they would depart three to six months later without a promise ever to return. Aside baffled girlfriends left behind, most townspeople did not question the migration as long as they paid their rent for the somewhat inflated lodging rates.

I had just started a new class when my name was announced on the intercom. "I'll be right back," I assured the students. Checking in with the department secretary, "He wants to see you," she said with a gesture at the director's office.

Anticipating another complaint from a student, as was the usual case, I stepped into his office sour faced. "How's it going?" he said, chewing on a cigar while avoiding my stare. "I hear you're doing excellent work in training. I thought about bringing you in with the engineering staff. Interested?" It was when he looked up to judge my reaction.

"You know what I want, dammit," I angrily responded, like several times before. "I want to be on the frontlines." Though Bob W. was considered God within the executive office, we had developed a special working relationship. It may have been my job skills, or personal openness, or both that formed our mutual respect for each other. As for me, considering his military career, Major General in rank, I always adored the man. All I had to do was imagine him seated behind the controls of the B-17 flying fortress bomber, soaring into enemy territory to deliver yet another bomb load in the name of democracy.

"Think about it," he said. "You'd be part of my staff. It's not every day I extend such an offer. With you out there in the field, I can't guarantee a position when you come back."

"I appreciate the offer, and understand your generosity, but I'm not cut out for an office job. My mind is on foreign territory, you know it."

He knew quite well of my interviews, and offers from the other computer manufacturing companies. I had offers from UNIVAC, RCA, NCR, HP, DEC, CDC, and a few more when I accepted the offer with Philco-Ford. He knew what attracted me to the job. It was the opportunity to travel overseas, to explore the world. It was my dream, and I could not afford to let it being shattered. We used to talk about it frequently with him telling me stories from his assignments with the Air Force as B-52 bomber pilot stationed in the Pacific—Guam, specifically.

"So, you say." He got out of the chair, picked up an opened envelope from the desk, and deliberately advanced in my direction with an outstretched hand stating, "Then today is your lucky day." He paused while I stared with awe at the notification addressed from the DISCO office.

"You mean…? I did not finish.

"Yes," he beamed. "Your clearance was granted."

I grabbed his hand with the most heart filled "Thank you" I could muster up. Despite the chance for losing me as a staff member his face lit up at my gratitude. "The world is yours," he said accompanied with a grin. "I felt the same way when I took command on the B-52."

With a Top-Secret certificate in my hand, I could wait no longer, "What's next?"

"I have a position open as field engineer, I can have you assigned to."

My heart skipped several beats while my mind was silently racing with euphoria. *Finally,* I thought, after years of anticipation, and waiting. "Where am I going?"

"Guam."

"Guam," I yelled out in disgust. "You can't do that. Not after what you've said about the place."

"Guam," he'd explained on earlier occasions, "is a rock. There's nothing there. It's an island in the middle of nowhere. There's nothing to do unless you're into playing golf." Now, in presenting this offer, he was hoping I would be discouraged from leaving.

"It's the only choice you've got. There's nothing else available." I knew right away he was lying because the company had a difficult time manning the overseas ASCs[14] quick enough to go operational at the scheduled dates. His body language confirmed my suspicion. Trying to avoid my stare, he squirmed in his seat. I demanded more. I had my heart set on the Philippines, Japan, even Vietnam, a conflict that had escalated into a full-fledged war by 1968.

"I'll quit," I said, and turned to exit.

"Wait," he called out. "Don't be so hasty. I'll make you a deal." I stopped, and turned to face him, waiting for how he'd get out of the trap. "You go there for the testing. It's only three months. After that, I promise you any assignment you want."

"Promise?" At least there was hope. Should I believe him. Regardless, it only took me seconds to decide. "Okay. I'll take it. But I'll hold you to the promise. When do I leave?"

"As soon as you can pack."

I knew the schedule well. I also knew that he had been trying to staff Guam as demanded by contract, but had a difficult time filling positions. I was not the only one that objected to an assignment there. From what I'd heard in the past year, everybody had the same idea: "Guam? Not me." Site acceptance testing was to commence right after the upcoming holidays. There had been already several delays with the opening

---

[14] Automatic Switching Center, the secure Intel facility housing AUTODIN.

of the site. First, there was Typhoon Agnes sweeping across the island in August, months earlier, leveling ninety percent of the island's housing. Then, with the holidays coming up, it was difficult for the company to find willing subjects to travel. Everybody wanted to spend Christmas, and the New Year with families back home. Bob knew I was single, and unattached. I was the innocent mark he had been looking for. I accepted with a silent mutter. *What's another three months?*

"Who else is on the team?"

"The site manager."

"That's it? Only the two of us?" It seemed incredible because the contract called for fifteen engineers, and technicians just for the testing phase alone. The full staffing would be ramped up to forty following site-acceptance on March 15th, the time the site would go operational. It gave me less than three months to prepare the system without additional help. I realized right away that I had fallen into Bob's trap. The normal debugging, repair, and testing timeframe allocated was six months.

"Don't worry," he said, sensing my hesitation, "the rest will be there after the holidays."

I knew right away that I would have to hustle day and night to get the site ready. But it was the opportunity I had been waiting for.

"Stop by before you leave."

I scrambled for the exit before he could change his mind, or something else came up to prevent me from leaving. It was not that I was ungrateful to even be employed here, or to have the opportunity to be an instructor on the world's most sophisticated computer system, the latest design in mainframes, the Philco Ford-built model-102, a modified series 2002 system, the defense monster running at the NORAD Mountain. The Model-102 had a more innovative design for the central processing system than competitive manufacturers. To begin with, the internal adder registers were of predictive design. To understand the function of the adder, take two binary input numbers the size of its internal registers (48 numbers in length), add both numbers and, depending on progression, hand off the results to the next processing stage. What made it unique was that the adder would read, process, and provide the result based on their logical input before the numbers were even computed through the registers, greatly impacting speed, and performance.

Another innovation was the means by which data, and information were transmitted across the ether. Where IBM, the leader in the industry, was communicating over Token Ring network topology, the other manufactured mainframe computers were connected via Star, Bus, Ring, or Mesh network topologies, transmitting data, and information in standard serial fashion. The 102 processor had a different approach. Its design permitted simultaneous parallel transmission based on a new design concept, a time-slice scanner. Each data segment, and information stream was dissected into one binary bit (alpha-numeric character) at a time, sent out to one subscriber channel within one time-slice element, ready to release another data bit to the next subscriber line 250 times (number of subscribers), providing uninterrupted streams of data and information to all destinations simultaneously. The concept may be too complicated to readily understand for the novice reader, but I assure you that the transmission speed was 250 times faster than its competitors. It was MIT, in conjunction with DARPA scientists that came up with this unique approach.

Being in a teaching capacity, I had obtained first-hand knowledge, and involvement into all aspects of leading-edge designs, and technology. The opportunity alone brought me to the forefront of knowledge, and skills in the area.

It took no time at all to find someone from the student body to take over my apartment lease while I was cleaning up my local affairs. The only things left were getting my travel orders authorized by headquarters, picking up traveler's checks issued by accounting, booking the flight, and packing two suitcases, and I was ready. I took the first available Pan Am flight destined for Guam. I still could not believe the good fortune, being on my first leg to adventure. It was how I had looked at the future. I knew that it had to be job or career related for such a lifestyle. I could not, and probably would have never been able to afford it on my own.

Seated in the comfort of business class travel in the Boeing 707, I realized then and there that the third milestone of my ambitious plans had materialized. With seatbelt sign just turned off, after being served a martini, I succumbed to the feel of heightened anticipation. It would be a long flight from Philadelphia to Guam, with refueling stops at Hawaii, and Wake Island. I did not care how long the flight would take. I was happy just being in the air with dinner served amid a couple more martinis. Stopovers were brief, only long enough to refuel, and take on additional passengers. I must have dozed off when "Fasten seatbelts," from the speaker sound seeped into my brain sixteen hours later, "we are getting ready for landing."

I had been dreaming. It was a repeating dream, played out in color of foreign lands, and cultures I had envisioned many times in the past. It was wheels touching the runway that jolted me from dream. The landing was announced by the stewardess: "Don't forget your belongings." I reached for my briefcase, headed for the exit, and with my first step on the ramp felt like I was being hit in the face by a board. It was the first time in my life I had been exposed to tropical heat. "Wow," I recall my first spoken words on Guam, U.S. Territory to Micronesia, central Pacific region. "Is it ever hot."

Considering where I was born, and grew up, hot was an understatement. Still shaky-legged after the long flight, I carefully made it down the mobile ramp. I checked the airport over; it was ground level only, with insufficient space for the recent growth in airline travel. Ever since the war escalation in Vietnam, travel to Asia with a brief stopover on Guam had seen tremendous increases. It would not take long thereafter for island contractors to build a new airport. However, it would be an airy terminal for some time to come, with arrivals subjected to the torrential rains prevalent to the region. Islanders had learned how devastating the annual typhoons could be to construction, and dwellings. It would take another decade or more to see modern construction flourish on the island, primarily funded by Japanese entrepreneurs.

PACIFIC RIM - GUAM

Stepping on solid ground, after a twelve-hour flight, to my surprise, I felt light headed not only in my mind, but in body as well. I did not feel my full 150 lb. living weight on the ground. It was exhilarating from the highpoint of the island's airport to see into the blue ocean in the distant horizon fading in with the blue sky above. I stood there in the midst of exiting passengers anxiously headed for the airport to depart while bumping into me. From the height of the airport location I took in the spectacular view. I could easily make out the crested swells breaking on the shores. I could even see a couple of towns in the distance hugging the shoreline. "How beautiful."

"Tamuning Bay," a person nearby pointed in the appropriate direction. "Rainy season just ended." A stewardess, as flight attendants were addressed back then, stopped to ask, "Where're you staying?" Slightly puzzled, though we had a couple of brief chats while in flight, I stopped to look at her, smiling pleasantly. I was not accustomed to being accosted by strangers in a rush to head for their destinations. "Hotel, I suppose," I said.

"You got reservations?" It may have been an invitation, but I did not recognize it as such.

"Not that I know."

"Then," she informed me, "you're out of luck."

"Why?"

"No accommodations. There's only one hotel on the island, and it's reserved for us—flight crew. Joy," she said, offering her hand.

I was startled at her unexpected, friendly approach. Up to this point in my life, my focus was mostly set on career, and foreign regions waiting to be explored. Opportunities for a possible relationships, at this time, were farthest from my mind. Though, what I realized in an instant was my dreams taking shape. I vaguely remember giving her my birthname, but my mind had already adapted to the transition confronting me from here on. I decided to leave the past behind, and start a new beginning, that of Alex Bauer, the long-suppressed pseudo identity of my dreams. I was determined to turn it into reality, and follow a path suitable for my future.

From this point on, I will refer to himself as Alex Bauer. It would be a change not only job, and career wise, but character, and personality wise as well. The persona I was born with had gradually morphed into Alex Bauer. At this moment, I had arrived on the threshold of adventure, Day One in my acquired identity.

"Alex," I said somewhat reluctantly, returning her handshake. "Alex Bauer."

"I thought you said…," giving me a once over.

"I know. My mistake. My mind was in the past."

Obviously satisfied with my appearance she said, "Look me up at the hotel. I'll be here three days." She was staying at the Cliff Hotel, located at Agana Heights, a place near the airport, as I would learn.

At this time, receiving travel cases on arrival was still conducted in the open. As soon as the truck arrived at the terminal to unload the pile of suitcases from the craft, travelers sought out luggage, and headed for the exit. It was a hectic affair. In Guam, though it was a U.S. possession, a custom-check was enforced. Only passengers arriving with U.S. passports were excluded from inspections. It became apparent that

Guam was subjected to smuggling from territory islands, and surrounding countries. "Where else would the local population get their merchandise," was my rationale.

"Bye. Hope so see you," were Joy's departing words before she was whisked away by the crew limo.

Not only did I make a friend, but she had mentioned her flight schedule to me. *What better introduction to the Rock,* I thought cheerily? The Rock will always be my label; Robert "Bob" W. had used the term to refer to Guam, and it stuck with me. Unfortunately, Joy, and I did not connect, not this time. I was swamped with a workload I had not anticipated. However, I received a call from her two weeks later.

"Remember me?" the cheery voice said on the receiver. What followed were pleasant times on each of her successive stopovers until one day the calls stopped. "She must have been reassigned," I rationalized. Being part of the flight crew was a nomadic life in the 60s, and 70s. So was mine, as it would turn out. I had no complaints. There would be many more opportunities to make friends.

Now, upon leaving the terminal, to my surprise, I spotted my name on a receiving card held high by an individual dressed in a sailor's uniform. "You Alex?" he asked when I approached.

"That's me."

"I've got your transportation."

"Terrific. Where're we going?"

"South. BEQ."

"BEQ? Thought the site was up north."

"Bachelor Enlisted Quarters."

"Aha." I was clueless, waiting for more explanation.

"Nothing else available. Typhoon leveled the island."

It did not take long to find out what he was talking about. Everywhere I looked there was devastation. Whatever places were still standing had their rooftops torn off. "There's no electricity. No air-conditioning either," I was forewarned. His words did not sink in until the first night, when I was trying to sleep at the place. It turned out I had to double-up in a small, whitewashed, but clean room without the slightest cooling or windows. For the next three month I endured the conditions; it was not a pleasant experience. I began to see what Robert "Bob" W. meant. Extremely busy with system analysis, debugging, testing, my work schedule was so demanding the three months went by in no time. The holidays came, and went without my noticing. Christmas, and New Years were hardly noticed on the island. The steamy topical climate did not inspire much for caroling, and seasonal holiday songs as back home. What I did notice was the date. I made the call.

"Remember your promise," I demanded, as soon as the distant receiver picked up thinking it was the director.

"What are you talking about," the unfamiliar voice demanded in return. "Who are you?"

I realized then that it wasn't the person I had expected. "Bob?"

"Robert W. is no longer working here. I took his place. Where're you calling from?"

"Guam."

"Ah yes. You're Alex?"

"That I am."

"What can I do for you?"

I was highly distraught. It was a turn I had not expected, especially not at the onset of a promising career. Anything could happen. *I could get stuck here forever, laid off, or even worse, get fired if my demands were not met,* went through my mind. But a promise was a promise, and I said so, "I called to find out about my replacement." If it was a newly hired, he had to be trained which meant several more weeks on the Rock.

"What replacement?"

"Replacement I was promised before taking the assignment on Guam."

"I don't know anything about it."

Hearing it, I became even more distraught. "But…"

"There is no 'But', the voice interrupted. "From the schedule in front of me your assignment is for two years."

"Two years," I yelled into the phone, and hung up. It was an unacceptable proposition I could not tolerate. I was fuming. It became apparent that there was either a communication break at the leadership level, or an intentional oversight. I was bound to find out. Checking my wristwatch, I realized that the office staff at HQs left work for the day. Since there was a fifteen-hour time difference, I had to try later in the day, around 5:00 pm, to catch HR in their morning on the east coast, 8:00 am. I kept checking my watch frequently for time. My day crew was just leaving when I made the call. The distant operator answered, courteous as always, "Whom may I direct your call?"

"Program director," I demanded, in a not overly friendly tone of voice.

"Please hold."

"Yes?" The same voice answered as earlier.

"I'd like to speak with the AUTODIN program director."

"Speaking."

"Listen," I said. "I was upset when I called earlier, but I need to speak with the person in charge of the program."

"That would be me. As I said earlier, Robert W. is no longer with the company. He quit last month. I am in charge now. You'll report directly to me. Do we understand each other?"

"I don't even know you," I objected, but submitted myself to the unfortunate change.

"Arthur C."

"Okay Arthur," I started. "Here is my plight…"

"Call me Art, and I realize your position. I spoke with HR to check on your schedule. You are right. I understand your dilemma, but there is nothing I can do to resolve."

"What do you mean by nothing?"

"There is currently no replacement scheduled for you. You are obligated to the contract."

"But that's not fair. I came here on good faith for the specific duration. Doesn't a promise mean anything anymore?"

"I did not make the promise. There is nothing I can do."

"We'll see," I said, and hung up once more. My mind was made up. I stormed to the front office to resign. "You can't leave," the site manager objected.

"You know I was here for three months. Where is my replacement?"

"They never sent anybody. I need you here," he pleaded.

"Not anymore," I said. "Consider it my termination." I abruptly left the site. It only took me two days to book a flight back, notify Naval Admin, and pack my belongings. The following morning I was on a Pan Am flight back to Philadelphia.

Twenty hours later, I checked into a motel near HQs, retrieved my vehicle from storage, and waited for the morning dawn. As soon as I walked into the building, people greeted me on recognition. "Where have you been?" I did not stop to chat. My focus was the director's office. Still steaming, I walked in without prior announcement.

"Who are you," Arthur C. demanded, him on the phone, and my eyes on the nameplate verifying his name.

"Alex Bauer."

As soon as I made the announcement, he hung up demanding, "What are you doing here?"

"I quit." Facing intentional consequences, it was the boldest statement I had ever made.

"Now just wait a minute," he stalled. "First of all, you did not leave the site unintended, did you?"

"Naval Intel is in good hands. I left a trained crew behind."

"Okay, but we still have to work things out. You can't just quit."

"I did. Want to know why?"

"You told me already. It means a lot to me, but I did not make the promise. What I do promise, we'll work something out. I don't want to lose you. You have the best reputation one could wish. We need to talk. Have a seat," he said with a gesture at the office table. Seated across from him I waited for what he had to say. "I can't replace you at the moment," he started. "I just don't have anybody that fits your qualifications."

"You could hire and train somebody."

"That's true but I have a contract with Naval Admin for a specific number of contractors qualified to operate, and manage the Guam site. They demand full complement staffing for the duration. It's why you can't leave, but I have an offer for you to consider. It's not a promise," he said. "It's a deal I hope you'll consider."

I had been studying his face and persona while listening, watching his demeanor. Facing me was a self-assured, friendly mannered, face underscored by strong leadership ability. He seemed sincere. I waited for the offer.

"From your skills, and performance, according to our pay scale, I see that you are underpaid. I'll give you a raise effective immediately. Not only will you have a pay increase, I'll provide you with a promotion you deserve. How does Site Superintendent sound to you?"

I remained silent because my mind was rapidly processing the information he just offered. Though it was not exactly what I wanted, it just may work out. While I spent the last three months on Guam absorbed with nothing but work challenges, I had notions on many occasions in joining the team with their frequent recreational activities. Once my team settled in, with their dedicated jobs assigned for the next two years, or longer, their lives adapted to the local environment for fishing, diving, golfing, bowling, and other recreation mostly centered on weekend beach parties. In the presence of my new boss, realizing it now, I had envied them all.

"I need a week to arrange to take care of personal matters," I said. I had to terminate my apartment here that I had kept up paying, find a storage place for my vehicle and other personal belongings I wanted to keep before taking off for the next two years. "Two year?"

"That's the condition. You in?"

"I accept." We shook hands solidifying the deal.

"Come back in the morning. I'll have your travel orders and checks waiting when you get here, and call me Art."

"Okay Art." I turned and left, for the best part satisfied with the way things turned out.

One week later I was back on the island once more. Word had already preceded my arrival. "Couldn't handle the World?", and "You missed the Rock?" were some of the return greetings. There was a slight misgiving from one on the team, my replacement, who saw his new position in jeopardy. I assured him that it was not the case. He retained his job as site systems engineer. There was one situation that still needed to be resolved. My space at the BEQ had been reassigned. I was out of a room. As luck had it, I found a more suitable accommodation much closer to work. It was Guam's only beach resort. When I checked at the place, as expected, I was told, "Room? Not possible. We are completely occupied, and have been since the typhoon came through." The host was amicable, but could not accommodate one more regardless of my begging. "I'll take any space. Just give me a closet, crawlspace, anything." He did.

"Now since you mentioned it," he offered. "There is a space under the staircase I could let you have, but it's not suitable for living."
"Just show me. I'll be the judge." One minute later I beamed at him, "I'll take it." After retrieving the key from the office, he opened the door to what I could only describe as closet. Fortunately, it was spacious enough to accommodate a small bed and night stand, tiny window, sink and faucet, no hot water, but cozy, and most of all, I would go to sleep at night by the pounding of waves from the beach only one hundred yards away. The following months turned out some of the happiest times I had. The host and I would become longtime friends. Shortly after I settled in, an island-wide warning was issued. "Typhoon imminent," the weather center announced. "Forty-eight hours."

"Not good," was all I could muster, considering the recent past, and hoping for the best. By now, the islanders had gotten used to the many warnings sent out during the annual typhoon season. There had been a total of twenty typhoons, and four super-typhoons, including thirty-nine tropical depressions during the preceding year, with each contributing more to the island's devastation. *No wonder,* I thought, *ninety percent of the island was flattened.*

Sure enough, a couple of nights later, it was past midnight when I received a phone call amid the roaring of winds. "Site is down." It meant the electricity was out. As if my workload had not been enough already, I anticipated the worst.

As soon as I stepped outside I was in the midst of the elements. No matter how I tried to rationalize against taking the twenty-minute drive to the site, I had to make the trip. It was my responsibility to restore power. Hopping behind the wheel of my rental, a 1960 Volkswagen Beetle, I took to the road. Minutes later, after leaving the town behind, I was hit full force by the storm. It was my first experience wresting with a typhoon, trying to keep the Beetle on the road. On several occasions I had to slow to a crawl to prevent from being swept off the road. If the conditions were not bad enough already, the rain was pouring from the sky. The windshield wiper quit shortly after, unable to clear the torrents of rain from the windshield. Leaning out on the driver's side, I had no choice but to press on while getting soaking wet in the process.

I finally arrived at the site in spite of several roadblocks, mostly fallen palm tree branches amid corrugated rooftops slicing through the air. Sure enough, the facility was doused in darkness. Taking an initial assessment, aside from electricity being out island-wide, Naval contact was lost with the 7th Pacific base, as well as the Polaris submarine fleets, in a total communication blackout. Fortunately, I found no lasting damages to mainframe computers, and support functions. But there was one obstacle I had to overcome first. The UPS system had shut down. Unfortunately, backup generators, supposedly on emergency standby, had not kicked in. It was up to me to restore the site. But not all was hopeless. Minutes later, the power expert, also a contractor, made it to the site.

The UPS system, the core in every critical operation, was designed for automatic switchover, but at times, due to component breakdown, especially in the tropical humidity, the transition from batteries to generators failed. To get the system started it took two people to activate the spark initiator, a foot-long, manually-manipulated lever. When activated, closing the contacts was accompanied by an explosion-like sound generating streaks of sparks shooting through the dark. The first generator spun up quickly, followed by four more in rapid automation, necessary for carrying the full load to the onsite equipment.

The site, 7th Fleet, Polaris subs, fleet headquarters in Wahiawa, Hawaii, Naval Command in Norfolk, VA, and JCS at the Pentagon had communication from the Pacific back again. Aside from fighting the prevalent weather conditions, my crew came out champions. In the years ahead, the event was the first of many situations I was tested on to fight, and resolve. It took many more hours of apprehensive standby duty until the winds calmed down. I faced bright daylight when I stepped outside, headed home to catch up with sleep.

"You've got a visitor," the site administrator announced a couple of days later on the intercom. As usual, I was busy with analysis, troubleshooting, and testing failed computer components.

"Who?"

"Don't know. Ace's his name. Says he's assigned here."

"Okay." It must be an additional crew member headquarters had promised. Sure enough, I met him by the guard shack. "Alex's the name."

"Roland C.," he returned. "But you can call me Ace. Everybody does. Was sent to work on the team."

"Ace? Kind of unusual."

"It's what they call me."

"Welcome aboard, Ace. Checked in at the Gate?"

"Not yet. Was told to see you."

"Let's do it," I offered, headed for security shack located alongside the secured perimeter fence. Each time upon entering or leaving the facility, one had to pass the armed, Marine-guarded checkpoint. High-level security at each of our facilities was strictly enforced. The reasons? Just in case. The results? Nobody was ever killed trying to rush the gates. Peoples' mindsets in the 60s, and 70s were different. Generally, people respected and looked out for each other on both sides of the fence, military, and civilian. Draftees were physically, and mentally conditioned for the services, with the free-spirited hippies, prevalent during the 70s, had not taken to violence. Their minds were mellowed from their daily drug dosage, fueled by expendable cash in their pockets.

"Where're you from, Ace?"

"Georgia. Just been hired on."

"Didn't see you at the training center."

"I was in the Air Force. Had done four years when I heard about AUTODIN."

"Word gets around, doesn't it?"

"Mostly rumors. Nobody knows much about the project. Heavy recruiting is taking place. That's the reason I'm here."

"I suspected it. Most of my trainees were ex-military. What skills do you have?"

"Computer programming. Trained on the job."

"What systems?"

"SAGE."

"I've heard about it, pretty complex. Well," I said, patting him on the shoulder, "you came to the right place. I sure can use your help."

"Glad to be here."

"You eaten yet?"

"Nope. Just got off the plane."

"Let's have lunch." With most local restaurants leveled by typhoons, there were only two choices of eateries, both located on base. It was either the Navy mess hall or the O Club. Since the mess hall was subject to dish clutter, the Officer's club was a better choice to talk.

Watching him attack a burger, and fries, it became obvious he had not eaten. Our dialogue was brief, interrupted in-between taking bites. "How many are on the team?"

"What team?" I said, letting him know the current manning status. "Just the two of us, UPS tech, and site manager."

"What?" He looked baffled. "I was told there was a team."

"For now, you are looking at it. It's you, and me, but more are promised."

"You mean you've handled the job by yourself? The analysis, debugging, repairs, and pre-test?"

"That's why you are here. I've been working sixteen hours a day, seven days a week nonstop. I'm lacking computer experts. It appears that everybody wants an Asian or European assignment. It looks like management has forgotten about Guam."

"The word is out," he confirmed, taking another bite.

"What word?"

"I was told you could handle the job by yourself."

"Yeah," I agreed, somewhat dismayed at the lack of headquarters support. "But even I deserve a break now and then." I was happy to finally have some relief with the pressing workload. "Let's find you a room. Probably need to recover from the flight. You can start tomorrow." He lucked out. Some rooms had become available at the BOQs, right here at the Naval base, where the site was located. "Not bad," he admitted when checking in.

"You're lucky," I agreed. "It's been a miserable three months."

"What's the working hours?"

"I start early. 7:00 am, take a late lunch break, with more work until 10:00 p.m. It still gives me time to grab a bite to eat, and a drink before the clubs close at midnight. Since you are here maybe I can get a decent dinner for a change."

"You can count on it."

"Meet me at the mess hall in the morning before seven. Bye," I said, headed back to the site, where much more work was awaiting me.

The following morning, as promised, Ace was ready for work, but I'd noticed a flaw in his appearance. "That what you're wearing?" He was dressed in casuals, a short-sleeved shirt, and sneakers.

He seemed puzzled.

"Dress code is formal."

"What? In this heat?"

"Headquarters' orders. No exceptions. We've got to match the customer's code of dress, and conduct. Navy personal dressed in neatly-pressed uniforms. We're required to wear suit and tie. Got one with you?"

"Lucked out. Packed the suit. I wasn't sure what to expect." He was back ten minutes later properly dressed.

While there were rumors about changes in the Navy, for now Air Force, and Army command still enforced inherited customs affecting discipline, behavior, and personal conduct according to long established policies. It would take several more years before the changes were instituted. Asserted by intense public pressure put on military services, the initial break to go casual, part of what the public called "antiquated customs," came with Admiral Elmo Zumwalt[15].

Up to that time, everybody working government contracts was required to dress up. For civilians it was suit, and tie. The only exception to the strict rules was while assigned to Guam, and other tropical places. Because of the constant heat, with the site not having air conditioning during construction, workers were permitted to remove dress jackets. Other than that, it was white shirt and tie, iron-pressed trousers, matching socks to polished shoes. When the changes finally come about, I was at a loss because on the one side, my crew demanded an immediate adaption while headquarters refused

---

[15] Admiral Zumwalt assumed duties as Chief of Naval Operations, and was promoted to full admiral on July 1, 1970, and quickly began a series of moves intended to reduce racism, and sexism in the Navy. These were disseminated in Navy-wide communications known as "Z-grams." These included orders authorizing beards (sideburns, mustaches, and longer groomed hair were also acceptable), and introducing beer-dispensing machines to barracks. Not all of these changes were well received by senior naval personnel.

to comply. I even had to fire some on my team because of non-conformance. It took another couple of years for commercial industries to accept and conform to the changes.

"Ready?"

"Let's do it."

Arriving at the guard shack, Ace was handed an ID badge, and in we went, with me giving him a tour of the site. He seemed impressed at what I had accomplished, and more so by what still had to be done. While partially-configured computers, switching gears, memory cabinets, drum-storage units, comm, and COMSEC equipment were ready for acceptance testing, many more were waiting to be debugged, and fixed. At least now I had support and was hoping to proceed more rapidly. One person can only accomplish so much while pressured by the schedule. It was either additional help or working extra hours, as was the case with me.

"See these cabinets?" I said to him with a gesture at a row of neatly-aligned equipment cabinets. "I haven't gotten to them yet. They are yours. You can check out a set of logic diagrams, and an O-scope[16], and whatever else you need with logistics."

"What's their function?" he wanted to know.

"Front-end processors connecting to the outside world." It was not that simple. There was much more hardware, equipment, and software connected in between, like tech-control monitoring consoles, COMM equipment, and patch bays in line with COMSEC, and crypto gear feeding channels to hundreds of subscribers located across the Pacific Rim, connecting with fleets, embassies, and Intel stations at places like the Philippines, Korea, Japan, Okinawa, Thailand, Vietnam, and other, more or less obscured places of conflicts, and war. Okinawa, though a Japanese island in the Ryukyu chain, was still under U.S. military jurisdiction at the time.

Internal to the primary complex was a cluster of six interconnected mainframe computers with dozens of associated internal and external memory banks, mass data storage units, and switching gear, providing multiple, operational redundancies via an interconnected matrix in case of equipment failure. There were not only one or two backup systems. There were six altogether. It may have seemed an excessive redundancy but with transistor technology at its infancy, breakdown of components[17] occurred frequently, almost on a daily basis. Once a system was operational, a technical team was assigned three shifts to maintain component integrity, and operation status to the site. The designers of AUTODIN had the foresight for automatic, seamless switchovers to standby equipment ready to take over.

Work proceeded more rapidly with Ace by my side. Because of the pressing schedule, we kept on working until most of the equipment was tested, repaired, and ready for acceptance. Relief finally arrived with additional help from headquarters.

---

[16] O-scope is an abbreviation for Oscilloscope, used to troubleshoot circuit boards, and computer, wiring, and back frame connectivity. Each, and every component subject to inspection becomes a visual electronic stream rendered on the screen to identify component functionality. It is the means to identify failed transistors, diodes, capacitors, etc.

[17] A component in this case was either a transistor, capacitor, or resistor, configured in multiple elements to each circuit board located within each piece of equipment by the hundreds. It took many thousands of boards to make up the system.

Assigned several leased cars from a local car rental, with four occupants to one vehicle, mostly dilapidated, and rusty from the ever-present humidity, the team was shuttled to, and from the work location, working long hours, after which a quick bite was assured before turning in to catch a few hours of sleep, our daily routine.

The day for the acceptance testing finally arrived. The annual monsoon season was over with the dry season on its way. Tropical places such as Guam had two seasons, wet, and dry, with day, and night time temperatures fluctuating only slightly. The sun rose, and set each day at the same time. Relief from the heat came after midnight. It was a daily cycle repeated with cooler air currents surging inland from the sea, reversing the following morning when the sun began to heat the island. Body, and clothes turned wet as soon as one stepped outside an air-conditioned environment. Although cooling, and climate control on the island were marginal, for buildings containing electronics, air-conditioning was a necessity.

At the beginning of March, a government-sponsored test team arrived from the mainland, taking over the facility to prepare for acceptance, scheduled for March 15th. It would take two extremely busy weeks of more debugging, and fixing for site equipment to pass final test before being turned over to operations.

"You did it," Arthur C., the program director said, shaking my hand. He had arrived a few days early for the turn-over ceremony. "You've made the company proud." Since there was uncertainty within corporate management about completing the task, I, despite several technical setbacks, kept assuring them of my ability to satisfy my first customer, the U.S. Naval Command, Pacific.

There is one important thing I had learned from working in Intelligence: "Intel is the best career anybody could attain. It teaches one to analyze an solve every challenge thrown across your path." But to attain it, strict prerequisite action is required to visit or take an assignment at an Intel center such as:

- The contractor requesting the clearance has to hire the prospective individual
- Access Clearance with a security processing agency was requested (*)
- When granted, the primary contractor is informed of the status (**)
- The individual is notified and prepared for location assignment
- Immunization shots and certificates are initiated
- A certificate message from the security agency is sent to the site
- The site security officer is notified of the new arrival
- After arriving on site, credentials and clearances are verified
- Depending on work assignment, if qualified, special access may be granted

With Autodin there were three special access section:

- Computer Center: Highest access category (i.e. SPECAT, SCI, or ESI) (***)
- Communication Section: Highest access category COMSEC
- Comm Security: CRYPTO
- Operations: ESI and/or SCI "Restricted for Addressee Only" (****)
- Power Station: SECRET

(*) Two options were available:

a.   Commercial Contracting agency
b.   Military Intelligence agency

(**) Depending on level of clearance it may take from six month to two years to grant a clearance. My Secret took nine months followed by Top Secret that took another 1 ½ years. Most times the clearance will be granted unless the individual is caught lying about their past or committed a serious crime.

(***) Highest security clearances bestowed by the Government:

- SPECAT (Special Category)
- SCI (Special Compartmented Intelligence)
- ESI (Extremely Sensitive Information)

(****) Granted and accessible to only specific individuals.

With the successful turn-over of the site completed, the place settled in to a daily routine managed by a full complement of jointly-manned Naval, and contractor operations personnel. I caught up with Arthur C. before his departure. "Whatever happened to Robert W?" I asked.

"Got promoted. He's managing several programs now. Couldn't come."

"It means from here on I report to you?"

"That's right. I'm your boss. I was told you did a bang-up job getting the site ready."

"I promised Bob W. I would."

"Well," he said, getting ready to board the plane to carry him back to the States, "take care of the Navy."

From here on, though there was the anticipated, frequent equipment failure, my life on the Rock turned pretty much routine. I showed up for work like everybody else around 8:00 am, took time out for a regular lunch break, and worked until 5:00 pm, to finish up the workday. Most times I was stopped at the exit by the departing shift with: "Join us for a drink?"

With the Chief's, and Officer's clubs on base nearby, I readily accepted since I did not enjoy drinking alone. Most evenings turned out pleasantly. There was only one thing missing from the scene: companionship.

Women, at the time, had not been accepted to serve in the Navy. There were reasons for it, but it would not stay this way forever. For now, for my time serving on the island, I had to fend for myself amid the other single men on the team and, worse yet, thousands of young, and able-bodied sailors, and marines hoping for a chance to tie up with a local girl. I don't have to point out that the situation caused much concern among the local citizens, especially the young Guamanian. It was visible with the frequent bar brawls over a local girl. She might have wanted a flirt with the sailor from the mainland, but the local competitor did not want her to. It was not until years later when entertainers were brought in from places like the Philippines and Korea to provide entertainment pleasures. Soon, the solution became so popular that a nonstop stream of performers followed suit with a main objective to obtain citizenship in Guam. Word spread quickly of such opportunity because, as a result, it provided automatic U.S. citizenship.

One week into live operations at the site, supporting the 7th Fleet as well as Polaris subs assigned in the Pacific, one early morning, I had noticed a new face on site pacing along the walls checking equipment, floors, and ceilings. I was observing him from a distance when Ace walked up. "He's been asking for you."

"Oh? Where's he from?"

"I don't know. Didn't say."

"Thanks. I'll check with him." Before I made the attempt, I had a chance to study the man. Tall, assertive, graying temples, apparently methodical in persona, he kept snooping in and around equipment, above ceiling panels, and beneath the elevated floors. Since I was in charge of the facility, I followed him slyly. Minutes later I could not contain my curiosity any longer, and approached him. "What's up, Mystery-man?"

"Your cabinets need dusting." I was startled causing an immediate emotional reaction, "How dare he criticize my equipment." I did not expect a newcomer to be critical of my maintenance crew. He then abruptly turned, and left the room. Angered at first at such boldness, I quickly checked myself with the notion, "Perhaps he's right." To find out I headed for the maintenance room. Taking stock, sure enough, there were no ladders, not even a stepladder. I realized then that it must have been an oversight when logistics, and facility tools were selected. I sought out the shift supervisor, "Haven't your guys been cleaning the top of equipment cabinets?"

"Can't reach high enough," was his ready response. "Don't have a ladder."

In retrospect, he was right. Nobody was at fault. I realized then that in subsequent visits it was Mystery-man's way for informing other site crews about the oversight. He was polite enough not to upset people in charge, but subtle enough to make his point. He was the only person tall enough to see over the top of computers. I gained new respect for the person I caught snooping my facility. I decided to get to know him better. Perhaps he had other, and more important suggestions I could apply to processes and procedures. I should learn soon enough that my assumption proved correct. There would be many more such encounters with Mystery-man.

To prove his point, I reached up, and ran my fingers along the edges of cabinets. I did not have to inspect the result. I could feel the grid of dust cling to my fingers.

Minutes later he was back deliberately eying me up, and down. "You Alex?"

"That's me."

"Call me Robert," he offered with an extended hand.

"Can I help you?" I replied.

"No!"

I was taken aback by the gruffness, and challenged him. "By the way, what are you doing here? What is your mission?"

"Checking for bugs."

"What? Roaches, mice, geckos?" I said, trying to be humorous. It wasn't every day some stranger showed up unannounced, not at this remote site.

"Intel bugs," he said, without volunteering further explanation.

"You want to explain?"

"There is nothing to explain. It's my job. You go about your business, and I about mine."

"Let me see your credentials," I demanded, irritated, blocking his path. "You better have a T.S. or I'll have you removed." I was ready to call security.

"No need to get hostile." He reached in his jacket pocket, retrieved an ID, and handed it over.

I took one glance at the card, and apologetically huffed, "Wow—always wanted to meet one of you guys." I was impressed. In bold lettering his office symbol read, "DARPA – Department of Defense." Mellowed out, I immediately changed my attitude, "Sorry. Had no idea."

"No offense taken," he said. "I get it all the time. People don't take well to the likes of me."

"Why?"

"Think we all are spooks."

"Can't blame them. Don't you think? After all," I reasoned, "nobody knows anything about DARPA. Want to enlighten me?"

I watched his mind churning with reservations, but instead he said, "Meet me at the O Club. We'll talk then. Six o' clock."

"I'll be there. You can bet on it."

For the next several hours I mulled over the unexpected visitor. While I must have come across as pretty insensitive, he displayed a certain confidence without having taken offense. It gave me a new meaning of fortitude. When I walked into the club, as promised, he was sitting at a table enjoying some wine. He spotted me by the entrance, and waved me over to the table. "Have a seat," then, "Drink?"

"Wine please," I ordered when the waiter stepped up. "So—Mystery-man," I prodded, unable to contain my curiosity any longer, "what are you doing here?"

"You German?" It was obvious he was stalling with personal questions.

"What gave it away?"

"The accent. I spent many years in Germany."

"Oh?"

"WWII. Flew the B-17 Fortress."

"Peace missions?" I could not help but rub in the damage the bombers did to the country I grew up in. He hesitated with the answer, clearly unsure how to respond. He eyed me sheepishly, then explained, "Just followed commands."

"A hell of a job you guys did."

"You started it, remember?"

"Well," I offered, "it's part of the past. I don't hold grudges. Besides," I explained, "I was a kid."

"Look," he offered, "I think we started off on the wrong footing." He reached across the table, and offered his hand. "Robert L. Krantz, Sr. I am here to inspect your place for Intelligence leaks."

"How formal. 'L' stands for Lawrence, I suppose?"

"Something like it." While he meant his given name, referring to the Lawrence Livermore Laboratory, a proper label in his capacity, my jest passed by unacknowledged.

"Actually," he explained, "I am with the engineering branch for DARPA.

"Now I understand," I said. "Brains cooking up all the secret projects."

"That's me."

"Tempest team?"

"Not exactly. They come later. I am here to look the place over. The specialty team is on its way. My job is to verify that everything is implemented according to the contract."

"You can trust me," I said, trying to put him at ease.

"So, they all claim," he responded in a somewhat cynical gesture. As was the case within every industry, contractors, especially inexperienced ones, when rewarded a government contract, were not always fully qualified to perform to the customer's satisfaction. Representing DARPA, it was his responsibility to make sure that the contractor had delivered as promised.

"I can assure you," I said, seeking out his face. "I only work above board. Always!"

"We shall see, won't we? But let's not quarrel. Would you care for something to eat? I'm buying."

Knowing the quality of food served at military clubs, it was an offer I would never turn down. I had gone through the menu selections more than once, and enjoyed every bite of it. "Ribeye for me," I ordered when the waiter showed up.

"Make it two," Robert confirmed. "Best cut of meat."

"I totally agree." To Robert, I said, "Tell me about your organization."

"You fully cleared?"

"Got the same credentials as you," I said. "It's the prerequisite for my position."

"Superintendent?"

"It's the label I carry when on site," I explained. "Otherwise, it's system engineer. I grew up with mainframe computers."

"I did some checking before I left," he said, with a slight grin on his face. "You are top-man in your field. It's why I'm out here."

"You mean," I prodded, "the gruffness was a charade?"

"I wanted to check you out first hand."

"And?"

"You passed. I had to do it. In this business you never know who you can fully trust."

"I'll drink to that," I said, raising my glass to him. "Salute."

"I want you to understand," he explained. "I need your full trust if we want to work together."

"You got it." In the years ahead, Robert, and I would cross paths many more times at places back home, as well as in foreign lands. He would always show up unannounced. He would spend only a few days, sometimes only hours at a time, on location, but I would always look forward to his visits. Since then, we had developed a completely trusting relationship with each other. We could openly share information, and data, political, as well as national defense issues. Through him, I learned much about the intricacies of who, how, and where Intelligence operations took place. For instance, though funded by obscured budgets, I learned about DARPA, and who created its innovative concepts, designs, and projects—an army of dedicated, brilliant PhDs, diligently supported by thousands of creative individuals spread across the many black projects.

Back to WWII, as a child hiding in the protection of our basement shelter during air raids, little did I know that one day, I would meet face-to-face one of the B-17 pilots twenty-five years later, who would become one of the invisible warriors himself, Mystery-man. It was he, that became my counterpart working within the domain of DARPA's defense parameters. Aside from DARPA and DCA, there were numerous other organizations and agencies we would interface with. Vietnam alone saw many such associations by virtue of U.S. military, and war-related support functions, in addition to numerous conflicts that followed near and far.

And here I was, thinking I held an important a position, that of "Superintendent." Regardless of my extravagant status, the job I performed was just as important, keeping a site operational 24/7, supporting military, and Intel operations Pacific-wide from Hawaii to the Indian Ocean, and from Alaska to Australia. It was my gratitude to give all my time and energy to the safety, and well-being of the services, and the country, while in turn, military services provided a save place for all of us citizens of the U.S. and its allies.

More suitable accommodations for living quarters came in the form of relief with the construction of a trailer park on the island. These were fifteen, double-unit trailers, 12 feet wide, by 50 feet in length, flown in from the U.S. mainland, specifically built, and installed for my team. It turned out to be a God-send for all of us, not only for the relief from a daily thirty-five mile commute each way, but for their air-conditioned environment.

The park, initially a desolate spot by the ocean surrounded by dense jungle, in time with the help of landscapers, turned out to be as I had always envisioned a tropical island to be: paradise. It became my home for the next two years, but I am jumping ahead again.

REFLECTION ONE

"Hey," Ace called out from the bar, waving me over. "Come, and join us." As usual, he was having a good time among other team mates. With rotating shift schedules, one could always find some of the crew at their favorite hangout, the NCO[18] club. I ordered my favorite drink, the Mai Tai cocktail, popular in the tropics. "Guy's been bragging about you," Ace added. "Is it really true you knocked a two-star general to the floor?"

"Well," I said, recollecting the incident years earlier. It was a time I had just started this job.

"It wasn't the best day I had. Got fired over it."

"Tell us more," he insisted, encouraged by the others. "Who saved your butt?"

It was at Ft. Monmouth, NJ, Army signal training center, a few years back. I was new to the project, but busy as hell trying to get the system ready for training. Since it was the AUTODIN prototype site, top official visitors came from all over the globe wanting to see the communications miracle devised by DARPA. I was moving swiftly between the mainframe cabinets, and system consoles up front debugging some final circuit problems. In my haste, turning one of the corners, I was suddenly faced by a cluster of visitors dressed in impeccably white uniforms. There was no room to sidestep my hasty pace. I collided with the first of the group, sending him sprawling to the floor. I was clueless about command rankings at the time. What made the situation worse, I did not bother to help him up or apologize, but kept on going on my quest.

Sure enough, five minutes later, I heard my name called over the PA, "Alex! Front office. Now!"

"Not good," I muttered on the way there.

"Is it true," the site manager demanded, "you ran a general to the floor?"

"I am sorry, but he was blocking my way. It was not intentional."

"It's too late for apologies. You should have done so with him. I'll have to let you go."

It was then when I realized the severity of my tactless behavior. I was fired on the spot. Driving back on I-95 from Ft. Monmouth to the home office in Willow Grove, PA, I had time to contemplate the situation. I did not realize how sensitive customer relations might be among high officials, and had to face the consequences of my rude behavior, which cost me not only my job, but my career as well. Losing my security clearance was foremost on my mind. If revoked, it would be the end of my dreams.

"Is it true?" Art C., the new program director demand, shaking his head. He had replaced Bob and was new in the office back then. "You knocked a NATO general to the ground?"

"I did," I admitted. "It was his fault for blocking my work, but mine for not apologizing," I admitted, then told the rest of the story.

---

[18] NCO – Non-Commissioned Officer. There were at least three distinct military rankings: Officer, NCO, and Enlisted men. The distinction between officers, and non-commissioned officers, was that officers required college graduation, and were trained to become career leaders. NCOs generally were promoted from enlisted ranks but could be elevated into leadership roles.

"Okay. At least you are honest enough to admit your mistake. This is what we'll do. I can't afford to lose you. Take a week off, and then see me."

"But the site manager fired me."

"Let me deal with him. I'll take care of it."

"A week later," I explained to my buddies seated by the bar, "Art hired me back, but put me on nightshift for the rest of the testing effort with a precondition to keep my face away from daytime personnel." I was forever grateful to him for having saved my otherwise shattered career.

"Wow," Ace exclaimed. "You sure lucked out."

"Then the rumors are true," another said.

"I never make up stories," I insisted. In my recollection, it was the first of many more incidents I would encounter over the next thirty years. Assigned to the frontlines of conflict, my life turned into never-ending challenges, not only with the authorities, but coworkers, and foreign officials as well. Along my future path, I had many confrontational encounters, including being drawn into destructive fights. It was the reason I became intricately involved with martial arts. Once my travels led me to Asia, I took the opportunity to join the best Dojos in the Philippines, Korea, Okinawa, and Guam. Kung Fu, popularized by Bruce Lee, was just emerging in Asia, and so was I. My life was directed by two interests: career, and survival.

MARIANAS ISLANDS

AUTODIN, as a whole, performed well even with the frequent breakdown of computer components. I had made sure that each electronic piece of equipment was thoroughly tested prior to switching it online. The basic configuration of the system was as follows: computer sector containing mainframe computers with their internal, and externally-connected memory banks, drum storage devices, interfaced via insulated cable groups to front-end data processors with its memories, and storage devices, and on to more clusters of computers each serving subscribers. From here, the digital data was handed off to the COMM sector with dozens of racks of COMM, and transmission gears whose function it was to convert digital data to analog, then forward the data on to the COMSEC room, the most critical aspect of the system, before sending encrypted information on via sub-oceanic cable trunks, implemented in the early part of the 19th century. Communication would be transmitted in this manner until satellite technology came of age ten years later, when transmissions were shifted from ground to space. Information coming in was received in the reverse order. Additional means for transmissions such as microwave dishes, and Tropo-scatters were applied in foreign countries where underground, shielded cables were not available. Those transmissions, however, were limited to line-of-sight to sparsely-populated areas. Energy used in this mode was very useful on flat terrains, but had its drawbacks. Concentrated into a solid beam created so much power it would heat up, and fry any living creature passing in front of the 30-meter dish.

With testing over, site personnel in place working three shifts 24/7, and visitors departed, I could settle into a semi-routine living. I had met my newly-arrived team members, ready to perform on a perpetually rotating work schedule, who had been set up comfortably at the 15-unit trailer park. With the team complement in place, my work load was drastically reduced. I could focus my time on activities other than just work.

"Let's go diving," Ace suggested, getting ready to leave the site. In only a short time, it had become obvious why he had acquired the nickname. He held up the true status of the title.

"Okay by me." I readily took to his recreational activities related to fishing, diving, surfing, and flying. It would take us weeks to get acquainted with Guam's numerous fishing, and diving spots. After taking a couple of drives around the island, 80 miles in circumference, I realized the potential for an outdoor, and water-based lifestyle. Before long, my first year on the island became filled with such activities. I must credit much of it to Ace, since he was a licensed diver, as well as experienced pilot. In only a short time we developed a dependency on each other, necessary for such actions. There were other recreations I was involved in such as joining the contractor's bowling team, taking up deep-sea fishing, taking spills on motor biking, and most importantly, the weekly beach parties. I began to like living on the Rock.

After a workday finished, on many a day, Ace, and I would take to the water dressed in diving suits, snorkels, face masks, and flippers with a spear gun in hand, taking a running start, and leaping into a ten-foot wave breaking across the reef. It was exhilarating fighting the elements once I learned how to dive into the wave without getting smashed onto the reef. To this day, I still have scars on my back carved by fire coral, injecting its poison into my skin. Once the breakers were cleared the ocean became a new world to explore. Having glimpsed the water only from above until now, I was completely mesmerized at the prolific sea life taking place below the surface. It was truly amazing.

"Stay away from these." Ace would gesture when I got too close to certain objects. Not all was safe to the touch. Especially dangerous were the stone and turkey fish, prevalent in these waters. It was not until either one was pointed out that they became visible to the diver. Where one would cling to the reef, blending in perfectly with the rocks, others would drift in schools nearby, like seaweed, seeking out prey. Both, when touched, would inject lethal poison into an unwary body, foot or hand, which would then have to be amputated to save an arm, leg, or life. I have witnessed this on several islanders, lucky to be alive, but permanently damaged with a deformed, or crippled foot or hand.

"The only means to stop the poison from spreading," I was told, "is putting the appendage into boiling water." Either way, skin, tissue, and muscles were destroyed. From here on out, being cautious, and aware of such living creatures, I exercised caution, though I felt brave enough to catch both species for my fish tank. Getting them to the surface proved to be a somewhat difficult venture without getting stung. The result was a tank filled with sea-born creatures, a miniature slice of sea life caught from the Pacific Ocean. One would not put a hand into the tank. Aside from the fun of diving, we had several close encounters with moray eels, as well as sharks. Prevalent to these waters was the white-tipped reef shark. Inexperienced as I was with diving, the first time I was confronted by sharks was pure thrill mixed with panic.

Ace had just signaled to head back to shore. Spending another afternoon amid the thrills of ocean life, I had ignored the time. It was getting dark already. He was in the lead when I was intercepted by sharks. My first reaction was the thought of flight, but that was quickly followed with reason. Flight would mean being chased with possible deadly consequences. I decided to take a stand to face the threat, and headed for the bottom. At least one side was covered: my back. It was a struggle to stay alive. Three of the white-tipped sharks headed straight for me, kept on pressing closer, and closer. The only means of protection I had was the spear gun, and knife tucked against one of my legs. First, I considered shooting the most aggressive in range, but the last second decided against. It would have triggered a feeding frenzy with me being part of their catch. The sub-surface environment was spinning with sharks until my senses sobered. After reasoning returned to my senses, I fended off the assaults by jabbing their noses with the spear. After repeated thrusts, they gradually backed off one by one long enough for me to head back towards the reef. Inching my way along the bottom in the direction of the shore, I huffed, "What a trip," and scrambled to safety on dry land.

"Where were you?" Ace wondered.

"You won't belief my encounter."

"Sharks?"

"Yes, sharks," I sputtered.

"I spotted them. It's why I signaled you. Didn't want to alarm you."

"Thanks. Swallowed more water than I had all week. Next time holler."

"Right," he said. We both wound up laughing.

There were more such incidents but without the close encounters. I had learned to keep my distance from their feeding grounds. Over time, I came to find out that sharks were territorial creatures defending their turf. At the time, there was hardly any information available on sea life, and its dangers one could encounter. A special thrill was a night dive for lobster. On one occasion, Ace was knocked over by a shark dodging between his legs from behind after he dove to the bottom to retrieve the speared lobster. I don't have to explain that the shark won out for getting the catch.

At other times I would join a fishing excursion out into the ocean to catch some of the regional fish. Common to these waters were tuna, bonito, sailfish, grouper, and snapper. All were excellent for eating. Among the teams were three fishing boats available with one taking off in the early morning hours most days. After gathering at dawn by the boat basin, it would be an eight-hour trip filled with fun and excitement for whoever was on the boats. How much partying preceded the evening before would determine how many faces would bend overboard after the first swells of waves washed over the rails. Fortunately, with exposure, and time, most got used to the sway of the boat without further sickness. The rest would remain on land, and refrain from further fishing excursions.

Once the favorite fishing ground was reached, the real fun began. Depending on species, each catch could be identified while still underwater. For this reason, different lures, and catching methods were applied. Cheering followed when a catch would reveal a tuna or bonito, everybody's favorites. Both were excellent eaten raw or BBQed for sushi, and steak.

To catch either one was not an easy task. First, the fishing grounds had to be reached. Depending on the season, the species would differ. But there was one spot off the island where a catch was guaranteed. It was the off-shore location where the Pacific Ocean met with the Philippine Sea to the north. It was a wedge-shaped region extending out from the island about forty miles. To enter these waters required extraordinary boating skills. Bordered by tumultuous crested waves, upon entering, the vessel would be jolted between the tops of waves only to drop vertically seconds later into the depths. I am sure there were silent prayers from my fisher buddies while I was usually elected to pilot the craft. Even I, at times, had doubts about whether we would make it back alive, but this always was accompanied by a rich catch. Some of it we would keep for the weekend beach party, and the rest would be sold to always present locals at the dock waiting for the boats to return. Back in the 60s, it was the usual means for the local population to get their daily fish, a staple for the islanders.

The following year, a couple of things occurred that almost cost me my life, both times. The first was a motorcycle accident on my bike, a 350-cc Honda, while I was tackling an obstacle track built on top of a mountain rim, 1450 feet high. The monsoon season had just ended when Ace and I decided to check it out. Driving to the top one Saturday morning, we jumped on the trail with Ace in the lead. Half way into the track, I watched him jump the first obstacle in the path, a diagonal trench cut by torrents of rains. Seconds later it was my turn. I revved up for the jump but fell short, resulting in the front wheel of my bike dropping into the trench. What followed next happened so fast it was beyond my control. With my hands tightly clutching the handlebar to keep the front aloft, the sudden drop twisted the accelerator to maximum throttle, in turn twisting my bike 45 degrees into the bottom of the washed-out trench. At full speed, the bike, and I shot over the edge of the cliff.

While my mind registered the rapid sequence of events, my reactions were too slow to prevent the inevitable, a vertical drop to the coral reef I knew was fourteen hundred-some feet below. The forward momentum lasted only a second, with me seated rigid in the saddle, until the bike began to drop straight down. It must have been by instinct alone that I released my hands, turning my body forward into a stretched-out position to follow the bike. When I saw the ocean swells breaking across the reef below, I had one last thought. It was not a pleasant one. I cussed into the incoming ground, "God damnit. What a way to go."

Seconds later, I saw the ground rush into my face. At the last instant I turned my helmeted head away from getting smashed in the face before blacking out. I don't remember how long I was unconscious for when I opened my eyes, the first action was to take in air but this proved unsuccessful. No matter how hard I tried, my lungs would not work. I blacked out again. Sometime later, it must have been after the muscle function from my collapsed lungs returned, I was able to take my first lifesaving breath of air. Still dazed, I was gradually winched up to the top of the mountain trail. Thirty minutes later, as I was bandaged up, laying on the hospitalized gurney, Ace relayed the information for what had happened.

Driving ahead on the trail he was able to jump the wash on his 125-cc Honda. Considerably lighter than my 350-cc, he had no problems. "I watched you follow a hundred feet back when one second you were there, and the next you were gone," he explained. "There was only one way you could have gone. Off the cliff. I backtracked to the trench, leaned over the edge expecting you a thousand feet below. But instead, I saw you had landed on an outcropping fifty-some feet below. Next, I was able to reach Tony"—a team member who I knew owned a Jeep with a built-in, front-end winch. "Thirty minutes later, we hoisted you up. That's when you woke up. We realized your lungs were collapsed, causing the blackout. Resuscitation partially worked, long enough until you reached consciousness."

"Man, am I glad to be alive. I thought it was the end when I saw the reef below. Don't know how I can ever thank you."

"You being alive is enough thanks," he muttered, in his ever so humble manner. To thank the team, several days later I hosted a party after being released from the hospital. In spite of a broken shoulder, ribs, knee, ankle, and foot, I was able to hobble along on crutches. I should point out that many injuries, while I was still young, for the most part healed up. It was years later when the injuries resurfaced in the form of aches, and pain. Today, hardly a day goes by without feeling past damage to bones, muscles, and tissue. Nights are especially troublesome.

The second event equal in intensity, only weeks later, happened in the air. It was a trip we had plotted for my flight training. I was scheduled for the aviation test to get my private pilot license. Due to the lack of land area on many islands, with a three-point landing requirement by the FAA, a minimum flight distance of 250 miles at the time, aside from Hawaii, Guam was the exception to the flight restriction about flying over open water with a student license.

It was the dry season. The sky was blue without any chance for clouds or rain. I plotted the course to land on Tinian Island, then fly on to Saipan, land, refuel, and return to Guam. It would be an easy flight in the Cessna 172 I had rented. As usual, Ace was by my side, qualified as a flight instructor. The guy was amazing for what he had accomplished at his young age. Checking the weather report, submitting the flight plan at the departure desk, following the pre-flight check that included topping fuel tank, external craft inspection, and engine oil level check. Next came mechanical functions check for elevator, aileron, and rudder controls. Final check was cockpit inspection comprised of altimeter setting to local ground reference, compass heading adjustment for flight direction, radio dial for departure frequency, and a request for takeoff. After a short drive to the end of the runway, with all checked out, accompanied by Ace in the instructor seat, I took the craft to the air.

Cruising at an 12,000-foot altitude, headed in a northerly direction, flight time at 140 knots for the 135 miles distance would take approximately an hour and twenty minutes including ascent, and descent. The flight, as I listened mostly to the drone of the engine, was a pleasure. The view below was a vast expanse of blue ocean, the distant horizon was hazy without any land in sight. Trouble did not start until an hour, and thirty minutes into the flight.

"I don't see the island." Ace broke the silence. I was slightly alert but not alarmed. Checking the horizon, there was no island in sight. I reached for the map to compare my flight plan with flight time, and compass heading. It all checked out.

"What do you think is going on?" I said. Ace remained quiet. Self-confident as usual, he seemed to contemplate the reasons for the discrepancy. The speed had held steady the entire trip without wind shift or air turbulence. By now, the arrival time had already passed by ten minutes. We should have been on a descent path fifteen minutes ago. Something had gone wrong neither he or I could figure out with time and fuel running short.

"I'm going to fly a grid," I said.

"We don't have enough fuel. We've only got one shot. Ten more minutes, and we'll have to ditch."

"Can't belief there's no island," I muttered. I was as puzzled as he was.

"We should be directly over Saipan. What did you do?" he shouted over the drone of the engine.

"What?" I swallowed hard.

"What's the compass heading?" I sensed his frustration with me being at fault. But there was nothing I could do but being humble.

"Right at 30 NNE." Shaking my head in doubt, I compared the compass with the map once more.

"Can't be." He was adamant. Even he was getting alarmed as time was running out.

"Wait a minute," I broke in.

"What?"

"I've got an idea," I volunteered, clinging to hope with only minutes remaining before we were forced to ditch.

"Out with it. There's not time." Although we succumbed to the inevitable, we had to keep trying to solve the mishap.

"The compass. What do you read?" My nerves were stressed to the breaking point now.

"Why? There's nothing wrong with the heading. I've flown it before."

"Give me the heading," I shouted out with an elevated urgency while fear set in for the waters below.

"30° NNE."

"The map," I gestured again.

"Should be 28° NNE," Ace corrected. "You're off by two degrees," he said with a hint of blame in his voice.

It did not make sense to me until I checked my seating position. My quick analysis revealed that during the initial flight check when setting up the compass, I was seated in the copilot's seat. From my point of view, the compass registered a two-degree difference from him, the pilot position. It was enough for a considerable course deviation over the 135-mile distance. Being a hazy day, and us high enough in altitude to canvas the horizon, the island should have been in view directly ahead, and below.

"I better call Guam flight control. They may have us on radar," I huffed with droplets of sweat streaming down my face.

"Naw," he replied. "We're too far out for radar." Though he did not let on, it was obvious he was trying to solve the same concerns I had, ditching the craft.

"I'm flying a grid," I insisted, determined to find the island. Being a pilot candidate, it was unthinkable for me to fail the pilot license before I'd even been certified. "Here goes one chance," I said, turning the craft 90 degrees west. It was the only logical heading that made sense to make up for the miscalculation. Still flying at 12,000 feet, an island, though hazy, and barely visible, gradually crept into view.

"We'll make it," Ace proclaimed with a grin, slapping my shoulder. I wasn't sure if it was a friendly gesture or one of reprimand, but I felt it to the bone. Sure enough, minutes later, he'd recognized and identified Saipan. We would make it, even if the craft would run out of fuel. We had enough height to glide to our destination ten miles out.

It could have turned into a calamity ending in injury, or worse, death. On our safe return, both of us headed straight for the club. It did not have to be suggested that drinks were in order. Both of us never spoke of the experience. He had his reason for trusting my navigation skills, and I blamed myself for not having enough flying experience. I learned that, while placing complete trust in the instruments, they are only as good as the navigator's alertness.

The two years for my contract obligation passed by too fast. At this time, I had acquired a passion for all the recreational activities I participated in. The job took care of itself once everybody on board acquired the necessary skills for performing their duties. Much of my days were occupied with performance liaison, personnel evaluations, and weekly status reports back to HQs and to fleet command. Hardware, and software failures still popped up but with less frequency. Much of my work I could delegate to the shifts. The more difficult systems problems I would handle myself. For these, sophisticated diagnostic programs were developed. Though I was intricately familiar with them, having been part of software development and diagnostics development teams, I preferred using my own techniques. I would insert a dozen program instructions into the mainframe registers, press the Enter button, and have data analysis on the printer within seconds. One look at the information returned would be sufficient to identify, correct, and solve the failure, which for most part would turn out to be another failed transistor. With computer technology rapidly evolving, components were becoming more reliable. Solving software challenges proved to be more difficult. For that, I had to set software traps followed with analysis work to catch the bug.

Speaking of evolving, I also detected changes on the island. The rebuilding of towns, and dwellings, destroyed by the typhoon the previous year, progressed just as rapidly. Not only did the island population experience construction growth all around, new business was attracted as well. Entrepreneurs arrived daily on flights from Taiwan, Japan, and the Philippines offering their respective skills, and investments. The Japanese's primary interests were in acquiring beach properties. Within months, new ground was broken all along the Tamuning shorelines. Having time on my hands, even I became involved. First, I invested in a resort complex developed along the beach, followed by the acquisition of two prime condo units, with a pristine view of the ocean and sunsets, even before property sales had closed. It became the start of the investment spirit I would carry through life.

Being tired of driving the rented Beetle, one day at the Governor's hosted party which I had been invited to, I purchased his car on the spot. He mentioned getting a new model and I took the opportunity. It was a black 98 Oldsmobile sedan, deserving of his status, which now was mine. Each day I drove it to work people would wave at me, thinking it was the island's governor. It helped me to become even more popular on the island. I was already member of the Executive bowling league, a team comprised mostly of business, and political leaders. The acquired status suited me well.

In hindsight, working decent hours supported by a well-performing crew, liaison to Naval Command, enjoying recreational opportunities, dinner invites, beach parties, my life could have been secured and successful. Who could wish for more? I did.

There was something gnawing at my mind. That something was the world. I wanted to explore it. It was what I set out to do years ago. I felt my dream slipping away. Taking stock over my two-year commitment one day, I was faced with a difficult decision. Should I stay, and continue life at its fullest leisure, or throw it all away, and move on? I still had several more months to decide. Pushing the thought aside, I pursued my daily life of sun, fun, and excitement, not wanting to face the pending decision.

"I'm taking a trip," Ace announced one day with the holidays coming up.

"Oh? Where're you going?"

"Home to visit my folks."

"How long will you be gone?"

"One week. Think you can live without me?" he said with an egocentric grin on his face. He knew quite well that it would impact my recreational activities since he was my buddy for diving, flying, and biking.

"I guess," I replied. "I have no choice. I'll survive."

One week came, and went without Ace returning when I received word from the home office that Ace had been detained by authorities. Which ones? Nobody seemed to know until another week went by when he finally showed up back on Guam. "Where in hell were you? People are looking for you."

"In jail," he confessed.

"But why?"

"I smuggled my firearm collection through customs, and got caught."

"What?"

"Remember the guns we bought?"

"I should. We bought them together." While I had acquired two handguns, a 45 cal. semi-automatic, and a 357 cal. Ruger Magnum at the Anderson AFB BX, he confessed that he had bought a few more weapons.

"How many more?" I said, surprised.

"Thirty-two."

"Are you out of your mind?"

"Hey," he said, almost yelling. "I'm a collector."

"What happened to your guns?"

"That's why it took so long. I was detained at Hawaii customs until I could prove ownership."

"But thirty-two guns?" I was still awestruck. "Did you get them back?"

"I did, but had to register them with the FBI."

It reminded me of my own purchase. "Guess I better do the same before I leave."

"You decided yet?"

I had expressed my desires to get off the island on several occasions. "I'm not staying if you're leaving," he would respond. I never found out his reasons for wanting to leave. Despite the buddies we were, with a dependency developed for life and death for each other, it still amazed me that we really did not know each other outside of our common sport activities. We may have been just too busy enjoying life to dwell on personal feelings and sentiments. We just lived the moment. Since, I have learned that women typically do a better job with that. He left the island shortly after, off to whatever venture he had decided on. Unfortunately, we lost contact with each other.

That was the turning point for me on the island. While there were a number of personnel on site with which to make friends, after two years, most had formed their own groups of friendship within their work schedules. It was then that the family spirit surfaced, keeping the common bond alive for the American overseas. No matter where or what the circumstances were, it did not take long to form a local community of home-based spirits.

I had several more weeks to go before my departure. Ace's leaving made up my mind. I was ready to move on. When word spread of my decision, I was surprised at how many others quit with the same response: "I'm not staying if you leave." It was an exodus headquarters had not expected. Begging me to stay on did not change my mind, even with the director paying a visit. I realized the burden it would place on the company. They had a contract with Naval Command. I was under contract, and so were the others. "But hey," I thought, "this is not a penal colony. We live in a free society." No matter how much Art, and the local command tried to convince me to stay, my mind was made up. "I paid my dues, two years on the Rock," I told him.

Fortunately, two other sites', Okinawa, and the Philippines, contractual obligations came to an end with the initial site management, operations, and support obligations of two years expired. Up for open bidding from other computer service companies, some locations changed hands, with some remaining in place. Guam was one such condition. What management did was bring in some of the released personnel from the two incumbent sites to replace the departing staff on Guam, resolving the issue I had caused. What my future with the company held for further assignments was up in the air, but I stood my ground. I would not let me be forced into another corporate breach of commitment with a promised replacement, as I had already experienced twice.

With staffing resolved, I was released to tidy up my personal affairs. My vehicle, and sporting equipment had to be sold among bidding my farewell to my personal connections I had established in the last two years on the island, thinking it would be the last time I'd set foot on Guam. Unbeknownst to me, the future had other plans. I would visit the place many more times along the journey I was about to embark on. There was one more thing I wanted to do before my departure: take one last flight over the island.

It was a Saturday morning when I stopped by the airport to check out a Cessna-150. Air traffic was light since most international flights arrived during evening hours. I did not file much of a flight plan since it would be a local flight exercise. Taking one circle around the island would take about forty minutes, after which I would be back for the landing. Taking to the air, I was always amazed at how serene things appeared from above. The only sound I perceived was the steady engine hum. Arriving back at the airport, I decided to finish with some practice runs. Checking with ground control, I was assigned the usual area for private flight maneuvers, designated ten miles off at an 8,000-foot altitude.

From a flight perspective, there were a few procedures one could perform. Most common was touch and go, landing, and taking off practice. Next common was instrument training, followed by cross country flight. The most undesirable performance was the stall. While required by FAA flight policy, it was not much practiced after pilot certification. The reason was obvious just by the term alone. The stall was considered an emergency procedure in case of an engine failure or running out of fuel, which could happen to the best of pilots. It was the reason why pilots were instructed to "always look out for a landing spot below," no matter what route one had plotted for the flight. The rule applied to me as well today. While setting the rule aside, practice flights were at an altitude, and area near enough to the airport in case of an engine failure. It would get most light planes back to the runway on glide.

I was not happy with my first practice stall. I had lost too much height, close to 120 feet in altitude drop. The next stall I exercised was much better. To the non-flyer, the procedure was as follows. Pulling the throttle to idle, the craft was taken into a steep climb, straight up. Within seconds, the weight of the craft would pull against the upward momentum of propeller, and engine power. The effect was the craft slowing into a motion where upward momentum stopped. The result, in an abrupt change, due to the craft's design, was that the plane's nose would drop forward into a straight dive, headed for the ground. It was up to the pilot to compensate for the sudden drop with rudder, and engine controls. Applying engine power with the flight control handle pulled in towards the chest, the craft should recover into level flight with merely a fifty-foot drop within seconds. If executed as described within the emergency recovery manual, it was a relatively simple maneuver. I had practiced the stall a dozen times or more with perfect results.

It was getting dark. Ready to call it a day after three such stalls, I had a thought. "What about a power-on stall? It should achieve the same results." Slightly apprehensive, I decided to give it a try. It was a decision I still regret to this day. "Here we go," I muttered over the engine sound. Pushing the throttle to maximum power, I pulled back on the controls with the engines roaring. The craft behaved much like a normal stall. There was only one difference: it kept on climbing upwards. Almost at the point where I was giving up the maneuver, it finally slowed its upward momentum, coming to a halt. "So far so good," I remember thinking. What transpired seconds later was completely unexpected.

Rather than the craft's nose dropping into the expected dive, the craft turned onto its left side into an ever-tightening spin towards the ground. My view straight ahead was a kaleidoscopic effect I had never experienced. Earth was spinning around its own axis at two seconds each turn to a point where dizziness took hold. Instantly, I became nauseous. Amid the sickening feeling taken hold on my body, my eyes were frantically watching the instruments spinning at an ever-increasing rate. Each time I checked the altimeter I'd dropped another five hundred feet. At this rate, my mind calculated, it would take less than thirty seconds for the inevitable crash. My mind was screaming for a solution when I recalled something, I had read in emergency manuals. But no matter how hard I tried to stop the spin by slamming the rudder paddles in the opposite direction against the spin, the craft did not stop spinning. With the craft spinning left, I punched the rudder to the right, perhaps twenty times. At the point of giving in to the inevitable, my eye touched on the power throttle. An immediate light went on in my brain. "Of course. That's it."

In the process of setting up the stall, with throttle at maximum power, the craft moved upward until it reached equilibrium in motion. For a second it hung weightless in the air before engine torque took over. It literally spun the craft into the opposite direction of engine motion, taking the body of the plane into a rotation with the left wing pointed to the ground.

With the most frantic move I have ever made, I yanked the throttle back to idle, reducing engine power. Next was stopping the insane spinning. With the next rudder slam to the right, a miracle happened. The spinning slowed, a couple more slams and the rotation stopped. At least my focus came back, but I also realized how much height I had lost. "Not going to make it," my mind registered with the ground shooting directly at my face. I was still in a straight dive down. A glance at the altimeter brought on the next shock. The craft had already exceeded the safety speed of the Cessna design, 250 mph. "There's no way the wings will hold," were my final thoughts but I had to give it a try. I realized that I was doomed.

With engine power at idle, I pulled back on the control handle, applying all my energy while I sat, and watched the wings dip past the crest of palm trees passing by my view. At less than fifty feet, wings straining under the controls, in the last seconds, I watched the craft finally level out to a straight flight. "I'm going to make it," my mind screamed with euphoria. For my next reaction, I applied engine power to regain flight height, and not soon enough. I barely cleared the terrain, including populated dwellings in my path. I realized that I would live, but not without the possible consequence of losing my license. I took my time to calm my nerves while circling the airport.

Minutes later, I called ground control for a landing request. "You're pushing it today, aren't you?" the voice from the tower controller operator shot back.

Glad to be alive, I had regained most of my senses, evaluating what had just transpired. Not wanting to put my pilot certification in jeopardy any further, I tried to be as calm as possible with my response. "Just practicing stalls."

I did not think he quite believed me, especially not if he had been watching my last maneuver. It did not take binoculars to see where I was practicing the stall. When passing by his flight desk, all he said was, "Just take it easy with the flying from now on. I've got other planes in the air." He was right. After all, Guam Airport was international with flights arriving though mostly for refueling stops, in addition to local pilots flying their personal planes.

I don't have to emphasize that it would be my last power-on stall for a while. I had decided to leave maneuvers like that to stunt pilots. I was not cut out for it. Perhaps in my younger years, yes. Either case required nerves of steel, and guts with a desire to face death.

It would be my last adventurous encounter before leaving the island, headquarters bound, hoping for a reassignment to the promised foreign destination. My mind was set on Asia.

The following day, I boarded the Island-hopping flight for one last time. Two hours later I landed at my immediate destination, the Philippines. I wanted to experience the place one last time in the company of my local business friends. Several days later I continued the flight to my final destination, Taiwan.

I would spend the greater part of the day contemplating what direction to turn for my future career when the phone rang. It was a Chinese friend I always visited when in Taiwan. I met up with him at the hotel bar for a couple drinks. While I would pace my alcoholic intake, he on the other hand did not. I was curious about one thing that I had noticed. Most Asian people turned red in the face when imbibing alcoholic beverages. It was not only a distinct visible sign, but it must cause a certain amount of discomfort to watch them scratching and rubbing their skin, which I'd observed on numerous occasions. When I asked about the symptoms, "Alcohol heats up my body," was the general answer. There was another thing I should mention. Asian people could, and would get drunk at any occasion, but would not develop hangovers suffering through the next day, as most white people did.

The reason was explained with a then recently conducted two-year study by Mellon University. Studying enzymes, and blood samples from dozens of human specimens, the secret finally surfaced. Asians lacked two enzymes in the intestines that white people have. It was these missing enzymes that prevented the digestion of alcohol, allowing a direct absorption into the bold stream. It would heat up their blood, resulting in their skin turning red, and heated to the touch. For now, I enjoyed my time in the company of the friend. I did not know if we would ever see each other again since the political tension between Taiwan, and mainland China was heating up. China wanted this island outpost back in their control which they had lost during WWII.

Bidding my goodbyes to my friend, I returning back to the hotel I was staying where the hotel clerk waved to get my attention. Approaching the desk, he informed me, "You have a message waiting," handing over an envelope. Tearing it open, I found it was an official embassy typewritten directive stating: "Report to HQs. Next available flight." Though it was an immediate change in directions, I still had to return to Guam to collect my personal belongings, and check out with Naval Command.

"Could you please call the airport to arrange a seat on the next available flight to Guam," I beckoned the manager. Thirty minutes later I departed for the airport. "Come again. Soon," the desk manager said, palmed the twenty I pressed into his hand while flagging the next taxi waiting for a fare. "Airport," I directed.

Two days later arriving at HQs, "Thought you'd slip away again," Art, with a sheepish grin on his face, greeted me as soon as I stepped into his Willow Grove office.

"Can't blame me for trying," I responded. Over the years, we had developed a close, but professional relationship. We each respected each other's status, his being the boss, and mine being his warrior for getting the job done on the frontlines. "Is Buzz here?" I asked. Buzz, the nickname he'd acquire, was suitable to his personality. He had been on the team the longest. No matter how many new members rotated through on their assignments, he was the core of the projects I was assigned. Much like me, he was a committed nomad, in for the duration of a career, inspired by contracting opportunities extended by the government. For the most part, we had become interdependent on each other.

"He's waiting for you."

"So," I demanded, "what's the assignment?"

"This one you'll like. It's close to your hometown, Augsburg, Germany."

"No kidding? I'll be able to visit my family." It had been ten years since I'd left Germany, and my family behind. I could already imagine how happy they'd be. Earlier that year I had received a postcard from my father, informing me, "I'm getting married again." He had promised, on my departure, to keep me abreast of family affairs. He also kept me informed about accomplishments of former friends, and schoolmates. I was looking forward of meeting his third wife, my new stepmother. Although Dad had his own agenda, and affairs, nobody would ever replace my real mom. Although her loss already a part of history, the fondness of my memories of her would vividly stay with me, always.

"Let's have dinner," Art offered. It was an invitation I would never turn down. The man knew how to celebrate. It would be a steak dinner at the best restaurant in town, accompanied by jokes, reminiscing, fine Italian wine, and after-dinner drinks. "Tell Buzz, and some on the team to join us." He knew exactly who would be seated around the table. His favorite allies. The gang he could always depend on, and took care of no matter what the prevalent situation.

"See you at six," I promised on my way out. As expected, the gathering turned out like many times before, filled with jokes, and laughter. The host, who else but an Italian, had grown fond of us, tolerating our somewhat, at times, noisy antics, but always appreciating our presence. He would happily instigate another round of drinks, in the process getting inebriated just the same as the rest of us, with the tab paid for by the Boss, as everybody called Art.

I should point out that getting high on drinks was not a norm for us. It was reserved for special occasions by the core team within the current program. Always a treat, nevertheless, being hosted by the Boss, everybody took advantage of such a distinct social gathering. Though plagued the following day with hangovers, alcohol was the method of choice for us. It would have been unthinkable, taking to drugs. Not in our career, as sensitive as substance drugs were treated back then. Subjected to a pledge in the name of national security, one infraction would have caused immediate termination from the job, ending one's career. Aside from that, drugs were not our choice of entertainment anyway.

A personal note: I had the opportunity to observe the results of drugs versus alcohol on projects on numerous occasions during my career, and came to the following conclusion. Where an alcohol user could be relied on to perform on the job as trained for a given skill level, a drug user could not. It must be the substance base causing the difference. Alcohol apparently stimulated brain cells, where drugs, in many cases, suppresses one's innovative capacity. I specified "in many cases" because I have observed individuals turn into genius-level creators while habitually using psychedelic substances, especially with software designers. But those were exceptions.

Two days later we were on the way to Germany with a promise from the Boss: "Keep up the good work. I'll visit soon."

"I'll be looking forward to it. Make it real soon."

"Wouldn't miss it," he called out, watching us head for the airport.

GERMANY

"Everybody make the flight?" I asked Buzz while he propped his body into the next seat. Like most flights in the 70s, seating was spacious. It would take another decade before airlines would gear up to accommodate the masses. For now, as usual with overseas flights, headquarters had put us up in business class. I was grateful for the special treatment especially since the arrival of the Boeing-747, and its world-class services. It was a time, pre-terrorism, where passengers could enjoy air travel. That would change with the first terrorist attack I would personally experience. But that was later.

"Nobody else is on the flight," he informed me. "Most on the team are newly hired. Left days ago, while you had fun in Taiwan."

"Hey," I protested. "Not much fun when you get called away after one night." He was well aware that hotel management on Taiwan had already planned for me to have a hostess serve as a tour guide while on the island. It was a common practice for arriving guests in Asia. Leave it to the Chinese—they may be a hard-working lot, but when it came to hosting a guest, no effort was missed for providing comfort. It was their way breaking away from a never-ending workload piled on much of the population. Where in the West, many laborious tasks had been mechanized and automated by machines, the Chinese laborer was still a link in an endless conveyor belt formed by human muscles.

"You've been to Augsburg?" he wanted to know.

"Once. Ancient city near Munich. You'll like it."

"Tell me about the place," he said.

"Built by Romans two thousand years ago like many cities in Germany. Walled, cobblestone streets throughout the city, you may still hear the clanking of horse hooves early mornings, and evenings resounding through your room."

"What about bars, and clubs? You know," he said, "the team's going to ask."

"Lots of restaurants, and bars."

"What about the beer? I heard it was different from ours."

"You'll get hooked on it like everybody else. I promise you." Most visitors— American military, vacationers, and businessmen alike—immediately take to the locally-brewed beer. While light beer had been brewed, and recently introduced by the Japanese, European countries were solidly clinging to their ancient traditions, beer, and wine included. "Nobody drinks this piss in Germany," were comments made when canned beer was introduced. Light beer was created to satisfy a world of ever-growing demand, but the Germans stuck to their traditional brewing process of a nine-month natural fermentation. Sadly, I must admit, even that culture was pressed into changes in the not too distant future. There came a time when I could not find a naturally-brewed beer in American liquor stores. But for now, I ordered from the stewardess, "Bottle of German beer."

"Make it two," Buzz said.

"You won't be disappointed," I promised. It turned out that we drank several more by the time we landed.

I had ample time to contemplate my life, and career as I usually did on a lengthy flight. Total travel time to Munich, our destination, would be an eight-hour night flight, arriving early the next morning. I was never able to nap in transit. The reason? I still don't know to this day. It did not bother me much. I could always catch up after I was settled in at the next lodging. Surrounded by the subdued hum of jet engines, my thoughts touched on the present, as well as the past. Whenever I was sitting idle, I dwelled on the past. My life had turned out more than I'd ever dreamed of during my childhood. My destiny had been limited to German's post-war predicament if I'd stayed on, but it had turned a most unexpected turn after my arrival in the new land, America. I was on my way to adventure, and it was the adventures I would reminisce on during my idle times. Though it may seem unproductive for the upcoming project, once I arrived in stress-free mode, it assured a satisfied client, in this case NATO Intel.

I had been informed by Art about the project waiting at the end of the present flight. "The building's just been completed. Your job," he'd explained, "is to install the equipment we shipped out, presently in storage, interconnect mainframes with all other equipment, troubleshoot, debug, test it all, and let me know when you get close to finishing. You've got three months."

"Anything else?" I'd asked, slightly annoyed at the pressing tight time frame.

"You can do it. Work overtime if you have to," were his departing words. "I'll be there," and that was it. My orders were to serve NATO for whatever their Intel agenda was.

Surprisingly, I dozed off for a couple of hours, and awakened when I heard the announcement from the flight attendant: "Thirty more minutes to landing…"

Buzz, and I were still drowsy when we collected our briefcases from the overhead storage compartment.

"Where to?" Buzz said after checking through customs, and baggage claim.

"Rental car." The rental was already waiting.

"Wow," Buzz exclaimed. "Beemer. Going in style." We were looking at a latest-design BMW in the stall, waiting for us to take possession. The day before our departure, I had instructed the travel agent of my preference.

"Let's go," Buzz said, anxious to road test the vehicle.

"Let's see what she can do," I said, stepping on the pedal. With Buzz clinging to the seat, even I was amazed at how much horsepower the Beemer developed when I opened it up on the Autobahn headed for Augsburg. It was thrilling to be able to max out the accelerator without fear of the police chasing you down.

"Where'd you learn to drive this speed?" Buzz appeared slightly tensed-up but impressed.

"I grew up here, remember?" It wasn't so much him being concerned at the speed. It was an inherited cautionary action with somebody else doing the driving. An hour later we checked into a guesthouse, the usual accommodation back then. Motels had not yet propagated to the "Old" country, as I usually referred to European places. Hotels were more of an establishment and also rare. And, if so, they were occupied by regional, traveling businessmen. We each lavishly received a single room, though it was customary to double-up at many places. It could mean a different stranger in the room each night. I had occasions of no sleep, listening to the snoring from strangers in the next bed, unaware of their personally induced intrusion, glad when the early light of dawn arrived.

What made lodging in Europe different from the U.S. was that a lavish breakfast was dished out, including a variety of coffee, tea, milk, creamer, bacon, ham, eggs, potatoes, butter, preserves, fruits, bread, and rolls, including ample assortments of cheese. It was the meal of the day, highly appreciated by the team burning three thousand calories loading, unloading, and staging heavy computer equipment, and cable gear. For most team members it was either heavy work and, when that was completed, followed with the tedious tasks of making interconnections with tens of thousands of wire strands, color-coded for continuity and connections. Each signal wire had its specific digital path from the originating processing register to the final connection at the crypto gear ready for transmission in the ether. The reverse was obtained for receiving signals from any location on the globe. It was the ingenious design of color codes that was able to accomplish flawless data processing across the distance without so much as one single data bit loss.

"Know where you're going?" Buzz was by my side, trailed by several rental cars, locally leased for the duration of the project, making sure nobody got lost.

"Place called Gablingen Kasern."

"What's that?"

"Name of town, and NATO Intel on the German army base." It was a fifteen-minute drive to cover the distance.

"Man, is it ever foggy." As soon as we left town, visions became impaired by dense fog.

"It's common early in the morning."

"Can't even make out street signs." He was right. I had a difficult time driving, but made it without incident by following the white center line, always kept freshly painted for this reason, looking for a left breakout in the road. You could not see more than ten feet ahead. Drivers were forced to slow to a crawl until the sun burnt off the heavy layer of fog later in the morning.

"Not the first time," I assured him of my driving experience in the land. I grew up in fog-layered valleys. I'd expected nothing less. Others on the team were not so lucky. There was the occasional fender bender but, fortunately, no serious crashes for the following months while work proceeded on schedule with a total team complement of about fifty in site engineers, computer/COMM installation technicians, manager, supervisors, logistics, and support personnel, overseen by NATO administrators, dispatched from SHAPE[19] headquarters homed at Belgium.

There were, however, two major occurrences worth mentioning. The first was immediately after site installation was complete. One day, a special Tempest[20] team

---

[19] Supreme Headquarters Allied Powers Europe (SHAPE), headquarters of the North Atlantic Treaty Organization's, Allied Command Operations.

[20] TEMPEST – Prescribe policies, procedures, and responsibilities for the Department of Defense to evaluate, and control compromising electronic signal emanations. The procedures implement national-level, and DOD policies to protect information from foreign Intelligence collection. It required that the application

arrived to inspect security leaks for the facility, as well as our work progress. I was busy with the usual analysis work and felt a presence nearby when someone asked, "How does it feel to be back home?" I did not have to look up to recognize the voice.

"Mystery Man," I muttered from behind the stack of computer printouts. "What are you doing here?"

"Checking up on you," he replied with a grin.

"You wish." I knew, no matter how pressing, and difficult a project he threw at me, there was never an issue of non-compliance or non-performance on my part. My team, the best in the world, and I always got the job done within the scheduled time, and under the allocated budget. "What's up?"

"We need to talk."

"The office?"

"Not secure enough," he said, hinting at the purpose of his visit. "Any place private nearby?"

This aroused my curiosity while my mind tried to come up with a place other than the site. "I know a spot in town." Ten minutes later we drove up to my favorite place, a cafe. A quiet place this time of day, though it never got noisy in evenings even when crowded. My favorite waitress was tending to us. "Alex," she said. "Taking the day off?"

We had been socializing on her evenings off, and she knew about my long working hours. Ever since my arrival in Germany, I had been busy with systems testing and analysis. "Yes. Special visitor."

"Hi," she greeted my company with a friendly gesture. "America?" Back then, an American visitor was always welcomed. It meant special courtesy on top of ample tipping. German customs did not provide for personal gratuity. Tipping was not expected, but welcomed, nevertheless.

"I was here before," he said, looking up at her. Addressing her directly was not customary for the Mystery-man. He tried to avoid eye contact whenever possible.

"Oh. When?"

"WWII."

Her demeanor quickly changed from friendliness to resentment. "Dropping bombs on us?" Although it had been already twenty-five years since the end of the war, the Germans still had a bitter taste.

"Let's not talk about the past," I reminded her. "Times have changed. Besides, he's my friend." It was the first time I suggested a personal friendship and was curious at his reaction. He appeared pleased by the smile he offered her. It seemed to have broken the WWII-barrier many Germans still harbored.

"What can I get you?" She asked with a friendly smile on her face.

"Try some German wine," I suggested.

"German wine it is." He seemed grateful to not have to explain his missions of destruction, already more than two decades in the past. I was happy that she didn't press further. "Listen," he said when we were alone. "We've got a problem at the site. A huge problem. We may not be able to go live."

---

of TEMPEST countermeasures be proportional, and appropriate to the threat, and potential damage to national security.

"What do you mean? Ever?"

"Yes, ever."

"You better explain." It was unthinkable for me to accept such an unexpected turn of events, not with the way the Cold War was escalating. Only recently, though demanded by NATO Command, the deployment of short range, nuclear-tipped missiles had been rebuffed by the U.S. Congress in view of threatened retaliation by the Soviet Union.

"The results from the Tempest team came in. They have located seventy bugs in your facility."

I was stunned and said so, "Holy shit." It was enough of a report to shake up everybody. In short, the team had located that many electronic spying devices implemented into the walls, and ductwork in the building. Getting to them was no easy task, for it required breaking through structures ready for operation, potentially causing unprecedented delays. It was no secret to us who the instigators were.

"What are you going to do?" For once, I had the luxury of putting the burden on him, and the government.

"Don't know yet. What I do know is what you are going to do."

And there it was. The responsibility shifted back into my lap once more. "What?"

"I need you to take each piece of equipment apart, and inspect it for bugs."

"But that'll take days, weeks," I objected. It was not that I objected to the delay. To begin with, my team would welcome some additional time since they were enjoying their time in Germany. Some experienced a good time alone while other had already teamed up with some local girls with a hint of promises for a future together, as was not an uncommon practice among allies. I had a professional reputation to protect, a flawless career.

"What would you suggest?"

I thought about it for a minute, then said, "I can take care of hardware, and systems, but what about the software?" I had taken a system apart before, and reassembled it while keeping it in operation, if only on a limited downtime basis.

"I've got that covered. Software team can handle it remotely." I understood, since I worked closely with DARPA programmers at the highly secure Ft. Detrick,[21] MD facility. As a matter of fact, I had been part of the sophisticated Utility Program[22] development, and testing years ago.

"How much time do I have?"

"Two weeks," he announced unceremoniously.

"You're Crazy!" I shouted out while detecting a smirk in his usually somber face. I knew that he liked throwing challenges at me. My success also assured his success. He relied wholeheartedly on my skills, and capabilities; I, on the other hand,

---

[21] The DARPA software development fell to a proprietary company, also primary contractor responsible for creating the AUTODIN operating platform, and applications.

[22] Utility Programs were a major part in mainframe computers and its associated equipment. It greatly aided in the analysis, and problem solving of computer hardware issues by localizing a failed component down to the individual circuit board. The basis was to break into each circuit on the electronic board, run the Utility test, incorporate the resultant error, reassemble the program, and continue to simulate the next failure, one circuit at a time. It may seem like an enormous effort but the result was a timely analysis during an operational mainframe failure.

appreciated him keeping political entities off of my back. "You're a slave driver," I manage to say, but agreed. "Two weeks it is."

"I'll hold you to it. Two weeks is all they'll allow. And," he insisted in a whispered tone, "absolute secrecy."

"You can trust me."

"Make sure to tell your team. We cannot afford a security leak on the bugs. We want to keep the Soviets believing their bugs are still in place and operation."

I fully understood.

The second incident occurred shortly after. One early morning, I received a call: "Emergency! Get your team on site. Immediately!"

On arriving, twenty minutes later, the ground floor was covered in water inches deep, pouring from an overhead ceiling-based sprinkler pipe. Broken in half, water was shooting into offices, and hallways. It called for immediate action by everybody, warding off waves of water by using brooms to slow the flow of water headed for the computer, and communication rooms below ground. It was a hectic effort to keep power, and electronics from turning into a fireball. It would have been a total loss, and caused permanent shutdown of the site.

The investigation that followed revealed that somebody had sabotaged the sprinkler system. It became plain that someone did not want the system operational. Who, and what entity was behind the sabotage was never officially disclosed, not even to me.

The result? I was served with letters of thanks by NATO authorities, the team came out heroically, accompanied with bonus incentives.

The completion of installation, testing, and certification signified the end of site deployments. The initial project effort, as envisioned by JFK, for a survivable communication system in case of an all-out nuclear war had come to a completion. The complex, as a whole, performed flawlessly. In its entire operation over the following decades, it proved invaluable to the U.S. Department of Defense. The protection of our citizens was assured, country wealth, and assets were protected while spying between the superpowers went on as usual, aided by NATO, all securing the necessity of the NORAD Mountain complex for protecting us from any surprise attacks by the Soviet Union.

Art showed up as he had promised on my departure for this project, months earlier. Yes, it was the first time I did not live up to my reputation, "project delivery within the allocated timeline." Delays were multi-fold, with some already stated above. It must be understood that my team and I were not the only participants for the NATO project. There were numerous contractors present, local as well as from the U.S. While some were still putting finishing touches on interior and exterior of the building, others were occupied with special tasks from sniffing out bugs, mounting transmission antennas, connecting facility cabling to the national grid, arranging supply lines with local and foreign suppliers, informing and coordinating process and procedures with the other Intelligence facilitates, keeping allied organizations abreast local and international, maintaining public relations with Augsburg's mayor and political affiliations, and more, all contributing to project delays. My hands were washed clean from taking any personal responsibilities.

I was grateful.

"Hey," I greeted him. "Didn't expect you here."

"I promised. Remember? I wouldn't miss the trip for anything. You ready to travel?"

"Where're we going?"

"Italy."

"Italy. Where?"

"Rome, and other places if we have the time." The break from contracting suited me fine. It had been some time since my last visit there. "This is what I want you to do," he said. "Lease a car for a week and get a couple more from your team. I'll show you a good time."

It reminded me of Art's heritage, Sicilian, as well as of his reputation for showing people how seasoned he was with entertaining friends and business colleagues. Much like myself and my team, he enjoyed the travel whenever he could get away from his office. There would be many more occasions when he would show up unexpectedly at the most unusual places.

From here on out, with site installation ending, much of the deployment team was disbanded. Some sought out more permanent employment, others switched jobs, but a core team prevailed with Buzz and me supporting the global system for the next thirty years, implementing many upgrades and enhancements, as fast as technology leapfrogged ahead. There were many such deployments, from moving the defense grid from the ground to satellites, replacing antiquated computers to more technologically advanced systems, in addition to COMSEC[23] cryptology advances. For the three generations contracting with the DOD, I basically wore three professional hats, that of engineer when at home base, systems analyst while on the road, and customer liaison with government and military, when on Intel sites.

"Your job is secured," I assured Buzz, who was asking about his status. We had developed a symbiotic relationship, looking out for each other while delivering superior products, and services to the government, defense department, and military services, assuring a sound and solid nation from possible, foreign hostilities.

In the 70s, nobody—not the scientists, inventors, engineers, or management— ever envisioned the speed, and scale technology would change, benefitting the nation in cost reduction, efficiency, and economic growth. It seemed progress was boundless in every aspect of rapidly-advancing industries. Growth was phenomenal. IT technology became the foundation for wealth, and prosperity. Primarily based in Silicon Valley, CA, much of the world's nations benefitted from its IT-based manufacturing, and marketing competences until countries became self-sufficient in their own manufacturing capabilities. The modern world, it seemed, was prospering without an end in sight. But, as is the case with most economic successes, they only lasted a specific time. In this case, our national prosperity was displaced through unrestrained outsourcing of technology, and manufacturing to many foreign countries.

---

[23] COMSEC – Communication Security. Provides national security systems support related to the function, operation or use of Intelligence, cryptologic, and classified storage, processing, and communications. It includes the solutions, products, and services used to ensure information availability, integrity, authentication, and confidentiality.

And thus, another industrial cycle had begun, prosper, and eventually collapse as a new building block for the next generation. Other than infinity, nothing is everlasting.

Two days later, five of us, crammed into a German Ford Escort rental with me driving, headed south to the border. All Autobahn and Autostrada, I made excellent headway on our journey, expecting to arrive in Rome sometime in the evening. There were only a couple potential events that could have abruptly ended the trip. Both times I was able to recover safely, but not without leaving tire marks in the wake. With everybody speeding, most of the times, I had underestimated my load. Driving mostly with two passengers in the car, I was not used to a full load the rental accommodated. The first incidence was in Austria forced off the road by a passing driver who lost grip on the passing lane, sliding into mine. The second time was in the Rhone Valley after entering a long-drawn-out curve, a similar condition again, forced me off the road. Traveling at maxed out speed, keeping pace with traffic, this time we landed on gravel. A push on the brake petal would have ended the journey in an instant, but due to my driving expertise, I eased off the gas and let the vehicle roll out with hands cramped to the steering wheel, silently praying.

We arrived in Rome late in the afternoon. On entering the outskirts, somebody in the backseat voiced an immediate opinion, "What it this?"

"What," I responded.

"The city. Still in rubble? After all the years?" I had noticed the same condition. No matter where we turned, Rome appeared to be in shambles. It seemed that the city had not yet recovered from the aftermath of the war. Heaps of brick and dirt could be seen obstructing sidewalks and streets, with heads protruding by workers diligently at work.

"What's with the rubble," I asked Art.

"You guys don't know anything," he shot back. It's not rubbish. It's excavations."

"What do you mean?" Even I was perplexed.

"City is being excavated by archaeologists."

"You mean the entire city?"

"Wherever Christians were hiding."

It then dawned on me. I read enough history on Rome and persecution of followers of Jesus to get the idea. What transpired here today, was unearthing historical artifacts for the onslaught of visitors from around the world to learn about Roman's rich and ancient history.

After we settled into a hotel, itself a historic artifact, the following days were filled with exploring some of Rome's invaluable architectures and artifacts on display at many of the city's museums. Most remarkable were the Colosseum and catacombs, permeating through much of subterraneous Rome.

It was a most memorable trip for all of us. The remainder of our stay in Europe, once we returned to Augsburg, was occupied with packing and arranging passage back on Pan Am.

PACIFIC RIM TWO

Arriving back home, since it was the start of summer, I spent the next few days at my favorite place, a vacation spot near Atlantic City, Wildwood beach resort, a two-hour drive from Philadelphia. Back in the 70s, the place was one of undivided leisure. It was a place not overrun by vacationers as is the case today. Atlantic City, back then, was still a small and quiet town, not even slightly associated with the gambling metropolis of today. In the serene surroundings of sandy beaches, light sea swells, and salty sea breezes drifting in from the water, I could relax, and dream about the times ahead. "Future looks great," was my definitive assumption, while dozing in and out of slumber, in between frequent cooling-off swims in the warming water.

Monday morning arrived with heightened anticipation. "Come on in," Art said, gesturing to enter his domain with a friendly grin on his face. "I've got good news. You are going places."

"So," I wavered, "I'm not laid off?" I already knew the answer, but wanted to stress my point of view, and its importance.

"Forget about that. All your men make it back safely?" He then laid out the impending process for the project I had been selected, and put in charge. "You'll take a team back to the Pacific."

"But," I immediately objected, "I just came from there." It had only been months since I'd left there, just prior to the NATO project.

"Hear me out first." It appeared he'd expected my reaction. "The contract is for Guam…"

"Guam? Not again!" I objected, perturbed at the mere mention of the place.

"Let me finish," he cut in. "Your assignment is to Guam, Japan, Okinawa, Korea, the Philippines, Vietnam, and Thailand. It's a six week stop at each place to integrate new technology."

"Now that I like." It was exactly what I had hoped for after all the years of uncertainties for a future I'd prepared for.

"You'll spend the next two weeks working with engineers at the lab to get familiar with the project. I already instructed HR to hire the necessary technicians. Your new crew is going to be a complement of twelve. Think you can handle it?"

"Handle what?" I challenged.

"The job."

"I was thinking more on the lines of the team," I explained. Since I would acquire new faces for this assignment, some newly hired recruits could be radical, and unsettling especially with the customer, in this case would be various military services over a number of Intel sites. I had witnessed some of their rowdy behavioral characteristics in action, and was watchful. The job, I suspected, would be challenging enough without having to worry about the team's personal issues. But after spending six years at various responsibilities from the design board to development, implementation, and managing teams, I felt confident to handle any rebel thrown my way. By now, I knew the systems in and out, no matter what the challenge, technical as well as staff-related responsibilities.

"That's why I picked you," he stated, notwithstanding an implied grin. My foreboding was justified. It would be a challenge, but not on the technology side. "Nobody else could handle the team."

And there it was again, payback time for my unauthorized departure from Guam. The project team was my penalty. I understood well when watching his face turn into a broad grin chewing on the ever-present cigar, while I maintained my silence. In spite of the unspoken reasons for payback, we both respected each other's status. I'll share my personal concerns here for the team change with my readers.

Though all of the members I was assigned were experienced engineers and technicians familiar with their jobs they were hired, not all were easily managed. Some were disappointed about their families and relationship left behind, where others had deeper seated anger, or even a special axe to grind, mostly with the authorities. Some were battle hardened soldiers where few were hired and trained from the streets, not easily conforming to discipline, as required, for me to exercise my position and contract obligations. There were times in the past where confrontations could not be avoided. It was those times when my physical training in fighting came handy. Not so much as getting physically involved, more so from a psychological factor. There was always somebody from the team nearby to diffuse the situation with a remark like, "Alex will kick your ass," or "he's got a blackbelt."

Being crammed in daily between workspace and closely configured lodging accommodations did not help either. Some male had to exercise their individuality in prowess and strengths while others measured their superiority against a team member or a stranger. Anger could easily turn into a brawl after a few drinks at some local establishment. Though my team knew the consequences, getting fired from the job, if things got out of hand, not everybody conformed to rules and regulations.

Regardless of potential implications, I had never lost a team member. I realized right from the start of handling teams, managing it was directly proportional to respect and understanding of the individual, no matter what background and past was attached to a person. There were only a couple occasions where I succumbed to the inevitable, give in and join the team. It usually resolved the confrontation at hand.

"When do I start?"

"Two weeks from now," he said.

"Okay," I said, reaching out to shake his hand. "It's a deal."

"No hard feelings?"

"No hard feelings. I'm indebted to you." The second I said it, I regretted the slip of the tongue. It would leave my future vulnerable in the company's favor in decision-making. But it was how I felt. It was Art that had looked out for me on my career path, not only once, but would several times more in the future. I had developed an unequaled trusting relationship with him. From here on, all I had to do was ask to get what I wanted. I was ready to tackle the future with all of its challenges while applying my vigor, and energy to its fullest, and Art knew it. I got what I needed, and the company, and customer, in turn, received mine, and the team's unrelenting dedication.

Unfortunately, my being assigned mostly overseas, at times for several months or even years, headquarters management changed on me a number of times. Each time, on my return from an assignment, it seemed like I had to deal with new faces. There even came a time when Art had left the company. It deeply saddened me when I found out. He was such as great manager, and personal friend. Fortunately, his departure was one of career advancement for him. I was able to touch base with him on occasions when visiting out east, the DC area, where he relocated. Our get-togethers would always be joyous in nature over a steak dinner, fine Italian wine, and lively reminiscence of the past. But these occasions were still in the future. For now, he would be my director for many more years.

GUAM

Arriving on Guam for the second time, this time limited to only six weeks, in charge of the project manifested as Memory Expansion, I was received by my former site team under new management with a cheering "Back so soon?"

"Yes," I promptly responded, "but not for long." I wanted to assure my replacement manager that I would not be a threat to his position.

"Let me know if you need anything," he replied on his way out. It was a cool, but courteous response. I had already learned that no manager or commander appreciated an intrusion on their territories, and responsibilities, especially not when it affected their career performance. In contrast, I never harbored any of these negative feelings. There was not one incident where I could remember retaining a negative thought or insecure notion on my disposition. In later years, through self-analysis after taking some psychology classes, I concluded that it was my self-assured attitude I carried through life, to a point of overconfidence, which at times would get me in troubles, but would also turn out to my advantage, career, and otherwise.

Back on Guam, the project turned out as well as could be expected. With the team holding up on the project effort as individually promised, twelve in all, I was able to carry decent working hours. Granted, there were emergency situations at times, such as an unexpected system crash, but to me, it was nothing unusual. I had prepared for it through redundancy procedures, assuring Naval Command of my flawless project performance, even though it was integrating critical, and untested technology while keeping the system operational at all times. Such was the situation I would face for the most part in my career, bold, and daring, but always courteous, and civilized with corporate, and customers. Whether executive, director, manager, or commander, doubts one may have had about my knowledge and capability in handling projects was soon swept away. I always came out a hero, no matter how difficult, and challenging the tasks. It may sound conceited on my behalf, but even to this day I still carry the same attitude, assuring customer success.

What led to this project were rapid advancements in computer technology. While the initial deployment of the AUTODIN system had ended, design, and development had not stopped. Command authorities, and corporate management realized from the onset how limited speed, and traffic deliveries were to get messages (email) delivered around the globe. High-priority Intel was delivered immediately, but created more and more bottle-necks over time due to escalated traffic volume. With the allocated $50 million spent, a new budget appropriation for a replacement system, the most expedient approach, was out of the question with taxpayers. Alternative means had to be met in the form of segmented technological integrations.

While still deploying the original systems, design engineers at DARPA had already been at work with alternative implementations. The next best thing they came up with was a memory expansion scheme that would quadruple data handling and throughput. To achieve it, additional racks of core memory banks had to be installed and configured into the current system, in addition to doubling the size of switching gears. The integration was not as easy as envisioned by the engineers. Out in the field, when on location, seamless integration would be critical without interrupting ongoing operations, and managing the system.

Consequently, the burden was placed on me to assure 100% operational uptime. It would have been unthinkable to take the entire site down even for one day, let alone six weeks. It would disrupt the Pacific Rim communication on which U.S. military, Intel agents, and embassies' lives were dependent. With the Cold War at its height, taking down a system was not an option. Notwithstanding management concerns, my team, and I pulled off what was considered by many "an impossibility," but it certainly pleased the powers-that-be. After establishing the initial success, we earned another "Attaboy" in the process while moving from location to location, interfering with site personnel with minimum intrusion on their hectic work schedules.

"Well, well. Mystery-man again. What are you doing here?" I assigned him the name for how he drifted in, and out of my life, much like the comic book hero.

"I've got to talk to you," he boldly stated without introduction. When we crossed paths, there were never casual exchanges with trivial niceties. It was direct, and to the point while still maintaining a professional attitude. Only on rare occasions would I catch him unguarded. Smoothing out an occasional affronting only took a couple glasses of wine at some quiet restaurant.

I stopped the task at hand, and followed him. He was already headed for a quiet spot, usually along a wall behind an array of COMM equipment. He always sought out privacy when he wanted my opinion, or share some secret project coming my way, and rightly so. Treading in the arena of top secret innovations, conceived by a slew of scientist PhDs, he could not afford information leaks. He knew he could trust me, for I carried the same security credentials aside from having established a full, trusting relationship. Back in the days, the 60s, 70s, and 80s, the security-entrusted workforce had a different mindset. Aside from an inherited human curiosity instinct, it was unthinkable for an individual to compromise the personal status of trust, honor, and truthfulness prevalent in those days. Unlike today, in many instances, as demonstrated through damaging implications to national security on a number of occasions, sensitive information was never compromised unless sanctioned by policy makers to deliberately leak information through disinformation dissemination.

"Shoot," I said, anxious to receive yet another secrecy conceived under the cloak of black projects.

"Take a look at this," he said, with a gesture at some newly-installed gear. "Recognize it?"

"Can't say I do. When was it installed?"

"Newest in satellite technology. Equipment has been here for some time waiting for you to test it."

"It certainly looks different from the ones I built," I said, accompanied with a smirk. He knew that I had built the first military satellites launched into orbit a decade earlier. It appeared that now was the time to have them interconnected into the AUTODIN grid. What took so long was the manufacturing of critical equipment to carry the highly sensitive signals around the globe.

"Transceivers, modulators, signal isolators, wide-band receivers, amplifiers, analog/digital converters, interface," he expertly explained with gestures at the array. It was all he had to say. I knew right then and there that we had entered a new era in data communications.

"Ready to test it?" He was already headed for the command console, the focal point in the tech control, and COMSEC sectors, with decoded signals waiting to be fed to monitor screens.

"What about the software?" I was not aware of any new applications on my system necessary to drive all the equipment.

"Already taken care of." A faint notion of secrecy swept my mind for the complexity of the system. While software was downloaded, pushed from the central development lab at DARPA, hardware still had to be installed on location. But even that would change in the near future where everything would be software managed, and remotely controlled. But for now, on Guam, I intensely watched test-pattern data sweeping across the console's monitor screen at an incredible speed. Mystery-man kept switching the instrument knobs through higher, and higher frequencies while we followed data transmissions between ground, and satellite hops.

Where up to now transmission speeds had been limited to T-3 (3 megabytes), ground-based cable quality, I marveled at the speed increase to 10 M-bites, then 50, 100, 500, up to 1 G-bites of data streams. Watching the incredible performance, awestruck, I muttered, "Wow. What speed."

"Thought you'd like it. Ready to go live?"

"Let's do it." He then walked off as briskly as he had entered, without a glimmer of glory. To him it was just another gadget successfully tested, and put into operation.

It only took minutes for COMM-techs to configure instruments and equipment. The effects were instantaneous.

"What's going on," the operator at the nearby computer room, jumping up from his seated position at the command console, shouted out. He promptly headed in my direction to get an answer.

"What?" I responded, momentarily startled, as everybody on the operations deck.

"Come and see," he said, hasty and out of breath. "Everything's disappeared."

He then explained, "I was assembling and feeding backlogged traffic into the system when 'Boom', everything was gone." His shout attracted attention.

"Let me take a look at it," I said taking the command seat, calmed him somewhat. It was not the first-time message traffic had disappeared in the past, but was recovered with each incidence. At times, with an equipment failure, traffic currently being processed would be affected and lost, but only temporary. Due to the failsafe system design, everything is recoverable from archived data, thus, AUTODIN, a store and forward system.

After a brief analysis, my conclusion and stated so was, "Consider yourself lucky."

"What did I do?" His concerns for losing data and information, including his Top-Secret clearance was clearly painted on his face. "Why lucky?"

"We just made your job a thousand times faster."

"I don't understand." I turned in his direction and became aware of shift personnel gathered closely around the console. Everybody was watching. Word had spread quick about the mishap of the rarest of occurrence, inconceivable loss of traffic.

Where the operator was currently managing a backlog of messages scheduled for delivery, at times taking hours, in a flash of a second, they had disappeared. They all had been processed instantly after Mystery-man and I switched the new COMM equipment online.

It was such events that kept me, and my team busy for the years ahead. Technology was changing at an ever-faster pace. In the years that followed I had to constantly reeducate myself on new items appearing on the platform. First, it was tested on my system and, after some time of classified operation, downgraded, and turned over to the public sector for commercial applications, traded for corporate profits.

As was the case with most projects I handled, time passed very quickly with my busy schedule. The time on Guam ended in no time at all with us preparing to move on to the next location, Okinawa. I should present a quick overview of this time on Guam. As short, and busy as the trip was, I dedicated the off-time to my favorite recreational activities, diving, and fishing. In recognition of my island presence, there was always a friend ready to offer his boat, diving gear, and an invitation to a local Dojo to satisfy my recreational needs. After dark, I usually joined the "Gang" at one or another social club at the growing number of hotels going up along newly groomed beachfronts.

As remote as Guam was, situated in the middle of the Pacific Ocean, the island was changing prolifically as the Japanese industry had taken leadership in technology. For the first time in modern times, the Japanese had money to spend, and spend they did. Lots of passengers arrived daily from Japan seeking new endeavors on Guam. It was this foreign influx building up the island's economy at an ever-increasing rate. New opportunities were presented for entrepreneurs, businesses, entertainment, fishing, and diving sports, and much more than the island could handle at a comfortable pace. Many islanders resisted to the rapid changes, but others welcomed them.

The end results?

The foreigners, though former enemies a couple of decades earlier in WWII, were here to stay. Where in the past, their ideological differences could not be resolved, today the value of money won the final peace. Two cultures, once fiercely fighting each other for territory, finally came to their senses for a peaceful coexistence achieved through travel, and trade. It was enough for now.

OKINAWA

Arriving on Okinawa heightened my expectations. My first time on a colonial territory to the United States, the island was still under strong American influence. It became obvious by the U.S. military presence, especially in the central region of the island. Kadena Airbase was the thriving hub for all sorts of interactions between the troops, and local population. Deemed an outpost island to Japan, this was not immediately obvious other than the similarity in Asian facial features, and local customs accompanied by the local language spoken. Enforced regulation by American was very much present as soon as one took to driving on the proper (Western) side of the street. But that was about to change. It was shortly after my arrival when I became aware of the daily demonstrations held on the island with issues, I was told, such as American driving policy.

Sure enough, one day soon after at midnight, I was awakened by the incessant sound of automobile horns blowing from city streets below. Leaning out of the hotel window at the Hilton I was staying in, it seemed the entire island's traffic had come to a standstill. It was total gridlock, or so I thought. Watching in awe, the entire traffic switched directions to the opposite lanes, aligning with mainland Japan's traffic rules, as was the case here prior to WWII. What was amazing by morning, was the orderly transition the islanders had executed without causing major accidents.

Work at Ft. Buckner, the Marine base proceeded very much like it did on Guam without any big incidents slowing the team's progress. Granted, there were the occasional human errors cropping up during the implementation and acceptance phase from missing a proper wire connection or faulty soldering job, but nothing that would delay the schedule. At this point, there was nothing but praise from the accompanied project COR[24], relayed back to his office at the Pentagon.

"How about dinner tonight?" Henry, the current COR offered. "You've earned the break. Bring the team."

"What place?" I asked.

I could not recall the name he mentioned but expected to dine on Japanese cuisine. As I drove up to the address that evening, to my surprise it was a Mexican restaurant. It then dawned on me that Henry was Hispanic. Curious at his choice, the evening turned out to be one of jokes, laughter, and joy. It was my first experience with Mexican cuisine. Dished out was an assortment of plates ranging from enchiladas to burritos, tamales, quesadillas, guacamole, tostadas, tacos, and refried beans, served with an abundance of salsa, and nacho crackers. Overwhelmed by the rich assortment, I tried them all in between profuse swigs of XX (Dos Equis) beer. I went to sleep happy that night.

Since it was Saturday night, I planned to sleep late into the morning without having to set an alarm clock. Sunday was the team's day off. Regardless of my

---

[24] COR – Contracting Office Representative. The implementation was accompanied by a government-assigned individual trained, and prepared to provide oversight for proper contract execution. He/she would remain with the current project through all phases from start, and implementation through final test, and acceptance, assuring that contract requirements were fulfilled. The COR was a service member or Department of Defense (DOD) civilian appointed by the contracting office.

intention for sleeping in, there was persistent knocking at my door, tearing me from slumber. I did not have to guess much as to who it might be.

"What's up for today?"

It was Buzz, my social buddy, running mate, and main man on the team. While I was a nighthawk, he was an early riser. I should point out my waking, and sleeping patterns. Ever since the day I began my career with the DOD, my internal circadian clock became confused. To begin with, there was never enough time in a day to complete all of the tasks thrown at me. Each day was filled with challenges, mostly project related issues. Involved with runaway technological advances, it seemed that I had to constantly keep up with the changes. On top of that, rushing from project to project in itself was a hectic life.

Working two shifts back-to-back on many occasions, I quickly learned that, if I still wanted to have a social life, the only way I could achieve it was by cutting back on my sleeping hours. Subsequently, I rationed myself to three hours of sleep during workdays. No matter where I landed in the world, my daily cycle was to be up at 6:00 a.m. followed by a quick breakfast before rushing to the workplace followed with a thirty-minute lunch break at noon, then back to the project, generally until 8:00 p.m. By then, I was ready to eat a decent meal either alone or in the company of some team members gathered at a restaurant or eatery.

Where some of the guys would retire by 11:00 p.m., my social time was only beginning. No matter what country I was in, whether there were curfew restrictions or not, I would seek out nightlife places either on base or at the local entertainment district. That was where I could mingle with the local population to absorb some of their customs, and language. To get the most out of the time spent among the crowds, I would make it my mission to quickly learn the fundamental basis of the local language to satisfy my needs I had set out, that of exploring the world's cultures. It was during those times I was in the element dealt to me which I had sought out since childhood. It was my time. It was my mission. I felt wholesome. But it came at a price. It surfaced with damaging consequences to body and mind, I shall illustrate at the proper times.

For today, my mind was set on: "Let's tour the island."

"Fine with me. When are we heading out?" Buzz was always ready to go, preferably on his terms.

"Guess I'll have to scrap breakfast," I muttered. It was obvious that he was anxious to get going. I could always catch up when we stopped for lunch. Though the island, the largest in the Ryukyu island chain, was only about 70 miles long by 7 miles wide at an average, it would take several hours to circumnavigate at the maximum allowable speed of 25 mph. On today's trip it would only be him with me behind the wheel, driving my Japanese rental car, a typical, junior-sized Toyota customary in those days.

Leaving Kadena headed south, I had just entered the main road. Fumbling for the air-conditioning controls I must have pulled the wrong knob because all of a sudden, accompanied by a crashing sound, our view suddenly turned dark. We were blind-sided by the hood popping up only to rap against the windshield with a metal-tearing sound. I immediately let off the gas pedal, slowly rolling to a stop. Fortunately, we were only driving at the speed limit when I had pulled the knob. Buzz, on the other hand, had no clue. He was dumbfounded until I explained to him my mistake. As usual, he could not restrain himself from making a wise crack while shaking his head in dismay, "You Kamikaze Kraut." I knew that the mishap had shaken him up, if only slightly.

We straightened out the hood as well as we could, tying the latch together with a shoelace from one of the sneakers I wore. My inspection revealed that the vehicle did not have a safety latch for the hood, as was customary back home. I had reached for the wrong knob under the dashboard. My intention was checking the handbrake. I had occasions with foreign rentals before, mostly with a stuck emergency brake that would heat up and incinerate with the heat once on the road. Twenty minutes later we were back in traffic once more without further issues. Driving along the shoreline, as the route took us, we circled the southern tip to head up north towards the far end of the island. In the process, we stopped at some of the memorable places marked by WWII events one would rather forget such as Naha, Bloody Ridge, Shuri Castle, and Suicide Cliff, where the bloodiest battles took place in the Pacific. Looking at the infamous cliff line, it was difficult to imagine how Japanese soldiers and civilians could end their lives with a jump into death, rather than face the aftermath of war. It's what cultural discipline can do to the population.

It was late afternoon when we headed back towards Kadena. Arriving at the central hills from the north end of the island, about 8 miles out, we stopped to admire the valley below. From our vantage point we had a clear view of the U.S. airbase, taking in the scenery for some memorable pictures. "Look at that," Buzz suddenly exclaimed. I pointed my camera in that direction, and snapped a scene right out of science fiction. We were stunned while watching an object approach the airfield from the south at high speed, preparing for a landing. "What do you think?"

Perplexed, I muttered, "Never seen anything like it. Ever!"

"Me neither."

From our spot the object appeared very much like a flying torpedo. We were even more baffled when a parachute popped out from the rear of the craft as soon as it had touched down. The craft slow to an eventual stop only yards short from the end of the runway. Asking around base personnel the following day, Monday, nobody seemed to know anything or had witnessed the unusual landing. Right away we knew something strange was going on at this distant airbase. Though in operation since WWII under American control, covert operations became obvious. What we witnessed was the landing of the highly-kept secret SR-71 Blackbird[25] stealth plane, a replacement for the U-2, just returning from a spy-mission over the Soviet Union. I believe it was a time when rumors of UFO sightings began to appear with the public. It would not be the only wave of such appearances. In the years to follow, rumors of many more such strange craft would be reported as UFOs. Not common knowledge to the public, new stealth crafts like the B-1, and B-2 bombers, F-17, F-22, and many more novel designs would make public news whenever one was sighted.

---

[25] It was not until 1976 when the SR-71 Blackbird was publicly announced after achieving speed, and altitude records exceeding 50,000 feet at 2,193 mph, but this failed to discourage people from reporting more UFO sightings.

The remainder of the stay turned out pretty much uneventfully. Okinawa, from an economic perspective, was somewhat different from mainland Japan. It did not have a thriving metropolis. While the native population worked very hard at their business, backbreaking chores in the fields were nothing new. Though covered with fertile volcanic soil, the terrain was rocky with many valleys at the base of steep slopes interspersed from the northern tip to the south of the island. Agriculture was still prevalent, mostly for rice growth, with the primary customer being the Japanese.

Culturally, the people were quite accommodating to foreign tourists. It was not the case with the U.S. military presence. There had been many demonstrations over the past decades to try to remove the remaining forces from the island. Progress was slow with the first step already accomplished by reverting traffic back under Japanese control, who's primary focus was for sharing mainland trade, and commerce with the island. At this point, most of the local businesses were geared towards tourism, which was not very prolific other than retired U.S. WWII veterans revisiting infamous fighting fronts. Watching documentary footage from U.S. forces trying to gain hold of the island in the later part of the war, with wave after wave of Marine forces thrown into battle, memories of the individuals involved still had strong connections with their fallen buddies, killed in action by the tens of thousands. It could only be truly assessed by the soldiers directly involved in fighting on the frontlines.

JAPAN

Next stop on the project was Japan. Despite the lengthy daily commute from Tokyo to Asaka, the location of the U.S. Army Intel site, work proceeded as scheduled. While the work location was only fifteen miles from Japan's largest metropolis Tokyo, it was a two and a half hour commute each way. Put up in Armed Forces accommodations, the Sanno Hotel, the day began quite early for the team. Alarm clocks went off at 5:30 a.m. with a hurried breakfast at the hotel restaurant, followed with a quick dash to the nearest station to catch a subway headed for the Tokyo main terminal, switching to a local train. At each stop, one was pushed, and shoved by trained Japanese people-herders into one of many neat columns of commuters arranged to jump on the train as soon as one arrived. In record time, commuters from inside each car were disgorged by the sheer force of the masses with platform commuters ready to jump on board, pushing, and shoving their way past the entrance, trying to claim a vacated spot in the tightly-packed train. Two dozen stops later, the train arrived at our station by 8:00 a.m.

During travel, one did not have to reach for a hold to hang on to or seek out a handle dangling from the carriage frame. As soon as the train started, the entire human load shifted backwards against the pull of the engine, and again forwards when braking for the next stop. The commuting routine was repeated at each station in twenty-second record time, loading, and unloading the daily workforce moving in, and out of the city, eight million commuters with a basic city population of only four million, swelling the daytime population to twelve million.

The same process was reversed for us after each workday by leaving the site at 5:00 p.m., and trying to make it back at a decent time for dinner at the hotel. While commuting was hectic, this mega-city provided ample nightlife activities for us. It did not take long for the enterprising to locate popular hang-out spots to get involved with the local population. The Japanese were highly proficient when it came to entertaining, and were just as inviting to foreigners by participating in their favorite activity: getting drunk. It would only take a few minutes before I would be approached, and invited by a group of happy drinkers to participate in their joyous Karaoke, then a newly emerged form of entertainment only recently originated in Kyoto. Being foreign, I would make my nightly round without having to spend any money since the invitations were accompanied with free, and ample drinks.

During all of my travels, I had never experienced a happier drinking bunch than the Japanese. It was a daily practice for the working class to head for a favorite sake club as soon as their twelve-hour work schedule ended. With four hours left until midnight, there was ample time to get drunk. Then all clubs closed for the day, with customers rushing to catch the last transportation home. Not all would make it. Many were left stranded at the station, crashing on the platform for the night, waiting to catch the first train ride home long enough to groom, have breakfast, only to rush back to the city and be at the office by 8:00 am for another long workday.

Once I became familiar with their language—I had signed up at one of the schools to take language lessons—interacting with the local population became an educational experience. Aside from learning much of their heritage, ethnicity, and society, I absorbed everything about their culture as readily as it was presented. There was one cultural drawback in this society that I assessed. Being a foreigner, though treated as a friend, one was never accepted into the home, and family. By tradition, it was a cultural code seldom broken. The code was an inherited safeguard against the many invasions experienced from neighboring countries over the past millennia. With the Japanese having lived for thousands of years in virtual isolation, they had developed a tightly-knit culture amid its secure island shorelines by shutting out all strangers. The result was an inherited distrust for anybody from outside.

Japan was not alone with being connected to a strong heritage. There were countries with similar caution for strangers in Korea, and China. Where their customs, written language and traditions were similar in nature, noticeably different was the spoken language. They may have been genetically related, but the differences may have been developed over eons due to geographical isolation in the case of the Japanese, ruggedness in terrain, and climate for the Koreans, with the Chinese being the dominant force because of its size and ancient heritage.

Regardless of the differences, each of their ideology was unique in the practice of the arts, architecture, music, dress code, individual conduct, as well as laws, if not adhered to. While human values seemed to have been neglected in many neighboring counties, here it was elevated on, and above the norm. Foremost in importance was the family. It always came first. Honor, pride, and cultural values amid these ancient countries were traits highly respected by the Code of Bushido, with the most disciplined among the Japanese society. For the Western world it might be difficult to imagine that such a harsh discipline as Seppuku (Hara-kiri), the art of self-inflicted suicide, was a mandatory act of self-justice if one dishonored the family or insulted a member of the Royal seat. Despite the code of ethics being as striking as it might appear, there were genetically inherited flaws to deal with, much like in the Western world: how to cope with the criminal elements?

The answer materialized in the form of Yakuza, a self-serving culture, much like the Italian Mafia. Bound by their own strictly-enforced ethics, it was a legitimate business for its families, and members. Thus, most populated settlements created their own Yakuza. Sanctioned by the law, the Yakuza served two principle needs, collecting taxes from businesses for the royal coffer, and keeping the criminal branch of society curbed, and disciplined. It worked for thousands of years until one day in 1853, when island harmony was disrupted by a foreign armada, that of Commodore Matthew Perry, American admiralty, enforcing their own rules, and policies onto the island population. Talking with people today, a society adapted to the fast pace of life much of the world was engaged, the young generation welcomed the changes with open arms while the elders were still desperately trying to cling to ancient practices with a quickly fading heritage.

Westernized attitude, and behavior may be considered as barbarous to these ancient worlds, and justly so, as we seem to leave a large footprint on whatever country we set foot on. Whether we, democracy, are doing the right thing to the world's population, history will be the judge. It may not always be readily visible as our forefathers had intended, but at least our society was based on freedom, and liberty; many may not yet understand, and appreciate the concepts of our constitution. The constitution is fair to all living beings, and animals alike, but it may take millennia for the world to appreciate, and accepts its doctrine. At least nobody could claim we did not try. In the meantime, political, and religious differences in policies, and faiths struggle on, dividing inherited ideologies, between ancient and modern traditions, customary to each place.

As for my personal vision, I will dread the day when a world council is formed, declaring, "As of today, all borders have been eliminated from the globe, and replaced by free trade, free speech, and unrestricted travel." It may sound like Utopia, a world finally peaceful in a place of free living, free speech, and shared wealth, but to achieve it will take much more time, and struggles. In contrast, it will achieve the complete opposite. What it will do is eliminate hundreds of distinct cultures that took millennia to create, nurture, and struggle to maintain. For this reason, "globalization" is not one of my favorite terms.

For now, there were more locally-oriented challenges, and issues to deal with. To get the present technology upgrade finished on time, as usual, I was forced to work many hours into the night. To avoid the lengthy and cumbersome commute from Tokyo to Asaka, I checked into a local hotel. Rural hotel, in today's terms, in Japan back then was an overstatement. It was a fairly good-sized home with the owners renting out spare rooms. There were no meals served. It was just a small room, miniaturized chair, and table, as they all were, and a closet to hang up a jacket, but the bedding was warm. Being there in the dead of winter, I welcomed the down covers. But not all was cozy. During one of my first day's stay, wrapped up in solving a persistent mainframe issue, I was forced to work past midnight. When I checked the clock, it was close to 2:00 a.m. I should have just worked through the night but was overtaken with sleep. I could hardly keep my eyes open any longer when I checked out with the night sentry. The path I was forced to take, stumbling through snow, was relatively short, perhaps ten minutes. When I arrived at the back gate, as I usually did, it was locked and deserted. Reading the sign was no encouragement. It said, "Gates closed after midnight." It meant I had to trod all the way back to where I had come from, take a route in the opposite direction, headed for the main gate, then backtrack once more. I finally made it to the hotel forty minutes later.

The place was dark, and deserted. "What shall I do?" I contemplated in the dark, not having checked out a key. I began knocking on the door. Nothing was stirring on the inside. I repeated the knocking, more forcefully, but to no avail. Faced with a decision I finally gave up. There were two alternatives: stay on until morning or turn back to the site. I was too tired to take another step, and decided to stay. Despite the night chills being winter, I sat down by the entrance and promptly fell asleep. I was shuddering from the cold when the door opened for the day; it must have been 5:00 a.m.

The first thing I did was ask for a key. "We don't give out keys," was the stern reply.

"Then," I said, "how will I get in?"

"House rule. You must return before midnight."

I've never heard of such a thing, and stated so.

"It is the custom here in Japan."

"Well," I muttered. "Now I know." From then on, I made sure I'd beat the closing time. Since it was a small town clustered around the army base, restaurants, and bars closed at midnight without exception. With the team residing back in the city, facing this town alone, I would schedule working hours accordingly, and took meals at appropriate times. I did not mind the adjustment. It gave me an opportunity to meet local town folks.

I made acquaintance with the proprietor of a nearby sushiya, a typical Japanese sushi place. Happy I had made the effort to learn to converse in Japanese, though broken, he understood my English. We had lively conversations following several shots of sake he used to offer as a wellness gesture. First time there, I learned to eat with chopsticks, but one thing kept bothering me. It was the incessant slurping of local customers sipping their soup right out of the bowl. When I asked about the queer custom, he answered, "It is our culture. It serves two functions. One, while served piping hot, it instantly cools the soup. Two, the sound serves as gratitude to the host."

"So much for etiquette," I thought. "Two slovenly habits settled within one serving." It took weeks before I got used to the slurping sounds emanating from every table. Even today when visiting an Udon (noodle soup) place, I am still annoyed. In my own culture, making eating sounds like that was not acceptable. One could get thrown out of a restaurant. Today, I suppose, internationally-oriented hosts back home are more tolerant with the prolific Asian travelers.

Notwithstanding local customs, I decided to test my host for his tolerance. Buzz was by my side one evening, when I ordered two Kirin beers, the size of a liter bottle each, which was referred to as combat bottles by the GI. As he usually did, the proprietor served. I was his honored guest, usually the only foreigner in the place. Today there were two. Gracefully striding up to our table, he handed us two glasses, considered miniature back home. Following the customary gesture, the guest picked up the empty glass raised to the host, who in turn, filled as many glasses as the bottle held, in our case two, followed with a common toast. It was an honorary, ceremonial gesture reserved for special patrons.

Inadvertently, I rejected his offer, reaching for the full bottle, and taking it directly to my mouth while watching his facial expression, clearly indicating that such an insult had never happened in his place. His jaws dropped open. Without so much as uttering a word he gracefully took the tray of glasses, and my bottle back to the counter only to return with a new bottle, and glasses to repeat the offering. This time, after realizing my mistake, I dared not repeat what was a gross insult in Japan, seriously offending the host. While customary in our country, nobody ever drinks directly from the bottle.

He even took his time to explain other mistakes customers made. Another insult, he patiently explained, was ignoring chopsticks protocol. As directed by culture, one should never scrape the wooden sticks together for shaving off potential splinters. It was an offensive habit some customers displayed prior to using the utensils. In addition, chopsticks must never be directly placed on the table. The pair specifically came in a paper wrapping serving as a resting prop, otherwise while eating, they must be placed on the dish in a certain order.

I should point out that certain customs have changed since then. Today, with prolific travels not only to Japan but other countries, many local customs, to the disappointment of the elders, have vanished.

During my many visits and repeated stays in Japan, customary quirks set aside, Japan, for me, became an unrelenting source of treasures, not only for artifacts, but for cultural riches inherited for thousands of years. The country, reliant on cultural values, much like other Asian countries, was subjected to westernized pressures previously unequaled. It was the cause for unwelcomed changes by much of the population resisting foreign influence. In the decades ahead, I would observe many changes the elders resisted while the young embraced a new, and unfamiliar form of life, adopted from the Western world.

Changes were not only reserved for the local citizens; they also affected my presence. The day after my arrival at the site, an Army Intel center, Camp Drake, located at Asaka, Mystery-man was anxiously pacing the floor. "Hey. What's up?" I greeted him. I could read from his expression that his unexpected visit was of extreme urgency.

"I have a proposition for you," he boldly announced. "I'm going to offer you a job, but I want you to think about it first. Don't make a quick decision. It's for the long term." It was a rare time where he actually held my direct eye contact. He was studying my reaction. From his position, I realized, he took a great chance in making the offer. There were two elements working against me. First, I did not hold a PhD credential, and second, there was still a distrust factor by DARPA against hiring a foreigner, regardless of my current clearances, and solid background investigation.

"What would I do?" I said, contemplating the offer.

"We have some exciting projects coming up. We sure could use your expertise in computers, and communications. I've been watching your work, and can't think of a better fit."

"What about the grade?"

"We'll give you an entry commission as GS-11."

"I am impressed," I replied. I knew well that it was not every day the government extended an opportunity to a new hire at a position equal to Full-bird Colonel. I took the offer seriously because I knew that most hires started at the GS-01 entry level, and would never reach the level offered me. "Give me a couple of weeks to decide. I'd have to consider, and train a replacement."

"Like I said, take your time. Now, let's talk about some of the projects ahead. How about dinner?"

"Dinner sounds great," I said, accepting his offer. As always, I would enjoy his company discussing innovative technologies I could only dream of.

"Six at the O Club?"

"I'll be there." I knew he was doing his best to soften me up in case I would have some reservations. Reservations may have been an understatement in my case. It would mean following the chain of command, endless strategy meetings, daily accountability, weekly reports, and these were only some of the considerations I would have to evaluate. On the other hand, the job would be guaranteed for twenty years with unequaled retirement incentives to follow. It put me in a quandary I would rather not have faced. Any other office, outside of DARPA, I would have blatantly turned down. My reasons were simple. I needed career challenges to capture my interest, and dedication.

Skeptical at first over dinner, after spending three hours at the club listening to his project schedules in the planning, wondering at future possibilities taking part in groundbreaking technologies, mostly stealth related, I seriously considered the offer.

Following our present Pacific Implementation effort, I had several more opportunities to visit Japan. Where most went uneventful, there was one worthy to illustrate. It was the trip I'd termed "Japan Immigration Incidence of 1984," after a personal Holiday leave back home. It may have had serious political consequences if the Japanese authorities would have pursued it, but the incidence was resolved eight hours later in my favor. It all began because I had filled out the immigration Landing Card erroneously by entering Business rather than Personal purpose for my entering the country.

Arriving at Immigration and Customs Check, on orders to "Open Case," expecting an array of personal belongings, my suitcase was filled with nothing but electronic computer parts. I had mailed my personals the day before through US/APO postal service. I was immediately detained by customs, as a result from smuggling illegal contraband, then handed off through several levels of authorities in the process, with agents unsure of what to do with my illegal entry with an inappropriate visa. Amid the ensuing confusion, I had an inspirational thought. I played ignorant and demanded to see the entry card to verified my mistake.

As expected, I had inadvertently entered the wrong visiting purpose. Realizing my mistake, I pulled out a pen I always carried inside my jacket pocket, stuck out the Business entry, and scribbled Personal instead while the flock of uniformed agents were watching. It must have been a "first" for everybody. What immediately followed was wild jabber in Japanese, accompanied with incoherent gestures at me, and the open luggage while the landing card wad handed between the officials.

I recognized shouts in Japanese repeated up and down official ranks, "He Changee Mind" (He changed his mind). Where they were dead serious, I, on the other hand thought it hilarious. My mood must have reflected on my face. I was immediately led to a detainment room by stern-faced customs agents. As expected, the event had turned into a serious major international smuggling incidence. I was about to be detained when I pulled out my trump card, a U.S. DOD identification. I deciding to let the authorities sort it out, which they did. To the demise of the customs agents, I was released 8 hours later free to go, including my black-market contraband with a warning not to come back into the country after the present tour.

"Cannot promise," I stated. I like your country. Been here many times. Have friends here." But the authorities already knew of my travel status from passport entries filled with ten years of customs stamp entries from many countries. The reason I was freed was following: Right from the onset of the affair, I displayed an "I don't give a damn" attitude. Japanese authorities did not know how to handle it. They are used to expect nothing but bows, courtesy and politeness. In my defense, I was at an advantage only I knew. I was ordered to take the suitcase of electronic parts on my return trip. It was an assortment of shortages the site had been waiting for. I could afford to be cocky, which I displayed to the demise of the authorities. My rational was, "let the governments sort it out." When this became obvious to the customs officials, my release was based on: he is nothing but trouble, hoping never to return. Though I was flagged as such with Customs Immigration, repeated visits back in the country would not be blocked. Political policies prevented such drastic measures.

KOREA

On to Korea. Up to this point, about halfway into the project, I was right on track with the pressing implementation schedule. Still considered an undeveloped land in the Western world, Korea was heavily influenced by its own cultural heritage and traditions, and technical limitation, but would soon follow Japan's current technological successes. Years earlier on my first travel to this country in 1968 while stationed on Guam, I was not familiar with the local language, and customs. Then, the airport was only a dated, provincial landing strip without the modern-day aircraft docking ports. One exited onto a mobile ladder pushed up to the plane's exit door, once on the ground, scrambled for the luggage eventually delivered at the main hall of the terminal, and passed through an immigration station only to exit into a chaotic parking lot. Cab drivers pushed, and shoved each other for the next fare in such a disorderly fashion it frightened many first arrivals. Amid the confusion, luggage carried by airport porters, was torn from the arriving desperately trying to hold onto individual valises amid orders barked at the potential fare in a strange language, hastily dragged to the next taxi in line. The race was on. Whichever driver reached his cab first dumped your luggage into trunk, unsuccessfully trying to slam the lid shut. Since taxi trunks were not large enough to accommodate a Western suitcase, the trunk remained open while the driver jumped behind the wheel, taking to the road whether you were in the taxi or not. Many arrivals lost their luggage this way. The trick was— but you did not know until next time—to firmly hold onto your luggage, and not let go no matter what forces were tearing at the valise's handle.

The airport was not the only place of chaos, and confusion. Many arrivals, as was the case with me, were traveling to an inland destination. The next challenge I faced was arriving at the downtown train station. Arriving from the U.S., living in an orderly society, I was faced with the second wave of confusion. Two suitcases and one attaché case clutched between hands and under my arms, I had to constantly be on guard to ward off potential thieves. Unlike at the airport, conditions here were even worse. I had to fend off a local onslaught of passengers, all trying to gain a seat on the next train out. With Korea facing overpopulation, many lived in small villages spread across the hilly terrain up and down the country with only limited road access. The railway seemed to be the best access aside from a single dusty road hewn into valleys, and mountain slopes.

Facing a dozen ticket windows, I tried to capture a familiar name for my destination, Taegu. The only thing I knew about the place was that it was a cluster of army bases centered in the middle of the country situated within valleys surrounded by mountains. Typical of such a location, it was hidden from the general population, away from traffic, transportation, and communication interference, with the function of the facility cloaked in secrecy to protect an ally. No matter how hard I tried to hold my position, I could not advance one foot towards a terminal window. While there were lines of demarcations separating the ticket windows, all were disregarded to make way for whoever pushed, and shoved the most. Finally, one uniformed ticked agent seemed to have pity on me. He must have observed my struggling against the mob, and left his window. I watched him approach, hoping he was help on the way. I was relieved as soon as he barked at me, "You. Where?"

"Taegu," I yelled over the insane turmoil.

"Come," he gestured, pulling on one of my suitcases. Alarm signals went off immediately as he pushed me towards the next window, shouting my destination at the ticket agent. Seconds later I had a piece of paper in my hands, and more hands tearing at my luggage. I departed with a "thank you" smile at the helping agent and rushed after the luggage handlers disappearing through the main station entrance. I had to run to keep up with them, each claiming one of my cases headed for one of a dozen trains scheduled for departure. Handing both a gracious tip, for I actually made it, they waved me off with thankful grins with the train already in motion to the next destination. Taking a deep breath, relieved, I felt safe anchored to the spot I had claimed next to the door. It was impossible to move, or even lose balance, and fall—that's how crowded the carriage was. Packed like sardines amid unhappy faces staring at me for having luggage, no matter how desperately I had vied for an empty spot, there was not one inch left on the floor or overhead bins. I was stuck like everyone else headed south towards Taegu. Scheduled for a four-hour trip, I sank into a complacent daze hoping for a station stop somewhere along the way.

One hour into it, I was pressed for the bathroom. It must have been the beer I had on the flight finally pressing for release. I only had two choices, peeing in my pants, or stepping up in line at the toilet door. I was already gnashing my teeth when one passenger leaned back and offered his place near the door in broken English. "You. Go next."

I had found a compassionate soul. Bowing with a courteous "Thank you," I did not dare check with the other faces in line. To show my appreciation, I made a quick entry and exit just as the train slowed at the upcoming station. With the carriage jammed packed, it became a mass of disgorging hordes as soon as the exit doors opened. What must have been cusses at me, and my luggage fixed by the floor, exiting passengers tripped towards the exit, having a difficult time because of the inrush of new passengers. I took the opportunity, and confusion to stash my cases overhead, and quickly popped onto an empty seat before being overtaken by the wave of undisciplined, and rude travelers. "Thirty seconds," I counted the time the doors were open.

I was glad that there were no other stops on the way to my destination. At least I could relax, and enjoy the remaining ride. As crowded an image as the world may have had of Korea, the land appeared barren along the way, only speckled by tiny villages all looking alike: dusty, one-level, dwellings, built with a mix of mud and straw, with gray-thatched rooftops mostly hidden by the barbed wire topped walls protecting the homes. I was curious about the security aspect of the construction, and soon learned the reasons. It all led back to the inherited distrust of the nation's people dating back to ancient times when invasions from neighboring marauding tribes were frequent. But that was centuries ago. Today, the reason was from prolific break-ins to ransack homes.

"Thieves wait until nightfall until after occupants are asleep before breaching the walls," I was told. Furthermore, spotters canvased neighborhoods to see who was moving. "It's easy pickings when people are exhausted, and tired." In the years ahead, I would experience such misfortune first hand when I lived here for a couple of years.

Taegu turned out to be a sprawling city in the central region of the country, but lacked the signs of a modern metropolis. On arriving at the station, I had thirty seconds while the doors were open to dislodge with the flow of shoving passengers. I lost my grip on my luggage a couple of times ripped from my hands in the rush for a taxi. Stepping out from the terminal, I discovered fetching a taxi was just as maddening as it was in Seoul. A dozen drivers homed in on every arriving passenger to snatch a fare. Then the haggling began. Prior to departing the U.S., I had been wise enough to purchase a travel booklet. There, among other suggestions, it provided suggested taxi fares in, and around the city. It greatly helped me not to overspend while on foreign soil, like many a traveler was pressured, and coerced into. Luckily, the station was located in the middle of downtown Taegu.

"Kumho," I directed the driver. He knew exactly where to drop me off. There were no high-rise structures. Again, only one color was prevalent, gray. Everything looked gray from businesses to restaurants, bars, clubs, apartments, and homes, including the containment walls surrounding each, and every structure.

The hotel was one of a few buildings with more than two floors. Ushered in, I experienced haste everywhere. It appeared that every task had its time limit. There was no indication for leisure. Everybody seemed to be struggling. "Maybe things are different at night," I pondered. But they weren't.

I was checked into a room on the third floor. After tipping the porter, I was inspecting the room. Though evening already, it was sweltering hot. The window overlooked the main street below. If there was air conditioning, I did not feel any. The sounds from outside were overwhelming. Craning out, I spotted mostly taxi cabs jamming the street and intersections. The noise was emanating from hundreds of cabs jostling for position while incessantly leaning on their horns. One could not get away from the tumultuous sounds. The second thing I learned that day was a nasty habit of forcing one's vehicle, whether taxi or private automobile, ahead in traffic with nobody, not the police, not the government, and not the authorities able to stop them. The sound prevailed day, and night. I closed the window, but only for a short time. "No way can I sleep in this heat," I said to myself, headed for the door. When I opened it, I checked the hallway for a porter, but did not see one. What I spotted at the end of the corridor was a Korean, handgun stuck in his belt, staring me down. I quickly shut the door to call the desk.

"Could you please turn on the air conditioning?" I begged.

"Cannot be done," I was told in perfect English.

At least I could communicate, I thought in frustration while curiosity took hold. I had to find out about not having the room cooled at the city's foremost hotel. I slipped into my shoes, opened the door, and headed for the guard. "Is there air conditioning in the building?" I said with a friendly smile.

To my surprise, he understood. "There is," he readily answered. "Central."

"Then," I begged in anticipation, "could you please have it turned on?"

"Not possible."

"Why?"

"Power conservation. Not allowed to turn on unless directed."

It was not only my face dripping with sweat; he had the same problem, but could do nothing about it either. "Maybe midnight. See the button?" I followed his gesture, and recognized a breaker box. "My job. Guard it. I get call from the front desk, I push the button." It was that simple. His job was guarding one item, the power switch. I noticed a hint of a smile on his face, thanked him for the explanation, and returned to my room. He was probably grateful to talk with someone, and receive an acknowledgement, though only from a passing guest.

In the days ahead, I learned that each floor was guarded in the same manner. In due time, hotel management had learned that during summer, and winter, guests would help themselves, depending on the season, to cool or heat their room. Korea, being an emerging country at the time, had a necessary policy to conserve electricity. In spite of the strictly enforced rule, brown-outs were a daily occurrence for most of the land.

Today, several years later, the summer of 1970, arriving at Incheon International Airport was a much different travel experience. Not wanting to face the same lodging accommodations as I had experienced on my first visit here, I sought out the military base headquarters. If they could not provide housing for the team, at least I hoped that they could recommend something more favorable than a non-airconditioned room. Besides, knowing the team, and their intolerance for inadequacies, I had to find suitable housing.

I immediately noticed on arriving that Taegu had experienced tremendous growth in the past years. The Kumho was not the only hotel in downtown anymore, but traffic was still as uncontrolled as ever, with the blearing sound of horns prevalent through the night whether in the city or the outskirts. It seemed a cultural custom nobody had been able to break. Clearly reminded of past accommodation inadequacies, I directed the taxi for Camp Henry, the headquarters base of my destination.

All the team members had arrived when I met them at the base cafeteria. It was close to lunch time. "Where've you been?" Buzz demanded in his usual impatience. He was not happy with me dumping my responsibilities on him during my early departure from the last site.

"Command headquarters."

"What's the deal?"

"We've got base housing." I had just returned from the local army command headquarters following a lengthy, but productive briefing.

I could see relieved grins on the faces for making the stay easy, and them not having to deal with local traffic, the language barrier, and foreign customs. Most members on the team did not have the entrepreneurial spirit to venture into unfamiliar territories as disorderly as here. Many visitors did not know that they had entered a war zone. Even as late as the 70s, South Korea was still at war with the North, both unable to come to terms with each other. Where the local citizens on both sides may have questioned the idiocy against a peace treaty resolution from the respective governments, the policymakers had their own agendas for keeping the conflict alive, already in its twenty-fifth postwar year. Even at the day of this writing, 2019, peace is still beyond reach, with border tensions on the increase to perhaps an inevitable, nuclear war. The future for North Korea still hangs on shaky ground, hinged on international forces pulling on a totalitarian dictatorship.

For now, other than technical work, issues had been solved. I was able to secure comfortable living accommodations at the nearby housing base, Camp George, with work conducted at Camp Walker, and restaurant, and social accommodations found at Camp Henry. All three camps were located in a valley surrounded by mountainous hills high, and isolated from the rest of the country and the city. It was the isolation U.S. Intel sought out in foreign places of conflicts.

Working diligently at the worksite, the daily schedule was shuttling between the camps to satisfy the team's needs, from eating to work completion, to the customary after-work recreations conducted either at an on-base, or a local establishment. Unfortunately, for customers, and entertainers alike, curfew was strictly enforced at midnight, a time everybody would scramble for a taxi home, or pay the fee to stay overnight at the local establishment. One was preferred over the other since no local visitors were allowed to spend the night on base. For civilians, the choice was easy. For the military serviceman not, for it required an overnight pass not easily obtained during weekdays.

Routinely, each day proceeded in a similar manner until the project was completed six weeks later, except for a now familiar face pacing the floors. "Mystery-man," I said with an extended hand. "You show up at the most unexpected places."

"It's my job, keeping an eye on you, and your team."

"I am glad someone is looking out for us," I replied with a grin, unsure what to expect other than contemplating my future career. I assumed he was here to follow up. With the tight schedule the project held, I had not taken the time to evaluate his earlier offer any further. I could use it as an excuse when the topic came up, as it sure would.

But as professional as he always appeared, first on his agenda was technology, and how to implement it in the most seamless way into the AUTODIN system. Where designers back at DARPA might have had specific initiatives about their newly contrived projects, somebody had to liaison with field engineers such as me, and that was Mystery-man. What was slightly unusual about his unexpected visit was the time factor. Half way into the project, it would be unproductive to change direction, no matter how pressing a project might be. It meant retracing to the other sites that were already completed, and implementing new changes, and doing the project over again, not an efficient means.

Again, my mind was jumping ahead of myself, for I did not even know the reason for his unexpected appearance. "Follow me," he said with a gesture towards his favorite talking spot, the back in COMM facility. Since all the sites were identical in construction, he would pick the same spot because it was quiet, with voices muffled from the sounds of internal rack cooling fans, and outside of other people's earshot. I would have liked to sit by the command console in the comfort of captain chairs, but he never trusted the position.

"What's up?" I inquired.

"Not the best of news," he replied. "We believe North Korea is elevating political pressure on the South. As you probably know, Cold War tension has escalated in recent months. It may affect the project."

"How so?" I was curious to hear though I had suspected something like this. Already, for weeks, my people, and I had been monitoring the airwaves on COMM monitors for amplified "chatter" from the North, a common jargon for a sudden increase in Intel communication. It was a means to evaluate tension buildup between nations, or conflict escalation from within. Either way spelled trouble, but I could not reveal my knowledge. Where Intel agencies may have suspected covert activities taking place on the frontlines, such as monitoring highly classified traffic, it was only tolerated as long as there was never a security breach. After all, it was field operatives, and people like us enhancing system performance that allowed for the protection, and safeguarding of collaborative countries such as South Korea, and adversaries like the North. My team and I, usually had firsthand knowledge on political events taking place, utilizing the miracles of advanced technology we were implementing in foreign territory.

I should point out that no matter how sensitive the Intel data shooting across wires, painted on monitor screens was, nobody talked about it other than a hushed comment or two among the site crews. It was this attitude that helped create the sound reputation for AUTODIN as being the most trusted, innovative system for its time. Unfortunately, and as tragically as his life ended, JFK could not participate in the success of his vision.

Where in past decades, with two dynastic leadership generations, North Korea may have had notions of possibly invading the South, it had always been ignored by the West as improbable or impossible. It was not until in recent years, through the young, and ambitious third dynastic successor when notion turned into a more likely reality with the renewed threat of nuclear-tipped rockets the North had developed. Backed by Chinese forces, a border nation and ally to the North, what used to be an isolated, economically-deprived nation depending solely on international aid, the North had turned a major power not pushed off lightly. While international diplomacy initiated by the West may delay the potential threats, conflict was inevitable in the near future. It was North Korea demanding equal status in world politics only achievable through the threat of a nuclear confrontation.

Presently, facing Mystery-man, he said, "You'll have to either cease the scheduled implementation, or speed it up to complete as soon as possible. It will impact your schedule. How do you want to handle it?"

Okay, so he had handed off the responsibility onto my shoulders, again. What else was new? The decision, involving the South and its population's safety, would be up to me. Since we had just started the project it would have been easy to terminate the schedule here, and move on to the next location, but it would severely impact U.S. and Korean Intel communication capabilities. I could feel the weight pressing on my shoulders, and sought his opinion. "What do you think?" He flinched at the shifting of the burden back onto him.

"It's still your decision," he stated, unrelentingly.

"Here is my decision," I said after a few seconds of assessing the importance. "I will double the shift and work weekends. We could finish up the project in two weeks."

"You will do that?" It was obvious he had not expected a workable solution with the limited resources at hand. "Can it be done?"

"I assure you success, but it would impact my promise to join your team."

"Oh," he said, rubbing his chin. "That'll have to wait. I need you here more than anywhere else."

It was official now. His offer for the GS-11 position had been postponed. Since I had not taken the time to decide yet, I could relax. I am sure he was unburdened as well at my solution with the time sensitive dilemma.

As promised, we completed the job in record time, two weeks. While the issue was locally solved, it would impact the overall schedule, nevertheless. I had a solution for that as well, and told him. I would grant the team some time off at the next location, the Philippines. I was sure it would be welcomed by my men.

Mystery-man even remained on site to see the project through, with periodic observations at the workers such as, "You guys are amazing," and "the government really appreciates your efforts."

Future follow-on projects were assured for both company, and team.

PHILIPPINES

A place located in the distant expanse of the Pacific, 7,300 miles west from the U.S. coast, on my first visit to this island group, I was awestruck. I only had a vague memory of the place from reading Pearl S. Buck's books, the British novelist, on foreign travels. Being the daughter of her country's ambassador to Asia, and Indochina, she also wrote about the Philippines. Though the islands had just been freed from one oppressor, Japan, another liberator took its place, the U.S. Her books dated back to the early 1900s, and so did the Filipino lifestyle. From her illustrations of the people, headhunters were still prevalent throughout the islands. Visitors still disappeared even later past my first visits in the late 60s, and 70s. I can imagine, and as rumors had it, that some of the Japanese were cooked, and eaten during their occupation.

It was the impression carried on my mind when the flight attendant announced our landing destination, Manila. First off, my mind was not prepared for the view as the craft descended onto the island's capital city. Looking out the window, I could not believe the sprawling metropolis coming into view. Expecting a horde of villagers on the run to meet our arrival, I was flabbergasted with thoughts such as "Whatever happened to the natives, the headhunters, the indigenous?"

The craft landed, but instead of a horde of natives carrying knives, spears, and blowguns greeting the arrivals, it was a horde of baggage carriers, hawkers, and taxi drivers demanding my full attention. Though guarded, I did not feel threatened. Much like the other places, I was rushed, shoved, and ushered into the city's top-rated hotel, the Hilton. In the process I lost grip on my suitcase several times, but managed to hang onto the briefcase. I did not want to lose it because it contained my passport and local currency, as well as a stack of traveler's checks.

Checking in at the front desk, I was instructed, "Passport please."

"Can I have it back?" I insisted.

"We keep it in the safe. It's better this way."

Losing the passport would present a problem. Rumors stated that it was a hot commodity in some countries in order to obtain the very sought-after U.S. citizenship.

"For how long?"

"Until your departure."

Alerted about a possible black market, I voiced my concerns. "What else should I know?"

"Keep your wallet in the front pocket."

"Okay."

"What room would you prefer?"

Not bad, I thought, having a choice. "How about the top floor facing west?" I always enjoyed sunsets.

"Room 2416. The porter has your key. I'm your concierge," he offered, "in case you need anything."

"I'm fine."

"I mean anything at all," he persisted with a wink of an eye.

I understood, and was whisked off by the porter lingering nearby. He had been waiting for the desk manager's sign that I was ready for business. Business in the land where anything was up for sale, purchased either with the local currency, the peso, with U.S. dollars preferred, gratuities were rendered for personal services, and anything else a person needed or desired. I quickly learned that the Philippines were a paradise for the single man, or woman, for that matter. I spent the weekend in Manila before departing to my final destination, some forty miles in-country.

Arriving at Angeles City Monday morning, the second largest city on the island of Luzon, the scene changed drastically. My first thought on arriving were, "Now that's more like it," recalling my distant impressions of the land. It was like it had been illustrated in Pearl Buck's books. Outside of the capital, poverty appeared present wherever one went. Though a city, it was more of a sprawling country populated by native people housed in makeshift, single-dwelling shacks, crammed against each other, built mostly from leftover WWII construction materials such as corrugated rooftops, and plywood mounted on mud-constructed walls, many without running water, and electricity, labeled Nipa Huts. Each place looked lofty without windows with the interior held up by bamboo flooring, I would come to learn at a later time.

The way of life here seemed at its simplest form that I had experienced so far. The city basically embraced Clark AFB, supporting all of the needs a U.S. military base overseas required and desired. Arriving in three rental cars I had checked out in Manila were Buzz, and three of my team crammed into the small car. Jammed in the second and third rentals was the rest of the crew. We had met during the weekend when most on the team arrived.

"It sure looks different," Buzz commented. Another chimed in with, "You got that right." Their focus was centered on the many bars, and clubs along the streets. "Going to have fun here," and "looks like Paradise," were additional comments made, anticipating ample entertainment for the single guys. Though it was mid-day, they had spotted local girls lingering around bars, and clubs waiting for patrons. I could only imagine what the nightlife would be like.

Asking for lodging accommodations, I was directed to Hotel Row, a lackluster dusty street covered by potholes amid stray dogs chasing the rentals. Arriving at the hotels, aside from an obvious lack of windows, the accommodations were quite comfortable. "Too many break-ins," I was told when complaining about the dark rooms. Checking out my room, it was accommodating nevertheless, at a total cost of $6 per day.

To simplify the daily passage through gates, and checkpoints, I traded two rentals in for a VW bus, readily offered by a local rental agency. It would provide ample transportation for the next six weeks, but not without a number of incidents, and mishaps.

The following day, Monday, rousing everybody from sleep, we had anticipated having breakfast at the base cafeteria or military mess hall. Being an Air Force facility, American food would be the choice for my team. The hotel we stayed in was located just a short distance from the main gate. After arriving minutes later, we encountered the first problem. Fifty yards out from the gate a warning sign was posted, "Stop." We were surrounded by dozens of activists dressed in slippers, shorts, and t-shirts topped by bandanas shouting and bellowing at us. It did not take much of an imagination to realize we were caught up in a demonstration preventing passage onto the base. "What now?" Buzz exclaimed, slightly annoyed

"Turn back, and celebrate," the team cheered.

"Not so fast," I objected. "I need to inform base command. They'll probably provide an escort."

"Shucks. Forget it. It can wait," the team objected. I knew well what was on their minds, and it was not the project. Unable to proceed further, our passage was blocked by fierce looking, shouting, and intimidating demonstrators. I was allowed to turn back, but not without menacing, threatening gestures not to return. It was enough of a threat to take seriously. We returned to the hotel with the team headed for the nearest bar across the street.

I checked with the hotel desk to negotiate a private call to mainland CONUS[26]. Since it was nighttime back home, I left a message explaining the situation. It was already evening when I received the call at the hotel. Explaining the local conditions preventing us from getting on base, I was assured a callback. Unsure about the demonstration, I checked with the hotel manager.

"What's the demo about?"

"They want the Americans to go home."

"Who are they?"

"Local businessmen. They want Japanese business investments like everywhere else in the Pacific." It became clear that other countries such as Okinawa, Korea, and even Guam demonstrated for the same cause.

"How long do the demos usually last?"

"One or two weeks."

That's bad, I thought. It would impact the schedule. I did not cherish the thought of explaining to the team about having to make up any incurred time slippage. For now, we were safe, after finishing up two weeks ahead of Schule at the last place, Korea.

The callback came several hours later. "Got a contact for you," the voice on the phone stated. "Got something to write with? Here's the number."

Grabbing a pencil from the hotel desk, I jotted down the number then I asked the desk manager, "You recognize the number?"

"Hmm," he contemplated, shooting a quick glance at me. "You must be important. Gonzales, commanding general, two-star. I know of him. Follow me," he said with a gesture at his private office. "Take your time."

I appreciated the courtesy of letting me use his personal phone to make the call.

"Base Command," the voice announced. "State your business."

"I need to speak with your commander. It's important."

"Please hold."

I probably was not the first person calling his office this morning. It took several minutes for the general to get on the phone. "What do you want?"

He did not sound friendly at all. Probably the situation at the gates, I presumed. "My team, and I can't get on base. I was supposed to start a project this morning, and was refused entry. Can you please help?"

"What project?" He sounded short-fused.

---

[26] CONUS – Continental U.S., a common abbreviation in the military community.

"Memory upgrade at the AUTODIN site."

After a few seconds of silence, he shot back, "Can't help you."

"It's important to get the project started today. I have a tight timeline."

"I told you already. I can't help you." The phone went dead. He had hung up.

It put me in a dilemma. I stepped out to see the manager, "Can I make another long distant call?"

"Of course. Go right ahead." I must have pulled some weight for lodging a dozen travelers at his place. He acted very accommodating.

"Headquarters," the operator stated.

"Let me speak with Art," I said. My director was well known at headquarters.

"Got a problem," I informed him. "Base command refuses entry to the base. I need immediate assistance. Here is my contact. Please get back to me." It was all I could do for the moment.

"Sit tight," Art said. "I'll get back to you."

"Thanks." I knew he would act accordingly. It was his responsibility to resolve any issues with DOD.

"Listen," I said to the hotel manager. "I'm expecting a call. Could you send for me? I'll be with my team across the street."

"Early's," he said with a grin.

"What?" I questioned his gesture.

"I know the place. Everybody in the neighborhood does. It's a place my guests hang out during the day, killing time until evening."

"What then?"

"Entertainment begins."

I'd heard enough, and headed across the street. "What's up?" Buzz said in anticipation when I pulled up a chair.

"We won't get on base." As soon as I made the announcement, cheers went up with "more drinks."

"Let's not get hasty," I reasoned. "The dispute may get solved by morning. I've got a call in with Headquarters."

"I'll drink to that." Buzz encouraged his buddies indicating a toast. The call did not come until the next morning. I had already canvassed the base perimeter, but was turned away by the demonstrators much like the previous day. Since there were no cell phones back then, I had to either stand by the phone or leave a contact. It certainly left me stranded while the team decided to explore the local territory.

"See you later," Buzz yelled out, driving off with a busload eager to scope out the native territory. I would have liked to go along.

The following morning, I met up with the team at our usual meeting place, the hotel cafeteria, for yesterday's firsthand briefing. "Mostly friendly territory," Buzz reported. "Drove up-country some ways, but had to return. Roads were washed out by the monsoon. Couldn't get all the way up north." I had brought along a map of Luzon to get an idea on the place.

"How far up did you get?" I had him point out the path they had taken. "Tarlac, and on to Baguio. Came back via La Union by the ocean."

The hotel manager walked up with, "How is breakfast?"

"Couldn't be better…excellent…just great," were comments from the table.

"Glad you like it. What's this, I hear you went up north?" He must have overheard the lively conversation.

"They are telling me of yesterday's trip."

"Baguio?"

"Yeah," Buzz confirmed. "Couldn't get farther. Roads are washed out."

"It happens after the monsoon. But," he cautioned with a serious look on his face, "I must warn you. Don't go farther north. We just received reports of some servicemen disappearing."

"What do mean, disappearing?"

"Like your people, they drove up north a couple of weeks ago. Never came back."

"Never came back from what?"

"Igorot territory."

"What's Igorot?"

"Local tribesmen."

I took it at face value because he had a serious expression on his face. "Headhunters."

"This day, and age?" I was as speechless as my team. "You can't be serious?"

"I'm telling you the truth. Just stay away from their land. It's fiercely protected by the natives. They don't want any visits from outside. Even our government people don't go there."

"You heard him," I cautioned the team. Sure enough, days later rumors began to spread about the disappearance. Though not admitting to any misdeeds, the Igorot chief issued another warning for strangers to keep off their land. As if the manager's advice was not enough already, he added, "Don't carry a wallet, watch, or sunglasses. You'll be prime suspect for getting robbed."

I should mention that the lawless customs dated back to colonial oppression when Portuguese conquistadores settled here. After taking possession of the islands the foreign intruders, at times, were fiercely fought off by local tribesmen. There were many clashes with one remarkable one-on-one duel fought. It involved local tribal chief Lapu-Lapu, who in 1521, refused to convert to Christianity, in the process killing Ferdinand Magellan, the Portuguese explorer leading the exploration.

In the years that followed, many more explorations took hold on the islands. In spite of heavily armored armadas forcing their ways inland, in trying to ward off the unwelcome intruders, the local tribes became more and more aggressive. One of their means was through pilfering, taking, and stealing anything that was not part of the ship while anchored at bay. The results were foreign ships leaving with much of their provisions absconded. Subsequently, over the years, the custom of taking was still prevalent without repercussion by the law. Taking something from a stranger, as much as from a careless local citizen, was considered "borrowing" only. My team could attest to this first-hand.

Being accosted unexpectedly, mostly at night, several lost such items as wristwatches, wallets, and even an entire week's pay. I was called on several times to present the theft to a local magistrate, but met without success. The advice was generally the same, "Tell your men to be careful when out on the streets."

Being keenly aware of the local conditions, after several incidents that could have led to a potential robbery, I successfully avoided them by being watchful at all times, especially during night-time hours. Regardless of petty crimes by a zealous thief who made it a living in a corrupted, economically deprived country, it was usually just simple theft. People here have always been poor, and would remain so for most of their lives unless government, and political policies adapt to enforcing the laws.

As predicted on our arrival, the protest demonstrations lasted two weeks. No matter how diligently I pursued getting on base, my attempts were ineffective. We were turned away each day after making another attempt. What I could not understand at the time was the ineptness displayed by the Pentagon. With as much power as the U.S. government wielded in this country, all it would have required was a minimal payout to the chief-in-charge of the demonstration to allow our passage. I could attest to the claim through my own experiences in the years to follow. You can get anything accomplished with a few dollars, paid in gratuity. In other words, adapt to the craft the country was built, and thrived on. It was something, especially when entering into a business arrangement in the Philippines, that one had to accept as a "way-of-life." I was not judgmental in my opinions since many visitors fell subject to the inherited way of life here.

Regardless of the legal perspective in the Philippine culture, theft was considered a give-and-take, depending on one's personal needs. One day, when one had extra money to spend, it was readily shared with other family members, and friends, resulting in everybody owing everyone something. The system worked well through most social classes, especially for the poor. For all practical purposes, the country never had a middle class. As was the case with many third-world countries, the two classes were the wealthy running the country, and the poor slaving to live another day. It would remain this way forever since there was no cross-over between the two castes.

Anxious to get the project under way, it seemed that I was being completely ignored by the Pentagon, as well as my own headquarters. My follow-up calls were either stalled or ignored altogether. It was puzzling. Two weeks went by with similar results when my calls were finally answered. "You are cleared to proceed with the project."

I was relieved as much as anxious to get started. As expected, my team was gathered at the breakfast room waiting for me to show up. "What's the scoop?" Buzz wanted to know.

"We are on. Get your things together."

"Give us ten minutes to finish," he replied while I headed to my room to gather the necessary project materials. From past experience, I had made it a habit to carry extra sensitive electronic components in my briefcase, just in case of a critical shortage in parts. Where printed circuit boards, the core of any mainframe computer, had proven pretty reliable, there was always the weakest link in the configuration. Although discrete transistor performance was improving by the month, manufacturing still had inherited flaws.

On our way to the site, we arrived early at the security gate. "IDs," the sentry demanded.

"Here," I said, handing over my travel orders. The orders, a document allowing temporary entrance into the command facility, would serve as passage. I watched him disappear into the gateway booth to make the call. Seconds later he emerged. Expecting the normal "Proceed" through an opened gate, to my surprise, he commanded, "Can't enter."

"What?" I shot back.

"You cannot enter," he repeated.

Angered about more delays, I stepped out from the driver's seat, demanding, "Get me the phone."

"Not possible. For official use only."

"I'm official," I argued.

"You're a contractor." He gestured at the papers. You have no rights."

That was it. I faced the inevitable, another unexpected delay. After getting back to the hotel I flagged down the manager. "I've got to use your phone."

"My office," he gestured.

Sounding off my anger at Art, I reported, "Refused to let us on-site."

"Standby."

I was put on a lengthy hold once more before his response came through. "Keep your men ready to move at a moment's notice. That's all I have for you."

I joined the team at the daily gathering place with, "We're on standby."

"For how long?" Buzz said, "and why?"

"Don't know. Nobody knows. Even headquarters didn't know." The protocol I had to follow was to receive orders from the contracting office that, in turn, would negotiate, and resolve any problems incurred with the Pentagon, the directorate-in-charge of the specific project while overseas under direct jurisdiction of the U.S. embassies. I was in a quandary for reasons unknown. By now, the day had already been wasted.

"Let's get going," Buzz demanded, checking for my approval.

What could I do, but say, "Check with me in the morning."

"No problem," he said, gathering the team for another scouting trip into the country. I was stranded again, facing the wasted day alone.

"Any news?" Buzz said the following morning. "What's going on?"

"Don't know. I'm still waiting for word."

"What about us?"

"Stick around for a while," I said, advising the team.

It was not for another couple of hours before the manager showed up. "Phone call."

Rushing to take the call, "What's the word?" I barked in the receiver.

"Commander wants to meet with you. One hour."

Ready for anything, I directed Buzz to the site. "Base Command." Ready to climb in the passenger seat, I noticed both side mirrors missing from the vehicle. "What happened?" I demanded.

"Got stolen yesterday."

"Where?"

"Our trip. I parked the bus. We went into a store. We came out, and the mirrors were missing."

"It's your responsibility. You get it fixed," I ordered, annoyed.

"Will do."

Like on previous days, we were stopped by the sentry. A quick check and directions gave us passage through the gate.

Arriving at Command HQs, "Only you," an orderly insisted, guiding me to the base commander's office.

"Hi," I said on entering, but all I received was, "You Bauer?"

"Alex Bauer," I replied with a friendly smile, but my gesture was ignored.

"What's the project all about?" I was taken by surprise at the unfriendly reception. I had been greeted with unrestrained welcome on all previous visits to Intel centers, so this was a first. I suspected something was amiss. I knew he had been briefed on the upcoming project weeks before our arrival, as was customary with the DOD. No project would commence without prior approval by the site. "Explain," he demanded.

"I am here to upgrade your computer, and communication systems."

"Nobody touches my equipment," he stated in a commanding voice. "Not you, not the Pentagon, and surely not a contractor."

And there it was. The contractor/customer relations conflict was out in the open. I had heard of personal disputes between Air Force commanders and contractors before, but never experienced it personally. I studied the person seated behind the desk—pompous, cigar stuffed between his jaws, staring me down to underline his resentment. I retained my composure, respecting the uniform, especially when I recognized the emblem clipped to his lapels, two-star general. Regardless of rank, I had a job to do, and handed over the paper. "My orders."

He only took a quick glance at it, got out of his chair, and guided me from his office, saying, "Orders don't mean anything here unless they come from me."

Standing undecided in the hallway for a moment, I heard the office door slam shut. It was apparent that the commander did not want my team on his site. I felt anger well up at being rejected so unceremoniously, but left without reservation to let others solve the issue. "We'll see," I muttered, headed for the rental, explaining the situation to the Buzz.

"Back to the hotel," I directed.

"What are you going to do?" Buzz said. "We can't sit here forever. I want to go on to finish the tour." While he was just as determined to see a successful implementation, the team, in contrast, did not object to the added delay. They completely enjoyed the localities with day-and-night entertainment, and added benefits provided for personal companionship. Dollar-spending patrons were readily welcomed in this part of the poverty-stricken country. The black market for U.S. currency was prolific, and went unchecked by local authorities, who, likewise, benefited from the readily accepted windfall. As a matter of fact, since tourism had not yet reached this part, the only means of income was from U.S. servicemen, supporting the local economy, an added benefit to the already allocated annual defense budget the country received from the Pentagon.

It would take several more days before the dispute between the general, and the Pentagon was settled. The call I received from Art went something like this:

"You can get on base."

"Oh. What happened?"

"You outranked the general." I must admit that on hearing that, I became slightly conceited. Though I was authorized the equivalent rank of full-bird colonel while on projects, it was not every day a contractor outranked a general, let alone a two-star.

"How did you manage to convince him?"

"It wasn't me. He was directed by JCS[27]."

"I can hardly wait to face him," I said before hanging up with a, "thanks for clearing the way. You realize I am three weeks behind schedule."

"Don't sweat it," I was told. "You'll make it up."

Again, the burden others had caused was up to me, and the team to make up. When I faced the general shortly after, his boldly-stated advice was, "I don't want any fuckups. You hear?"

It became apparent that he had been concerned about my interfering with his career as I would find out later. Fiercely refusing to cooperate with my contracting office, after several days of refusal, he was given an ultimatum by JCS: "Either let the contractors do their job or face immediate retirement." He might have had the ultimate decision-making powers throughout a glorious career, hoping to join the upper Pentagon echelons, but he realized he had screwed up badly. But now, with this imbecile contractor standing before him, I could read his thoughts: his future was in jeopardy. My deduction proved correct during the following weeks while performing on his site.

He would show up unexpectedly on occasion to check on the team's progress. "How much longer?"

"Another couple of weeks," I said. I had sped up our progress by having the team, including myself, work daily overtime, and on weekends. This must have pleased him because he admitted, "So far you haven't caused me any downtime. Can you guarantee it for the rest of your time on my site?"

"I can guarantee my personal performance, but cannot do so for each team member."

He stood silent for a time before responding. "My career depends on your performance, and don't you forget it."

Two weeks later, after completing the project, I conducted the customary out-briefing. "Mister Bauer," he said locking eyes with me, "I don't ever want to cross path with you again. You caused me a lot of grief."

"I didn't mean to but we had a job to do. You understand?"

"The only reason I'll let you go is because you upheld your promises. Otherwise," he swore, "I'd have you locked up."

"No amount of personal conflict is worth fighting over," were my last words with him. He refused my extended hand, turned, and abruptly left, releasing me. I never had to deal with the general again. Whatever direction his career took, I never heard his name mentioned on the rosters when reporting to the Pentagon. I harbored no hard feelings with him because I respected the uniform, and rank of all military service

---

[27] JCS – Joint Chiefs of Staff was the uppermost echelon level in the hierarchy of military services. Many generals strove to be on the panel but would never achieve this heralded position. There was only room for the best qualified commanders from within each service—Air Force, Navy, Army, and Marine—appointed by virtue of personality, diplomacy, and personal achievements.

members. After all, they were an honest, and tough breed commissioned into service to protect our country, and the safety of the citizens.

Getting ready to depart for the next assignment, Vietnam, I was faced with one last dilemma. On one of the team's nightly outings to one of the local clubs, the VW bus was further vandalized. When informed the following morning, I saw the damage caused by thieves. When I inspected the vehicle, aside from the driver side seat, I saw that missing were all three bench seats in back, the radio, license plates, and spare tire. The bus was stripped of all parts that were removable. All I could muster was shaking my head when faced with returning the vehicle to the rental place.

"I have bad news," I proclaimed at the rental office.

"Accident?" I watched the leasing agent's face turn from bad to worse.

"No accident. Theft. The vehicle was stripped by thieves." He promptly headed for the parking lot. Spotting the bus all he did was keep shaking his head while inspecting the damage. Pacing around the vehicle several times, checking inside, and out, he started laughing uncontrollably, stammering, "This is not my bus. Tell me it's not. This is not the same VW you leased."

I had to repeat, and assure him that it was, followed with an offer for having my insurance company pay for the damages. Reluctantly, after I signed the contract, he dismissed the whole lot of us with, "I don't want to see you again. You understand?"

"I understand," I muttered. Then, "I need transportation."

That shook him up. He had thought he was rid of us. "Where?"

"Manila Airport."

"How many?" he said, counting the team.

"Three vehicles should do it," I volunteered, expecting his denial.

"It will cost you."

"Government pays for it."

It must have struck a positive note because he let us have the three requested vehicles. Though reluctantly, because he did not offer the best of rentals. In spite of it all, he took the courtesy to shake my departing hand.

"That went well," Buzz voiced with a relieved breath of air.

Though damaged from potholes, scrapes, and bumps, the vehicles got us safely to the airport four hours later. It closed another chapter on our contracting obligation. It would not be the last.

VIETNAM

Impressions I had after touching down on the tarmac in the Boeing 707 at Tan Son Nhat airport, Saigon, brought back distant memories out of childhood. With uniforms hurrying to service incoming, and outgoing aircraft, and support crews shuttling cargo from the coast inland to war zones, though fairly well organized in a country at war, on my first arrival it may have seemed chaotic. Where the dispatched soldier was met by a detachment from his combat unit, a contractor, on the other hand, whether government or civilian, was on his own, felt misplaced. Stepping off the gangway onto solid ground, in the midst of tropical heat, one felt in another world. It appeared a world of haste, confusion, and bewilderment. For the moment, I followed the other emerging passengers rushing to collect their luggage. For all practical purposes, the airport was a neutral zone. Heavily surrounded by armored military vehicles, one could feel safe, outside of the initial confusion. Gazing around the bustling facility, one was struck by the colors, or lack of. What the eyes perceived was one color, olive green, back then the popular paint for the Army. Headed for the receiving entrance, one was met by a cooling rush of air created by humongous generators feeding the complex. "What a relief," I muttered, inhaling the cool air. The sound from arriving, and departing jets was muffled once inside. "What next?" I thought, seeking out the 'Arrival' sign for luggage, and customs check. "Over there," I saw with relief.

"Anything to declare?" the uniformed official demanded. To my surprise, facing me was what I presumed a Vietnamese agent with facial features much like the Chinese, but slightly darker in skin color. He was gauging me with distrust, as many customs officials did. Slightly offended, I thought, "Can't you read my honest face," but instead said, "No. Nothing to declare." Regardless of my negative response, he ordered, "Open." To which I promptly complied. He took a brief glance at the contents of my two-suiter, fingered between my neatly folded personals, and closed the suitcase. Next, he handled my briefcase with equal swiftness, and efficiency. Waving me off, I was free to go on. But where? First, I checked on the team. Some were still processing through customs lines.

"What a trip," Buzz remarked. "Never saw such rush. Wonder what they're looking for."

"Beats me." I wondered the same. I could not imagine anybody smuggling anything into this country other than a fist full of dollars. I had heard about the thriving black market for U.S. currency, and its inflated value at warfronts.

"Should have brought some." He sniggered. Because of the way we were brought up by our parents neither he nor I were prone to illicit activities. We fully trusted each other. It had paid off at times when we had to rely on each other.

As was the case with most individuals assigned to a war-torn country, prior to departing CONUS, the individual was usually indoctrinated on Status of Forces Agreement (SOFA) policies. What this meant was getting briefed on a list of "Can, and Cannot Do's" while in the foreign country, with who to seek out when in trouble or injured, what foods to avoid, especially local drinking water, refraining from dealing in the black market, and a number of additional basics to protect the American citizen from getting into trouble, one may regret. Where the soldier was subjected to the rules of military policies, the civilian contractor was not. However, they could get help from the military support services if complying with SOFA agreements. But, as was the case with many rules, and regulations, they could be broken, and in a war zone; they always were. One may have had good intentions to comply with stated policies, but opportunities in the form of goods, services, and pleasures, readily offered at a minuscule price were always present, if paid in U.S. currency.

Although both of us were experienced travelers, Vietnam was a first. Since we had been traveling several months already, for the team to not get indoctrinated was an oversight by our headquarters. Gathered at the arrival lounge, questions were fired at me. "Where to, Alex? Where's our contact? What do we do next?"

Since I was in charge, it was up to me to make connections to appease the team. "You stay put where I can find you," I instructed them. "And don't wander off. We are in a war zone."

"Don't take too long. I'm hungry. I need to lie down," my team replied. I knew well how tiresome travel could be, and ignored the complaints.

Gazing around the terminal my eyes fell on a prominent sign, "MACV," in small lettering explaining its function, "Military Assistance Command, Vietnam." Since it looked official, I headed for the desk, and proclaimed, "I need help."

"Got orders?" the sergeant said. I put the briefcase on the counter to retrieve the papers, and handed him the copy. "Nha Trang," he responded. "You're going up north."

"Where's up north?" I said.

"Near the DMZ."

"When's the next flight out?" Since we were presently at Saigon's commercial airport, taken over by the U.S. military at the onset of war, there was no flight board posting flights. As I would experience over time flying in, and out of Saigon, depending on the priority status of orders, with mine stating the highest bestowed to a civilian contractor, I was usually whisked away with the first craft scheduled for takeoff, with mission, and type of craft subjected to availability. For this reason, I have been part of the flight crew on the C-129, C-135, C-141, C-5, C-17, numerous helicopters, and even an F-4 Phantom fighter jet, which I did not mind at all. Most times, a loadmaster did not worry much about timetables. Schedule changes to cargo deliveries were inevitable, and common. Generally, troops ordered into action had priority over everything. A brigadier general had rank over me, but only if I was not on an emergency mission, in which case I had to pull rank. It usually left a very unhappy general loudly voicing his dismay by cussing after me, "Damned civilian..."

Another thing I had learned was where Army, and Naval personnel always appreciated my callings, Air Force personnel alleged they were a special "know it all" breed. Since their educational level was generally superior to the other service members—I am talking about enlisted men—I never held any grudges, and appreciated their assertive attitudes. However, not meaning to be disrespectful, through my many visits to Air Force Intel sites, they quickly learned that there were others who knew just as much or more about the job.

In contrast to the Air Force mentality, Naval rankings were known for being "specialists in nothing, but masters in all." It meant that they had to be self-sufficient while at seas for months at a time, and capable of fixing anything, and everything that needed repairs.

Regardless, my support visits were always appreciated by the ones that counted, commanders, and decision makers.

Today, on our arrival, we wound up spending the night in Saigon. Hitching a ride on a troop carrier, we were dropped off at the Continental Hotel located in the heart of the city. My first impression was that of a city in shambles. The military had taken over every commercial complex, communication system, government building, and even hotels. A continuous arrival of servicemen, Intel agents, reporters, and civilian contractors presented a lodging problem that was never solved. When rooms were available, the soldier was put up for the night, and, if not, was transported directly to the warzone allocating the space to the civilian, separated into two major categories. Government officials, and reporters were put up at the Caravelle Hotel, while Intelligence, and contracting personnel lodged at the Continental Hotel. Both were spacious, much like palaces, built years before for vacationers while the country was under French colonial rule. Though constructed in palatial style, neglect was clearly visible due to local conditions from war, and terrorist attacks.

What struck the visitor first was the smell of garbage as soon as one entered the city perimeters, and fittingly so. The city's refuse, and garbage were dumped by the residents daily onto major street intersections, fermenting by the sun, and heated air. The stench was inconceivable to the newly arrived, and so was the sight. Dogs, cats, and rats were seen feeding on the heaps of garbage piled twenty feet high, causing all kinds of sickness, and disease. Cholera was rampant, and so were dysentery, and amoeba infestations to men and animal alike. I had never seen a more dreadful-looking lot of scavenging dogs as in the streets of Saigon with tails, and patches of skins missing, hobbling along on three legs, only to be overrun by a taxi or private vehicle aiming directly for the poor creatures, sold to local restaurants for the meat. "But," I was told, "that's war."

Checking into the Continental was as routine as back home with a slight difference. "Passport, please." The desk manager was courteous, and accommodating after verifying my identity, then secured the document at a safe in the back office. A porter lingered nearby, waiting for the signal from the desk clerk to carry the luggage. My room contained one spacious guestroom, and shower stall almost of equal size, all white-washed, bright, but clean for the most part. What struck me as odd were the sizes of the rooms. It was colonialism throughout from wall to wall, and floor to ceilings that must have been twelve feet high. "Leave it to the French to create personal space," I thought.

All together there were two pieces of furniture, a king-size bed, and a stand-alone closet containing a couple hangers to accommodate coat, and shirt. Even though it was a warzone, U.S. dress code was still enforced. It was suit, and tie worn during travel with tie shed at the job location. It would be unthinkable today for the American traveler to be dressed in suit and tie at a tropical location.

I propped the suitcase on one side of the bed, leaving space to sleep on the other half near the bathroom. Checking around further, I located a miniature bar of soap by the showerhead with enough space to shower an entire squadron at the same time.

I took a shower. I needed it. Before even stepping off the plane at the airport, one could feel the cabin warming up while in flight thirty minutes before landing. It's how the tropical heat impacted the environment whether airconditioned or not. Everybody felt, and appeared sweaty, at all times. Taking a shower was not so much about scrubbing clean; the sweat took care of that. It was to cool off the heated body. As was the case with most lodging accommodations in Vietnam, city, and country alike, there was no hot water. Taking the local conditions into consideration, on my future trips here, I would make travel adjustments. First, and foremost, no heavy suitcase. I planned to travel light with my briefcase only. It would contain my passport, a full-size bar of soap, toothbrush, and paste alongside a stack of traveler's checks. There was still space left for a change of briefs, to justify the purpose of the hand-carried case. Where else would one carry shorts, but in a brief case.

Since it was early afternoon, I sought out the in-house restaurant located on the top floor. Once the elevator door opened, I stepped into the space serving as club, bar, and restaurant, lively with patrons, and hostesses. On passing, I called for the waitress, and had my first education in the country. "We don't have waitresses. We are all hostesses."

Well, it set me straight, knowing what to expect at the end of a day. Overlooking the Presidential Palace through the glass-enclosed penthouse club at the city square not far off, I very much enjoyed my first bottle of "Ba Muoi Ba," Vietnamese beer brand "33". The brew appeared much like a watered-down substance. Thinking it would be a light brand, which I never enjoyed, I was taken by surprise when my vision became blurry minutes later. It suited me fine. It put me at ease so much that I order a second bottle. Ten minutes later I staggered into the elevator, entered my room, and propped my weary body into bed, happy. Ready to doze off, I heard a knocking at the door. Reluctantly, I opened it to a well-dressed porter. "You got laundry?"

"No laundry," I replied. I was ready to close the door, but was interrupted with, "Just put it outside."

"Outside?"

"Put outside your door in the evening." He then explained that most guest had the clothes they wore during the day laundered, and pressed during the night neatly stacked by the door. It was a custom created for the soldiers taking advantage of a one-night pass into town. I went to sleep.

Sure enough, come midnight, I was awakened by a persistent knocking. Sleepy-eyed, I opened the door to a friendly, smiling young hostess from the club. "You want company?"

I was startled by the boldness, and politely declined at the strangeness of the offer. I had grown cautious during my frequent travels, not to trust anybody, especially not in a war zone. At the time I did not know the alluring custom of hostesses trying to stay over at the hotel. It was a preferred method against having to scramble for a taxi, trying to dash home before curfew set in at midnight. I would also learn that it was almost impossible to flag a taxi that late even though cab-sharing was mandatory. Another thing I would learn was that many of the hostesses, and families had fled the countryside to escape the VC[28] mercilessly pushing south and, in the process,

---

[28] Viet Cong (VC), in full "Viet Nam Cong San," in English, "Vietnamese Communists," the guerrilla force that, with the support of the North Vietnamese Army, fought against South Vietnam (late 1950s–1975), and the United States (early 1960s–1973).

overrunning and burning many villages, if not complied with their demands. Though a farmer's life was filled with hardship, the Vietnamese were a free society released from slavery by the French colonial government, housed mostly at oceanside cities along the South China Sea.

The following morning, the message light was blinking at me. "You have a message waiting at the front desk," the operator said when I picked up. Orders had arrived from MACV to report to the air terminal by 10 a.m. I roused the team, and we headed out shortly after. Arriving thirty minutes later, the airport was bustling with arrivals, and departures to, and from every landing strip in the country, collecting, and delivering cargo, supplies, and soldiers. Our flight, a C-130 cargo craft, arrived an hour later to take us up-country to Nha Trang, our destination. The flight was noisy, and bumpy the entire time while everybody was facing backwards, "in case of a crash," we were told. It was the customary seat configuration for all military flights in, and out of the war zone. The flight attendants, a couple of uniformed servicemen, were firm in all instructions but polite, nevertheless, served piping hot coffee in paper cups along the flight.

An hour later we landed at our destination, anxiously waiting for our luggage that never arrived. "How could they lose the luggage?" Buzz, and others exclaimed. All twelve of us witnessed it get loaded on the craft in Saigon. There were no stops in-between. Because of the extended stay in Vietnam, some brought along high-end stereo gear recently purchased in Japan. Others, including myself, had invested in tailor-made suits, and shoes. We decided to take matters into our own hands by rushing to the tarmac amidst warning commands fired at us by military police guarding the terminal with sub-machine guns aimed, and ready to fire. Disregarding the shouts, and warnings we charged a truck ready to depart with our luggage for unknown destination. It was our turn now to shout "Stop" commands at the driver.

My foreboding about our luggage had come true. It was on the way to the black market, a common practice with arriving passengers from the U.S., I was warned beforehand to always keep a close watch on luggage, and belongings. To the dismay of the luggage custodians, we forced the driver to halt the truck. Local airport support personnel, Vietnamese, dressed alike, loosely fitted black garb and trousers flopping around in sandals, had taken possession of our belongings. We took control of the military truck with some of us jumping on the running board while others, including myself, scrambled up the back of the vehicle. Despite fierce interference from approaching MPs, we won the battle by getting our belongings back. It was our first experience with illicit dealings in a country surviving mostly on goods acquired through black marketeering. It was also a first experience for airport MP military, and U.S. command guarding flights and airport. What nobody had expected was an arriving team taking possession of transported luggage. Our action was considered an act of hostility to local authorities, as well as U.S. forces personnel, stations at the airport. All we did was trying to protect personal belongings from falling into the hands of black marketeers. News got around about our daring act, but faced no repercussions or disciplinary action. Where black marketeering was generally condoned in a warzone, as part of reparation for being in the country, my team an I had a different view. After all, we were warriors much like the soldiers called into action, though mostly invisible to the enemy.

Once the luggage was in our hands we could proceed to our quarters, a gated, walled, guarded compound, the Nautique Hotel. Before the war, Nha Trang was a popular French resort some hundred yards from the most beautiful beach in Vietnam, by the South China Seas. The beach would become the off-work gathering place, and hangout for the team for the weeks ahead.

The following morning, the first day on the jobsite, we found ourselves in the midst of war. From that day on, daily, we witnessed nearby artillery fire shelling the countryside, in retaliation for destroying hostile launch locations, set up, and timed during night time by the Viet Cong to go off during the day, aimed mostly at strategic locations such as our Intel site. It was no secret to the North Vietnamese that the place we were assigned, was Army Intelligence gathering data, and information on NVA[29] troop movements, and VC infiltration.

Even though daily war action took place in, and around the city, the contrast between the workplace, and resting at the beach was an epic experience. Young, and enthusiastic as we were, getting hurt never entered our minds. It was only after witnessing someone getting killed that reality set in as a reminder of how precious, and short a life could be.

Once our project commenced, I began to explore the country, most times on my own, and after dark. Much like the previous locations, I wanted to learn the language, and land. After work ended the team usually gathered at the on-base canteen or all-ranks club. As was the case with most war zones, all installations were built in a tactical manner, temporary, to be abandoned if overrun by the enemy, or closed at war's end. In most cases, the base with its facilities were turned over to the victor, as was the case in May of 1975, when the North took over the South, thus ending the 20-year war for the U.S. For us, at present, the war effort was at its height, lasting a few more years.

Some of the team remained at the base club until the 10:00 p.m. curfew, while others gathered back at the hotel club for a few beers. Where curfew in Saigon was rather lax at midnight, near the warzone it was strictly enforced at 10:00 pm. My aim was the city. To get there, I walked dark roads passing several checkpoints along the route manned by Korean special forces, the White Horse brigade, commissioned to fight for the South. In my recollection, the division was trained back home prior to being assigned as a security force to guard traffic, and to protect U.S. forces against VC attacks in, and around the city. Other functions they performed were VC interrogations, along others not publicly disclosed.

"Stop," the sentry sergeant bellowed out as I got close to the shack, usually manned by four sentries. "Friend or foe?" It was the standard warning call.

"Friend," I called back from the dark with my arms raised to my shoulders. The first time, I was stopped, and thoroughly frisked. Satisfied with my explanation—

---

[29] The North Vietnamese Army (NVA) was a military force much like the U.S., drafted, and commissioned. The Viet Cong (VC) was an army, and political movement that infiltrated South Vietnam, and Cambodia during the Vietnam War. It was comprised of both guerrilla, and regular army units, as well as a network of cadres who organized peasants to support their liberation cause in the territory it controlled.

Coming from the O Club,—following an ID check, I could proceed to the next checkpoint. Passing on an alert call of my coming, passage there would be quicker. Several days later, after similar checks, my face became familiar to the sentries who would just wave me on. It was during one of my nightly walks when I became aware of a shadow following me about fifty paces off in the dark. Being curious, and enterprising, I halted several times to let the shadow catch up, but in vain. The shuffled steps silenced just the same. Puzzled, I continued my walk.

Though guarded, I still watched the brilliance of stars shining overhead, partially illuminating my path. That's how dark the countryside was. Only distant artillery fire against the horizon would illuminate the hills whenever an observation plane flying overhead would alert nearby artillery batteries to hone in on suspected VC ground activities. I was keenly aware of the swishing projectile sounds overhead launched into hills.

Days had passed. One evening I had stopped in the shadows of a building when the body of a person slowly materialized from the dark. To my surprise, it was a woman dressed in the customary ARVN[30] uniform. She cautiously approached with, "Where're you going, GI?"

"You should know," I replied. "You have been following me for days. By the way, I'm not a GI."

"I know."

"How would you know?" Curious, I watched her while she talked. Almost my height, twenty-some, I guessed, well-groomed, and pretty, educated in language. The purpose of her shadowing? I did not know, but I planned to find out.

"Your hair is long, and you don't wear a uniform," she said.

"Come," I encouraged her, pulling her into the shadows. "You talk. I listen. Why are you following me?"

"Orders." One word could mean nothing or explain all.

Now, I was really curious. She had all of my attention. "Orders from whom?"

"Embassy. American."

"You work for the embassy?"

"Not work. Assigned."

"Who assigns you?"

"Intelligence."

"Who's Intelligence?"

"South Vietnam."

"But why?" I did not understand why I had been singled out by foreign Intel.

"Your mission. Important."

I was beginning to understand. It was not the first time I had been watched. I knew well that my phone conversations were monitored, as was my personal life. In the Philippines, for instance, there had been an incident where I had been approached. One day, identifying as Naval Intelligence, two agents came knocking at my hotel room door, demanding a private audience. "You are breaking policy," I was told.

I was speechless, and exclaimed, "What?"

---

[30] ARVN – Army of the Republic of Vietnam (South).

"Cohabitation."

"You better explain," I demanded.

"You have been reported as having a foreigner staying with you."

It all fell into place now. It was true. I had met a nice Filipino woman who had become attached to me. After a few days of seeing her, she desired to stay over on more than one occasion. Innocently, we had a lot of fun sightseeing, and visiting places. While I remembered reading the Intel portfolio on cohabitation, I had not realized its importance. There were three major factors Intel was looking out for. Cohabitation with foreigners, gambling to incur possible debts, and homosexuality, all prime suspect for compromising national security. Regardless of infraction, any one was subject to immediate dismissal from the job. Once that happened, reemployment with Intel would be out of the question, forever. Many had succumbed to the infractions through breaching national safety policies. It was not only the spying that could land you in prison when caught.

"What do you suggest I do?" I had also learned that one could repair a compromised position as long as one was honest about it. Lying would only make the situation worse. It is what security is all about, honesty.

"End your relationship. Drop her like a hot potato."

And so, we learned. I had to comply or my career ended. "You have my word," I'd promised.

It seemed to satisfy the agents. They left as promptly, with an unspoken promise that I would be watched for a time to come. The occurrence was a warning I would not forget, but it put me in a dilemma. "What about my personal life? My desires? My physical urges?" No matter what promises were made, I was a young male filled with unbound energy. There was a compromise that I did not like. It was to either get married to an American national or solicit prostitution. Chances for the first option were pretty slim. My lifestyle, and field of operations did not leave many options open for meeting an appropriate woman. As for the second option, I made a modification I could live with while on foreign soil, which was engaging a hostess or escort company. There were ample opportunities in certain countries, where girls working in the entertainment industry was an accepted, and sanctioned way of life.

My thoughts had wandered off, sidetracked from the immediate encounter at hand. "Tell me about your function, life in the warzone, your family. I want to learn about your culture. It's why I'm here."

"Really?" It must have put her somewhat at ease, for she said, "Where are you off to tonight?"

"You tell me," I replied, open to suggestions.

Pulling me by my arm, she said, "Come, I know a quiet café. We can talk there."

Now, that's something new, I thought, considering the area we were in, the middle of a warzone. I had yet to find a quiet place. Because of that, I had trouble getting sound sleep. Bombings, artillery fire, and shooting took place all day, and night. The only way I could get a few hours of sleep was after having a couple bottles of 33. I had learned something about the beer which was not common knowledge. It was laced with codeine, a mild sedative, but a drug nevertheless. Where drugs were not permitted in Vietnamese society, dealing in them was something else. Many a local official became rich during the years to follow. Though the war had already been going on for years, battle escalation was imminent, as dictated by my presence here.

Ten minutes later we were settled at the café. As she had promised, it was a quiet place in a somewhat secluded neighborhood not entirely ravaged by war, yet appearing much like a back alley in Paris. "Now," I suggested, "tell me about yourself." I had always been interested in people, their upbringing, what they stood for, their views, as well as their motivations, especially uprooted as the population here was. The local situation reminded me very much of my own childhood, growing up during a war with its aftermath, trying to rebuild an economy left in shambles.

"Lucy," she offered with an outstretched hand. "You are Alex."

"Of course," I replied. "You know everything about me."

"Not everything. I want to know more."

"I can't tell you much. I am married to my job." With respect to the limited liberty of my work, I had never felt comfortable talking about myself. This time was no exception, but there were always the customs, and cultures I could delve in to explore. It suited me well. She seemed not to mind. We spent the next few hours discussing just that, her people, and her land. Though I was very informed about the present, and past war activities in her country, I would learn quite a bit about its impact on the people.

Saigon, like most other cities in the country, had absorbed much of the population, driven from their lands, and properties by the encroaching VC. Vietnam, like most of Indochina, existed on rice crops, vegetables, and fish, the basic staples for sustaining their daily lives. Without electricity, and running water, even these life-supporting substances had to be gathered daily. As a result, cities had grown by a tenfold, and more. What was not visible to the foreign visitor when passing the many shanties hastily erected along every sidewalk was the hidden life taking place within the dwellings. Where the original homes were built a hundred years ago as spacious as hotels, business centers, and the imperial palace, now they were occupied by the hundreds, comprised of three generations. With dwellings lacking doors, and windows, street noise, dust, and waste were ever-present. One could not imagine ever getting used to the stench from cooked food in the midst of garbage pails. Dogs, and cats did not help the situation either. Shoppers, headed for the markets, passing up sidewalks in the early morning, and late evening hours, would witness the cleansings of semi-naked bodies with remnants of droplets squeezed on the head from well-worn rags, trying to wash off soapy sweat. Shopping at the marketplace, in the early hours, would fetch the products fresh, whereas in late evening, one could get the left-over goods at a greatly reduced price. The trick was to use old, and tattered clothes while pushing through market stalls to appear poor. It was the shabby appearance that would determine the final cost haggled from the vendors.

It turned out that her father was an official with the U.S. embassy, enjoying certain privileges not extended to the common citizen. It had provided her with an education, jumpstarting a potentially rewarding career. It gave her the opportunity to do something positive for her country, interacting with the current colonialists, as she called the American presence. It was not the first time her country had been ravaged by invading forces. Her people knew not much else but neighboring, as well as distant powers taking control of her people, dating back thousands of years.

Lucy, poised across the table, was eyeing me expectantly for my attention. Every so often, my mind wondered about the local situation, and my presence in the land. I would have preferred roaming the country on a motorbike at will, and at my own leisure rather than being strapped to a specific arena of action. Regardless, I always found ways to steal away for a few hours at a time, roaming villages not yet overrun by the North. It was my way of exhilaration to satisfy my inherited curiosity.

"Alex? Are you with me?"

"I am listening."

"Are you a spy?" The question took me by surprise. I had to think a moment about how to answer her.

"No," I said. "I am not a spy."

"Then," she said expectantly, "what are you doing in my country?"

"I built the infrastructure so spies, spooks, and people like you can do their work."

"But why the frontlines? Nha Trang is not a safe place for you."

"I maintain, and support field operations, and places like the embassy where you work."

"Doing what?"

I figured she already knew about my mission, but wanted to keep up the conversation. "Tie in your command headquarters with the Pentagon, and Intel services to help direct the war effort."

"Thank you. Now I understand."

"I knew you would. You are a smart person. What about you? Why are you following me?" I had wanted to shoot the question at her ever since we met.

"We received reports that you tend to wander off on your own. I was ordered to watch over you." The conversation ended when she said, "I go now." I was left with my own thoughts, contemplating if the woman was truly working for us, or if she was a potential spy for the North. *I will have to put her to a test.* But how remained to be seen. I was confident I would come up with some scheme. We parted with her planting a small kiss on my cheek, feeling the contours of her body pressed against mine ever so slightly. I felt better already, but was not yet convinced about her sincerity. I would make it a point to find out if, or when our paths would cross again. No matter how pretty, and intellectual a person she might be, I could not, and would never put my career in jeopardy. A thought crept into my mind: "What about her safety?" She might have been secure while her country was still under control of the South. What would happen to people like her, operating for the U.S. government, if her country was overrun by the North? Consequences would be severe, most likely ending in execution.

Personal note: Saigon, as the city was known then, was conquered in one day by Ho Chi Minh's army, the city cleaned up of millions from overpopulation, and sent back to the countryside where most came from, reverting back to farming the land once more. My assumption back than was correct, that many of the Vietnamese collaborators to the U.S. were rounded up, confined to jail, until executed. The process was short, without publicity or ceremony. Today, Vietnam is under loosely managed, communist control from the North with Saigon relabeled, Ho Chi Minh, city.

The following morning, I had just finished showering when there was an urgent knocking at the door. "Where were you last night?" It was Buzz pushing his way through the door. He had taken the room next door, and checked up on me daily. He was well aware of my nightly wanderings. I would rather have investigated places during daylight hours, but with my presence needed on location this proved impossible.

The place we were put up for our stay was a motel rather than hotel. Ever since the start of the war, sentries had been placed outside the gate which was secured after 10:00 p.m. to guard the complex, basically a town-sizes square of one-level dwellings set up as vacation place decades ago for the French vacationer. The buildings were raised a few feet above ground level, accessible by a few stone-constructed steps. It kept bugs, and vermin from entering the rooms, everybody was assured when checking in. But, as I found out, this was not always the case. I had my first encounter, as did others, by something scurrying across the bedsheets. I was lying awake listening to my portable Walkman, a faithful companion during my travels. In actuality, it was a Panasonic miniaturized stereo system I had purchased while in Japan, Akihabara specifically, a traveler's candy store for every conceivable electronic "Made in Japan." One could purchase a computer of every kind, as well as gadgets from latest model stereo to calculators, VCRs, and more.

Switching on the desk light, I watched as the tail of a rat disappeared into the shower room. Jumping to my feet, I chased after. To my surprise, the stall was empty. Looking around, I spotted the opening leading through the outside wall where the shower water drained onto the courtyard. "So much for privacy," I muttered, slightly perturbed. As anticipated, additional critter visits would be a nightly occurrence as soon as the lights went out. There were two choices for facing the unexpected, either pack up, and leave, or accept the intrusions with revered tolerance. Since the first option was not possible, I reluctantly accepted the second, ignoring the nightly visitors as a way of life. An entire population did.

"Squeezed in just before curfew," I said. Buzz understood only too well. Where he was apt to seek out the comfort, and security of the compound, and base clubs, he knew of my personal escapades, putting my safety in jeopardy.

"Just watch yourself. How did it go?"

Being my only permanent friend, I kept him informed about my whereabouts just in case I did not show up one morning. I told him about the nightly shadow. "I finally met her. She's an amazing person."

"What'd she looked like?" He was eager to hear.

"Well groomed, intelligent, and friendly."

"I mean her body."

"My height," I explained. "Pretty, and shapely."

"You're a lucky dog," he muttered. It was not every day one would meet someone as tall as people in the West, in Vietnam. Affluence had never been part of the population. "You see her again?" I figured he was anxious to meet her.

"Don't know," I said, shrugging my shoulders. "Topic didn't come up."

"You serious?" He shook his head. "No phone number? No address?"

"Nothing."

His inquest ended with the semi-truck driving up at the courtyard. It was a daily occurrence for us to be picked up to, and from the worksite, escorted by a squadron of guardsmen, mostly MPs, and special forces commanded by a sergeant. They had been especially assigned for the task, and with time became friendly for invitational get-togethers on weekends, attending our hosted BBQ parties either at the beach or, when it rained, on the compound. A quartermaster always showed up, carrying a carton of prime rib or T-bone steaks appropriated from a ready supply of first-grade food items supporting troops assigned overseas. It was an important incentive for the warrior fighting for the cause of the country. "Give a GI three squares, and a cot, and he will fight to the death," was the wartime motto.

Each day turned out much like any other. Arriving at the Army Intel site, the team jumping from the truck-bed was dismissed by the squad leader with, "Pick you up at five." Next, checking in through gate security with our IDs, then handed off to an on-post security officer. As stated, security was tight, not only for our safety, but against our being captured. Where the soldier was trained to endure interrogation, and possible death, if captured, the civilian contractor was not. It would be up to personal endurance as to how much torture the individual could tolerate. At the end, both were treated in the same manner entrapped in the warzone, facing execution. The enemy was not prone to democratic notions, and showed no mercy to our constitutional rights. A life in the Orient and Asia was plentiful, cheap, and expendable. Many times, unappreciated by the foreign nation asking for help, it was these conditions we were fighting for: their freedom while preserving ours.

Several days went by before one late evening, well after curfew, a slight, but persistent knocking at my door woke me up. Drowsy, and sleepy-eyed, I opened it. "Surprise," the voice cheerily announced, squeezing by the entrance. It was Lucy. I was stunned not only by her unexpected visit, but more so at the time she'd arrived. There was only one way she could have entered the compound, through gratuity or by ordering the sentries. I did not bother to find out. No matter what was on her mind, I welcomed her presence. It aroused my arduous spirits.

"I need a drink," she said. I readily complied. Like in most places I travelled, an alcoholic beverage was never far from reach. I generally kept a bottle of Kentucky Bourbon, and Coca Cola on hand. Ice, when available, was a precious commodity. Since there was no refrigerator in the room, the tempered mix had to do.

"Cheers," I toasted her, then, "what brings you here?"

"You," she said with a hint of a smile on her face. "I couldn't get you out of my mind. You are most intriguing."

"What do you have in mind?" I could not help but be charmed.

"Get to know you," she said while getting comfortable on the bed. Since bed, and closet were the only furniture in the room, there was no alternative. Again, I did not mind. What followed was romance, and sex, that simple. Her actions were just, and very much appreciated. With the restraints placed on my social activities, I was completely satisfied except for one issue, and I stated so. "What about you, and me? Your, and my safety? Our discretion?"

"Don't worry," she stated. "It's okay. Everybody knows."

"Who is everybody?" I demanded, highly concerned. "Who knows?"

"Embassy."

"Embassy!" I exclaimed, alarmed at compromising mine, and her positions.

"Don't worry," she insisted with a laugh. "This way, the authorities can keep an eye on you."

I felt entrapped, but enjoyed this woman who claimed her name was Lucy. I was not sure anymore, but enjoyed her presence for what was left of the night. Just before dawn I felt her stir then hurry for the exit, saying, "See you tonight. Yes?"

"You know where to find me." I was exhilarated, and worried at the same time, wondering where the encounter would lead. "All part of the war," I appeased myself at the promising times ahead. Intriguing as the encounter was, it lasted during my stay in the country.

"You are my hero," Buzz admitted on not only one occasion. He was duly impressed with my involvement with a foreigner, and getting away with it.

What else could I say but, "It's not cohabitation unless the person lives with you."

"Smart move," he agreed. "How did you find this loophole?"

"Actually," I explained, "it's common sense. It's a means around policies. You don't think that everybody in Intel suddenly turned Puritan?"

"I guess not."

It'd turned out that I was not the only one personally challenged by the current environment. It seemed that war brought out the worst, and best in people. I'd learned that others had been romantically involved as well. Not so much the fighting soldier, but more commonly, officer rankings. It was them that attracted the local girls, for they had the opportunity for possibly providing the sought of, U.S. citizenship, as some had the fortune to obtain through marriage.

"Alex," the intercom announced one Monday morning. "Report to the front office." My ears perked up at hearing my name. It was not the first time, and always caused a slight reaction of anguish, especially in a warzone. It could be anything from the enemy on approach, an imminent bombing alert, or a number of personal issues from a team member. I promptly left, headed for the office. To get there, one had to exit through an array of electronically-controlled, airtight-sealed double doors. This served two purposes. One, it prevented unauthorized entrance in case of an enemy attack, and two, it prevented classified information, and digital data from leaking to the outside world. It was almost guaranteed that the enemy had sensitive listening devices nearby snooping for Intelligence. How did I know? We did it to them.

"Colonel Otsuka." Commander, 1st Signal Brigade, I acknowledged the uniformed person sat by the desk. He was field commander for Army Intelligence, responsible for me, and my team among his brigade operating in Vietnam. He was clad in combat fatigues, sleeves rolled up to present a casual appearance. I waited for him to address me. "So," he said, turning to face me full on, "I received more complaints about your guys this morning."

"What is it this time?" I said, anxious to find out. There had been not-so-pleasant run-ins before between my team, and the sentries guarding the compound.

"Please instruct your people not to crash through the gate." With a stern look, he further advised, "This is a serious matter. One of these days the gate guards will take it as a personal affront, and start shooting. We don't want your people to get hurt. Do we?"

I knew that he was sincere, but also dead serious. I had some stern talks about the unruly behavior with my team before. It seemed that some were disregarding safety measures the Army had in place. The only thing I could come up with was the one thing they had in common: they were ex-military themselves. Regardless of past commitments, whether disgruntled, and resentful, it did not give them the right to put theirs, and soldiers' lives in jeopardy. Aside from personal safety, their actions were a direct insult to the colonel, and his staff.

"I will have a talk with them," I promised once more.

"Make sure they understand. I can only curtail my soldiers for so long."

"Well," I informed my team, addressing the specific individuals I knew were causing the problem. "You have been put on notice. The next time you crash the gate, you'll be shot."

There were immediate objections. "You can't be serious."

"Dead serious," I underscored the warning. "From now on you will respect the guards, and comply with their orders. Is that so hard?"

"We'll see about that," was one response from one aggressor. I could detect suppressed anger surface. Whatever personal gripes he had with the Army he would not voluntarily disclose.

"Will it matter when you are dead?" It was my final message, hoping it would sink in this time. What puzzled me was the persistence at the subordination some individuals conducted themselves with in contrast to better judgement. There was already enough chaos fighting the war without creating additional confrontations.

In retrospect, what they had pulled off back then in the 70s, they would have been shot at the first occurrence in today's world, with its ever-present terrorism threat. Unfortunately, there were more incidences caused by my team, but not with the severity of a possible loss of life. Most were brawls after too many drinks. I would like to mention that individuals causing trouble caught up in a warzone were not necessarily bad people. It was that their minds were conditioned to follow orders, regardless whether they made sense to the individual or not. There result was a stimulated hatred against the enemy, whether justified or not, without a means to be resolved by the individual. The frustration level, heightened during the day from nothing but orders, was usually softened down, and drowned with the intake of alcoholic beverages, imbibed during evening ours, only to be repeated the next day, and next, until rotating out from the frontlines.

The end results? Many individuals, at one time straight, returned as alcoholics.

The alternative? Abstinence of Drugs. But getting involved in drugs presented yet another matter with long-term implications our nation is still trying to resolve.

In spite of the incessant spectacle the fighting front experienced from incoming mortars, and rockets set off by the VC, the implementation project progressed on schedule. Where most of the Intel sites around the globe operated below ground, here the facility was set up in a tactical fashion. It meant that it could be vacated, and destroyed on an hour's notice in case of an enemy takeover. Though our superiority was assured by sheer size, and technology advantage over the North, a consolidated push from combined enemy forces could occur at any time. It was only a matter of armament, and manpower concentrated on the focal point of action.

A typical example was demonstrated in February of 1968 when the North Vietnam army unexpectedly advanced on the South and, in doing so, overran the fortified defense perimeter set up by the Vietnamese defense forces. Such a push may have been anticipated from an increase in communication activities (chatter), but the day, time, and location came as a surprise. It was too late for the South to relocate their forces to the enemy's specific target, Nha Trang, our place of work. We were alerted from sleep with the break of dawn by an onslaught of an entire enemy regiment. Their initiative was to capture the city to honor Ho Chi Minh, his birth place, and North Vietnam's leader for his communist cause. The attack was executed with precision by gaining hold over a major part of the city.

Fortunately, the combined U.S., and South Vietnam military forces were able to fend off the attackers over the following days to successfully regain the enemy-acquired territory. It was a serious lesson learned, not to take the enemy for granted. But situations changed after many years of fighting. Defense posture might be down, soldiers weary from fighting, or command temporarily rendered ineffective after a tactic or strategy change, subsequently weakening the war effort.

While fighting battles was not a pleasant experience because there were always casualties, it might become necessary after negotiations for peaceful intentions broke down. Aside from the calamities on the battlefront there were many other hostile actions taking place within the country. Terrorist factions emerged with bombing attacks on the civilians, allies, and enemy alike. There was no country that appreciated foreign occupation, a byproduct of aiding a nation in despair. If the war could be kept short, and effective, the citizens were gratifyingly thankful. If the fighting went on, prolonged over many months, or even years, as has been the case with most recent wars, eventual protests emerged from the populace, and resistance factions formed to drive the occupants from the land.

With soldiers fighting at the fronts, police, and internal security forces were protecting the citizens, keeping up order. As a prerequisite, one was always aware of the overhead surveillance planes flying a grid pattern while observing, and reporting trouble spots below. Concentrating their efforts in cities, and populated areas, there were never enough resources on hand. Black marketeering, as well as general crime, was a byproduct of any conflict. Criminal elements took the time of confusion to their advantage in conducting unlawful activities. In essence, where established citizens pursued their daily routines with business, or their place of work, others sought out opportunities for the sake of survival in an economy interrupted throughout every sector of industry and living. Many people lost their jobs as a result of the war, and grasped every chance they had to live yet another day in a poverty-stricken land.

To assure safety for the citizens, checkpoints were set up throughout the cities, and connecting roads with warnings that any person not complying with security policies would be shot. Whether the warnings were effectual, and taken seriously or not, I personally witnessed numerous VC suspects being shot by security forces off their speeding vehicles, mostly the 98-cc Honda motorcycles, while trying to escape. Whether a suspect turned out to be a potential enemy or just someone trying to get away with minor contraband was unimportant. Those cases were eventually registered as part of a lateral casualty count.

Four months into one of my assignments to Vietnam, one Monday morning I could not get out of bed. Aside from having severe stomach cramps I felt miserable, and too weak to get up. After a brief knocking at the door, Buzz stuck his head in the room. "You're late." It was six thirty in the morning, and I had not shown up at the gate. The reader may wonder how one could just bust into the room. As was customary throughout Vietnam, doors were kept unlocked. As was common in a GI-centric environment, many overstepped their "duty call," and had to be awakened by a buddy. It was for this reason that doors were kept unlocked. To provide security, the place was fashioned in a motel layout, surrounded by a twelve-foot high wall topped by barbed wire, mostly to keep out thieves. Theft, and vandalism were rampant in the country.

"Can't make it today."

"What?" Buzz said, somewhat surprised. I could understand his reaction for I always made it to work no matter how I felt. My presence was required to schedule the day's tasks with the team and liaison our working progress with HQs.

"You'll have to manage today. I'm too sick."

"What's the matter?"

"Don't know."

"Hope you'll feel better by tomorrow. I'll check with you in the evening."

He was gone. I was left with my own misery for the next ten hours. The maid showed up some time later, but I had to wave her on. I must have slept the day away when Buzz returned in the evening. "Guess what?" he stated. "Braddock didn't show up either. Claims to have similar symptoms. You guys ate at the same place yesterday?"

"Not that I know off."

"How're you feeling?"

"Same as this morning."

"You going to make the call in the morning?"

"I'll hitch a ride to the dispensary. I've got to see a doctor." Daylight came, and I did not feel any better. I had to pull myself together just to get up. Too weak to shower, I dragged my body to the pickup point, and was pulled up to the truck bed, and twenty minutes later deposited at the dispensary, a temporary makeshift tent.

I could see from the activities that sickness must have been a common routine. My team mate Nieman Braddock was there as well, complaining with the same misery. He had been my jogging, and workout partner for months, and looked awful. I must have appeared in the same condition as he stated, "You don't look so good." We compared our conditions, and tried to find a common source for our plight while waiting to see a doctor.

"Can't find anything wrong with you," the doctor said after administering several tests. As far as testing went, it was a brief physical examination followed by taking a blood sample to be ready the following day. Since there was obviously nothing wrong with me at the moment, I was handed an arm full of medication, and sent off with, "Come back tomorrow."

It would become a daily routine each time we visited the field hospital, with both of our conditions worsening in the following weeks. The medications we were prescribed were numerous, containing antibiotics, anti-dysentery, anti-depression, anti-this, and anti-that. In spite of my misery I went to the job site, if only to direct the project, and so did Braddock. Several days later, the only food intake we had was the medication, in the process losing weight, pound after pound. Weeks later, completely emaciated, and at the point of passing out, we both quit going to work, but continued our semi-daily visits to the dispensary only to refill the prescriptions.

Since there was no improvement in our conditions, doctors stopped seeing us. Rumors had it that we were faking our sickness to get out of the warzone. It was common practice by soldiers to be assigned a rear-position, safe from the frontlines, but my intentions were far from this. I would have traded my misery with any position on the frontlines; that's was how miserable I was, and Braddock was the same from what I saw.

One day, while at the dispensary, I peeked at my medical chart. It stated, "psychosomatic condition." I had seen enough. Not even the doctors believed that I was really sick. It was time to make changes to my health before I became a collateral casualty. I put Buzz in charge of the project, and called it quits. On the next day, Braddock, and I were on a flight back to Saigon. From there, we went separate ways. He booked a flight to Frankfurt, Germany while I returned to Philadelphia, my home base at the time.

Since I had relinquished my apartment to someone else attending computer training classes, as was common practice among project teams waiting to be assigned to overseas locations, I was forced to stay at a hotel. Checking in with headquarters I took medical leave until my health condition was diagnosed.

The following day I was admitted into Thomas Jefferson Medical Hospital, the best health facility in the city with the finest reputation. Sure enough, tests revealed a severe dysentery infection localized in the intestines. Confined to the hospital bed, suffering from starvation symptoms, I was administered liquified medication. When taken, it felt like my throat, esophagus, stomach, and intestines were self-destructing. The medication was burning its way through my body, repeated daily for the next two weeks.

Since eating was out of the question—I was too weak to eat anyway—I was kept alive intravenously. In my dazed condition, I wondered at time how Braddock was faring. He'd preferred a hospital in Frankfurt, to be close to his German girlfriend he had met during his last assignment there.

As promised by the medical staff, treated as a special guest returned from the warzone, I was released two weeks later feeling much better. All I had to do from here on was rebuild my body to the condition it used to be, agile, and superior in strength. Working out, running, biking, and spending time at gyms would be the path I would take for many years to come.

Several days later, I was called into the office with sad news. My boss, Art, had received a telegram from Braddock's mother that he'd passed away at the German hospital. It was the saddest news I had received, aside from my mom's death decades earlier. I really liked him. Well balanced with a great spirited attitude, everybody took a liking to him. To this day I still miss the guy. Dying at such a young age, in his thirties, he had not been extended a fair chance at life. It made me even more appreciative, knowing how precious, and unpredictable life could be.

Though cut short one assignment, I would return to the war zone several more times, but with shorter duration. While I enjoyed the excitement of travel to burning points like Vietnam, I became more cautious in my behavior after what had happened the last time. But no matter how carefully I planned, traveling to places such as Indonesia, and other primitive, exotic jungle regions, sickness, and disease were never far, as I would experience several more times.

Personal note: I consolidated several of my travels to Vietnam, over a period of years, into one section, as illustrated above. The reason is to simplify my experiences into one focal point. Although I had many more encounters with Lucy, war-torn environment, and local conditions with an escalation of terrorist attacks on the population, I was traveling alone without a team. In contrast to present-day terrorism, initiated by groups such as Al Qaeda, ISIS, and the Taliban, as we experience in our own country, terrorist attacks have occurred many times before, mostly as a result of prolonged war. Not to be judgmental, and to be fair to both sides of a conflict and war, both sides are fighting for their own justification. Whether it is a fight initiated over territory, resources, or humanitarian causes, when viewed for the cause of it, justification is generally due to both sided.

It also holds true for terrorists. Most begin with the purpose for protecting their own people from domination by another culture, justifiable in intentions, then culminating into sporadic attacks on the intruders, eventually elevating into conflict and full war, as was the case with Vietnam. We were not the first nation asked for help in solving the colonial conflict Vietnam was facing. There were the French before us, preceded by numerous other countries infringing on the sanctity of a jungle-based region, the Indonesian natives inherited from their ancestors. Where their quest was to maintain a life in the harmony of their own befitting culture, surrounding nations did not necessarily see it this way.

What followed was Vietnam Royalty asking for our help in removing the French government from further colonizing their land. To justify our involvement, initially based on our democratic, humanitarian spirits, human development in modernization requires resources, whether human, animal, or plant life. And resources require land to harvest and for digging them from the ground, generally as compensation for aiding a country's plight. What essentially transpired, over years and several administration changes, the ideology we harbored for humanity changed to greed by overzealous industrialists, always willing to jump in to provide the shortages in war.

At the end, everybody lost. The French lost their dignity and another of many of their previously conquered colonies. The South Vietnamese lost another chance for freedom, relinquished to the North and Communism. The U.S. lost a long-established reputation for world leadership, on top of precious resources, not to mention thousands of precious lives that never had a chance to enjoy the splendors that earth has to offer.

THAILAND

"Another playground," somebody on the team commented, stepping off the gangway into the sweltering heat upon arriving at Bangkok International.

"You're not kidding," I muttered on the way through customs check.

Arriving at the terminal, looking at the status boards displayed we were as much confused as other international arrivals. Much of the information signs were displayed in Sanskrit, as would be the case throughout the country, we'd learn. But, being part of the travelling world, Thailand was no exception; one could always locate an English-speaking official.

"Korat?" I asked the uniformed agent. "Where?"

"Korat... Korat?" Just by the troubled look on his face it was obvious he was confused. Besides, he was scratching the back of his head. It must have dawned on him when he finally announced, accompanied by a brightened face, "Nakhon Ratchasima."

"What?" It was my turn to be puzzled.

Buzz came to my rescue with, "I think he said Nakhon Ratchasima."

"Never heard of it," I said.

"My uncle was stationed there. I remember the place from the postcards he sent the family."

"Lucky us," I muttered. "How do we get there?" I asked the agent.

"Bus or taxi," he said with a gesture at the exit gates.

Luggage in hand, the team was already headed for the exit while I handed a ten dollar note to the appreciative agent with a customary thanking gesture, both hands clutched into prayer position. *Must be highly religious,* I thought while rushing after my team.

"Holy Moses," Buzz exclaimed, watching the tumultuous crowd clambering up windows, and rooftop on already packed buses lined up by the dozen ready to depart. People were clinging not only to the running boards of the departing busses, but more desperately, their belongings on top of the roof rails. "It'll take an hour to get a seat. Let's take a taxi," I suggested.

It took three cabs to accommodate everybody, but the service was effective, and efficient. When word reached taxi drivers of our destination, everybody wanted to get in the game. "Four hours," I was told by the driver when I asked the driving time, and upcountry we went, three cabs in a row. The driver came with the vehicle. It turned out to be a thrill-ride all the way. Our cabs were weaving in, and out of the two-lane country road, barely missing oncoming traffic which was just as aggressive. Even leaving the airport, and city behind, the smoke billowing from buses, and trucks was overwhelming. In addition, the sound of blaring horns added to the chaotic traffic conditions. "Air conditioning," I demanded from the driver.

"No have," was his apologetic reply. "No spare parts." It was a common expression I would hear many more times in the weeks ahead.

Along the route I took the time to absorb the local environment. Immediately, it became apparent that the country had to deal with the change of times. Thailand was a typical example. Where the country still followed strict religious, and secular practices, very visible throughout the land with pagodas, temples, and shrines everywhere, their cultural struggles were quite severe, resulting in many of the male population turning to priesthood, and monastery living at any age. Wherever one turned, yellow-clad monks could be seen morning, noon, and evening, carrying baskets while trotting from house to house begging for the daily meal. "It's a way of life," I was told.

As a matter of fact, I had been approached, and invited by monks to join a monastery. Taking on the offer one day, I took the opportunity to stay at the indicated monastery for a weekend. It gave me a chance to evaluate the lifestyle of the monk while taking a weekend off from my hectic schedule. I was ultimately faced with a monumental decision: become a monk, and live in harmony for the rest of my life, or remain in modern society only to struggle through it until my life's end. After serious consideration I eventually choose the latter when the thought of giving up the many pleasures I had felt, and tasted that life had to offer.

The end results?

I became a more tolerant person to challenging situations, and to follow other people's demands.

The alternative?

I would become intriguingly involved in the Chinese martial arts.

Four hours later, thirsty, hungry, and sweaty, we arrived at the country's second largest city, Nakhon Ratchasima. It still puzzled me about how we Americans derived the name Korat from it. We checked into the only modern place in town, the Korat Hotel, a five-story complex. "Meet you in the lobby in an hour," I yelled after the team while paying off the taxies.

"Right," Buzz replied, just as anxious to cool his body. Surprisingly, checking into the top floor, as I always did to get as far away as possible from street noise, the room, again very spacious, was airconditioned. "First things first," I muttered on the way to the shower stall while tearing off my clothes. "What a blessing," I thought, with the cold water cooling off my heated body. It was exhilaratingly refreshing. Like most places I had stayed on this trip, I propped my suitcase on one side of the bed to leave space for my body. Hotel management must have anticipated such antics since many hotels had no place for hanging up your jacket, and shirt. It seemed everybody travelled light with only one set of clothes. As I had experienced in other places in Asia, clothes were left at outside of the room evenings, and neatly stacked, and laundered collected mornings.

An hour later, refreshed and invigorated again, the hotel manager was as accommodating as expected when asking for a taxi. At many of the foreign countries, agents were educated in several languages to accommodate international travelers from a multitude of countries.

Minutes later the taxi I'd requested drove up with the driver speaking in the language I could understand. "Where to?"

"U.S. air base," I ordered, clambering in to the passenger seat. Americans were used to spacious cabs, but accommodations in foreign lands were largely scaled down in size, and comfort. Back then, it was mostly French vehicles mixed in with a miniature-sized Toyota Corolla just coming on the marketplace, with a maximum of three passengers crammed in.

"Wow," Buzz exclaimed on the way to the base. "It's hot here." We had just passed a 30-meter microwave tower hugging the ground.

"Kind of low position for microwave," I agreed at the direction the tower was aimed. It must have been the local terrain to where the dish was pointed, almost horizontal to the distant target receiver fifty miles away. From the technical perspective, the aim of the dish was unusual, but who was I to criticize the government.

We had just passed the arrival checkpoint, and were cleared to proceed by the sentries, asking the drivers to stand by. Buzz, the first to enter the building, unexpectantly stumbled back into my arms, exclaiming "What the hell!" The team, as well as I, were startled by the sight greeting us. It was a fully-grown, overshadowing, gesturing bear squeezing his way through the entrance. Lucky for us, the bear was accompanied by what must have been his handler, who welcomed us. "He's harmless. It's our mascot," he stated with a grin on his face. He already knew the reaction he received from other visitors. While slightly shaken by the reception, he explained, "We caught it as cub, and have raised it ever since." In more detail, nobody at the site expected it to grow into a 10-foot adult when standing upright, but it was as docile as a pet. All it wanted was to hug us new arrivals. Free to roam, it became obvious that it exceeded the limited space for getting in, and out of the building. The situation, while humorous, was also of concern to government officials when inspecting the facility. "Get that thing out of here," were the usual orders, but they were ignored for the most part. Since the animal was not a danger to anyone, nevertheless, serious considerations were given to home the bear at some zoo. For now, it became a daily talking topic when the team got together in the evenings at a local establishment over a bottle of Singha beer, everybody's favorite.

During the following days commuting to, and from work, an Air Force Intel site, it was someone else's turn to complain, "Wow. It's hot out here." It was several days later when it dawned on me. "It's the damned tower." When asked, I explained my theory.[31]

"What?" someone said. "We may get fried?"

"We'll be okay," I explained, "but don't ever go walking here. You'll be well-done in minutes." It explained the reason why no domestic animals were seen grazing in the empty, but lush, land. Since the cow was a holy animal in Thailand as much as in India, it was revered equal or more than the human being. Cows roamed freely within cities, and towns, readily supported, and fed by the neighborhood, a ready gesture to gain religious merit.

The project implementation proceeded without any additional bizarre incidents. While remotely located, the city turned out to be a cultural treasure-trove for the exploring individual. While limited on language skills, I learned much about Thai society, and its cultures, and customs as well. It was intriguing. "Want to go

---

[31] Microwave transmission towers, I recalled from taking radio, and microwave certification classes at CIT, generate so much power that it will literally make your blood boil when exposed to the dish. For reasons of human safety, most towers are elevated, and aimed at a distant receiver of equal dimensions, mostly hill or mountain to transmit data. Because of the present terrain we were in, Thailand's central plateau, the next tower some 35-mile distant was mounted also at ground level, and so was the next to cover the transmission range necessary throughout the land. It was an effective means of military communications, but also had its dangers to man, and animal if one should linger nearby a tower.

sightseeing?" the hotel manager volunteered the following weekend. I had dismissed the taxi drivers for local car rentals. It would be more convenient than relying on a driver, as was customary with contractors.

What are some of the tourist places?"

"Angkor Wat."

"What?"

"Angkor Wat. It's a place not far from here I am sure you would like," he said, enthusiastically explaining the route, but also warning me, "You must be careful. There is a war going on."

Having been to Vietnam months earlier, a neighboring country to Thailand, I was well aware. The next day, when informing the team of the place, several expressed their desires to visit, especially after learning more about the world's ancient, and largest temple complex, supposedly built eons ago dedicated to the country's god Vishnu. Early in the morning the following Sunday, crammed in two rentals, some of us took to the road for some 250 miles in moderate traffic. Halfway there, our passage was blocked by a heavily-armed, ready-to-fire squadron. Checkpoints were common in a land of conflict, not only at the place of war, but the surrounding nations as well. It was a precaution against possible enemy infiltration. "Hope they won't shoot," Buzz muttered in the tense atmosphere. Though battle educated, we all were aware of the immediate confrontation.

"Stop," the squad leader ordered. He was mean looking, with a submachine gun pointed in my face. I have to point out that most, if not all, of the sentries I encountered were as mean faced as a junkyard dog. Much like the Pitbull back home, they must have been bred, and trained that way. Very seldom one encountered a friendly face guarding a border crossing. "ID." Luckily, everybody had remembered to bring along their passport. Rifling through my specially assigned, 48-page blue-covered passport filled with many foreign stamps, he barked at me, "Why so many countries?"

"Contractor, U.S. government," I replied watchfully.

Scrutinizing the team through the open windows, he gestured at his squadron to collect all the passports, then disappeared into the shack, leaving us wondering about our safety.

"What if they detain us?" Buzz worried. We could be sent to prison for spying, if the authorities questioned our trustworthiness.

"Can't help it now," I said, concerned as well, intensely watching the squad leader making a call to contact his superior at some military headquarters. Minutes later, he emerged. "Where you going?"

"Angkor Wat." He disappeared again for another ten minutes reemerging once more accompanied by his superior, identified by additional stripes on the uniform, barking at me, "You have no visa for Cambodia."

"Cambodia," I shouted at him. We don't want Cambodia. We want to visit Angkor Wat." We were warned to stay out of Cambodia, as well as Laos, up north. While the war, officially had not involved the neighboring counties, rumors had it that the CIA was heavily involved at those places. It was an effort, though highly covert, that would hound the U.S. government for many years to come.

My reaction may have struck a chord with the squad since none of them resorted to their ready and aimed weapons. I was trying to stall, for what I did not know at the moment. I could sense from the leader's unfriendly posture what it was he wanted: money. Experienced from past similar encounters, I fished for my money clip, and handed him a twenty-dollar bill, asking, "We go now?"

Tensions were high while he palmed the money, handing over our passports with a warning. "Angkor Wat only. You return today." It was a chilling demand after the three-hour ride once we got there, only to face another three hours to get back on the same day. I nodded, complying with the demand. Three hours later, exhausted, and parched, we arrived at the mystical sanctuary without any further problems.

Parking was ample on the entirely deserted grounds. "Where're all the people?" It was not only Buzz being curious. Others voiced similar concerns.

"Consider the location," I said. "We are in a warzone." Presently not involved in the conflict, that would change soon with American B-52 bombers unloading their loads over the country. We lucked out this time from being detained as potential war criminals or even spies.

As it turned out, we were the only visitors at the place. Emerging from the vehicles, numb-legged, and thirsty, we attempted to enjoy the holy presence. At first sight the place looked like what it was, the largest religious relic from an ancient past. From the distance it appeared a complex in ruins. Getting closer, though weathered by age, the actual structures took on individual shapes. Stumbling, and climbing the many ruins to the interior, the shapes became colossal. Words, when spoken within the empty chambers, were hollow echoes bouncing off in shallow reverberations, returning hints of secrets from glorious times well past. It was up to the individual imagination to wonder how, why, and who built this glorious temple complex. Within the silence of the walls, one could easily imagine ceremoniously garbed holy men celebrating another national event to placate one of their many godly spirits, with Hinduism[32] as their principle spirits.

"I can feel the spiritual energy," Buzz said. "Can you?"

Whether the impression was only a personal perception or for real, everybody agreed on it.

"Maybe there is a spiritual realm after all," I muttered, taking another few snapshots with my recently purchased Japanese-made Minolta camera. It was already afternoon when we took off for the return drive. The visit, as brief as it was, with everybody taking pictures, left a deep impression on me to a point where I would return two more times during my visits to Asia. The return trip went uneventfully for the most part, other than dodging in, and out to pass colonies of trucks, the main transport carriers in the land. It did not matter that everybody was speeding on the two-lane highway. What mattered was your vehicle burning up extra fuel to squeeze a couple more miles of speed from the engine to pass another bus or truck, and not to get stuck behind inhaling the billowing blue unburnt fuel most vehicles expelled.

---

[32] Before Hinduism, and Buddhism were introduced into Thailand, only one religious belief was prevalent. The belief was that a spirit world existed as a mighty, powerful, and controlling entity termed Animism, manifested in the form of spirit worship. To call Animism a religion may not be correct. It is better categorized as a spiritual belief, but without a doubt it was the oldest form of worship known to mankind, practiced long before all the popular world religions were conceived.

Road safety rules, it seemed where none existing in Thailand. The norm was everybody passing everybody, only to be interrupted by the leading vehicle squeezing back into respective traffic lanes, fractions before colliding.

"Hurry up," my passengers would encourage me for another pass. I could feel the carbon monoxide pressing on my lungs as well.

"I'm trying," I would reply, eager to get in front like everybody else on the road. Despite racing all the way, it was midnight by the time we got back to the city, just in time to fetch a couple of Singha at the hotel lounge. Unkempt, grimy skinned, tired, parched, and famished, we kept celebrating our successful visit to Cambodia until the place closed at 2:00 a.m. For us contractors, each day was pretty much a repeat at the end of a workday. Many evenings, for a change in venue, we would head for a nightclub nearby. I was surprised to find that modern rock music had made its way to such a remote location, but from the popularity I observed, at the time in the psychedelic genre, heavy metal sounds seemed to be welcomed by every young generation, no matter what restrictions the culture dictated. In time, I would learn that the general population was struggling to maintain its identity in contrast to a very confusing religious past.

It was on one such night out that I would become a personal target as a mugging victim. I had just left one of the nearby clubs, headed home for the night. Walking along the darkened sidewalk I was suddenly confronted by three Thai thugs emerging form the dark. Unexpectedly, one came from the front, sporting a broad smile, and throwing a greeting at me. "Hi Joe." At the same time, two rushed in from the back, grabbing both my arms. Though mellowed out after a couple of drinks at the club, and unprepared, I realized in an instant their intentions. *I'm being robbed.* From the corner of my eyes I took in the immediate scene. Like every night, there were young people milling in, and around the hotel courtyard I stayed at, guests making out with local hostesses. It was the central gathering place in town.

As soon as the initial confronter uttered the first word, the three went into action. Everything took place within seconds. One tore the watchband from my wrist, another sliced the back pocket of my trousers open to retrieve my wallet, and the third tore the 24-carat gold chain I wore from my neck, all in one swift motion. It took this long for my mind, and body to react. On instinct, I delivered three punches to the first assailant's head, chest, and lower abdomen, watching him sink to the ground. Turning, free from his helpers in back, I delivered more kicks, and punches before I realized my 24-karat watch was missing from my wrist. I froze a moment with the ominous feeling that other items were missing. Sure enough, I realized what else had been ripped from me. An instinct later my body went back into action. The thugs suddenly realized that I was not easy prey. Two took off running towards a speeding truck headed in my direction while the other was too stunned to even get up.

I yelled at him, "Where's my wallet?" He looked at me dumbfounded, and opened his empty palms with a gesture at his fleeing buddies. I landed another punch on his body, then turned to watch them jump on a canvas-covered truck bed with the driver picking up speed. The only thought on my brain at the moment was, "My wallet, my ID." In a split second my subconscious mind took over and decided. I took off running to intersect the speeding truck headed my way. The next action the watchers at the nearby hotel perceived was me jumping for the passenger handle alongside wildly swinging into the back of the truck, ready to fight. Since it was nighttime, the inside was completely dark. As soon as my feet landed, my body was battered with kicks, and punches from the two escapees.

By now I had somewhat sobered and was ready for combat. My first reaction in the dark was to fiercely ward off the attack, followed by retaliation. Despite both kicking, and punching, I beat the crap out of both and, in the process, got my belongings back into my hands. But it did not end there. While the fighting continued, I was able to get my hands on one neck, trying to extract him from the accelerating truck. Because of the tropical heat, my hand slipped off his neck in frustration, clutching only the collar of his shirt. The next action my spectators witnessed was me flying out of the darkness from the truck, hanging onto the empty shirt. I landed hard on my back in the middle of main street traffic. As soon as I landed on the pavement, I rolled over to the curb to prevent my being run over. It was here that the fight ended with the truck rapidly disappearing in the dark.

Getting on my legs I could hear cheering from the nearby spectators. Some approached with, "You sure taught them a lesson not to fool with us." It was an American serviceman patting my shoulder. Dusting off my body, I readily accepted his invitation to the hotel bar where I had to tell the story.

"How were you able to fight off three attackers?"

"Martial arts training."

"But three at one time, and coming out unharmed."

"Third-degree blackbelt."

"Where did you learn to fight?"

"I earned my degrees in the best Asian Dojos."

"Man, I don't want to cross you the wrong way," he said with admiration.

"Can you teach me?" another asked.

"I'll tell you what I can do," I offered. "You meet me at the base gym, and we'll start with the basics."

"What style?"

"Shaolin Kung Fu."

"Wow. Can't wait to get started."

After agreeing on a day, and time, it was only one of many such interactions I had much of my career. Initiated into martial arts since my first time on Guam, it was there, when Bruce Lee, a famous Chinese martial arts action actor, introduced his fighting style to the world. From there on I attended some of the best martial arts schools in the Philippines, Okinawa, Japan, and Korea. I even started my own Dojo in 1971, the Guam Dragon, immediately attracting students, and editorialized in the local paper to promote my style, and skills. However, it was not until I lived in Korea that I mastered the arts to become a fearless warrior.

Spending many hours at base gyms, I was always a focal point for martial arts action. No matter where I traveled, word would precede my arrival. Only a few days would pass before I was approached to teach a class to ever-willing students ready to try out their fighting skills. On the other hand, I was always willing to teach the ancient Chinese arts of combat. I even acquired skills in weapons fighting of all sorts from sword to scythe, spear, shuriken, and nun chuck.

While weapon fighting may have been fun it held no match against the ever-growing, trigger-happy thugs carrying concealed guns, pistols, and semis, ready to shoot on the whim of individual notions. Unfortunately, the days for one-on-one combat, matching bodily skills, seemed to be part of the past. Where fights before the turn of the century were rarely fought over life, and death, in today's world it seemed to be the norm.

It was 3:00 a.m. by the time I made it to my room. On opening my door, another surprise was awaiting me. "What the hell?" I blurted out at the couple having sex on the bed.

"I'm staying here," the apparent GI stated. "Booked the room earlier."

"Sorry," I said apologetically on my way out. "Must be on the wrong floor."

Back in the hallway I headed for the elevator. Stepping inside, I pushed the button for my floor but the door quickly closed, and reopened. It was here that I realized that something unusual was afoot. Checking for the correct floor, I trotted back to the room I had just left, inserted the key, and reentered.

"Hey," again in the middle of the sex act, the young GI shouted. "Get out!"

"Wait a minute," I insisted, this time I held my space. Quickly glancing around the familiar room, sure enough, I spotted my suitcase propped by the wall. With a gesture at the case, I proclaimed, "This is my case." The other thing that was missing from the night table was my radio where it had been plugged into the wall outlet. "Where's my radio?"

After seconds in surprise, he said, "My buddy took it."

"Okay," I ordered them from the bed, "it's time to go." They must have understood because both jumped from the bed, fetched their clothes, and hastily got dressed, leaving the room. With the bed in shambles, I reached for the phone.

"Front desk," the night clerk answered.

I told him the situation, and my demands. "Change the bedsheets. Now."

"Be right up," was his response. In less than a minute a couple of youngsters showed up with new bedding, and promptly replaced the soiled sheets.

"What's going on here?" I demanded, but only received a shrug.

"Don't know. Talk to night manager."

It was exactly what I did. Headed for the lobby on the ground floor, I spotted a young guy sitting on the floor listening to a radio. I walked up, and recognizing my property, took it from him, turned, and headed for the desk. "The manager is out," I was told. Since he did not object or follow me, he must have understood, and left the premises. I was satisfied. I hold no grudges.

Three hours later, the alarm clock woke me from deep sleep. It was time for work. On the way, I put in a complaint with the desk manager. "So sorry," he said, with a promise, "I will talk to the night shift."

What I would learn later that day was that it was common practice for the night clerks to temporarily rent out rooms to short-time interludes with visiting GIs from the field trying to have some fun for a few hours, regardless of prior occupancy. Most did not care whether the room was occupied or not by another guest, as they must have deduced from personals placed around. My theory was reinforced by talking to GIs at the site. "Yeah," I was told. "We do it all the time." The mentality behind the practice, dishing out a few bucks to the clerk, was much cheaper than renting a room for the night.

"You sure caused a stir last night," Buzz announced in the morning on the way to the cafeteria, our gathering place prior to the ride to the site. Since today was Saturday there was no rush or time table. Most showed up later, or not at all, depending on severity of hangovers. Since Buzz, and I did not party much outside a casual beer or two, we did not have the general weekend suffering others did.

"You saw?"

"I woke up from the commotion, and watched from the window. Wow," he said in admiration. "You are quick. Where did you learn Kung Fu? I'd heard about your skills, being fearless, and all, but this? Last night's exhibition I did not expect."

"You should come to the gym with me. Would do you good."

"I know how to take care of myself."

"I'm sure you do, but most non-trained fights turn into brawls. They don't last long. Neither will the fighters. On the other hand," I explained, "being trained, no matter what type whether boxing, taekwondo, or other skills, you are focused with each punch, and kick."

"I can land a punch," Buzz defended himself.

"But you also run short on breath. You guys forget to breath in the process of a fight. How long do you think the average brawl lasts?" I was putting him to the test.

"Oh," he thought. "Five minutes."

"Have you ever watched a boxing title match?"

"Many times, on TV."

"Thirty to forty minutes."

"I give up. There is no winning a verbal match with you."

"Sorry. Didn't meant to patronize." It was a reminder for me to shut up. When it came to explaining skills, and technique, many got lost, or were not interested.

"Forget it. What are your plans for today?"

I thought about it for a minute than came up with something unique. "Want see something new?"

"Sure."

"You ever been to a snake farm?"

"Never," he said. I detected curiosity in his eyes. "You?"

I had been to Thailand before, and heard about them. Apparently, there were many such places, but mostly visited by locals. To them it's like cock fighting back home.

"Let's go. Should I get the others?"

"Probably can't roust them. So, it's just you and me?"

The hotel manager pointed us in the direction of the most popular farm in the area. We took off as directed.

I had the pleasure of driving. "Oh no," Buzz exclaimed. "The Kamikaze himself."

I had been known to drive like many did in the country, especially taxi drivers. Similar to most Asian countries, drivers were extremely impatient, and aggressive. Most visitors avoided driving as much as possible. Personally, I thought it exhilarating trying to ace each other out in traffic. What happened on the main streets was against all traffic rules back home.

Many city street signals only had two colors, green, and red. That's how impatient drivers are. When traffic lights changed at an intersection from green to red, drivers on approach rushed to the innermost lanes with the drivers taking position much like at a racetrack, lining up grill to grill across the entire width of the street, curb to curb, in the process blocking all lanes from oncoming traffic. When the light was about to change green, you could hear the revving of a dozen engines trying to beat each other out by forcing the vehicles back onto the proper lanes. It was a rush unequaled in civilized countries. If the move back to the proper driving lane was unsuccessful, vehicles directly facing the oncoming traffic would be forced to stop or crash into each other. This was played out at many intersections. When in the mood, mostly in the mornings, I was among the aggressors. The same was true in other less chaotic countries. Take Korea, for instance. Drivers behaved in a similar manner on entering, and exiting a traffic circle, with comparable results.

For those travelers visiting Thailand, and India, there was another eccentric behavior I would like to point out. Highways outside the metropolis were saturated with trucks, and buses, all speeding to get passengers to their destinations as quick as possible. Apparently, drivers were paid by the load, and time delivered. On the road, when approaching a bus or truck, the driver seat always seemed to be vacant. I was puzzled when I saw it for the first time. "Driverless vehicles?"

Since most drivers were tall, and skinny, the driver's upper body was twisted by ninety degrees, pressed against the driver-side door, making it appear that the driving wheel, and seat were empty, with their feet barely able to touch the pedals.

"What the hell?" I huffed the first time I saw it.

"It's like this in our country," a taxi driver explained. "We allow space for Buddha. He is a much better driver than us. He is all-knowing." Buddha had left his mark wherever he set foot. The entire nation hinged on his wisdom.

We had arrived safely at the snake farm. Ushers in red jackets tended to arriving vehicles. After we paid a small fee at the entrance gate, the usher led us around the various demonstrations held at dedicated areas. With the snakes safely contained within the many glass tanks, one could watch every kind of snake from the Orient waiting to be handled, with the most sought out being the cobra. Much like in dog fights, snakes went after each other, trying to deliver a deadly bite within the allotted fighting time. Most handlers did not want to lose their snake. That meant spending money they did not have on a replacement. Fights were mostly for show. Snakes, much like the cows, were protected by the law. "It is why there are so many snakes in our country," our guide explained. "Do you want to handle one?" We both nodded. "Come," he said, leading the way.

He led us nearby to another spot. Striding closer, we could make out what appeared to be logs lying around the ground. Upon getting closer, they took on shape. Pythons of different sizes, and weight were awaiting us. Unless one was used to handling these creeping creatures, it brought on an initial chill. For once, even I felt my skin crawl. More so when invited to step up and touch. Next, our guide reached down to pick up a sizable snake, and handed it over to me. "120 pounds," he said in broken English.

As he handed me the squirming python, its head reached out for me. Though cautiously squeamish, I took hold of its neck, and gradually draped it over my shoulders. I could feel the weight press down on my body but also felt like a hero. "Want to try?" the handler offered to Buzz while removing the writhing snake from my shoulders.

Another handler followed my gaze toward other beautifully colored logs gradually moving around the grass. He led me to one specimen returning my stare with expressionless eyes, just begging for food. Since I was an adventurer, willing to try anything more than once, he handed me the head of the snake. "175 pounds," he said. I believed him as soon as the snake's body wound itself around my shoulders. The snake was so heavy that I had a difficult time holding its weight with both hands clutched around its throat. I must have choked it. In the next moment I felt the reptile's body tighten around my ribcage. I instantly realized its strength. It could crush me in seconds. Short on breath, I released my hold at the throat, and felt it relax, but with an audible snort that sounded much like a horse. I held it up long enough to have some pictures taken. If I did not already have an admirable respect for reptiles, the experience would have made it so.

And so, the adventurer was educated on foreign customs along the voyage. There were many more similar incidents I would encounter with some turning out humorous, and funny, but others were not so pleasant, ending in more serious consequences.

Six weeks later, we returned to the Philadelphia headquarters to tackle the next assignment. The current project had ended, but not without us having gained a wealth of knowledge along the way. Some were looking forward to the next adventure while others would seek work on more solid ground near home base. Foreign travel was not cut out for everyone. It called for adjustments in conveniences, accessibilities, and lifestyles with sacrifices made to familiarity, and comfort. Where some of the places turned out to be playgrounds for the young, and adventurous, others turned out to be nothing but hardship, especially when on the frontlines.

With travel over until the next upgrade, I was curious of what management had in mind. For the most part, since I was paid from government funds, my assignments depended on my being contracted out. For now, I expected to be home based, hopefully not for long. While back at CONUS, I usually reverted back to engineering working with the designers for the next system upgrade, which was fine with me. It presented a firsthand knowledge for new technology.

GUAM

With travel focused mostly in Asia, I had adapted to many of the diversities of their foreign cultures. With the exception of modern electronics some countries had to offer, the basic way of life appeared pretty much the same, hardship, and struggles in trying to catch up with the Western world, such as the United States, a leader in innovative achievements. I wanted to get to the core of it. I wanted to learn more. With this year's hectic implementation schedule coming to an end, it was this inherit desire driving my following decision. I wanted to stay within an ancient culture. I had to find a means to satisfy both worlds: the world of contracting obligations, and a world filled with wonders.

Presenting my decision to management upon arriving at headquarters, Art said, with a grin, "You're in luck. I think I can accommodate you, but first, let's have dinner." I usually spent an hour briefing him on a project's success while I received his update from the corporate, and economic perspective. Interested in my personal escapades, knowing my desires about foreign cultures, he gave me free rein as much as the contract would allow. At times, he would receive complaints from the field about my team's unruly behavior, which he ignored most times. He knew well the sacrifices each of us were forced into, working many hours, in turn forfeiting amenities, and the luxury of living back home. Once we got biz talk out of the way, we could devote the evening dinner to adventurous events. I could read it in his eyes how much he missed out being stranded back home. But it had been his choice to climb the corporate ladder rather than remain project oriented, as I am sure he did in his younger years.

Dinner time would prove to be another memorable event. Everybody on the team was looking forward to the invitation. It signified the end of a project, hoping for the next opportunity. There was no guarantee that all, or anyone, would be picked up again for another project. It all depended on the next contract, corporate budget, and government sentiment on how the company, management as well as employees, performed as contractor. So far, we had lucked out for five years now, for two reasons: one, the demand for AUTODIN as a vital link to national defense, and two, the skills we brought to the program. Developing, and implementing the size of our current project helped us acquire knowledge not readily available in the industry. But, for now, we pushed career issues aside to enjoy the dinner party.

As usual, my seat was reserved next to the boss. As he listened intently to my foreign experiences, he casually presented an offer. "How would you like to be assigned to Guam?" I could read from his demeanor that he had been waiting for the right moment. Though there were others qualified within the company for taking on the assignment, managing an operational Intel site, he had held back until my return to give me first choice of refusal. He knew I would be the best qualified, if accepting his offer, while others would most likely reject it. Nobody in the company knew the island as well, with its diverse, but challenging opportunities, like me. One had to

---

[33] PCS – Using military terminology, Permanent Change of Station was a permanent job assignment as opposed to TDY, Temporary Duty, a timeframe less than one year.

make serious lifestyle adjustments to fit in, and be comfortable on a small island isolated thousands of miles from any mainland. There was no such thing as, "Let's take a drive in the country," or "let's spend the weekend in the city." When on the north end of Guam, by craning one's neck one could make out a distant speck of land, Tinian, but that was it.

Tinian, I should point out, was best known for assembling the atom bombs dropped over Hiroshima, and Nagasaki that eventually ended WWII. Other than that, there was nothing but calm waters, at times swelling to destructive turbulence, sweeping the island during typhoon season.

This time, I did not take much time to accept the offer. "How long?"

"As long as you can stand it," he said with a sheepish smirk. It was a payback package extended for my turning down his earlier offer to join his management team back at headquarters. Earlier in the year he had offered, "I've got a manager position reserved for you. Why don't you join me at HQs?" It was not a surprise. He had hinted at it occasionally, waiting for a commitment that never came. He thought this time I might accept since there was only one alternative left: Guam. We had come to an unspoken agreement that the management position would always be open until I accepted. For now, my eyes were still set on Asia, and the Pacific.

"What's the job?"

"You'll be in charge of the center, keeping up communications with the 7th Fleet, Polaris submarines, U.S. Embassies, and whatever conflicts need military support. Your sphere of operation will be the Pacific Rim."

"That's some trust you put on me," I said, contemplating the offer. "You can count on me."

"I knew I could," he said. We departed with a handshake that would last for two years before we met again.

Two weeks had passed since my arrival at headquarters. I mothballed my personal vehicle to long-term storage, packed my two suitcases, bade my farewells to friends, and took off on a Pan Am flight headed for the west coast, then on to Guam.

Leaving L.A. airport in the evening, it would be a night flight all the way. Twelve hours, and four drinks later, I stepped into the familiar heat of the tropics. Flagging a cab, I knew exactly where to head. "Tamuning," I instructed the driver. It was my favorite stretch of beach, in recent years populated by hotels, and condos. A few years back, during my initial stay on the island, I had the opportunity to invest in the island's first condo complex. Built right on the shore, the view into the sunset was spectacular. I bought two units then, one reserved for my own living when on the island, and rented out when I was absent, with the second leased out permanently. During leisure times I would sit on the balcony, absorbing sun, and sea breeze with a view I had always dreamt of. During my initial visit here, I had considered it a desolated Rock in the middle of the ocean, but now, three years later, it had become my paradise. I was the happiest person alive.

In buying the condos, my first successful investment paid off. Unfortunately, not all of my endeavors were successful. It seemed that each time I went in partnership-related business ventures, I would lose out. But each time I sought out an investment on my own, I came out a winner. In hindsight, I would like to share a personal tip on the matter.

Not all businesses can be operated by one person, especially with today's corporate business structure in the U.S., but I suggest to conduct your business and investments without a partner. You will have less headaches while giving yourself a chance without having someone being a drain on your investments as well as business success. There are many business opportunities today conducted through the Internet without the enormous expense of operating a corporation with its demanding payroll and expenditures. One more thing. Investing in a brick and mortar type of business, one usually has to commit to a five-year lease in office space, hire permanent employees, pay utilities, on top of payroll whether successful or not, payment must be met. The alternative is a failed attempt.

The difficulty when forming a corporation, not everybody puts up the same share of investment, as should be the case. One must be aware of the partner that only offers his/her share in unfunded contribution, but demanding equal partner and share distribution. By that I mean an offer to be the organizer, expert, and such without the usual monetary commitment. It is this person that will screw others out of their investments, if things don't work out. The moral for a corporate or partnership is: "There is always somebody willing to spend your hard-earned savings."

After spending many years living in hotels, and eating at restaurants, I suddenly realized what had been missing from my life: my own domicile. The condo would become my preferred home while in the Pacific for a number of years. All I needed now was pleasant company, but before that happened, I had an appointment in the morning to brief Naval Command. Assigned primarily to act as liaison between Command, and headquarters, the meeting went as well as expected. My sphere of support to Naval Command was from Alaska in the north to Australia in the south with Hawaii to the east, and the African coast to the west, a total of 63,800[34] square miles. I appreciated the assignment, and added responsibilities very much. It would extend my professional horizons by a sizable magnitude not everybody ever had a chance to reach.

Into years of proven, and stabilized computer technology, I found my new haven an operational breeze. The workload, from the technical perspective, I would resolve in minutes. Software-related issues I could turn over to site programmers, a joint civilian, and government team. Operational challenges I handled myself. The first day on the job I'd noticed something new, and unusual. Curious, I asked the site's operations chief, "What's with the chicks?"[35]

He could not suppress a grin when he said, "ETs."

"ETs?"

He explained, "Electronic technicians."

It immediately made sense. Earlier that year, I had come across an intelligence report issued by the NSA stating that a new breed of technicians had graduated pending

---

[34] The Pacific Ocean encompasses approximately one-third of the Earth's surface, having an area of 63,800,000 sq./mi—significantly larger than Earth's entire landmass of some 58,000,000 sq./mi.

[35] Chicks, at the time, was not a derogatory term. It was a reference applicable to young girls, in this case unusual for a Naval installation. It would take decades more before women were accepted to serve on naval vessels.

assignments. It further stated the reasons, and purposes for their training: "Listening experts trained in various languages."

Enough said. For Pacific assigned, it would be gathering information on China; while stationed in Europe, it would be Russia. ETs, though unheralded and clandestine, they spearheaded what was the first step for the woman to become an intricate part through all military and defense related services.

With job assignment under control, and personal career advancing rapidly, I could dedicate my leisure time to sports, and water-based activities. Between fishing, diving, and parties spent beneath the beauty of coconut tree forests at one of the most remarkable shorelines, Tarague Beach, time passed by rapidly. Since Guam lacked the four seasons, the passing year could not be judged like back home. Years of aging, not readily visible, slowly, but gradually left their marks. Everybody was getting older without noticing the change. Settled in, picking up my favorite sports in martial arts, and windsurfing, I was given access to local gyms, and provided with the desired equipment, including with hotel-franchised surfing gear at no cost, as long as I would surf along the beachfronts. It provided free advertising for hotel management while giving me the thrill, and pleasure needed to make my life wholesome.

With the war in Vietnam ending, my frequent travels there lending support, ended as well, allowing more time spent on the island. I made new friends. I picked up invitations from influential businessmen, and local politicians, attended briefings with Naval Command, submitted my weekly reports to headquarters, kept in touch with DOD contacts, and had my calendar marked off daily. "What else could be better?" I occasionally questioned myself. There was one constraint of which I became aware. It was the limited freedom of travel, commonly known as Island Fever. Travelling was a natural function most people enjoyed. I always wondered why there was so much air travel in and out of Guam with only a population of 75,000, with major airlines, stopping to refuel, dropping off, and taking on new passengers. The entire population, I was told, travelled to several of the surrounding countries at least once a year on a one-month, one-price ticket extended by the airlines. Many took advantage of the offer. I did too after learning about it.

Where many of the islanders could only afford the round-trip expense once a year, I took advantage several times with the usual stop, and layover in the Philippines, Japan, Korea, Hong Kong, and Taiwan. It seemed wherever I went, I made business connections. It was on these trips that I learned about creating a corporation, conducting business, and trading in inter-island commerce. There were many products to buy, sell, and trade. Some were successes with others ending in failure. I tried a number of different goods, and products, such as planting a mango farm on some acreage I had leased from the Guam government. I did some research on plants that would grow on the rocky island ground, but was misadvised. It seemed that mangos needed rich volcanic soil to prosper. Seedlings I had imported from the Philippines took root, but grew poorly, I'd learned from horticulturists, but had to give it a try. The rewards would have been prosperous in the long run. The venture ended in failure.

A more successful endeavor was imported products from Italy. Guamanians are fashion-conscious, so I went into partnership with a local friend who took on the management in the business. What we created was "Moda Italiana," a high-end designer shoe store, successful for several years while it lasted. Unfortunately, it was a time where foreign entrepreneurs were investing heavily on the island. Strip malls, and stores sprouted up everywhere, competing for business. The following year we were forced to close shop. Initially a short time success, but another failure.

Another venture I started was the opening of a martial arts school, the first on the island in my Kung Fu style. A couple hundred students signed up right from the start. My partner, and I managed it until both of us left the island years later. I landed in San Francisco, while he took a position with a law firm in L.A. The reasons for our eventual departures were several, with one being growth on the island getting out of control. Just within two years, island population had doubled, then tripled. Economic development could not keep up with population influx, bringing along undesirable elements with an escalation in crime quick to follow. Living there was not safe anymore. It was time to leave, and move on to safer grounds. Besides, my term on Guam was up. I was recalled back to headquarters with new projects on the way.

KOREA

It was late 1972. I had just returned from Augsburg, Germany, looking forward to spending Christmas holidays back in the States. While I had paid several appreciative visits to my dad living at Lake Constance in the southern part of the country, my brother residing in Hamburg, and my sister, married, with her family living in Austria, it was time for a more stable life. Though adventurous, constant travel overseas could be demanding work, and lacked permanency, and stability. One was subjected to a life driven by urgency on a daily basis, keeping up schedules to get the project done on time within the allocated program budget. Besides, the NATO effort had come to a successful completion with most of the implementation teams released, and only the operational site crew remaining. While I had been requested to stay on, my desires were focused on Asia, so I turned down the offer. As far as I saw it, my job in Germany was done, and I bid everybody goodbye. We had worked hard each, and every day with an occasional Sunday off. "You can take off sightseeing after the project is done," was the usual response by the site manager when someone requested time off to enjoy a bit of Germany while there. The result was that some were bitter about missing out on desirable travel destinations. Two days later, I checked in at headquarters, decorated in the seasonal holiday spirit.

"You've got one week to get a team together," Art said with a welcome gesture, shaking my hand. "By the way," he stated. "Thanks for doing a great job for NATO. Corporate is really happy about your performance." He diverted the attention from my pending departure.

"Is that the thanks I get sending me overseas on the holidays?"

"Not my decision," he said, sour-faced. "Pentagon asked for you specifically. Korea is going hot next week. They need an operational team on site."

"How big a team?"

"Twenty-five."

"That's impossible. How do I get somebody to leave on a holiday, let alone a couple dozen?" I objected. "Nobody in their right mind will take off to leave wife, children, and family behind. You know that."

"Try your best," he ordered with finality. "I'm depending on you."

And there I was, the infamous pushover, sucked into a time schedule somebody else had dreamed up. Regardless of the impossible situation, I went to work making intrusive phone calls to my contacts. Surprisingly, I was able to drum up three for the team with Buzz as my faithful companion. "How did you get away?" I asked after meeting him at the Philadelphia airport Christmas day.

"Wasn't easy," Buzz, Nate, and Mitch replied, the most dedicated, and reliable engineers employed with the company. It was the core team the company relied on the most. Where Buzz was taking care of computer systems, Nate's principle job was software engineering with Mitch managing COMM operations.

"Who else is coming?" Buzz demanded.

"Guys," I said, headed for the departure gate, "this is it. The four of us. The rest of the team will trickle in after the holidays."

"How're we going to explain it to the government?" Nate was just as concerned.

"All we can do is promise a full complement after New Year's. Best I can do." The flight, with a brief stop-over in Anchorage, was long but comfortable. Because of the holiday, the flight was practically empty. We had the entire flight crew to ourselves, serving us whatever our hearts desired. We were in pleasant company all the way, on a sixteen-hour flight. Even the pilots stopped by to chat, wondering what idiots would commit to a job on that day. Coffee, champagne, and wine flowed almost nonstop amid the best quality dinner, and breakfast being served. Airlines back in the 70s were still traveler oriented. Profit, and bottom-line earnings were still subjected to government regulation limited to a ten percent profit margin for publicly-held corporations. Cabin space was configured for nothing but comfort, making travel a pleasure all around.

"Prepare for landing," the sound of the attendant's voice seeped into my world of dreams. I, like my companions, managed several hours of sleep after getting drowsed up with champagne. Reality set in quickly as we landed in Seoul, our intermediate destination. We still had to catch a four-hour train or, if luck was on our side, a local flight to Taegu, the end of our journey.

"No flights today," we were advised at the in-country ticket desk. We understood, and rushed to fetch a cab to try, and catch the next train south with a parting, "Better hurry!" from the airport ticket agent.

Palming the ten dollars I'd pressed into the driver's hand to get us there in time, "Don't worry," I was assured. "Can do," and he did. In record time. Not so much for taking care of us, but he was looking forward to spending the day with his family, like any other sane person would. Though Christmas was not a national holiday in Korea, commercial enterprise had taken root in many other countries, with the population welcoming Western holiday practices, in addition to their own.

We were loaded up, and cramped, with luggage protruding from trunk, windows, and seats. Our driver even had to drive crouched against the steering wheel, but did not seem to mind. "Record time," he boasted after a forty-minute reckless drive to the train station located in downtown Seoul. Aside from the inexpensive tariff, I tipped him double the fare, receiving a grateful, "Thank you very much. Have a good trip."

As scheduled, four hours later we arrived at our destination. "Taegu," the female voice sounded. "You have one minute." It was enough for us, as well as the other departing passengers, to scramble for luggage, and other personal belongings. I watched farmers pulling caged chickens, and ducks from the overhead compartments, perhaps presents from friends, and families.

"Now what?" Buzz said, anxious to get out of the chilling cold while slapping both arms around his body. Since there had been no time for me to make hotel accommodations on the short travel notice, the only option we had was Camp Henry, the Army's administration base for the location, within a cluster of three Intel bases within a three-mile radius. With our international flight timed to arrive in the early morning hours, luckily, it was still late afternoon. Though it was holiday season, I was able to track down the administrative sergeant. I gave him the name of my contact. Several minutes later, he announced, "Somebody will be here in ten minutes."

Travel-weary by now, in a strange environment with everything shut down for the day, all of us were looking forward to stretching our bodies, and some rest. As promised, our contact, a tall, uniformed individual, direct but friendly-faced, walked into the room, "I've been expecting you."

We shook hands as I introduced the team, followed with, "At least somebody had a mind to notify you of our coming." I was grateful for being welcomed in spite of my predicament.

"Where's the rest of your team?" It was an embarrassing question I faced. I could see from his ranking, warrant officer grade IV, that he deserved an honest answer.

"It's only the four of us. The others will arrive in a few days," I stalled.

"COR is not going to like it," he forewarned me. "He'll hold you responsible to the contract."

Just before departing headquarters we were told, "Your obligation in Korea is two years." The news was surprising, but not entirely unexpected. With the completion of successfully implementing all Intel sites contracted by Ford Aerospace, primary contract holder and my current employer, direct support functions for the duration of one to five years were assured while specific military services would gear up to eventually take over site staffing, and support. Whether it would materialize or not, that was the plan. For now, we faced at least a two-year assignment here.

"Let's go," he said, leading the way.

"Where are we going?"

"You can have dinner at my place while I try to get lodging for you guys." I was grateful for his offer. It was not the first time I had been stranded without a place to stay. Securing lodging could be trying in a foreign land, especially up-country where strangers were not frequent, or welcomed. The American in Korea was not exactly a friend. Rising demonstrations to expel U.S. forces proved my point. We met our host's wife, gracious as she was. "Have a seat," she said, gesturing at the ample table settings. Our timing was perfect, participating in the delicious Christmas turkey dinner she had prepared. I will never forget our hosts, and am forever grateful for their effort to put us up in the chill of the Korean winter. Our host, in the meantime, had arranged for us to secure rooms at the nearby Cp. George BOQ, the camp's officer housing.

The following day, Monday, I met with the COR representative assigned as Korea liaison between myself, and the DOD. While the complex was an Army-specific Intel site staffed with U.S. civilians, the Department of Defense had overall responsibility for our performance. "You are late," were the not-so-friendly words uttered by my opponent. I could see from his face that he was angered for some reason.

"Why do you say that?" I responded, displeased at the introduction. There was no extended hand for me to shake. It was hostility at first sight.

"You were supposed to be here two weeks ago," he said, demanding justification.

"My team, and I were in Germany," I explained respectfully.

"Your management will hear about it. Besides, where is the rest of your team?"

"They'll be here after the holidays." That really set him off.

"I demand your team on site tomorrow." We both knew that was an impossibility, and I stated so.

"I don't want excuses. You will meet my demands."

I was getting angry at his unrealistic insistence. "You're a complete idiot," I was about to say, but kept quiet, considering the time ahead. After all, I had to work with this imbecile for the next two years, and could not afford starting a fight. Though I was required to report to him weekly, we never saw eye-to-eye for the entire duration. He made my life miserable whenever he could until an event the following year. Unfortunately, he was an alcoholic, spending most of his time at the on-base officer's club until one morning, when someone found him drowned in the gutter. The following inquest report stated that the man died from drowning while exposed to torrential rains during the night. I did not wish him the misfortune, and will not mention his name for the potential disgrace to his family. Henry, his replacement, turned out to be a joy. We would have many good times together in the years ahead.

"Nice place," Buzz commented after we settled in. The quarters were clean, and spacious, accommodating all of us exclusively. It turned out that most visiting army personnel preferred to lodge in the local economy for the following reasons. Renting a house in Korea, if one could come up with the monthly tenancy fee for an entire year up front, would be cost free. The fee would be returned at the end of the prepaid year. It was an offer many could not refuse. The landlord, in turn, would invest the funds in one of the locally-operated investment firms, guaranteed a thirty percent return, the norm for Asian investor payouts. Thus, both parties benefited. The visitor lived rent-free, the proprietor earned his thirty percent profit on your money.

Though I was here before during prior system upgrades, it was during summer. Korea, I quickly learned this first winter, was a harsh country. It did not snow much, but the cold winds blowing in from the Siberian Steppe chilled the country, and its people to the bones. "No wonder the Koreans are such a sturdy breed," Buzz would comment when the topic came up. Talking about the people was never far from our minds. The harshness was clearly visible in their red-tainted faces: runny noses from the ever-present winter cold seemed to last the entire season, fists balled to retain body heat, stomping the ground for the same reason while performing their daily chores, regardless of the harsh weather condition. I would truly experience the cold of winter when three of us moved into a local place. We leased a mansion-like home when we were forced to move from our temporary, but comfortable BOQ housing.

"Military policy," we were advised when questioning the order to vacate. Apparently, occupants were only permitted to stay up to one year at on-base housing.

As for local homes, most houses were heated by inserting specially formed, pressed charcoal briquettes into a round opening along the outside wall, at times hourly, or as soon as the coals burnt down, a process repeated whatever time the briquettes would last to. The process was customary in Korea. Homes were constructed with heating pipes running throughout the home for heating the bamboo floors.

Rather than putting up with the time-consuming chore, we had decided to go without heat for most of the time, especially towards early morning hours. Indoor heating water was just as cumbersome. A kitchen stove had to be fired up, and wood or coal fed into the opening to heat the kettle, which was not large enough to cleanse the three of us. I would rather take a bucket of cold water, step in the tiled washroom, vigorously scrub some heat into my body, and douse myself with the bucket of icy water shocking me awake, repeated daily. It was a way of life one had to get used to, or seek alternative lodging at an expensive downtown hotel, not recommended because of the problematic commuting one would face.

But not all living was as challenging. To keep warm, one could as easily walk into a restaurant, or bar, order a drink, and sit by the fireplace until closing time. It was the practice many on the team preferred, including myself.

"Where are you off to?" Buzz would ask many times at the end of a work shift. Managing a flawlessly run site operation required my daily attention.

"Dojo," was my standard response. Shortly after we settled in, I signed up for martial arts training. After being refused by every Dojo in town, one day, after meeting the Army's regional radio announcer, James, we acquired memberships in the country's best martial arts school, which taught Shaolin-style Kung Fu. It'd turned out he, and I were the only foreigners ever allowed to join. When querying the Master instructor, Dong Hack Soo, we were told, "Americans lack discipline." I had wondered why Asia had the best trained fighters in the arts. The fact became clearly visible when watching the combatants in action. It was pure discipline instilled by instructors before the student could advance to the next level of skills. Where in the U.S. martial arts was popularized in the early 70s, by movie actor Bruce Lee, local Dojos had been around for eons. Fortunately for us, James, and I accelerated rapidly, demonstrating that a foreigner could be worthy of propagating the ancient fighting practice.

Exclusively taking up my off-working hours spent at the Dojo, time in Korea passed quickly. On Sundays, with Dojos closed, I could dedicate my time to browsing the many souvenir shops located at every corner in a city block. Speaking could be a challenge, and learning to read Hangul, the Korean script, was another, but highly appreciated by the citizens for making the attempt to communicated effectively. It seemed that studying was my destined occupation while in the country, but I enjoyed every second of it.

Beforehand, I was clueless about the antagonism some Koreans displayed towards the foreign visitor. Strolling along sidewalks window shopping, I was bumped into many times by an aggressive youth or two, staring at me while I was forced to sidestep the rude behavior. "Cultural practice," I was told by my language teacher. Koreans liked to measure their strength against the foreigner, an inherited practice dating back centuries as a result of many invasions by the Chinese, and other warring nations. Koreans have effectively learned to protect themselves from foreigners trying to dominate and change their culture. The American presence was no exception.

Almost from the first day after arriving, I had been challenged for one reason or other. Being Christmas, with most facilities closed, I was fortunate to locate one place open for business, the Officer's club. As soon as I walked in, I found business an overstatement. Glancing around the room, aside from the bartender, I could see I was the only guest. The conversation he started was light with the usual small talk, "Where are you from," and "when did you get here?" As was the case with social functions on base, some of the staff, after having caused some minor infraction, resulted in Kitchen Duty, and Latrine Patrol being assigned by the squadron leader. Sunday duty was one such consequence.

"Somebody is waiting for you," the bartender interrupted.

There was a slight stirring from the far end in the room. Taken by surprise, "Waiting for me," I muttered at the person slowly making her way to the bar.

"Hi," she said with a forthcoming smile on her face. "I am Miss Lee. May I join you?"

"Of course," I said with a gesture at the barstool alongside me. At one glance, I assessed the person as Korean, almost my height, long auburn hair flowing to her shoulders, well dressed and groomed, sporting a pleasant smile, and speaking excellent English. "You have been waiting for me?"

"Yes," she affirmed, and added, "I am not an escort girl."

"Drink?" I offered with a gesture at the bartender.

"Wine would be fine," she ordered.

"Coming up."

Eying her in anticipation, I opened the dialogue after the drink was served. "You have been expecting me? Nobody knows I am here."

"Three people know," she said. "You, me, and my fortuneteller friend."

"What?" I was baffled.

"Yes," she went on to explain. "I was told to meet you here today. I was almost ready to leave when you walked in, and here you are, and I am not disappointed."

I returned her smile, but my curiosity was heightened to a level I had never experienced. My mind was churning with questions. To begin with, I did not believe in psychics, clairvoyants, or fortune tellers. It was a realm beyond my way of life. My entire existence was anchored in a world of science, logic, and reality. There was no room for spiritual, and mystical means in my world. "Tell me more," I demanded, despite my negative attitude.

"Already weeks ago, my friend, who is a psychic, kept telling me to be at this place on this specific day to meet my future partner," she claimed in a subdued, pleasant voice.

"What?" I exclaimed. "How could that be?" *The only way*, I silently reasoned, *is that there must be a hidden world in society propagating information on specific individuals targeted as easy prey.* That was my belief when the topic of fortune telling came up. There could be no other explanation. Having psychic abilities was beyond my realm of understanding. "It's all a hoax," was my usual comment on the subject. I had absolutely no interest in cosmology.

As for the situation at hand, I believed that she was putting me on to meet someone, anyone, on this lonely day.

"You don't believe me," she claimed, somewhat saddened. "I will take you to her."

"I'm not interested." I wanted to terminate the subject matter.

"In me or her?" she asked, waiting for my answer.

"Let's not fight over it. I am still interested in you," I assured her. Aside from the absurdity at hand, I wanted to talk very much about her culture, and people, and stated so. "What brings you to this town?"

"I was born in Pusan," she claimed. "It's a city south of here on the China Sea. My father..." She commenced to illustrate her path from early life to the present. "Interesting..." was my general comment. We spent the next several hours seated more privately at a table with her doing the talking, and me the listening. I would learn about her education, her mom dying shortly after her birth with her dad being one of Korea's last renown philosophers, traversing the countryside giving lectures on a more glorious time before the two countries, the North and South were split up by the war that started in 1952.

"So, you are interested in history?"

"It is my passion."

Asking specifics about her country, what she explained next was intriguing, seemingly a history buff myself. "The earliest known Korean pottery dated to around 8000 BC, the Neolithic period began after 6000 BC, followed by the Bronze Age by 800 BC, and the Iron Age around 400 BC."

She sure knows her history, I though while she talked. *Probably through her father.* There was something else I learned, just as intriguing. Where there had been many dynasties through the ages, at around the 14th century, Korea as a nation split up into two kingdoms, the Northern, and Southern regions. As it happened, the southern part was ruled by the royal Lee dynasty with the northern seat ruled by the Kim dynasty. A country split with irreconcilable differences resulted with all people inheriting the respective royal surnames within the two given regions. Consequently, surnames were reduced to only two, Lee, and Kim, still predominant to this day. It explained why everybody in the region I resided, the South, was named Lee. However, due to trade, commerce, and migration, a recent study indicated additional surnames introduced to the land were Kim, Lee, Park, Choi, Moon, and Jeong.

Though most had individual first, and middle names, with surname inscribed first, it was customary to maintain cordial respect by formally being addressed as Mister, Missus, or Miss.

"Can I see you again?" she asked as we parted just before the midnight curfew. The bartender was anxious as well to close the place for the night.

"I'll tell you what," I offered. "You know Camp George. I stay there. Stop by the gate, and tell the guard to let me know. I'll meet you then." We parted with her extending a friendly hug.

I didn't expect to hear from her, shrugging off the encounter as passing trend. Several evenings went by when I suddenly became aware of someone trotting a few yards behind me. I had just left a local club, a usual hangout by the team after work. I waited for her to catch up with, "Well, well. If it isn't Miss Lee."

"Where have you been? I have been waiting to see you," she greeted me. I explained to her that I usually returned from work through another gate, at the opposite end of the base closest to my workplace. While I had a rental car, and hired driver, I preferred to walk the two-mile distance to, and from Camp Walker, my place of work.

"Come with me," she insisted, pulling me along. "My friend wants to meet you."

"Friend?"

"I told you about her."

"The psychic?"

"Yes. She is waiting to meet you." With heightened expectations, I followed her to a private home nearby. After a brief knocking, a steel gate opened revealing a lady I estimated to be in her 40s. "Anyong Hashimnikka (please be welcomed)," she invited us in with the customary greeting expression in Korean, stepping through the gate. I should explain that homes in Korean towns, and villages were clustered from four to six, fortified, and protected by a twelve-foot wall topped by barbed wire with a single entrance, a four-foot high steel gate one had to stoop under to get inside. The miniature entrance fashioned within a normal sized dual gated closure, I was told, served two functions. One, it kept burglars out, and two, it was to show humbleness to the host through stooping on entering, both an inherited customary practice.

In the days there, I had already learned rudimentary phrases, and replied with the same greeting to the host. Once seated in a stove-heated room, plain but comfortable, I was offered cookies, and tea, the customary brew made from burnt barley rice. Though quite different in taste than green or black tea generally found throughout Asia, because it was cheap, Koreans preferred this home-made product for every-day consumption. Once used to it, it tasted quite pleasant. I enjoyed it while the lady began muttering in her language. "What's she saying?" I asked my companion.

"She's awaking the spirits."

"Spirits?" I was as doubtful as ever, but inquisitive, nevertheless.

"Pssst." With index finger touching her lips, she cautioned me to maintain silence. The psychic's chanting went on for at least twenty minutes before she broke the otherwise silent presence. "She wants to read your palm," was the next request. Still hesitant, and doubtful, I reluctantly complied. While I could not understand what she was saying, my companion began to interpret. After another monotonous, and lengthy deliberation, as in a trance, the lady suddenly stood up, and walked to the kitchen range to retrieve a heated pot of tea. "She's reading tea leaves," I was told. The session finally came to an end. I shot a brief glance at my wristwatch, and was surprised to find two hours had passed. At the indication, the session had ended, puzzled but mystified, I reached for my money clip to pay her the standard fee of $50 U.S. for her services, but she graciously refused payment. My companion and I left with the explanation, "You were a special guest in her house. She normally reads to U.S. servicemen once a month. But more important," she emphasized, "you received every service from palm, to tea leaf, to psychic readings, all at no cost."

"Why," I asked.

"Because her and I are friends."

"How does she do it?" Intrigued, but doubtful I clarified, "The chanting. Who was she talking to?"

"Your grandfather's spirit."

I was even more mystified. How would she have known that he was dead? "What about palm, and leaves?"

"She reads the layout of leaves when pouring tea to the cup, and the lines in the palm of your right hand."

"What about my left?"

"Right for men, and left for women," I was educated.

Regardless of purpose, and resolution of an uncertain future, I got what I had asked for, a reading for five years. Impressive, as formal as the reading was, it was permanently chiseled in my brain, gradually revealing over the next five years as my future unfolded, herewith exemplifying her pertinent, and more important milestone readings.

Reaching the base gates ten minutes later, the sentry, firm but courteous ordered, "IDs." I complied. "Her ID," he demanded next. *That,* I thought, *could be a problem.* When we were initially checking into our quarters, all of us were instructed that there were no visitors allowed on base without prior authorization. Surprisingly, after showing him her personal ID, we were allowed entrance. From the gist of the verbal interchange between my companion, and guardsmen, I guessed that she was no stranger. My assumption would prove correct in the times ahead. Once we settled in my room, I handed her a bottle of Coke stating, "I want you to know that whatever your friend said I won't believe," I said, explaining my position with psychics.

"Maybe not today, but you will in time."

"So, tell me."

"Her predictions went like this," she began. "You will leave your job in two years."

"What?" I was completely taken aback by the revelation. "Impossible!"

"Why impossible?" she wanted to know. In her mind, the prediction was infallible since she believed everything her friend revealed. As blinded as I was at the time about predictions, over the following five years everything she stated would come true. But, for now, seated comfortably in the coziness of my room in her company, I was as doubtful as ever.

"There is more," she indicated. "Much more."

"Go on," I encouraged her.

"Some is good but others not so. You sure you want to know?"

"Tell me everything your friend said," I insisted. "I can handle it."

"Okay," she agreed hesitantly while I still pondered about quitting my job. It would be inconceivable for me to terminate a career I had solidly built, and cherished. *What about the adventures, and unfinished explorations I have planned?* I thought.

As incredible, and nonsensical as it sounded, I wanted to hear more. The direction my career had taken with the position I had achieved, there was no way I would ever quit. It confirmed my belief on the whole fortune telling gambit. "Go on."

"You will travel to another country…

A country she believed to be the Philippines…

You will meet your future wife there…

You wife will bear three children…

No boys only girls."

"Wait a minute," I objected. "Marriage is not in my plan. I don't plan to ever get married."

"You have no control over your destiny. It is written in the book of life."

"You believe whatever you want," I insisted. I had been studying her face, and body gestures while she talked. Though I am not clinically trained in psychology, I had taken courses in human behavior but could not read her signals. "Is there more?"

"Yes," she went on. "There is more, but you will not like it."

"Tell me anyway."

"You asked for it. Right?"

"Yes. Please."

"You will become involved with foreign business partners…

You will get sick in the first year…

You will lose your investments as a result…

You will be paralyzed…

It will take years to fully recover…

When well again, you will return to your country."

I thought that I had heard enough, and stated so, when a thought hit me. "What about you? Why were you sent to meet me?"

"We are meant to meet. We will be together as long as you are in my country."

Cohabitation, I thought. *Another impossibility, and there it is. Whose destiny is it now?* "Mine!" I decided right then, and there I had to prove it. I had complete control over myself, and my future. As friendly, and accommodating as Miss Lee had been, I decided not to see her anymore. It would prove my point. "You have to go now. It was nice meeting you. Come," I offered, getting up from the comfort of the sofa, "I will take you to the gate."

"When will I see you again?"

I hesitated with my answer. We lingered by the gate, but for different reasons. Her, wishing to see me again, and I, forcing my hand in destiny.

"Ask your friend." That was it. I watched her disappear into the alley. I decided a stroll through town would clear my head from all that I had heard today. I tried to push thoughts about her from my mind, but they kept returning. Recollecting the evening, "She is pretty," I decided. "And smart too. I sure would like to get to know her."

What kept gnawing away at my brain was the determination she had extended to the psychic. Thoughts like that stayed with me until I finally went to sleep, interrupted by upsetting dreams. More trouble was infringing on my life in the days ahead.

As limited as news broadcasts were at an overseas military base, world events eventually found their ways there. Racial discrimination, in later years termed ethnic struggles, to be politically correct, after emerging in the U.S. during the 60s, did not appear at military bases overseas until the early 70s. On most days I would spend the early part of the evening at my favorite Dojo training for the first-degree black belt. My sparring partners were the Dojo's Master instructor Mr. Do, and my new friend James, who had already earned his third-degree months earlier. Having been in Korea on military assignment already for two years, he had gained a certain popularity, not only as radio announcer, but more prominently, as the best fighter in the company. Not only was he fearless facing the enemy, he also performed personal feats acquired through martial arts training not many could match.

"I'm done," I huffed, exhausted from another grueling match. "See you tomorrow." Though surrounded by a body of about thirty local students of lower rankings, the high point of the evening was usually the three of us sparring with each other, the only blackbelt holders in the Dojo.

"Where're you headed?" James said.

"Back to quarters."

"Why don't you meet me at the club?"

"What club?" Though there was only one club on base with joint military rankings, off-base clubs were numerous.

"Bat Cave. I'll see you around eight."

"Bat Cave it is." While I was pretty confident in handling myself in trouble situations, I did not feel quite comfortable at his mentioning the place. It was an all-black nightclub. I had not met one white that had ever been at the club. Close to the appointed time I left my quarters for the ten-minute walk to the club. As usual, a dozen or so patrons were milling around the front entrance chatting, drinking, and smoking in the company of cheerful bargirls. As soon as I walked up slangy trash talk was flung at me. Disregarding the remarks, I pushed my way into the club looking for James, who had not arrived yet. Headed for the bar, I ordered, "OB." It was the only beer brand in town, produced by the Oriental Brewery.

I could see the bartender making no attempt to fill my order. Checking over the place I became aware of an air of hostility. Minutes later I was crowded in from both sides of the bar demanding in not so friendly voice, and gestures, "What are you doing here, white trash?"

"Meeting a friend."

"No friend of yours in here," was his reply, followed by, "Who's your friend?" I could smell and feel the escalating tension in the air breathing in my face from stale alcohol and smoke, getting ever so closer. The imminent fight was only seconds away. It all depended on who would flinch first.

"James Cook."

"He's not going to save your ass." They did not, could not, and dared not make the connection between me and James to meet here in view of recent, violent clashes played out on the very spot I was standing. I was prepared to defend myself when James casually walked up, asking, "What's the problem?"

"This guy claims to be with you. That true?"

"I invited him."

"How could you bring white trash in here? You know they're off-limits."

James did not hesitate when he said, "You all know me. You respect my judgement. Don't you?"

"Well, yeah. But…"

"He's on our side." It was a true statement since I had spotted several familiar faces from the site's shift personnel, but were conveniently ignoring my presence. "Besides," he went on, "you don't want to mess with him. He'll whip your butts. All of you."

"In that case," I was told, reluctantly, "you can come in." They had backed off.

I watched scorn immediately turn to tolerance. While I was accepted into the club, I would never become friends with some of the regular patrons. It was different at the worksite. Faces I recognized at the Bat Cave during the standoff, would treat me as part of their culture on and off the job.

The dispute was settled even though I was the only white guy ever to set foot in the Bat Cave. I realized that James, as smart as he was, had played me as trump card to squash local racial tension at an ever-increasing frequency. He managed to dissolve further clashes in the region before they started.

"I wondered why me, and why now," I said, shaking my head.

"Somebody had to teach them a lesson," he said with the wink of an eye cast at me. "You paid your dues."

"Could have paid a high price," I complained, "if you hadn't showed up."

"I was in back watching over you."

I should mention here that I had been observing racial tensions for a number of years while overseas. As far back as the late 60s during my first assignment to Japan, I was surprised at frequent clashes between military units living on base. With multilevel units clustered closely together, apartments brightly lit after dark, in passing I could perceive what sounded much like crashes propagating throughout hallways, rooms, and floors.

"Why doesn't anybody manage it?" I wondered many times. What I could not understand was the lack of discipline in not reprimanding the soldiers living together in close quarters. Even though there were generally no weapons in use, fights were fought through amplified stereo equipment, the boombox, and whatever audio system would produce the overly excessive sounds reverberating through many rooms and halls. It was these intrusive sounds fought between blacks[36], and whites cranking up soul, R&B, Motown, and country western music that eventually escalated into cultural clashes.

At the time many of the technical staff on site were white, but almost all of the operations functions were managed by blacks. It was an unintentional divide contributing to the tensions. Individuals were indoctrinated by the Army, chosen by skills, and experience. There may have been bias between the two cultures coming from different backgrounds during service recruitment, but it was not the only issue demanding attention. There were other issues such as female coexistence in the service, female battle assignments, and more, not only with the Army but throughout all services.

What James resolved that day was the beginning of a somewhat more tolerant community educated in living, and working together while tolerating, and respecting each other. It was a peace treaty achieved for the military communities at Taegu, that even the Korean governments between the North, and South have not been able to solve to this day. Where James, and I became lifelong friends, a synergetic ambience developed among shift, and management personnel at the isolated military bases. It seemed that ethnic tensions had been replaced with a workable coexistence.

After things had settled to a more peaceful phase, I was able to focus on the job for which I was contracted. The team finally made it, but not without delays. The site, installed, and tested weeks ago by a special crew, was finally ready to cut over for real-time operation. Where some of the team had been trained at headquarters for their specific functions, the remaining I could handle locally, assigning appropriate positions following training. On the day of the cutover, everything went as planned. Verifying that all computer, and COMM equipment was functional, Tech Control personnel enabled subscriber[37] lines as quickly as they could be tested. With tensions heightening between the North, and the South the site was of utmost importance for the Cold War threat. Where North Vietnam was supported by Chinese insurgencies from Hanoi, North Korea's support came directly from the Soviet Union, our superpower adversary.

New hires had been trained for operational functions, but they were not necessarily indoctrinated to an assigned task. Some were clueless about their

---

[36] On a personal note, it is not my intention to single out color or creed as special designation to an ethnic group. It is the label chosen by African-Americans as a result of decades lacking social identity.

[37] Subscriber was the user ranging from a CIA outpost to military commands, embassy, and other classified functions related, and linked to the Korean theater of operations.

functions, and responsibilities, resulting in the question most frequently raised, "What am I here for?"

To get a better understanding for the reader as to our purpose overseas, I will describe a typical function for site operations, and management without getting entrenched in details with classified materials. Though overseas locations were managed by separate military branches serving various countries, as a whole, all sites were linked with the Pentagon, and the White House through landlines, and subsurface cables through the 60s, subsequently moved to satellites in the 70s. To gain access to a site, working personnel, as well as visitors, needed to be cleared Top Secret. In addition, after Intel communities tied into the system in 1972, special access clearances were required, publicly referred to as "Above Top Secret."

While the primary functionality for an AUTODIN site was supporting war efforts, conflicts, and political tensions, the underlying infrastructure was to support military command, and control, government contracting personnel, embassies, and Intel field agents deployed to fight, guide forward firepower, provide political diplomacy, and gather Intelligence on the enemy. It may sound simple and direct, but for the system to function as a whole, a totally committed staff, and support personnel was needed. The typical site was manned by three rotating shift crews of approximately 125 highly-trained individuals from management to computer maintenance, operations personnel, communications and crypto specialists, logistics, and UPS support. Each sector was staffed 24/7 with one crew on break. While all Intelligence functions were automatically processed by computers, monitoring the system, with local interventions by the local staff were necessary.

In today's world, contrary to the classified Department of Defense operation decades ago, public data, and information are processed as email, texting, imaging, and voice carried over unsecured wire, HiFi, and wireless media.

With today's enormous demand for communication needs, technology, and speed has increased tremendously. In the early days of computer-managed operations, the speed at which technology leapfrogged ahead was unimaginable not only in the scientific community, but the business world, entrepreneurship, and government as well. Nobody back then had envisioned the demand, and growth seen today. Communications, whether embraced or rejected, is a marvelous thing. Within each industry sector, everybody in the modern world depends on it, and so do Intelligence, national defense, military, cyberspace, and investigative services.

Once the initial haste for getting operational had passed, personal life gradually took hold. With shifts in place, working responsibilities sorted out, liaison established for an effective interaction between contracting personnel, and government, everybody proceeded in accordance with Intel policies, and military regulations in a system owned by the government, but operated by the commercial contractor. A dependency developed much like parts in a well-performing machine while Intelligence gathering prevailed under military commands jurisdiction, monitored by joint services. Traffic priorities ranging from routine delivery to ops immediate, flash, and flash override were handled, processed, and delivered according to importance, and criticality. Without questioning, following strictly enforced guidelines, information was sent, received, stored, and processed as directed by policy makers. Essentially, I was able to dedicate my spare time to more personal ambitions.

While mostly dedicated to martial arts, I sought out alternatives. I tried out the International Wanderers organization, which originated in Germany and spread worldwide, but found out that club activities were too challenging. Koran pathways cut into mountainsides were crowded with locals at all hours of the day, and especially on weekends. Water-based sports at my location were nonexistent. The solution came through my driver, who one day approached me with, "Could you buy me a model airplane, please?"

I had already observed some clusters of enthusiasts grouped at spacious fields not only trying out their home-made planes, but model cars, and boats as well, tested in nearby fields, and lakes. He was a most courteous, and accommodating Korean individual, attending to the team's and my transportation needs. His primary function was to shuttle my people to, and from work locations in-between running errands.

"What did you want?"

"Could you buy a plane, and a car model kit? I will put it together for you."

"Fine," I said, promising the items which I purchased the following day at the base model, and craft shop. He was the happiest I had ever seen a person. Days later he came up, asking, "You ready to test it?"

I was ready when he drove Buzz, and me to the field. I had bought two models; one was a fighter craft remotely operated, and the second was a trainer controlled by wire. He promptly demonstrated his flying skills, remotely, and expertly executing climbs, dives, inverted flying, and loops ending in a safe landing. It was my turn now. I took the second craft to the air at maximum speed the model engine allowed, manipulating similar maneuvers, but managed from wires attached to flight controls. The craft performed well, but was limited by the length of the wires. The sound of miniature engines buzzing at high speed had attracted nearby villagers, and kids curious about our activities. No matter how much my driver, and I cautioned the crowd to back off, they kept encroaching on my flying space.

"Stay back," Buzz kept yelling at the spectators, but was ignored the same. Ten minutes into flight, I knew fuel was about to run out. Seconds later, with the engine sputtering, and stalling, the flight ended abruptly.

"Watch out," I yelled out to alert everybody. It was my final warning just before the plane took a dive, headed straight for the belly of one kid. With terror-stricken eyes, he let out an ear-piercing scream when the model hit him, assuming he was about to be killed.

"I told them," I said, voicing my frustration. My driver had already rushed to aid the youngster. On inspecting the kid's body for damages, we found only bruised skin formed at the place of impact. Amid threatening gestures, and chatter by the townspeople, we hastily departed to avoid possible implications.

Other mishaps followed in the days ahead, including damaging the model car by being run over by one person on the team who had a personal vendetta with my driver. He did not appreciate the sound of model engines buzzing his quarters. As restitution, I went back to the store and bought a model boat. The first time we tested it on the lake, again, we were soon crowded by onlookers, but this time the boat was out in the lake without endangering others, but inflicting pain on myself.

The incident happened just as we decided to quit for the day. It was time for my driver to beach the boat. While I watched the boat riding the shallow waves in, I walked up to the shoreline, squatted down to retrieve the boat, and was jolted by Buzz's warning call. "Look out!"

It was too late. I promptly squatted onto the needle of the syringe my driver had placed carelessly by my feet. The needle was used to fill the fuel tank of the super-charged craft. I felt a piercing penetration into my right buttocks with kerosene injected into my body. Minutes later, I could feel my leg turn numb.

"How're you doing?" Buzz said, concerned when I turned pale.

"I don't feel well." It was time to head home. Apparently, the kerosene was picked up by my blood stream and carried through my body. On inspecting my back, the point of entry left a dark spot, festering an infection for weeks. To this day I can still spot the tainted spot on my skin. As one can see, not all battle scars are earned by bullets.

After the issues, I considered models a waste of time while Mister Ko, and others continued to fly, and test more models. An entire land was waiting for me to explore. It came in the form of Miss Lee. One evening I spotted her familiar face lingering by the main gate. I slowed my strides as I considered turning back. I had put her from my mind as "too much of a challenge," but thought better of it after she had spotted my approach. Since I perceived her to be too involved in the spiritual realm, I did not believe that we would have much in common. "What the hell," I'd decided. "I'll at least find out what she had to say."

"Hi," she said with a bright smile as the sentries watched us.

"What brings you here?" I said, just as friendly. Glancing at her at close proximity reminded me how pretty she was.

"I was in Pusan, visiting my dad."

"Nice. Any brothers, and sisters?"

"I am the only child."

"So," I asked. "What brings you here?" I was not trying to challenge her. I was just curious since we had parted weeks ago on somewhat strange terms.

"You," she said. "Remember the promise?"

"Your friend?"

"Yes," she said, even more determined. "It was prophesied."

"You know my position. I don't believe in it."

"You cannot be smarter than what is directed by destiny."

Okay, I thought. *So be it. Have it her way.* Religion, and faith were personal issues. So far, I had always managed to keep my distance from getting involved with these personal, yet highly controversial, subjects. Almost everybody, unless closely related within a likeminded community, either inherited, or grew up with a different belief system. For me it was Roman Catholicism with its strict inheritance. I looked at it as a taboo topic for personal discussions since it usually turned into clashes. Not knowing much about Korean secular, and faith practices, *maybe I can learn from her,* was my immediate thought.

"You will have to explain."

"Can we go somewhere? Perhaps a nearby club?"

"Lead on," I offered.

"Soju," she ordered when the hostess stepped up. *The Lady drinks,* I took notice. *Can't be all bad.* Soju was a rather potent alcoholic beverage made from fermented barley. "Cheers," she toasted at me.

"Kanpai," I matched her toast, literally meaning, "empty the glass."

We sat in silence with both of us eying the environment. The place was quiet, rather unusual for Korea where prolific chatter was the norm. Noisy sounds did not seem to bother people much. My first time here, I thought everybody was out to pick a fight until I had learned it was a cultural behavior to be heard. Korea was a rough country, and so were its people.

"How come you are avoiding me? Have I offended you?" she said after we were seated.

Our eyes met, and locked for a fleeting moment. I let her speak. "Do you like it here?"

"Yes. Like you said, it's a quiet place."

"I meant Korea."

I hesitated before I spoke. "I don't know much about your country. I would like to learn more."

"Maybe I can help if you let me." It was an invitation I would have to consider. "What are your interests?"

"Your customs, your culture, your people. It's mostly why I came here."

"What about your job? Don't you have to work? By the way, what kind of work do you do?"

"Not important. Let's not talk about work." She seemed satisfied because the work topic never came up again.

"I want to be your tour guide," she offered.

"How much do you charge?"

I must have struck a sour note, because she fired back, "I am not a bargirl. I don't charge for my time. I just want to be with you."

"So sorry. I didn't mean anything by it. Just wanted to compensate you for your time." To expect a gratuity for services rendered was a common practice in Asian countries. It was part of an economic system justifiable where much of the population was poor on a level of starvation. Only a very small percentage were blessed with wealth, mostly royalty, and business tycoons.

"You are forgiven." With an extended hand, she offered, "Tell me what you are interested in, and I will explain or take you there. Agreed?"

"Agreed.

"My people…" She went on to explain. We sat for hours with her doing most of the talking on every topic I was interested. It turned out Miss Lee had been educated at the country's best schools, and had acquired limitless knowledge on her heritage, and its people, resulting in us getting together more frequently in the months ahead. I considered myself fortunate to have met her, while she felt similarly, and thankful to her friend, the psychic, for bringing us together.

The following two years turned out to be happy times for the both of us until the day I announced, "I am leaving Korea."

I could see her world crumble. It was not an out of the blue decision. My time here had come to an end. The contract was up for open bidding with another contractor being awarded the service support for the next five years. Many of the current personnel would be picked up by the new service provider, but I was ready to move on to enrich my knowledge in other cultures.

"You are coming back. Are you?"

"Don't know, but I will try," I promised.

"Marry me. Please. I want to come with you."

"We talked about this, remember?"

"I know…I know, but I want to see your world. I want to live in America." Like most people I came in contact with, the dream was for a better life. Nobody could blame them. Having had the same desires since childhood, I considered myself as one of the lucky ones. My dreams, and aspirations had come true. *What about all the others?* I silently questioned. *What about her dream?* I avoided her pleading eyes. It was too painful to watch her world of hope, and dreams dissolve into emptiness.

"I will be back," were my final words when we parted. We both knew it was an empty promise, but it kept the sense of hope alive. Knowing, and believing what her friend predicted, she knew I would not come back.

Completely forgotten, I had suddenly realized that her prediction was about to come true. "Could there be substance to psychic premonitions?" I pondered, stunned at the revelation. My life had been directed by reality for so many years that I was left completely confused at my spiritual ignorance, but for the time being, I deferred judgement to the future.

I had never seen a more desponded person, as I watched her disappear in the dark. It was a rare occurrence, that I felt saddened with deep regrets. In spite of my pursuit in adventures, my life went on as predicted, I would learn at events as they would occur.

Being freed from bondage to the two-year assignment in Korea, Buzz, I and the team were dispatched to the new location, the Philippines.

PHILIPPINES

The yearend holidays had just passed when I stepped off the plane at Manila International, ripping off the winter coat I wore. "It's supposed to be winter," Buzz gasped amid the crowded terminal. "Where are all the people coming, and going from?"

"We'll find out soon enough," I said, having read in some travel brochure that Filipinos have a large community in the U.S., Canada, and Australia. It would explain the high-volume travel. It appeared we weren't the only ones wearing winter clothes. I made a mental note to buy light apparel as soon as I'd settled in.

"You've got the contact?"

"Why don't we stay in town for a couple of days?" I suggested.

"What about the site?"

"Work can wait. It won't kill them to run on skeletal shift."

"Fine with me," he said, headed for the first taxi in line. Again, we were crammed in the cab by our suitcases. Fortunately, it was only a ten-minute ride to the Hilton, where I had made reservations. "You want company?" the cabbie asked on arriving.

"Here we go again," Buzz muttered while I paid the fare. By now, I had gotten used to being hustled at every landing in Asia. It seemed the entire economy was run on entertainment. I largely ignored the solicitations since most international arrivals were targeted, the ones with money to spend. I would also soon find out where business was conducted. It wasn't at the office. It was in saunas, tennis courts, and nightclubs, many times in the company of hostesses.

I spent an enjoyable weekend seated mostly in the air-conditioned top floor suite at the Hilton overlooking Manila Bay amid ample offerings of snacks, fruits, and refreshment drinks. A five-star hotel, it was my favorite accommodation in the country. I knew management well. The reason I was given first choice was that I could afford the high rate of $25 U.S., paid by the contract. Compared to a rate of $250 U.S., or more extracted in today's world, it seemed a steal. But, back then, it was considered the highest rate charged for the guest at most countries. It's how much inflation has crept into the worldwide economy. Unfortunately, not all pay scales have kept up. Buzz was sitting beside me, also enjoying the view. "Doesn't look like cargo ships," he stated with a gesture out at the distant bay.

"Gambling casinos," I informed him. "Gambling on land is prohibited."

"I wonder why," he contemplated.

"Let me tell you about the Filipinos," I offered. He sat back to listen to one of my monologues he'd grew used to over the years. He usually did not mind to listen while I expressed my inner self. "They are hardworking laborers when there is work to be done, or available at all. But when work is finished, many take to gambling. It's one of the reasons why they are poor."

"We gamble back home."

"We do it more for recreation. With them it's in the blood."

"How do you know?"

"I know Filipinos, and I've been here before, remember?" I was not trying to judge the local population for their recreational preferences. They had theirs, we had ours, with visions of my prior trips to Las Vegas. My aim was to share my experiences and knowledge with others.

"What do you want to do today?" Buzz asked. I was more inclined to, "what I wanted to do when?" Though the present serenity was hard to break away from, there was much exploring to do.

"Let's take a walk along Rojas Boulevard. But first, I need something light to wear."

"Me too. You know a place?"

"Come," I said, leading the way. "You'll love it. It's a shopper's paradise."

As was the case with many cities in foreign lands, market places were generally within walking distance in downtown. Some shops were covered with solid roofs while others conducted commerce beneath makeshift tents, mostly to keep vendors from getting scorched by the sun, amid endless lines of shoppers passing by hundreds of tables bedecked with Filipino-made artifacts of every kind. It was fun to just watch the shoppers briefly stop at a table, select the items sought, and begin the process of haggling for a mutually acceptable price. Where Westerners were not comfortable with bartering, it was a necessity here. Barter was an accepted way of life. Without it, one was considered a fool, I was told.

"Like you said," Buzz admitted on arriving. "Shopper's paradise."

He was as impressed as I, pacing along the many stalls with vendors dashing in and out blocking your path, with, "New from Italy, latest from France," and many more copied designer clothes.

"Are these for real?"

Designs, tags, and make, looked like the original items fabricated in the Philippines, whether licensed or not. For designer items manufactured in the country of origin, one had to visit the Shoe Mart, the country's only shopping mall, but you expected to pay ten times the price offered here. The Philippines was a country of contrasting lifestyles. There were the few wealthy who could afford anything, and everything under the sun, and then there was everybody else, the oppressed citizens with only dreams, and wishes for a better life. There was no middle-class in the previous century. Today, I would like to state that things have changed, but a visit there would probably tell me otherwise. The masses still struggle daily to gather the few Pesos it takes for a bowl of rice, and some fish for soup, basic essentials to survive.

For Buzz, and me, our trip was paid for by the U.S. government. We were the fortunate ones who could afford a purchase at both sides of the aisle, poor or affluent, but preferred the economically offered merchandise, real product but fake label. I will explain the situation in favor of the poor. The merchandise bought in these markets most likely were genuine since many fashion designs from Europe, and other industrious countries was outsourced to be manufactured in the Philippines, and other deprived nations in the region.

"You sure you want to buy this?"

"Don't feel guilty," I educated Buzz. "Outsourcing cost the U.S. economy millions of jobs with billions in revenue. The guilty ones already have enough wealth without depending on our contribution."

"If you insist." It was the last thing to be said. An hour later we both were loaded down with bags of personal designer wear suitable for the climate. The remaining days we spent exploring the nightlife, with its never-ending opportunities for pleasure. We would have liked to remain a few more days in Manila, but duty called for us being up-country.

Arriving at Clark Airbase, this time, there were no strikes preventing us from entering the base. We were welcomed by the new commander without misgivings. What our work entailed was supporting the Vietnam War, escalated to new heights with nonstop B-52 bombing runs out of Guam unloading their destructive loads. Intel had become a necessity to military command, and control, as well as to save our soldiers' lives, aiding in the effort. With Vietnam unsafe due to the bombings, we provided remote communication connectivity to the Pacific region from the Intel site at Clark AB.

Being another PCS assignment, it usually took a couple of weeks for everybody to settle in. If available, temporary quarters were authorized on base for a few weeks, but had to be relinquished to permanent housing, which was our responsibility to locate, and occupy. Since our daily monetary living allowance to spend was $7 per diem, with an additional $12 for lodging accommodations, most choose to stay at one of many hotels located around the base perimeter. The choice was for safety reasons since hotels provided security guards stationed around the clock.

Once settled, with the work schedule assigned, the job became rudimentary. Supervisors, programmer, engineers, technicians, and operations personnel were manning every station 24/7 as required. Only management had the luxury of working daytime hours, which Buzz and I were partaking in. It left evening hours, and weekends to explore the land. With Buzz by my side whenever he was off-shift, we took advantage of travel whenever possible, as inexpensive as it was in the Philippines. We explored places such as nearby volcano Mt. Mayon, erupting every so often, Mt. Pinatubo, currently dormant but smoldering, Baguio, Mt. Apo, Taal Volcano, all in similar conditions, ready to spew fire, and ashes at will. With Manila sixty miles away, we spent numerus weekends in the city enjoying sights, markets, and restaurants with an endless variety of local cuisine. One of my favorite dishes was Britohon Bangus, deep-fried fish. It was also the place I was introduced to eating lobster. I took to it like a cat to sardines. With the first bite I could not suppress sharing my enjoyment with Buzz. "How could I have missed out on it all of my life?"

The answer was simple. Americans, generally, did not develop a taste for it until the 60s. On my arrival in the States, there was only one seafood restaurant in Philadelphia, usually lined up with Jewish patrons only. It was not until years later when the Holiday Inn, I recall, introduced the weekly fish and seafood fares on the menu: "All you can eat."

Not only was the lobster exquisite in taste, in the Philippines the price was also right. For $3, one was served two one-pound crustaceans on an oversized dinner plate. Young, and full of energy, in-between bites, we managed to finish the plates with frequent sips of Sam Miguel, a locally-brewed beer.

Stuffed to the hilt, unable to hold an intelligent conversation afterwards, the limited comments between Buzz, and I were, "Boy, am I stuffed," and, "me too." Between work, excursions, and dining, month after month went by, mostly uneventful until one day one of the team came up asking for my help. It turned out that he had been swindled out of one month's pay. Prior to my travels, I had the foresight to subscribe to the first credit card issued, American Express, but others had their paychecks mailed out via APO. Either means of payment was expertly handled by one of numerous local banks. However, as was the case in conflict regions, black market currency exchange flourished. The Philippines was no exception. Though illegal under U.S. status of forces laws, one could easily exchange a personal check at any street corner for double the value in local currency. Money hawkers were everywhere, promising high rates, but not all of them were honest. Several on the team lost their earnings, but only once. Most wised up to the vendors' game plans.

"I need help," he said, explaining his dilemma. The following day, we sought out a local law firm. Explaining to the lawyer what had happened, the final advice was, "There is nothing you or I can do. Filipino law has no precedence on the matter." It was the end of any further street transactions by the team. They had learned their lesson at an unforeseen expense.

BUSINESS VENTURES

Months later, on one of my weekend trips to Manila, this time staying at the Intercontinental Hotel, I met a local businessman in the lobby. While he was waiting for others to arrive for a business meeting, we talked, with him carrying most of the conversation. I learned he was a successful entrepreneur with ownership in several local operations. After his guests arrived, I was introduced around, and invited to join. The meeting turned out to be a most interesting affair. Situated at the top level, on leaving the elevator one entered directly into the conference room, taking up the entire floor. The panoramic view into Manila Bay was spectacular. One could even make out Mt. Mayon in the distance. I sat, and listened, becoming more, and more intrigued. What I was invited to turned out to be the monthly meeting of the country's Petroleum Club, the most prestigious, and influential enterprise for the region. What it meant was members of the country's wealthy deciding on where, and how much petroleum to import in the months ahead. I could not believe that I had stumbled into the nation's elite. It was a new experience that would soon change my life.

Not only was I introduced to the attending members, I was promptly invited to the board of directors with several other enterprises. One such prominent business was the largest cement mining operation in central Luzon. Another, an offer to join a mainframe computer implementation for the country's largest supermarket, the Shoe Mart. Still another was a joint venture for opening a sporting goods store featuring the latest recreational equipment imports. As I would learn in due time there was a reason for it all. After accepting corporate membership, I was automatically extended a business visa to the Philippines.

It appeared that good fortunes were literally falling into my lap throughout my entire career. First, there was my childhood dream come true. Then, contracting offers by the U.S. government to partake in satellite development, space launches, creating the world's first Internet, generation one, and two, and now this. I was faced with a dilemma. A huge one that would impact my future since I was still under contract with the defense department. On the one side, the site was putting pressure on for my return, and on the other, my new business friends wanted my commitment. To sweeten their offer, I was invited to join the local Chamber of Commerce, all while still on my extended stay in Manila. To my surprise, I met Ferdinand Marcos, then president of the Philippines, who hosted some of the meetings.

Having been technically oriented for most of my career, I was somewhat overwhelmed at the attention I had received, and my introduction to a world of international businesses. My dilemma was solved by headquarters several days later. I was ordered to return to the U.S. for other assignments. It was felt that my present job at a permanent location would be a waste of time for my skills that could otherwise be employed more productively, in favor of corporate headquarters. I took the opportunity to beg off from any assignment for the time being by requesting leave. After working non-stop projects for several years, I had accrued six weeks of vacation time I was ready to take. Since there were no rejections by headquarters, I felt free to pursue the business opportunities extended. At least, I promised myself, "I must try the once-in-a-lifetime opportunity," and accepted the business offers.

As soon as I had committed, I was delegated to head off several innovative projects to the Philippines. First, I was tasked to develop the country's first computer training school, and curriculum. Next, I joined the team to computerize the already mentioned Shoe Mart. Next, one of the partners, and I opened the sporting goods store, and initiated channels for importing foreign sporting goods products. Then, I led a team of draftsmen to design, and build a mobile home manufacturing plant. It was enough of a workload to keep me busy every waking hour. There was more to come. My sporting goods partner invited me to join the local archery club. Since guns, and rifles had been outlawed by the current president, with everybody required to surrender personal weapons, many took on an alternative means, that of taking up archery as a form of recreation.

Since I had trained with foil, dagger, and sword during my college days, in addition to a variety of Chinese weapons through martial arts, I had acquired a liking for weapons fighting. After the first archery shipment arrived from the U.S., June, my partner, came up and said, "You ready to try these?"

"Lead on," I said, promptly headed for the shooting range with an assortment of bows, arrows, stabilizing rods, sighting gauges, and whatever other parts were needed.

"Here," he suggested, handing me a recurve bow indicating 40 lbs. It took that much force to pull the string, and arrow for successful release. Though I was at the prime of life, I struggled with it, trying to stabilize my focus on the target, 25 yards out.

"Too strong," I said. "I need something less powerful."

He understood, and handed me a 25 lb. bow. It felt more comfortable in my hands, something I could handle. "You've got to develop arm, and wrist muscles," he suggested. In no time, I was ready for the 40-pound equipment. From then on, archery became pure bliss. June hired a store clerk to free our time, and off we headed for the range almost daily. "You are getting to be a real pro," he would say. Whether it was inspiration or encouragement did not matter much. I had fun. I felt that I had mastered the sports by persistently scoring bullseyes. "You ready to teach?"

"What?"

"See these young archers across the field?"

"The girls?"

"They are training for the Olympics. I need a hand with the training. They are too many for one instructor." It turned out that June was one of the best shooters in the country, not only in archery, but in handguns, rifles, and machine guns as well. Much like the present shootings in the States with riots many places, the Philippines had their time of gang wars escalating to an unacceptable, and unsafe level to the public. It was that situation that caused the president to step in, and outlaw personal weapons, which may happen in our country if effective gun control and/or local law enforcement will prove ineffective. Though I am a strong supporter of the second amendment, there is no reason why a civilian can acquire a fully automatic weapon to satisfy personal needs or killing desire. It must be stopped before military, and police must step in, and confiscate personally-owned guns from innocent owners. Historically, the above stated misdeeds, and actions were strong indicators to trigger a civil war that nobody wants. Aside for tightly managed hunting licenses, weapons sports should be reserved for fun, and recreation only.

June, and my training efforts payed off. The Philippine archery team came in first in the following Olympics. I was proud of my achievements not only in archery, but in the other endeavors I was committed to. Unfortunately, President Marcos declared martial law the following year, turning the country into chaos with an immediate decline in commerce, trade, and prosperity for the following ten years, after which he, and his family were exiled from the land. It proved that citizens could only take so much poverty, and starvation while the ruling power acquired all wealth without so much as sharing a portion. My opinion on such a matter was that the ruling class forgets who produces, and provides the means for a strong and healthy economy. It was due to this fact that all dictatorships in the past ended up in failure with either getting exiled or killed.

While historical archives contain a nation's accounts in success, and failure, the guilty will not learn to regard, and respect proven laws set up to provide an honorable birthright, that of being free from slavery, and oppression. It is this sentiment that mankind will have to struggle through generation after generation.

With all the activities I was involved in, the weeks of my requested contracting leave had passed. While in the country, I had no reliable address to receive personal mail, and corporate correspondence. To assure delivery from headquarters, and Pentagon contacts I sought out the American embassy, but was told, "We don't handle personal items."

"Well," I thought on departing the grounds, "I'll have to find other means."

Walking towards the car park I spotted a secluded building nearby. Curious as I was, I could not resist. I entered. "Yes," the desk clerk said.

"I wondered if you could help."

"Can I see your ID?" I readily complied by handing over my DOD credentials.

After a quick glance at my picture ID she said, "Wait here," and left for a private office identified by the sign, "Station Chief."

"What is this?" I pondered. "CIA?"

Sure enough, I was introduced to the Philippines' head of CIA operations. "Come on in. Have a seat." A most friendly face gestured at a posh armchair. "What can I help you with?"

"I have a favor to ask."

"Sure."

"It seems the embassy is not equipped to handle personal mail. I am temporarily in the country, and need a contact for my headquarters', and personal mail."

"Who is your employer?" he tactfully replied.

"DCA," I said, hoping it would expedite my request.

"Well, of course. I also report to the defense department." He shot a quick glance at his watch, and said, "Care for lunch?"

It appeared he was as genuinely curious about my activities as I was in his. "I'd like that," I said. Over the next couple of hours, spent at the CIA's private club along Rojas boulevard, I learned quite a bit of their operations while I informed him of my present business ventures in the Philippines. In the time I spent in-country, we became social friends as well, while getting updates from headquarters. My affiliation with his agency would prove an important connection in the times ahead.

"Hey," Buzz had left a message at the hotel. "When are you coming back?" In the heat of my newfound ventures, I had forgotten about my responsibilities with him, who I had left in charge of the team. I promptly returned the call. "Sorry," I apologized. "Didn't meant to leave you stranded. Why don't you come here, and spend the weekend? Make it for breakfast. We must talk. I'll reserve a room for you. Afterwards, we can explore the city."

"Fine. I'll be there." As promised, he showed up to enjoy a late serving at the breakfast room. "So," he said. "When are you coming back? HQs' been asking for your report." As a contracting requirement, I had failed to submit my weekly updates. Since I had no access to a typewriter at the time, I solved the problem with, "It's your responsibility from now on."

"You're not coming back?" Buzz was shocked. I did not get the feeling that he was happy.

"Well," I explained. "I was offered an opportunity that I just cannot refuse." I then proceeded to tell him my decision for taking time out.

"For how long?"

"I don't know. Maybe forever. My future career could depend on it."

"What about me, and the team?"

"I informed headquarters about the change. They don't have to send anybody. I'll put you in charge."

He remained quiet for a time then agreed to it. He deserved the post as superintendent I had vacated. "What about us?"

"You ready to take a walk?"

I paid the bill on the way out, headed in the direction of the local supermarket, and said, "See this place?"

"Shoe Mart?"

"Yes. It won't be a Mart much longer. My first project is to computerize their operations. The owners have plans to expand countrywide, but can't do it without the computer."

"I thought that many of the companies had computers."

"That's true," I agreed. "But they don't have any trained programmers. It's my job to initiate the first school."

"Wow. I had no idea." I then explained the reasons why technology lacked support in Asia. In the early 70s, IBM, the most prestigious computer manufacturer, had sales agents solicit their systems, the popular 360 Mainframe, around the world. The result was that many large companies, and governments, bought the system at a cost of one million dollars, only to have it sit idle for years. Aside from internal IBM system developers back home, the company had no teams available to be deployed overseas.

Consequently, the systems were sitting idle, only running on internal operating software. Unbeknownst to the customers prior to the purchase, business application software had yet to be developed. Some software programmers made initial attempts in getting their systems operational, but this proved too expensive for many businesses. When Shoe Mart executives heard of my computer experience, they had decided to present me with an offer. After I had accepted, a local team was hired with one of their executives to manage the project for getting the effort underway.

"Now I understand."

"It's just one of several projects I am involved in," I explained to Buzz.

"In a way I envy you," he stated. "But I wouldn't want the responsibilities."

"You know I crave to finish what I started." He knew how I felt about the job. Any job. "Now you see that I have to follow through to finish what I started."

"I understand, but you're coming back? Aren't you?" With years of contracting projects together, we had developed a strong dependency on each other, work-wise as well as socially. "I'll miss you."

"Here is what I will do," I offered. "You come down here anytime you can manage. I'll have a room reserved."

"That," he said, apparently satisfied, "I won't turn down." We saw each other frequently. It was always a pleasure being in his company, strolling through city avenues followed with a few San Miguel at one of the many establishments.

While he returned to Clark airbase during weekdays, I kept expanding my scope of activities. The various businesses I was involved with began to flourish. In contrast, the political situation in the Philippines rapidly diminished. It was not long after when, one day, unexpectantly, the president publicly declared martial law. In anticipation of such drastic measures, my friend, as well as many of the affluent, buried their personal weapons, and hired personal protection squads.

MARTIAL LAW

Because he couldn't have a third term, and didn't want to give up power, President Marcos found a way to get around the rules through martial law. As a precursor, secretly initiated by Marcos' regime, rapid social conflicts developed at the southernmost island in the Philippines' 7000 islands, Mindanao. Conflicts were nothing new to the island, situated close to Malaysia, and Indonesia. The Philippines was an island group introduced, and influenced through Catholicism, forced on the islanders by Portuguese conquistadores hundreds of years before, with Malesia, and Indonesia inheriting Muslim cultures from the Middle East. Clashes were unavoidable at times, but were usually solved in a peaceful manner for some time.

On Marcus' orders, first militias, then government troops, were dispatched from Manila to squelch the growing fighting that had escalated into a full-fledged conflict. When the fighting could not be stopped, Marcos attached the country's military forces as presidential defense under his command. With this first phase initiated, the country became subject to military takeover. Once that was accomplished, the president enforced an NDAA[38] act. It meant the confiscation of all personal firearms owned by the citizens, with ownership prolific. A specific date, and time were set for Filipinos to surrender their weapons. I recall the day when the act went into effect. 50-gallon drums had been set up in, and around every city, and town by military units to collect firearms with the ultimatum expiring in thirty days. When counted, only a total of approximately one million, or ten percent of the weapons had been submitted. It fell far short of an estimated ten million firearms still in the hands of citizens.

Kept secret until the specific day, the connected, upper class, became aware that a coup was being planned. No secret remains secret for long. No matter how tightly controlled it may be, it will eventually leak. The compromise usually followed a predetermined path. The involved will carelessly or inadvertently disclose the upcoming event to an immediate family member who would spread the secrecy to a friend, who further propagated the rumors within the elite class. The elite could prepare beforehand, but the public did not have the means. At the end, it was the common citizen falling prey, paying the price of getting fired, incarcerated or, worse, executed without a trial.

Prior to the enforced act, since I was associated with the affluent, I became aware that many expected the worst. In the months ahead, they accumulated semi, and automatic weapons for personal defense squads for their own protection. When things turned serious that faithful night of the takeover, many buried their acquired arsenals in backyards, jungle patches, and hills. With the people defenseless for the most part, it was an easy takeover for Marcos' military when he announced martial law. The economy collapsed soon after due to corruption, and exploitation by government officials. Black markets sprouted up overnight, and so did crime. Marcos' reign of power was assured indefinitely under the protection of national military and local police forces. Not only was he the ruler of the nation, he went as far as confiscating every major, and successful business operation in the country. It was the beginning of

---

[38] The National Defense Authorization Act would allow the military to arrest citizens in their own back yard, without charge or trial, if personal fire arms were detected on the property.

the end of my business affiliations, but not for another few more years ahead. Personal events overtook my business success.

It was close to the end of my first year in the country when one of my business friends came up with, "What plans do you have for the holidays?"

"Take a break," I said. I had been busy more than my body could handle. I needed some time off.

"Why don't you come with me to Cebu? I'll introduce you to my family."

Though reluctantly, with him insisting, I eventually agreed. "When are you leaving?"

"Tomorrow."

Somewhat relieved, because my heart wasn't on holiday travel, I said, "Probably can't get a ticket on such short notice." Holidays were the busiest times for travel.

"Don't worry," he assured me. "I've got it covered." Asian countries operated differently for the affluent. Everybody with the means had a personal contact in every office of every organization, especially the airlines. For them, no reservations were necessary. If seating was fully booked, depending on demand, one or more passengers were bumped in favor of an affluent friend or family member. Again, the common citizen suffered, but everybody was aware of it without complaint. "It's a way of life."

My reprieve was short lived. The next day I was on the flight, seated next to my friend in a tightly cramped seat. It did not matter much. The flight only lasted a little over an hour. After arriving, and flagging a taxi, ten minutes later we arrived at the home. We were received with whole-hearted welcomes. I have to admit that no matter how rich or how poor a family might be, a stranger in the Philippines was always welcomed. It created a sense of celebration no family would refuse, especially not the visitor.

From the start I was treated with celebrity. Every family member in town stopped by to meet me. I would learn that the American was revered with great respect. It was many a family's desire to make acquaintance with a visitor from the most successful country in the world. Even to today the sentiment prevails, with many desiring to have a chance at immigrating to the U.S. It must have been the result of us treating the Filipinos with respect, and reverence when our armed forces liberated the country from Japanese oppression after WWII.

I was introduced to every family member who was willing to share a toast of Tuba (coconut vodka), a locally fermented, and brewed beverage made from the coconut flower. I must admit, I had not been this relaxed in ages. During an evening of celebration, I had an idea. Since the family, I gathered, was below average income, I invited everybody to the beach the next day. Immediate cheering followed, especially from the many children gathered around. It would be my tribute to the host's affectionate accommodation I was extended.

It was not long after when the head of the household, the mother of the clan, sidled up on the seat next to me. She was a well-groomed, esteemed lady, soft spoken with a thoughtful but friendly look on her face. I could see from the corner of my eye that she was perusing me. Minutes later, she spoke. "You don't want to go to the beach tomorrow."

It was a declaration I did not expect. I was taken aback, quietly evaluating a possible reason for such bold statement. "Why not?"

"Don't go to the beach," she repeated.

"You mean to say," persistently, I said, "nobody goes to the beach on Christmas day?"

"You don't. You'll get sick."

"What do you mean by 'get sick'?"

"You can't walk."

I tried her to further explain the reasons, but she remained silent for the rest of the evening. It may have sounded like an ultimatum with certain intentions on her mind, but I could not detect the slightest discontentment or maliciousness in her. Whatever her reasoning, I shrugged it off as meaningless while the celebration continued into the night. In hindsight, I should have listened to the well-meaning mother of ten children when unforeseen events took over my life for the holidays, and following years.

FATAL CONSEQUENCES

As planned, the following morning, Christmas day, the three jeeps I had hired showed up at the gate. Surprisingly, none of the children I had promised the outing to were present. "Where is everybody?" I inquired.

"Went to church," my friend said.

"I guess we wait." There was no reason for me to take to the beach by myself, I thought.

"No need. They decided not to go, but me, and a friend will come along." I was perplexed. To have all the children turn down my offer was puzzling. Despite the failure of my well-intended gesture, feeling despondent, I accepted.

Dismissing two of the vehicles, the three of us headed for the beach, a twenty-minute drive. While it was winter in the northern hemisphere, here, closer to the equator, it was the dry season of the year, a temperate climate with moderate humidity. It promised to be a warm, and sunny day to enjoy the outdoors. Where the local population may have embraced the coolest times in the year, to me it was still a hot day once we arrived by the sea. The China Sea, a large body of an ocean extending south to the equator, never changed its temperature. Entering the water close to the beach felt like taking a hot bath. It was not refreshing. Regardless, I jumped into the shallow, swell-free water, swimming out. I welcomed the exercise.

Twenty minutes later I returned to the shallow beachfront. I lingered ten more minutes in the shallows, soaking up water in the heat of mid-day, when I suddenly felt tired. It was not the usual tiring of the body after a swim. Intense sleep clouded my mind. Within minutes, feeling completely exhausted, I muttered, "Better get on shore." The beach, to my surprise, was still deserted. Not one soul was present. My friends had left the scene for whatever place they may had chosen.

I promptly fell into deep sleep, unconscious to the world. "Alex…Alex," a persistent voice entered my dreams. I opened my eyes, and recognized my friend bearing down on me. "Go into the shade," he said. "You are completely sunburnt."

"What time is it?"

"Four in the afternoon."

I jumped to my feet, and promptly collapsed. "I'm too tired to walk," I said.

"Let's go," he insisted, helping me to my feet. "You are dehydrated. We'll get something to drink. Man, do you ever have a sunburn."

I could care less about any sunburn. All I wanted to do was go back to sleep. Sure enough, I was in, and out of sleep as soon as we arrived at the house. "What happened to him?" I heard some of the folks ask, concerned about my looking all blistered. My lips were cracked. My body ached. My mind was incoherent. My feet fell asleep. What else could I do? I laid on the couch, and went back to sleep.

The afternoon had turned into evening when I was awakened with, "Dinner is ready."

"I'm sick," I admitted to my friend. "I don't feel like eating."

"Here," he said, pressing a beer into my hand. "It'll make you feel better." The coolness of the beer quenched my thirst, and relaxed my mind. I started to feel a little better after the second bottle. "What happened to you?" he asked once more.

"I don't know. I went for a swim then came back to relax. Ten minutes later I felt weak."

"You are not used to the sun. How do you feel?"

"My feet are still asleep." I tried several times to walk off the prickling feeling, but no matter how hard I stomped the ground, it did not go away. Every step I took felt like walking on broken glass. It was the weirdest thing I had ever felt. Despite the happy environment, a house full of festivities, I became concerned about my health. "What can I do? What should I do?" I made the decision. "I've got to go."

"What do you mean?" My partner, and his girlfriend tried to persuade me to stay. "Where would you go?"

"Back to Manila. Tomorrow. First flight." It triggered more concern when word spread about me deciding to leave, but people understood. I must not have looked at my best.

Early the following morning, my partner drove me to the airport, and checked my luggage, bidding me goodbye. "Take care. I'll be back next week." Minutes later I was in the air headed back to Manila. In the one-hour flight I took the time to analyze my personal condition. "What is happening to me?" At dawn, after getting up, I hoped that I would be better, but to my disappointment, my feet were still numb but the rest of my body functioned fine. "Gotta see a doc," I promised myself. "First thing tomorrow."

It was then that I remembered the psychic prophecies years earlier. "Could it be true?" I questioned again. "Could prophesies be for real? Naw. Impossible." Curious but in denial, I kept questioning the unexpected events. "If it were true," I thought, "I would have already met my future wife." Recollecting all the people I had talked, and met while in Cebu, ten siblings, and their many cousins, it seemed unlikely. The ones not married already were still too young. Concluding my analysis, I pushed prophecy out of my mind, and spent the remainder of the day resting at the hotel, hoping to feel better by morning.

Arriving back in Manila arranged by June, I had a photo shoot scheduled. The local sports magazine was writing an article about our success with the archery team at the Olympics. I was appointed to pose for pictures by the Manila harbor while demonstrating my personal archery skills. It made for good advertising for our sporting goods business. My sports partner June met me at the docks. He was late. The writer, and photographer had already been at work writing editorials, and taking pictures while I was struggling with my equipment. For some reason, I had a difficult time. No matter how hard I tried, I could not pull the bow to release the arrow. Today's promotion was about us going shark hunting in the ocean with bow and arrow.

"What's the problem?" June said, watching my struggle.

"I don't know. I feel weak."

"Try again. We need the pictures."

And so, I posed several times more in vain, to the disappointment of everybody. June, who realized I was in trouble, came up from behind, helped pull the string and arrow back, and then quickly retreated long enough for me to hold the position for a few seconds, posing for several shots before relaxing. "Think we've got all the pictures," was the final comment from the photographer. "Prints will be in next week's issue."

We all left the docks. With my feet still numb, walking much like a zombie, June asked, "What's the matter with you?"

"I don't know. I got sick over the weekend."

"Where did you go?"

"Cebu. I was invited." As soon as I said it, my legs gave way. I stumbled, and fell to the ground.

"What…?" perplexed, he said. "Come. I'll take you to my doctor."

I could not have agreed more. I barely made it to his car. I stumbled, and fell a couple more times, feeling weaker by the minute. Not having control over my body was something completely foreign. It was scary not knowing the reason. I felt helpless like I had never felt before, hoping that the doctor would have some answers. Then reality hit when I realized that the third prediction had come true.

First, I quit not only my job, but a lifetime career. Second, I left Korea for the country predicted, the Philippines. Third, I came down with the predicament of "not being able to walk anymore." I felt devastated by the very thought. *What if it is true?*

I dared not dwell on it until I saw the doctor. Twenty minutes later we entered June's personal physician's office. The doctor, after a thorough examination, prescribed some medication. "Here," he said. "Use it for a week. Come back if your condition does not improve." Thankful, June, and I left, not any wiser about my condition.

"I'll take you home," he said, appearing seriously concerned.

"What about my vehicle?" It was still parked by the docks where I'd left it.

"Don't worry. I'll take care of it." By the time he dropped me off at my apartment my stride had turned into a shaky gait. Still puzzled, I could not understand why I kept losing balance without an obvious cause. I was alone once more, left with troublesome thoughts. The day turned into evening. My stomach was growling at me, demanding food. I had not eaten since my return from Cebu. Feeling weak and exhausted, I tried to stand up by the bedside, but collapsed. After several unsuccessful steps I let my body sink to the floor, and crawled to the kitchen, where I could get some food from the refrigerator. Reaching for the handle, I pulled on the door. It opened enough to reach some cold cuts, and bread. Famished, I stuffed myself. But not for long. In the process of chewing food, I sputtered, and gagged. It seemed the food had become stuck in my throat, unable to get pushed past the esophagus, into my stomach.

June stopped by on his way to the office. I heard the doorbell, and yelled, "Hold up." After ringing the doorbell several times, he was about to leave when somebody from the building let him in. "What are you doing on the floor?" he said, a bewildered expression on his face when he entered the room.

"I can't stand up anymore." Just about that time, I passed a stream of wind, completely embarrassing, that lasted for close to a minute.

June wrinkled his nose. "What did you eat?!"

"Nothing," I sputtered, embarrassed. I had never imagined that the organ could hold this much air. "I got food stuck in my throat."

"Come," he offered, helping me out. "You are going to the hospital." Thirty minutes later we arrived at the city's foremost medical facility, South Western Medical University. "I'll check on you tomorrow," he promised, and quickly departed. Gratified that I was in capable hands I submitted myself to whatever modern examination techniques were available. When delivered to the hospital, my vision had deteriorated and, worse yet, my mind lost coherency. I was hallucinating. Drifting in, and out of consciousness I saw new faces dressed in white coats bending over me.

"Don't know… Check his heart… What about his vital fluids… Loss of muscle functions," were some of the words seeping into my brain. I became aware that people were at work trying to find the cause of my affliction. Within days, I had become a human vegetable, lifeless, and incapable of coherent thought. With this thought in the recesses of my mind I succumbed to sleep. But not for long. Seconds later I would wake up, desperately gasping for air. I tried to yell but the muscles to my voice box did not cooperate. Other than gasping I was unable to create sound. It did not stop there. I lost control of my lung function. Deprived of sleep, each time I closed my eyes I would jolt awake, suffocating from the lack of oxygen.

I rang the buzzer by the bed to alert the staff. Seconds later two attendants rushed to my side checking monitors. My condition must have registered on the screen. Minutes later the doctor on duty stepped up. "What is the problem?"

"Can't breathe," I sputtered.

"You are doing okay right now," he said, keeping an eye on the monitor.

In-between gasps, I was able to relay to him, "It only happens when I try to sleep."

"Stay with him," he instructed the orderly. "I'll check something." An eternity went by before he returned. "We're trying to locate a life support unit. Stay with me until then." He was in, and out of the room without a sign of encouragement while the clock kept on ticking. The clock, mounted on the opposite wall, was the only thing I could focus on. It kept me awake.

"Is this how I am going to end?" In trying to stay awake, my thoughts drifted in, and out of the past, trying to recall a life destined for success, but cut short by a, yet to be determined cause. It was during one of the recollections when I remembered the psychic's prophesy: "You will get very sick." I had instructed my Korean friend to interpret the monologue for more information, and she had said, "It is up to you to survive."

Two years ago, it had not made much sense. But now, lying mortally sick, two weeks had already passed without hope or cure in sight. The psychic's words began to sink in. Whether it made sense, or not to my feeble mind, I did not have much of a choice. By this time, I had kept myself awake for two whole weeks.

"Sorry," the doctor had said, shrugging his shoulders. "We have not been able to locate a life support system." Later on, I learned from June, who stopped by periodically to check on my health, that the only two "Iron Lungs," as the system was called back then, had been dead-lined "awaiting spare parts."

So much for modern medicine. I had kept myself awake, thinking, "What's another couple of weeks of waiting?" By that time, I was sure at least one system would be shipped from the States. It turned out to be wishful thinking. Days went by, followed by weeks. In the meantime, more doctors, and specialists stepped in and out of the room, trying out all sorts of fluids dripping through my veins via intra-venous injection, keeping me alive.

"His sodium level is low," one diagnosed, resulting in them pumping salinized fluid through my body until salt came oozing through my tongue, eyes, and skin. It did not help or improve my condition.

"Let's try a spinal tap," another suggested. Since I was permanently bedridden, laying on one side of my body, they inserted the tap into my vertebrae for days with staff periodically checking my vital fluids for protein changes. Once the tap was in place, I relinquished all further objections. "Protein level is normal," was one of many remarks. Much like the clinical specialists, I felt completely hopeless in the weeks to come. Occasionally, I received phone calls, and visits from faces I did not recognize. What I did hear were comments such as, "He looks terrible... Can hardly recognize him... Only skin, and bones... Think he's dying?"

I endured most of my misery with my eyes closed while consciously forcing one breath of air after another into my lungs, and staying awake. I did not have enough strength to keep my eyelids open. Besides, my eyeballs were burning from dryness. When I tried to speak it was mostly incoherent babble.

"Hallucinating," a voice would mutter. What I did not realize was, all of my body muscles had ceased to function. It was most visible to staff, and visitors by my facial features. Following extreme muscle atrophy from a lack of nourishment my face was drooping to an unrecognizable feature. I had become a vegetated body without an identity. Only the staff, and I knew who I was. To the amazement of the hospital staff, they could not figure out why I was still alive. I say that because none of the doctors or clinical staff ever thought of inducing an IV containing a body's most vital minerals to stay alive, fluid.

To this day, I can't explain how difficult it was to stay awake hour after hour, turning into days then weeks without a wink of sleep. During the first few days, it was the body itself that kept me alive. Each time my mind shut down into sleep, oxygen deprivation by the lungs forced my brain into action. Jolting from a few seconds of unconsciousness, air was sucked into my lungs. The reflex action was so violent that, to prevent a repeat, I forced my brain to maintain consciousness. It's how I managed to keep focus on my lung functions. To my amazement it worked. It kept me alive for the following six weeks. After the initial two weeks in the hospital, time had become meaningless.

On the next visit from June I gestured for him to come closer. After he bent down, I whispered in his ear, "I am dying. You have to get me out of here."

I could read his facial expression. My words were no surprise. He only nodded, and briefly disappeared. He was accompanied by the staff physician, hospital manager, and accountant. Next, June picked up my limp body, turned, and headed for the exit, on the way out handing over cash to doctors, staff, and hospital management, the means with which bills were paid in the country. Because corruption was prevalent, nobody trusted the banks, not even bankers themselves. Transactions took place—in one pocket, and out the other—for purchases, and services rendered.

"Where do you want to go?"

"Clark Airbase," I whispered.

"Know anybody I could call?" I gave him my buddy's contact number. He made the call then informed me, "Buzz is coming to pick you up tomorrow. Your apartment?" It was good enough for me. At least I would be with a friend for my final days.

As promised, Buzz showed up the following morning. "My God," he exclaimed, "what have they done to you? If it wasn't for the sound of your voice, I wouldn't have known you."

"Bathroom. Let me have a mirror," I said. I took one look in the mirror, and quietly muttered, "This is how I'll die."

"What should I do?" Buzz asked, at a loss for answers.

"Clark hospital." It was the only alternative I could think of. It was a decision that ultimately saved my life. Getting there was not without incident. June provided his personal limousine, including driver while Buzz followed in his own vehicle. Day had turned to night while I dozed in, and out of consciousness. Speeding there for most of the two-lane highway, we encountered head-on traffic, blinded by many vehicles. As was customary in the country, drivers kept headlights at high beam while switching lanes to alert oncoming traffic. There was one event that almost took our lives. With traffic in, and out approaching our lane, the only means to avoid disaster for June's driver was to swerve to the right, shooting off of the road while getting clipped by an oncoming truck. The vehicle flew in the air only to land twenty feet down a ravine. We hit the ground nose first. After his inspection in the dark he came back inside. "Hood, and fenders are damaged." On turning the ignition, the engine seemed okay. He stepped on the pedal, yelling, "Here we go." Careening up the slope, squeezing into a tightly held traffic flow, we made it to Angeles City and Clark AB.

Driving up at the hospital's emergency entrance, with Buzz by my side, within minutes I was whisked in, deposited in a neatly made-up bed, injected intravenously with fluids, and was informed, "Doctor's on his way." I felt safer already with the knowledge of how advanced American medicine was over a third-world country. A glimmer of hope touched my brain. It was close to midnight. Minutes later I became aware of person dressed in hospital whites asking questions. I was too weak to respond, but Buzz gave him an account of my health as much as he remembered. It became apparent that my affliction was beyond the present staff to administer any kind of aid.

"He needs a neuro-specialist," was the immediate diagnosis. Followed with, "We have a problem. Our specialist is out of town. He won't be back until the morning."

Buzz checked with me, and I whispered, "Fine."

"I'll be back in the morning," were his departing words. By now, following the many weeks I had kept myself awake I thought, *a few more hours won't matter.*

CLARK AIRBASE

It was close to 7:00 a.m. when the hallways illuminated, stirred into action. The door to my room promptly opened with a person entering. "Good Morning, Mr. Bauer. Sorry I wasn't here when you were submitted, but let's take a look at you." I anxiously watched while he examined me. Highly professional in appearance, very assertive, confident, and efficient, I determined. Only minutes passed before he announced his prognosis, "I have good news, and bad news. Which do you want to hear first?"

After weeks of nothing but bad news, I only took a second and whispered, "Good news." Could it be that there was a glimmer of hope? I had to hear it first.

"I will have it confirmed in the lab, but from what I can see," he said, "you have what is known as Guillain-Barre syndrome." As far as I was concerned, he could have just as well spoken in a foreign language. I was clueless, but he'd sounded positive. "Now for the bad news. Since you are still alive after keeping yourself awake all this time, you will live." I thought about it. What he said did not make much sense. He must have noticed the clueless expression on my face. "Let me explain," he volunteered. "The common expression for your symptom is better known as a combination meningitis, and encephalitis."

Still, it meant nothing to my feeble brain.

"You have a bacterial infection in the brain as well as the spinal cord that has a fatality rate of ninety percent, if not treated. What medication did you have?"

"Nothing as far as I know. Nobody there was able to identify my condition."

Next, he said, "Thank you for being in my hospital." I must have had another puzzled expression on my face when he explained, "I always wanted to meet a patient with your affliction face-to-face. I'm a neurological specialist doing my internship in the Air Force. I consider myself fortunate for meeting you."

"What about the bad news?"

"I'll come to that. There is no cure for the disease."

"Nothing you can do? Am I going to stay paralyzed?" It was my condition I was concerned about. I was paralyzed from head to toe without being able to move one limb.

"Let me explain. Since you survived this far, your survival is assured. Most people die from asphyxiation, as you have experienced. I commend you on that. As far as I know, nobody has ever survived without a life-support system. You are the first one."

"I assure you I'll be honored once I get better," I muttered. "But what can I expect?"

He pulled up a stool, and sat beside my bed. "What I'm going to say will not be a pleasant experience." He took a deep, compassioned breath then continued. "First, we have to start shock treatment."

"Wait. You mean electric?" The thought alone jolted me into alertness.

"Yes. Electric. It serves two purposes. One, it stimulates the nerve system, and two, we measure progress response time."

"How long will it take?" Though there was hope I did not look forward to electricity shooting through my body. I had seen documentaries about such treatment. They were horrifying.

"Weeks. We will begin tomorrow, but first," he suggested, "you'll need sleep." He then gestured at the staff that had gathered around the bed when word spread about my unusual affliction. It seemed that everybody on staff wanted to get a firsthand look at what, until this day, had been an elusive disease. I was promptly supplied with a respirator device strapped to my face, and an IV needle inserted and taped to my wrist. The doctor bid, on his departure, "Have a good rest."

They were the last words I heard before blacking out. I went into a deep sleep that lasted for close to 24 hours. I opened my eyes to early sunrays warming my face. "What's this feeling?" I thought, rubbing my lower abdomen. It was pressure on my bladder I had not felt in six weeks. It then dawned on me. "I've got to go." Fully awake, I tried to get out of bed to head for the bathroom, but was restrained by tubes, and wires strapped to my body. "Nurse!"

Orderlies, busy with other patients rushed over to help me unplug. It felt great when taking my first steps with their help. My mind kept urging my legs forward, but they refused to function. I sank to the floor after the first step. "You need a pan," one said, helping me back to bed. "You can't walk yet." While I was laying there, relieved, I marveled, "I am feeling my body again. Could there be hope that someday I will walk again?" Six weeks had gone by since the last time I went to the bathroom. I remembered now how unceremoniously my intestines collapsed. It made sense now with the IV.

My doctor stepped in with a cheerful face. "How are we feeling today?"

"Weak but alive."

"Are you ready for some exercise?"

"It depends. I don't have much energy."

"Don't worry about it. We'll let machines do the work. Orderly," he called out, "I need a gurney here." I was transferred from the bed, and promptly wheeled to a room down below in the basement level. I had an ominous feeling something not so pleasant was about to happen. Nervous, but not scared, I submitted my body to whatever was about to transpire. Two attendants were busy attaching wires to my head, limbs, and torso, twelve in all, while the doctor was busy reading my charts. He must have obtained the medical records faxed over from the Manila hospital. Ten minutes later he said, "Are you ready?" I had no choice. I was securely strapped to the table by several leather belts. Not waiting for my answer, he went on, "Here is what I'm going to do. See the machine over there? It'll induce electric current into your body."

Having worked with computer electricity, and AC power for most of my adult life, I had been shocked a number of times with 110 volts. The shock effect was always greater than the potential damage unless one was caught up standing in water. I needed to know what to expect and asked, "How much?"

"400 volts."

He averted his eyes when I sputtered, "400 volts DC? It'll kill me."

"Sorry. You ready?" he alerted the attendants. Without a reply one pushed the prominent, red button. My limbs would have flown straight off the table if my body had not been tied down. With current surging though my body, from the neck down arms, and legs, and back up to the head, I felt like letting out a scream, but could not. Even if I could, screaming and crying were never part in my life. As a child while growing up, after I had gotten hurt, and was ready to cry from pain, my dad used to say, "Boys don't cry. Bear it."

For the following twenty minutes, the process of inducing current into my body repeated every thirty seconds. With each jolt my arms, and legs struggled against the restrains. What I felt was current burning each, and every nerve strand in my body, tearing at skin, flesh, and muscle tissue at an incinerating rate. Short of smoldering, I felt like I was burning up from the inside out. My jaws were so tightly clenched my entire head hurt. I could not focus my eyes. My mind was in disarray, waiting for the next command of "Go."

Though pure torture, it finally came to an end. I was exhausted. I felt close to death when I heard the doctor's words. "That's enough for today. You did well. I'll meet you in the gym." He had left the torture room. I had many questions, but could get not one answer from anybody. Each following day, I silently begged that it would be the end of the treatment. With probes, and wires removed, I was wheeled upstairs once more, but to the exercise room. On entering, I realized that it actually was a gym, fully stacked, but reduced in size, like those normally found in schools, and clubs. He was already waiting at one end of the parallel bars. This one extended to a length of at least twenty-five feet. I had arrived in a wheelchair placed at one end. My attendants pulled me upright, with the doctor directing, "I want you to walk to the other end."

"Well," I thought, as weak as I felt, "I can do it," Clutching the bar with both arms, my intentions were stronger than my muscles. It was a monumental effort to just keep my body upright. "Go," I heard the doctor, with attendants by my side, say, "keep going." Cringing, wincing, and huffing with my body feeling aching, and on fire, I managed to drag myself to the far end. It seemed to take forever. I had felt excruciating pain several times in my life, but this was different. I felt it throughout my entire body from head to toes. At the far end I collapsed into the wheelchair, ready to remain in it for the rest of my life.

At times we are quick to judge; at this moment, so was I. After being wheeled back to the recovery room I had ample time to think, and evaluate my future. I could have just as easily succumbed to remaining in the vegetated state I was presently in, perhaps medicated for the rest of my being to ease pain, but it would not have been me. With my brain beginning to function again I was able to contemplate every possible alternative.

I always thought, when it came to pain, that I was tolerant. Falls, and mishaps endured through childhood, causing cuts, bruises, and infections, were nothing new. As the saying goes, "Time heals all wounds." But time is a relative factor, as I should learn, solely depending on the effort I was able to endure pain. In short, what I had to endure for the next three months was excruciating pain, and stress, followed with five more years to complete recovery, driven by my sheer will to regain my body functions.

For the next two weeks every waking hour was a repeat from the previous day, much like the movie "Groundhog Day."

"Wake up," I was ordered. "Have to make up the bed."

"I can't. Too painful."

"Doctor's orders!"

"Well," I would contemplate, "if the doctor said so." Though reluctantly, I would comply, if not for my own benefit but for his wisdom. He seemed to be the only person in my feeble world who had answers. With the help of an orderly, I gradually made it to the bathroom. "What for?" I would ask. I had not eaten in many weeks. Besides, my stomach, and intestines were not functioning. There was no food to process.

"Wash your face." Since there was no tub or shower, I took soap, and water to my face as ordered.

"Here is something to eat."

"I'm not hungry." My body, other than IV liquid, was rejecting solid food still jammed in the esophagus. I had learned that the human body functioned much like the human brain. It sought the easy way out.

"So," my doctor enquired as he did each morning. "Have you eaten?"

"No."

"Here. Try this." He handed me a dish I knew well. It was a plate topped with my favorite fruits cut in small pieces: mango, papaya, and pineapple. To my surprise, my throat and stomach accepted it.

"Good. You need your strength. We need to build up your body." As busy as he may have been as a neuro-surgeon, at the time the only one in the Philippines,[39] he took his demanding time to watch my progress. In a way, as he would prove in the following weeks, I was his guinea pig. The daily routine was his challenge. He recorded every step of my progress.

Twenty minutes of shock treatment that I absolutely abhorred. No matter how much I begged, he would insist on it, and not back down.

Strapped between parallel bars, dragging my body across the length, and back, more frequently each day as I improved.

Walking exercise up and down the hallways.

Force-feed myself three times a day while listening to groaning, and moaning from half a dozen other patients in the room. At the time of my submission, the Vietnam war was at its height, about to be lost, with fierce fighting ending in many casualties. I should mention that the primary function for Clark Airbase was supporting the war, specifically with casualties injured in the field flooding the hospital in the weeks and months ahead. One such day, a paratrooper was delivered whose parachute had only partially opened on landing, resulting in internal injuries. In a coma when he was submitted, two days later he finally gained consciousness, to everybody's demise. Let me explain.

I don't recall his general affliction, but he suffered from persistent hiccups. Every few seconds, with each hiccup, his body would bounce up, and collapse back down shaking up the bed with every mattress spring squeaking, and squealing. It was so annoying, nobody in the room was able to sleep. On the third day I remembered something from the past, and suggested it to the attending nurse, "Why don't you put a paper bag over his face?"

She looked at me, dumbfounded, stating, "We don't want to kill him."

I took a few minutes to explain to her what I had learned as a kid about "oxygen shock effects." Without consulting anyone else she took my suggestion and, sure

---

[39] On the day I was delivered to Clark Hospital, he had been on an emergency call to Manila. It so happened that the president's son was involved in a vehicle accident that rendered him unconscious, and in a coma. It was my doctor treating the son, with daily trips to the Marcos' residence after my treatments.

enough, after just a minute of breathing air from the bag he was hiccup free. As a result, I was treated as a hero by my fellow bed mates, promptly falling asleep.

Thus, one week after the next went by with my physical strength gradually improving. Though tedious, and painful, I could slowly feel my body gaining its balancing functions back. Where I could only crawl weeks ago, now I was able to hobble around on my own on crutches. Three weeks into the routine, my hero came in one morning, and instructed me to get dressed. "What? I'm being released?" I did not know whether to laugh or cry. That's how happy I was.

"Not just yet," he said, then left with, "I'll be back in an hour. Be ready."

He came back at the stated time with an attendant pushing a wheelchair, and ordered, "Ready? Let's go." I was promptly taken down to the ground floor, arriving by the entrance hall with a sign proclaiming, "Auditorium."

Comfortably leaning back, I thought I was going to be treated to a play or perhaps a movie. Instead, I wound up on the middle of the podium, exclaiming, "What?"

"You'll see. Just follow my instructions." Curious, and amazed, while I watched, the seats down below began to fill up with doctors, and specialists dressed in white coats as well as formal suits. Left alone on stage I felt deserted, but curious, nevertheless, when the inquisitions began. It would prove to be a weekly repeat ending in the same results. What transpired was this. My doctor would ask the attending physicians, invited from other hospitals, and clinics in the Philippines, to "Take a look at the patient, and give me your diagnosis based on his appearance, and behavior."

The silence was interrupted by nervous coughs, and shuffling of feet while hands were raised, followed by educated suggestions. I missed most of the clinical terms, but quickly learned his reasoning for the quest. After the initial session he sat by my bed to explain.

"As I told you already," he began, "I consider myself a lucky person for being here to take care of you." What else could I do other than extend him a thankful smile.

"When you were submitted into my hands, I took one look at your face, and knew the answer, Guillain-Barre. You had the classic symptoms for the disease." He paused, and corrected, "I can't call it a disease because we don't know anything about it. It is a syndrome detected by two French physicists, hence the name, only occurring at about three cases annually, worldwide. The fatality rate is close to ninety percent because most times the symptoms are not recognized. Without any research conducted, because of its rarity, and lack of funding, we know absolutely nothing."

"What about my condition? How long will it last?" I was keenly aware of it every time I looked in the mirror. First off, I did not look like myself. Even my friends had quit visiting. To them, I must have appeared like a lost case. Since my brain tissue, and nerve system were attacked by a bacteria and eaten away, none of my muscle tissue was in working order, resulting in a severely distorted face. As if this was not enough, all my body muscles had waned into atrophy. I weighed 85 pounds with nothing but skin stretched over bone. Worse yet, I had lost all of my body hair from top to bottom from the lack of minerals, and nourishment. I did not recognize myself anymore. If this was not my inspiration to rebuild my body, the accompanied pain from tissue rubbing against bone was an instinctive drive to get better.

"It's entirely up to you, but I should warn you," he said. "Nobody has ever regained full body function." It was a most discouraging statement. In the years to follow, it became the most important factor in my daily routine, reminding myself, "You can do it."

In recollection, it took greater than five years to fully recover, and rebuild my body to its full capacity as it was before I had taken ill. Only I know how much effort and pain it took. Losing every muscle in my body, followed with rebuilding through extreme exercise, felt like I was on fire. From morning to night every strain of muscle was tearing at my body. It would make each muscle strain physically jump and quiver after a stretch of exercise. I could also feel strength surging through my veins with each protein shake I took in. Liquids, at the time, aside from fruits, were about the only substances my stomach would readily digest. But, over time, every one of my internal organs began to function again. I felt stronger with each month, especially when I began jogging, followed with running.

Buzz visited often. A lifetime companion, he was by my side providing inspiration, and updates whenever he could. Without TV or radio in the room I was dead to the world. Global events went on without my services. As far as he was concerned, as was the case with everybody else paying me a hospital visit, it was only a matter of time to see my end. To them, just by my physical appearance, what my friends told me later, I was declared "dying."

RECOVERY

Two years had passed since I arrived in the Philippines. Word had reached headquarters about my affliction, and I was granted leave until I was fully recovered. When I was finally released from Clark Hospital, my two-year contract obligation had also come to an end. Buzz, including the team, were preparing to leave the country. "Hey," Buzz said as soon as he stepped in. I was staying at the Hilton again since I had lost the apartment.

"Hey," I returned his salute. "Heard you were packing up. That true?"

"Yep. Leaving tomorrow."

"Where're you headed?"

"Got assigned in California."

"Where?"

"Palo Alto."

"Never heard of it. What's there?" The world had not stood still while I was laid up at the hospital.

"Headquarters packed up, and moved to the West Coast, lock, stock, and barrel."

"Really! Everybody?"

"The entire division, as far as I know."

"Give my regards to Art. Tell him about my condition. I haven't talked to him in years. Tell him I'll be back soon."

"What about your business? I thought you were going to stay here."

"Not anymore. Lost most of it to Marcos, and his gang of gangsters." That's what the public called him. He had taken his dictatorship too far for the likings of the people. They were ready to oust him at the first opportunity. Demonstrations has escalated to new heights with many members of the military joining in for the protection of their families.

"Look me up when you get back," he said with a departing handshake. There was nothing more to be said. Since both of us have never liked small talk we never lingered on sentiments.

"I promise."

The site, as specified by contract, had terminated, and been turned over to Air Force management, staffed with military support from within units. Out of work, and short on funds I turned to my Manila business partners. While I was hospitalized, certain events had taken place in the local economy. What had transpired was even beyond my associates' control. Marcos had taken over the business world and annexed all successful operations, resulting in us losing forty percent of all of our businesses. Though my partner's wife was friends with Imelda, Marcos' wife, it proved to be no exception. What followed was a mass exodus with Filipino businessmen looking for a better future elsewhere, primarily in Australia, New Zealand, and Canada. My partners had left the country as well. I was caught up in the process, not only losing my investments but company stocks as well. With them gone I had no income. Still recovering, I was not fit to travel or take on a new project. Fortunately, through a mutual acquaintance, I met someone. It was not difficult to meet other Americans in the Philippines. One only had to lounge at one of the international hotel lobbies to make connections. An American entrepreneur, presently managing a logging operation in the jungles of Butuan, in the northern part of Mindanao, had just returned from the field for a weekend home.

Learning of my dilemma, being without a job, broke, and having no place to stay, he readily accommodated me. "Why don't you stay at my place? This way, you can keep an eye on the place while I'm gone." Filipino apartment management had a habit of double renting a place to short-timers while the occupant was out of town. I was grateful for such unusual hospitality. He went further yet, and offered me a job as soon as I was back on my feet again. I readily accepted. We spent the weekend with me getting updated on world events, and him being informed of my purpose in the country. He left, and would not return for another month. The place during his absence was mine. Spacious, modern, and cleaned by a daily custodian service, I felt like a million bucks. Life was beginning to make sense once more. Taking my time, I started to go out, met new people, and socialized in the evenings, making connections with business friends who had remained in the country in spite of losing their businesses to Marcos' henchmen.

One such day there was a knocking at the apartment door. Curious, I opened it to a young, and friendly face. Somewhat hesitant, she said, "Remember me?"

"No." Trying to recall the face, I could not make the connection, and said, "But do come in."

"Annette," she said with an outstretched hand. I was curious, but had also lost much of my memory. My sickness had affected not only every part of my body, but my organs as well. The only organ that had remained functional, though barely, was my heart. Doctors had to probe for a usable vein when taking my blood pressure. In the years to come I had to learn, and relearn much of the technical aspects I had acquired in my career.

"Who are you?"

"Don't you remember Cebu? I am one of the sisters you met. I am grown up now."

"Ah yes," I recalled, distended memory coming back about her family. "You have really grown up. Whatever happened to all of you?"

"What do you mean?"

"The beach outing?"

"Oh that. We were ready the next morning but Mom told us not to go. You had left the next day. We all missed you. You were so much fun talking with me, and my brothers. They all wished they had your job, travelling the world, and all."

"Well, yes. I lucked out."

"What happened to you?"

"You want to come in?" I offered.

"Yes. Thank you."

"Can I get you something?"

"Water, perhaps?"

"I've got soft drinks too."

"Coca Cola?" I knew from my visits that it was the preferred drink, a special treat.

"Coming right up. I'm on leave," I explained. "I was sick for the last two years." I then told her of my ordeal, and trying to get back to a normal life. "And here you are. How did you find me?"

"It was not difficult. Most foreigners stay at the American Apartment. It's the most modern place in the city. I remembered your name, and called."

"What brings you here?"

"I just started my internship at a local hospital, and thought to say hello."

"Such a surprise. I'm glad you did. How's the rest of the family?"

"Dad is at high seas, my older brother just finished pilot training with Philippine Airlines, and my older sister just started work as stewardess with the same airline." Hearing reports of family successes spurred an interest in me.

"What's your dad doing?"

"First mate. He works for Everett Shipping lines. Travels around the world."

"Sounds like your family is doing well."

"Not always," she explained. "Dad didn't get paid much working for local freight ships but held up his promise to Mom when they got married by sending all of his children to college."

"I admire such commitment. How many are there?"

"Ten in all."

"Wow." I could not suppress my surprise. "Tell me about them."

"Six boys, and four girls, ranging from twelve to twenty-five."

"Your mom is a commendable woman for having these many births. How is she?" I clearly recalled her warning, *don't go to the beach.*

"She told me to say hi."

"Tell me," I said. "Did she ever explain why we couldn't go to the beach that day?"

"No. But she is psychic. She had a vision about you."

"I wish I could talk to her someday."

"You can always come, and visit us, but for now," she said, "I am living here in the city."

There was another knock at the door. I opened it to face a tall, young, well-groomed Filipino asking, "Is my sister here?"

"She is. Come on in."

I watched him curiously inspecting the apartment. "Nice place. You ready to go," he urged his sister to leave. He had just come from applying with the airlines, and was ready to head home, back to Cebu Island.

"It was nice to see you well," she said on the way out.

"You are welcome any time," I offered with sincerity.

"You wish," her brother replied in an unfriendly tone. As was the case with brothers in the Filipino culture, he was overly protective of his sisters. Most girls, when out, were chaperoned by their brothers. He eyed me with suspicion, and promptly left the building while she shot a quick smile back at me. "What a pretty girl she turned out," I though, watching both headed for the elevator.

In the following months, Richard, the owner of the apartment, came back for another weekend. We went out together. He introduced me to some of the hostesses at the most popular nightclubs in metropolitan Manila. There were many. Some classy, other not so much which I learned to stay away from. Chatting with a girl at the club was not mandatory, but expected. It was part of the free services offered, with many hoping to meet someone nice for companionship.

The following day he said, "You ready to go to work?"

I was startled at the offer but readily accepted. I had grown bored sitting home alone most nights. Besides, I felt much stronger, ready to tackle anything. "Where're we going?"

"Mindanao." He then explained his function at the southernmost island. Already for several months he had been in the jungles of northern Mindanao collecting data and information on lumber logging. His plan was to computerize the operation for taking orders, accounting, processing, delivery, inventory, and salary. What he lacked was a computer software specialist with my skills to put it all together automating the process. He was pleased when I accepted. I had a job but it did not last long.

Weeks later we lost the project, "Due to economic conditions," we were told. Most corporations either were forced to scale back on expenditures, or closed their business to protect themselves from being further subjected to Marcos' greed. As was the case with many dictators, not only had Marcos acquired much of the nation's wealth, he had begun starving the people into submission to eradicate the middle class. He was not satisfied with taking only forty percent of the country's businesses; he was looking to enrich his family through aid from world nations, mostly the U.S., taking advantage from nations apt to support starving countries. It was what greed did to a country.

I was jobless again. One evening, there was a slight knocking at the apartment door. On opening, it was Annette. "Hi," I said, slightly surprised, and gestured for her to enter. "What brings you back? Everything all right?"

"I wanted to see you."

"No big brother," I said, craning down the hallway.

She understood too well. "I'm alone."

"How have you been?" I said. "Make yourself comfortable." We spent the next several hours in pleasant, uninterrupted conversation while Richard bunked on his yacht, anchored in the nearby bay. He was preparing to head to sea again after taking an offer from an oil exploration company as an "emergency standby" vessel somewhere in the South China Sea. Before he left, he begged me to take over the lease on the apartment. Though unemployed at the time, I readily agreed in anticipation of landing a job sometime soon. "Where are you staying?"

"At the hospital dorm," she said. It turned out that the hospital she interned at was located in Quezon City, about ten miles distance away. It was getting late in the evening, and I was expecting her to depart soon. I did not anticipate what she said next. "Can I stay the night?"

I was taken by surprise. I viewed her as a young girl just entered adolescence. My being in my mid-thirties, I hesitated. "You sure?"

"I don't like it in the dorm. There are too many people crammed in one room." I had heard how crowded places of lodging could be in the local economy. I understood, and offered, "Of course you can stay. How are you going to work?"

"By bus. It's only an hour."

"Ten miles taking one hour? There's something wrong here," I said, calculating. I also knew that Manila was too crowded: too many vehicles, not enough streets, growing poverty with people subjected to air so polluted you could cut it with a knife. I considered myself fortunate to have an apartment by the sea. All I had to do was open the balcony door and windows to feel the refreshing ocean breeze. "You sure your family won't mind?" I recalled the protective nature her brother had displayed.

"They don't have to know. Besides," she explained, "my sister flies out of Manila. She'll check in on me." Her sister, I would learn, was more receptive to a foreigner. She was dating an American herself who I would soon meet, and become friends with.

Although she did not move in, she spent many nights, and weekends at my place. Some mornings she was late, and I would drive her to work. I learned that it would take close to two hours to go the relatively short distance. Most days traffic was gridlocked during rush hours. Besides, not having an income, I was dependent on my dwindling savings. Regardless of my financial status, I terminated the current lease and took an apartment near Annette's workplace. It worked out for the better. Richard, I learned, retained the job south for several years and was grateful not to be burdened with the upkeep of the apartment expense.

Still recovering, with her support, I would spend many hours in the pool, the place I felt most comfortable, while Annette had only a short walk to work. Soon after, I started jogging again. With her taking care of me, her being a clinical nutritionist, my health improved rapidly. We were both content with our living arrangement, enjoying a happy relationship. She flourished into a woman while I was on the way to full recovery.

The year was 1977. Annette was getting close to finishing up her internship. On several occasions I had expressed my desire to return to the U.S. Having lost all my investments in the Philippines, with partners relocated overseas, Marcos in power for God knows how long, she understood. One day, on a weekend morning, she sidled up to me with, "We need to talk." It was something I had expected for some time. I had sensed her desire to accompany me to the States on more than one occasion by her remarks. Much like my dreams at her age, it was many Filipinos' desire to come to the States. She was no exception. As I would learn later on, her family was backing her one hundred percent.

"What is it?"

"I want to come with you."

"What about your career? The internship? Your family?"

"I thought about it all. Don't worry. I'll finish up soon."

"Are you sure?"

"Nothing could stop me. You know I love you."

"I know," I said. I was a coldhearted individual. I had just never fallen in love. It was my protection against compromising my career. She sensed my reluctance in committing to marriage. I did not know at the moment how to approach the subject. Buzz, much like myself, never discussed our jobs or activities. We strictly obeyed our sworn secrecy. Disclosing national security would never be compromised. Everybody on the program—there were thousands over the thirty-year period—submitted to DOD policies, and rules. It was unthinkable to place the system, people, and country I cherished so much in jeopardy, aside from losing my security clearance. It had been my ticket to freedom, and success.

"I need to think about it," I said, watching tears trickling down her cheeks. She seemed heartbroken. "Let me tell you what I will do," I said, renewing her hope. "I will get you to the States. It may take some doing, but it's a promise from the bottom of my heart." It seemed to calm her. I could read it in her expression that there was hope.

Over the following weeks, the promise I had made weighed heavy on my mind. Since I had lost two years to a business venture that never materialized into success, I was forced to return to a career I knew best, one I could not compromise. My career would be on the line. How could I compromise my future? I weighed my job against marriage. "I'll find another way," I decided, yielded to the promise. My first stop the following morning was to the American embassy.

"Your passport please," the Embassy employee requested when I approached the desk. I had already passed inspection by the smartly dressed Marines by the entrance. "What can I help you with?"

"I want to return to the States," I said. "What do I need?"

"How long have you been in-country?"

"Three years."

"That may present a problem."

"How so?"

"You are here on a business visa. I can't help you."

"What do you mean you can't help?"

"You need an exit visa issued by Philippine authorities."

This came as a complete surprise. "Can I talk with somebody else?"

"Maybe the ambassador might have a suggestion." She dialed an in-house number. Within minutes I was led to his office.

Friendly, and accommodating, he tried to help my situation. "Here is the problem. You came here on a U.S. government contract. You applied for a business visa. You were in business for several years. You need an exit visa only the Philippine Embassy can issue. Here is the address."

The place was my next stop for the day. As soon as I stepped through the entrance, I could see a difference in atmosphere. Where the U.S. kept their environment, and official offices clean, and organized, the place here seemed chaotic. People rushed in and out, passing several desks occupied by women dressed in casuals; uniforms must be a luxury item the government avoided. Local citizens arrived continuously asking for help. It was apparent that the place was overloaded with applicants wanting visa extensions or exit visas to numerous countries. First on the preferred list was the U.S. followed by Canada, Australia, and Europe. Contemplating my dilemma in the confusing environment I was approached by a runner (assistant).

After explaining my reasons for being here, it was his job to direct me through the maze. "But first," he demanded, "I need twenty pesos." I willingly handed him the note. I expected to be led to the proper office, but he demanded more. "I need twenty pesos for every office stamp, symbol, and signature."

I had heard about payoffs demanded at every government office, but did not expect this. I was wondering if I had enough money in my pocket. "How much?"

"This building has four floors. You will be required to stop at each floor."

"So, eighty pesos will do it?"

"If you want anything done, you must hire me as your guide. Two hundred pesos." I realized why the disorder, and confusion. No visitor could find their way around this place without a guide.

"Okay," I agreed. "Here," and off we were to the first office. I had to explain my problem at each floor we visited to get a rubber stamp slammed on the passport page to finally get to the head of the embassy for his signature. It took four hours before I was able to face the top man. Slouched into a posh chair, he invited me, "Have a seat." My guide courteously waited by the entrance. Apparently, he was not allowed in the office. I handed over my passport, politely requesting his signature.

Looking over my passport, he took his time before he spoke. "This is worthless," he said while leafing through the pages.

"What do you mean?" I said, expecting the worst. "My guide here took me to every office for the required stamps." I watched while the ambassador assessed me. I could almost hear the 'Cha Ching' turning wheels in his brain. The whole system was built on payoffs.

"First I have to see an NBI[40] report. Then you need a local police clearance from your residing district. Next, you'll have to deposit thirty thousand U.S. dollars in the national bank."

"What?" I yelled at him. He must have been used to the response because he did not blink an eye.

"To guarantee your employees get paid for one year."

"That's outrageous! I don't have the money." It would have been useless to explain to him why not.

"It's the law. Get a lawyer," he suggested on my way out. I was outraged at such demands. As he had suggested, I solicited legal advice. Just as the ambassador he explained, every step was necessary. I was also told that it was Marcos' doing to assure his share of the immigration proceeds.

It took one month to get all the documents prepared, and signed but, I did not have the required bank deposit. "What are you going to do?" Annette said, when I explained my dilemma.

"I'll find a way. I promise," I reassured her once more.

"I hope so. I don't want to stay here either." We were aware of the country's chaotic conditions. Not only was the economy permeated with corruption and disorder, for Marcos to assure his reign in the police state, he created more chaos in the south. He had sent troops there to fight so called Muslim infiltrators on his land, secretly instigated by him, and executed by his military. It was a tactic that had been used by other leaders in the past.

"I want you to come along tomorrow."

"Where're we going?"

"To see the U.S. ambassador. I'll explain the situation. I am sure he can help."

As planned, we headed out early. On arriving at the embassy, I asked to see him. As before, we were ushered into his office.

"It seems so organized here. Is it like this in the States?"

---

[40] NBI – National Bureau of Investigation. The U.S. equivalent of the FBI.

"Most places," I assured her.

"I hope we get lucky. I can't wait to get there," Annette said in wonder.

"Have a seat," the ambassador offered on entering his domain. "What seems to be the problem?"

I explained the run-around I had gotten for the past month, complying to all the official requirements. Annette listened attentively, getting more discouraged by the minute. I had asked her along just in case. I wanted her to hear the outcome first hand.

"There is nothing we can do here," was his eventual conclusion. Annette was in tears. I could not blame her. All hope had dissipated into emptiness. What could I say but, "So sorry." We left the grounds. On the way to the gate I remembered something. "Come." I gestured for her to follow. As I had done each month, I stopped by the CIA headquarters to collect my mail.

"Is he in?" I asked the office administrator.

"You want to see him?"

"Yes. Just want to say goodbye. I'm leaving the country." I did not want to skip out without informing him of my pending departure.

"Come on in, Alex." He gestured with a gracious smile. "And who is this young lady?"

"My friend. Listen," I said, "I'm getting ready to leave the country. There is no future here for me."

"I know. I know," he said. "You lost your business."

"Not only one but several ventures." It then occurred to me to ask for his help. He listened attentively to my ordeal in trying to get an exit visa. "I don't think I can ever get the visa." I did not have to ask.

"I can help. I know the ambassador well." A glimmer of hope began to emerge.

We sat quietly for some time before he finally spoke. "This is what I can do for you. Let me have the passport." He promptly stamped the page, put his signature next to it, and wrote a short personal note to the Philippine ambassador, declaring, "Alex Bauer is reassigned and is leaving the country. Please expedite his departure." He had boldly declared my affiliation with the CIA in a way I had never expected. *It's not only the Philippines where anything can get done with the right connections,* I thought.

"Wow," I stammered, thanking him profusely.

"I'll make arrangements for your transportation. Be at the airport at 1:00 p.m." We parted, shaking hands, with him bidding, "Keep in touch. Look me up in case you change your mind." Over the years we had become friends. I would miss his, and his wife's company a lot.

"What about me?" Annette said. In one way she was happy for me; in another, she was terrified that my promise had not come through.

"I'll leave tomorrow, but as I already promised, I will find a way." It was the last I would see of her. With tears in her eyes she went back to the dorm, expecting not to hear from me. My heart was also filled with sadness. She had brought so much joy to my life. Aside from taking care of me she had stood by my side through all my misery.

As planned, I showed up at the airport on time. Checking the airline schedule for arriving flights, I was gravely disillusioned. There were no flights. The schedule board listed arrivals, and departures only for mornings, and evenings. With suitcase in hand, I was undecided as to what steps to take next. There were no phones in the departure launch to call the ambassador, and cell phones had not yet been invented. I sat down in the launch, and ordered a drink. My situation had turned hopeless. I had to do some thinking. I had lost my businesses, given up the apartment, sold my car, had my visa canceled and, worse, I was short on money. Years before I could ask a number of friends for help. But now they all had left the country. For the first time in my life I had no plan. With such thoughts on my mind I suddenly heard my name on the intercom. "Alex Bauer, report to gate five."

With an overstuffed suitcase in hand, I rushed to the gate where an attendant anxiously waited to check me in. I had noticed something else reflecting through the windows, a B-747 passenger liner with whining engines sitting on the tarmac signified KLM. I was rushed up the mobile ramp, and met by the copilot. "Hurry up. We can't stay. Want to sit in the cockpit?" he offered.

I was dumbfounded but readily accepted. There were no other passengers leaving or loading.

"I got the call on the way to the States from the local CIA office to pick you up," he said. "Where're you headed?"

"San Francisco."

"You'll have to take a shuttle. This flight goes to L.A."

"No problem." I laughed, happy to have made it out of the Philippines, greatly enjoying watching the cockpit crew at work. I was safe, looking forward to an organized life. It would not be the only flight to take me on as an emergency passenger. There had been some in the past, and there would be more to come. It was part of my job to be prepared on a minute's notice. My immediate destination was to get my job back.

"Damn." Listening to the soothing drone of jet engines, it suddenly hit me. "Could the prophesies be true? Are they for real? What about spiritual realm?" I questioned. The answers, I figured, could be hidden in ancient scriptures. No matter how hard I'd tried pushing thoughts like this from my mind, they kept returning almost daily.

"I've got some reading to do." Where in the past, if I had the time, I was absorbed by reading technical documents, that would change soon.

BACK IN THE STATES

"Hey! Look who's here," a familiar sounding voice shouted from the far-end cubicle on my entering. I had stepped into the office unannounced. Heads popped up over space dividers, quickly followed with hugs, and handshakes. "Man," Art, my boss, headed my way with his face set in a broad grin. "It's good to see you. I thought we'd lost you."

"It was touch, and go for a while," I replied. "I guess Buzz kept you informed? By the way, where is he?" Art turned to gesture at the entrance, with Buzz headed in our direction.

"Speaking of the devil, there he is." I had spotted him as well.

"I'm really glad you could make it," Art said. "We need you. Step in here," Art said, addressing us. "Both of you. We need to talk." As usual, he was chewing one end of a cigar. It was his signature of authority, and prestige. A sore point for me, and the environment, I had tried for him to stop his habit a number of times to his response: "My wife tried. Why do you think you could?" Years before, when smoking was still accepted by society, he would stop by the lab, dump cigar ashes into whatever vial was within his reach. I always had to clean up after him. It was his way of exercising authority, I figured. It was his only flaw that I knew of. Otherwise, he was the best manager anyone could wish for.

Once seated in his office, he began, "Okay, here's the deal." He then explained the reasons, which I already suspected, for the company's move west. The sole purpose was to get away from entrenched teamster unions prevalent on the east coast. One could ask any free-thinking individual what they thought of the union. In response, personal opinions were usually suppressed, accompanied by clenching of jaws, and gnashing of teeth. The reasons for uncommitted opinions were ever-present union members reporting any insubordination. One would be fired no matter what skills, and expertise would be lost. What made matters worse was that the unionized constraints severely impacted regional economies. Only union members received a fair share through boosted salaries.

"No unions?" I could not, and would not subject myself to further insults of being restrained every step taken while doing a job. Neither would anybody else in the department anymore. "How many came with you?"

"Most of the division," I was informed. "First off," he said. "I'm glad you're back on the team, glad to see you healthy. Here are your assignments." From what he indicated, not much had been accomplished other than the relocation process. I had not missed much. "Our task is creating Net Two."

"What does it entail?" I asked.

"Moving from mainframes to supercomputers."

"Wow," I exclaimed. "About time."

"It's your team's job to test, and develop it. It's my job to see that it gets done, but you'll have several managers to deal with."

"What? You now I don't work well following the chain-of-command."

"I know too well," he said, underscored by a grin. "I've had my share of complaints about it."

"Why the change?"

"Too many managers, not enough projects." It turned out that each department had an assigned manager, in addition having to deal with the vendor supplying supercomputers.

"So," I said. "What's the deal?"

"You two will report only to me." I was glad to hear the reprieve. It assured my place as well as him maintaining control. I suspected that he had a number of managers competing for his director position. My assumption proved to be correct sometime later.

Well, with job, and responsibility laid out, we went to work. Short of designing new computer systems, the company had solicited technologies developed at MIT. All we had to do was put the systems together, and make them work in accordance with government specs. From a technical perspective, things went well. From an economic one, the move to California proved to be a major mistake. The division move to the "Western Development Labs" could not catch up to the local economy. Our east coast inherited pay scale was way below that of compatible earnings in Silicon Valley, the Lab's location. We could not afford prevalent living conditions. Cost of local living had grown out of proportion with the technology boom in the Valley.

Division management was already looking for new working ground at other geological locations across the States. But it would take four more years to materialize relocating. In the meantime, life at the Lab was extremely busy with technical challenges while our personal activities were just as demanding. Us singles would get together on weekends for social events, and private parties. One had a great selection of restaurants, bars, and clubs up and down the peninsula. I spent a great deal of time getting to know the city of San Francisco, regardless of the hour's driving time across the Dumbarton or Oakland Bridge.

Though thrilled by the city display, I felt that there was something missing. I could not share my excitement with anyone. Seeking a quiet spot by the docks, my thoughts would touch on Annette every so often. I felt lonelier the more I thought of her. In addition. promises I had made were gnawing at my conscious. I had to do something about bringing her into the country. I sent her a brief letter. In it, I asked, "You still want to come here?"

Within days, to my joy, I received her response. "How soon can you get me there?"

It was the assurance I needed to initiate the process at the immigration department. Making several visits to San Francisco, I eventually obtained her entry clearance. Fortunately, I was presently not on an assigned government project. It would have hindered my sponsoring a foreigner. I voluntarily kept proper Intel, and investigative agencies informed of my personal choice and, in response, received their blessings without possible future implications. Regardless of strictly enforced security policies, as long as your intentions were honorable, the agency would sanction certain conduct, if submitted up front. It was the denial of an act that would jeopardize a top-secret clearance.

The day of Annette's arrival was a joy for the both of us. I watched her briskly striding through the arrival gate at the airport, searching for a familiar face. The second she spotted me, her face immediately lit up much like switching on a chandelier. She had arrived in the new world, a world filled with possibilities, like I had felt years earlier.

I should mention, prior to her departing the Philippines, though I had tried to get her an entry visa for permanent residency, it'd turned out to be impossible. The only way possible was through marriage. When I relayed the requirement to her, she was only too willing to comply. With me making the necessary arrangements on this end, Annette, and her mom complied with preparations at hers. As a temporary measure we were married, at large, by the respective embassies, her passport to the States.

Once we settled in an apartment in the nearby town, Mountain View, with my support she could relax and make eventual plans for a successful future. Within weeks she landed her first job, and appeared blessed, and thankful. Over the next several years I was taking on several field assignments within the DOD, sometimes accompanied by her while preparing for a future family environment. She blessed me with three beautiful daughters, who, in time, would provide a meaningful future for my otherwise wasted personal life, but successful career. It was much later that I remembered the predictions revealed years earlier. All had come true as prophesized.

Resuming government contracting opportunities, I traveled many more times overseas. The next times I visited Korea, I would make attempts to locate the fortune teller. But my searches proved unsuccessful. When finally connecting with a former friend I was told that she had quit giving prophecies at age forty-four. I wanted so much to receive her wisdom for the remainder of my life. Although there was one revealing element, I wished I had not received. The last question, expecting an evasive answer, I had asked her, "How long will I live?" She was honest to the core.

My Korean interpreter relayed my terminal point. At the time, young, and full of vigor, it did not bother me but, over time, I became keenly aware of the prophesized end to my life. She proved to be correct about my age with one exception: I survived the prophecy, but not without multiple physical, and psychological issues I was forced to overcome, which I will illustrate in later chapters.

For now, I had many more years filled with personal, and professional challenges, some humorous, and remembered, others with sobering effects impacting my life, as well as people dear to me, resulting in problematic events I try not to remember.

For now, I am burdened with the knowledge. I should warn, or rather, advise the reader: if you ever get your future read don't make the same mistake I did. Don't ask for how long you will live. It will be a burden you carry with you for the rest of your life. Be happy just to be alive.

Imagine you did not exist to begin with.

It's impossible. It's like trying to figure out who, and how the universe was created. We don't have enough knowledge and insight into the workings of creation. We must accept this miracle as much as accepting the possibility of there being a spiritual realm. Though I am a skeptic, and was a nonbeliever in the spiritual, after experiencing certain unexplained events, I have given in to the possibility of there being a God or creation by intelligent design. Whereas one is spiritual, the other is mathematical based by design. Millenia from now, if mankind still exists, we may have a better understanding.

FOUR YEARS LATER

The year was 1980. I was not surprised when the company announced, "Prepare for the move to Colorado."

"What do you think?" Buzz said, probing for my decision. "Are you going?"

"I'll let you know later." I was married, and wanted my wife's opinion because we had sponsored her parents, and some of her brothers, and sisters to immigrate to the U.S.

"I am moving. I hope you will come along," he brusquely announced. He had been married just the same and realized that we were barely making a living out here. Paying our earnings for apartment rent, or cheap housing, at the end of the month there was only money left for food.

When I discussed the impending move with Annette, she agreed. "My parents can follow us to Colorado." We had received a notice from the Philippines immigration department that their application was approved, but could take up to five years to process. In contrast to her siblings, it was dependent on a twelve-year waiting list.

"We are moving too," I informed Buzz the following day.

"It'll make my wife happy," he said. Our wives had become friends along the way. Six weeks later, corporate presented each employee with a one-week travel ticket to Colorado Springs, our future home. Within the allocated time, everybody took the invitation to spend a week house hunting at the proposed destination with the executives taking first choice. Advanced contact notifications brought on a myriad of real estate brokers, and agents only too happy to accommodate us. Temporarily set up at the Four Seasons hotel, at the south end of town, at the end of the week, I still had not closed a contract. Annette, as well as our agent, were beginning to get frustrated. Though we looked at a number of homes, daily, up and down the I-25 corridor, there was nothing that caught my eye. As we prepared to return to California the next morning the agent suggested one more look at his computer listing at the office. "Maybe something came up today."

On the brink of giving up, he eagerly announced, "A new listing just got posted. Want to check it out?"

Ten minutes later we arrived at a home-owners, managed settlement. Driving up the yet unlisted home, my agent did not have to make the slightest attempt to close the sale. "This is it. I'll buy it if we can afford the payments," I excitedly proclaimed.

"You can afford it," he said, erasing my concerns. He had seen the listing price in the computer. It was listed within my income range. We lucked out. The owners were home for us to inspect the place. Everything fell in order just like the place was meant for us. Thirty minutes later, we closed the deal as proud owners of what I would term, "Our Castle." It was a remarkable place. Built in Swiss-style chalet architecture, four-bedroom, two-level, it was spacious with large, embedded windows, and balconies all around. One neighbor to either side, with an unobstructed common property view extending into the valley. I could not wait to move in. Three weeks later we took possession, and invited our friends to the housewarming party. There would be many more parties in the years to come with us proudly hosting our guests from behind a sunken wet-bar, stacked with every kind of beverages from champagne, to liquors, brandy, Scotch, and imported wines, and beers. They proved to be our happiest years.

At our newly occupied Ford Aerospace HQs in Colorado Springs, corporate mergers, and acquisitions were not immune to our operations. Before long, we were taken over by Loral Command, and Control, followed by brief associations with Western Development Labs, White Trucking, Goodyear with an eventually merger with Lockheed Martin. The main thrust of the company's operations was directed at NORAD, the Mountain, with its space asset control, operations, and management.

Taking possession of two newly-constructed buildings, one reserved for headquarters' executive management, and the other for operational support, and computer system, testbed function to maintain our extended AUTODIN design, development, implementation, and support functions.

Buzz, as usual, took on the responsibility to build out testbeds, and keep computer systems in functional order. He took great pride in providing his skills, and expertise for all sectors of operations, maintenance, and support while I was assigned field support overseas directed by the DOD. I knew that my, at times, lengthy assignments would create a problem for my family of two daughters, with another one on its way. But, as was the case with all of my assignments taking me away from wife, and children, we always seemed to manage. All of our precious daughters grew up into responsible adults.

JAPAN

1983, my team had been waiting months for the next overseas assignment to Japan, taking on short projects at the Mountain, and other local auxiliary locations in the meantime. Directed by headquarters to get an advance team of six together with twelve more members to follow some six weeks later, the project called for a two-year assignment. When the greatly anticipated day finally arrived, we boarded a flight in late November, two weeks before the holidays, destined for Tokyo. The route took us to Denver for a change of plane, then on to Anchorage for a refueling stop with a one-hour layover. I called Annette, who had left weeks before for San Jose, CA, where she settled into an apartment awaiting her parents' arrival. I called her from Anchorage to say my final goodbyes when she commanded, "You don't leave until you select a name for our daughter," whom we expected to be born four weeks later. "You promised."

I had forgotten about it. To uphold the promise, I stalled with, "I'll call you back." Pressured, and short on time, I paced the airport halls while running names for girls through my head. I had trouble coming up with anything suitable when it suddenly hit me. "That's it." I made the call. "Guess what? I think you'll like it." I relayed the first, and middle names to Annette. She was happy, but in tears because of my lengthy departure. Taking care of her parent's needs, who had arrived, she promised to join me after the current schoolyear finished in May, which she did.

Unfortunately, our marriage did not last all that long. Though we were married in 1977 by the Philippine embassy, with a church ceremony that followed a couple of years later, we only lived together for six years. Terminating the marriage was a joint decision between the both of us. It took place after my return from Japan.

Unfortunately, neither she nor the children took to Japan. It was not so much the language barrier or living conditions, it was the daily two-hour commute each way from Yokota AB, the location of my assignment and our apartment, to the DOD school in downtown Tokyo. For first, and second graders it was up at 4:30 a.m. only to return by 7:30 p.m. The bus ride proved too much for our daughters. I completely understood their complaints, but the DOD school was the only option we had short of us moving to Tokyo, out of reach for the expense with what I was being paid.

"We are going back to San Jose," Annette announced two months later. There was still time to register the girls in schools' back home. Besides, her parents were happy to see them back. Although I regretted her decision, I understood. Not everybody was cut out for overseas living. I was on my own again.

In the meantime, for the first six weeks, work proceeded as I had planned. On arriving at Yokota AB, a U.S. Air Force base, some twenty-five miles from Tokyo, the six of us were put up in temporary BOQ quarters. During my briefing the following day with AF Command Headquarters, I was informed that the building was not ready yet to be occupied. "Construction is completed but the interior it not yet finished."

"How long before we can move in?"

"Six weeks," I was told, then, "We set up a temporary workplace for you. Tarmac tent."

"Neat," I could not suppress my delight.

"What's neat about it?" Buzz jumped on me. Even the commander was baffled at my remark. He had expected a complaint rather than approval.

"I like airport activities." What I did not mention was the environment I had worked in for one year prior to leaving Germany in 1961. I had sought out a workplace intentionally to get some language and cultural exposure prior to immigrating to the States. Employed by the German civil service, I had been assigned to the Coleman Barracks, a U.S. military airbase near Manheim. It worked out for the best. It was the place where I met my sponsors through a young G.I., their nephew, doing a four-year tour of duty in Germany.

It was settled. We moved into the tent. It would be our home for the weeks to come. The job was not an easy task. It entailed dismantling six mainframe computer systems, and removing all electronic parts, and power sources to completely strip the systems to their core frame to be refurbished. It was a task decided on by the DOD, approved by the government accountability office, to be accomplished by my team. The job was necessary because the systems had been in storage for several years, exposed to tropical humidity. No matter how polished electronic contacts may have been leaving manufacturing, in time even gold-plated contacts become tarnished.

I should mention the reason we did not implement the supercomputers tested in California. It turned out too costly for the government to purchase and maintain. The cost alone was exceeding congressional budget approval. On top of 24/7 staffing expenses, supercomputers at the time required internal freon cooling at additional cost of one million dollars annually, for each system. As a result, existing hardware and equipment assets in storage for several years, was used for the added Intel installation at Yokota.

The workplace was what I had envisioned. Aircraft, civilian, and military alike, were taking to the air, and landed throughout the day and evening. It was a busy place on Japan's Honshu island. It was not work only. We took a break every so often, following airport activities whenever a craft pulled up close by. The move-in day to the permanent building finally came for us to pack up, schedule the move, and have transport loading up equipment.

"What in the world…" Buzz exclaimed, as soon as we set foot in the new building, an Air Force Intel complex. Considered a secure, and hardened building, the structure housed computer, and electronics below ground for signal shielding with administration, and office spaces located above ground. We had just taken possession when Buzz applied power to the equipment.

"What?" I was alerted, and stepped up.

"Take a look," Buzz said with a gesture at the power panel.

It immediately became apparent that something was not wired right. Testing more circuit breakers, where power should have turned on when switched online, it shut the equipment off, not only to computers, but centralized air conditioning, lighting, and emergency signs as well.

"Let's go," I said with an ominous feeling creeping into my stomach on the way to the command office. "We have a problem down below." It only took seconds to spur action into command. Rather than giving a lengthy explanation, my policy was, "demonstration by example."

One on the team was already busy checking out wiring. "Like you said," he confirmed with a gesture at the swish panel. "Everything is wired backwards."

"How could it be… Who did this?" Finger pointing was quick to set in. Watching, and listening to the grievances, an idea came to mind that I had learned while taking Japanese language classes. My question to the instructor had been, "Why are your traffic lights red to get traffic going, and blue to stop?"

"It's the way our system works," the instructor had said.

"What about the colors?"

"Our primary colors are *Aka* = red, *Kuro* = black, *Shiro* = white, and *Aoi* = blue," she explained.

"What about green?"

"There is no green in our language and culture."

It was as simple as that. The local electrical contractor that did the installation used the local color code, not only for power, but equipment switches, and indicators as well. To begin with, all switches, and indicators were wired reverse. "On" was red, and "Off" green. Though the green color matched our U.S. code, it was still labelled 'Blue.' The color green was slowly implemented over time after U.S. forces insisted on the color change with the occupation.

When I presented the facts to headquarters, it caused the expected uproar. There would be more delays not accounted for, but it could not be helped. There were two solutions: one, rewire the entire building, or two, accept it as is, and have instructions ready for maintenance personnel to be advised of the discrepancy. "Not acceptable," was my response when solution two was presented. The impact of rewiring was not as severe as had been anticipated. It took place with us moving in, and staging computer systems. After that came interconnecting equipment followed with testing for operational preparedness. By the time we went operational, the system had been rewired, and functioned according to U.S. standards.

"Where to?" Buzz asked, as usual, at the end of a workday.

"Tokyo," I would say. Where I was apt to explore the land most on the team would gather at the O or NCO[41] clubs to pass evening hours. Since the young Japanese were very socially oriented, it was not difficult for a foreigner to make a connection. Since many of the young spoke English, preferred language elect in high school, it was not a barrier. But it was almost impossible to become involved because of their strict inherited cultural heritage. From a social perspective, for the young, and unattached U.S. serviceman, contractor or businessman, chances of landing a date were slim, but not impossible. If by chance one should develop a friendship, the visitor most likely would never be introduced to local family, and friends for the stated reason.

Setting off on the trip to the city was always an adventure. It began with a brisk walk to the railway station Ushihama (Cow Pasture), the town we resided near the airbase, then hopping on a local commuter, transferring in Tachikawa to an Express train, and on to the final destination, either Shinjuku (Pearl City), Ginza (Restaurant

---

[41] At the time, military ranking separation was strictly enforced. Officers had their own social facilities as did Non-Commissioned Officers (NCO), and enlisted men. Today, many bases are consolidating recreational facilities under one roof to curb spending. Adjustments had to be made for service policies to allow for a salute free facility.

town), Akihabara (electronic city), or Roppongi (entertainment district), where many of the clubs, and restaurants were located. Either way, Tokyo was a fun city. Though crowded, and overpopulated, dwellers were conditioned to put up with each other in packed conditions.

Establishments were busy, as were shops, clubs, and restaurants—sushi, soba, sukiyaki, yakitori, and a number of other popular cuisine places. Dining in Japan, unless one was invited to a formal night out, was different from other cultures. Most places serving food were specialized to carry only one type of dish, but in a number of varieties. For instance, a sushi place only served raw fish while a noodle place (soba) carried only noodle dishes, etc. For this reason, Buzz, and I, like everybody else, would usually stop at three places to complete dinner. It was an affair that would take at least two hours, then end at one, or another of dozens of sake places. The Japanese were prolific drinkers. The business day for the Japanese man began at 8:00 a.m., and ended at 12:00 a.m. midnight, just in time to catch the last train or subway home. Since Tokyo was mostly businesses, and shops, everybody commuted, in the process moving millions of people in, and out the city, daily.

If, by chance, one missed the last train, which happened to us frequently, the only option home was to take a taxi, almost an impossibility since most were already occupied with other people that had missed the last train. There were times we would miss the ride home only to wind up sleeping at the station until 5:30 a.m. when the first train pulled up, taking us back home, and on to work.

Weekends were just as hectic. It seemed that the entire country was on the move. Where many headed into the mountains, where most temples were located, others, on warm days, took the train to the shores. Japanese men dedicated six working days to business, but the Sunday was strictly reserved, and dedicated to the family. Though the man was the principal household earner, he never carried cash or a wallet. The predominant means to pay a tab or fare was through *Meishi* (business card) on credit. It was the wife's duty at the end of the month to visit the places the husband frequented to pay off creditors.

On other weekends, Buzz, and I would head into the mountains. There was one event not long after we arrived in Japan, the annual fire-walking ceremony at Mt. Takao. Monks would gather from many of the regional temples to attend the affair. We arrived at 4:00 p.m. just when the fire was started. It was not just an ordinary log fire. It had taken several days to build a hill of tree trunks, and branches fifty feet in height, and even wider—to one hundred fifty feet in length. It took four hours to burn the wood heap into a bed of red-hot ashes one-foot deep, burning into the night. Monks would gather barefooted, and line up in rows a quarter mile long with a dozen walkers aligned side-by-side.

Buzz, and I, as well as a few others on the team, were present to witness the once a year event. It had even attracted CNN for their first ever overseas event coverage with Dick Cavett reporting. I had the pleasure talking with him on the fire walk.

"What do you think?" I said to Buzz with a gesture at the ceremony.

"Are you crazy?" he responded. "I'm not going to burn my feet."

"Come on," I pestered him. "You can do it. I will."

"You going to walk?"

"Follow me." I gestured, instructing one team member to take pictures while the rest fell in line for the one-time adventure, regardless of outcome. I spotted the CNN anchor striding through the fiery coals nearby. Fire walking was not new to me. I had done so once in Hawaii. But this one was a huge bed of smoldering wooden cinder; one could feel the heat singeing the body from fifty feet off. My anticipation heightened with each step closer. I remembered the instructions from my prior walk: "It's all in the mind."

"I don't like it," Buzz objected, watching other walkers in front stepping onto the red-hot bed of coals. Not everybody was determined, and fearless. Some, after taking the first few steps, began to run across the fiery bed screaming like hell. They were the ones without faith who had lost control over their minds and body.

"Follow my footsteps one pace behind," I reminded Buzz. "Don't run. Think of something pleasant."

He remained silent as I took my first step into the inferno. Step by step we solidly made the one hundred-fifty feet to the far end. Proud to have conquered such extreme action, Buzz, with a sweaty face, shook his head. "Can't believe I actually did it."

I will describe my experience. Getting closer, with each step my mind calmed into emptiness. I did not think or fret about the environment. With shoes, and socks in my hands, pant legs rolled up to the knees, and the many monks' yellow tunics flowing over the coals ahead, nothing caught fire. After taking the first step I was surprised at how cool the coals felt on my foot soles. Though surrounded by intense heat it did not burn any part of the body. Aside from the runners, the walkers kept a steady pace from one end to the other. It was close to midnight when we left, feeling euphoric for having had the opportunity to participate in the extremely challenging ceremony.

"You look as I feel," I said with a glance at my buddy.

"Content?"

"Yes. Some will not believe your walk, but you'll always remember your triumph." I had run into non-believers when, at times, I would tell the story. It did not matter. There were no words to convey the actual experience. One has to live through such an event.

My times in Japan were never idle stays. When not busy on the job, I was interacting with the local population. To do so effectively I had taken Japanese language classes. This ancient language, from a compositional structure, was surprisingly similar to German grammar. Where the difficulty became noticeable in Japanese was that three different languages merged into every-day reading, and writing practices.

The Japanese population, having been isolated for millennia before modern commerce, was first visited by the Chinese, but they were limited to one annual stop at Kyushu Island. Known as Black Ships, the sailed schooners were only allowed to trade the sought-out Japanese silk produced, and used to fabricate the Kimono, for their increasing demands for formal customs wear, in turn traded for spice products from China.

Where other countries had been building sailing vessels for thousands of years, Japanese Royalty had forbidden the construction of ships, other than for localized fishing vessels. That is how close a society the Japanese were. It was not until 1853 when American Commodore Mathew Perry, with a fleet of four ships enforced trade relations with the Japanese, thus taking over their long-standing relations with the Chinese. Though dominance only lasted one hundred years before American liberation took possession of Japan following WWII.

Originally, before trading with China, the Japanese spoke, and wrote only in their cursive native language, Hiragana. To effectively trade with the Chinese, the native language proved insufficient, which led to their adoption of Kanji, the Chinese symbolic characters. When Captain Perry forced trade on the Japanese, again, the combined hiragana (46 phonetic symbols), and kanji (greater than 50,000 phonetics) proved insufficient, spurring a third adaptation, katakana (71 symbols). From then on, newspapers, books, signs, and printed materials included all three language forms as used today. It is this mix that makes it difficult for the foreigner making the effort to learn the Japanese language, with kanji being the most challenging. It takes years of writing, and reading practice to become proficient. As for me, it took several months to memorize 600 kanji symbols, the fourth grader learning level. What made learning even more challenging was the spoken format, where mostly women spoke hiragana, with men mainly using katakana, and kanji to conduct business.

During my conversations with Japanese men I was periodically reminded, "You speak like a woman." Rebuffed initially, it began to make sense because of how I acquired the language, taught in classes by a woman teacher.

I never ventured into the business world in Japan, but I still met influential entrepreneurs inviting me to special events. To be able to converse intelligently in customs, and culture, I took several courses in Bonsai training, and Japan's most revered tea ceremony. A bonsai is a tree raised, and kept in a pot, stunting its growth; its branches are forced by wires formed into exotic shapes, as desired by the owner.

By contrast, the green tea *Matcha* ceremony is a personal deed acted out, usually following a severe personal mistake or indiscretion made by one or the other dating, and marriage partner. What makes it a special treat was the method, and effort which is required to carry it out. A special, privately-arranged affair, it takes hours of preparations, followed by a secluded, precisely-executed performance in reparation to the insulting misdeed. The ritualized preparation, and serving of tea are very simple, with simplicity being the basis for the apologizing partner. However, each step of the preparation, with accompanied utensils is fixed, and placed by precisely executed motions amid a ceremonial setting while kneeled on the tatami mat. It is the serving of tea, drinking from the cup accompanied by traditional ritual for depth, silence, and serenity that makes up the damaged infringement.

Before I had realized it, two years had passed. Our contract obligations came to an end. "What are you going to do?" Buzz, like me, was faced with departing soon.

"I need a couple of weeks to work things out with my family." It was my responsibility to make sure things were all right. "I'll be in San Jose."

"I'll be back at headquarters until I hear from you."

"Fine." It may sound like we had become inseparable, but one never knew what plans the DOD had in the workings. Though I considered myself a "loner," I had to admit that being with the right company was a better option. There were times you had to rely on somebody. A friend was better than a stranger to watch your back. "See you back there."

I bid my farewells with the team departing Japan, headed back to Colorado, since my destination was San Francisco. About to board my flight, I heard my name on the PA. Checking with the departure desk, I had a message waiting. "Report to headquarters for new assignment. Urgent!"

"So much for family," was my thought. I had planned to take a couple of weeks break, but it was not meant to be. I would check in with headquarters once I'd reached the mainland. The ten-hour flight gave me time to contemplate my future, and family obligations.

With my DOD contracting obligation there was not much I could contribute to a sound family environment. Initially, where I was looking for a travel companion, Annette was mostly interested in having a full-time husband, and children, permanently set in a happy home. I would have to face her head on. In spite of HQs urgent calling, I decided to make the visit in San Jose.

Arriving at her newly acquired home, I was received with open arms by all. Inspecting the home, I saw that there was enough room to accommodate her newly arrived parents, as well as the occasional visitor, me. I bunked with my daughters in the top floor attic rooms. It was fun listening in on their chatting each other to sleep. Facing Annette with the marriage problem went fairly well. She had accepted the fact that I was married to my job more than to her. "I am busier than you can imagine," she proclaimed. In addition to taking care of our three daughters, and her parents, some of her siblings, her parents had sponsored, were also on the way. Leave it to Filipinos; they will always find a way around the system, in this case a twelve-year immigration waiting list.

The two vehicles Annette, and I owned were not enough once her brothers, and sisters landed jobs. I turned mine over for family use while looking for a new purchase. With demands for vintage model cars at their height, I had always desired to own a muscle car, a Pontiac GTO specifically, since I had missed the 50s period in the States when they were popular. Checking daily newspaper ads, I could not locate the precise model since many had been purchased the years before while I was living overseas. I finally located a 1974 AMC Javelin at the cost of $2,100. 1974 had been the last year manufacturing muscle cars in the U.S. The chassis was in excellent shape, but the engine, transmission, brakes, and gears were not. The previous owner, a spoiled, rich kid, within only two years had managed to drive the vehicle into the ground.

I had enough time to have the vehicle transported to Colorado, where I planned to rebuild and refurbish it. Annette, and I parted as friends, with me visiting the girls as often as my schedule would permit. In hindsight, it was not the most ideal of arrangements, but in the end, it worked out to the best. My daughters grew up into responsible adults, which may not have been the case within an unhappy environment. There was a maxim to both Annette's, and my personal lives I wanted to share, as inscribed in a poem by Lord Alfred Tennyson.

"It is better to have loved, and lost, then never to have loved at all."

I had rented out our home in Colorado for the two years I left, and took possession once I had arrived. Living alone in an empty home was not the easiest. I dearly missed the family, and visited them often over the following years, flying out over a long weekend, or driving the thirteen hundred miles nonstop for a week or two.

Checking in with headquarters after my arrival back in Colorado, Buzz, and I were assigned a five-year contract with Army, Air Force, and Naval Intel services. What it entailed was constant travels around the globe with a two week visit at each place, including England, Germany, Italy, Korea, Japan, Okinawa, and Guam, followed by a two-week break back at headquarters in Colorado Springs. The cycle would be repeated several times a year for the next five years.

Leaving for Europe to continue east to Asia, we travelled on TWA flights. Return from the Pacific would be with Pan Am via Los Angeles or San Francisco. I would spend the two weeks break with the family before starting the next travel cycle. This way, I was able to see them on a regular basis, and was received with welcoming arms. In return, I would bring presents back from many of the places I had visited. I did not stop exploring foreign cultures, and met many new faces in the process.

Buzz, as always, was by my side, sharing my adventures. While in Europe we took side trips to Switzerland, Austria, France, Luxemburg, Belgium, and Lichtenstein. On the Asian leg, we made stop overs to Israel, India, Hong Kong, and Hawaii. There were many other places I would have liked to visit, but with a T.S. clearance, they were off-limits to us. Some were communist countries while others were fighting conflicts with neighboring countries.

It may sound like we were neglecting the job, but that was not the case. It always had priority. After all, the government was paying our salaries, travel, and lodging expenses. I should mention an important fact. Working as government employee or contracting was by far less compensating than working for a commercial company. Though both sectors, public, and private, had their advantages, and disadvantages. One advantage for working with the government was that your job, and retirement were secured. The disadvantage was that one would never get rich. Working for the private sector, career, and salary advances were abundant, if one had the energy. In the times to come I would learn the mechanics that drove corporate ambition.

It took me some time to have the Javelin restored to a classic model, but could not do it completely on my own with the hectic travel schedule. Buzz came to my help. It'd turned out that his son, Brian, took up automotive trade while in high school. His acquired expertise and training were readily applied with me appreciating his effort while carrying the cost of the restoration into a pristine show car.

To this day, I tremendously enjoy the monthly ride to car shows, showing off my pride, and joy in my possession. With an exception of a Christmas present at age five, a spring-powered Mercedes, model 300SL, red-colored toy, the Javelin is the only toy I can remember owning. I'll probably cling to it until the end of day.

DEFENSE PROJECTS

"You ready?" Buzz said, preparing for the road to the next location for the trip. You could say trip because this project would be a combination of work, and leisure. For once, I could plan things out for each destination. While career, and work had kept me trim for most of my life, there was no substitute for exercise. With body kept in shape on the job, I had not much need for a gym. My eyes were set on the abundance of beauty each place had to offer, and for the most part beauty could mostly be appreciated in nature, out in the open. Joining the International AVA, a Volksmarching organization, we took to walking Europe every opportunity. Despite the organization having spread across the globe, it was most prevalent in Europe, its birthplace. It gave us an incentive on weekends to get to know a country, and its neighboring lands, in the process walking thousands of miles over the years. One kept track of walks with the register pass issued when joining up, receiving a stamp entry for the event and distance with each walk.

"I'm ready."

"Got your passport?" Buzz was a stickler when it came to details. Somebody else might have been upset by his prodding, but I appreciated it. It was a trademark that had made him successful on the job. Together, we were an effective team, always welcomed by the military on our trips around the globe. This way, we would show our faces six times a year each place, keeping the customers pleased.

"Passport?" I fished for it in my pocket. "Sure do. Let's go." We took turns driving. To get to the walks we generally had to drive some distance of up to fifty miles. Being the most popular activity in Europe on weekends, Volksmarching, since its inception decades ago, had turned into an annual affair for a specific town. Each weekend one could find an event within 30 miles, no matter where one resided. Central, north, south, east, west—it did not matter. There were always scheduled walks at 5, 10, or 26 miles, the marathon, if one had the time, and energy. What made it so attractive to folks was that at each place was an annual affair organized by the town or city in similar fashion, though on a smaller scale, to the October or Wine festivals, served with meals, and drinks, and supplemented with cakes of all kinds. It was the latter that attracted me. While a cool mug of beer was attractive to some, a home-baked cake was my incentive to walk. The extra pounds put on through beer, and sweets was the incentive to walk again the following week.

In reference to Buzz's passport reminder, I couldn't blame him. One of the weekends we decided to take our first walk in France, then move on to Luxemburg for the next walk, and to finish our last for the day in Belgium. The time was before terrorist bombings became a threat. With borders relaxed between Germany, and France at minor border crossings, one could expect nobody guarding the borders early mornings, and late evenings, if at all. Thus, we entered France, did the walk, moved on to Luxemburg, and finished in Belgium. It was afternoon when we arrived at the German border.

"Passport," the sentry ordered. Buzz handed over his, but I did not, or rather, could not. I must have left it at the hotel.

"No passport?" The next command was clear. "Pull over."

What followed proved to be a fiasco. We were detained. I could read it from his face, Buzz was pissed. He left without saying a word. He had to drive back to our town, have the hotel manager retrieve the passport from my room, and return here, a turnaround trip of 120 miles. It was late in the evening when we finally made it back. To make it up, aside from buying him dinner, I paid for a few rounds of beer. Recalling the event among other past incidents, we both retired on shaky legs, happily.

Not every trip turned out well, and humorous. Another time around, at the same place in Germany, but this time with another travel partner since Buzz had remained back in the States, detained by a family emergency, the incident was more severe. In the end it turned out okay, but it could have had lasting consequences. As was the case with many of our trips, somebody from local command was always willing to host our present visit. At each place we were revered as a result of the services we provided. Reporting directly to NATO headquarters, 5th Signal Command, the commander, located in Worm, Germany, usually came into town for a first-hand report, and to meet with us. We—us, and some of his local subordinates—were usually invited to dinner by a family-owned, mutually acquainted, authentic German restaurant host. I would never turn down such an invitation, and neither did my partners.

As always, dinner turned out to be a lively affair hosted by the proprietor, and his wife. After the customary patrons had left, they dedicated the rest of the evening to us. My temporary travel partner displayed the common trait of feeling tired after several rounds of drinks. Suppressing a yawn, he leaned in my direction, and said, "I need some sleep." One look at him, it became apparent.

"Go get some sleep in the car," I suggested. He readily accepted the offer, and I was glad not to have to break up the lively party among friends. He politely excused himself, and made his way to the exit. Two hours later, by 2:00 a.m., the party broke up with an invitation from the hosts, "Let's do it again soon." He, and the wife had enjoyed, and welcomed our periodic appearance. On our earlier arrival, we had to park the rental at a curb some distance away, rather than the guest parking, which had been taken up by earlier patrons. Arriving at the rental after a two-minute walk or, rather, an unsteady gait to the darkened, and quiet street, I spotted my partner's head sticking out of the opened driver side of the rented German VW-Beetle, with feet extending into the street at the traffic side. Six feet three inches in height, there was no space comfortable for him other than across the reclined front seats.

To get behind the wheel, I was forced to lift up his upper body, and position him in the passenger seat. Next, I had to tackle his lower body. Stooped down, reaching for his legs, I was about to lift them inside when I became aware of rapidly stomping boots headed in my direction. My mind was focused on the challenge of getting him positioned into the rental, while my brain became aware of the ensuing commotion, accompanied by orders shouted at me, "Hands up. Hands up."

Still mellowed from drinking and busy with my buddy, I turned in surprise at the approaching squadron shouting German commands. Seconds later, I was overwhelmed, and overpowered by half a dozen commandos wearing tactical uniforms. Taken down, and promptly cuffed with tie wraps, my partner was yanked from the car, and treated with similar force. Awakened, they forced him to the ground while he struggled to free himself from the shackles. Dragged to an armored squad vehicle, we both were promptly tossed inside, and locked up.

"What in hell is happening?" Not used to being manhandled he struggled trying to free himself. Sobered, and dumbfounded by the sudden turn of events, I was speechless, groping for answers. We were stared down, and surrounded by fierce looking commandos as the armored vehicle sped off. While chatting among themselves the squad leader kept bearing in on my partner in German. "Where are you from? Why are you here? What is your mission?"

More passive in appearance, I was mostly ignored. I should point out that my companion was Hawaiian with Samoan ancestry, tall in stature, pleasant, but with a powerful presence. He must have looked the part of their profiling. With us still contemplating our demise, the vehicle slammed to a halt in the middle of town. "Raus mit Euch" (Get out), was the command shot at us. While on-route, listening in on their verbal exchange, I understood what was said, and also read the emblems displayed on their lapels. We had been captured by an anti-terrorist squadron. Apparently, someone had called the police, and, based on the report, they in turn had called the anti-terrorist office. We were promptly arrested, and landed in jail, locked up for the night, or so we thought. An hour into being detained, voices emerged from the front office. Minutes later, the familiar face of my commander appeared at the cage we were contained in.

"What happened with you?" he said, not overly friendly. "I had just gone to sleep when the phone woke me up, and here I am. What did you guys do?"

I could see from the expression that he was not happy. I explained the condition I had found my partner in, and what transpired shortly after. Somewhat calmed, he understood, and quickly left with the promise, "I'll get you out in the morning."

Several hours later we were released, but not without the following consequences. In the hours since, the commander explained, dozens of phone calls were initiated from local police headquarters to 5th Signal Command, relayed to the Pentagon, corporate headquarters, and back several times over until there was enough evidence that we were not terrorists. The following morning apologies were extended to us by the local Army Base command, the 5th Signal Command, and police headquarters. With a sheepish grin on his face, my commander friend bade us farewell, begging, "Stay out of trouble."

I promised with, "I'll be back." He just laughed it off, but was satisfied. Prior to our departure the police commander held a small ceremony, offering both of us an official shield, German ID, and signed certificates declaring the both of us were official members of the German police force. It was his way of paying respect for causing us, and NATO Intel unnecessary grief. All in all, nobody was hurt, nobody was cited, and no criminal records were initiated. But it certainly created an interesting story, told occasionally during happy hour gatherings. Aside from an interrupted journey, the incident shaped our relations even tighter between U.S., and NATO ally command in Europe.

One may think that constant travel eventually would get tiresome. It was not the case with us. For the most part, other than in England, and Korea, every place else was not far from metropolitan areas. The work location in England, for instance, was near the college town of Oxford, a historic, and idyllic place in the British Islands embraced by Ireland, Scotland, and Wales. Also, what impressed me were the many canals crisscrossing the land. Canals were everywhere one travelled. Though relatively narrow, passage, and locks could be tricky when encountering another boat.

Britain has many places worthy of a visit. A prominent one is Stonehenge, which archeologists believed was constructed between 2000 BC, and 3000 BC, and are still debating its purpose. I visited there several times. Strolling within the colossal stone erections could be overwhelming with a sense of awe. Today, the complex is roped off to keep the busloads of daily tourists at bay from touching the artifacts or inscribing their initials, as was an innocent practice at times.

As far as London was concerned, other than Piccadilly Square with its high-end fashion stores, clubs in the Soho district, and the West End theaters, and shops, I kept my distance. Like many international cities, it was what it was, a cultural mix from around the globe. The original Brits that had settled the islands had lost much of their country in the 70s to foreign investments when the land almost went bankrupt. Whether privately or government owned, upkeep, and taxing the many castles became too much of a burden for the proprietors.

Korea, and Seoul were not much different other than being heavily influenced by Chinese ideology. The country had as much history from the Asian perspective with one exception. Itaewon with its nightlife was well known around Seoul, as this was an area that drew throngs of tourists year-round, usually a multinational group, in addition to a U.S. presence from nearby military bases.

With U.S. Intelligence presence in many countries, they were mostly a joint operation with local Intel utilizing existing military ally facilities. For this reason, much of the population was unaware of our presence. The five-year contract obligation for my visits became pretty much routine. On the first day I would conduct an in-briefing followed with an introduction to section chiefs. It was a necessity for getting to know new faces because military personal kept rotating in, and out throughout the year. Also, the same day, I queried section supervisors for problems experienced since our last visit. Most turned out to be minor unless there had been a major power outage, or software uploads. It was these that usually proved problematic to sensitive computer hardware, and operating systems. Following analyses, and troubleshooting hardware, software, and system problems kept us busy several days over the following two weeks. When everything was corrected at the end of the second week, I would conduct an out-brief with local command, who was generally extremely satisfied by our non-intrusive presence. The end result was an uptime, and readiness guarantee of 99.99% in operational performance.

Software related problems were generally resolved with monthly updates, and annual version change uploads. With technology evolving at a runaway pace, system enhancements, and upgrades were frequently necessary. Security, with hacking not yet fashionable, was not a problem other than professional spying conducted between countries. With the foresight JFK had in protecting the nation from political, and government adversary-inspired intrusions, AUTODIN, being a closely guarded system, had not one incident with security breaches during my thirty-year career. While many were curious about the Intelligence carried across transmit wires, the mindset back then was different—curious, yes. Destructive, absolutely not.

With the incorporation of new technologies, the cost of operations, and support increased as well, but not beyond the annual military budget allocation. Nobody, not the designers, not the developers, not the government, and certainly not the contractor, ever imagined AUTODIN in operation past ten years, the usual lifespan of a government system. The same belief held true for the teams of specialists, support, and operations personnel assigned to the program. Regardless of the congressional approved budget expenditures, with today's economically extravagant spending, the benefit of national security outweighed costs a thousand-fold. Added benefits from the system, aside from superior survivable communication during war, and border conflicts, were reliability, speed, performance, and growth demands, but these could not be truly assessed until the system was turned over to the public in the early 90s. It was here where the system was put to the test by connecting every computer, and network-ready appliance in the world into a system to benefit everybody on the globe.

Was John F. Kennedy's vision in 1962 a good thing? I'll let the reader be the judge.

With the five-year lucrative contract, I brought to the table for Ford Aerospace, my success with the company was assured. Once Buzz, and I had established a baseline for our periodic visits with the multi-service Armed Forces—the Army, Air Force, Navy, and NATO Intel—we established a flexibility to where we could enjoy each country's culture during the visits. We were not trapped into an eight-hour presence at the sites once all issues had been resolved.

Where in today's world of hardware, and system reliability demands for 100% operability for the lifespan of the equipment was the norm, in the days of mainframe computers, such was not the case. Aside from environmentally induced manufacturing flaws, which were a constant problem, transistors, and other discrete components had a limited lifespan due to a high bias voltage load applied to computer components. Today, bias voltages are measured in milli, and micro volts designed to switch a transistor state one molecule at a time, an unimaginable achievement in the world of 60s technology. One circuit board, then, would be limited to four circuit components; the same physical size today is comprised of millions of components on the sub-atomic level.

But this will not be the end. There are new designs already being put to the test in quantum computing with resultant performance specs not easily understood. Imagine a task performance where the results are available even before the operation is executed, at speeds much greater than the speed of light. The internal mechanics may still be beyond the experimenters understanding, but have already become reality in today's world of science.

The current service contract presented system issues generally beyond the onsite technical expertise of permanent technicians, but many issues presented challenges mostly for system designers to solve. This was where Buzz, and I stepped in. With onsite military personal rotating in and out of a specific field assignment, generally three years in duration, they would not necessarily get a chance to become experts in the field of computers, and electronics. Facing challenges for me was a daily occurrence, but not the only thing. What I obtained was visibility, and contacts with personnel from a variety of other organizations, and agencies. Once my reputation was established, word proliferated among the powers-at-be, and with that came opportunities, not only technically related, but personally, and socially as well.

There was a time, I recall, in the 80s when I was extended an invitation. "How would you like a personal tour in the White House?" The invitation came from the head of the secret service assigned there. Who would turn down such an invitation? Nobody.

The day came, after arriving at the nation's capital, when Buzz, and I were escorted through the personal sanctuary of our country's leader, President Reagan. He would spend much of his time at his personal ranch in Bel Air, CA, so aside from the permanent staff, we had the White House to ourselves for a few hours. At other times we accepted invitations to personal, and public affairs hosted by prominent individuals in one or another capacity of influence. In summary, our lives, bestowed with special considerations, turned out gratifying. We were on the best way for career recognition, but destiny had different plans beyond our control.

It was during Reagan's second term when political, and subsequent economic conditions forced the nation's changes, triggered by the Iran-Contra affair, which, as it turned out, was not very popular with U.S. citizens. Drastic budget cuts followed by a trickle-down economy proved ineffective. After experiencing several economic recessions during my career, I saw the writing on the wall. Our five-year commitment with Intel services came to an end not long after. Regardless of the outcome, events such as illustrated above presented everlasting memories greatly appreciated in the days ahead.

Even the best in innovative designs, advanced systems would eventually meet their end. Advanced being a relative term. As soon as AUTODIN turned public, it would not take much time before it would turn into a competitive system. Though the government turned the system over to public use after declassifying it from top secret to unclassified, the core of AUTODIN was retained with an eventual change from analog to digital. The conversion was necessary to keep government, and military services isolated, and secure. Due to budget cuts, most of the AUTODIN centers in-country, and around the globe morphed into the public Internet, with autonomous nodes replacing functions that used to be performed by thousands of personnel, drastically reducing operating, and support costs. The nodes were completely self-contained, and maintained, so most occurring problems would be resolved remotely from one centralized office location.

Like many times before, Buzz, and I were facing the same question: "What will be next?" We knew our careers would take a turn with the automation.

"Let's not worry," I said, not overly concerned.

With more budget cuts initiated by President Reagan, the country was forced into massive layoffs through all government, and military ranks. First on the list of attrition typically were contractors. The ensuing unemployment was felt through all industry sectors, affecting technology branches the greatest. Us being employed by a major government contractor, in addition to having flawless careers, we had high hopes for continued employment.

Returning from our final trip, saddened, Buzz remarked, "Guess this' it." The past five years had been exceedingly rewarding for the both of us, not so much monetarily, more so for professional, and personal gratification. Every place we visited, and revisited became an unwritten success story within the secured environments for government, military, and Intel activities. We were among an army of dedicated citizens diligently working for one common goal, to protect our national wealth, and the safety of its citizens from being compromised by hostile forces with adversary intentions, not only to the U.S., but other vulnerable allies as well.

SPECIAL ASSIGNMENTS

Contractors with the defense department, military, and Intel organizations did not always have smooth sailing. There had been many unexpected, and unforeseen emergency calls. That was the reason for my 24/7 on-call standby status. The tradeoff was a deserving break afterwards while sacrificing a two-week annual vacation time each year. As I did at times after such a call, I took a few days off for hibernation at one of my favorite places such as the Philippines, Taiwan, Hong Kong, or Hawaii before checking in with headquarters. Management, though tolerant, did not like my disappearances, but learned to accept them. There were many years where I would forfeit vacation time while jumping from one place, and project to the next. The last time, no sooner had I checked into my favorite hotel in Taipei, after spending one night, then the desk clerk handed me a telegram in the morning. "American Embassy want to see you." I thanked him, and made the call. It was not the first-time headquarters or the Pentagon had tracked me down. I would learn later about the tracking, and investigative capabilities of our Intel, and FBI services.

Since I had no permanent place of residence my home could be Guam, if supporting Naval Intel, the Philippines, Korea, Japan, England, Germany or Italy. It did not matter much. When directed to change location, I would forward my stereo system, pack my two suitcases, and hop a flight to the new destination. Life could be hectic, but it was the one that I had chosen. There was a time through the 70s, and 80s when I owned, and operated four vehicles between the Philippines, Guam, Germany, and back home in the States.

Vietnam was a different situation. When called up I was given first priority on the next military flight scheduled, or if delayed, could take a commercial airliner destined for Saigon. Often, I had the privilege of being invited into the cockpit, or flying first class. Back then, it was not unusual to find a civilian in the cockpit of a military craft. There were no commercial flights into the frontlines. Battlefields such as the Delta, and DMZ called for a variety of craft from a C-5A to a C-141, and other non-specific transport. Pilots did not care whether their passengers were CIA, DIA, or a contractor. They just followed orders, and mission commands. Based on individual behaviors, I suspected many were high on drugs, especially chopper pilots, and crews headed into, or out of battle fronts. I was stunned when I learned about the high addiction rate, but could not blame the individual for fighting a losing battle, as most knew they were.

This call was for an emergency which developed in November of 1983, during Ronald Reagan's reign. He was scheduled to address the Korean National Assembly in Seoul, with a visit to the U.S. troops deployed in the country. What transpired one week prior to his departure, officially, was that the main communication trunk (underground cable) running between Seoul, and Taegu, our Intel site, was cut by road construction work, jeopardizing his visit. Unofficially, it was an act of sabotage to undermine Reagan's visit. Without links provided by AUTODIN, Intel, military, special forces, secret service, and local security detachments were without communication.

To reestablish, I was dispatched as part of an emergency team trying to repair, and restore the network. Since it would take weeks to fix the damaged trunk[42], and there was no time to reschedule the president's trip, we had to find alternative means. What it entailed was the rerouting of land-based connections to satellite operations for a temporary support function, and reconfiguring through AUTODIN sites located in the Philippines, Japan, and Guam for subscribers in Korea, and Reagan's party to be tied in with the Pentagon, and White House. This would provide the president, his staff, and local 9,000 security coverage instant access to secret service, Intel, and military support functions. The solution was challenging, but we accomplished it on time.

Short of reuniting the two troubled nations, the presidential trip turned out to be successful for U.S., and South Korean relations. North Korea, on the other hand, kept struggling for independence from communist dominance, still at war with the free world to this day. With the current leader building up his nuclear-based ICBM arsenal, it clearly expresses his adverse sentiments, portraying the United States as an unrelenting, demonic nation. Unless China, and Russia step in to resolve the personal conflict with the world, peace will not be achieved soon.

It was not long after the Korea incident when I was called upon again. This time, while assigned in Japan, an issue had developed in Italy. With the Cold War with the Soviets escalating once more, the site desperately needed a technological upgrade. The question became, "How to implement the outdated AUTODIN site with new innovation without interrupting vital, and critical mission operations?"

Coordinating the strategy with design engineers, we worked out the most logical approach. Where the fully operational site needed to be scaled down during the initial eight hours, to service only the most critical subscribers, Intel, and Military command, and control systems, I would assure operational readiness within the allotted time to local command.

On the day of the project, I had just arrived by plane at Pisa two hours before. Picked up by a waiting military vehicle I was driven to the hotel I usually stayed at. I registered at the hotel desk, and was about to check into the room when the driver objected, "No time for that. Commander is waiting for you."

"Could you please take care of my luggage?" I asked the desk manager.

"No problem. It'll be in your room when you get back."

The next second, I was whisked off to the Army Intel site, a twenty some-minute drive. "We've been waiting," the base commander greeted me with an outstretched hand. The team had already arrived the previous day from the States.

I briefed the commander, "The integration strategy is a challenge, but it will work."

"Can you assure continuous system operation?"

"I can." In my mind, as far as I was concerned, though complicated, the task was flawless. All I needed was buy-in from local command.

"Okay. Let's get going." The commander seemed satisfied. It was not the first time he had witnessed my performance. Since four of the mainframe computer's

---

[42] A standard trunk cable would contain fifty thousand pairs of wires that had to individually be rejoined.

functions were backup operation in case of primary system failure, though it would shut down subscribers for eight hours, mostly support functions not too detrimental on a holiday weekend, they would be the initial stage for the upgrade. Once completed, primary could be switched to the integrated system, freeing up primary for upgrade. It was that simple. Or was it? Shortly after, I would be faced with opposition from an unexpected direction.

"Hey." Buzz walked up. He appeared irritated. "Where were you?"

"Sorry. Not my fault. I got here as fast as the airliner could fly."

"Didn't think you would make it. Don't let me hang like this in the future."

"Won't happen again. I'm glad you are here. When did you guys get here?"

"A couple of days ago. Thought I'd have to lead the project. Headquarters was ready to cancel the project, and here you are, showing up at the last minute."

"Are you kidding? I wouldn't miss this project for anything. What's the state of the site?"

"Primary system is stable. The rest could use some tweaking, but will hold up for the switchover."

I usually had to rely on him to back me up with a heavy workload. But this time, headquarters decided to send along some heavy goons from the engineering department. Even the boss had made his rare appearance, pacifying the commander, and assuring success to site personnel. "Speaking of the devil," he said, walking up. "About time you got here. Where've you been hiding out this time?"

"Japan, and I wasn't hiding." I had been managing the implementation at the Air Force Intel site in Yokota when I received the call. He knew it, but was giving me a hard time for getting here late.

"You ready?"

"I am. Let's pull the plug." It was the team expression for kicking off the project.

I had arrived Saturday morning after a twenty-four-hour flight from Japan. Already late for the start, the deadline to get operational capacity back was less than eight hours away. Though my mind was focused on the job at hand, I could have used some sleep. While traveling on a plane I was never able to sleep, not even a wink, unless I had a few glasses of champagne to dull my mind. Because of the criticality, and urgency, I had decided to keep a clear mind. The pending task required teamwork. It entailed a heavy workload from everybody, not only for the initial eight hours, but the following two days as well. Each mainframe computer had to be disconnected from the system, certain sections replaced, tested, and repaired to be returned to operational status, one unit after the next, six in all. With the system technology as dated as it was, many interconnecting wires would be broken in the process of replacing cables, and sections with components that had to be tested, repaired, and reconfigured.

Minutes short of 4:00 p.m., the deadline, the commander firmly strode up. "Are we ready?"

"Just a minute," I stalled for a few additional minutes. "You are welcome to watch."

"Wouldn't miss it for anything," was his reply. Having an entire system switch over or come live was a spectacle most of the site personnel would not miss. It entailed activating hundreds of mechanical relay switches driven by the primary system while configuring, and interconnecting every piece of operational equipment. The process, accompanied by the latching of relays, would take up to two minutes in a silenced computer room.

"Here we go," I said, initiating the process. As anticipated, the autonomous configuration went into action. It was a pleasure to hear the sound of mechanical relays connect. Like musical clockwork, when it worked, one piece of gear after the next came on line. As agreed with the commander, the first fifty subscribers, most mission critical, were returned to fully operational status.

Watching success on the command console, operations team, and visitors alike were momentarily distracted. Footsteps quickly approached the command console. Pulling me aside, the site manager, with a frustrated look on his face, said, "We need to talk."

Slightly annoyed at what seemed like success, he led me to the commander's office. Once inside, waiting was the commander, and COR, a watchdog specifically sent by the Pentagon to oversee the effort for the project, who boldly announced, "You can't go operational."

Immediately, alarm bells went off. My annoyance turned to frustration. It meant halting the configuration process. "Why not?" I demanded. Not only did it appear a most irrational demand, it did not make any sense at all.

"Pentagon's orders," the COR stated, holding steadfast.

"You better explain," I demanded, frustrated, and short fused by now. There was absolutely no reason for such an act.

"You cannot go live until every subscriber is fully operational."

"But," I vehemently objected, "it'll take three days."

"I don't care," he replied. "You can't go operational." The boldness of the demand even puzzled the commander, and his site personnel. "Please excuse yourself," was his next command directed at only me. Angered, I left the office, wondering about the unreasonable demands. Whatever private conversation took place between the two, I could not contemplate. Sure enough, ten minutes went by before the commander reappeared on the floor. "Shut the system down." Even he was puzzled.

Sworn to follow the chain-of-command, the commander's hands were tied like mine as well as the team. Questions were fired back, and forth. "What's going on?" I had no answers, and waited for the commander to explain. He never did, not even privately. I did as commanded. I shut the system down, muttering, "To hell with them."

Word spread immediately amid the Intel communities. Visitors arrived from headquarters, German signal command, and whatever commander was curious about the ensuing outage. Not only did it affect Italian operations, the outage affected NATO, and every U.S. presence in Europe. With me, and the team diligently at work, around the clock, official negotiations took place over the next several days. I was kept up to date by the site manager. When asked for a status, "No change," would be his answer while calls initiated back, and forth with the Pentagon gave no sign for positive results. My current operational status reports, and demands to go operational were ignored. In spite of the situation, not understanding the delays, every available hand on site, from managers to supervisors, and local crews, pitched in to expedite the effort. Word had leaked out that for some political reasons I was being prevented from going operational until three days had expired.

It was the evening of the second day. Everybody on the team was kneeled, crouched, or otherwise busy, diligently working alongside each mainframe with cables, and computer parts strewn across floors. The whole system had been torn apart. My entire implementation plan had gone to hell. There was no need to stage the work in an orderly, sequential fashion since the entire site was deadlined without any solution in sight.

Busy with fixing solder connections, I barely noticed the footsteps, but immediately recognized the voice. "I hear you've been having some problem."

"Well, well. Mystery-man is here. I sure hope you can do something about it," I said, jumping to my feet to greet him. "COR won't give one inch. You know what his problem is?"

"Political," he said, slightly shaking his head. "Nothing you or I can do."

"Why not? You run the project." I had to let him know about his responsibilities.

"Not after it's assigned to the field. It's out of my hands."

"I don't like it. It's going to reflect poorly on my performance, as well as the company's."

"Can you get away?"

"Now?"

"Yes, now. Let's get something to eat. I hear you haven't had a break in the last couple of days."

"I sure could use a bite, but am afraid I might go to sleep."

"Don't worry. I'll keep you awake."

"I was afraid of that."

"Let's get Frank, and the team to come along." Frank was the new project manager who had replaced Art. Frank, and I had worked several projects together as engineers. He had moved up the ranks to become department director. I was glad for him. He'd deserved it.

We were gone for the next several hours visiting our favorite restaurant in this part of the world. The proprietor knew us well, and hosted us accordingly. There was only one difference this time. I did not touch the customary wine, and after dinner drinks. I would have been useless for the rest of the project. I was too exhausted, and couldn't wait for dinner to end to get back to the site. The challenge for the job at hand was keeping me awake.

Since my presence on site was required nonstop, I forfeited sleep for 72 hours, in addition to the 24-hour flight time in route from Japan. By this time, I was not only exhausted, but dead tired, on the brink of passing out. During the entire episode I noticed team members disappear to eat, and get a few hours' sleep. To assure project readiness following the three-day delay, I made it my mission to be present at all times. I did not want to be the cause of added delays.

Three days later I finally got clearance by the COR to switch to operational. I did not stay around for an out-briefing. I left the site in total disgust, headed back to the hotel, chauffeured by an army sergeant.

I made it as far as the lobby, sought out the nearest chair, and promptly collapsed. The lobby was dark, and deserted. The clock indicated it was past midnight. Hours must have passed when I felt a tapping on my shoulder. "Please wake up." It was the desk clerk. Unperturbed by my behavior, the manager had let me sleep without being interrupted. It was noon time with vacationing guests arriving for lunch. I had slept for close to twelve hours. Awake, and refreshed I checked into my assigned room to take a desperately needed shower, called the site manager for status, and headed for the restaurant. I had only taken time out that one evening with Mystery-man to eat, but that was already two days ago; I was famished.

He was seated at the restaurant table as I walked in, waving me over. "Let me buy you lunch. The least I can do for the trouble we caused."

"What do you mean? Did you know about the delay?"

"I did. It was a last-minute decision by GAO[43]. Couldn't be helped. Even you are not immune from politics."

"I don't like it. You wouldn't either if your reputation was on the line. Would you?"

Though he didn't reply, we enjoyed the time together. "When are you headed out?" I said.

"This afternoon. I just wanted to talk with you before I left."

"I feel honored."

"I don't know when I'll see you again," he said, hinting at an uncertain future.

"Why? You bailing out?"

"Not me. You."

"What do you know that I don't?" I was taken by surprise at the revelation.

"There are changes about to happen."

"For who? The government or commercial sector?"

"Both. I might even be retired."

"You can't retire. What would I do without you? You are my inside man. We've worked together for twenty years." Robert, and I had a special working relation. Though we both worked at the same playing field, we played in different sandboxes, he at DARPA engineering with me at DOD systems. "Don't leave me stranded out there."

"I'll stay in touch." They were his last words when we parted. It would be anybody's guess if, and when we would cross paths again.

It was weeks later when I would learn the details for the site mishap. As indicated by Mystery-man, the unnecessary delay was purely political in nature forced on me personally, in turn, affecting Europe's communication capabilities instigated by the COR. Apparently, after years of flawless performance, my team and I had become so efficient that the government had a difficult time awarding AUTODIN service contracts up to open, competitive bidding. We had worked ourselves into an indispensable position. To give other contractors a chance to bid on future contracts, an example of incompetency had to be made. I had been declared scapegoat. It would be the only flaw in my thirty years contracting with the government. It served as a reminder for my distaste for political issues.

The reason for competitive contract biddings were to keep GAO budget expenditures at a minimum. In the long run, changing the contractor usually proved less effective, with additional cost impact incurred from teams needing to be trained

---

[43] Government Accounting Office provides fact-based, nonpartisan information to Congress. Often called the congressional watchdog, GAO investigates, and enforces federal spending, and performance.

on the system, in addition to logistics support changes. Also, and costly, new security clearances had to be issued, preceded by lengthy background investigations. It may sound like a simple process, but it was far from it. Each individual was investigated by the FBI, and local authorities, involving manpower, and costs for agents tracing your history, and path back to childhood. Only individuals without a criminal record would be able to obtain a T.S. clearance. The process was a one and a half year effort to be finalized, and granted. In the meantime, each subject pending the process was sitting idle at headquarters getting paid while awaiting assignment to an Intel site.

I completely understood the need for giving taxpayers a break. What I objected to was the underhanded means by which it was accomplished. Long after the incident occurred, my hope was to face the individual that had caused my grief at least once more, but fate did not allow me the pleasure. I was desperately looking for a chance to get even. I had also learned the status, and position of what I termed "my career enemy." He was of high ranking in government circles with direct connections to the executive branch.

Completing the project in record time, notwithstanding cut short, I felt I would deserve a couple of days privacy. I needed the time to assess my position, not only within the corporate environment I had been working in, but more importantly, my career at working government contracts. A number of years had passed since I had started out as novice working with government, military, and Intel. "What do I want out of life, career wise?" I'd asked myself.

Personally, I had achieved pretty much what I set out many years before, fulfilling my dreams. As far as career was concerned, I had been bypassed by colleagues into echelon rankings within the government structure. But those were special circumstances not extended to just anybody. Connections, and timing were essential for unique opportunities, elevating one upwards in status, and position.

Sometimes I wondered what would have been if I had accepted such offers. In recollection, I had turned down two such opportunities. The first time I was assigned to Guam. I was offered a GS-12 position from Pacific Naval Command. Another time, not that long ago, it was for a position at the same status with NATO, Germany. The reason I declined was simple. I could not envision myself strapped behind an office desk following instructions, submitting reports with endless meetings. On the positive side, I could have escalated into an executive position, well paid followed with comfortable retirement incentives. In hind sight, knowing what I do now, I could kick myself in the butt for not jumping at the offers. They did not come along often, especially when the standard entry into civil service begins with a GS-01, taking decades to elevate to the GS-09 level. To be extended an entry of GS-12 grade, and higher takes extraordinary skills almost impossible to obtain. But life is too short to dwell on what ifs.

Since I had checked in at my favorite hotel along the beaches of Livorno, a resort beach near Pisa, for the next few days I decided to enjoy the warm waters of the Mediterranean. It felt great baking in the afternoon sun watching bathers dogging waves. I must have dozed off before I became aware of someone cussing in a language I understood well. Fully awake, I propped up on my elbows to watch an unfamiliar unfolding scene. It was so comical I laughed out loud. It must have distraught the surfing pioneer for he dropped his gear, and strode over in my direction. "You think it is funny?"

"You don't look comfortable," I replied, avoiding his stare.

He ignored my irrational behavior, and proceeded to explain, "I am from Austria. I am here to test this new design."

"What's it called?"

"Windsurfer."

What I had witnessed was him trying to execute what looked like a beach start. Each time he took a running start by jumping on the board while grabbling the boom, and sail, he fell into the water off the opposite side of the board. After several tries, he became desperate enough to let out his frustration. I got up from my sandy blanket to inspect the gear I had never set eyes on. Brand new in the industry, it was a sport just introduced that year.

"Want to try?" he said with an encouraging grin.

"Naw," I declined. "Just had fun watching."

"No really. You try it," he kept insisting.

When I did, it was his turn to laugh. Sure enough, each time I stepped on the unstable board with sail in hand, trying to balance my body, I fell off like him. Short of cussing myself, I thanked him for the offer, and returned the board. After several more unsuccessful starts, he finally gave up with a final cussing, "Damned thing is no good." Little did we know that windsurfing would take the world by storm.

I thought it might have been the end of the sport until the following summer, when the boards showed up at sporting goods stores. Bold enough, I bought one. Despite the many ditches that followed, I fell in love with it. It took several months to become proficient enough to handle the rig comfortably. After that, I was literally sailing the seven seas. I took to it every chance I had. I shipped the board as freight along my overseas travels wherever there was water.

The following year I watched a Yahoo commercial, and completely amazed at another new sport come to life. The commercial was some mountain climbers skating down a hill on what was to become inline skating. Within seconds I'd decided, "This for me," and promptly went to the store. Unfortunately, I had to wait another year before the skates showed up in stores. I totally enjoyed both sports activities to the fullest for many years to come.

Meanwhile, back in Pisa, I took the time to get to know what I had missed out on prior trips, the Roman arts with its rich classical culture. On one such fine day I decided to have lunch at a local restaurant. Since it was summertime, the population took to the terrace, gardens, and sidewalks.

Sunny, and bright all summer, it was nice sitting under an umbrella overlooking the city. Before long, I had a visitor. It was a raven landing on my table. Both curious, we kept eyeing each other for some time. When the waitress showed up, she said, "Oh. It must like you."

"Why do you say that?"

"The bird only stays with certain guests."

"What does it do?" I was curious.

"It steals money," she said with a smile on her face then went inside the restaurant. I decided to put the raven to a test. I put some Lira coins on the table, and waited. Sure enough, the bird took a coin, and flew away. I watched it disappear through a window not far off, then reappeared minutes later only to snatch up more coins. It then dawned on me. The bird was trained to fetch money for his owner. Italians could be crafty at times. I was entranced by it, and put up more coins, but this time placed them under an inverted water glass. I watched the bird land by the glass, fiercely pecking at it, but it could not dislodge the coins from beneath.

"What's next?" I thought while watching. It seemed the bird understood my intention of playing with it. The next thing it did was land on my shoe and, with its beak, untie the laces. Then it hopped to the next foot, and undid the other shoelace.

"How clever," I thought. "The bird can think." When the waitress reappeared with my bill, she said, "It is not nice to tease the bird."

"The bird started it," I complained. "It took my money, and untied my shoes."

She then told me the whole story. Apparently, the neighbor a few houses over specifically trained the raven to steal to compensate for a measly retirement. It was his way of making a living. So, not all of my life was without humor, and fun. There were many happy times especially when the team got together for a party. Things, at times, got out of hand, but in hilarious ways. In all the years managing projects I could not recall one incident where a fight broke out or I had to squelch a potential skirmish. It's how tight the team spirit was.

Back to my stay in Pisa. It was not the first time I was tested. There had been other challenges thrown across my career path to test my technical skills, but I would never let it bother me. One such time was years before. I was approached by Art with, "They want you in Georgia." Georgia being the Army Intelligence training center, located within the perimeters of Ft. Gordon Army base. I readily agreed, but wondered, "Why me?"

"They specifically asked for you."

I thought it was a teaching position. Though challenged at times by some "know-it-all student," I enjoyed instructing classes on technology, but did not look forward to a lengthy teaching assignment.

"What's the catch?" I'd asked. There were other prospects at headquarters jumping at the opportunity just to get away from the home office.

"No catch."

"What's the job?"

With a slight grin on his face, Art stated, "You'll find out after you get there. It's only for a week." I figured he knew what it entailed, but just did not want to divulge.

"Okay. I'll be on my way."

My travel orders were cut, and ticket ready when I stopped at the accountant's office. "Have fun."

"I always do," I called after her, headed for the airport.

It was a Sunday when I left. Arriving at Augusta, GA, I checked in at the Holiday Inn. The following morning, waved through the gate after an ID check, I was ushered to the commander's office. "He's waiting," the orderly said.

After I entered, he came right to the point. "We are all set."

"Set for what?" I said, somewhat surprised.

"You don't know?"

"I haven't been told."

"Okay. Here's the job. Signal school is conducting a reliability, and performance test to evaluate the students. GAO requested me to perform the evaluation. It's your job to see that it gets done. You have five days."

"That's it?" Though unexpected, I was ready to start on whatever had been arranged.

"That is all. Test conductor is waiting at the site."

I was whisked to the training center, a complete complement of an AUTODIN complex with a scaled down version of only a four-mainframe computer system. I was very familiar with the configuration since I had put the system in place years earlier. Moving the Army Intel school from the previous location at Ft. Monmouth, NJ, to Ft. Gordon, GA, was my first participation in 1966.

This morning I would be tested for my skill, I was told. Whatever they had in mind, I had five days to complete. I went to work. What it entailed was the following. Training instructors would induce arbitrary bugs (failure-induced circuit cards) into the system only known to the instructors, three sharp individuals conducting the tests. Arbitrarily in mainframe, and associated equipment, each would insert a defective circuit card into the system. It could be the mainframe, memory unit, processor, storage device, front processing, or switchgear. It was up to me to locate, and replace the defective part, and run a test program to verify.

It was sheer fun on my part in contrast for the instructors. I kept them busy, swiftly moving between storage, and computer rooms to retrieve the next bugged circuit card. At noon, we broke for lunch. I went to the break room vending machine for a sandwich, and the instructors were called into the commander's office. Not knowing the reason for the private meeting, I continued the rest of the day with pretty much the same routine that I had dictated throughout the morning, with one difference. There suddenly appeared to be more than one bug through the system. Fixing one problem would cause additional errors in the system. Puzzled after an hour's troubleshooting I challenged the instructors, "What are you doing to me?"

I'd noticed several red-faced, belying innocence. Whether intentionally, as I had suspected, or unintentionally, I was challenged. Calling their bluff, after correcting all errors testing the system, I restored the training site to its operational status. Expecting to get on with testing, though by now it was close to quitting time, 5:00 p.m., the instructors gathered around the command console where I sat, stating, "We don't have any more bugged cards." As unbelievable as it may sound, I had used up all fifty defective test cards prepared for the week in only one day.

The challenge had become personal. The earlier delays had been intentional. Whether it was planned or initiated during my analysis, and testing efforts was up for speculation. As I was preparing for departure I was called in to the commander's office for the out brief. "You sure kept my instructors busy. If I had not watched your performance, I would not have believed it."

"I didn't mean to. It's how I work"

From my perspective, I had achieved what I had expected to. From the government administrative offices', I was officially disqualified from future evaluations. Ensuing rumors began to circulate within the Intel community: "Test was fixed… Students did not do their job… He knew of the bugs… Test was cut short," and other comments.

I feel compelled to explain my position. It was never my intention to embarrass the signal school, the government, or its administrators. I had been called on to do a job. If I excelled, it was only due to my skills, and expertise. Others may have had a life; I did not. I lived to work. My entire life was dedicated to my career. It did not come naturally. It took one hundred percent dedication. Where others may go home from work, and forget about the job for the day, I was advancing my knowledge on technology in my off hours as well. I arrived at a stage where computers had become a toy, and game rather than a struggle. I could analyze, identify, and solve any issue, no matter how difficult, in the briefest time, within minutes, while others might struggle for hours or days. I had accomplished the ultimate in expertise, thorough understanding of the internal workings of computer hardware, software, applications, and systems. Much like a Rock guitar player, I had reached the pinnacle of my career. I was looking for new challenges.

It was not long after when I received a call from headquarters. "You've got a new assignment. How soon can you get here?" Unfortunately, it was not Art directing me. The voice was unfamiliar.

"I can't take on another project. I'm under contract for another year," I replied. Only four years had passed since I took the five-year contract obligation with the DOD, traversing the globe.

"We'll get you out of it," was the reply.

"Suppose I won't?"

"You have no choice."

"I can always quit," I said, holding my ground.

"You could do that, but it would be your last job with the government."

To this day I do not know if the threat was a bluff. *At least*, I thought, *I'll give it a try*. "What's the project?"

"Can't tell you on the phone. You have to come in."

"Where?" I had no clue where the call was initiated from.

"Lockheed headquarters."

"Colorado Springs? I'll be there in two days. Soon enough?"

"It'll do. See you then. By the way," he added. "I'm the program director. You'll report to me."

"What's your name?"

"Call me Jim."

MISSILE DEFENSE

The year was 1988. I was not surprised at the new boss, Jim, but regretted that it was not Art, my friend, and mentor. What irked me more was the prolific corporate mergers, and hostile takeovers through the 80s. I started my career with Philco Ford, the consumer division for Ford Motor, in the 60s, which not long after became Ford Aerospace. That I understood. It was a move for Ford corporate to get the AUTODIN contract award. What transpired in the 80s was entirely different. It was corporate greed driving owners to eliminate competition. I could hardly keep up with the changes. On my four years around the world tours serving the Intel communities, it seemed like each time I returned to headquarters, the company, as well as management, had changed hands.

The initial transitions directly affecting my employment, from what I can recall, began with Martin Company taking over American-Marietta to become Martin-Marietta. Sometime later, Loral Command & Control, a newcomer to the defense industry, took over Ford Aerospace. In between, Ford Aerospace merged with Goodyear, then White Trucking Co., and Western Development Labs. Finally, Lockheed merged with Martin, and acquired Loral Command & Control systems, taking over missile defense systems. Whereas Lockheed had been heavily involved in rocket building for space flights, it eventually turned that effort over to Boeing, creating the ULA[44], with its own primary focus on the nation's defense, and Intelligence support. It was this situation I would face in the following years.

"REACT – Program Office," the sign above the doorframe said when I knocked on the door.

"Come on in," the manager said. Stepping inside, he gestured to a chair. "Have a seat."

The office was a relatively small space. I would have thought a director with his responsibility would deserve at least a corner suite. *Budget must be tight,* I thought, looking around the bare office with only a few personalized pictures, and college plaque fastened to one wall.

"Jim," he offered with an outstretched hand. He was about my age, impeccably dressed in suit, and tie, well groomed, with a flare of sophistication. I immediately took a liking to him. I could relate to his presence, emerged from the same establishment, the 60s. He did not seem to fit the general profile for its day of a director with the usual cigar dangling from lips, belly stuffed in dress pants with coffee mug not far from reach.

"Bauer," I said, returning the gesture. "Alex Bauer."

---

[44] United Launch Alliance is a provider of spacecraft launch services to the United States government. It was formed as a joint venture between Lockheed Martin Space Systems, and Boeing Defense, Space & Security in December 2006 by combining the teams at the two companies. U.S. government launch customers include the Department of Defense, and NASA, as well as other organizations. With ULA, Lockheed, and Boeing held a monopoly on military launches for more than a decade until the US Air Force awarded a GPS satellite contract to SpaceX in 2016.

"I've heard about your success. It's the reason Corporate called you back from the field." He then abruptly left his office, but not before shoving a manual across the desk. "Here. Take a look. I'll be right back."

My eyes were focused on the framed pictures hanging from the walls. Like many managers in the industry, they represented career histories of the person occupying the office. "Impressive," I muttered. Jim, much like myself, seemed to have had a rich career. The only difference was that I had no office, no pictures, and no secretary. I reached for the manual to get an idea of what was in store for me. "Rapid Execution, and Combat Targeting," the cover stated in bold lettering.

"Wonder what that's all about," I thought just as Jim reentered.

"Sorry about that. Had to step out for a minute. Now," he said with a smile at the manual, "let me fill you in."

"What's REACT?"

He thought about it, then said, "I'm new to the program. I just started here a couple of weeks ago. Don't know much about it either. Let's do this," he said, getting up from the chair. "I'll show you. By the way," he stopped for a second, "you'll be reporting directly to me."

"We'll see." As usual, when faced with a new element, I proceeded with caution. I did not commit myself to anything until I was familiar with the project. I did not want to get stuck with something not befitting my skills. I'd learned that many years ago. It was the cause for many career failures in the world of corporations, and decision-makers. Many newly-hired, when offered, accept a corporate level, too advanced for their competence, leaving disgruntled employees in their wake. With a position change generally came along new responsibilities that had to be learned and acquired. Not always an easy task, especially when sensing resistance from competing subjects vying for the same position.

I was led down a lengthy corridor before we turned left, then down another passageway, arriving at an entrance protected by a cypher lock. He pushed a few buttons then opened what appeared much like a vault. Being led inside, the first impression I perceived was that of a sterile environment taking up space the size of several offices. The room was humongous, filled with dozens of filing cabinets, and an array of printers, and plotters, without anybody present.

"You see all this?" Jim indicated with a sweep of one arm across the room. "Consider it yours."

"What?" I was dumbfounded. There was more reading material stored here than at the national archives.

"It's yours. All yours," he said again, accompanied by a grin.

I was looking for signs of humor in his face, but he seemed dead serious when he stated, "You have full access, twenty-four seven."

"What makes you think I would want any of it?" Appalled at such a bold presumption, I felt like stepping in a hornet's nest.

"You have no choice," he replied, stern-faced. "Corporate's already decided."

"Let me get this straight," I stalled. "I am ordered?"

"It seems that way, doesn't it?"

"I need to talk to somebody in charge." I was upset all around, not so much about stepping into an empty vault void of employees, but more because of the way I was treated. Although I appreciated the confidence extended, I should still have a saying in the matter when my future was at stake. After all, my career, and life were on the line if I failed. I had no inkling about the program, or what the job entailed.

"As I already stated," Jim said once more, "I'm in charge of the program."

I stepped up to a filing drawer partially pulled out, rifled through the folders, and arbitrarily picked one out. "Nuclear Testing – Bikini Island, 1953."

"What is this?"

"Most of the material stored in the cabinets are test results conducted by Westinghouse following WWII," he explained. "The company was commissioned to record all tests conducted at Kwajalein. It was the baseline for the design of our missile defense systems. It's going to be your baseline."

"I don't know anything about nuclear physics or science."

"Neither does anybody else." He then explained that the company, as large as Lockheed was, notwithstanding an employee resource pool of 120,000, worldwide, had not been able to locate anybody with the experience necessary for the project. "Scientists, and engineers that developed, and built the missile defense either retired or passed away years ago," he stated.

"What makes you so sure I'd accept?"

"Like I said, you have no choice. The company picked you."

"What are my options?"

"I promise you that much. You complete the job, you can name any place, any position you choose in the future."

"Guaranteed?"

"Corporate decision."

"What about people?"

"You get whatever you need. We've had people waiting for months."

"How many months?"

"The program is one year behind schedule."

"Who's the lead engineer?"

"You'll be it."

"What?" I objected. Not only would I be in charge of development, worse yet, I would be redesigning a system for a program already indebted. "Who's the customer?"

"BMO – Offutt AFB."

"Never heard of it."

"Ballistic Missiles Office. Not many have. So," he pressured, "what do I tell Corporate?"

"What about clearance?"

"You'll need atomic access."

"What makes you sure I'd qualify?"

"Listen," he said with finality. "You were picked to handle the project. You'll get whatever is required. Satisfied?"

"I'll let you know." I had made the decision, but wanted to get a feel for the task. The best way for that was to get familiar with the archived material.

"I need a commitment now." He was adamant. "They are waiting."

"Okay." I finally succumbed to the inevitable. I had been selected, but I was no pushover.

He was preparing to leave the vault when I stayed behind. "You coming?"
Short of an air of hostility, I said, "I've got a lot of reading, don't I?"
"Now?"

"There's no better time. Check with me in the morning." I closed the doors behind him. Being custodian for the material stored here, I would spend the following two weeks reading nothing but blueprints, test results, and classified reports. It would be my domain until I would emerge. The first several days I would take a break a couple of times a day to visit the cafeteria for coffee, and a sandwich. It was a meager subsistence, but I was used to eating only when necessary, especially when under extreme pressure. On one such trip I ran into a familiar face. "Buzz?"

Startled, he exclaimed, "Alex! What are you doing here? When did you get here?" Many questions followed, but only some of them I was able to answer. For now, I replied with a question. "What are you working on?"

"REACT Testbed," he said with a shrug of his shoulders, indicating his task. I realized with him on the program we could not fail. Buzz was the best, and most qualified individual for the environment. Others from the team would soon join. He then explained his function. I was happy to hear he was assigned on the same program. At least I had reliable backing. We sat while he reported. It'd turned out that the company, unsuccessfully, had made serious efforts in trying to locate anyone with skills, and expertise in warhead designs. Where launch facilities, and silos had been kept in an operational state of readiness for decades by trained missile crews, since the SALT[45] treaty, nobody had envisioned that it would ever be activated for a possible launch. Without any requirement, universities such as MIT[46], and SRI[47] had stopped offering curriculums

---

[45] SALT-I, common name for the Strategic Arms Limitation Talks Agreement signed on May 26, 1972. SALT-I froze the number of strategic ballistic missile launchers at existing levels, and provided for the addition of new submarine-launched ballistic missile (SLBM) launchers only after the same number of older intercontinental ballistic missile (ICBM), and SLBM launchers had been dismantled. SALT-I also limited land-based ICBMs that were in range from the northeastern border of the continental United States to the northwestern border of the continental USSR. In addition to that, SALT-I limited the number of SLBM capable submarines that NATO, and the United States could operate to 50 with a maximum of 800 SLBM launchers between them. If the United States or NATO were to increase that number, the USSR could respond with increasing their arsenal by the same amount.

SALT-II was a series of talks between United States, and Soviet negotiators from 1972 to 1979 which sought to curtail the manufacture of strategic nuclear weapons. It was a continuation of the SALT-I talk, and was led by representatives from both countries. SALT-II was the first nuclear arms treaty which assumed real reductions in strategic nuclear forces to 2,250 of all categories of delivery vehicles on both sides.

[46] The Massachusetts Institute of Technology (MIT) is a private research university in Cambridge, Massachusetts, United States. Founded in 1861 in response to the increasing industrialization of the United States, MIT adopted a European polytechnic university model, and stressed laboratory instruction in applied science, and engineering. The Institute is traditionally known for its research, and education in the physical sciences, and engineering, but more recently in biology, economics, linguistics, and management as well. MIT is often cited among the world's best universities by various organizations.

[47] Stanford Research International (SRI) is an American nonprofit research institute headquartered in Menlo Park, California. The trustees of Stanford University established SRI in 1946 as a center of innovation to support economic development in the region. The organization was founded as the Stanford Research Institute. SRI formally separated from Stanford University in 1970, and became known as SRI International

in nuclear science, and physics. Nuclear science in the U.S. had fallen by the wayside decades ago. The army of scientists, and engineers who had built the missile defense system in the 50s, by now, were either retired or had passed away. With MAD doomsday policies in place, neither the U.S. nor the USSR policy makers had ever thought of a need to possibly launch ICBMs at each other. But times changed, and so did politics. Nothing was ever guaranteed to last. The Cold War had escalated to new heights.

To clarify, when President Reagan ordered the Space Based Defense Initiative (SBI), better known as Star Wars coined by the public, with the Soviet Union, our adversary, unable to appropriate a budget to create an equivalent defense system, in retaliation, developed and built bigger, and more destructive nuclear warheads ten times, and greater than our present missile payloads.

Our military quickly realized, in case of a direct hit on our missile launch centers, and silos, that we had no protection against such devastating power. As a result, Lockheed was commissioned by Air Force (SAC) to build suitable protection. Several alternatives were considered such as the rail garrison, a railroad-based missile launch system. While most promising, it was scrapped for one reason or other. Due to severe budgetary restraints, the only means available was to upgrade our existing systems. This was the time when I entered the picture, to come up with a feasible design for warding off adversary initiatives from possible all-out nuclear attack.

It was at this point when I had an inspiring thought: *why not give Mystery-man a call?* After all, being head of DARPA's engineering branch, he might have access to PhDs with possible nuclear backgrounds, and knowledge of missile design. I made the call.

"Alex," he beamed. "How is it going? You on the project yet?"

"You knew. I'm on the program. Missile defense. Redesign new technology."

"It's about time. I always wondered if it's still effective. What's your function?"

"Lead engineer."

"They got the right man. What can I do for you?"

"I am looking for nuclear design experts. Know anybody there?"

"Are you kidding? Nobody left anymore. Can't help you. Sorry."

"Guess it's up to me now."

"Well. Do your best. I know you can do it. Let me know your progress."

For the time being, with me strapped to the defense program for the next several years, and him on only God knew what black project, it could be some time before I would see Mystery-man again. I had one consolation, though; I received help in the form of the chief rocket scientist liaison to Lockheed's Titan missile design headquarters out of Denver, though with one restraint. While he would periodically check with me on my progress, he informed me that, "I won't be much help to you with the nuclear warhead."

"But I still report to you?"

---

in 1977. SRI performs client-sponsored research, and development for government agencies, commercial businesses, and private foundations.

"We can work this out together," he assured me. "You design the protection and I will give you the best rocket you need." I appreciated the gesture, but it was not a rocket I needed. What I needed was an innovative design protection against EMP, and nuclear pulsing. I sobered up to the recognition that it was up to me now.

My design, with the support of qualified experts from the corporate pool of engineers, aside from applying Westinghouse' extensive test parameters, turned out relatively simple. Short of disclosing stated parameters for security reasons, my challenge was to find a company that would manufacture the necessary components. There were none in the country. Following an extensive trade study, I was able to locate one company that qualified. To negotiate possible fabrication, I wound up at a most unlikely place, Germany. It turned out that it was Siemens AG, headquartered in Munich, that could manufacture the solution.

"Want to take a trip?" I asked Buzz. As long as I was part of it, he was always ready for the road.

"Where're we going?"

"Munich."

"Germany?" He said with an anticipated grin on his face. From his expression, he could taste the naturally brewed beer already, and so could I.

"Thought you'd like it."

After arriving at their plant, and presenting the design specifications, it only took a few hours for Siemens management to agree with a promise of gearing up tools, and personnel. While they had not been involved with EMP directly, their components, while similar in nature, were used in large power plants susceptible to severe lightning strikes. The nature of a strike may have been different on the electrical grid, but the resultant damages were similar to a nuclear strike on the defense system.

The rest of the week we spent our daylight hours sightseeing at some of Europe's worthy tourists' spots with our nighttime's spent at the city's famous clubs in Schwabing, the city's international entertaining district. At any night, in any club, one was able to rub shoulders with high-profile actors and actresses from around the globe. It was a place Eva Gabor got her start of fame.

Five days later, back at headquarters again, we had our work cut out for us. Many months behind schedule, I drew on engineering resources, as much as I needed for blueprints, circuit designs, graphics development, component values, and more. I was even allocated the first IBM PC, up to then only issued to management. My initial workaround was sneaking in the director's office, and preparing the weekly progress reports on his computer. He must have gotten tired of it because one morning I had a unit sitting on my desk.

The PC, or personal computer, in my opinion was one of the biggest inventions for advancing the world of modern business. It cut down time wasted on correcting typewritten documents, accessing databases, researching in archives at libraries, and many more business-related functions. It was a glorious moment for me when I installed the newly developed software application AutoCAD. It allowed me to design EMP protection into the REACT system with extraordinary speed, and efficiency.

It was getting close to the date for my first design presentation with BMO. Top brass from Offutt was expected to attend. On the morning of the presentation, the head of the engineering department rushed into my office cube. "How do we stand? Are you ready? What are you going to present?"

Obviously highly nervous about the event, he wanted to make sure that nothing went wrong. No matter how much I tried to placate him, it did not help. He was as anxious as could be, sticking his head in my cube every five minutes. I finally got tired of him because he would not let me focus on the material I had prepared. What bothered him most was that I had been tasked by management to make the presentation whereas it should have been his responsibility. To make things worse, I had disregarded corporate policies by not following the chain of command. One day he confronted me. "Why can't you report to me?"

I gave him an honest answer. "I'm not about to waste time explaining my designs to everybody."

"I'm head of engineering," he'd complain. I asked him on more than one occasion to make the presentations. His response was, "I can't do it. I don't know the design." In my defense, I could not, and would not waste my time to educated others in the nation's most critical work handed to me on a program already many months behind schedule. I had a job to do without additional interference. In retrospect, he congratulated me at the end of my success on the program with, "I could not have pulled it off. You did it." We parted on respectful terms.

He was in his rights to do so. What he could not accept was that I only worked directly for the executive level, better known as Mahogany Row. There was always a place reserved for me, if I elected to do so. But that would not have been me.

The presentation went well. The brass was extremely pleased with my progress. They should have been. After I familiarizing myself with thousands of documents collecting dust in filing cabinets for fifty years, I was ready for the design. Fortunately, one of my former colleagues, Al, volunteered to help me with the designs. We split the effort into two categories. He would take on Minuteman while I could concentrate on Peacekeeper missiles. We would compare notes whenever necessary, making great strides. I had known Al U. since my early days when he taught computer science at the Army signal school. Though we had crossed paths on occasion, our spheres of responsibilities were worlds apart. Where he had been assigned to support the European theater, my focus was in the Pacific.

As for the REACT program, we worked well together without having to waste time with strategy meetings. Management left us alone, assured that we would get the job done. Though grossly outdated in technology, the missile defense system was diligently kept up by Missileers[48] through rigid testing. There was never any doubt about that. We both knew technology in, and out. If there was a question, we knew where to find the answer. There may have been nobody left alive from the original designers to get answers from, but we had the archived documents.

The teams supporting us were just as proficient in their work, and deliveries. We delivered the design months ahead of schedule, ready to be tested. There were many elements within blueprint, and project parameters. Some of the major ones were the command and control console, tactical acquisition and targeting software, new

---

[48] A missile Combat Crew (MCC) is a team of highly trained specialists, often called Missileers, manning intermediate range, and intercontinental ballistic missiles.

hardware, and antenna hardening against a direct nuclear strike, as well as missile silos, and power feeds. Each part not only had to be software tested but hardware tested against shock, impact, and nuclear pulsing as well, with the comprehensive test plan I had developed. Three years into the effort, Al U. and I turned all project elements over to management, stating, "That's it. We are finished here."

"Terrific… Well done… Outstanding job."

"Guess I can move on now," I proposed. To what, I did not know at the time. I had been too busy to keep track of economic, and political developments. *I could take time off from contracting*, and similar thoughts crossed my mind, but reality had a different plan.

"Not so fast," Jim insisted. "We are not finished yet."

"What?" I was dumbfounded because there had not been the slightest indication of additional work. I would have known about unfinished business. For all I knew, they must have kept it a secret for some specific reasons.

"There is one more task waiting for you." Regardless of type or scope I remained in the executive suite to listen. "This one is highly classified."

"I'm listening."

Deliberately shoving a few contract pages across the table, "Here is the task order," Jim said with a serious face. "We are nine months behind delivery."

Delays or not, I read the addition to the original contract, and could not help, but exclaim, "Man! This is serious business."

"You are not kidding."

I understood why management had held it back. Rumors alone could have shifted the balance of power. It was not part of the SALT treaties. It could have triggered serious consequences if our adversary caught wind of it.

Following was what the order entailed: Build a tactical (mobile) control console into a portable suitcase, one for Minuteman (with backup), and one for Peacekeeper (with backup) missile launch capabilities, to respond with immediate retaliation in case of an all-out preemptive strike by the adversary powers."

I could have refused. I could have objected. Instead, I accepted the order. There were a number of reasons for not taking on the assignment from a moral perspective to my limited knowledge on missile launches. One, I had never worked with radio spectrum frequencies, and two, it was an assurance to eliminate mankind from the face of the earth. I will explain.

Where the current missile defense system was restrained by SALT to strategic (fixed), identifiable locations know to each adversary, the U.S. and USSR with nuclear-tipped, targeted ICBMs centered and targeted at each other for annihilation. In contrast to using portable launch consoles, the operator could launch from any protected location, when selecting proper frequency, launch one to ten missiles, regardless whether strategic launch centers still existed or had been destroyed by enemy warheads.

Where I was faced with the same challenge at the start of my REACT participation, this proposal was serious. It impacted humanity and morality for a possible annihilation. It had become personal. Did I want to tackle the project or pass on it? I felt like making a decision implicating every person alive on the planet. Consequences could be too terrifying even to think of. Then a light went on in my brain. "U.S. policy makers could not have overlooked this possibility." I knew that we had the best strategists in the world working at the Pentagon. "What if the plan was to shock the Soviets into submission with the revelation for having backup during an all-out nuclear exchange?"

Jim detected my hesitation, and stated, "You have no choice."

"Sounds familiar," I huffed. "Doesn't it?"

"We have nobody to do the job. Besides," he explained, "it would take too much time to hire and clear a radio frequency expert."

"So," I challenged him, "what's my baseline?"

"You'll have to decide." He leaned back with a sigh. His job was done. Mine was only beginning. "Try to do your best," he said, indicating the end of the discussion. Aside the friendship we had developed, attending social affairs, BBQs, and periodic dining out, I felt a certain compunction for him. He was as trapped as I was for the success of the company, the world's largest defense contractor.

I did not only try, but delivered the product, two prototype built-in launch panels in a record six weeks. To accomplish the task, I shut myself out from all management interferences aside, from an occasional query: "How are you coming along?" I responded with, "It's coming." As a penalty for dumping such a world-changing challenge on me I let them guess, and speculate. For getting the job done I asked for Al, and Buzz's commitments, who, as usual, helped me out of the jam. We were an effective team willing to take on the world if necessary. I designed the electronics packaged into the aluminum case, while Buzz handled the hardware acquisitions, and Al U. built the actual cases. To accomplish the job without interference from the outside we acquired a specially reserved mini-lab with private access only to the three of us. Luckily, the required parts needed were available at government surplus stores. What proved a challenge was creating the spectrum of frequency modules capable of triggering, and launching the array of missile silos contained below ground at the various classified locations spread through Wyoming, Montana, and the Dakotas.

"Ready for the test," Al announced on the given day. "How do you want to do it?"

We had been faced with similar conditions months before. Where Al, and Buzz had handled shock, and impact testing at the Army's proving grounds at Dugway, NV[49], I selected the specific radio frequencies necessary to trigger, and launch missiles, if required, in a last-ditch effort to save the U.S., and its citizens from annihilation.

---

[49] Dugway Proving Ground, located southwest of Salt Lake City, Utah, is a U.S. Army facility established in 1942 to test biological, and chemical weapons, and as training range forming the largest overland airspace in the United States.

Note: My intentions are not to disclose classified data to the reader or to the world. Where in the past some of the material within the author's writings has been held as classified information, in the world of today, though uncommon knowledge, all could be verified as public data through FOIA, with Google, and other search engines. Many years had passed since the original designs with much of the materials having been declassified on public demands.

Proving it would be a challenge: how to effectively test a destructive device with its delivery system live. It would have to be closely coordinated with participating defense command, military organizations, NORAD, missile crews, the Pentagon, and the president. It could take days, as long as there were no obstacles or objections from command positions. In either case, the tests would have to be conducted in absolute secrecy. If, by chance, a missile would be triggered inadvertently, hell would break out from Soviet Union command, anticipating a direct launch aimed at their nation.

How could we prevent such possibility?

My engineering team, and I tossed numerous scenarios at each other to be prepared for any potential mistakes or failure. It was not an easy task. It took intricate knowledge of system hardware, software, performance, and simulations, with its politically charged policies. Any inadvertent error could be held as a declaration of war. To make certain that the testing was conducted in a failsafe manner, we had to consider all possible variations before executing. All components were tested live, and only the actual missile launch would be simulated. Rocket engines had to be disabled from firing just prior to being triggered.

To redesign hardware, software, and systems took months to prepare, more time to verify, and test, in addition to develop a sound test plan that included not only step-by-step parameters, but policies, and procedures in accordance to military and defense specifications. Designing, and engineering were the foundation for any technological creation, but when it came to document each element, and step, everybody shied away from the responsibility. There seem to be an aversion, in general, to tackle the tasks for recording process and procedures. However, they were responsibilities specifically spelled out within every government contract, down to the last detail.

Where it was not a steadfast requirement in the commercial sector, where most projects are winged based on budget, and timeline, government factions made sure all requirements were met. The purpose served two important factors. One, accountability to the taxpayer, and two, continuity of operations, especially pertinent with critical missions. What it meant is seamless transition of technology, and procedure within the periodic, and frequent transition of personnel.

For some unexplained reason, most times, either I took on the responsibility, or I was designated to generate the required documentations whether test plan, presentation materials, processes and procedures, and whatever else was required to record, and archive data. In recollection, I must have had an unconscious foresight to acquire writing skills applied to writing novels in later years. Though, the experience creating documents is not nearly enough to become a published author, it certainly helped to gain the fundamentals, as was the case with me.

My time with the REACT program was coming to an end with all contractual obligations met. In the three and a half year I achieved something I had never expected, successfully redesign the nation's missile defense system in preparation to a potential retaliation from a superpower attack. Where the stage was set to implement the system into the defense grid, several unexpected events took place affecting the world, resulting in dramatic changes.

Initiated in Europe, a sequence of actions were taking hold changing the cold war. It all began in November of 1989 with the Berlin Wall being stormed by a group of East German freedom fighters taking advantage of an unexpected turn of events.

The Berlin Wall was a guarded concrete barrier that physically, and ideologically divided West Berlin from the East from 1961 to 1989. Constructed by the German Democratic Republic which began on 13 August 1961, the Wall cut off West Berlin from virtually all of surrounding East Germany, and East Berlin. Once in place, it divided Eastern Europe from the West for some thirty years not only effecting political, economic, as well as social relationships between a once united, but now severely separated people, and culture. The wall had cut off all possibility to ever unite the people again. In case of a border breach by courageous individuals trying to cross the border, punishment was severe with most lives ending in death while the world watched in horror without being able to help the unfortunate. Many have tried and paid for it with death.

Then, I clearly recall the day of liberation. I was on one of my missions assisting NATO Intel, enjoying another fine German meal at my favorite hotel restaurant, when a news flash came across the screen mounted against the dining wall across my vision. The event took place late in the evening. I could not believe what I witnessed. A group of young nationals on the East German side of the Wall were taking possession of the main border crossing by force amid completely confused border guards. To mine, and the organizers surprise, there was no resistance or retaliation. When one, then several, followed with more courageous individuals passed guard posts, more, and more joined in to an eventual torrent of liberators forcing, pushing their way into the West, lasting through the night. West Germany was taken by storm in November 1989.

What followed days, and weeks after was witnessed in awe by the world. News headlines became a daily experience while watching more, and more people pushing their way West while East German, and the Soviet Union governments permitted the crossings. Weeks later, it became obvious that the Cold War was destined to come to an end as result of Presidents Mikhail Gorbachev, and Ronald Reagan, who initiated events months back with the following statement: "Mr. Gorbachev! Please tear down the Wall."

The wall's demolition officially began on 13 June 1990, and ended in 1992. The barrier included guard towers placed along large concrete walls accompanied by a wide area that contained anti-vehicle trenches, "Fakir beds," and other defenses was being demolished. The Eastern Bloc, portrayed by the Wall originally built as protection from fascist elements conspiring to prevent the "will of the people," creating a socialist state in East Germany, was crumbling. In practice, the Wall served to prevent the massive emigration, and defection that had marked East Germany, and the communist Eastern Bloc during the post-World War II period. The results were dramatic, affecting East, and West.

Ronald Reagan, at the time, was facing the end of his career as presidential leader. With the public generally satisfied with his promised accomplishments, he wanted to maintain his acquired popularity for posterity. Following are some of his accomplishments:

He changed the course of the Cold War through the Reagan Doctrine.

He introduced the Strategic Defense Initiative.

Ronald Reagan played a key role in ending the Cold War.
His economic policy resulted in a considerable decrease in unemployment, and inflation.
Reaganomics led to one of the largest peacetime economic booms in U.S. history.
Reagan took unprecedented firm action when PATCO went on strike.
He introduced strict legislation for drug offenses.
Ronald Reagan is considered one of the most influential presidents in U.S. history.

On a less positive note, while the heralded economic program utilized during the Reagan administration emphasized low taxes, decreased regulation, low social services spending, it caused and high military spending. It contributed to low interest rates, low inflation, but large budget deficits. Some of the major legislations passed during his presidency included the Economic Recovery Tax Act of 1981, the Tax Equity, and Fiscal Responsibility Act of 1982, and the Tax Reform Act of 1986.

The Tax Reform Act obtained an overhaul of the income tax code, which eliminated many deductions, and exempted millions of people with low incomes. At the end of his administration, the nation was enjoying its longest recorded period of peacetime prosperity without recession or depression. Success, however, had no guarantee to last forever. Budget cuts affected some economic sectors, and others suffered as result.

As for myself, and the team, faced with a career decision in 1993 with the end of the REACT program, in addition to the Berlin Wall events, the U.S. defense posture was at stake. With all test elements in place, the day arrived when I announced to management, "The job is finished." As before, there was surprise as well as praise. The ultimate challenge in my, and my colleague's careers had been accomplished. "What's next," was the question of the day.

It was the end of our five-year contract obligation. Transition from here, not only us, but for many in the defense sector, would become necessary. Since corporate was apt to provide jobs for every one of us facing the end of a project, under normal circumstances, it would not present an issue. The company was large enough to assure continuous employment somewhere. Some were relocated while others sought out possible employment elsewhere, if the job offered was unacceptable.

When I was faced with the decision about my career future, no matter where I looked within the parameters of government contracting, there were no challenges left to capture my interests. Besides, being technologically oriented, there was nothing new on the immediate horizon. Shortly after I made the decision, and walked into Jim's office. "I quit."

"But why?" was his immediate reaction. "You are so successful."

"Tell me this," I countered. "Why are you here?"

"What do you mean?" he said with a puzzled look.

"I understand that you have had challenging programs."

"That's true. What are you getting at?"

"How come you are here? You should be at Lockheed's principle headquarters."

"Didn't have a position for me."

"You get my drift?"

"As a matter of fact," he said with a look of confession, "I'm thinking of quitting."

"Now you understand," I explained. "I have no future here."

"There will be other programs. You are still young." We were about the same age, in our 50s.

"So are you. I can't wait around for things to happen. There are no challenges left with the government." I would be proven wrong, but for that to happen, it would take another decade.

"Let's get out of here," he suggested, getting up from his chair.

"Where're we headed?"

"I'm member of a club. We can discuss the future there." The next few hours turned out to be quite pleasant. "Ever had Remy Martin?"

"Not that I recall." It was a brand many people talked about, but could not afford. Not only did I have the best lobster lunch in town, but best brandy as well.

The day turned out well with both of us getting to know each other on a social level. I learned that he had just been divorced after a successful marriage, was drifting aimlessly through the day, felt lost in a successful career cut short, and was looking to get a handle on life. It sounded much like my life. Both of us had arrived at a point in life imminent for changes. I supposed this was what was meant by "midlife crisis."

Since I had spent most of my time overseas, my quitting was not a monumental affair to headquarters management. It appeared that I was one of several retirees in similar positions exiting most months. While Reagan's political success as president was undeniable, budget cuts were imminent, especially with government, and military spending. Rumors of RIFs within government circles were circulating. If true, it would place 100,000 Air Force, and 200,000 Army personnel into retirement, burdening commercial job markets. There were no new programs on the immediate horizon. As far as the Intelligence community was concerned, black project funding was still off in the future. For now, my options were with the private sector, hoping new commercial technologies would emerge.

The year was 1994. On a Monday morning, which was supposed to be a working day, I woke up early as usual. Following a thirty-year career with government contracting, in addition having been on call 24/7 on a minute's notice, dispatched to one of many burning points on the globe, I was overcome with a strange feeling, one of desolation. I had not felt like it before that I could recall. I always followed a plan worked out months, and years ahead or drawn into spur-of-the-moment situations occupying every waking hour of the day, many with three hours of rationed sleep. "What am I going to do today?" Where my mind was at a loss the body had the solution. I had slept in late. I had not realized how run down I was physically, and mentally. Realizing that, I decided to take a break from chasing computer, and software application bugs. "Tomorrow's another day," I muttered just before sinking into another round of sleep.

I let several days pass in the solitude of my Castle, letting each day slip by uneventfully. There was one task I followed each morning, checking the job market on an Internet-based career site. Websites in 1994, aside from Intel, and Microsoft, were not many. But as a result of Ronald Reagan's "Trickle-down Economy," the job market was getting saturated with 300,000 ex-military personnel taking priority in job openings. Fortunately, there was one sector emerging, Silicon Valley. However, in order to land a job, one had to have current software developing experience in Cold

Fusion, Java, and Visual Basic. Any one of these would assure immediate employment.

I realized right then that I was behind the technology curve, and had some rapid catching up to do. The question was, "Where to get the experience?" My scholastic timeline was outdated by years. "Did I want to go back to school? I guess not—at least not at the moment," I'd decided. I had money saved to last at least one year as long as I stayed away from any major purchases. Though mortgage payments were due at the beginning of each month, I managed to live within my allocated budget and savings.

There was something else that kept gnawing at my mind. Several years ago, on a trip to Korea I had acquired a hernia that had been a bother and needed fixing. Overloaded with suitcases while rushing to catch a train, reaching for the overhead rack, I had felt the pop. An abdomen hernia had broken through once more. It did not call for emergency surgery right then, but over time, it kept bothering my performance, and wellbeing. Eventually, I paid a visit to the doctor's office, and had it repaired. The surgery went well, but left me sore for weeks. Restless, and idle, Marek, a windsurfing friend of mine in town, checked up on my daily needs. Aside from providing company he went to the store to replenish food, and beverages.

On one of his visits, he suggested, "Why don't you start a book?"

"What do you mean?" I responded, somewhat startled. It had never occurred to me.

"Write something, anything. You've got the time."

Lying awake in bed, after much contemplation, I considered the idea, but had no idea for how to go about it. "Take some classes," he further suggested. "You can take abstract mathematics if you are interested."

I laughed at him. "You crazy?" It was the specialty subject he was teaching at UCCS. Though taking his advice to heart I did sign up several days later, but in literature. Since it was late spring, it was in the midst of the semester. There were only a few selected classes available; I chose psychology. Taking the course not only provided me with a window into the minds of mankind, but it presented additional opportunities. I focused on an intriguing subject, the practice of hypnosis. After ending UCCS classes with credits in psychology with professionally-trained skills in hypnotism, I was left dry, nevertheless. The question I faced was, "What do I do with it?"

As specialized as the vocation was, my application would be very limited. Out of three disciplines—clinical hypnosis, regression hypnosis, and self-hypnosis—my practice would be limited to qualify for only one, self-hypnosis, and that's what I pursued.

In the following weeks and months, I spent most of my time practicing hypnosis. I must admit that I became quite good at it. I even offered free sessions to friends with some declining, and others giving it a try. There was one thing about the process that kept bothering me. It was a time-consuming effort to lead the mind into a comatose state, taking ten to fifteen minutes. Consequently, I experimented with various trial and error approaches, taking into consideration counting process, followed with scale of depths, focal point, and various other means to minimize induction time.

The results were amazing. I was able to cut the time to minutes, and even less to achieve the hypnotic state. The question still remained: "What to do with it?" The answer came to me shortly after. "Why not writing a book?"

That's exactly what I did. At least, I had a topic to write about. I did not want to wait for another semester three months away. Since I had no learned writing skills, what I needed was inspiration. Residing in Hawaii, Glenn, a friend from my contracting days currently assigned to a long-term project in Japan, offered his condo. "Come on out, and stay as long as you like."

Who would turn down such an offer? Paradise for the affluent. I immediately accepted. Arriving one week later, I settled in at the place in the midst of Waikiki. Each day, as I made my way to the beach, I felt like King Kamehameha himself, riding the waves, and sailing the prevalent winds of Oahu. In the morning I would write, afternoon, and evenings I would relish waves and winds amid palm trees, and sandy beaches, getting a tan like a native. My writing, rudimentary at first, progressed with time on a book titled, "Ultimate Solution." It was a work of healing body, and mind from life's daily drudgery and ensuing afflictions, using self-hypnotic practices. After six months of writing about hypnotism I was amazed at how beneficial both could be, the writing as well as the hypnotic practices. While it was not a solution for all ailments, many disorders could be cured.

Again, the question surfaced: "What do I do with the product?" Should I have it published or should I try self-publishing? About the same time, I was creating my first website, a tedious task in those days. First, one had to learn HTTP[50], the web developing language. Photoshop, a miracle in graphics development, had also just been introduced to the market. Unlike in today's world with sophisticated Web developing, and canned solutions, using Microsoft Scratchpad for uploading text, data and images, online testing, correcting mistakes, and repeating the process for each element took much time, and effort. A time where there were no Internet merchant accounts, and direct bank transfers, I created an FTP connection for book sales. It worked, but was a timely process, with a prospective buyer sending an email request to purchase a copy, and depositing a personal check to your bank account, thus enabling the download of a printed copy in PDF format.

Regardless of the time-consuming process, I could claim to be one of the first publishers selling my work on the Internet. Though I did not sell many copies, most sold to colleges, and universities. About two years online I decided to discontinue sales after receiving several threatening emails. Though a very small percentage, some readers were highly upset about works of hypnosis being unethical, immoral, or even fiendish. With attitudes like those, I decided to quit with, "Who needs the aggravation?" I pulled the files, closed the website, and shelved my literary work. If at a future date someone was interested in publishing my work, the manuscript was still available in my archives. For now, I had other fiction volumes in print with more to follow. Thanks to Marek, I am happy with the sales, and means my writing skills have turned out to provide.

---

[50] Hyper Text Transfer Protocol.

In closing, I feel compelled to state a few facts about the subject of hypnosis. Hypno-therapy works. It is not a miracle cure. One has to personally work and admit on it. The reason it does work is because healing comes from within one's mind, and body. Whatever invisible energy forces there may be, the mind, in conjunction with personal efforts, does the rest. I have proven it to myself on numerous occasions. Experimenting many times over the cause of five years of diligent practice, I could assure you that there is truth to professional claims, but with limitations. Where, for instance, the individual could heal some mental affliction or persistent pain, hypnosis cannot mend broken bones.

In contrast to hypno-therapy, demonstration practices with subjects under hypnosis, highly claimed by practitioners, has no merit. Watching a hypnotist putting one, a dozen, or an entire audience to sleep, for the most part is bogus. It may seem to work, but only with the willingness of participation from a group, or audience being manipulated into a fake trance.

Worse yet, regression practices are even less effective. The hypnotists, in clever ways, trick the subject into thinking the particular event had occurred or, through leading the victim, into believing a past event took place. The novice, much like the expert, knows the limited powers of hypnosis, but are never willing to ever admit to its limitations. The only disproof one has is a legal one. Hypnotic results, regardless of guilt or innocence to a committed crime, could never be admitted, or submitted in the courts of law.

No legal system was willing to take the chance of uncertain testimony by convicting a subject by the uncertain results of a hypnotic prognosis. The reasons I cite the beforementioned is to inform the interested or innocent victim to be guarded against getting misleading results, or becoming a willing subject of fraudulent intentions, and scamming.

Hypnosis has to come from within, and only works if the person is willing to apply interest in self-healing. While hypnotism has developed into a profitable profession for many practitioners, lasting success is still up to the individual. Other words for hypnotism would be inspiration, enthusiasm, and self-motivation.

SPECIAL PROJECTS

Prior to taking the five-year roaming project from 1984 to 1989, assignment with NATO, following the corporate relocation to Colorado Springs in 1980, I had worked from a newly constructed headquarters building, the first in an eventual industrial park development. Rather than interfacing with DOD, for the time being, I was placed under direct Ford Aerospace management pursuing new projects. With Cold War tensions growing to new heights, in spite of President Reagan's pleading with Soviet leadership, there was no lack of military program awards. Adversary nations were expanding into the Western world, infringing on our country's safety. Aside from Soviet pressure, internal trouble developed in the Mid-Eastern monarchy when Mohammad Reza Pahlavi, better known as The Shah of Persia, Iran, came under severe pressures from within his own country.

Mohammad Reza gradually lost support from the Shi'a clergy of Iran, as well as the working class, particularly due to his strong policy of modernization elevating his country into the modern world. Several other factors contributed to a strong opposition to the Shah, among certain groups within Iran, the most significant of which were U.S., and U.K. support for his regime, clashing with Islamists, and increased communist activity. By 1979, political unrest had transformed into a revolution which forced him to leave Iran. Soon after, the Iranian monarchy was formally abolished, and Iran was declared an Islamic republic led by Ruhollah Khomeini, known in the Western world as Ayatollah Khomeini (Shiite religious leader of Iran). Facing likely execution should he return to Iran, the former leader, The Shah, unceremoniously died in exile in Egypt, whose president Anwar Sadat had granted him asylum.

It was this monarchic change in Iranian leadership that would eventually draw the U.S. into a conflict still fought, and unresolved to this day. Although I was not directly involved at this time with Mystery-man, and DARPA, many more projects surfaced from within various government sectors. One such project was the International Space Station (ISS), initiated by President Reagan, and the Strategic Defense Initiative (SDI), coined and publicly known as Star Wars.

It seemed that congressional budget approvals for many of the upcoming innovative programs were limited to 50 million dollars, at the time still a considerable amount of money. People did not think in terms of billions yet. Two projects commenced about the same time shortly after Reagan's election. He had a vision unequal to several of his immediate predecessors, still plagued with postwar Vietnam issues, and other conflicts in development. While JFK had provided the means to launch man into space, Reagan took it even further. He developed mankind's first space platform as threshold into the galaxies.

The international space station, at the time known as Space Station Freedom[51] was born, supported by every major government contractor on the congressional

———————————————

[51] Space Station Freedom was a NASA project to construct a permanently manned Earth-orbiting space station in the 1980s. Although approved by then-president Ronald Reagan, and announced in the 1984 State of the Union address, Freedom was never constructed or completed as originally designed, and after several cutbacks, the project evolved into the International Space Station program, a combined effort between

budget. Using exploratory results from Mercury, Gemini, and Apollo-Soyuz, resultant successes were applied to the ISS, and space shuttle developments. Ford Aerospace's engineering pool was commissioned to develop the power plant necessary to sustain the space station, connected to an array of solar panels extending into space to collect energy from a perpetually fueling sun.

As a precursor for my involvement in the ISS initiative, with the Apollo program winding down in the late 1960s, there were numerous proposals for what would follow. Of the many proposals submitted, large, and small, three major themes began to emerge. Foremost among them was a manned mission to Mars, using systems not unlike the ones used for Apollo. Next, a permanent space station was considered, both to help construct the large spacecraft needed for a Mars mission as well as to learn about long-term operations in space. Finally, almost as an afterthought, the idea of a "space logistics vehicle" that could cheaply launch crews, and cargo to that station appeared to make sense.

In the early 1970s, Spiro Agnew took these general plans to President Nixon, who was battling with the deficit. When Agnew presented the three concepts, Nixon told him to select one. After much debate, NASA selected the space logistics vehicle, which by this time was already known as the space shuttle. They argued that the shuttle would lower the costs of launching cargo so that it would make the construction of the station less expensive.

From this point forward, these plans were never seriously challenged, in spite of dramatic changes spurred to redesign the shuttle concept. In the early 1980s, with the space shuttle completed, NASA proposed the creation of a large, permanently manned space station; in some ways, it was meant to be the U.S. answer to the Soviet Space Station *Mir*.

NASA plans called for the station, dubbed Space Station *Freedom*, to function as an orbiting repair shop for satellites, an assembly point for spacecraft, an observation post for astronomers, a microgravity laboratory for scientists, and a microgravity factory for companies.

Reagan announced plans to build Space Station *Freedom* in 1984, stating: "We can follow our dreams to distant stars, living, and working in space for peaceful economic, and scientific gain."

In April 1984, the newly established Space Station Program Office at Johnson Space Center produced the first reference configuration. The design would serve as a baseline for further planning. The chosen design was the "Power Tower," a long central keel with most mass located at either end. This arrangement would provide enough gravity gradient stability to keep the station aligned with the keel pointed towards the Earth, reducing the need for thruster firings. Most designs featured a cluster of modules at the lower end, and a set of articulated solar arrays at the upper end containing a servicing bay. In April 1985, the program selected a set of contractors to carry out definition studies, and preliminary design. Various trade-offs were made

---

numerous nations including Russia, France, Italy, Germany, and several other technologically emerging countries.

in this process, balancing higher development costs against reduced long-term operating costs.

Shortly after, late 1986, NASA carried out a study into new configuration options to reduce development costs even further. Options studied ranged from the use of a Skylab-type station to a phased development of the dual-keel configuration. This approach involved splitting assembly into two phases. Phase One would provide the central modules, and the transverse boom, but without keels. The solar arrays would be augmented to ensure 75 kW of power would be provided, and the polar platform, and servicing facility were again deferred. The study concluded that the project was viable, reducing development costs while minimizing negative impacts.

Underestimates by NASA of the station program's cost, and the unwillingness of the U.S. Congress to appropriate funding for the space station resulted in delays to *Freedom's* design, and construction. It was regularly redesigned, and re-scoped. Between 1984, and 1993 it went through seven major re-designs, losing capacity, and capabilities each time. Rather than being completed in a decade, as Reagan had predicted, *Freedom* was never built, and no shuttle launches were made as part of the program.

By 1993, *Freedom* became politically unviable. The administration had changed, and Congress was tiring of paying yet more money into the station program. In addition, there were open questions over the need for the station. Redesigns had cut most of the science capacity by this point, and the Space Race had ended in 1975 with the Apollo-Soyuz Test Project. NASA presented several options to President Clinton, but even the most limited of these was still seen as too expensive. In June 1993, an amendment to remove space station funding from NASA's appropriations bill failed by one vote in the House of Representatives. That October, a meeting between NASA, and the Russian Space Agency agreed to the merger of the projects into what would become the *International* Space Station. During congressional budget debates for the ISS, an additional program was initiated by Reagan, the Space-based Defense Initiative (SDI).

Career opportunities emerged once more, not only for the defense related workforce, but for myself as well. When offered a job taking on the challenge as member of our engineering department, I readily took it. I became part of the workforce facing a new epoch in the U.S. government taking on space.

STAR WARS

As with prior government initiated programs, I was extended the opportunity partaking in the challenge. The Strategic Defense Initiative (SDI) was a proposed missile defense system intended to protect the United States from attack by ballistic strategic nuclear weapons (intercontinental ballistic missiles, and submarine-launched ballistic missiles). The concept was first announced publicly by President Ronald Reagan on 23 March 1983. Reagan was a vocal critic of the doctrine of mutual assured destruction (MAD), which he described as a "suicide pact," and he called upon the scientists, and engineers of the United States to develop a system that would render nuclear weapons obsolete.

Timeline:

On 23 March 1983, President Reagan delivered his "Star Wars" speech, stating "I call upon the scientific community who gave us nuclear weapons to turn their great talents to the cause of mankind, and world peace: to give us the means of rendering these nuclear weapons impotent, and obsolete."

In 1984, the Strategic Defense Initiative Organization (SDIO) was established to oversee the program, which was headed by Lt. General James Alan Abrahamson, USAF, a past director of the NASA Space Shuttle program.

In addition to the ideas presented by the original Heritage group, a number of other concepts were also considered. Notable among these were particle-beam weapons, updated versions of nuclear-shaped charges, and various plasma weapons. Additionally, the SDIO invested in computer systems, component miniaturization, and particle sensors.

By 1986, many of the promising ideas were failing. Edward Teller's X-ray laser, code name Project Excalibur, failed several key tests in 1986, but was being suggested for the anti-satellite role regardless of results. The particle beam concept was demonstrated with failed results, as was the case with several other concepts being tested. Only the Space Based Laser seemed to have any hope of developing in the short term, but not without certain limitations not solvable at the time.

The American Physical Society (APS) had been asked by the SDIO to provide a review of the various concepts. They put together an all-star panel including many of the inventors of the laser, including a Nobel laureate. Their initial report was presented in 1986, but due to classification issues it was not released to the public (in redacted form) until early 1987.

The report considered all of the systems then under development, and concluded none of them were anywhere near ready for deployment. Specifically, they noted that all of the systems had to improve their energy by at least 100 times, and in some cases as much as a million. In other cases, like Excalibur, they dismissed the concept out of hand. In a best-case scenario, they concluded that none of the systems could be deployed as an anti-missile system until into the next century."

For the SDIO, when set up within the United States, the Department of Defense was to oversee development. A wide array of advanced weapon concepts, including lasers, particle beam weapons, and ground-, and space-based missile systems were studied, along with various sensor, command and control, and high-performance computers that would be needed to control a system consisting of hundreds of combat centers, and satellites spanning the globe. A number of these concepts were tested through the late 1980s, and follow-on efforts, and spin-offs continue to this day with cyberspace defense systems.

SDI was highly controversial throughout its history, and was criticized for threatening to destabilize the MAD-approach, and to possibly re-ignite "an offensive arms race." SDI was derisively nicknamed "Star Wars" by the media after the popular 1977 film by George Lucas. By the early 1990s, with the Cold War ending, and nuclear arsenals being rapidly reduced, political support for SDI collapsed. SDI officially ended in 1993, when the administration of President Bill Clinton redirected the efforts towards theater ballistic missiles, and renamed the agency from Ballistic Missiles Office (BMO) to Ballistic Missile Defense Organization (BMDO). Years later, BMDO was again renamed to the Missile Defense Agency (MDA) in 2002.

One may ask, "Why all the program changes?"

The answer is quite simple: "To acquire the budget for a new program." Congress, and taxpayers would not be the wiser.

My career, at times uncertain with the periodic program changes in government, and military, charged by political differences, was redirected once more. Regardless of changes in directions, I gained inside into new technologies, as well as political machinations.

STRATEGIC DEFENSE INITIATIVE

Following the damaging report by the American Physical Society, and the press storm that followed, the Strategic Defense Initiative Organization (SDIO) changed direction. Beginning in late 1986, General Alan Abrahamson, who served as a designated astronaut, Associate Director of NASA, and former director of President Ronald Reagan's Strategic Defense Initiative, proposed that SDI would be based on the system he had previously dismissed, a version of High Frontier, now renamed the "Strategic Defense System, Phase I Architecture." The name implied that the concept would be replaced by more advanced systems in future phases.

The Strategic Defense System, or SDS, was largely the Smart Rocks[52] concept with an added layer of ground-based missiles in the U.S. These missiles were intended to attack the enemy warheads that the Smart Rocks had missed. In order to track them when they were below the radar horizon, SDS also added a number of additional satellites in low altitude orbit that would feed tracking information to both the space-based "garages" as well as the ground-based missiles. The ground-based systems, operational today, trace their roots back to this concept.

While SDS was being proposed, Lawrence Livermore Laboratories had introduced a new concept known as Brilliant Pebbles. This was essentially the combination of the sensors on the Garage satellites, and the low-orbit tracking stations on the Smart Rocks missile. This combination was made possible by new sensors, and microprocessors that allowed them to be packaged into the volume of a small missile nose cone. Over the next two years, a variety of studies suggested that this approach would be cheaper, easier to launch, and more resistant to counterattack, and in 1990 Brilliant Pebbles was selected as the baseline model for the SDS Phase 1.

While SDIO, and SDS was ongoing, the Warsaw Pact was rapidly disintegrating, culminating in the destruction of the Berlin Wall in 1989. One of the many reports on SDS considered these events, and suggested that the massive defense against a Soviet launch would soon be unnecessary, but that short, and medium range missile technology would likely proliferate as the former Soviet Union disintegrated, and sold off their hardware. One of the core ideas behind the system was that the Soviet Union

---

[52] Brilliant Pebbles was a ballistic missile defense (BMD) system proposed by Lowell Wood, and Edward Teller of the Lawrence Livermore National Laboratory (LLNL) in 1987, near the end of Cold War. The system would consist of thousands of small missiles, not unlike conventional air-to-air missiles, which would be placed in orbits so that hundreds would be above the Soviet Union at all times. If the Soviets launched its ICBM fleet, the pebbles would detect their rocket motors using infrared seekers, and collide with them. Because the pebble strikes the ICBM before the latter could release its warheads, each pebble could destroy several warheads with one shot.

The name is a play on the idea of Smart Rocks, a concept promoted by Daniel O. Graham as part of the Strategic Defense Initiative (SDI). This used large battle stations with powerful sensors, carrying dozens of small missiles, the rocks. To keep enough missiles above the Soviet Union at any given time, a minimum of 423 stations would be needed. The United States Air Force pointed out that this would require an enormous space lift capability, well beyond what was available. In meetings with Graham, Teller dismissed the concept as "outlandish", and vulnerable to attack by anti-satellite weapons. The SDI Office (SDIO) was similarly dismissive of the concept.

would not always be assumed as the aggressor, and the United States would not always be assumed as the target.

Ballistic Missile Defense Organization (BMDO) Specifics

In 1993, the Clinton administration further shifted the focus to ground-based interceptor missiles, and theater scale systems, forming the Ballistic Missile Defense Organization (BMDO), and closing the SDIO. The Ballistic Missile Defense Organization was renamed again by the George W. Bush administration as the Missile Defense Agency, and focused onto limited National Missile Defense. Under new direction, numerous potential weapons, conceptual, and in design, underwent evaluation, and testing. Some of these directed-energy weapon programs were the following:

1. X-ray Laser
2. Chemical laser
3. Neutral particle beam
4. Laser, and mirror experiments
5. Hypervelocity Railgun

At this point in my career, I was as confused as many members in congress, and defense sector about the future of our country, while the threat from the USSR was escalating in an ever- increasing magnitude. I will recap some of the confusion parameters for untested technology, and proposed projects with the reader in Appendix A. The following examples are initiatives proposed by the defense sector, and its supporting contractors, in conjunction with the country's scientists, to evaluate, and test possible technologies untried at the time. The process of selection is tedious, time consuming, and expensive to the tax payer, but necessary as well, for the protection of the nation.

As the reader can envision from the various defense systems under testing, with only partial positive results, the entire SDI system was scrapped as ineffective. Where the public was kept uninformed about the programs, and testing efforts, due to the critical nature of the defense systems, inversely, information, and data for complete successes were purposely leaked to the adversary superpower, the Soviet Union.

More specifically, operatives responsible for the design, and applications of the tested systems knew well into testing that none of the systems would perform to their projected functions, none more so the laser system. While much value had been placed on laser defense readiness, scientists, and engineers knew otherwise. At the time, since laser technology was at its infancy, and only laboratory based, no laser would be capable for use as an effective defense weapon in cyberspace. But that information was kept highly classified from the public, adversary authorities, and the world.

As a matter of fact, the disinformation of "successful testing" released by the U.S. to the Soviets had adverse consequences. Unable to come up with a defense budget to match the U.S. SDI program, due to an economic recession, and an unwillingness of the country's citizens to be taxed, already stressed to a maximum, Mikhail

Gorbachev[53] decided to amass, and increase his already superior ICBM missile arsenal from a 5 megaton tipped warhead to 50 megatons, and larger. When our foreign policy makers realized the counter action, the U.S. was suddenly faced with having no effective retaliatory powers. Our nuclear defense system had suddenly turned obsolete.

It was at this stage in 1988, that Al U. and I were commissioned to redesign our antiquated missile defense system. Our mission was to protect communication, and power systems for survivability against a direct hit on the underground launch centers, and silos for the Minuteman, and Peacekeeper systems.

The cited projects above were not limited to the technological experimentations. There was one that would outperform all in the times ahead as explained in the next section.

---

[53] Mikhail Sergeyevich Gorbachev, born 2 March 1931, was the seventh, and last General Secretary of the Communist Party of the Soviet Union, serving from 1985 until 1991, and the last head of state of the USSR, serving from 1988 until its collapse in 1991.

ARTIFICIAL INTELLIGENCE (AI)

From the 80s through early 90s, following the relocation from California, I had been working from my home office, the Ford Aerospace headquarters in Colorado Springs, reporting to Mahogany Row, executive management, in-between travel demands overseas. Early one morning, I received a phone call from an unfamiliar (202) prefix number from Washington, DC. "Bauer," I answered, waiting for a response.

"Can we meet?"

"Mystery-man? Where are you?" I readily recognized his voice.

"Getting ready for the flight. Meet me at the airport. Two hours."

"Colorado Springs?" Since I had not heard from him in some time I was surprised.

"Yes. We need to talk." He hung up before I could reply. Cleaning up my work space before departing, I had plenty of time to meet his flight. It was a thirty-minute drive to the airport during which time I mulled over his unexpected visit. Evaluating the state of current economic, and political conditions, the height of the Cold War, I speculated without viable results. I had to wait until meeting face to face with Mystery-man. With the local airport relatively small compared to the overseas destinations I was used to, arriving passengers were processed swiftly without passenger, and luggage inspections.

"Thanks for meeting me," he said with an extended hand. It was an unusual gesture since he would always pop in from nowhere without formal introduction. In past encounters I would normally sense his presence seconds before hearing his voice.

"Good to see you," I replied, anxiously awaiting the reason for his visit.

"Let's have lunch," he suggested. "I don't have much time. My flight leaves in three hours."

"Going back so soon? Why don't you stay a day?"

"Can't. Have to be on the West Coast tomorrow." I had an idea where he was headed: Lawrence Livermore Labs.

I drove the short distance to a nearby hotel I knew had a restaurant. "So," I invited him to talk after a waiter had taken our orders, "what deserves your special visit?"

"We are kicking off a project that will change mankind." He certainly captured my full attention with such a profound statement.

"That I'll have to hear. What's the classification?"

"Proprietary access. It is in the research state, expected to employ many scientists and engineers. There is no time for lengthy background investigations. Congress put on a time limit of five years. After that," he emphasized, "we either have a product, or it's the end of the initiative."

"Another initiative, eh? Must be big."

"AI."

"Artificial Intelligence?"

"That's the one."

The label was not new to me. It had been tossed around the scientific community for some time. While I was familiar with the basic concept, for the underlying mechanism, I was not.

"Biggest ever if we can get it to work. Let me fill you in on the project." He proceeded to explain the general outline over the anticipated five years ahead. From my action-oriented career baseline, spending most of the time on the frontlines, the program did not seem very inspiring. But, from a research perspective, it would be the ultimate challenge. Mostly listening for the next few hours, I was fascinated by the technological approach he presented. I had a difficult time imagining only a marginal probability for the survival of mankind.

Aside from unequaled challenges of a potentially successful development in AI, if it could be accomplished, the results would not only affect every human being on the planet—it would endanger mankind itself. On a positive note, the potential was there to replace all of our tasks, and chores with machines. On the negative side, machines could take over, and eliminate man, if we were not careful. It was up to us to make sure we would never lose control over the machine.

"You know how critical it all is," I said, expressing my personal concerns.

"This is where you come in," he said, holding my eye contact. Though we had known, and worked together for many years, I knew he was assessing my trust base. "This is what I need from you. You'll be my eyes and ears for the duration of the project. You'll report directly to me. I need to know sentiments, viewpoints, methods, tactics, approaches, and progress by your company."

"You know," I said, reminding him of my personal edicts, "I don't spy on people." Immediately, I could see a caution flag reflecting on his face.

He quickly responded with, "It's not spying. We already discussed the critical aspects of the program. You are not my only informant. Aside from every national laboratory, there are a dozen companies involved. All major aerospace companies, and government contractors have a stake in it. That's how big the effort is."

I understood. A national involvement changed the entire picture. I was impressed not only in his trust, but confidence in my capabilities as well.

"How do you want to handle it?" He knew that I had accepted his offer.

"First, and foremost," he said, "I need to be informed of caution flags."

"Such as?" I had an idea, but needed to hear it from him.

"Potential research breach with ill intended consequences. You know," he emphasized, "for putting man's future in jeopardy. There are many who would take control over the globe through the force of machines. The objective is to create a safe environment for everybody to benefit. It can be done, but only if everybody works together. Since this is the most critical program ever initiated, we need to ensure a successful outcome. Otherwise, our days will be numbered."

"We've lived through critical programs before," I said, reminding him on the atomic age.

"I know. Atom bombs. But this is different. Nuclear devices are designed with limitations. They need man to be launched. They are not built with sophisticated software endangering our existence. That's where AI poses the greatest danger. If we are not careful, from what I saw on the drawing boards, they can, and will eventually reprogram themselves to take control. It's what AI is all about, machine education, and learning every bit of knowledge conceived by mankind."

He checked his watch for time. "Have to go now. I'll have you placed on the program. I'll keep in touch. Do your best." He promptly left for the departure ramp, leaving me with troublesome thoughts. As the reader will come to learn in Appendix B, the concept of abstract thinking was nothing new. The chronology briefly describes the concept, and evolution in the quest for Artificial Intelligence which in recent years began over 70 years ago with the idea that computers would one day be able to think like us. Thoughts of Artificial Intelligence had been around since antiquity. It was Greek philosophers, and mathematicians that first conceived the notion, but it did not materialize until WWII when a practical application was sought with the invention of the computer.

As it turned out, I was attached to the engineering department, but only in a provisional capacity. My task was to attend weekly status, and special progress meetings. Since there were no prototype, and engineering tasks other than software development, within the capacity of current technology, it was soon realized that project development was way too premature. It became clear that to achieve a workable model simulating just the basic concepts of AI, and its potential capabilities, much more computing power was necessary. It would not be for another twenty years that the program was picked up once more, but this time with viable results. Though still very limited in applications, AI proved workable as long as it was segmented into special, industry specific applications. To make the whole AI concept work, and effective for all possible phases of life, many more innovative ideas were needed. Until such time, we could breathe freely with the life bestowed on us for being superior to machines. Or so we thought.

The answer is not as simple as that, much like Google in the first twenty years of its existence. Its amassed data, and knowledge from every database on the globe, complemented with proprietary information, was stored on personal, business, and research computers, building the world's greatest knowledge-based system owned by anyone, housed within tens of thousands of computer servers, staged around the globe. Initially, to be effective, big data software was used to acquire, and manipulate every possible marketing advantage, and business scheme. In recent years it has become even worse.

AI developers, using Google's infinite knowledgebase, successfully built its AI self-learning neural networks into a foundation containing every bit of knowledge of the entire human race. Designed as an open, and progressive system, there were no limits as to AI's ultimate capabilities, and goals, making every decision for humankind. The question is not "if it could be done." The question is, "How soon can it be used."

There are already large segments in use, and applied to various industries. For instance, in hospitals, survivable critical surgery is already performed by AI programmed robots performing more efficiently than humans could. Pharmaceuticals are not far behind in AI technology, and so are a few dozen other companies experimenting with AI capabilities. If it would stop there, the usefulness of AI could benefit every sector of the industry, and satisfy every need of man. But, similar to mankind's ingenuity, the time will come when AI instructs itself in learning to supersede mankind's knowledge limitation including thinking, and decision making for its own purpose to propagate, and perpetuate itself into an omnipresence, we believe, that could become the new creator of the universe, become God.

If one believes in the Big Bang, one must also consider the possibility of AI becoming the creator of all things. With the self-creation of an all-knowing robot connected to a self-learning neural network superior to man, we could eventually face a new cycle of universal rebirth. It is not unthinkable that the Big Bang had already seen many such cycles.

Aside from keeping Mystery-man abreast in AI results, for now, my skills were applied to an earthlier mission, that of partaking in the development of a tactical battle management system desperately needed by the U.S. Army for the upcoming Gulf War, an involvement with more destruction of man. Also, a time for me to seek a more stable career environment.

My career as a contracting employee would come to an end, but not without personal reservations facing the commercial sector for the change. Rather than having taken some time to evaluate the consequences of working in a new arena, the decision for change, I recalled, was a snap decision. It was based on the previous day's discussions I had in the company of several colleagues including Frank, current project manager, about the benefits of early retirement. All of us came to the same conclusion: it was better to retire early at an eligible age 55, while the opportunity was still offered by the Supplemental Security Income (SSI), for reasons of logic. Taking the maximum available compensation at age 75 vs 55 meant giving up 20 years of supplemental compensation that could never be recovered. Since we, the core team of AUTODIN, started out at about the same age, most of us quit our government jobs within the following year.

Where some retired altogether, and others took local employment at computer repair shops, and such, I would eventually find contracting opportunities with Microsoft, and its profitable client base headquartered in San Francisco. It would prove to be the right choice for me since I could start earning an income I deserved with my acquired career skills which was unmatched by working for the government. There were, I would find out, certain drawbacks to working in the commercial industry.

Right from the start I noticed the lack of structure the government demanded. In government, every project needed accountability to the Accountability Office. Everything was documented to its smallest details from blueprint to budget, and daily tasks. This was not the case in the corporate world. Here, everything was winged. Nobody took the time to record even important activities. People, if given a choice, did not like paperwork.

I took upon myself to document my every action. Aside from acquiring writing skills, it was very much appreciated by the executive boards. I usually received first cut for projects, was allowed certain liberties, and received compensation rewards beyond my expectations. But that would have to wait for a couple more years. In the meantime,, I took on short-term projects based out of Colorado Springs while taking care of two of my daughters living with me.

Regardless of my future commercial successes, I will always miss the structured environment, and established hierarchy with the government. What I did not like was the direction the government had taken in recent years. Notwithstanding character assassinations during election processes, it seemed that government control had shifted from a respectable entity to a business model with too much personal ambition by many members in congressional office. Coming from a disciplined, and structured background, I am having a difficult time accepting the liberties of free enterprise. At one time the markets were effectively managed by the government, but in today's world, corporate America is directing the economy.

Regardless of personal sentiments, democracy is still the best form of governance.

FAMILY VISITS

I retired from Lockheed in 1994, with high hopes for getting into the commercial job market. First, I sought out several locally-based, technology-oriented companies with one specifically pioneering in something innovative, and novel. The defense department had already launched twenty-four GPS satellites into orbit, but mobile units for public use were lacking. For one reason or another, the job application I submitted went unanswered. Another prospect went as far as a personal interview with the project manager for systems development with Digital Equipment Corporation (DEC). When I learned who was in charge, the job was guaranteed, or so I thought. On the day of the interview I was greeted with a joyful welcome. "Alex," he exclaimed with a surprised grin on his face. "How have you been?" It'd turned out that some ten years earlier, while managing the NATO contract in Augsburg, Germany, he had been sent by headquarters to work for me. Today, the tide had turned.

"Retired from Lockheed," I responded, equally surprised. "I sure could use the work." We spent close to two hours reminiscing, and speculating about where technology was leading. With him managing DEC projects, being leader in the computer industry at the time, me getting onboard seemed only a formality. I was proven wrong. When the topic for my visit finally came up, he promptly turned me down. I was completely taken by surprise when he explained the reasons. "You don't know Token Ring technology."

"What?" Stunned at the moment, I was speechless. "Token Ring," I protested. I knew more about network protocols than anybody in the business. "I worked in network development," I countered. "Remember AUTODIN?"

"Yes," he said without a hint of consideration. "But it's different."

No matter how much I assured him of my capabilities, and knowledge, it proved fruitless. At the end, I did not depart on friendly terms. I should explain the reasons for getting turned down for the job. It would have been ideal since it was directly in line with my many years of technical experience.

In the world of PCs, networking, as it is termed within IT, is the basics for computer communication. It gives the Internet its popularity. Without it, the computer is only a standalone metal box as smart as the applications loaded. That was before wireless, a fairly recent development. Personal computers for the first ten years were mostly used by software geeks, and gamers playing Pac-Man, Gallagher, and Mario Brothers. I was one of them during my spare time.

Back to Token Ring. It was a network protocol developed by IBM. It was the simplest of network configurations among computer connectivity. It was no challenge in terms of design. In contrast, along numerous network topologies, the design I helped implement, and configure with the defense department was the sophistication of inventions, better known as time slice principle. With most computer company designs, the computer serviced one user at a time, though at the electronic speed (speed of light), before switching to a next user task, with Transfer Control Protocol (TCP) as the network carrier, later extended to TCP/IP for Internet Protocol.

The design I worked with was innovative in nature with all users being serviced simultaneously, one time-slice apart. What this means in layman's terms is that the system operated at the maximum performance technically possible, short of quantum mechanics, which was still years away from being invented.

Today, many years later, quantum mechanics is still in its infancy at this writing, presenting an unimaginable leap in technology development not yet realized to its fullest potential. Once perfected, and implemented, it will present the solutions even before the process of infinitesimal computations is completed, greatly advancing technologies in sciences, and applications such as astronomy, sub-atomic particle physics, genetic engineering, and many more for the benefit of mankind.

By now, one year had passed since I had left Lockheed, but not in vain. I had company. Pleasant company. It was the end of the schoolyear when, out of the blue, I received a call from Annette, my ex-wife. She sounded upset. Without any introduction or explanation, she boldly announced, "It's your turn to take care of your daughters. They are on their way."

I was speechless. At first, I did not believe her. It took seconds to compose myself. I remembered years ago, when the subject of custody came up, Annette had said, "You cannot raise children." I had understood. Without a permanent place to hang my hat, constantly traveling around the globe, and gone from home most of the time, I had no moral or legal right to take a stand. Where I miserably failed as father, Annette did a terrific job as a mother. In retrospect, given the chance, I would have excelled as father, I believe, like I did in most things in life I tackled.

"What do you mean by 'on their way'?"

"Just what it means. They are on their way."

"What? Today?"

"You can pick them up at the airport." She then gave me the flight number, and arrival time at the Colorado Springs airport. Apparently, she had waited to the last possible moment to tell me, forcing me to accept without reservations. No matter what my condition was at the time, unemployed, no income, it gave me no alternative to object or refuse. "What a proposition," I contemplated. Of course, I welcomed both daughters with open arms. Considering how family-oriented Annette was, I was just surprised at her decision out of nowhere.

Settling in at their new home, I realized right from the start that both Liz, and Tracy had been somewhat spoiled. Born into a large family on their mother's side, being very popular during their growing years, they had become the most favorite among the families, showered by their aunts with presents, and treats at every occasion. Out of work, without an income, I explained my situation. "Girls," I remember saying. I presently don't have an income, but I do have some savings. The problem is, it's only enough to pay for mortgage on the house and food. I don't have any money for you to spend."

"No problem," they said. "We'll work." I was grateful at the suggestion. Though unrealistic at their present ages, sixteen and fourteen, it released some of the pressure from my mind.

Days later, when I mentioned the surprise addition to my household to a German friend of mine, Joe, he said, "I could use some help." He was looking for some help running a part-time business. While he was teaching computer science at UCCS, he was also a part-time owner at a Manitou Springs motel. He offered both my daughters jobs cleaning rooms.

Working was a first for them. I was surprised at the enthusiasm they applied to it. Each day early in the morning I would drive them to the workplace while chatting about the previous day's events, and I would pick them up in late afternoon, six days a week. Handing them an initial allowance, once they earned on their own, they were only too happy to spend their earnings on personal necessities, which was not much. I went to pick them up by 4:00 p.m., and stopped at a sandwich shop or McDonalds on the way home, where they would change into sweats for our daily workout, martial arts. I had prepared one room with weightlifting equipment for rainy days. On dry days, we would spend hours under the spacious deck where I had mounted punching, and kicking bags. Liz, the elder, took to learning the Chinese art of fighting much like I had done one generation earlier. In between, I would teach them shooting handguns, as well as archery. On other days, one would find us shooting hoops at a basketball court or chasing each other around a parking lot with inline skates strapped on. Skating rinks for rollerblading had not yet been allocated. Consequently, we made ample use of parking lots, school yards, and other vacated premises we thought fit.

Evenings we would spend playing chess, discussing worldly events, or just having a good time. It must have been a novel experience for both being educated on what I considered valuable things. I still relish the thought of having had the opportunity to pass on my acquired skills they would otherwise never have had. A mother, I understood, looked at raising daughters from a different perspective. There had never been the slightest grumblings or complaints. I expected the visit to last three months during the summer break, but when consulting Annette, she said, "Keep the girls."

Though overenjoyed by the prospect, going back to school in August was an imminent challenge. Luckily, the home I bought fourteen years earlier was located in school district 20, accessible to the U.S. Air Force Academy. I enrolled both at the high school as a freshman, and sophomore respectively.

It turned out to be the happiest time in my life. I adjusted to a point where I could easily imagine myself as a single parent, but there was one problem. I ran short on funds after one year without work, and an income. Where I had minimized on personal expenditures to a bare minimum, mortgage payments went on with each month, and so did child support, a necessity if I wanted to keep the home, and custody. The only thing I had asked Annette was to reduce the obligatory payments. She agreed with one stipulation: "Repay me once you find work."

I agreed. As time went by the day came where I had only enough money left for one more mortgage payment. I felt pushed against the wall. Landing a job became critical.

Another month went by before I was called to a crucial job interview with Raytheon, one of the top ten aerospace companies. The interview was for a technology upgrade at the INS, and Coast Guard headquarters, both Miami-based. I accepted. The program director, Ted, hired me on the spot. He, and I became social friends for the years to follow. After the project's completion we both moved to California, with him taking on a director's position with TRW at McClellan AFB, Sacramento, and I contracting with Microsoft as business solution provider assigned to San Francisco, but that was still another year in the future.

The job was confirmed, but there was a problem: it was out of town. I was faced with a decision. Who would take care of my daughters? It was solved by a Lockheed work colleague who had just returned from the field. As he was looking for a place to stay, I offered my home with the condition to look after my daughters during my absence for six weeks. He was grateful, and happily accepted. I informed Annette of my decision hoping for her approval. But no such luck. She immediately shot me down. Explaining my financial dilemma did not help. It was either find a job in Colorado Springs or send the girls home. The choice was taken out of my hands when she, and her sister showed up the following day to take them home, removing them from the best high school in the nation. I had gotten used to a family life, and did not want them to leave. The next day they were gone. I felt lonelier than I had ever felt. What saved me from grieving was the job ahead.

The Immigration & Naturalization Services (INS) project was finally announced to commence. I knew what the project entailed, but would not learn the specifics for the delays until later. Microsoft had some final issues with developing Windows 3.1, their first fielded operating platform, an advanced prototype for Windows 95. The following week, I met the other members at the airport, one dozen engineers bound for Miami. Work was assured, if only for six weeks.

MIAMI BEACH PROJECT

Although winter was still present in Colorado Springs, with April being the driest months there, stepping from the plane in Miami felt like summer. We were met by a limo driver accommodating us dozen arrivals with, "Housing accommodations are waiting." He knew exactly where to drop us off. To our great surprise two mansions were waiting which the contractor had reserved for us. Seven on the team elected to stay at the larger complex with the remaining five of us being ferried to the second place, our temporary home. The team split-up turned out perfectly. Where the seven made friends among each other, us five applied our energy mostly on planning, and scheduling the work ahead. It did not mean the absence of fun. There was plenty of joking, laughter, and drinks being passed around. We had fun times, especially after getting acquainted with our inherited house guest, a resident mouse.

It was an unusual creature, the largest mouse any of us had ever laid eyes on. A most beautiful thing, if you could call a mouse that, light gray in color, long legged, stiff-eared. It would prance across the kitchen counter bidding us good morning, and good night each, and every day to let us know who owned the place. I should point out that it was no ordinary creature, not a pet either, but clever as hell. The place must have been empty for some time because the creature had taken up permanent possession of the place, and did not want to share, it seemed. It considered us an intrusion on its privacy to freely roam in, and out rooms day or night.

The project itself, once started, went rather well. What it entailed was Microsoft's first ever computer platform rollout with and advanced copy of Windows 95, still in final development. We were pioneering the deployment, an innovative technology for its time. We were observed by many projected agencies, and corporations also scheduled for deployment. Weeks later, finished with the INS[54], we went to the next client, the Coast Guard headquarters. We were initially delayed from fighting rat infestations residing beneath roofs; after the pest was eradicated work proceeded as expected. After dozens of dead rats were removed from our workspace, we proceeded with running connection cables across ceilings. Coast Guard officials, and administrative personnel on duty turned out to be a joy to work with. They were an energized, and people loving bunch we had not expected.

Our next, and last job on the consolidated project was unexpected. It turned out to be a rollout deployed to the largest prison built in Florida. Just finished, it was anticipated to house ten thousand illegal detainees from across southern borders. When the complex was started the previous year, the U.S. government had good intentions for enforcing immigration policies, but priority had shifted after a new INS administration took over.

The prison, in the midst of Alligator Alley, a centrally located, and completely isolated place, was surrounded by fifty miles of swampland. Modern in construction, but with minimal security without detainment walls, and towers, was enough. No sane person would ever want to escape the place. Any flight would be guaranteed to meet with disaster. To prove the point, on our daily commute through swampland on I-75,

---

[54] Immigration and Naturalization Services.

we spotted dozens of alligators alongside waterways, swamp embankments, and on streets warming up their bodies for the day. On the rise in numbers, back then, they were hunted legally for the sale of belts, and footwear popular at the time.

Back at the mansion, my hunt for the mouse continued. I had made it my daily mission to catch the creature. What began as a mission turned out to be pure play. It was wits played out between a mouse pitted against my human intelligence. My daily hunt began with a stated arrogance: "I'll get you yet." What was I going to do after the capture? Probably let it lose again to roam its mansion after teaching it not to mess with my brain. Over the following weeks I had built a number of contraptions to capture it, but in vain. Each morning, whoever was up first would report, "It ate the cereal." It was a mystery to us how it had escaped again, and again from my foolproof contraptions. Regardless of my repeated, and failed attempts, I was regarded as "Mouse Hunter."

Where I had only playful intentions it must have struck the critter seriously. It began one night around 2:00 a.m. when I was awakened with a thud on my chest. Startled, I opened my eyes just in time to watch the mouse scurry across my bed, and disappear behind the headboard. I turned on the lights. Still drowsy, I pulled the bed from the wall, and could not believe my eyes. A hole had been chewed through the wall large enough to pass a basketball through. On inspecting closer, I noticed a heap of drywall powder on the floor six inches high. My immediate thoughts were, "What have I done? I disturbed the mouse's domicile, and destroyed the mansion."

Contemplating my choices, short of losing my rationality, I knew one of us had to go. Having failed numerous capture attempts, three quarters into the project, I decided it was time to pack up, and leave. Unbelievable as it sounds, the mouse had won. I had lost. Imagine a human brain matched against this tiny, innocent creature. Innocent? I think not. Against my rational thinking, notwithstanding my honorable intentions, I was taught a lesson I would not forget: "Don't mess with the animals." Inferior, or so we believed, they were living beings to be treated with deserving respect, and dignity.

The day before my departure, a Sunday, I was soaking up the sun at Miami's South Beach one last time when the team leader for the project walked up. He had spotted me from the distance. "Sorry to see you go."

"Well," I said. "Project is almost done. You'll see to it through testing without me."

"You did a great job routing out, and running cables."

"We had a great team. I'm going to miss them. By the way," I said. A thought had just occurred to me. "What are your plans for the future?"

"Don't have any. Going back home, looking for more work."

"How about this," I suggested. "We form a company, and list it on the Internet."

I did not have to wait long for his answer. "I like it."

"Give me a call after you get back in town. We'll figure out something." My thoughts were on setting up a business in the emerging, and rapidly expanding computer industry. Living in a corporate environment in the U.S. business world, proprietary, and partnerships did not work anymore. It would be corporations all the way.

"Will do. Have a safe trip." He walked off.

Brad was never much for chitchat. He was strictly technology oriented. Coming from Hollywood's film industry, he had planned on a career change when he took this gig, as he used to call a project. A man of genius with great work ethics, and discipline, there had never been a project he had not finished with superior quality. His career reminded me much of my own but performing in different theaters. Having served four years in the Navy, exploring the world serving the country on the Eisenhower carrier ship, he landed in the midst of the nation's foremost film making capital, Hollywood. Being a musician of superior skills in instruments, and song writing, he signed up with some of the famous rock bands playing session guitar. After achieving the ultimate level in the profession, he had decided on a career on more solid ground. It was at this junction that we met at Microsoft's INS rollout. We worked well together, first on planning out the job, followed with implementing, and testing the system for our extremely satisfied clients.

SILICON VALLEY

Home again with several thousand dollars in the bank, I could plan out a future career. It had bought me the time I needed to pay the mortgage, and land the next job. Walking into an empty home, I had a difficult time adjusting to the loneliness. Loneliness had been the greater part in my life. Having had a recent taste in family bonding was not easy to shrug off. I determined right then to seek employment in California to be closer to the family, but the question still remained, "How to relocate without an income?"

The answer came in the form of a call from Brad. "Remember what we talked about?"

"Future business?"

"Are you ready?"

"Hell yes. The sooner the better." I suddenly felt the weight drop from my shoulders. It was always better to share a burden with a friend.

"Why don't you come over to my place, and we'll figure out the strategy."

It did not take much of a discussion for both of us to agree on one thing: "Let's do it." From that day on we would meet daily to develop the website, and work out a marketing approach. One day not long after, Brad received a call from Silicon Valley. It was from a business broker who had followed our INS performance. It turned out that Microsoft was looking for experts in Windows, and server technologies to organize, and implement another rollout, this time in the commercial sector. He accepted the project on the spot at the negotiated offer of $40 per hour, plus paid lodging, and living expenses.

"I'm getting a team of twelve together," the broker said. "I have seven commitments from here, but need five more experts. Can you handle it?"

"No problems," I heard Brad reply."

"How soon can your make it out here?" the broker said.

"We'll be there by Monday," Brad responded, and hung up with a broad grin across the face.

"We are on?" I was busting with anticipation.

"We made it. I need to get three more for the team. Who should we pick?"

"What's the project?" I said, highly energized, mentally browsing through faces we'd worked with in Miami. We selected the best of breed.

"Computer rollout staged out of San Francisco secured for nine months." It sounded like the start we had hoped. If it was good enough for Brad it certainly was good enough for me. It only took one day to get three more members committed for the team complement we were promised.

The five of us left the same weekend for San Francisco. Stepping off the plane I was euphoric at the opportunity that had fallen into my lap. "This is going to be home," I muttered. I had been waiting for greater than a year for something like this. Now, that it had happened, I was ready to tackle any new technology. I completely felt at home having arrived at the hub of innovation, and inventions. The driver of a limousine with a sign held high, "Microsoft Team," was waiting at the arrival gate. Collecting our suitcases, we were shuttled to the renowned Ramada Inn near San Bruno, only yards from the calming waters of San Francisco Bay. Requesting the top floor, prime accommodations awaited every one of us. It would be our home away from home for the next nine months.

Still vague at what the new project entailed, we received an in-briefing the following morning. In addition to deploying Windows 95 to desktops, and laptop computers, we were tasked with installing clusters of computer servers loaded with Microsoft's latest operating system driving desktops to the corporate client, Levi Strauss, and its design headquarters. Microsoft would become our contracting employer not only for nine months, but for years to come. When asking Microsoft's program director for the reasons for employing our team he boldly stated, "The business world was watching your performance at the INS with great anticipation. After the successful completion," he explained, "you won the pending rollout effort hands down. The world of business will be yours."

The following day, we showed up at Microsoft's first business client, the Levi Strauss designer campus. From that day on I knew that Microsoft technology would be my new career. I would be part of the pioneering technology serving the world with business solutions. While applications were still limited, new companies sprouted up in the Bay from San Francisco to San Jose, and on south, developing software needed to serve the business world. Silicon Valley would become the hub of a nation, vied, and sought after by the rest of the world as trend setters in technology advancements. The greatest incentive for Brad and I was, we had first cut to all of Microsoft's present and future innovations.

The campus was a pleasure to work at. Located by the piers, a five-minute stroll brought me to the Bay. I would spend lunchbreaks, and evening hours relaxing at the piers, watching sealions snapping, and barking at each other with fishing boats, and pleasure cruisers departing, and returning amid swells generated by ships' hulls. The scene was incredible. I could have not asked for more. Evenings, and nights with many quaint places to frequent were just as enthralling. For the time being I was content at how my life had turned out. I was able to visit my daughters on weekends or invite them for a day in the city.

The workplace turned out a busy place for us working around employee's work schedules. Most of the tasks were accomplished at the end of the workday after desks, and PCs were vacated. We went to work replacing Monochrome terminals with modern desktop computers. Depending on individual usage, the team would load up required software, provide connectivity to the network, and test the system. To perform the required tasks, the team was divided into three groups—installers, testers, and troubleshooters—each working different hour to assure readiness by the time employees arrived at the work place. Lucky for Brad and I, we were task to provide Level-3 server support. It meant working daytime hours.

The project proceeded well, but not without issues. Where hardware, and software problems were resolved as quick as they were identified, personal conflicts were not. Only days into the project I was faced with a personal challenge. It so happened that Levi's project manager was an inexperienced woman in management, as well as technology, dictating task schedules resulted in delays, and problems. Within days she caused discontent within the twelve-member engineering team. When word leaked to upper level management the response was swift. The following morning, stern faced, the female manager stormed into our breakroom, demanding, "Who is making trouble?"

Apparently, word had reach management about her incompetency. I watched her gaze scan across the room, trying to read our silent faces. When her eyes landed on my face, I immediately knew that I was singled out for whatever action she had planned in retaliation. Being senior on the team I was elected as scapegoat. It may have been my age, my European accent, or whatever else. She promptly turned, and stormed off.

Not more than fifteen minutes had passed before I was called to her office. I was not surprised when she made the announcement. "You are fired." Sickened by my new career being cut short I abruptly left without a response, headed back to the team anxiously awaiting my report. Unbeknownst to me, the team must have sensed the manager's discontent for me for days already. Questions like "What did she say," and "What went on?" were shot at me.

"I'm fired," was all I said, getting ready to depart the premises.

"Not so fast," Brad insisted. "There must be something we can do." Somebody in the team boldly stepped up and stated, "If you go, I'll quit too." I could not believe my ears when Brad stepped in with, "We'll all quit. Right?" I was surprised at the unrelenting support I received. I had never envisioned such loyalty. It may have sounded judgmental, and ungrateful on our behalf, it'd turned out that none on the team liked to work for her. Reason expressed were mostly in the way she handled the project. With all of us being seasoned engineers, having worked years in the industry, other than daily reprimands, nobody was getting credit and recognition by her.

After some deliberation the team decided to make the announcement to management first thing in the morning. We had to deal with two management factions. Actually, there were four. There were the Microsoft executives, Levi Strauss executive management, the team's project manager, and the customer project manager with the woman manager in the focus of our discontent.

It was not only me that had been frustrated since the start of the project. The team felt the same. The problem we faced was simple. Each morning, the woman would hand out the day's tasks for each team in a piece-meal type fashion. Since every member on the team was seasoned with computer and networked related projects, it was an insult to the competency for the contracted team, us. At the end of the day, the result was confusion to a state affecting our progress and reputation. Apparently, the manager was clueless of the importance of the project schedule or timeline, resulting in Levi Strauss employees showing up for work unable to perform their tasks.

The comments some of us made, causing my getting fired. Which brings up the question, "What happens to incompetent managers?"

Rather than correcting their inefficiency, they get promoted out and up to the next level. The following morning, as anticipated, the "Colorado team" gathered at Levi's executive office to announce our intentions. "If he goes, we will all quit."

A fifteen-minute recession was called with a request for us to standby. Right from the start of the project, the twelve-member team was split into two factions, the Colorado team containing five members, and the Bay-area team with seven. The split, seemingly unnecessary at first, greatly benefitted overall progress. It spurred on team competition, and performance pride not expected by management.

"You can all stay. We made a mistake," the executive announced shortly after. Then, he added, "You will report directly to your new project manager," who was also present. Conducting a brief speech, he dismissed us with, "You all know your jobs. There won't be any more interference. I will make sure you will be briefed daily on your progress."

As promised, the teams were briefed on every aspect of the project including issues, justification for delays, and possible resolutions. From here on, both Microsoft, and client were extremely satisfied with our progress. My career had been saved. Hours later rumors were circulating that the woman had been removed from her position. The Levi Strauss owners, Haas twin brothers, had admitted their mistake by placing their heiress into a technology position she could not handle.

After this, the Windows 95 rollout proceeded better than anticipated. It proved the point that a project effort was only as good as its managers, directors, and executives. Since I could claim getting experienced in both sectors, public, and private, I was able to gauge both industries for their differences in conducting businesses. My assessment is following: in the public sector, much like the government, every aspect of every task is documented, and precisely spelled out in accordance with the contract, but this was not the case with the private sector, the commercial industry. Here, most decisions were passed from the executive level down through the ranks only verbally. It was left to the program, and project managers to see that the job got done. It went even farther than that.

Once the project was on its way, I utilized a sophisticated application, Project Manager, a trial version only recently furnished by Microsoft. It would hand the burden for the project off in the employee's hands. It shifted responsibilities, and issues to the employee for both fault, and incentive. Completely software-driven, it worked well if properly managed. It freed up time for managers to deal with the overall performance without being troubled by project details.

Once the team had settled into work's routine, to avoid the daily commute from San Bruno across the Oakland Bridge into the heart of the city, we moved to more convenient accommodations readily available in San Francisco. We took possession near our place of work at a popular high-rise building located at the base of famous Lombard Street, acclaimed to be the world's most serpentine street. Taking apartments on the top floor, the view was spectacular. Stepping onto the balcony I had a panoramic vision from the Bay Bridge to the Golden Gate Bridge, and everything in-between, with Alcatraz, and Treasure Islands centered a few miles off. In addition, I could also make out the shoreline curbing Sausalito, and Tiburon in the far distance. To this day I still dream about being able to afford my own home at either one of those places.

From that day on I completely enjoyed life in the City by the Bay. I would skate, jog or walk along piers into the night after the tourists had retired. At times unable to sleep, I would jog the nights until I tired. I found the city inspiring, and free from crime. There may have been pickpocket occurrences as found in other metropolises, but that was all. The years living there, though piers were prolific with tourists, I never witnessed or experienced crime.

Not only did I enjoy the city, but so did everybody else on the Colorado team. It was unthinkable for our present life to end in nine months. When gathered at one or another café, tossing ideas across for, "how to prolong our current lifestyle," Brad came up with the solution. "Let's take Microsoft courses." Everyone agreed. What this meant was going back to school for one purpose, to learn Microsoft technology in its entirety. Courses were offered in every aspect with the most sought out business solutions provided by Microsoft.

Our ambition was to become MCSE,[55] but it required a nine-month commitment to take evening, and weekend classes. Both teams jumped at the opportunity when Microsoft opened a training facility right the middle of Market Street. Fortunately for us, management was tolerant enough to let us work daytime hours to 6:00 p.m. when classes started. Team members not interested in taking the classes were put on evenings and night shift to deploy desktop computers, and software configurations, ready for operation when the employees showed up in the morning. After studying Microsoft's Internet-based technology, the job became a breeze, especially when the mobile phone made its appearance. From then on, the team would spend the time resolving project issues either from the campus grounds, piers, and other places of preferences. It became the ultimate in working environment for our time. Telecommuting was born.

Silicon Valley was just emerging, but limited to manufacturing. Back then, it was nothing compared to what it offers today. For any technology-minded individual, it was the "place to be," with company names like Apple, Google, Facebook, Intel, eBay, and more becoming leaders in their respective industries. The high-tech hub for the world, in conjunction with many occupying a corporate office on Market Street, provided career opportunities for geeks as well as managers.

Having lost career connections with my former employers, and teams, I sometimes wondered about Buzz. He was not happy when I left Colorado. While I took the opportunity for early retirement from government contracting, he took an assignment with JPL in Pasadena, CA, but eventually returned to Colorado Springs. We would not see each other for the following twelve years until my return. But that was still years in the future. In the meantime, I prospered as a Microsoft Solution Provider to Fortune-500 companies, followed by an offer from PacBell I could not refuse, and on to MCI, and numerous other companies in need of Microsoft business solutions. Reaping the fruits of my success, an expert in leading edge technology, I spent my earnings wisely which had escalated from an initial $40 per hour to $65 with the next project, then $85, and on to as much as $110 per hour. I applied most of my earnings in emerging company investment, and several thousand dollars that went into the purchase of new computers.

My vision was to join the best of breed in renowned solution providers for Microsoft technology. To achieve it I had to become familiar with every software operating system, and business application offered to industry by the company. For a

---

[55] A Microsoft Certified Solutions Expert (MCSE) certification proves your ability to build innovative infrastructure, and data solutions on-premises, and in the cloud. Through certification one earn an MCSE in Server Infrastructure, Desktop Infrastructure, Private Cloud, Enterprise Devices, and Apps, Data Platform, Business Intelligence, Messaging, Communication and SharePoint server, one element at a time, greatly expanding skills.

contractor, as was the case with me, there was only one means to achieve it, creating my own business environment. I had to purchase computers to create my private, corporate network with services for accounts, databases, Web farm, applications, mail, VPN, DHCP, development, staging, and workstation servers, in addition to gateway, firewall, ports, switches, hubs, and monitors to make the network complete. Some software applications came with the systems, others I purchased. During my government contracting days I mostly worked with systems based on one proprietary compiled software, but here, I had to become familiar with JavaScript, C+, HTML, database architecture, Active Server, and numerous services, such as creating, and managing user accounts, and emails, developing presentations, spreadsheets, documents, figures, charts, and tables, all for the support of work, and career.

It even became more complicated when I took the job with PacBell at their corporate headquarters in San Ramon. Unlike my first project involvement with Microsoft's Windows 95 rollout, this effort was much more of a challenge. It involved the deployment of Server 2000, New Technology (NT), with software engines that would support front-end desktop, and laptop computers, in addition to today's smart phones, iPads, and hand-held gadgets.

However, this deployment was not as simple. When Microsoft figured out the time it would take to deploy 700 computer server platforms including Windows 2000 applications across PacBell's 12,000 employees, at HQs alone, it would take three years at a 24-hour workday to complete the job. It was not an acceptable solution. Directed by Microsoft, our task was to shorten the deployment with the aid of corporate experts. My new team was comprised of another dozen engineers skilled in various aspects of hardware, software, and system development seeking a viable solution.

The first step was to get our hands on the original Microsoft source code for the operating platform, the Server 2000, and Windows 2000 application everybody in the industries had been waiting for. As with various previous clients, PacBell became a testbed for the development. To work effectively, we were assigned a facility visible to employees, and visitors alike, in the headquarters entrance, a cathedral-topped hall three stories tall. It was a pleasurable place with ample lighting, and space all around.

Everybody on the team was assigned a special segment from operating platform to database, Web interface, security, application processing, and other aspects necessary to make the operating system work. My responsibility fell on legacy computer interface everybody else avoided. What it entailed was developing a software interface conversion between outdated mainframe systems to modern Microsoft technology. The reason why the business world preferred Microsoft in place of IBM, and other major computer products was the cost factor. It took millions of dollars to purchase, service, and support mainframe and supercomputers, where the cost for Microsoft products provided a solution at a fraction of cost. It not only reduced hardware, software, and systems expenses; it allowed small businesses to emerge, and flourish, the true reason for Silicon Valley to exist, and expand. But there was one problem. Most well-established businesses were not willing to scrap their inhouse developed mainframe systems. Connectivity and linking between management, employees, internal accounting, manufacturing, etc., was too complex for an easy transition, let alone replacement cost. The solution that Microsoft proposed was to leave mainframe systems in place while adding its technology on the front-end, mainly for business processes. It may sound simple, but proved challenging, when implemented without disturbing employee and corporate business functions.

Six months later we presented Microsoft with the product of our work, a streamlined operating system, specifically tailored to every business need in a deployable time of ten minutes per computer. Until now, a Windows platform installation time took a minimum of forty-five minutes, with additional hours to configure it into the corporate network. What it equated to was PacBell having a completely new business-based system installed, tested, and operational within six weeks. Though it took us many months to streamline, and configure the operating software, the end results were dramatic to the computer industry.

Reporting directly to the corporate director for the Pacific region, most of us were offered jobs within our specific disciplines. I would have gladly accepted, if it had not been for something much bigger awaiting my career success. Brad, who was not on this specific project, but contracted with MCI out of Napa, and I decided to form our own company. It could have been a failing endeavor if it had not been for the location, and contacts we had established. With the newly developed business applications, there was an emerging need for corporate, and network security. It would serve as the foundation for our business entity.

Much of our funding came from well-established San Francisco-based companies such as ION Systems, Intel, MCI, and others for getting our first application off the ground. In only a short three years, specializing in the design, and development of secure business and network applications, we became a million-dollar company. With a core of a dozen regionally based, skilled software specialists, we solicited working resources from India supplied by a contracting broker with offices in the U.S. At the time, unbeknownst to us, we had become just as much at fault for what would have dire consequences for the American economic future, better known as outsourcing. Ignorant at the time, like everybody throughout the industries, companies began to flourish based on two factors. One, the cost of development by hiring a foreign workforce was paying thirty cents on the dollar. But, more importantly, work could be accomplished around the clock. We worked twelve-hours daytime in the U.S., and our resource pool located in Madras, India, developed the product during their daytime hours, our night time.

With the Indian broker interpreting our designs, and blueprints into Hindi, each product segment was delivered in record time. Five years of operation elevated us into the corporate forefront. Initially, while on the Microsoft team, I was treated with extraordinary courtesy. It must have been the previous success with the successful Windows 3.1 version deployment to the INS. While Microsoft was the supplier for the Web hosted software, it did not provide direct support to the company performing the implementation. With Levi Strauss being Microsoft's first official customer, the team was provided with paid monthly trips home, shuttles in private limousine services to and from airports, paid lodging and living at the city of my dreams, San Francisco, a completely different lifestyle than the government could provide.

Microsoft took it even further when I formed my own company with a couple partners. They offered us direct partnership for the duration of the business. Unfortunately, all good things do not last forever. Ours ended with the collapse of

Silicon Valley. It was a tragic moment when in 2007 the stock market plunged following the sub-prime lending fiasco, taking with it banking, mortgage, and lending institutions impacting U.S. and world economies for the next ten years. We, as well as many Silicon Valley based companies could not sustain operations without clients and were forced to close business.

Unfortunately for us, and the industry, our successes ended abruptly when Silicon Valley collapsed. Our future would have been assured if it had not been for three events that occurred in rapid succession: the 9/11 terrorist attack on the New York Trade center, the economic recession as a result, with a final blow from sub-prime lending instituted by Wall Street, causing the collapse of the housing industry in 2007, affecting not only the existence of Silicon Valley, but more devastatingly, an economic collapse felt around the globe.

To save the business Brad, and I decided to move our development effort to a more economic region, Lake Havasu City. Unfortunately, it proved to be only a temporary fix. Our business never recovered. Two years later we decided to close operations, and went our separate ways with the lingering knowledge of what could have been a successful future. Our corporate success turned out to be only temporary, and was not meant to be in our future. It would take ten years for Silicon Valley, and other business parks to revive, and rebuild into what it is now, a haven for the young, and upcoming entrepreneurs.

I envy Apple, Google, Facebook, Intel, eBay, and others that have taken over where we left off. I especially miss the business hub of Market Street, docks, and piers with their barking sealions, quaint city clubs with their international patrons jabbering in foreign tongues, Coit Tower with its spectacular view, the Golden Gate Bridge, and parks, Columbus avenue with its many restaurants, and cafes, Bay Street with its multi-cultural shops, city bustle, and traffic sounds heard by day, and night, but most of all, I miss the sound of fog horns emanating from ships traversing in and out of San Francisco, during the nightly fogs.

The year was 2008. Having sold my original home in Colorado Springs, when I returned after a twelve-year absence, I was faced with a dilemma. Housing, what used to be an economically stable foundation, had collapsed, leaving a real estate mess in its wake. Probing the housing district of Rockrimmon once more, nothing was available for me to purchase. All sales had frozen with the national housing collapse. The reason, I'd learn, was lack of ownership and title proof. In short, what led to the collapse were banks, and lending institutions gambling away U.S. property titles and holdings at Wall Street, and commodity trading exchanges. Without the slightest knowledge by home, and business owners, American assets were being sold to foreign investors worldwide. Foreign banks, and institutions, mostly Russian and Chinese, were only too happy to acquire U.S. assets. It put us in an economic vulnerability never seen before. All of a sudden, foreign countries owned 40% of our wealth, putting us at an extremely vulnerable economic disposition felt to this day, one decade later.

Fortunately, working with a real estate company in town, I was able to locate one home up for sale, a registered short sale, pending title search. As luck had it, I was offered a temporary occupancy rental until the title was located. While I was prohibited from renovating the place, pending ownership, I was able to stage my corporate computer complex in the basement, turning it into my new command center. Setting up network, and COMM links, I was able to communicate effectively once more with the outside world, colleagues, government, and Intel contacts.

It took nine months of title searches before it was located, spread over several banks with principle ownerships at Banks of China, Bank of India, and Bank of Shanghai. Fortunately, with housing prices at a low, I lucked out to acquire a title free purchase, for the home I still occupy to this day.

HOMEBASE

Several days after arriving back in Colorado Springs, "Alex!" Buzz sounded when I called. "Where are you?" It had been years since we last talked. After being successful for much of my career I did not relish admitting failure from a once-thriving business.

"I'm back," I said.

"What do you mean?"

"Back in town."

"You moved back?" He had not expected that I would ever return.

"It had to be done."

"But why?"

"There are several reasons. Can we get together?"

"I'm on the job right now, but I'll stop by your place after work."

"What time are you getting off?"

"Four. I'll see you there."

I had a cold beer waiting for him.

"You're looking thin," he said, checking me over.

"Been busy," I replied, then explained.

"You closed the business? But why?"

"The Valley went under."

"So, I've heard. This place is not exactly thriving either. Couldn't get a job if you tried. So, tell me why you came back. The last time we talked you were doing well. You could have waited it out there."

"I don't think so. It'll take ten years for the country to recover."

"You think so?"

"Take my word."

"What are you going to do now?"

"Well, at least I am in better shape this time without an income. Financially." We sat for hours catching up. The government, as I expected after 911, had terminated many contracts, resulting in many job losses. He'd been laid off and, like me, had returned to Colorado to wait it out. Unlike me, he had kept his home. I told him the problem I had with the title search, and finding a place. It turned out that he was offered the same job back with Lockheed supporting the Mountain. As critical as national defense was, NORAD had survived the budget cuts.

"What plans do you have? Thinking of coming back? The company sure could use your skills."

"I suppose so, but I probably don't know anybody anymore." He knew I was referring to management.

"You are right. Things have changed here. Many moved out East, the Beltway, where the jobs are."

"Guess I'll take a break from business, and wait it out here. I've made a lot of business connections in the country. I have met executives from different sectors. I'll find something. Another beer?"

"No thanks. Have to go. The wife will have dinner waiting. Let's get together again in a week."

"Sounds good. See you."

The following day I checked in with a former contracting friend Leon, who also lives in town. He was part of Microsoft's rollout team with Levi Strauss, and several other projects. While I had veered off on my own business, he had returned. He was surprised to hear from me, and more so when I told him I was back in town. "You ready to go to work?" he said. He was not much for social talk, and always focused on current projects he worked on.

"You've got some work for me?"

"It depends. How soon can we get together?"

"Tomorrow soon enough?"

"Meet me for lunch. Chili's on the Academy." I knew the place well. We used to hang out there years before.

"Hey," I greeted him after five years of separation.

"So, you are back," he said in a halting expression. "What are your plans?" Leon had acquired management experiences at the executive level. He always came directly to the point.

"Not sure. I don't see any future in California for at least ten years."

"Why don't you come with me? I could use your help."

"Where?"

"DC."

"Tell me about it."

"I'm headed off on a project I know you'd fit in." I listened patiently for the next hour as he explained what it entailed.

"What's the timeline?"

"Oh, five, six months."

"What are my responsibilities?"

"I direct the project from here. You'll work wherever you are required. When can you start?" It had already been a couple of years since my last income, though I was not apt to take just any job. With Leon directing the project, it did not come any better. We would make a sound team.

"How soon do you need me?"

"How about tomorrow? You can work at my place. We can work out the strategy from there, and then move to the field."

As it turned out, he had been looking for the right person to work the project. Mostly homebound since his return from San Francisco, he needed someone in the field he could trust. As agreed, I showed up at his place, which I call a cliff hanger. His home, spacious with a spectacular view, was built on top of a ridge overlooking the valley. I had always envied him for it. Like me, he had his own business network connecting a cluster of computer servers. For the next two weeks it was our workplace with him delivering a monologue to get me up to speed on the project, and me taking mental notes. What the project entailed was as follows.

In the capacity as Project Director with Discovery Communication, the multi-channel entertainment complex headquartered in Washington, DC, he had full authority for this as well as other projects. Where he would direct all phases of tasks, including customers, and field teams, I would gather information for timelines, schedules, and parameters from a variety of the company's operating locations.

What I liked about Leon was the mode of operation he worked in. Much like me, he was one of few effective managers, and directors that would guarantee a project completion on time, and within the allocated budget. Where I had been trained in Germany through industrial discipline, his training was through command action in the Air Force. As we had proven time, and time again in past years, we made an effective team. On that premise, I was hired for the project without reservations by Discovery. His word was his trust with any corporate executive panel.

The project entailed moving Discovery's program scheduling systems, based in London, England, to a new, and secure location in Washington, DC. Discovery's most vital system had become critical in recent years due to the increase in terrorist attacks on European facilities. Corporate executives had decided that it was high time for the relocation despite the difficulty of the effort. Since London was the program scheduling, and processing hub for the company's European, African, and Mid-Eastern multi-media entertainment, the transition had to be performed flawlessly without interrupting live TV broadcasts, and program viewing.

The first thing we did was direct London engineering to build a second computer system to run in parallel. It would become vital for the eventual switchover. Next, the current operating, and servicing software had to be duplicated, and loaded to ghost (run in parallel) with the primary system. This guaranteed that every program, and advertising slot was running in sync to the split second. It was our job to assure that no interruptions occurred before, during, or after the transition. Since Leon knew planning, and operations, and was familiar with management, engineering pools, and operations personnel, I prepared transition schedules, and test plans for each segment. Over the following weeks, and months, we went over the plan many times to close any loopholes still open, and unfinished.

Five months into the project, our preparations were finally put to the test. There was one more task to verify. We had to inspect the new location that would house the system once it was relocated. Working mostly from Colorado Springs, aside from a monthly status briefing at headquarters in person, we took a last flight to Dulles airport. We checked out a rental car, and headed for Sterling, VA, the newly constructed hosting facility located nearby.

A highly secured building complex, we were issued ID passes, and authorization. Escorted along brightly lit passageways containing individually secured and locked cages, our escort guided us to one prominent space containing the new system. As we strode up close, the initial sight was awe inspiring. Centered in the middle of its allocated cage towered the world's most expensive computer system designed by man with a cost in the millions. My first comment to Leon was, "I've got to get me one of these."

"You are not kidding," he said, equally impressed.

Whatever engineers at Sun Microsystems had concocted this monstrosity, the Sun Fire-F6800 was an engineering marvel, and for its time the most powerful Unix-based computer system in operation. It seemed the entire building was constructed around the monster computer. It was Joshua[56] for its time. We were satisfied with the hosting location, and returned to Colorado the same day. With another recent bombing attack on London, the timeframe had become critical.

Though staged, and consolidated within Sun Fire, there were many elements to the system to drive Discovery's business, TV productions, and program schedules. Aside from highly qualified engineering, and operations pools coordinating the effort in Europe, Africa, and the Middle East, it was up to the two of us to test the system before, during, and after the transition from England to the U.S.

Scheduled for a weekend, the day for the switchover had finally arrived. Leon, and I sat at his lofty home, him Godlike on the phone, and me, the executioner, intensely watching Sun Fire making all-powerful decisions in a world of newscasts, broadcasts, programs, documentaries, and other entertainment, propagated throughout the globe, with world population watching dozens of Discovery channels, unaware of a flawless switchover without experiencing the slightest interruption to live programs propagated over satellites, and wireless.

"Was it worth it?" I said, interrupting Leon's concentration. "All the effort, and expenses?"

"Time will tell." Still focused on today's events, he responded once more, "Time will tell."

Time did tell. In only a short few months a wave of ISIS attacks broke in over London, Paris, and New York. It appeared that Jihad extremists were expanding their terror through much of the Western world.

What Leon, and I had just accomplished, in the year 2007, would be the last project in my career. While the commercial field was gearing up publicly, into a civilian life driven, and centered around social media, the government was still plagued with a lack in budget allocation, further inundated by the new political administration.

How my professional future will turn out is up in the air. Still unemployed in 2018, I occupy my time with writing novels and, recently, my autobiography, Invisible Warrior. I dearly miss my involvement with challenging projects, corporate, and government alike, and I relive my past adventures, and team spirit through the days spent writing.

---

[56] Joshua was the monstrous system watching over the North American continent, breathing live into NORAD's underground home base, the Cheyenne Mountain.

HOMECOMING

Now that I had time again after neglecting friends, and family, I gave Buzz a call. "Where have you been? Haven't seen or heard from you in months." I felt a twitch of guilt, and decided to be more considerate from now on. I had spent most of my waking hours with Leon, but I was back at my own home again. Even my computers, and home network had been neglected. I could spot the thin layer of dust settled on equipment casings. I had missed the spring cleaning. It would be my next scheduled household chore.

"Sorry. Been busy out east."

"You are not thinking of moving, are you?"

"Nothing like it. Just finished a project with Discovery."

"TV Network?"

"The one. But I am back again."

"Want to get together?"

"Now?"

"Yeah," he said. "Got a beer waiting for you."

"I'll be right over." After a fifteen-minute cross-town drive, sure enough, a can was waiting cooled in a cup holder. Once we were settled comfortably in easy chairs, it was reporting time. He kept me abreast with news from the Mountain, a mystery place to the general citizen, while I presented updates from projects near, and far. It always made for lively, at times, controversial discussions. They were the happy times since neither one of us were very talkative, a product of our jobs.

"By the way," he said after replenishing drinks. "What ever happened to your daughters? I haven't seen them in years."

"Liz, and Tracy?"

"Actually," he said, "all three of them."

I had not kept in contact with them for months. I made a mental note to call. "Oh," I stalled, trying to recollect my last contact with them. "Thanks for reminding me. I haven't either."

"You have three, don't you?"

"Still do. Liz is living with her family in Napa. She's got a full-time job. The same is true for Tracy. I never know what she's up to until she calls in, which is not frequent."

"What about the youngest daughter?"

"Danielle? Taking care of her mom, I suppose." My youngest daughter was born in 1983 just days before I left for the two-year contract assignment to Yokota, Japan. Though all three daughters came to visit me during summer break the following year, I never got to know her well. It was the time Annette and I separated, with her mom's eventual remarriage to her second husband, who, as stepdad, had full custody.

Buzz had his own children. When he and I used to be absent from home for months on end, our wives became friends, and kept up family ties while raising our respective children. Today, I am sorry to say, it is only Buzz, and me still in contact. It was a reminder of the society, a free world, we lived in. I knew well that we did not live in a family-oriented country as many third-world cultures did. Here, when children reached adulthood, they were expected to move on, and create their own world.

"Yeah. Listen," Buzz said, suppressing a yawn, "I've got to get up early. Job, you know."

I understood. I needed to make some calls anyway. "We'll talk again."

"Make it soon. See you."

Back at my place again, I called Liz to reconnect. Our talk was lively as usual with her putting the kids on the phone, and me giving updates about my recent silence. We spent our usual two hours catching up with a promise to visit soon. Tracy was not as easy to locate. I usually wound up leaving a message on her mobile, or was it a cell? I don't know what the young call their gadgets these days. From what I can make out, the young generation is creating their own world of Internet space, and language. Ever heard of such things as Frenemy, Selfie, Spotify, Lyft, LOL, ICUMI, and hundreds more? I could not keep up with the rapid changes forced on us by the young. It must be the times we live in. I cannot fathom the speed at which young minds operate. Where during my life, time had gradually accelerated with age, and wisdom, I questioned many times what the future for the young would look like. Subjected to a world of stress, and demands exerted by mainstream media, I was glad to have a private sanctuary I was able to hide in, and shut out a world gone crazy.

My thoughts were interrupted by my cell buzzing from the nearby table. I reached over to retrieve the gadget to check caller ID. I usually ignore Robo calls or numbers I don't recognize. I decided to take the call since it was a San Francisco number, a region where some of my family lived.

"Alex," I answered. There was silence. I was ready to hang up when a distant, almost imperceptible voice came forward. "Dad."

I was not sure at the moment which of my daughters it could be since all had similar sounding voices. "Yes?"

"Danielle," the voice said, more assertively. I was completely taken by surprise. I had not heard from her in years. We had never really connected since Anette, and I were divorced about the same time. California based, she was raised by her mom and stepdad. Getting the highly unusual call, I was certainly curious.

"How have you been?"

After another hesitant pause, she said, "I wondered if I could visit with you."

Now, it was my turn to impose silence. I tried to evaluate her request, as strange as it sounded. My mind was churning for a plausible answer, but needed an immediate response. "What do you have in mind?"

"I wanted to talk with you. There are things I need answers to."

"Business not doing well?" I had just recently learned that Danielle had started her own Internet-based fashion store. I suspected it might be the reason she wanted to talk.

"That's not it. I am kind of at a loss." Another pause. "I have no goals, no clear focus on the future."

At least I had the reason for her visit. I am not as family oriented as most, with anybody just dropping by on short, or without notice. For the greater part of my life I had been living alone. Loneliness I could accept, but an unexpected visitor, I usually avoided. Though estranged from my daughter, I would welcome her.

"Of course, you can visit. When?"

"I'm not working these days. I can hop on any flight as long as I am welcomed."

"Of course, you are welcomed. You can visit any time."

"Okay," she said with an audible sigh. "Next week. I'll text the flight info."

"Fine. I'll be glad to see you."

"Bye." The phone went silent, but not my mind. It turned over with questions, and sentiments of guilt. Not so much for guilt of neglect or such. More so for not making the initial effort to establish a lost family connection. Regardless of estrangement, she was still my flesh, and blood, and so, for the rest of the week I pondered until the day of her text, "arriving Colorado Springs…", followed with a flight number, and arrival time.

My curiosity was heightened to new levels as I waited for passengers to emerge through the arriving gates. I recognized her face as soon as she stepped from the ramp. My heart beat almost doubled as she approached with a friendly, "Remember me?"

Danielle looked as stunning as my other two daughters. It must have been a healthy mix from both sides of the gene pool. Since a handshake was out of the question, I greeted her with a reserved hug. "Of course. I never forget faces," I responded. "You got luggage?"

She had a fashionable bag slung around one shoulder, which she indicated with a gesture. "No. Only this."

"You hungry?" It was close to lunch time.

"No. Had a snack in flight." We left the airport grounds headed for home. On the way north, in between light conversation, I pointed out some of the prominent landmarks in the area. "Peterson AFB, Cheyenne Mountain, Pikes Peak, Air Force Academy," and "we're almost there."

A few minutes later we drove up to the home. "Big place," she said with an approving nod. Many families living in California, due to overpopulation, crowdedness, and high cost of living, were crammed into small, and somewhat dated homes, but Colorado still offered ample living space.

After a brief tour through the new Castle we sat on the deck to enjoy the afternoon warmth. "Quiet place you have," she remarked, checking out my domain.

Since it was a sunny day, as usually in the Rockies, we settled outside on the deck. "Now," I probed, "what is on your mind?" After all, it was the reason for her being here.

"Dad, if I may call you that, there is something on my mind only you can explain."

"Go on." It heightened my curiosity especially when one could just Google information on the Internet, but I held my tongue. I quietly sat, and listened to give her all the time she needed.

"There has been something on my mind I don't understand, and need clarification. I thought, since you are involved with the government, you would know."

I remained silent, and just waited for her to continue at her own pace.

"What do you know about UFOs?"

I felt like my head was hit by a board. Though rumors about ETs, and UFOs had been prolific at times with the public, in general, the mainstream media kept silent, resulting with a public tranced in ignorance. True, some radio stations carried programs about the subject, after a sighting occurred, but in my mind, it was mostly bogus information generated by conspiracists. I needed time to think, and instead stalled, "How about a drink?"

"You have wine?"

"White or red?"

"What do you drink?" It was an indication that she was not prone to drinking alcohol.

"Cabernet."

"Sure. I'd like to try some."

Minutes later, after retrieving one of my finest from the basement suitable for the occasion, I was ready to listen.

"Why do you ask?" I maintained a reserved disposition. I had to find out more.

"I am confused about it all. Some people claim to actually have seen, or been in contact with Aliens, and even been abducted. Is it true?"

"What do you want to hear?"

"I want the truth," Danielle insisted. "I had hoped you could provide it."

I avoided a direct answer, and instead said, "How long are you planning to stay?"

"My ticket is good for five days."

Because the demand was so unusual, I needed time to figure out an approach. Though I had been asked at times for my opinion on the matter, I usually stayed distant for discussing what I considered, "a motive for clashes with people." Much like with religion, and politics it was a topic to avoid. From my experience, it only caused discontent with people. More so, entire families, and friendships had been destroyed over the difference in opinions. Though I savored the occasion of her visit I still stalled for my answer. I would rather plead ignorance than commit to what could damage the fragile relationship I already had with her. I tried to ignore her request. But, knowing my daughters, as level headed individuals as they were, they never accepted a brushoff. Danielle probably felt the same way, given the reasons for her requested appearance.

"Now, where were we?"

"You were going to give me an answer."

"Ah, yes. ETs, and UFOs." I silently groaned, hoping she would change the topic. But no such luck today.

Staring directly into my eyes, she kept pressing on. "Well?"

"Okay. If you insist. But I must warn you that whatever the outcome, you'll have to accept it at face value without reservations."

"I promise."

"Have you ever heard of 'Full Disclosure'?"

"I have, and it's the reason I am here," she said, indicating the importance of her sitting across the table.

"It's where the president will publicly announce the secrets about UFOs."

"Yes. You are killing me with suspense."

"Not so fast, young lady. First, I will have to tell you about governments."

"I know about the government, spending, taxes, and all that."

"I did not mean to imply that you didn't. But there is much more to it than a simple, and ready answer."

"Okay then. If you must."

"I must," I said with an underscoring grin. Though her impatience was obvious, for her to get the full picture I decided on a timeout. It would take some time to explain. "Let's take a walk. We can talk there."

I needed the space to think. I was not sure at the moment what, and how much I was willing to disclose. I clearly recalled Mystery-man's warnings about it the last time we had talked not that long ago: "Don't do anything irrational you might regret. Those guys are merciless."

Where much of the general population was not aware of the prolific undercurrents questioned, speculated, and discussed on nightly radio talk shows regarding Alien and UFO phenomena, a small, but highly persistent percentage, in the tens of millions, nevertheless, are in constant pursuit of the truth. Nothing less will satisfy these followers, other than a "Full Disclosure" announcement by the government. Suffering from sleeplessness, for much of my adult life, I am one of the nightly listeners entertained by the various radio hosts with call signs such as Coast-to-Coast AM, Ground Zero, Darkness Radio, Black Vault, and a dozen more. Though quite entertaining to me, whereas much of the listeners are dead serious about the nightly controversial topics of supposedly government coverups, speculations, and whistleblowers calling in to contribute to the mysteries, it provides an alternative perspective on life. I am always amazed, and grateful, at the boundless dedication and energy, talk show hosts apply night after night. They are a special, honest, breed of operatives, applying their unique skills to benefit man through an otherwise miserable night plagued with insomnia, only to keep myths and legends alive.

Where I differ from the general listener, I know the facts, as Volume II sections will explain. Though I wanted to share information, I needed collaboration from the only other person I knew who would harbor the truth. My longtime friend at DARPA, Mystery-man. He, and I, not for curiosity reasons, but from necessity, had shared many secrets in the past. What puzzled me most to this day is, we never touched on the subjects of UFOs and ETs. I decided to give him a call. I needed his irrefutable backing.

VOLUME TWO

FULL DISCLOSURE

BRIEF HISTORY

For the readers not familiar with UFO events, I will present a brief history in this section. When the contemporary UFO phenomena started at the onset of WWII, it initially shocked the public to its very foundation. But the shock effect was short lived once Orson Wells, playwright for the 1938 radio scare, "War of the Worlds,"[57] revealed the truth behind the announcement. It was a daring play that would hound him, and the producers of the play for many years. It would set off an alertness in the public unlike ever before. From then on, UFO sightings were reported with so-called crashes, human abductions, alien encounters, bodily manipulations, and many more. While fictitious in nature, made up by overly sensitive minds, the people found a new frontier, that of the skies. An awareness of the UFO phenomena was created that would last to this day.

With an increase in UFO reporting of new sightings by the public, the government became alerted to a point where a decision became necessary for how to treat the phenomena following the early, but persistent, sightings briefly listed here:

DATE	NAME	CITY, STATE	COUNTRY
1909	Mystery airships	Otago	New Zealand
1917	Miracle of the Sun	Fátima	Portugal
1940s	Foo fighters	Berlin, Germany	World War II
1941	Cape Girardeau UFO	Cape Girardeau, Miss.	United States
1947	Kenneth Arnold	Mount Rainier	Washington
1947	Roswell UFO Crash	Roswell	New Mexico

It was the Roswell UFO crash that spurred the government into taking ownership. Early sightings were important enough for the government to take notice. Projects Sign, and Grudge were created in 1948 by the Air Force, but were short lived. They were terminated in 1949, and replaced by Project Blue Book, headquartered at Wright-Patterson Air Force Base in Ohio. From there on it was the Air Force that took responsibility for recording UFO sightings, researched, and evaluated by the Robertson Panel.

It was a time where the public had become keenly aware of UFOs, but were unable to identify the rapidly changing shapes of flying objects skidding across the skies, ranging from disk shaped to cylinder, cigar, boomerang, doughnut, balloon, and many more shapes in the times ahead. Most popular at the time was the disk shape, catching the eyes, and the term "Flying Saucer" was coined. Sightings, initially spurious, kept increasing, and growing to where the Air Force eventually distanced itself, letting the

─────────────────

[57] The War of the Worlds was an episode of the American radio drama anthology series The Mercury Theater on the Air. It was performed as a Halloween episode of the series on Sunday, October 30, 1938, and aired over the Columbia Broadcasting System radio network. Directed, and narrated by actor, and future filmmaker Orson Welles, the episode was an adaptation of H. G. Wells' novel The War of the Worlds (1898). It became famous for allegedly causing mass panic, although the scale of the panic was disputed as the program had relatively few listeners.

public handle the recording with MUFON, NICAP, NUFORC, and other private, and public centers.

Brief History of UFO Reporting

In popular culture, the term UFO—or unidentified flying object—refers to a suspected alien spacecraft, although its definition encompasses any unexplained aerial phenomena. UFO sightings have been reported throughout recorded history, and in various parts of the world, raising questions about life on other planets, and whether extraterrestrials have visited Earth. They became a major subject of interest—and the inspiration behind numerous films, and books—following the development of rocketry after World War II.

Flying Saucers

The first well-known UFO sighting occurred in 1947, when businessman Kenneth Arnold claimed to have seen a group of nine high-speed objects near Mount Rainier in Washington while flying his small plane. Arnold estimated the speed of the crescent-shaped objects as several thousand miles per hour, and said they moved "like saucers skipping on water." In the newspaper report that followed, it was mistakenly stated that the objects were saucer-shaped, hence the term flying saucer.

Sightings of unidentified aerial phenomena increased, and in 1948 the U.S. Air Force began an investigation of these reports called Project Sign. The initial opinion of those involved with the project was that the UFOs were most likely sophisticated Soviet aircraft, although some researchers suggested that they might be spacecraft from other worlds, the so-called extraterrestrial hypothesis (ETH). Within a year, Project Sign was succeeded by Project Grudge, which in 1952 was itself replaced by the longest-lived of the official inquiries into UFOs, Project Blue Book, headquartered at Wright-Patterson Air Force Base in Dayton, Ohio.

From 1952 to 1969 Project Blue Book compiled reports of more than 12,000 sightings or events, each of which was ultimately classified as (1) "identified" with a known astronomical, atmospheric, or artificial (human-caused) phenomenon, or (2) "unidentified." The latter category, approximately 6 percent of the total, included cases for which there was insufficient information to make an identification to a known phenomenon.

The Robertson Panel, and The Condon Report

An American obsession with the UFO phenomenon was under way. In the hot summer of 1952 a provocative series of radar, and visual sightings occurred near National Airport in Washington, D.C. Although these events were attributed to temperature inversions in the air over the city, not everyone was convinced by this explanation. Meanwhile, the number of UFO reports had climbed to a record high. This led the Central Intelligence Agency to prompt the U.S. government to establish an expert panel of scientists to investigate the phenomena. The panel was headed by H.P. Robertson, a physicist at the California Institute of Technology in Pasadena, CA, and included other physicists, an astronomer, and a rocket engineer. The Robertson Panel met for three days in 1953, and interviewed military officers, and the head of Project Blue Book.

They also reviewed films, and photographs of UFOs. Their conclusions were that (1) 90 percent of the sightings could be easily attributed to astronomical, and meteorological phenomena (e.g., bright planets, and stars, meteors, auroras, ion clouds), or to such earthly objects as aircraft, balloons, birds, and searchlights, (2) there was no obvious security threat, and (3) there was no evidence to support the ETH. Parts of the panel's report were kept classified until 1979, and this long period of secrecy helped fuel suspicions of a government cover-up.

A second committee was set up in 1966 at the request of the Air Force to review the most interesting material gathered by Project Blue Book. Two years later this committee, which made a detailed study of 59 UFO sightings, released its results as the Scientific Study of Unidentified Flying Objects—also known as the Condon Report, named for Edward U. Condon, the physicist who headed the investigation. The Condon Report was reviewed by a special committee of the National Academy of Sciences. A total of 37 scientists wrote chapters, or parts of chapters for the report, which covered investigations of the 59 UFO sightings in detail. Like the Robertson Panel, the committee concluded that there was no evidence of anything other than commonplace phenomena in the reports, and that UFOs did not warrant further investigation. This, together with a decline in sighting activity, led to the termination of Project Blue Book in 1969.

Other Investigations of UFOs
Despite the failure of the ETH to make headway with the expert committees, a few scientists, and engineers, most notably J. Allen Hynek, an astronomer at Northwestern University in Evanston, IL, who had been involved with projects Sign, Grudge, and Blue Book, concluded that a small fraction of the most-reliable UFO reports gave definite indications for the presence of extraterrestrial visitors. Hynek founded the Center for UFO Studies (CUFOS), which continued to investigate the phenomenon.

Aside from Project Blue Book, the only other official, and fairly complete records of UFO sightings were kept in Canada, where they were transferred in 1968 from the Canadian Department of National Defense to the Canadian National Research Council. The Canadian records comprised about 750 sightings. Less-complete records have been maintained in the United Kingdom, Sweden, Denmark, Australia, and Greece. In the United States, CUFOS, and the Mutual UFO Network in Bellevue, CO, continue to log sightings reported by the public.

In the Soviet Union, sightings of UFOs were often prompted by tests of secret military rockets. In order to obscure the true nature of the tests, the government sometimes encouraged the public's belief that these rockets might be extraterrestrial craft, but eventually decided that the descriptions themselves might give away too much information. UFO sightings in China have been similarly provoked by military activity that is unknown to the public.

Possible Explanations for UFO Sightings, and Alien Abductions
UFO reports have varied widely in reliability, as judged by the number of witnesses, whether the witnesses were independent of each other, the observing conditions (e.g., fog, haze, type of illumination), and the direction of sighting. Typically, witnesses who take the trouble to report a sighting consider the object to be of extraterrestrial origin, or possibly a military craft, but certainly under intelligent control. This inference is usually based on what was perceived as formation flying by sets of objects,

unnatural—often sudden—motions, the lack of sound, changes in brightness or color, and strange shapes.

That the unaided eye plays tricks were well known. A bright light, such as the planet Venus, often appears to move. Astronomical objects can also be disconcerting to drivers, as they seem to "follow" the car. Visual impressions of distance, and speed of UFOs are also highly unreliable because they are based on an assumed size, and are often made against a blank sky with no background object (clouds, mountains, etc.) to set a maximum distance. Reflections from windows, and eyeglasses produce superimposed views, and complex optical systems, such as camera lenses, can turn point sources of light into apparently saucer-shaped phenomena. Such optical illusions, and the psychological desire to interpret images are known to account for many visual UFO reports, and at least some sightings are known to be hoaxes. Radar sightings, while in certain respects more reliable, fail to discriminate between artificial objects, and meteor trails, ionized gas, rain, or thermal discontinuities in the atmosphere.

"Contact events," such as abductions, were often associated with UFOs because they were ascribed to extraterrestrial visitors. However, the credibility of the ETH as an explanation for abductions is disputed by most psychologists who have investigated this phenomenon. They suggested that a common experience known as "sleep paralysis" may be the culprit, as this causes sleepers to experience a temporary immobility, and a belief that they are "being watched."

The above stated accounts reported by the government only reinforced, and supported my analysis on the UFO phenomena. It is up to the individual now, to take my accounts as factual, and at face value as written by me, the author. Setting the record straight, once, and for all, I will leave it up to the individual reader whether to accept, and adopt my declaration of facts, or take the recorded accounts by Ufologists as reality. At the end, it does not matter. Folklore, and legends will continue to be created regardless of time, and epoch, conceived by man's imagination. Where in the past it was visions from heaven, nightmarish gargoyles, outlandish effigies, or mysterious UFO abductions, tomorrow may bring new enigmatic images by the inspiring sci-fi minds solely created for the entertainment of mankind.

Facts will remain facts steadfastly linked to science where mythology is subject to speculation; two factors separate facts from fiction, with the latter perhaps never being verifiable. In the world of today, with the passage of time, though the UFO phenomena still prevails, the public pretty much has accepted UFO sightings as part of our daily lives. Though curious, nobody gets shocked over it anymore. We as a public have been gradually educated in the matters of UFOs, and ETs through sci-fi, action based, and comic-book type entertainments, with our visual, and audio senses being prepped to accept just about any form of mystical, supernatural, and paranormal events.

Whether one likes, and accepts the reality, or not, it all boils down to one factor, that of an unsubstantiated phenomenon at this time. However, it will not preclude that it will remain this way forever. With the expanding deep space exploration by scientists, and entrepreneurs, developing means to travel space, and time, the future will hold endless possibilities to meet the unexpected.

As far as "Full Disclosure" is concerned, it is an episode created through events instigated by the public, but promoted, and propagated by the government to suit its purpose for various reasons, and needs not readily disclosed.

As for today, in a world where much of the population is educated, "whose responsibility is it to reveal the facts?"

"The Government's."

But this comes with a catch. Several generations have passed since the first modern UFO sightings, and with them, responsibilities. Where the original members involved in setting up, and recording the various supernatural phenomena, by now, are mostly retired, some incapacitated, and the rest have passed on. There is nobody left to take responsibility for the phenomena in the name of the government to the public. Consequently, the sphere of responsibility, and ownership has been lost over the past 70 years. As a result, UFO issues are being passed from department to department without anybody aspired to take back ownership, and responsibility, opening a void between government, and public.

It was this indecision that triggered my mind to do something about it without infringing on national security secrets. As the readers will see, they will learn the truths, and facts behind the world's greatest coverup. They will also learn that no matter what the consequences of my revelation will be, the public, as well as the government, deserve the truth. As stated, many in the government are as confused about UFOs, and Extraterrestrial subjects as the general public.

I don't want to sound disrespectful to anybody, not the government, not the military, and surely not defense and Intel organizations but, I felt, it was up to me, with the backing of a few dozen DOD contractors still alive, to set the record straight. In the end, it will be my sole responsibility to bear the burden in justifying the myth of extraterrestrials, hoping that the government will come clean with UFOs with the understanding that national security will not be compromised.

GOVERNMENT DEFINED

To get a better understanding of governments, and their workings, one must delve into historical accounts dating back millennia past the Roman Republic, Greeks, Egyptians, and earlier. However, it was Aristotle, Greek philosopher, that conducted extensive studies into various forms of governments, and constitutions.

A constitution may be defined as an organization of offices in a state, by which the method of their distribution is fixed, the sovereign authority is determined, and the nature of the end to be pursued by the association, and all its members is prescribed. Laws, as distinct from the frame of the constitution, are the rules by which the magistrates should exercise their powers, and should watch, and check transgressors.

In modern Europe, written constitutions came into greater use during the eighteenth, and nineteenth centuries. Constitutions such as that of the United States, created in 1787, were influenced by the ancient Greek models. During the twentieth century, an increasing number of countries around the world concluded that constitutions were a necessary part of democratic or republican government. Many thus adopted their own constitutions.

Different forms, and levels of governments may have constitutions. All 50 U.S. states have constitutions, as do many countries including Japan, India, Canada, and Germany. It is also common for nongovernmental organizations, and civic groups to have constitutions.

In its ideal form, a constitution emanates from the consent, and will of the people whom it governs. Besides establishing the institutions of government, and the manner in which they function toward each other, and toward the people, a constitution may also set forth the rights of the individual, and a government's responsibility to honor those rights.

Constitutions, whether written or unwritten, typically function as an evolving body of legal custom, and opinion. Their evolution generally involves changes in judicial interpretation, or in themselves, the latter usually through a process called amendment. Amendment of a constitution is usually designed to be a difficult process in order to give the constitution greater stability. On the other hand, if a constitution is extremely difficult to amend, it may be too inflexible to survive over time. For instance, the ongoing evolutionary nature of constitutions explains why England may be described as having a constitution even though it does not have a single written document that is designated as such. England's constitution instead inheres to a body of legal custom, and tradition that regulates the relationship among the monarchy, the legislature (parliament), the judicial system, and Common Law.

The former Soviet Union, for example, created the 1936 Constitution of the Union of Soviet Socialist Republics, also known as the "Stalin Constitution," but that document did not establish a truly constitutional form of government. Joseph Stalin, the ruler of the Soviet Union from 1924 to 1953, could not be formally penalized, or called to account for his actions, no matter how heinous, before any other government official, any court, or the people themselves. The Soviet Constitution also claimed to guarantee freedom of speech, press, and assembly, but in practice the Soviet government continually repressed those who sought to express those freedoms.

In the United States, individual state constitutions must conform to the basic principles of the U.S. Constitution—they may not violate rights, or standards that it established. However, states are free to grant rights that are not defined in the U.S. Constitution, as long as doing so does not interfere with other rights that are drawn from it. For this reason, groups or individuals who seek to file constitutional claims in court are increasingly examining state constitutions for settlement of their grievances. In the issue of school desegregation, for example, groups such as the National Association for the Advancement of Colored People (NAACP) began in the 1990s to shift focus to the state level, with the hope of finding greater protection of rights under state constitutions.

The Principles of American Government are republicanism, popular sovereignty, federalism, limited government, separation of powers, checks, and balances, unalienable rights, and the concept of democracy. All of these ensured that the power of the government came from the people, and that any powers given to the government were limited.

As I have stated before, though unethical, and against the law, "rules, and Policies are there to be broken." It all depends on the foundation of the country, and how strong the people feel about its constitution. We could analyze any country on the globe. Each went through several forms, and cycles of governing. It seems that a specific form of government, on the scale of human existence, only lasts a short amount of time before the system breaks down. There are several factors responsible, with one major contributor causative to social breakdown. I will cite two examples, China Cause, and U.S. Cause, which most of us should be aware of.

Though China has experienced many upheavals through past ages, it has always recovered, but not without rebuilding the nation through war. War, historically, seemed to be the only answer to reestablish social order. The major contributor to the collapse in first place, most times, was related to neighboring differences followed by infringements on customs, and culture, seeking hold on the country, and its people. The young might accept the changes, but the elders did not. They clung to inherited morals, and ethics everybody once valued without reservation. However, the once-revered values by the population were slowly pulled apart, bit by bit, adopting, and accepting the changes, first by few then followed by the masses.

In the process of changes, governments might change hands through various forms from democracy to republic, and on to monarchy, communism, fascism, capitalism, socialism, with the final blow dealt by dictatorship, or anarchism tearing the nation apart. The end result was always war. As the War of Independence, Civil War, and Mexican War demonstrated, we in the United States were not exempt from the perils of war.

In China the reasons for recent changes may have been through the preservation of its ancient ideology, but in contrast, the U.S. had no culture to preserve. It was too new a country for the settlers. What it sought was freedom from oppression, the same cause many left the old country.

It seems that in today's world in the U.S., our country is on the brink of changes subjected to the same cycles prone to follow history. While the general population may not be aware of any changes, an undercurrent of dissention is in the making. Mainstream media may not always inform the general population of things to come, especially when it serves their own interests. But rest assured, dissidents, and factions resisting the present government are on the rise. It is only a matter of time before patience from both barriers, government, and law enforcement, are pitted against a growing number of dissentions under the guise of "freedom fighters, resistance movement, fight for independence," or other factions. Success would be assured to the people if military, and law enforcing agencies were unprepared for an organized coup, overthrowing the current government with its flailing leadership.

"Why does the potential threat exist in today's world of affluence, and prosperity?" one might ask. The root cause blame is with the government. There is no excuse why the blame goes to the respective party we support, and depend on. In recent times, our government has acted mostly on responses exerted either through national disturbances, or from foreign nations exerting pressure on our country. There were wars we supported with opportunities for enriching industrial entities through armament, and weapons manufacturing. We sent troops overseas to suppress border clashes, and hostilities. We built up our armed forces to be prepared for any unforeseen hostilities, and encroachment on our own borders. Then there are fears for potential internal aggressions directed at our government. The results are a government, and military grown too large of a burden for the citizens and taxation to support the ever-expanding demand for power.

There are other contributing factors for increasing the financial burden, dating back decades. First, there was the monumental expense developing national defense with its exorbitant cost in nuclear technology development. Then, there were burdens put on the national budget with the inception of the ARPA (today's DARPA), and its evolving technological demands funded by incremental budget allocations for black projects. There were congressional budget approvals to fund many nations which had succumbed to natural disasters in a world expecting the U.S. to aid, and foot the expense. It adds up to one common denominator. Our government grew too large to be sustained by our industries, especially since the industries grew large alongside, a product of "Free Enterprise."

We do not want to linger on whose fault it is. What matters most is how to fix it. How to fix a government, and a budget deficit that has outgrown its constitutional boundaries as setup forthwith by our forefathers.

ROOTCAUSE

Back to the present. During the duration of my daughter Dannielle's visit, many more questions came up to satisfy her genuine curiosity. Where she generally was a quiet person, I'd learned, one such question was, "Why do governments fail?"

"Let me explain," I said. "To get a better understanding about a failed government is simple. It is run by the people. People are people, no matter how sophisticated, or complex their minds work. The differences between a successful one, and unsuccessful one, is the inherited intellect, and acquired cunning the mind is capable."

Next, there are the political issues, and ambitions with one such driving factor, "There are winners, and there are losers."

"Could you clarify it for me?"

"Certainly. In simple terms," I went on, "there are the ones with leadership qualities where the rest of us are followers. Where one faction is comprised by a very small body, the other faction makes up the difference by following the leader, and their enforced rules, and with it their inherited, or enforced policies. In dictatorship, and totalitarian form of oppression, an entire generation could be deprived of their birthrights."

"I can see that," she said in agreement.

"With the given conditions it is our choice to grow, and prosper, and if prevented in doing so by the rulers, we will have to endure reprimand, and possible punishment. The causes date back to a time when human development was still in its infancy, evolving into social bonds. It was human nature to flock together for security. Couples clung together, families formed, neighborhoods developed followed with settlements, towns, cities, and regions staked out, and demarked by boundaries. To make an economy work, it was slavery first, followed with communal obligations, partnerships, corporate entities, eventually grown into conglomerate industrial complexities. Every group sought growth."

"I understand."

"Governments are no exemptions. Organizations are created, agencies followed, people are promoted, causing an ever-increasing inflation factor. Initial prosperity is soon traded for acquired wealth, greed eventually followed with power as the ultimate goal. Growth is not a matter of ethics, or opportunity alone; it is purely a question of power supported by an army of dedicated workers relying on a growing pay scale in proportion to the inevitable inflation that is sure to follow, or lead.

"Whichever came first," Danielle said, questioning ethics.

"That's still subject to debate." I said, presenting some examples. Where most prospective employees in the government start as GS-1, the lowest paygrade, it would take a career life to achieve a possible GS-9. For this reason, higher education was desired. It could offer a jumpstart into the GS-9 level to rapidly grow upwards to GS-13, a level within the reach of many with rewarding pay opportunities to match. Everything above, usually GS-15, required congressional approval, or presidential appointment.

From a historical perspective, no matter what form of governing a country chose, war inevitably followed. It may take decades, in rare times a century, but ultimately, war is assured. No matter how careful a country was planned, as was the case with the

United States, creating a constitution through the country's most economically, and politically oriented minds, war could not be avoided. Policy makers were well aware of the possibility, but it may have surprised the inhabitants in the United States when war was declared, first for independence then quickly followed by a civil war. We cannot deny the facts: Mankind is a warring species.

It may not have been obvious at first after the new nation was created. But ever since WWII, the United States has been continuously involved in conflicts, and wars. Our policy makers believe that we have to go to war with every possible opportunity. Though unjust for the taxpayer, and unrealistic with a prosperous economy, it keeps the ever-increasing military might in operation. It is military business all around. It is exactly what our founders tried to avoid because they had seen it all.

I truly enjoyed Danielle's presence. She not only stimulated my intellect, she also provided the company I so dearly missed. Aside from going days, and at times weeks without talking to anyone, other than cussing at the TV screen with its mindless shows, and sit-coms, I keep tuned in for company, I relished her company, and inquisitee with questions like:

"Why does mankind keep killing itself? Is it for survival?"

"Hardly. We have enough resources to keep us going for a thousand years."

"Is it for riches?"

"More likely, but not altogether."

"Is it for ambition?"

"Now, you're getting warmer."

"How about greed?"

"That's it," I hailed. "But there are more elements involved. Power, for instance. Necessity, for another."

It takes a powerful nation to keep the diversity of humankind under control, especially when providing uninhibited liberty for most of their social desires. Where internal desires of the individual used to be kept in check by cultural guidelines for conduct, and behavior, mostly taught through discipline at home, and in school, in the modern world of today, the public is quick to object when their rights are infringed upon. There has to be a limit, nevertheless.

"For instance," I explained further. "Where government employees used to be limited or prohibited from initiating, and partaking in striking, today, enforcing such law seems ineffective. People do whatever they desire. Historically, the end result is obvious. Our country is doomed to failure, like many nations before us, headed for collapse."

I have one more question for today, "Have we learned from history?"

"No," I insisted. "Not in a society where many people have lost interest in reading." It may sound like an unjust statement, but it holds true with many societies today. Where reading used to be an only form of entertaining and informing, for thousands of years restricted to candle light after dark, in today's society, there is no restriction. Other than parents insisting on playtime restrictions for their children, people can watch television, and play computer games day and night without interruptions. The young, as much as the adults are at fault in the same way. For many, there is no set time separating distinct hours for work, play, and sleep, as was mostly the case in prior centuries.

I felt that I have reached a point in my quest for Full Disclosure where I needed some encouragement, or some support to go any further. I suddenly felt lonesome, isolated from the general population. One question kept seeping into my brain more frequent in recent weeks, "is it worth all the trouble I am going to face? What reaction will there be from the public? Will they believe? What about the government?"

There was no easy answer. From here on out there was no turning back. It was either let things be as they have been already many decades, propagating more confusion without an end, or take the big leap into the unknown of possible ridicule, as others did before me. I felt that I needed some support if only with lip service. I knew enough people in the government I could trust, at least to provide me with their personal opinions. The problem was, "how to approach the individuals."

Since the topic of UFOs was a highly sensitive, and personal matter without anybody committing to anything within the walls of government, and Intelligence, establishing contact would have to be treated with caution. My plan was taking shape. There were several contacts I planned to call. Each would require a personal visit. Since they were located in the general area, the Beltway, I could accomplish my mission within a couple of days.

Author Note:
For the reader to get a feel for my hesitations, and at times doubts, whether to proceed with my plan for "Setting the Record Straight," or not, I want to point out that I am not the only individual troubled with this highly sensitive matter. There are many others questioning the sanity, or insanity of the UFO phenomena. Where the majority of UFO specialists on the inside are sworn to secrecy for life, the ones with executive powers bare even greater responsibilities. Rather than recreating some of their sentiments, and concerns, I will, in short extracts, briefly illustrate environments, and activities from within their operations sectors. To achieve it, in the next four chapters, THE PENTAGON, CENTRAL INTELLIGENCE, NATIONAL INTELLIGENCE, and NATO INTELLIGENCE, I'll present a few paragraphs from my prior novels, taking the reader inside of the nation's Intelligence, and Defense organizations, to get a feel for the operative responsibilities.

THE PENTAGON

20 years earlier. The first call was to my longtime General friend in the Pentagon. Since we had not talked for some time it was more social than business. "How are things?" I said when Hank picked up.

"Alex. Good to hear from you. How're things back home?"

"Pretty quiet for a change. How about out there?"

"Been busy with all the terrorist activities."

"I can imagine. Read it in papers almost daily."

"You planning to get involved?"

"I don't know. What do you think?"

"You know," Hank suggested, "I could always use your help. Why don't you come out here so we can discuss it?"

"Sounds good. Give me a week. I'll let you know the day."

"Bye."

That was it, brief, and concise as usual. I was looking forward to the visit. Contemplating if I should accept another contract with the DOD, I decided, "Guess I'll play it by ear." What I really wanted to discuss was, what had been on my mind. I had to be absolute certain not to make a fool of myself, but more importantly, not compromise our friendship. Refusing would not only close any future contracting possibilities, it would cost me his friendship. One could never be sure about the sensitivity within government circles, especially when it involved national safeguards.

As for now, what I did most days when not on a trail jogging or cycling, I tuned to my favorite news stations. Most times I would watch RT, and CGTN programs, foreign correspondences to get an unbiased perspective on world events. Following U.S. broadcasts, for the most part, made me cringe since it had been nothing but politics, and scandals lately, viewed much like what used to be soap operas. I had no patience for it. With spirits boosted about the upcoming trip my mood had picked up in anticipation. It gave me a renewed focus on life. Things around the Castle had been relatively dull recently. I sat in front of my workstation typing up a few notes of discussion points with Hank. It helped to put pertinent materials on paper that I wanted to talk over. With my mind clear of worries, I got up, donned my cycling gear, and headed for the hills. Similar to honing my mind, cycling kept my body in shape.

It was Monday noon. After arriving at Dulles, leasing a rental car, and headed for The Pentagon, forty minutes later I parked at the visitor parking lot. A picture ID was waiting for me at the front desk. Hank always accommodated special guests by having proper credentials ready. Since I was familiar with the Pentagon, and its halls, I did not need an escort.

"Alex," he greeted me, getting up from his desk chair. "Come on in." We met at the doorway, "Care for coffee? Let's talk at the cafeteria." Ground Zero was still the safest place from snooping in the complex, more so than the office. One never knew if the spy network had placed another bug in the office in the middle of night.

"Fine with me." It was the place to be not only out in the open, but surrounded by renowned personalities of their times from military circles, and government alike. Where most people will only get a brief glimpse of the nation' power brokers on news wires, here, one could rub shoulders, or even make a connection. Ground Zero was an informal place, a "No Salute" space. It seemed they all knew the general.

"How are the daughters? They haven't been in the news lately," he mused.

"Liz is back with her family. As for Tracy, your guess it as good as mine."

"I sure miss working with them. Any chance either one would work here? You know I could arrange an assignment for either of them. The same goes for you."

"Don't worry," I assured him. "With the way things are going, they'll be back."

"I know," he agreed. "Terrorism is here to stay. Won't be long before they'll breach our shores again. But rest assured, as long as I am in charge here, they will be dealt with severely."

"So," he said without further delay. "What's on your mind?"

I shot a quick glance around the space, busy with chatter. Regardless, I kept my voice subdued. "I'll come directly to the point," I opened. "I want to be absolutely certain that there won't be a compromise between the two of us."

"Shoot," he directed with a guarded face.

"I don't know if you keep up with current events within public undercurrents. Do you?"

"You mean Weather Underground[58], and the likes?"

"Exactly. Just want to be sure we are on the same page. The question I have for you," I said, shooting another glance around the place for absolute privacy, "Do you believe in Aliens?"

"You mean ETs?" Hank, usually in charge, and commanding, appeared uncomfortable with the topic. I knew he would rather not discuss it, but forced the issue anyway.

"Yes. ETs, and UFOs."

"Why do you ask?" It was obvious he was stalling.

"One of my daughters wants an answer."

"Which one? Liz? Tracy?"

"Neither."

"What do you mean? You have another daughter?"

"I do," I affirmed. "You don't know her. She was brought up by her stepfather."

"I didn't know."

"Not many do. She just recently entered into my life. Says she wants to be a part."

---

[58] The Weather Underground Organization (WUO), commonly known as the Weather Underground, was an American militant radical left-wing organization founded on the Ann Arbor campus of the University of Michigan. Originally called Weatherman, the group became known colloquially as the Weathermen. Weatherman organized in 1969 as a faction of Students for a Democratic Society (SDS), composed for the most part of the national office leadership of SDS, and their supporters. Their political goal, stated in print after 1974, was to create a revolutionary party to overthrow U.S. imperialism.

With revolutionary positions characterized by black power, and opposition to the Vietnam War, the group conducted a campaign of bombings through the mid-1970s, and took part in actions such as the jailbreak of Dr. Timothy Leary. The "Days of Rage," their first public demonstration on October 8, 1969, was a riot in Chicago timed to coincide with the trial of the Chicago Seven. In 1970 the group issued a "Declaration of a State of War" against the United States government, under the name "Weather Underground Organization" with an active ideology in communism, Black Power, Black nationalism, Anti-imperialism, and the New Left.

"How old is she?" Foster displayed some interest since she was part of the Bauer clan.

"Young generation. You know how they are. Want to know everything."

"I can only guess."

"It's the reason for my visit."

"Well," he admitted. "In a way, I don't blame them. Nobody seems to speak the truth anymore. Whether it's politics or policies, everything is clouded."

"You understand, don't you? It's not only my daughter that wants the truth. I have my doubts at times." It was not so much a doubt about the phenomena, it was about collaboration by a close friend.

"So," locking eyes, he said. "Where do you stand on the subject?"

It was obvious he was stalling by putting the burden on me. I responded, "As far as I know, it's all conspiracy based. But with governments playing the public I am not sure anymore. I need confirmation from you."

"What makes you so sure I could be of help?"

"You should know. People report to you."

"Alex," he said, staring directly into my eyes with a hint of warning. "You don't want to touch this. The subject is off limits."

"You better clarify."

"Nobody talks about it openly. It's too sensitive a topic. Even for me."

"What are you afraid of?"

"My career."

"Enough said, but I still need confirmation." I took a minute to collect my thoughts on how to approach him, then suggested "This is what we'll do. I'll ask you a question, and you confirm with a nod if true, or remain silent if not. Fair enough?"

"I can live with that."

"First question. Are there aliens living among us?" There was no response.

"Have we ever been visited by extraterrestrials?" No response.

"What about UFOs?"

He did not respond immediately, but said, "That's up to you to find out."

"What do you mean?"

"Alex," he said, hinting at the answer. "You already know. You worked enough classified projects to have inside information. That's all I have to say."

"Enough said. That's all I needed." Though nothing was revealed, or exposed, to me, everything was stated as clear as today's overhead sky. Delineating his barrier, from here on we could proceed without compromise.

"I really appreciate your time, and frankness."

"We have known each other for a long time. You deserve the truth. Now," he suggested. "How about lunch?" Half an hour later, with him taking the rest of the day off, we both left the complex with me driving the rental, and the general asking, "What do you want to do?"

"How about the Smithsonian?"

"Suites me fine. Haven't been there in ages." Hank, like many residents of D.C., took the nation's rich antiquities for granted. It was mostly visitors inspired to stroll into history.

For me, the visit with him was completed. On to the next office. I was trying to get as much confirmation as I could arrange from The Top. At least, I would have some backing, if things got out of hands. My visit was not about getting the facts about the ET/UFO subjects, I have known the facts since the beginning of my career with DOD. It was backing I needed, from the top echelon level. Though I did not expect and would not rely on any of it if things got out of hands, from a legal perspective, at least I would not get side swiped with the unexpected.

CENTRAL INTELLIGENCE

I was let into the director's office by his office secretary. On my entering, I realized he was on a call, most likely private as most calls were in the current environment. He gestured at the table nearby. "Keep them damned reporters away from me," Harry fumed at the office secretary who was unshaken by her boss' outburst. It was not the first time she had experienced his rage. He did it every time the subject of UFOs, and Aliens was forced on him. "Whoever allowed FOIA[59] should be put in jail." He knew exactly who had initiated the policy, but needed the verbal onslaught to let off steam.

What he referred to was government policy that anyone could request classified information, including U.S. citizens, foreign nationals, organizations, associations, universities, and all agency records that were created, or obtained by a federal agency. This included print documents, photographs, videos, maps, e-mails, and electronic records. In addition to releasing information upon written request, stated agencies were required to publish instructions on how to make a FOIA request to receive published information at their "online reading rooms." The process included records that affected the public such as regulations, policy statements, and staff instructions, as well as information that was, or was likely to be frequently requested by the public.

While any information could be requested, government agencies could withhold anything determined to fall under one of nine categories that were exempted from FOIA. The categories, as outlined by the Electronic Frontier Foundation, were as follows:

1. Classified information that would damage national security
2. Internal information involving personnel rules, and agency practices
3. Material specifically shielded from disclosure by another law
4. Confidential commercial, or financial data such as trade secrets
5. Records that would be held privileged in open litigation processes
6. Information related to government regulation of financial institutions
7. Information that would invade someone's privacy
8. Certain geological/geographical data
9. Law enforcement records.

While policies may be outlined in simple terms, the actual delivery of declassified materials was not in the least. To the utter frustration of researchers, and investigators delving into classified materials, many of the requested documents received were either incomplete with lines, and sentences only partially exposed, or blacked out with markers in their entirety, leaving more questions to the public's disappointment.

Frustrated, at times beyond comprehension, there was one topic that would drive Harry into rage where he kept cussing out everybody living under the public sky by the slightest mention of UFOs. Where at one time it was the Air Force's responsibility

---

[59] Enacted in 1966, The Freedom of Information Act (FOIA) is a federal law that established the public's right to obtain information from federal government agencies. It was mostly researchers, and investigators digging into national archives.

to record any such sightings under the doctrine of "Project Blue Book,[60]" since its closure in 1970, the whole pile of dirt fell into the hands of the CIA.

"Why can't they just log on to the 'National UFO Reporting Center,' like the rest of the lot, and leave me alone," he practically yelled at me, referring to one of numerous reporting centers on the subject matter hosted by likeminded enthusiasts, recording every possible sighting whether legitimate or imaginary. From his perspective, as well as everybody else's working for the Intelligence community, the answers were simple. All they required were sound judgement, and common sense nobody in the country seemed to possess anymore. He had decided years ago, judging, "Public's gone UFO crazy."

It seemed that he realized just now who had entered his office, "Well, well," what brings you here, Alex?"

"I need some information," I stated, hoping he would be accommodating.

"Can't help you," he blatantly rejected out of hand, "otherwise you would have just called. Right?"

"You are partially right," I said, giving him credit for his intuitive nature. "But if I can't have an answer, at least hear me out. I would be happy with your suggestion."

"Okay. Let's hear it."

I already knew the answer, but hoped for his support no matter what his reaction would be. In his mind, the whole UFO matter had fallen prey to conspiracy. It was them that constantly pushed the limits for making his life miserable. His time with the agency used to be a simple one: spy on foreign countries, dispatch operatives to burning points, take out an adversary, or dictator, and plead innocent when caught. Today, any slightest infringement on the public caused an outcry. Congress saw to it by tying his, and his staff's hands and feet to where nothing, legally or illegally, could be accomplished anymore. The safety of the nation, his nation, had gone to hell with every adversary, and terrorist pressing on his borders. No matter how hard he pushed Congress for reform to allow him, and his agency more liberty, he was shut down with each administration change.

"Damned politicians," he cussed to let off steam.

"I feel for you," I said with a sympathetic gesture. "But, it's not why I'm here." I forced his focus back to my visit, and came right to the point. "Do you believe in Aliens, and UFOs?"

His eyes became piercing daggers locked on mine when he responded, "You too?"

"Me what?"

"I thought only the public, and reporters have gone mad," he bellowed in my direction. "Now, I find out that my friends have gone mad as well." Where I should have been upset, and dismayed, he had said enough. I knew the answer. His reaction affirmed the facts. There were no Aliens among us. UFOs may have been another matter, we both knew.

---

[60] Project Blue Book was one of a series of systematic studies of unidentified flying objects (UFOs) conducted by the United States Air Force. Started in 1952, it was the third study of its kind with the first two being Projects Sign (1947), and Grudge (1949). A termination order was given for the study in December 1969, and all activity under its auspices ceased in January 1970.

He knew well what the problem was. There was a time when he decided on "what was right, and how much he could get away with." But in today's world, his hands were shackled. He was only allowed to play by whatever little Congress would allow. It was always "play by the rules," and "observe international policies." It was a restraint he questioned daily: "Who in the world can operate like this?" Countries that used to respect United States' leadership, today, they crapped all over his nation. They showed no respect. Conditions had reached a point to where they disrespected, and disregarded everything the nation stood for, liberty, and justice for all, not to mention freedom from subjugation.

"I'll show them," he muttered an unspoken vengeance, that only I was privy to. For now, he paid lip service like many other agency directors curbed from doing their jobs. "My time will come again," he silently gloried in the sanctuary of his domain.

"Looks like my time is up," I said, headed for the exit. He was as frustrated as any operative would be with both hands tied behind the back, but acknowledged my visit with, "Sorry about the outburst. I shouldn't let it out on you. Can I make it up? How about Sushi?"

It was close to lunchtime, we headed for the place we used to frequent during better times. "Fine with me."

NATIONAL INTELLIGENCE

"Home in on Grid J-3," Jack, Director of Operations, NSA, instructed the operator. He wanted to get a firsthand look at North Korea's nuclear test launch only ten minutes away. Although the test was illegal with every government, there was nothing he could do to prevent it. Whether the launch went off successfully, or not, it did not matter much to him. What mattered was that they would allow it in first place. If it were up to him, he would have retaliated at the North when the launches started. Now, outside of a preemptive attack by his people, it was too late to teach them a lesson without getting severe repercussions from world councils, or "Spineless Chicken Governments," as he called them. What really bothered him, subconsciously mostly, were the restraints placed on him, and his agency by his policymakers. For all he knew, he had been sidelined from taking part in making national decisions. Whistleblowers, and the public saw to it. "What good is all of the firepower at your fingertips," he complained, as he did often, "without so much as a trial shot."

He, and many of his buddies at the Air Force, and DOD, were itching to test the newest weapons arsenal, acquired, built, and launched into orbit for decades already. "But no," he griped. "Can't reveal anything to the public, and potential enemies." While he was silenced, he knew the true reasons. On the one side, trillions of dollars were spent for the development of advanced technologies, and weaponries. On the other, as usual, secrecy prevailed. While the Air Force took ownership over all space-based defense systems, weapons included, the NSA was tasked with global surveillance over all friendly, and hostile activities. This was what bugged him most, not being able to make major decisions, or even participate.

"Damned system," he cussed again, referring to the liberal-minded policy makers. "Hope the next administration will do better." He had been saying it through several administrations over decades with nothing changing other than a shameful display of bickering, and slander. "Politicians," he spat out in disgust. "Should fire the whole lot."

"Target in range," the operator alerted him.

Jack squinted his eye to get clear focus. "Damned vision," he muttered at his failing eyesight, but refused to acquire glasses. For the greater part of his work he did not need to wear any. So far, squinting helped to regain focus. "Give me ground level view," he directed the operator, not happy at having to deal with the novices they kept hiring. "Budget cuts," was the excuse given by the Federal Accountability Office. On the one hand, trillions were spent, and on the other, people kept bitching about the cost of peanuts going up. "But," he muttered while keeping an eye on the launch already in countdown, "that's the system."

"Five-four-three-two-one," the North Korean count sounded over the PA. No matter who, or what was launched, with each time he tremendously enjoyed the fire, and flame spectacle displayed on an array of monitors. Five minutes into the rocket flight he growled, "Bastard's getting closer to us with each launch. Another six months, and they'll hit the West Coast." In a way, he was counting on it. It would shake up the politicians with their idiotic diplomacies, and excuses not to get involved, and strike first. He had seen enough. "Another wasted day," he huffed.

Striding back to the office, he had a thought. Rifling through his desktop filing cards, an antiquated appliance, he knew, but handy within instant reach when needed, he found the name card he was looking for: Tracy Bauer. "Why not give her a call?"

It had been many months since he'd heard her name on newswires. There was a time when she was heralded a heroine by the public for heading off a direct enemy attack on the nation. "Chinese," he recollected. "Boy," he muttered, "how quick political climates can change. Now they are our allies."

"UFOs on rapid approach," the operator called out. No matter how many times Jack had heard the alert, it always perked his interest to what new designs the people at DARPA had come up with. Turning to the monitor he made out a cluster of lightning fast objects crossing the skies headed out over the Atlantic. "Getting bolder with each year," he stated with a grin on his face. The boldness of these pilots gave him infinite satisfaction for how they maneuvered their hypersonic craft. Too fast for the average man's thinking process, he knew it was AI, that had control over the sophisticated technology. "We've sure come a long way since the U-2," he gasped with admiration when checking the speed on monitor readouts, marveling, "Mach-22," and "why these things don't burn up in space?"

Sure enough, a slew of phone calls followed. He was glad that he didn't have to deal with it. He had a special UFO reporting staff to handle the calls, at times daily, but mostly at night when sightings were more prominent. Though taking place around the clock, the majority of objects flying in the sky were not visible unless through closeup encounters. Ever since the Air Force had terminated Project Blue Book, the burden had been dumped on his agency to report the detested sightings. But that was decades ago. Today, he could not handle the flood of reports, and had his staff refer them to privately-managed commercial reporting sites. His agency was fully tied up with issues internal to the nation. While global satellite monitoring still went on, in recent years, listening had taken priority over sightings, and shifted to within U.S. borders. It was eavesdropping on individuals that today's policies called for.

He understood why the changes. Threats on the nation did not only originate from hostile factions; many had emerged from within our own borders in recent years. While psychologists, and specialists still tried to figure out the reasons for such occurrences, the public came up with a simpler answer: "Nut Jobs." Regardless of the source, the problem was here to stay. To Jack, it seemed that every decade brought on new events he had to deal with, and the agency could hardly keep up. His workforce was shifted from one task to the next on the whim of the public. It was public demands directing his job, and he did not like it. There was no stability in his, and other Intel organizations anymore. "Hell," he complained at times, "you can't even build a career in Intelligence anymore. One day you are hired, and the next you are fired." He was just in his complaints, considering the constant turnover of appointees within government circles.

Having a seat at the NSC, he was kept abreast of all black project developments, whether experimental or ready to be deployed. He was assigned shared responsibility between the NSA, and NORAD to keep track of sightings, and reporting on everything that crossed the U.S. skies. He did not blame the public for their confusion. It was the government, and military causing it with their innovative designs applied to modern technology.

"Pass it on," he instructed the operator on the sighting. "They know what to do." That was it. Jack had done his duty, passing along reports that usually lasted for days to follow. It seemed that one such sighting was enough to create a flurry of likewise, or similar objects speeding across the country side. It was always the same trend, one spotted object in the sky made the public look up in anticipation. "Mass hysteria," it used to be called, he recalled. Today, people got used to spotting these phantom objects, appearing, and disappearing in the blink of the eye, only to reappear at another spot. Hysteria had long since passed. Today, it was "Idiots," as they called it in the inner circles.

Fortunately for him, there were appropriate organizations that had sprouted up on the Internet in recent years with names like:

> National UFO Reporting Center
> UFO Reporting Center
> UFO Reporting Hotline
> UFO Research Network
> UFO Files
> NUFORC
> MUFON

For the more serious UFO aficionado, there were a slew of websites, and radio stations available for different interests like:

> AboveTopSecret.com
> CoastToCoastAm.com
> Beyond Belief.com
> Earthfiles.com
> UFOEvidence.org
> UFO.Wipnet.org
> UFOCasebook.com
> CrowdedSkies.com
> Darkness Radio
> Ground Zero

There were more, many more. One only had to insert "paranormal", and "supernatural" search tags into Google to get connected. Though, regaining popularity with almost every generation, UFOs, and unexplained sightings were nothing new to mankind. Sightings had been reported dating back to the second millennia BC with ancient historic names like:

> Fiery Disk
> Torch in the Sky
> Ships in the Sky
> Signs in the Sky
> Mystery Airships
> Miracle in the Sun

With more recently assigned names like:

> Foo Fighters

Ghost rockets
Kenneth Arnold Sighting
Betty, and Barney Hill
Roswell Crash
Green fireballs
Ft. Monmouth Case
Lakenheath Incidence
Ubatuba Explosion
Kecksburg Incidence
Andreasson Abduction
Travis Walton Abduction
Phoenix Lights

…and many more too numerous to list. As of today, there are about two hundred sightings reported to the UFO Reporting Center weekly, on average. The interesting thing is that where most, if not all, were considered first-hand sightings, around 2012, the reporting changed from "UFO Sighting" to "UFO Phenomenon." What brought on the change was the emergence of orbs, and spheres, either floating, hovering, or shooting across the skies, turning an individual event into mass experience, spurring scientific research institutions, and psychology experts into action. Regardless of such increase in popularity, mainstream media kept silent. One could but wonder, "Why?"

"Well," Jack mused, at times restraining himself from disclosing the government's most well-kept secret of all time. "There's a plausible explanation for it all." He knew better than to share the massive amounts of knowledge stored within the vaults of the agency with a purposely held ignorant world.

While contemplating the wealth of knowledge in his hands, a thought had just occurred to him. "Yes. Why not?"

With one stroke on the keyboard he brought up the employee register displayed on the computer screen. "Must give her a call," he muttered while reaching for the phone, but he decided to postpone the call. There were more pressing things in his email directory at the moment, awaiting his attention.

NATO INTELLIGENCE

Emmett W., Four-Star Commanding General, NATO, Allied Forces Europe, had been busy since he was elected commander over all forces, and detachments in the European theater, and there were many: Albania, Bulgaria, Canada, France, Germany, Greece, Israel, Italy, the Netherlands, Norway, Poland, Portugal, Romania, Slovenia, Spain, Turkey, the United Kingdom, and the United States. Though NATO dated back to WWII, when it was created for the purpose of strengthening war efforts, today responsibility focus had shifted primarily to deter terrorist aggression, and border clashes. He had inherited much of Middle Eastern countries prone to conflicts. Conflicts, he'd learned in history classes, were nothing new. They dated back to Genesis, and even the pre-deluge era.

Reading history, his favorite subject, he would have thought that mankind would learn over millennia of struggles, but not so. In his mind, there were no substantiating reasons why people in today's world, with humanitarian support, should still be fighting for survival. "But," he surmised, not everybody was prone to honesty, especially not the organizers managing world support, and operations. Statistics had it that the greater percentage of all support action funds went to management, and pilferage. It was a way of life for many of the countries in his sphere of responsibilities, with Allied Air Command at Ramstein, Germany, Allied Land Command at Izmir, Turkey, and Allied Maritime Command at Northwood, UK, a mandate for Commander, Allied Joint Force Command Naples. It was his responsibility to conduct the full range of military operations throughout the NATO area, and beyond, in order to safeguard freedom of the seas, and economic lifelines, and to preserve, or restore the security of NATO nations.

"What's the status with the tour?" he queried his adjutant, whose responsibility it was to schedule this week's visits to COM MC Naples. Since the reorganization in 2008, the MC Naples had become one of three subordinate commands of Joint Force Command. Located at the Bay of Naples, it was commanded by an Italian three-star admiral with staff assigned from 17 countries. He would be busy trying to appease everyone expected to attend since it included maritime operation, and combat piracy off the Somali coast to World Food Program chartered vessels.

"All set," he was assured. "Limo is waiting to take you to the airport."

Seated comfortably in back of the quiet, spacious limousine, he took the time to reflect on his position. He considered himself one of few fortunate ever to acquire top position for a major government branch. Where most of his peers had been, and still were, struggling for position, he had been advanced at an accelerated rate unequal to its times. He could only contribute the facts to "being at a place at the right time, or perhaps," he chuckled, "my good looks." There was a certain truth to it. Reading historical accounts, many prominent leaders had two qualities in common, statue, and appearance, the qualities of successful statesmen.

Total flight time today would be two hours, enough for a brunch served by a friendly flight crew. Slightly distracted by the attendant's youthful beauty, he recalled a time long past when he would have tried a personal advancement. It was a time when charm, and cavalier were still acceptable values in society. He was well aware that these values were rebuffed by the woman of today. "Living in difficult times," he sighed, forcing his mind on the upcoming mission.

His periodically scheduled visits normally entailed resolving issues of troubling events, but this one was different. It was a subject of great sensitivity that had to be handled with extreme caution without upsetting world leaderships, or worse yet, the public. It only took one slight mistake, or an unintended slip of the tongue for mainstream media to jump in, distorting the intended meaning. In the flight time remaining he mentally went over the topics he was about to address in today's summit.

There had been a time when he was as gullible as many in today's world with its citizens intentionally kept ignorant. It was a world held together by discipline, honesty, and integrity, detrimental values to a livable coexistence, seemingly lost to the past. He relished those times of innocence. It was also a time when one could plan ahead for individual goals, and prosperity. One could close a deal with a handshake, and honor its value without reservation. "What happened to the values?" he questioned. It was rhetorical. He knew exactly what had happened. The once honored values had been replaced by personal greed, and individual ambition. He could see the trends propagating not only through the Western world, but in cultural-preserving countries as well. "Who was to blame?" Again, he knew the answer: "Governments."

It was governments not performing their directed duties as intended by their respectively devised constitutions. The basis for a constitution in the Western world was a concept related to the Roman Republic with faith-related ideologies emerged through biblical origin. Though simple concepts, they were difficult to enforce by any member of society, the very reason why the government was born. It was supposed to keep balance between two major forces, preservation of heritage, and striving for progress. Mankind, with a brain exceeding that of animal, and plant life, needed both. Without it, life would become stagnant. One could equate it to paradise lost, with Adam, and Eve blissfully happy, but also still unclothed, and exposed to the elements. Much like animal behavior, we would still compete for survival of the fittest, killing or be killed, hunted for food.

Governments were supposed to look out for civility, protecting citizens, and keeping aggressors at bay; in return, they were compensated with a portion of the nation's wealth through taxation. It was an easy proposition when observed, but not when disregarded by the enforcing arm, responsible for keeping balance. The problem was, no policy lasted forever with every rule eventually being broken. "The root cause?"

"People!"

It would take a restrictedly-programmed robot to blindly follow roles, and to enforce policies. Unfortunately, mankind has exceeded a once-limited knowledge to earthly things. We have already entered the age of AI.[61] It would be impossible for future minds to maintain policy restraints, no matter how protected hardware, and software was in advancing computer Intelligence, and sophisticated application developments. We have already sold out to a world of robotic dominance.

---

[61] AI. – Artificial Intelligence is based on mathematical concepts of learning from data, initially programmed into the computer by a scientist, and in time superseded by the learning process of the software program itself.

Emmett W., he suddenly realized, was drifting in the wrong direction. "I've got to concentrate on the summit," he reminded himself. "What was it again?" he fleetingly thought. "Ah yes. The increase in recent UFO sightings." It was a topic he would have rather kept distant. He could already envision the audience, expressing their frustrations through shouts of accusations: "You keep lying," and "we want the truth."

The outbursts would demand what the public, in recent years, had coined, "Full Disclosure."

"What in hell were they thinking?" Fletcher silently protested. "Putting me up front, on the chopping block?" He could see it now. Years ago, when national security was pushed to the forefront with an increase on spying on each other, securing national wealth, and public safety became of utmost importance. Security clearances were dished out much like place cards without thorough due diligence by the FBI on personal background checks. With UFO, and extraterrestrial sightings on an exponential increase during the 70s, he recalled now, NATO was assigned the highest obtainable security clearance, that of COSMIC. Back then, he questioned such need as unethical since his organization was considered subservient to major nations like England, the U.S., and Russia. China had not emerged yet as major player. "Why COSMIC?" he contemplated, with no other country bestowed what was considered the highest privilege.

Today, it all fell into place, consolidated into one expression: scapegoat.

The major "Three" had the foresight that one day someone had to make the announcement about what everybody had kept under cover for so long: "Reveal the real reason" for what was behind the many sightings.

Amid government communities, the ones "in the know," sworn to secrecy, kept silent to protect their own interests, career, and livelihood. The rest of the forces, the "uninformed," rumors notwithstanding, kept silent for the same reasons, job, and livelihood.

Ignorant of the mission at hand until today, only hours away, he had been delegated to reveal the truth to the world. The thought alone already made him sick. "Wonder how I'll hold up on the podium," he said, questioning the insanity he was about to release. Regardless of the outcome, newswires would burn for days with the public split into two factions: "I told you," and "I don't believe it."

After today, his job would be done while the rest of the world would be stunned for weeks ahead. Emmett W. was thinking of retiring. He did not want to face the aftermath of blame, and accusations. "Let them figure out how to extract themselves from the mess they have caused."

Satisfied at having come up with a personal solution, he leaned back into the seat, ordered another martini, and listened to the soothing drone of twinjet engines taking him over the spectacular Alps passing slowly below, muttering, "What a wonderful world."

Author Note:

Having authored several books over the past six years, I have learned the facts of both worlds in my research, supernatural, and reality. Consequences or not, I was prepared. I knew exactly how to proceed on the subject matter, but first, I feel compelled to explain some of the major UFO, and Alien events, illustrated in the following section that were prime contributors to the public confusion.

For researchers, the facts are registered in numerous data bases, and data banks with numerous organizations, public, and private, one can dig into days, and weeks searching analyzing facts. The problem will soon surface, "What to believe." The key to the right path is to locate the original response documents released by the credible government organization, in the UFO, and Alien cases, the CIA, and Air Force.

To the pursuers of truth, it will become obvious that both agencies never initiated a report issued to the public. They only publicized findings based on their investigations which seemed to be factual within the parameters of their knowledge base. Whatever else surfaced on, and above factual evidence was the making of the public, for the most part left in the dark with black projects. It is no wonder, after receiving stacks of documents released through FOIA, with much of the information blackened out, it instilled doubt and distrust to the honest citizen. Consequently, the public cannot entirely bare the blame for the confusion created through rumors, and speculations that followed each, and every paranormal event.

However, anyone still in doubt about UFOs and Aliens, should read three books, essential to the confusion. A devout researcher, investigator, and author, Philip J. Klass, over decades spent more time analyzing important cases then many other researchers and investigators to unravel the myth. The results are clear and plain. His books, though out of print are still available second hand, at a reduced price.

1.   UFOs EXPLAINED, published 1974, by Random House
2.   UFO ABDUCTIONS: A Dangerous Game, published 1989, by Prometheus Books
3.   ROSWELL Crashed-Saucer Coverup, published 1997, by Prometheus Books

I am not trying to sell the books of Philp J. Klass, who, unfortunately passed away in 2005. I just want to pay him my tribute, posthumously, to the enormous effort and energy he spent in researching subject matters of UFOs and Aliens. With massive amounts of printed materials available on the Internet and libraries on paranormal related topics for the reader to enjoy, not much is offered containing facts. It seems that most people would rather forfeit facts, then infringe on imaginary events left to dreaming and fantasizing. There is nothing wrong with it. We all do it, in the name of science fiction. But to know real facts is worth something to some.

EXTRA TERRESTRIAL PHENOMENA
DO UFOs EXIST

On December 16, 2017, the *New York Times* published two stories that read almost like science fiction. "For at least five years, the Defense Department housed a $22-million, clandestine program to investigate UFOs. Military pilots had sent in reports of objects they observed that moved in unfamiliar ways; the mission of the Advanced Aerospace Threat Identification Program (AATIP), as it was called, was to investigate those claims to see if there was truly something otherworldly behind those sightings.

"American culture is steeped in depictions of what would happen if sophisticated aliens visited Earth, from *E.T.* to *Arrival* to *Independence Day*. Some are more hackneyed than others; some are downright terrifying. But outside the clear genre of fiction, most conversations about UFOs happen online, and with varying degrees of vehemence. Let's face it—believing in the paranormal has become shorthand for crazy.

"It's unclear just how many reports pilots had filed to the Advanced Aerospace Threat Identification Program,[62] but people who have come forward about the program have made it clear that there would have been a lot more reports filed if it hadn't been for one thing: stigma.

"The sightings were not often reported up the military's chain of command, former senator Harry Reid said, because service members were afraid, they would be laughed at or stigmatized.[63]

"There was absolutely no solid evidence that meets any standards of scientific 'proof' that UFOs exist. That's why people can't take it seriously," Sara Seager, an astrophysicist at MIT who studies exoplanets, and was quoted in the *New York Times* article, tells Futurism. To some, in the end, evidence doesn't matter. "I am not a UFO supporter in any way. It's just like why do people believe in God? There's no way to scientifically prove the existence of any God or gods. People just want to believe."

I have pondered the same questions in my early years after arriving in the U.S. when hearing not only of unexplained UFO sightings, but more serious events of close encounters, and abductions:

- Do UFOs exist?
- What is the Alien agenda?
- How many Aliens are among us?

———————————————

[62] The Advanced Aviation Threat Identification Program (AATIP) was a secret investigatory effort funded by the United States government to study unidentified flying objects, but it was not classified. The program was first made public on December 16, 2017. The program began in 2007, with funding of $22 million over the five years until the available appropriations were ended in 2012. The program began in the U.S. Defense Intelligence Agency. Although the official AATIP program has ended, a related group of interested professionals have extended the effort, founding a nonprofit organization called "To the Stars Academy of Arts & Science."

[63] For the *New York Times*' full report see Appendix C-1.

- Do Aliens intend or have committed harm to us humans?

Some questions will remain unanswered while others I can satisfy. For instance:

Question: How many people in the U.S. have heard of UFOs?

Answer: A recent National Geographic Society poll reported that 36 percent of Americans - about 80 million people - believe UFOs exist. Only 17 percent do not, and the rest of the people were undecided.

Question: How many people in the U.S. believe in UFOs?

Answer: (CNN) -- Nearly 50 years since an alleged UFO was sighted at Roswell, New Mexico, a CNN/Time poll released June 15, 1997, shows that 80 percent of Americans think the government is hiding knowledge of the existence of extraterrestrial life forms.

While nearly three-quarters of the 1,024 adults questioned for the poll said they had never seen or known anyone who had seen a UFO, 54 percent believe intelligent life exists outside Earth. Sixty-four percent of the respondents said that aliens have contacted humans, half said they've abducted humans, and 37 percent said they have contacted the U.S. government. The poll has a margin of error of plus or minus 3 percentage points.

But only 9 percent said they believed there were aliens near the Hale-Bopp comet, which recently passed close enough to Earth to be seen with the bare eye.

Some "Ufologists" believed a spacecraft was hidden near the comet, and members of the Heaven's Gate cult committed suicide, believing that they would be taken aboard the craft, and returned "home."

What happened in Roswell?

As for the Roswell incident, nearly two-thirds of the respondents to the poll said they believed that a UFO crash-landed in a field outside the New Mexico town 75 years ago. In one of the most famous UFO "sightings" in U.S. history, Roswell residents in 1947 saw lights in the night sky, followed by a loud explosion. A rancher found the "crash site", and removed a large piece of debris, storing it in his shed.

A few days later, Air Force officials from nearby Roswell Air Force Base inspected the site, and the debris, and issued a press release announcing the recovery of a "flying disc." The Air Force quickly retracted that statement, and claimed the debris was from a weather balloon. But countless statements, some from military personnel, appeared to contradict the Air Force's revised position, and several "witnesses" claimed to have seen bodies of dead aliens whisked away by the military.

Roswell today capitalizes on its fame as a UFO crash site, whether or not it actually happened, and celebrates the event each year in the first week of July.

Friend or foe?

Most people, 91 percent, told the pollsters that they had never had contact with aliens or known anyone who had. A similar number, 93 percent, said they had never been abducted or known anyone whisked away by beings from another planet.

But if they do meet someone from a galaxy far, far away, 44 percent said they expect to be treated as friends, while 26 percent think they'll be treated as enemies. Thirty-nine percent don't expect aliens to appear very humanoid, although 35 percent said they probably look "somewhat" human.

Regardless of numbers, and figures, a full disclosure by the governments would not matter. Normal life would go on for the average American, and human being around the world. It was mostly the conspirators believing, and propagating stories, whether substantiated or not. People attached to paranormal occurrences conveniently disregard facts and logical thinking, to further the propagation of paranormal mystique. Ever since taking psychology classes, I have been educated to become aware of human behaviors. Most times, when approached, or when at gatherings, I would study faces, and mannerisms for signs of normal, and abnormal conduct.

When involved in discussing the topics of UFOs and Aliens, I am partial in my responses for one reason. It is to respect every person's opinion, whether false or justified. I am not a judge, nor am I a fool. I know what I have seen with my own eyes to be factual. But so, do many others with similar claims. There is one difference, I, and a couple dozen software engineers and database architects had access to the source of it all.

FULL DISCLOSURE

Back to the present day, to my daughter Danielle's visit. After the drive to Garden of the Gods, Colorado Springs' renown tourist attraction, we stepped on the trail. Depending on one's mood or energy, several trails were available. The daily tourist crowds gathered at prominent highlights such as Red Rock peaks, Balanced Rock, Kissing Camels, and Trading Post, but trails, and paths, for the most part, were left to the local hikers, and runners. Since we planned to talk, I decided on an easy trail. A few hundred yards into it, I decided it was time to address her concerns, and share the government's most highly guarded secret.

To get a sense of her interest on the subject, I needed to feel her out. "How much do you know about history?"

"Oh," she said, noncommittally, "as much as anybody, I guess."

"You're not really interested in history, are you?" I suspected something like that. Today's generation had other interests. History was something for historians to research for writing biographies, and documentaries.

"I am," she replied. "But you have to understand that I am busy with creating a future." I must have touched a sensitive nerve, and reminded myself not to be judgmental. I realized then, and there that I had been way too isolated from social interaction. I knew the danger signals. When being alone too much, one had the propensity to become opinionated and, perhaps even worse, have eccentric behavior.

"Yes. I understand. I only have one recommendation for you," I suggested cautiously. "Don't forget to read."

"I read."

"I mean books. History books. They contain most of the answers."

"What about extraterrestrials?"

"Even that, if you dig deep enough."

"Really?"

"Sure. I could cite you phrases from the Old Testament, but this is not the time. I want to share with you what goes on in the real world. Today's world. Your world."

"You live in this world. Don't you?"

"I don't," I replied.

"I don't understand."

"I live in the past," I explained. "I have a difficult time relating to today's rapidly changing world. It's the reason I dwell in the past. Past memories keep me company, and maintain my sanity."

"I don't understand, but go ahead. I'm anxious to hear the truth."

"I want to be perfectly clear on this," I started. "The information I am about to disclose is classified Top Secret." I could sense her tension by the deepening of her breathing. To put her at ease, I clarified, "But much has been declassified through FOIA in recent years."

"FOIA?"

"Freedom of Information Act. It's researchers, and scholars periodically forcing the government to release data to the public. They deserve to know. After all, they are the ones paying for it all, but information is slow to be released. Sometimes, it takes years to get the files into public hands. For the questions you have," I explained. "You may never see a response from the government."

"Why not?" I could see her attitude change from inquisitiveness to slight hostility, and rightly so. People deserve more than being kept ignorant, especially when it came to fabricated secrets.

"Because it serves policy makers to keep it that way."

"What do you mean by policy makers, Dad? Whose policies?"

"Ours?"

"Americans?" She had a puzzled look on her face.

"Mostly. Ever since WWII, we," I quickly corrected, "the United States, took the lead in world leadership."

"I thought it was the United Nations."

"Not really. They took on the responsibility for keeping peace among third-world nations. It's a fulltime occupation just to resolve disputes, whereas we seemed to get involved in the middle of every conflict with arms dealings, and weapons smuggling."

"Are you saying that we fuel conflicts?"

"Pretty much so."

"Aren't there laws?" She shook her head in disbelief.

"There are, but people find ways around them to enrich themselves by selling armaments. It's big business for industrialists."

"You mean all countries?"

"The ones getting there first to make their biddings. It's like this," I explained. "Wars are part of humanity. They have been around since antiquity. They will be around into the distant future. It's part of our genetic makeup."

"You can't be serious. You don't really believe it? I don't feel this way."

"Like I said. Read the Bible—the Old Testament." It might be difficult to grasp, especially for the young who were taught mostly contemporary biblical accounts in Sunday school. Preachers stay away from ancient scriptures, and mostly teach the New Testament. In contrast, I kept my distance from the New Testament. It was not my intention to teach religion. Besides, my daughters knew more on spiritual aspects than me, since they were raised by a religious-conscious mom.

"By the way, Dad, what are you?"

"I consider myself an agnostic."

"Why not atheist?"

"I am a skeptic by trade. I believe in a higher power, but question everything that's not scientifically proven."

"Were you raised this way?"

"No. I come from a strictly Christian background."

"Then," she contemplated, "why didn't you ever attend church with us?" She was absolutely correct. Though prodded by their mom, I could only recall one time when the family, as a whole, went to church together.

I explained, "After I grew up, things happened that made me question the Word, and validity of the Bible. One has to have a blind belief in the scriptures to maintain faith. But let's not dwell on it. I will have to deal with the sacred issues when the time comes."

I checked my watch for time. In between short pauses to catch our breath, we had been walking, and talking for almost an hour. "How are you doing, energy-wise?" I said. Tracy, and Liz had always been in top physical condition, but I wasn't sure about Danielle. Most new arrivals to this altitude became winded after exertion. It took several days to get used to the thin air.

"Never felt better," she said.

"Any more questions?" I asked. She had taken the lead. At times the path narrowed to a single file with me dropping back. That way I could talk without having to turn my head.

"I haven't even begun. Let's sit for a while," she beckoned.

That suited me fine. We rested on a nearby bolder warmed by the sun. It felt great to just relax, and watch the surrounding scene. "Peaks look familiar," she said, pointing in the direction of the Kissing Camels cliff formation a quarter mile away.

"They should," I said. "We climbed them on your last visit. You were only six." As was usually the case when her two elder sisters visited from California, their mother's primary residence, I took them here. On one of the visits, all three spent a week with me, insisting on getting to the top of the red-shaded peaks. From the front view it seemed impossible to climb without gear, but we found a way climbing to the top along the edge. For some stretches they were too little to reach the next ledge. I had to lift them up. But that was before the region was restricted to only mountaineers with climbing gear. Now, with the flood of tourists arriving daily, one could only look at nature without being able to touch. *What a shame,* I thought in the quiet. *Children grow up without the feel of nature.*

"Dad," she broke the serenity. "Are we alone?"

"What do you mean?"

"I mean, are their Aliens among us?"

My muscles tensed by the boldness of the question. It prompted me to the purpose for her being here. It was a topic I'd tried to avoid for most of my career. To begin with, I never initiated the topic conversation. It always led to disputes. Much like religion, one had a strong belief for whatever denomination was taught them during childhood. I needed more information. "That's an odd question for someone brought up with close ties to Catholicism."

"That's what I mean," she said. "I don't know what to believe. I am totally confused. Mom says one thing, but people insist on something else."

"What people?" I knew exactly what she was leading to. Ever since the 70s, books, and literature had become prolific in the subjects of visitors from other worlds. Strange, and unexplained sightings in the air with supposed abductions, and many other encounters caused even more confusion. I was not the least surprised at the confusion exerted on the public. While I had clear focus, most of the general public was left to individual speculation. I cringed every time I read some author's work speculating on the topic, but taking ownership for their stated facts. Most claimed it to be factual, but it was all conjecture. It was no surprise people were struggling with the subject of UFOs.

"The family, friends, coworkers."

"Don't listen to them. They are all confused."

"What about you, Dad. Are you?"

"Not in the least. I don't listen to what people have to say on the subject. I did my own research."

"Why not share it with me?"

"You are right," I said, being reminded of the reason we were here. "The answer is not as clear-cut as you would like it to be. First," I said, "we need to clarify certain things."

"Like what?"

"ETs, and UFOs," I volunteered. "What do you want first?"

"UFOs."

"Okay then. UFO. Unidentified Flying Object. That's what it is. No more, no less. They're strange objects people are not used to seeing. Unfortunately, conspiracists have associated all strange objects observed in the skies with extraterrestrial origin."

"Aren't they?"

"No."

"How can you be so sure when the whole world thinks otherwise?"

"Though logical approach. Have you heard of SETI?"

"Search for Extraterrestrial Intelligence?"

"Yes. It's the science station at Arecibo, Puerto Rico, the world's largest observatory. Ever hear of Carl Sagan?"

"Wasn't he a scientist?"

"Cosmologist. He took the lead in 1982, probing the universe for life with the aid of an array of radio telescopes."

"I heard there were signals received."

"Nothing more than cosmic noise. True, there were a couple of times cohesive signals were recorded, but they were explained away as generated from an earthly origin. I don't want to go into specific details. You'll just have to take my word."

"What about all the sightings. Are they for real?" I detected a slight doubt in her face. Who could blame her for all the propagated nonsense initiated out of ignorance?

"They are," I assured her, and explained. "According to recent surveys, there are approximately 250 UFO sightings worldwide recorded each week, but most can be explained."

"How so?"

"Through numerous computer applications developed to watch the skies."

"Computers watching?"

"Yes, computers. Most people are not aware that there are about 80,000 professional, and amateur astronomers watching, and listening day, and night through optical, infrared, and radio telescopes from the home through sky-tracking software developed by Microsoft, and other vendors. The software is so sophisticated it filters out stars, planets, aircrafts, birds, space junk, plasma lightning, electromagnetic effects, and other oddities in the sky that cause people to incorrectly assume we are being visited from outer space."

"What about all the individual sightings, and reports?"

"I assure you," I said, "they don't come from the astronomers. Those people are educated, cool-headed, honest individuals only interested in reporting facts. They only have one passion, finding answers for all of mankind. Along the same lines, other agencies such as NASA, the government, and Intelligence monitoring services listening, and observing—not one had been able to identify life other than from our own earthly presence."

"What makes you so sure?"

"I am one of them. I keep close track of their processes, and progress."

"I didn't know you were so deeply involved."

"Not many do. For the most part, I live an isolated life. It's my choice."

"That's why you hardly visit us."

"Hey," I said. "My doors are always open to you, and the family."

"I'm here, am I not?"

"It's a good start. But let's not quarrel. You hungry?"

"I could use a bite."

"What's your choice? My treat."

"Any Chinese restaurants in town?"

"Chinese it is. I know a quiet place not far from here."

Thirty minutes later we arrived. It was close to dinner time already. We had spent all afternoon hiking, and talking. I was looking forward to a beer. "Tsingtao," I ordered from the waiter. Though the chart listed ten brands, it was the only brand I recognized from my earlier travels to Asia. "Tea, please," Danielle ordered, looking over the menu.

A couple of minutes later he reappeared. "What will it be?"

"Fried rice," she selected.

"Try something else," I suggested. "You can eat rice anytime."

"What would you recommend?"

"Dim sum[64]," I said. "Make it two."

"Never had it," she remarked.

"You won't be sorry." With most Chinese dishes Americanized in the U.S., it was difficult to find a genuine dim sum place. For the experienced, it was the top of the line Cantonese dish. Seconds later, he came back, pushing a cart close to the table. My mouth was watering already at the assortment of dishes presented. My selection was shrimp, BBQ pork, and shumai dumplings. I took my time savoring the selection with several more orders to follow. "What do you think?" I had been watching Danielle's expressions.

"Excellent choice. I like it. Where have I been?"

"It's not easy to find a place. Maybe San Francisco."

"I'll have to check on it. I'm glad you introduced me to this fine dish."

"You want to talk some more?"

"Actually," she said, "I am kind of burnt out with UFOs, and ETs. Maybe tomorrow?"

"Suits me fine." I let her talk for the remainder of the evening. It was light conversation with her telling me about her Internet-based business ventures, and reporting on the family. I was glad she had made the initial move to visit. It had been several years since I had seen her last. I was beginning to warm up to what used to be

---

[64] Dim sum are specially wrapped dumplings, steamed, and containing either shrimp, lobster, vegetable, pork or other ingredients. What makes them special was the time-consuming process for the staff to prepare.

a stranger. *But then,* I supposed, *I was never close to family, and children.* Growing up the way I did, alone for most part after my mother passed away, I surprised myself with the patience I was able to exhibit.

The second day of her visit I had breakfast waiting. "Morning, Dad. How nice," she said. "Bacon, eggs, potatoes, and coffee too, the whole works."

"Well, yeah. It's not every day I have company. Might as well enjoy it while it lasts. By the way," I announced, "Tracy called, checking up on you. She might come here."

"Great. When?" It was exciting news. They had not seen each other for some time. Neither had I, for that matter.

"She'll let us know. What do you feel like doing?"

"We talked a lot yesterday, but I still have many questions you didn't address."

I stalled with a question for her. "Have you ever been up Pikes Peak?"

"I have not."

"Want to take the drive? It'll be a nice daytime trip."

"Oh, yes. I have never been on a train."

"Unfortunately," I had to inform her, "rail management decided to discontinue the train."

"For how long?"

"Maybe forever. Infrastructure has worn down to be potentially unsafe after 126 years in operation."

"Bummer. I sure would have liked the scene." It was disappointing for both of us. I had been to the top several times, but it was always by car.

"We'll take my car. Bring a jacket along."

"Beemer?"

"Yes. It'll be a joyride, but it's always cold, and windy on top." In between comments on the beauty of the Rockies amid green valleys, and crisp air, we were at the peak in less than an hour. As I had anticipated, the air was too chilly to sit outside. We found a corner table at the inside restaurant with a panoramic view into the plains.

"You are fortunate to live here," she said with a gesture to the horizon. "Look at all the open spaces. It's pretty crowded where I live."

"I used to live in California, remember?"

"You're right. Too bad we weren't together then."

"Your stepdad would not have liked me in the picture."

"Why not?" she objected. "He is an honorable man."

"Yes, but it's not an acceptable situation in our culture. Once you are divorced, it's pretty much final goodbyes. By the way, how was growing up with a stepdad?"

"It was okay. I didn't know anything else. I was glad about having sisters. How come," she prodded, "you, and mom separated? Mom never talks about it."

"We should have never been married. We were not compatible to build a future together."

"Oh?"

"I wanted a travel companion to see the world together, but her priorities were having a solid marriage, nice home, and fulltime husband for raising a number of children."

"You could have managed."

"We did, but it only worked for a few short years. She finally got tired of waiting for me to come home—sometimes for weeks, sometimes for months—especially after you came along."

"So," she said. "I was the case for the divorce?"

"Don't be silly. It would have happened anyway. I am just happy you came along when you did. I could not have imagined a life without you girls."

"Dad," she said, "let's change the subject. I want to know more about what we talked about yesterday. Do you believe UFOs exist?" It always startled me when directly approached on the subject. It required an answer. And the answer was always final. I generally did not like it. It made one feel presumptuous, in a world of confusion. Her eyes reflected genuine curiosity. How could I not tell the truth? My problem was, revealing something that might prove compromising to national security. While I wanted to set the record straight for the general public, I had no intention of ever winding up in prison for disclosing closely held government secrets.

"I'm going to tell you two real life stories," I stalled. "I'll let you decide." She straightened out in anticipation with her attention on me while I described my first encounter.

"Your sister Tracy was about fourteen years old. I was in business in San Francisco when she came to visit one Sunday morning. A friend had dropped her off at my apartment for the day. We spent most of the time walking the piers, watching sea lions bark at us, tourists hastening from one spot to the next, in between eating at Ghirardelli Square, and snacking sweets served at the docks. The day went by fast, and before we knew it, it was 6:00 p.m. It was summertime, and still light for several more hours, but she had promised your mom to be back before dark.

"We left the city in my pickup, headed south on I-280 for San Jose, your home. About fifteen miles out, closing in on I-380 intersecting from the SFO Airport, we could see air traffic departing about three miles distant to the left, and below. Since I-280 travels on top of San Andreas ridgeline, we had clear vision to the airplanes taking off towards the Pacific. I slowed the vehicle to get full view of planes passing overhead at no more than five hundred feet up, each leaving a smoky exhaust trail. Then something startled the both of us.

"We clearly saw something unusual coming our way. It was a single object, green in color, disc-shaped in size much like a traffic light. While it followed the general air traffic pattern, it accelerated at a much greater speed, but slightly above the departing aircraft traffic. The disc-shaped object jump-skipped in a ram-jet type fashion increasing at a high rate of speed directly in front of our vision ahead to disappear a second later over the ocean."

"Did I hear you correctly when you said green disc?"

"That's it. Just the disc, but there was more."

"How could there be more?"

"I will explain. During my travels I have been close to tarmacs, and hangars numerous times. I am familiar with what a craft looks like, and how it behaves on takeoff, and in the air. I have spent time in cockpits of all sorts of craft, military, and commercial."

"I get it. What happened?" She was getting impatient.

"Tracy, and I looked at each other in wonder of what had just taken place. While the craft was directly overhead, for a split second, a reflection of the ground terrain appeared next to the green disc, much like an apparition. If that was not enough, we spotted the heat signature, the exhaust vortex trailing the phantom craft."

"What exhaust when there was no plane?"

"That's just it. There was no plane, but there was a plane."

"It's a paradox. How could that be?"

"The craft was there, but it was invisible. We only made the ID from the signs it left. Anybody else spotting the disc from a distance would have called it a UFO. Now, here is my logic. The craft was U.S. built with cloaking intentions to be hidden from public view, I suspect, with mirror-like concealment coating. Flying across the road, the ground reflected on the underside of the craft. It wasn't the only sign, but I cannot prove it."

"What do you mean?"

"Traffic coming from the south on the other side of the highway, from San Jose, would have seen a red disc."

"Navigation lighting?" Danielle suggested.

"Yes. That's my take."

"Ingenious, if it's true."

"Oh. It is true, I assure you."

"How can you be so sure?"

"I have an idea where the government spends the money. I worked on black projects."

"If I were to ask," she prodded, "would you tell?"

"Not a chance. I swore secrecy on my life many years ago."

"Don't know if I could handle it, a life led in secrecy," she said, shaking her head.

"It's not for everyone, and it doesn't happen overnight. It comes on gradually with different projects. So," I said, in conclusion of the story, "what do you believe?"

"I don't know. I didn't see it with my own eyes."

"Fair enough. Now you understand why there is so much confusion."

"But why keep it a secret? It's not fair to the public."

"But it is," I assured her. "Many people couldn't handle the truth. That's why conspiracies are prolific. It's been like that for ages. The mystical, folklore, paranormal, and supernatural have been around since the dawn of man. You want to hear more?"

"You promised two stories." I had noticed, through the windows, that the sun was at its peak. It was close to noon. "How about a snack?" I said, headed for the service counter. The selection was limited, but tasty. With burgers wrapped in paper we stepped out for a few minutes to enjoy the view. On top of Pikes Peak, the vantage point could not have been better. It presented a 360-degree panoramic view with a north/south dividing ridge clearly visible, in addition to mountains to the west, and flattened plateau to the east, with wind blowing from the north. "Too chilly," Danielle said, amid her shivering. "Let's go back inside."

While she could feel the coolness of thin air, I had been acclimated to the altitude for ten years. It felt breezy, but still comfortable. Seated back at our table, she said, "I'll miss this view when I'm gone. Didn't know it was this spectacular."

"You know," I offered, "you could move here. You'll have much more space, but also a slower pace of life. You young may think it boring."

"We'll see. I'll think about it. Thanks for the offer anyway. Now, what about the story?"

"This one is a bit personal. Think you can handle it?"

"Dad," she said with a hint of annoyance, "with all the shows on TV there is not much I haven't seen, or heard."

"It's been some years already, but I've had a relationship with an Alien woman."

This forced an instant reaction from her. "I thought you don't believe in aliens. First you tell me they don't exist, then you tell me you met one. I don't know what to believe anymore."

"Now you understand why the whole world is confused. Stories like this are recorded almost daily to reporting centers. But it will make sense once I explain."

"Sorry. I didn't mean to imply..."

"Don't worry," I cut her short. "You'll understand. As I said, I had an encounter."

"How was it?" The curiosity in the woman was taking hold.

"Beyond expectation." My response caused her to grin.

"What did you do?"

"I totally enjoyed it while it lasted."

"What about her? Her looks, her body, her demeaner? I want to know about the other species."

"Hispanic looking, full bodied, with all the trimmings."

"Dad," she said with a sly grin. "You are making it all up."

"I'm dead serious," I insisted.

"How long did it last?"

"Six weeks."

"Six weeks!?"

"Calm down, and let me explain," I said. "And keep your voice down. People are looking." Listening to my story, she remained quiet. What I had to say, though both were real, was more of an education than an encounter.

"It began gradually enough one late evening. There was a slight knocking at the door. I opened it to a gorgeous woman standing in a somewhat demure pose, asking to enter. Slightly doubtful of her intentions, since my guard for the unexpected was always up, I let her into my home. She was not a talkative person. We rather communicated through facial, and bodily expressions. It suited me fine since she was leading the advances. Amorous for the most part, her being the aggressor, from a purely sexual encounter, the night turned out to be incredible. It was an experience any man could ever hope for. I awoke by daylight, and she was gone. Not a trace of her having spent the night remained."

"What did you do?"

"I was totally confused. First off, I did not want it to end, and secondly, I wanted her to come back, but had no contact information. I spent the day in a hazy daze, but wholly satisfied, just the same."

"You ever see her again?"

"Weekly."

"What made it end?"

"I'll tell you." I took a minute to recollect events. "It did not take long before I realized her appearances were an apparition. Though real in its true sense, there were no physical remnants left in the mornings other than a sweaty bedsheet."

It brought on a sly grin on Danielle's face when she said, "You hound." We both laughed.

"Let me tell you the reason the encounter brought on."

Turned serious once more, she said, "This I'll have to hear."

"Are you familiar with vivid dreams?"

"I dream a lot."

"It's not the same."

"You'll have to explain."

"With a regular dream a story unfolds. Sometimes in color, at other times in black, and white, but always disjointed. When you wake up you realized it was only a dream."

"That's my experience."

"Well," I said. "Vivid dreams are different. Much different. They are so real you can't tell. If it was a pleasant dream you wake up longing for more. If it was traumatic, you wish not to have another experience."

"Really?"

"You don't know unless you have a vivid dream experience. It's that real."

"How come some have them, and some don't?"

"It took me a while to figure out the reasons. They are all drug induced."

"You don't take drugs," she protested. "Do you?"

"That's right," I agreed. "But there was one time I did. You see," I explained, "when I first moved to California, I developed severe nasal congestion. I was unable to breathe freely, unable to taste food, and unable to sleep. It was sleep deprivation that forced me into taking. After repeated doctor, and specialist visits, they all came to the same conclusion: 'You are allergic to dust mites.' They then explained that it was an affliction many arrivals in this part of the state suffered, suggesting, 'You'll have to learn to live with it,' prescribing different supplements, and medications to see what would work."

"What did you do?"

"As suggested, I learned to live with it, but not without health consequences. I was dependent on medication." Back in the 90s substances known as medication, today are considered drugs.

"What's the name of the medication? I want to get some."

Slightly startled at her remark, I told her anyway. "Ambien."

"I have heard of it."

"You don't want to get involved with substances that have psychedelic effects."

"It sounds enticing the way you've described."

"It may have, but let me warn you," I cautioned her. "There are after effects that are not easy to deal with. It's why there are so many suicide cases with people taking drugs."

"What about you? How did you react?"

"Once I realized the problem, I quit taking it. It took days of withdrawals, and sleepless nights. It's not a pleasant experience, I can assure you."

"Tell me about withdrawals?"

"After taking the substance, you develop severe insomnia. Next thing, you can't put your mind at ease."

"Why is that?"

"Your body craves the substance. There is nothing else on your mind, but another pill. Later, severe cramping sets in, starting at the gut, then migrates through the rest of the body."

"What kind of cramps?"

"It's difficult to explain. It's a combination of pain, throbbing, shortness in breathing, and in severe cases I read, throwing up, followed with unconsciousness, and even death."

"You went through all the stages," she said, voicing her concerns.

"I didn't throw up or go unconscious. I quit cold turkey, and dealt with the side effects for a few days."

"What about your sinuses?"

"After I left for Colorado the symptoms were still with me. Just by chance I ran into a former colleague of mine who claimed she had the same condition."

"How did you overcome it?"

"She told me how she was able to cure her affliction. Her remedy proved to be simple, and inexpensive. I acquired the required gadgets, and ingredients, available over the counter at Walmart then, available today on the Internet, and saw immediate results, but it took many months for it to completely clear up."

"What was it?"

"The remedy?"

"Yes."

"Are you familiar with the Neti Pot?"

"I've heard of it. What does it do?"

"It's a nasal rinse kit."

"You bought it?"

"I did, but it was too cumbersome to handle. There are better products on the market."

"What?"

"It's sold as 'Water Pik,' a sinus irrigation system, with nasal wash attachment. You'll have to know that the head contains eight sinus cavities of different sizes. It'll take a stream of water pressure to reach them all."

"By the way," she asked, "what do you think the problem was?"

"Misdiagnosis by doctors." I said, still fuming at the years of discomfort, and endless sleepless nights.

"But how could they all be wrong?"

"Inexperience, carelessness, too many patients with not enough professional healthcare, assuming a diagnosis rather than research. I don't blame the physicians for the misdiagnosis. Many in California are Asian, and not necessarily familiar with environmental conditions in the U.S., assuming that many causes for symptoms are alike."

"What was the final diagnosis?"

"I researched my plight over many weeks, and came up with a self-diagnosed solution. It was remnants of the Asian Flu I had contacted years earlier that kept festering in my sinus cavities. It could have been an early fix if a doctor would have performed an internal sinus inspection. But no," I fumed some more at the neglect, "It was always dust mites." Today, thanks to my friend, I was symptom free. I could breathe freely again.

"What are dust mites?" Danielle wanted to know.

"They are prevalent in some areas where the soil is arid. Floating with the wind, you breathe them in unhindered. They can only be detected under the microscope."

We were interrupted by the PA. "Ten minutes to closing." I felt blessed by a day spent in the company of my daughter surrounded by an unforgettable view. Forty minutes later, on arriving back home, the message light on the phone was blinking. I listened then announced, "Tracy is arriving tomorrow."

"Why doesn't she text your cell?"

"Must be on assignment. Cellphones can easily be traced with GPS."

We spent the rest of the day on light conversation, but not without one last comment by her on today's topic. "I am more confused today than before."

"We'll clear it up tomorrow."

"Morning, Dad," Danielle greeted me the next day on the way to the kitchen. "Want coffee?"

"That'd be great." I had been busy watching newscasts, and data coming across the wires. Minutes later she appeared with my favorite mug, a souvenir I had picked up at Italy's Leaning Tower of Pisa, emanating the familiar aroma of freshly brewed coffee.

"What's new?" she inquired, taking a seat nearby.

"ISIS is on the rise again. Found a weak spot in Syria."

"Will they ever quit?"

"Not as long as there are people alive."

"What's their objective?"

"Kill every Christian."

"You can't be serious." Raised, educated, and living in California for most of her life, Danielle was partial to liberal ideas. I understood their objectives, and did not object to their views. While many had a harsh political disposition for any party opposing their idealistic beliefs, I accepted both factions. It must have been my analytical training at work, looking at all sides before forming an opinion, or passing judgement. With conservativism, and liberalism, as was the case with the other political factions, they were needed for the power of balance. The alternatives were dictatorship or totalitarian, forms of governing I would not tolerate after living through it in post-WWII Germany.

"Read the Koran," I suggested. "It holds the Islamic doctrine."

"You have a copy?"

"Sure do."

"Can I see it?"

"Not now. It's time to pick up Tracy. Why don't you take the Beemer to the airport?"

"Great. I've always wanted to drive a sportscar."

"Good. Just watch the speed, will you?"

"I promise," were her trailing words on the way out.

THE TRUTH

"The truth will set you free," was an ancient saying, and is still true, more so today. It was the basis for this book. I ponder often about life, but linger mostly on lost values, one in particular, the truth. When I grew up, telling, and being taught the truth was a natural thing. One did not have to think of an answer when asked a question; it came naturally. Today, it seems, people hesitate when faced with a question. Since the young were born into this age, they may not be aware of the cultural changes I have experienced. To prove my point, all I have to do is direct the reader to one of today's popular TV shows aired daily, *People's Court*. Given, there was a reason for the litigants to be in front of the judge with disputes over personal rights. What troubles me the most when watching is that, in many cases, both plaintiff, and defendant, either one, or both sides were not telling the truth. The end result? Judgement falls to the side exerting the least lies told. Not an easy job for the judge to decide. In my analysis, it is not so much as lying or telling the truth. Personal admittance, it seems, in recent decades, is based on getting an edge on material things, the very cause for our cultural change.

There was something I had to do before my daughters arrived. I needed positive confirmation from the one, and only individual in the government I could completely trust on a topic we had never discussed in all the years we have known each other. I made the call.

"Well, well," the voice said on the distant end. "Alex Bauer. Haven't heard from you in ages. What gives me the honor?"

"Your fault for not calling me," I said, placing the burden on him. It had always been up to him to establish contact. "How are things with DARPA?"

"Political," Mystery-man hinted. "Things slowed down quite a bit since the end of the Cold War, but project wise, we are busier than ever."

"What's in the workings?"

"Can't tell you. All I can say is keep your eyes to the skies."

Though his reply was quite ambiguous, I understood. Black projects, I suspected. There were enough UFO sightings reported, and floating around nightly talk radio shows to make you ponder with conspiracists at their best. While the subjects may have not been common knowledge to the general citizen, unexplained sightings in the U.S., as well as other places, were factual events to the Ufologist community.

"Can we talk?" I broke in.

"We're talking now."

"I mean secure."

"Just a second, I'll switch." There was a brief silence with a confirming click followed. "Now, what're you calling about?"

I came right to the point. "Something we've never talked about. It's about UFOs, and Aliens." There they were, the world's most controversial subjects. Out in the open. The line went silent. I waited for his response. I could almost hear his brain grinding.

"Why do you ask?"

It was the response I'd expected. I was prepared. "In all the years we worked together why did the subject never come up?"

"Because you never asked. Why bring it up now?"

"I need to know your position. Do you believe extraterrestrials have visited earth?"

"Why do you want to know? It doesn't matter either way, does it?"

"I see your point, but need to know." I could tell him my reasoning, but held off, waiting for his admittance, or denial, which may, or may never come.

"You're not going to do anything stupid you may regret, are you?"

"Such as?"

"Like blowing the whistle. It would kill your career."

"I'm still waiting for your answer." I was not going to be brushed off.

"What is your opinion? What do you believe?" As usual, he had shifted the burden back to me.

"My opinion is immaterial. I want to hear it from you," I insisted.

"I will only tell you my take on it. Understood?"

"It's all I'm asking."

"I don't know."

"What don't you know," I said, waiting for clarification. I could not, and would not accept his answer.

"I just told you, I don't know."

"You, Mystery-man himself, don't have the answer?"

"That's right. Now, can you drop it?" It became apparent that he was uncomfortable talking. Perhaps it was the caution he exerted while on the phone. Perhaps he just did not know. I had to find out but decided to wait. Deducting from his response, it seemed, I had exceeded my welcome. "I'll talk to you later," I said, aware of the sudden silence. He had hung up.

"Hey," I greeted Tracy when she, and Danielle walked in. "Where have you been? I missed you. We all missed you." Dresses in latest fashion designer clothes from head to toe, she appeared as self-assured as always. "Travel becomes you. You look great." As usual, this earned me a kiss on the cheek. She, as well as my other daughters, were at an age where time seemed endless for them. You could come and go as you wished, get into all kinds of trouble, if you chose to, explore the world, coming out unscathed without so much as aging a wrinkle. There was a time when I went through a similar lifestyle, careless about what the future had in store for the individual, and rightly so. Life should be explored to its fullest, as long as it is lived within the boundaries of the law.

"Care for lunch?"

"It depends on what you have to offer."

"How about your favorites?"

"Eggs Benedict?"

"So be it. Make yourself comfortable. Brunch will be ready in thirty minutes."

Danielle helped me with the preparations while we talked. "Where does she get her strength? The independence, her self-confidence."

"Comes with the territory, exposure, and training."

"I wish that I had such opportunities."

"It's your choice. Just let me know what you want out of life. I can arrange the direction."

"Really?"

"Did it for both of your sisters."

"But," she replied, "don't you need opportunities first?"

"Don't worry. They will be there. Troubles tend to follow you."

"Could you get me connected?"

"I'll see what I can do," I offered. "Fair enough?"

"Fair enough. Ready to serve?"

"Call your sister."

As always when in company, especially the family I was blessed with, my life seemed wholesome. Watching the girls enjoy my dishes, I completely savored the moment. I could have easily been a chef since I liked cooking, especially foreign cuisines. Sometimes I wonder how my life would have turned out working in a simple world, serving customers, surrounded by people. One thing was certain, I would not have been alone so much. It's the only regret I had.

"Danielle told me about the conversations you've had over the past days. Want to explain?"

"You know me," I said. "You ask, and I tell."

"How come you never talked about it with me?"

"What?

"Aliens and UFOs."

"It never came up."

"What? In all the years I lived at home?"

"That's right. Nobody ever mentioned it." It puzzled me as well, but the past years were not exactly a holiday, especially with al Qaeda first, followed with ISIS, and Jihad on the move.

"I wonder why," she pondered.

"People are afraid of making fools of themselves. That's why."

"You can't blame them, can you?"

"You ever wondered?"

"Many times, but always brushed it off as nonsense. I remember your saying."

"What?"

"Only believe what you can see with your own eyes."

"It still holds true, but people have gotten bold. They have become outright demanding. They challenge things even from the government. Nobody is afraid of the law anymore. All you have to do is follow the news. Killings have become a part of our daily lives."

"Unfortunately," she agreed. "That's true."

"Hollywood production trends are effecting the public."

"Positively," Tracy agreed. "Hell, even I can see the changes in people's behaviors. They are getting brasher with each year."

"Let's change the subject," she said. "I want to know your opinion on the subject of UFOs."

"It's not an opinion," I corrected her. "It is based on pure facts."

"Okay. Let's hear it."

"Danielle?" Since it was the purpose for her visit, I handed the topic off to her.

"We have been talking for several days about it," she admitted. "But there are many more questions I have. For instance," she stated with a nod in my direction, "Dad seems to have all the answers."

"Well," Tracy offered, "let me in on some of it. I could use some truth for a change." It was her indication of the state the world was in.

"The truth is with the past," I said. It was a reminder to keep focus.

"Why the past?"

"It holds the answers."

"I don't understand," Tracy said with a puzzled look on her face.

"Projects I worked."

"What projects?"

"Net One, and Net Two."

"The Internet? You worked on it?" she exclaimed, not sure of what to believe anymore.

"I was part of software development, and afterwards led deployment teams."

"That's not proof."

"But it is," I insisted.

"You better explain before I completely lose my mind. There are too many secrets I don't understand."

"The proof is that there is no proof."

"Now you are talking in riddles." I must have totally confused both girls. I didn't blame them. Anybody listening to my dialogue would have thought, *he's getting senile.*

"Not at all. Let me explain." I took my time to focus, then continued, "To connect the world there was a need to access, and interconnect every defense, and Intel database. Because legacy data was so convoluted between mainframe manufacturers, we needed access to database architectures, data structures, and contents information. Datamining was not yet in use, but data analysis was. Data contained in legacy databases had to be restructured into newly developed systems. In the process of analysis, we had direct access."

"What did you find?" Tracy asked.

"There is no shred of evidence on the existence of extraterrestrials."

"What about all the sightings, and supposed first-hand encounters people claim?"

"Self-serving fabrication."

"You better explain."

"Yes, Dad," Danielle chimed in.

"People became aware of certain objects flying in the sky they were not familiar with, and reported them to the Air Force. This was before UFO reporting centers existed."

"It must have been before my time." Tracy snickered.

"Ever heard of Project Sign? Project Grudge? Project Blue Book?"

"Blue Book, Yes. The others, No."

"That was then when the CIA became involved. People just would not stop."

"Was it ever resolved?" Danielle wanted to know.

"It never was. All they would do was either ignore the reports or respond vaguely."

"What about you? Did you believe?"

"At first, sure. But that was before I became involved with Intel organizations."

"What about now? You still believe any of it?"

"I will let you be the judge."

"Why put the burden on us?" Tracy objected.

"Because," I stalled, taking a few seconds to formulate an intelligent reply. "I don't want to be known as a 'whistle blower.'"

"Wow. Now I understand. You know," she cautioned, "you could go to jail for telling."

"Believe me," I assured her. "I thought long, and hard about it. That's the reason I am careful when discussing the alien question, but I am safe. I don't disclose anything. There is not the slightest bit of evidence to disclose. There is little to whistle. There is nothing to blow."

"Then I don't understand why all the secrecy."

"It's defense, and Intel business. Their models are based on secrecy. It has to be this way for the sake of national security."

"Here we go again," Tracy challenged. "The excuse is always national security when the government is trying to hide something."

"There is more to it," I insisted. "It's to keep adversaries in check."

"I don't understand."

"One side builds a mousetrap," I explained. "The other side improves on it. It's the same with every invention." I had to clarify, "The name of the game is staying ahead of the other side. Let them keep guessing. It gives you the advantage over the next conflict or war. Ever heard of 'The Art of War'?"

"Not that I can recall."

"Sun Tzu, ancient Chinese battle commander and strategist better known as 'Master Sun,' developed, and documented the art of fighting wars dating back to the 6th century BC, still followed to this day."

"That's it? Is that all there is to the Alien and UFO craze? Nothing?"

"Not the least," I offered. "There is more, much more, but it'll take time to explain. I don't want to bore you with specifics. Maybe later?"

"I need a break," Tracy said.

"Me too," Danielle agreed. It gave me a chance to clear the table of dishes.

"What do you girls want to do for the rest of the day?" I could use a break as well.

"Let's go to town," Danielle suggested. "I have never been downtown."

"Great," Tracy said in wholehearted agreement.

"Who's driving?" I did not mind giving up driving privileges to my daughters, knowing how much they liked my sportscar.

"I am." I tossed the keys to Danielle.

The day turned out well. We visited some of the historic places in town, stepping in and out shops selling their wares, and just had a pleasant time catching up on local events. I realized once again how quick time was passing with the many tourists in town. It was not that long ago when there were hardly any visitors. Colorado Springs had been an old western town held dormant until just recently when tourism was mass marketed. The results may have been beneficial to the shopkeepers, but not so much for people like myself, thriving on serenity, quiet, and the beauty of the surroundings, the Rocky Mountain range.

SOCIAL UNREST

We live in difficult times. Though living this day, this decade, this century we are not singled out. Hardship has been part of mankind since the beginning of time. It seems that every generation born had its own challenges to cope with. There is only one principle difference between then, and now, that of a runaway evolution. Driven primarily by technology, the pace of life appears to increase at an exponential rate. This, however, is only a perceptional awareness. Cosmic time still behaves as it always has, ticking away with universal accuracy as measured by mathematical standards. What is different in our lives today are changes in our behavior patterns.

Another day in the serenity of crisp air, and sunshine was on the rise. I was busy tending to my Castle guests gathered on the deck amid light conversations enjoying the view into the Rocky Mountains. "How did you sleep?" he asked.

"I don't recall sleeping these many hours in a long time," Danielle acknowledged. "What about you, Tracy?"

"Slept like a baby, as usual. What about you, Dad? Still suffer from insomnia?"

"I don't think that will ever change. It's been with me since my 40s."

"What happened?" Danielle said.

"A couple of things," I volunteered. "Curiosity, and pleasures of life."

"You care to explain?"

"There is not much to explain. As a child I already thought the days were too short to satisfy my curiosity. With the after effects of the war, and shortage in electricity, families mostly depended on daylight for reading, the only entertainment available. It got worse over time. To get the most out of life I rationed sleep to three hours."

"Three hours," Danielle exclaimed. "I don't think that I could survive on that."

"You may be surprised at the conditions a body can endure. Just think of the detainees at concentration camps going without food, and medical attention for days, weeks, and months plagued with body pain and no medication allocated. The poor souls were purposely kept at a starvation level."

"We are lucky grandpa wasn't Jewish," Tracy reflected. "We would not be here."

"True," I said. "You may not know, but he wound up in a concentration camp as well."

"How come? He was German, wasn't he?"

"He was," I assured her. "His problem was insubordination to Hitler's causes."

"I'd like to hear more," Danielle said.

"First, he was part of the engineering team on the Hindenburg, and other airships."

"I thought they were built for recreational use," Tracy said.

"That was true before, but at the onset of war, the German defense used them as observation platforms. But that's not why he was detained. When the war started every abled man, and woman, and later children, were required to join a party. For the ones not drafted into the army, the other choices were Hitler's SS, the Nazi party, or Hitler's Youth movement. Since my dad was working directly for the war effort, building airships followed by bombers, he thought it unnecessary. The SS did not. One day, they hauled him, and everybody he associated with into detention. His social circle was extensive with mostly engineers, and educators. As a result, they spent many years in confinement."

"That's not a valid reason," Tracy noted.

"They were difficult times manipulated by a dictator. In his mindset, in addition to the Jewish problem, everybody that posed a threat to the regime was removed, temporarily or permanently."

"I never quite understood the Jewish issue. Could you explain it?"

"I don't have to tell you when it all started. It began in biblical times."

"That part we know." Both daughters nodded in agreement. "We learned it at Sunday school."

"Though a pre-Christian era, Jewish people were just as much at fault for fighting border clashes with their neighbors like most of the tribes. To exist, for millennia, it was killing or be killed. But eventually, people figured out that there was a better way to coexist."

"But, Dad," Danielle said, "what was the real cause for their problems?"

"Too many gods."

"What?"

"There were too many idols people worshiped. Reading the Old Testament, as you may have learned, the country was filled with temples, and shrines practicing idolatry. Everything important in nature was considered initiated by a god. It was a time when icons like Amon, Artemis, Asherah, Hermes, Zeus, with deities of Baal, Bel, and Molech, all in contention with each other, only separated by regions."

"What about Neptune, and Poseidon? Aphrodite, and Venus? What about them?"

"All the same gods, only different languages. One is Greek, the other Roman."

"I always wondered. Now I know," Tracy admitted.

"It was not until Moses, a descendant from the house of Abraham, showed up that things changed."

"Ten Commandments?"

"Not only the Ten Commandments, God's law. He gave us God. One God. Ever since, the Jewish people turned into a peaceful culture, but in turn were persecuted, and prosecuted. It was not until towards the end of WWII when the Jewish culture was finally accepted by the world with equal values."

"What about you, Dad? How do you feel about them, being of German ancestry?"

"My dad affiliated with them. He had no problems whatsoever."

"Then," Tracy pondered, "why was Hitler, and the rest of your country in such an uproar?"

"You have to understand Jewish ideology. The reason they were persecuted through all the ages is that they were smarter than the rest of the world. They were the educated ones. They excelled in literature, finance, business, the arts, and many other faculties. They became the most disciplined people in the old world. Their eventual mission was to acquire knowledge, live by principles, and teach righteousness."

"I never knew," Danielle said.

"Neither did I," Tracy agreed.

"Do you still want to know my position on the Jewish plight?"

"You explained it well."

"I like what they represent, and contribute to life, especially their culture in as much as lifestyle. That's the reason I have friends, and even business partners that are Jewish."

"I did not know," Danielle said with a questioning glance at her sister, who was shaking her head. "Where did you get all of the information?"

"I read. It's what I do if I'm not writing. It keeps me sane. Sane in a world filled with misgivings."

The world, as seen through my eyes, was a runaway world driven by an increase in demands for games, appliances, and conveniences to satisfy immediate cravings, and gratifications. It seemed the engaged, the producers, demanded compensation for the energy they expended to benefit others. Their attitude was not "Let's see what it will bring," it was "How much can I get for it?" The objective in today's economy is "Profit," no matter how it is derived, or who suffers in the process. To assure success, three elements are needed: prosperous times, affordable product, and marketing means, the standards for the industrious. Without these, unless the idea is unique, it most likely ends in failure. Novelty always sells, no matter what the gadget. For those who still remember the "Pet Rock," and "Hula Hoop," instant success was assured. The concept idea, though taken as an insult by many, for its inventor was instant success at a minimal effort. Gather a few rocks along the riverbed, clean them up, toss them in a basket or not, and put them on the store shelves. Energy, and effort expended? Little. Time used? Leisure.

For many, it has been an attitude adopted ever since. Given such opportunities, who needed long hours at the office, the perversity of commuting, insults endured from boss, and clients, correcting mistakes, schedules, and delivery conflicts?

"Who needs it?"

"You need it. I need it. It is you demanding it. It is all of us demanding it."

As I had always done so, I questioned everything, the source, as well as cause. It helps to formulate an opinion whether it proves correct or marginal. It is a necessary process to exist without being washed over by the never-ending onslaught of information. With mainstream media, at times disregarding the rules of ethics, ignoring events for factual evidence, to get to the truth one has to investigate, and make judgments on their own. While the majority of the population follows mainstream media to obtain information, I lay awake nights to follow talk radio tuned in on alternative news, of which there are many, to get a better perspective. A better perspective is not always the truth or factual either; those sources have their own flaws, and faults. But for the most part they present the truth, an important factor for me. I look at a mix of programs presented from a reality point of interest, but to other listeners it may well be viewed as gospel.

Paranormal listening audiences make up the majority discussing unexplained events, in turn impatiently hoping for a plausible explanation. It works for many, but not for all. There is always one element missing, an important element. It is the element exclusively held by the government. It is the element of Full Disclosure that everybody hopes for, but never materialized. The question still remains, "Why?"

"Why keep something a secret that has become so visible to everyday life?"

The answer has been there all along. The answer is as simple as it is complicated, making denial the best of choices. Denial means security. Deniability is the all-encompassing way out from the jam. But who has the privilege of playing this most important trump card? The government.

To assure compliance for something so covert, something that must be kept from the public at all cost, takes an enforcement body. It takes a body with all the power in the world to assure compliance for successful suppression of data, and information deemed classified, unfit for the public to know.

"Why all the secrecy?" one may ponder.

The answer is just as simple. "Preventing leaks from being revealed through gossip, slip of the tongue, self-serving interests, and other personal notions such as monetary compensations, individual esteem, and more, a notion better known as compromise."

That brings us back to the issue of Full Disclosure, the world's most sought-after secret, waiting to be revealed, but one that would never come. Shocking? The response may be shocking, but it is a simple one.

Presidential elects, and political leaders will never be stupid enough to make fools out of themselves. It would be political suicide.

Much of the public is not aware of the nightly broadcasts propagating fairytales, folklore, myths, and legends presented as real facts, and actual events. One imperative example would be the "Flat Earth" theory. In the minds of some of the paranormal spirited, it constitutes as being factual. In the minds of the average human being it is pure nonsense. The same holds true for most paranormal events. Revelations about extraterrestrials, UFOs, Big Foot, ghosts, unexplained sightings, aberrations, fear mongering, and supernatural experiences can all be explained, justified, and rationalized as earthly sightings, hoaxes, drug-induced visions, and lucid dreams. But, in the eyes of the susceptible, gullible to tales, they will always hold true as real, and believable events.

That leads as into the annals of Hollywood, a world of fiction and make-believe. Who could have ever believed that one fabricated show could have changed our lives forever? I am referring "The War of the Worlds,[65]" delivered by Orson Welles.

---

[65] "The War of the Worlds" was an episode of the American radio drama anthology series *The Mercury Theatre on the Air*. It was performed as a Halloween episode of the series on Sunday, October 30, 1938, and aired over the Columbia Broadcasting System radio network. Directed, and narrated by actor, and future filmmaker Orson Welles, the episode was an adaptation of H. G. Wells' novel *The War of the Worlds* (1898). It became famous for allegedly causing mass panic, although the scale of the panic is disputed as the program had relatively few listeners.

The first two-thirds of the one-hour broadcast was presented as a series of simulated news bulletins. The first news update interrupted a program of dance music to report that a series of odd explosions had been spotted on Mars, which was followed soon thereafter by a seemingly unrelated report of an unusual object falling on a farm in Grover's Mill, New Jersey. Martians emerged from the object, and attacked using a heat ray during the next interruption, which was followed by a rapid series of news reports describing a devastating alien invasion taking place across the United States, and the world. The illusion of realism was furthered because the *Mercury Theatre on the Air* was a sustaining show without commercial interruptions, and the first break in the program came almost 30 minutes into the broadcast. Popular legend holds that some of the radio audience may have been listening to Edgar Bergen, and tuned in to "The War of the Worlds" during a musical interlude, thereby missing the clear introduction that the show was a drama.

In the days following the adaptation, widespread outrage was expressed in the media. The program's news-bulletin format was described as deceptive by some newspapers, and public figures, leading to an outcry against the perpetrators of the broadcast, and calls for regulation by the Federal Communications Commission. The episode secured Welles's fame as a dramatist.

My declaration may upset many, but as stated previously, I live in a world of logic with scientifically proven facts that are based on mathematical formulas, verified by the world's most brilliant minds. In contrast to reality, nobody has ever come up with a mathematical formula proving that a spiritual realm exists. However, as farfetched as many claims may be to the contrary, having had "first-hand experience in the unexplained," I am just as confused. I spend many hours trying to come up with an explanation for how prophecies, and predictions may interact. It is a mystery that may not be solved in my lifetime.

To this day, there is no physical evidence that a spiritual world exists, other than artifacts dug from the ground as proof of an ancient civilization. Objects such as apparitions, ghosts, mystical phenomena, all are fabricated by overactive imaginations, and perhaps, wishful thinking. There is nothing wrong with it as long as one maintains reality. What I repudiate is not the material created by the mind, it is the ownership adopted by the individuals making such claims. Since there are many stories fabricated, and adopted daily, taking claim does not matter much. What matters is that the entire issue is confusing the world population and, in the process, influencing the population, confusing them what to believe in anymore.

With all of the multimedia entertainment available, ghost, and phantom stories have moved to the forefront in entertainment. To follow the production of the many research, and investigative teams scouting day and night through the so-called hot zones of mysterious ghosts, and bigfoot activities, one should but wonder why nothing is ever captured on film, or presented in actuality. It's because there is nothing to catch; otherwise, there should be fossil evidence as was the case with dinosaurs.

I thought it was time to clarify some of the misconceptions circulating the globe. It is not only the U.S. population making such convoluting claims. There are many countries affected, and since we are leaders in the world, we should have the means to prove it. We should set an example for separating facts from fiction. It is up to us to keep the people informed on worldly events; however, as already stated for reasons of self-interest, it will not happen anytime soon, or ever.

FACTS OR FICTION

A new day had broken over the Rockies. It appeared that my daughters had decided to sleep late. That was fine with me. I could spend the time catching up on email responses, and news feeds. They finally showed up by the deck, my favorite place in the mornings. It gave me the space I very much treasured with the view of the Rockies, and pristine air to breath. "Morning, Dad."

"Morning, girls." I still call them girls. In my mind they will always be such. Aside from being responsible adults, when caught off guard, I could still detect the playfulness of a girl's trait. "What do you want to do today?" I said.

"Shopping," Danielle said.

"I could use some new jeans," Tracy agreed.

"Then let's have lunch downtown. I know a local brewery that serves native dishes."

"Native dishes?" Danielle questioned.

"Mountain oysters[66]?" Tracy grimaced. From the expression on her face she must have had a taste of them, or at least had heard about the dish, local to the Rockies. "You won't like it," she commented to her sister.

"Buffalo burger," I announced. "Nothing drastic."

"Good. Always wanted to try it," Danielle agreed. A twenty-minute ride later we were in the midst of the city. Parking was ample since it was off tourist season with the town relatively quiet. Shopping was never a challenge at Tejon street, the town's main thoroughfare. Aside from several suburban-based malls, downtown was the place to shop. One could stroll up on one side, and back on the other with stops in between for the desired purchase. An hour later we entered Phantom Canyon Brewery.

"Beer," we all ordered. As was the case with most local breweries, an ample assortment was on hand to choose from, either draft, or bottled from lager to pilsner, light, flavored homebrewed, and the favorite of most visitors, Weiss bier. Glancing over the refreshment chart I clearly recalled the simplicity of life back in Germany. When it came to beer, in my time, there were two types available: lager, and pilsner. One was German made, and the other was imported from the Czech Republic, introduced with WWII. Somewhat bitter in taste, made primarily from hops, Pils had always been my preference.

Exposed to Californian lifestyles, my daughters were apt to sample flavored beers. Seated comfortably, Danielle opened the conversation. It seemed she could not contain her curiosity any longer. Inquisitive as my daughters were, there was hardly a minute without conversation. "Dad," she said. "You promised us secrets."

"What secrets?" I had told them what I knew. But, as curious as my daughters were, it would never be enough. From here on, it would be a topic for conversations, at times lively conversation, while at one time deemed Top Secret, now declassified. Those secrets, today mostly uncommon knowledge, would not infringe on national security.

"Yesterday. You know, UFOs, and ETs."

---

[66] Rocky mountain oysters, a delicacy of the Western hunter, and followers. They're bison testicles, which many visitors venture to taste.

"Girls," I explained. "They are no secrets. They are all around us, have been for millennia."

"What about freedom of information? What about disclosure? Will the government ever reveal its secrets?"

"I can only tell you what the public reports."

"What about the CIA? The NSA, and DOD?"

"They stopped listening, and recording with the closure of Project Blue Book."

"But people still report their sightings," Tracy insisted.

"That's true," I agreed. "But only to public reporting centers."

"What centers?"

"NICAP, MUFON, and NUFORC."

"I've heard about NICAP, and MUFON," Tracy said. "But not the other."

"NUFORC? Online database providing direct access for the public. You can do your own searches."

"But, Dad," Danielle objected. "We want to hear it from you. We know you tell the truth."

"Okay then. What specifically do you want to know?" I had no reservations to their demands since I was well aware of what information had been released to the public, and what had not.

"Everything you know."

"It's too broad a field. We'll be sitting here for days getting drunk. We wouldn't want that, would we?"

"We don't mind, Tracy said, supported by a nod from Danielle.

"If you insist." I sighed when a thought occurred to me. "By the way, any of you still read?"

"I read," Tracy hesitatingly admitted. "Novels."

"I read," Danielle volunteered. "Mobile, Facebook, and Twitter news."

"I meant historical accounts." Both kept silent. I was not surprised. It was the world I helped create. Whether we, my generation, liked it or not, it was us that had to bear the responsibility for how future generations would turn out. I could only hope that the government fessed up to its part, their responsibility for keeping check, and balance in a world of insatiable runaway technological demands.

"Rather than bore you with reported, and archived data, I'll give you my historical researched findings," I suggested. Much like during their growing years when I would tell a story, both their focus was concentrated on everything I would reveal. I lapsed into my usual semi-monologue, occasionally interrupted by either one.

"With the onset of mankind millennia ago, there have always been unexplained sightings. People then believed that every occurrence in nature was directed by some god. In ancient times there were as many gods as there were natural events. One could only express sightings in simple terms such as 'The Thing.' There was no wheel, balloon, or man-made object to compare. It was only much later when man learned to write that things could be explained in broader terms, mostly biblical. The 'UFO,' for instance, could only be associated with birds, and cloud formations, and 'ET' in simple visionary images. Yes, visionary images." Delving into history, one will also learn that all was not altogether a sober existence. Although brewing beer had been around for thousands of years, drugs, and psychedelic substances had been for much longer. The ancients knew where to find them, process them, and how to use them. Much like in today's world, drugs had same, or similar effects on people. They caused visions many took as reality. The world of dreams contained the secrets of life, the universe, and creation.

"Historically, it seemed that every generation added more labels, and images to unexplained real or visionary sightings. Medieval, and feudal years created their own world of gargoyles, and effigies. When man took to the air, flight created even more possibilities for images, and sightings. Man, as simple, and clear minded as most were behind the controls of a craft, had imaginations that were prolific, especially when the horizon was intercepted by some unfamiliar object. Where it was FOO Fighters in WWII, the visions changed to flying saucers followed with discs, and objects of every make, and shape, especially with the onset of balloons, aircraft, satellites, stealth technology, and spaceships, all contributing to more confusion. One might think people were prone to being gullible, but there is more to it.

"All could be explained in earthly terms if everyone involved with creating innovative objects, and images would divulge essentials, and state the facts. But, as long as there are nations competing for technology, and economic advantage, it will never happen. The consequences are that we all have to accept, and learn to live with the strangeness of things with more in the future, much more. With the rapid advancements in science, and technology it will only get worse. Much of the world population, for one reason or other, has accepted unfamiliar objects flying in the sky, or moving submerged, but the diehards thriving on conspiracies, paranormal, and supernatural will not."

"Dad, wait," Danielle interrupted. "You meant to say that it's all a hoax? The sightings, the close encounters, the abductions?"

"Not necessarily."

"Now I'm confused again."

"I'm trying to make you understand possible reasons for the phenomena. While some are real, others are purely imaginary."

"But, Dad," she complained. "I know when I imagine things. I also know what I see."

"Well, yes," I admitted. "But many people reporting sightings, and events are not necessarily sober, or free from drugs. With the overindulgence of today's population in drug use, many daily, and even hourly, objects perceived by the mind are not always for real."

"But," Tracy objected, "there are too many such sightings to just ignore."

"Girls," I said, keeping my calm. "You have no idea how many black projects there are." Fortunately, appeasing my own curiosity years ago, I had been involved with several such programs, so I could explain many of the sightings, and visions people report as UFOs, and Aliens. I felt the need to clarify. "But," I said, "I cannot do it for innovated projects of recent years. Not since I retired from government contracting."

"It's good enough for me," Danielle said with an assuring glance at her sister. Both nodded in agreement.

"For you to understand the broad spectrum of UFOs, I will explain the most major sightings, visions, mutilations, and abductions. You have to accept the sample cases. There are thousands more recorded with organizations, and agencies, too many to cite them all."

"We understand. Go ahead, Dad."

UFO SPECIFICS

"Let's take the most highly publicized cases. Every one of them illustrates the experience, and involvement of government, and citizens, but does not explain causes, and facts. Each has their own explanation that may or may not ever be completely revealed. Depending on the thoroughness of investigations by government authorities, and military, many are explained as misinterpretations by the witness or witnesses, or just plain made-up stories by individuals seeking notoriety, with many coerced by novelists and writers. Based on mine, and many other truths seeker's research, on close examination the records state both, facts, and fiction. Where science, as well as my own interests are purely focused on seeking out facts, conspirators, and paranormal followers present their fictional interpretations. Following is a sample list, and brief explanation stating facts for most popularized events:

"Aurora Crash, TX, 1897; Maury Island Incident, WA, 1947; Roswell UFO Retrieval, NM, 1947; Mantell Case, KY, 1948; UFOs over Washington, DC, 1952; Hill Abduction, NH, 1961; Billy Meier's Encounter, Switzerland, 1964; Incident at Exeter, England, 1965; Kecksburg Crash, PA, 1965; Pascagoula Abduction, MS, 1973; Piedmont Missouri Case, MO, 1973; Travis Walton Abduction, AZ, 1975; UFO Intercept, Iran, 1976; Valentich Disappearance, Australia, 1978; Cash Landrum Case, TX, 1980; Rendlesham Forest, England, 1980; Japanese Air Flight 1628, Over Alaska, 1986; America West Air Case, TX, 1995; Phoenix Lights, AZ, 1997; Chicago O'Hare UFO, IL, 2006;, and Stephenville, TX, 2008."[67]

Specifics:

Aurora Crash, TX, 1897
Hoax fabricated by the Mayor of Aurora based on political self-interests.

Maury Island Incidence, WA, 1947
Kenneth Arnold report of flying discs. An FBI investigation concluded that it was a hoax initiated by a certain Crisman, and Dahl, two harbor patrolmen boasting an imaginary sighting.

Roswell UFO Retrieval, NM, 1947
Cover up. In mid-1947, a scientific United States Army Air Forces research balloon crashed at a ranch near Roswell, New Mexico. Following wide initial interest in the crashed "flying disc," the U.S. military stated that it was merely a conventional weather balloon. Interest subsequently waned until the late 1970s, when Ufologists began promoting a variety of increasingly elaborate conspiracy theories, claiming that one or more alien spacecraft had crash-landed, and that the extraterrestrial occupants had been recovered by the military, who then engaged in a cover up.

Mantell UFO Incident, KY, 1948

---

[67] Direct Internet links to each case are provided in Appendix C.

Mantell misidentified a United States Navy Skyhook weather balloon as planet Venus. The balloons were a secret Navy project at the time of Mantell's crash made of reflective aluminum about 100 feet (30 m) in diameter, consistent with the description of the UFO as large, metallic, and cone-shaped. Since the Skyhook balloons were secret at the time, neither Mantell nor the other observers in the air control tower would have been able to identify the UFO as a Skyhook.

UFOs over Washington, DC, 1952
At 11:40 p.m. on Saturday, July 19, 1952, Edward Nugent, an air traffic controller at Washington National Airport, spotted seven objects on his radar. The objects were located 15 miles (24 km) south-southwest of the city; no known aircraft were in the area, and the objects were not following any established flight paths. Nugent's superior, Harry Barnes, a senior air-traffic controller at the airport, watched the objects on Nugent's radarscope.

Air Force Major Generals John Samford, USAF Director of Intelligence, and Roger Ramey, USAF Director of Operations, held a well-attended press conference at the Pentagon on July 29, 1952. It was the largest Pentagon press conference since World War II. Press stories called Samford, and Ramey the Air Force's two top UFO experts. Samford declared that the visual sightings over Washington could be explained as misidentified aerial phenomena (such as stars or meteors). Samford also stated that the unknown radar targets could be explained by temperature inversion, which was present in the air over Washington on both nights the radar returns were reported.

Hill Abduction, NH, 1961
According to a variety of reports given by the Hills, the alleged UFO sighting happened on September 19, 1961, around 10:30 p.m. The Hills were driving back to Portsmouth from a vacation in Niagara Falls, and Montreal. Just south of Lancaster, New Hampshire, Betty claimed to have observed a bright point of light in the sky that moved from below the moon, and the planet Jupiter, upward to the west of the moon. While Barney navigated U.S. Route 3, Betty reasoned that she was observing a falling star, only it moved upward. Since it moved erratically, and grew bigger, and brighter, Betty urged Barney to stop the car for a closer look, as well as to walk their dog, Delsey. Barney stopped at a scenic picnic area just south of Twin Mountain.

Their strange story, controversial as it unfolded over several years through many hypnotic sessions, can best be explained with the adaptation into the best-selling 1966 book, *The Interrupted Journey.* The publicity it received was so overwhelming it revived the modern UFO phenomena, producing many books, and literature to follow. What may have appeared as a real event to the Hills, through many subsequent hypnotic sessions conducted by various psychologists eventually brought about changes to the original account. There are many more such cases, too lengthy for the reader to digest, listed in Appendix C, labelled *More Sample Reports.*

"Dad. I've heard enough," Danielle complained. "I get the idea."
"Me too," Tracy said. "It all boils down to one common cause."

"Which is?"

"People are unreliable."

"Not all," I corrected. "There are many sober-headed individuals dispersed through the world, approximately 80%, based on latest statistics. While some may have doubts, at times, they never loose hold on reality. The rest, aside from having a vivid imagination, believe what entertainment, and mainstream media projected. To cite one example: Facebook was designed to keep up public, and personal interests within an openminded community, but in recent years, it has turned into a carrier of fake news, and vindictive assaults on all kinds of matters."

"It may seem that way, doesn't it?" Danielle was still doubtful. I felt additional clarification was necessary.

"People cannot be entirely blamed for their misjudgments. If they had a basic knowledge to compare the many different objects shooting across the skies, there would hardly be questions raised. Take for instance the blimp or airplane when they first took to the air. They were great novelties for their times, but only to the observers who had been informed through news, and word. People living in foreign countries, uninformed on technology, were sure to wonder about the object's origins. One can clearly understand why there is so much confusion over UFO sightings just from the handful of cases we examined. Imagine reading hundreds of such cases reported each week. While they are only brief extracts from lengthy reports, the cited cases did not even include the thousands of abductions, and various degrees of close encounters, let alone the millions of reported visions, and vivid dreams imagined, but perceived as factual."

"How come you never talked about it?" Tracy questioned.

"For most of my career," I explained, "I was too busy with technical issues. True, there were the occasional news articles on UFO sightings, and speculations on Alien encounters, but most people took them as hoaxes."

"What about you?" Danielle wondered.

"I knew better. I had access to information to the contrary, remember?"

"Ah yes, databases."

"That's right. Even thought there was no verifiable data, and information on extraterrestrial accounts, disclosing the fact would have been a security breach. Governments back then were extremely strict about Intel policies. One infraction, and you were out of a job, never to work on classified projects again."

"But," Tracy objected, "there was Project Blue Book." Project Blue Book was one of a series of systematic studies of unidentified flying objects conducted by the United States Air Force. It began in 1952, and was the third study of its kind. Because of the unreliability of the reports, a termination order was given by the Air Force to end the study in December 1969, and all activity under its sponsorships ceased by 1970. But it did not end there. Reports still flooded in weekly, directed to the FBI among other government services.

"Project Blue Book had two goals," I explained. "One, it was to determine if UFOs were a threat to national security, and two, to scientifically analyze UFO-related data. Thousands of UFO reports were collected, analyzed, and filed away. As the result of the *Condon Report* in1968, which concluded there was nothing anomalous about

UFOs, Project Blue Book was ordered shut down with the Air Force concluding its findings with a summary of its investigations:

1. No UFO reported, investigated, and evaluated by the Air Force was ever an indication of threat to our national security;
2. There was no evidence submitted to or discovered by the Air Force that sightings categorized as "unidentified" represented technological developments or principles beyond the range of modern scientific knowledge; and
3. There was no evidence indicating that sightings categorized as "unidentified" were extraterrestrial vehicles."

"Then," Danielle questioned, "why do people still believe in it?"

"People like to believe in the mystical, and magical. Stories about the unknown provide a break from the daily drudgery of life. It provides stimulation for thoughts, and discussions."

"I'd call it gossip, and rumors."

"Whichever. It's part of mankind's existence."

"Is it the reason why all documents have blacked out text?" Danielle asked.

"That's the reason. But people still won't accept the facts. Ultimately, Project Blue Book stated that UFOs sightings were generated as a result of:

A mild form of mass hysteria

Psychopathological prone

Misidentification of various conventional objects

Individuals who fabricate such reports to perpetrate a hoax or seek publicity."

When researchers, and investigators request information, and data on specific cases through FOIA, most times, much of the text is heavily redacted, (censored). According to the CIA's library:[68] This collection cataloged CIA information on subjects from the 1940s through the early 1990s. Most of the documents concerned CIA cables reporting unsubstantiated UFO sightings in the foreign press, and intra-Agency memos about how the Agency handle public inquiries about UFO sightings.

"So," Danielle hinted, still doubtful about my explanations. "There is no concrete proof?"

"But there is," I insisted, with an unshaken conviction.

---

[68] For the most recent CIA information on UFOs, see the article "CIA's Role in the Study of UFOs, 1947-90" at the Center for the Study of Intelligence website:
   https://www.cia.gov/library/center-for-the-study-of-Intelligence/index.html

Articles can be located in On-line Publications under the "Studies in Intelligence" section, specifically semi-annual Edition #1, 1997. Among the numerous documents found in the vast UFO archives of the Central Intelligence Agency, there are a number of sinister-looking images of mysterious unidentified flying objects, and very detailed reports of sightings all around the planet. The CIA claims: "We've decided to highlight a few documents both skeptics, and believers will find interesting." One report says: "Less than 100 reasonably credible reports remain 'unexplainable' at this time. It is recommended that CIA surveillance is continued. It is strongly urged, however, that no reports of CIA interest or concern reach the press or public."

The official link from the FBI vault can be found here:
   http://vault.fbi.gov/UFO/UFO%20Part%201%20of%2016/view

"I am dying to hear. After all, it's the reason for my visit."

"You will understand after I'll explain the facts."

"It seems," Danielle agreed, "that the UFO issue is getting more confusing by the decade."

"Well," I said, clarifying the issue. "Everybody has an agenda. The government in not exempted. Let me give you a couple examples. It will help you understand."

"By the time Project Blue Book ended, it had collected 12,618 UFO reports, and concluded that most of them were misidentifications of natural phenomena clouds, stars, or conventional aircraft. According to the National Reconnaissance Office (NRO), back then the most secretive agency, a number of the reports could be explained by flights of the formerly secret reconnaissance planes U-2, and A-12. Though a small percentage of UFO reports were classified as unexplained, even after stringent analysis, the UFO reports were archived, and available under the Freedom of Information Act, but with names, and other personal information of all witnesses removed."

"Why is that? What's the purpose?" Danielle, as many others have questioned before, was no different when things went against logic.

"The next example, as it was published in the news, will explain."

"Interestingly," I went on to explain. "In recent years, a number of governmental agencies have come out of the dark, and disclosed a number of images, and documents which directly imply that our civilization isn't the only one in the known universe. According to a report from the Federal Bureau of Investigations, "our planet has even been visited by 'beings' that belong to another dimension."

"What?" She exclaimed with doubts. "How can anybody trust the government?"

"Now you see the conflict public has to deal with. It gets worse," I proclaimed, promising even more. "For instance: A special agent of the FBI, a lieutenant colonel whose identity remains anonymous because of 'national security,' gathered data on the UFO subject after interviewing, and studying the phenomena for years. According to reports, and 'Declassified' documents," he claimed, "we have been visited by a number of extraterrestrial species, some of these are not only from other planets, but from other dimensions. Some of these beings originate from an ethereal plane coexistent with our physical universe. These 'entities', which could 'materialize' on our planet appeared as giant translucent figures."

"It reads like something out of science fiction."

"I agree," I said.

It seems we have entered a new era where governmental agencies simply cannot suppress their studies, and 'classified' documents about Alien Life, and the UFO phenomenon any longer. While most of us still approach some of these sightings, and reports with a degree of skepticism, that some of them are anything but ordinary, it will take an open mind to fully understand what the reports of the CIA, and FBI are really describing.

"Dad. What is it? Deception? Disinformation?"

"Both," I said. There was so much doubt written in her face, I had to tell her the truth. "In recent years," I explained. "Many credible people, and agencies have come forward with claims of UFO sightings, such as famous astronauts, professors, and even scientists, who you would think are working against their own principles, proof. But there is a catch most people miss."

"What do you mean," Danielle said, pondering what may sound like doubletalk.

"Reading journals, and reports on the subject," I continued, "there is one element missing."

"You are killing me with suspense," she complained. It became apparent, she had become impatient with my delivery, but in my defense, it was necessary to have her full attention. Where I was tuned into subjects of UFOs, most people, including her were kept in the dark. That had to stop, if only for the benefit of my daughters, but more importantly, for keeping my own sanity.

"Aliens," I almost whispered. It was enough to cause the expected reaction.

"Dad," she complained, in an accusingly tone of voice. "I thought it's what we've talked about all along. Are you leading me on?"

"Not at all. I am dead serious."

"Then, you better explain."

"When I ask you the question," I proposed. "Do you believe in UFOs? What comes to your mind?"

"Flying objects, and extraterrestrials."

"Right," I agreed. "Most people will. But this is where the problem comes into play."

"What problem?"

"They are two different things."

"What?" Immediately, I detected astonishment in her face.

"Let me explain. No government official, and scientist in their right minds would admit to the Phenomena, as it's called in recent years. Where Aliens, and UFOs used to be one subject matter for many decades, in today's world, it had turned into a Phenomenon, but with distinct differences. Where Alien is still a subject of extraterrestrials, UFOs have become earthly objects, and it is this separation that separates fact from fiction."

"I'm beginning to understand," Danielle said, still somewhat doubtful, but beginning to realize facts. "What you are saying," she volunteered. "Government, and Science came up with a solution both worlds would accept, that of mainstream media, and people."

"Informed people," I insisted.

"I'm informed," she objected.

"I'm talking about UFO, and Alien education."

"Then," she pondered. "When the government is backed into a corner by the media or people, they have a way out without compromising themselves."

"That's it. Now you understand."

"How did you come up with the answer?"

"Because I always knew. Remember," I reminded her. "I was on the software development team."

"How do you know your theory is correct?"

"By the complete lack of evidence. There has never been one shred of evidence about Alien visits to earth."

"What about UFOs?"

"Plenty of evidence."

"You mean nightly sightings?"

"Yes. Night, and day, but crashes as well. All kinds of crashes. Burnt space vehicles, space junk reentries, experimental craft, balloons, Chinese lanterns, searchlights from helicopters, aircraft landing lights approach, and many more dubious, and nonconvention objects, and if not, disinformation."

"Disinformation?"

"Disinformation to confuse the unsuspecting citizens."

"Why does anyone want to confuse us?"

"Self-interest."

"But that's completely unethical, isn't it?"

"You have to understand the way government, and politics work. They are tired of begging congress each year for more, and more funding. The public is getting wise to the ever-increasing budget deficit."

"I've been meaning to ask about that," Danielle said, breaking her patience to only listening. "It's in the trillions?"

"In excess of $21,000,000,000.000. The numbers are staggering."

"I can't even comprehend."

"Nobody can. Not even federals, who issue funds."

"How will the budget ever be balanced?"

"Never. The whole world is doing it. Other than world currency collapse, or direct war, there is no means ever getting out from being buried."

I could see fear in her face as I've seen many times before when discussing the subject of war. Though, living in the U.S., our generation never had to defend borders from direct onslaught by an enemy, many could imagine the trauma associated with such an attack, if only from watching movies. But, being caught in the middle of turmoil defending family, and home, is a completely different affair.

"But nobody is talking," Danielle objected. I knew the reference she made about our soldiers returning from the battle fields completely frustrated about the complacency back home. It's the major reason so many are taking to drugs, and alcohol. It's one way to dismiss, and forget the lack of interest. Sure, there is local media coverage from homecomings, welcoming returning soldiers, but it's where interest stops. For those who had never been on the frontlines, it is understandable. The spheres of fighting a distant war, and being at home are quite different, too far apart to envision, and completely understand.

THE PROOF

"Let's get back to the topic at hand," I suggested. I felt that I had drifted too far. There was one crucial factor I felt I still had to share with her.

"Proof?" She understood.

"The lack of it," I said. "It's the lack of proof from an Alien visit all around that should indicate that all is fabricated, make-believe."

"What about reengineered alien advancements, and such claims?"

"Untrue claims. It's all our inventors, scientists, and engineers at work.

"What about whistleblowers claims?"

"The worst form of misinformation."

"You mean disinformation?"

"Both. One is premeditated, the other is deliberate. Either one is unacceptable, and should be punished."

"Kind of drastic measures," she proclaimed. "Aren't they?"

"Depends of your perception if you'd like to have life based on reality or folklore."

"Now I am clear. I completely understand your point."

"Do you?" To my frustrations, I've heard similar responses before. "I want to hear you."

"There are no Aliens among us, but UFOs are for real."

"Now you are talking my language," I stated, proud to have one victim convinced enough to accept reality.

"And now I know."

"I feel compelled to clarify one point," I said, once more disrupting her sanity, hopefully for the last time. "Are we alone in the universe?"

"Dad, please." Again, instant doubt crept into her face. "No more confusion."

"It's an important one," I insisted. Since there was no response I continued. "Don't close your mind against discoveries. Disregard rumors, but follow science. We have not even begun exploring Galaxies, and the Universe."

"What about archaeological findings?"

"All earthly discoveries. No exceptions."

"You sure?"

"What have we been talking about the past hours?"

"I forgot. I have to get used to reality, but I need some time."

"I understand. Most people do after I lay out the facts."

"How come," she said. "Nobody is talking about it?"

"They are. There are many concerned citizens, but keep quiet."

"Ridicule?"

"Exactly. Nobody wants to make a fool out of themselves. The ones that do, you don't hear about it."

"Which ones?"

"Folks that live by radio. Nightly talk radio shows that address the very issues we talked about."

"I had no idea."

"You have to live the night when others are asleep."

"Like yourself?"

"Among all the others plagued by insomnia."

"How can you cope with it?"

"Tolerance, and submission to sleeplessness."

"You ever take sleeping pills?"

"Never. I tried a couple of times, but side effects are too damaging."

"All of them?"

"Every one of them. If not side effects, then addictions."

"Opioids?"

"Exactly. It's what's been in the news lately. It's what the government is trying to change."

"What about the ones that need it. You know, for chronic pain?"

"Those are the ones that deserve it. But you don't hear their complaints. It's the addicts that keep bitching."

"You are not very sympathetic," Danielle claimed. It made me wonder about her habits, and I said so, "You on drugs?"

"God no," she proclaimed. "But they are people too."

"I understand. I also understand that addictions, no matter whether drugs or alcohol, are plagues to society.

"But everybody is doing it," she objected, justifying the needs to relax.

"That's the problem. The ones giving recreation a bad name are addicts. It's addicts that cause problems. All you have to do is follow crime."

"Why only crime?"

"Where do you think the young get the money?"

"Working."

"Not a chance. Maybe a small percentage. But addiction is not curbed to one level. Dosages need to be increased to achieve the same level of euphoria. Besides, there comes a point of no return, and it's this point that causes all the crime. People at this level cannot keep a job. The only thing on their mind is 'where to get the next fix.'"

"How do you know?" The question made sense. I realized that I may have overstepped my boundaries. I had to curb my conviction on the subject, and stated so.

"I managed many teams in my lifetime, mostly young recruits. Most were straight, and dependent individuals I could rely, on and off the job. It did not hold true with habitual drug and alcohol users. But enough on the subject."

"I agree. I need a break. How about a drink?" she said, accompanied by a sheepish grin with pun on the addiction.

"I could use one." It signaled the end of my education on Aliens, and UFOs. It wasn't completely, by no means. We had numerous follow-on talks about the subject, but most were additional clarifications on specifics. There is already too much confusion instilled on society to readily accept reality. Some will believe while others insist on minds already made up. I did not blame the individual. I blamed the system. A system not easily accepted by the truth seekers.

In retrospect, one had to respect ideas, and suggestions hinted by the acclaimed notoriety. As an example, as the great Carl Sagan once stated, "Extraordinary claims require extraordinary evidence, and it might just be that documented data are, in fact, the extraordinary pieces of evidence we have been waiting for since the first UFOs in modern times were reported. One thing is sure, it is very unlikely that we are the only intelligent beings inhabiting the universe."

Where such claims are prolific, even substantiated by members of science, proof still has to be discovered. It is the primary reason why governments, and private organizations initiate space exploration, searching for life on other planets, galaxies, and the Universe.

The reading audience could deduct from the preceding dialogue with my daughter that Intel agencies were getting weary of responding to the increase in public requests for information. No matter what responses the public receives from the various organizations, nothing satisfies the conspirators nor will rumors ever stop. Conspirators have been on Earth ever since intelligent life appeared. Thus, the struggle to seek the truth will continue from one generation to the next.

What deepens public suspicion even further are the occasional whistle blowers coming forward to tell the so-called truth, supported by doomsday mongers always ready for self-glorification. Many of the conspirators read an idea someone puts on the Internet, claim ownership, and propagate it further, only to cause more confusion, disorientation, and bewilderment amid the population.

Conspiracies will prevail, and go on as always as they have through the ages. I cannot completely blame them for what, in their minds, was important. Where I had distanced myself from reading such materials, I must agree to the facts that life without the myth would be pure boredom for the conspirators, and doomsday mongers. I may write about fiction, but I don't read materials other than historical accounts, and documentaries. Though I have created accounts with a number of websites, I do not follow Facebook, Twitter, or other social media communities. I just don't have the interest, or the time it takes to enjoy the various public entertainment platforms.

The reason to the above illustrated confusion is not limited to the government, defense department, and national defense agencies, but encouraged, and propagated in the dissemination of UFO reports for serving their own interests, "to cloud experimental technologies, and black projects."

When asked, "Who should carry the blame for such confusion?"

"Nobody is to take blame," I would suggest.

For the benefit of the government, conspiracies serve to confuse enemies, hostile nations, and radical extremists from assessing current, and "Free World" technology conditions. For the public benefit, the contradictory stories serve as justified disinformation to keep the general citizen ignorant of national budget spending. From the national security perspective, the dissemination of misleading information serves to protect the country's wealth, and prevent harm to the citizens from ill-minded nations. They are all sound justifications.

"Then," Danielle remarked. "What the public wants and demands does not matter?"

"Right. It doesn't matter. Not in this political environment. Hell," I underscored my point. "Just watch political issues on the news to get the idea."

Confusing the issue even further, in past times, some presidential elects running for office promised the public to disclose Alien secrets once elected. They were empty promises mostly to obtain votes from a large conspiracy constituency of 15 million plus voters. The public plays right into the hands of the politicians to suit their agendas. Presidents, once elected, are briefed about the true presence of UFOs, and Aliens, but also informed that both are not of extraterrestrial nature. No president or government official would put themselves into a compromising position. It could mean the end of the career, or worse yet, possible impeachment. At the end, the means of all the confusion is justified.

"Is it?" Danielle understood well.

"Hardly," I muttered, answering her question. I realize now, after reading many books, and reports published by credible researchers, and authors, that prolifically publicized events are impossible to be erased from public access, and whatever is anchored in their minds. I would easily have fallen prey with the same flaws. Where I differ is spending much time in researching archived materials. While there is too much data, and information for any one individual to read, and analyze, I take the liberty of using consolidated researched materials as my baseline for establishing credible proof. I read, and evaluate events from many witnesses claimed as factual, interviewed over a period of 75 years, as documented proof, to only extract information that makes sense from a realistic perspective. I can see from my investigations where all of the confusion comes into play. There are two major reasons for it. One, people's memories fade with the passage of time, and two, many seek fame and notoriety for themselves, an escape from the daily drudgeries of life. It's also the reason why we read books, and watch TV shows.

The result, no matter how enthusiastic I may feel about writing this book, intended to present my life, as factual as I could recall through a promised biography to my daughters, I presented much material to the reader to make up their own minds about UFO, and Alien issues. Unless one was there to witness in person when the events occurred, most stories depend on the interpretation of other individuals.

One important fact to remember:

- Proof is the "Lack of Evidence." In other words, there is NO evidence.
- No evidence is the "Lack of Proof." The problem herein lies in "cause without proof or evidence," which is not obvious with all of the confusion created through deception over the past 75 plus years.

In the case of UFOs, and Aliens, no matter what the personal opinion may be, an event witnessed by one individual passed on to the next, the next, and on, may easily turn into rumor, folklore, legend, and the mystical, in time, subjected to tales of long ago, even though there is no evidence, or complete lack of proof. I can fully understand enthusiasms people display on such events, but when it comes to present visual evidence, I may be different. From my long-time contracting work with the DOD, system analysis work, and monitoring effort over thirty years, nothing but sound evidence, and proof is accepted by organizations, and agencies paying for my work. In contrast to my personal policy, in the make-believe world of script writers, and Hollywood producers, everything is possible, and presented as evidence, and proof, called Science Fiction.

While I do not enjoy Sci-Fi personally, for the general public, it is a major part of the insatiable desire for more, and more action it desires. For this reason, I hope that my purpose for writing "Full Disclosure" does not destroy the desire for the individual seeking pleasure in well researched documentaries, intuitive movie productions, and imaginative Sci-Fi actions. Whether factual or inspirational, there is sound entertainment for everybody. I hope that with this book I managed to "set the record straight," if only for the realistic minded individual.

Danielle's visit was an eye opener for me. Not only for her personality, and social standing, but personal issues as well. I had no idea that she had the intellect to follow what I present, as did my other two daughters. I was glad, and proud at the knowledge, and understanding they had acquired. Hopefully, I thought with anticipation, they will stay connected with me. I haven't had a social bond for many years, let alone the family. That brought up the question, "Why?"

I have no answer, but am set to find out. I wanted to get to the cause for, why I thought self-imposed isolation. Perhaps, I contemplated in the solitude of my home, it's not the lack of social interaction, it could be me. It could be my personality that shied people away. There was one way to find out. I would put my buddy, the person close to me, to the test.

I planned to give him a call.

A CASE FOR NATIONAL DEFENSE

No matter how I twist, and turn it, taking such drastic steps as "Full Disclosure," will certainly cause some disturbance within the Defense, and Intelligence communities. It is not so much about the disclosure itself, since there is no evidence to expose, and secrets to reveal. As I have stated already, the proof is in the lack of evidence. For me, it did not present a problem with infringing on national secrets, since there is no data, and information, but to others, perhaps the government, it may be an infringement on their political agenda. I considered all possible alternatives, but could not come up with a violation to national security breach, and here is why.

To understand defense posture, I will present the most recent publication, *Summary of the 2018 National Defense Strategy,* released by the Defense Department on the direction of their initiative with respect to protecting the country. The report, fourteen pages in lengths, may be excessive information to some. For this reason, I will cite a few short paragraphs from each critical section. The full report can be viewed on following Internet link:

https://dod.defense.gov/Portals/1/Documents/pubs/2018-National-Defense-Strategy-Summary.pdf

STRATEGIC ENVIRONMENT
"The National Defense Strategy acknowledges an increasingly complex global security environment, characterized by overt challenges to the free, and open international order, and the re-emergence of long-term, strategic competition between nations. These changes require a clear-eyed appraisal of the threats we face, acknowledgement of the changing character of warfare, and a transformation of how the Department conducts business."

"The central challenge to U.S. prosperity, and security is the reemergence of long-term, strategic competition by what the National Security Strategy classifies as revisionist powers. It is increasingly clear that China, and Russia want to shape a world consistent with their authoritarian model—gaining veto authority over other nations' economic, diplomatic, and security decisions.
China is leveraging military modernization, influence operations, and predatory economics to coerce neighboring countries to reorder the Indo-Pacific region to their advantage. As China continues its economic, and military ascendance, asserting power through an all-of-nation long-term strategy, it will continue to pursue a military modernization program that seeks Indo-Pacific regional hegemony in the near-term, and displacement of the United States to achieve global preeminence in the future. The most far-reaching objective of this defense strategy is to set the military relationship between our two countries on a path of transparency, and non-aggression."

"Concurrently, Russia seeks veto authority over nations on its periphery in terms of their governmental, economic, and diplomatic decisions, to shatter the North Atlantic Treaty Organization, and change European, and Middle East security, and economic structures to its favor. The use of emerging technologies to discredit, and subvert democratic processes in Georgia, Crimea, and eastern Ukraine is concern enough, but when coupled with its expanding, and modernizing nuclear arsenal the challenge is clear. Another change to the strategic environment is a resilient, but weakening, post-WWII international order. In the decades after fascism's defeat in World War II, the United States, and its allies, and partners constructed a free, and open international order to better safeguard their liberty, and people from aggression, and coercion. Although this system has evolved since the end of the Cold War, our network of alliances, and partnerships remain the backbone of global security. China, and Russia are now undermining the international order from within the system by exploiting its benefits while simultaneously undercutting its principles, and "rules of the road."

"Rogue regimes such as North Korea, and Iran are destabilizing regions through their pursuit of nuclear weapons or sponsorship of terrorism. North Korea seeks to guarantee regime survival, and increased leverage by seeking a mixture of nuclear, biological, chemical, conventional, and unconventional weapons, and a growing ballistic missile capability to gain coercive influence over South Korea, Japan, and the United States. In the Middle East, Iran is competing with its neighbors, asserting an arc of influence, and instability while vying for regional hegemony, using state-sponsored terrorist activities, a growing network of proxies, and its missile program to achieve its objectives. Both revisionist powers, and rogue regimes are competing across all dimensions of power. They have increased efforts short of armed conflict by expanding coercion to new fronts, violating principles of sovereignty, exploiting ambiguity, and deliberately blurring the lines between civil, and military"

DEPARTMENT OF DEFENSE OBJECTIVES

"In support of the National Security Strategy, the Department of Defense will be prepared to defend the homeland, remain the preeminent military power in the world, ensure the balances of power remain in our favor, and advance an international order that is most conducive to our security, and prosperity. Long-term strategic competitions with China, and Russia are the principal priorities for the Department, and require both increased, and sustained investment, because of the magnitude of the threats they pose to U.S. security, and prosperity today, and the potential for those threats to increase in the future. Concurrently, the Department will sustain its efforts to deter, and counter rogue regimes such as North Korea, and Iran, defeat terrorist threats to the United States, and consolidate our gains in Iraq, and Afghanistan while moving to a more resource-sustainable approach. Defense objectives include:

- Defending the homeland from attack;
- Sustaining Joint Force military advantages, both globally, and in key regions;
- Deterring adversaries from aggression against our vital interests;
- Enabling U.S. interagency counterparts to advance U.S. influence, and interests;
- Maintaining favorable regional balances of power in the Indo-Pacific, Europe, the Middle East, and the Western Hemisphere;
- Defending allies from military aggression, and bolstering partners against coercion, and fairly sharing responsibilities for common defense;
- Dissuading, preventing, or deterring state adversaries, and non-state actors from acquiring, proliferating, or using weapons of mass destruction;

- Preventing terrorists from directing or supporting external operations against the United States homeland, and our citizens, allies, and partners overseas;
- Ensuring common domains remain open, and free;
- Continuously delivering performance with affordability, and speed as we change Departmental mindset, culture, and management systems; and
- Establishing an unmatched twenty-first century National Security Innovation Base that effectively supports Department operations, and sustains security, and solvency."

STRATEGIC APPROACH

A long-term strategic competition requires the seamless integration of multiple elements of national power—diplomacy, information, economics, finance, Intelligence, law enforcement, and military. More than any other nation, America can expand the competitive space, seizing the initiative to challenge our competitors where we possess advantages, and they lack strength. A more lethal force, strong alliances, and partnerships, American technological innovation, as we expand the competitive space, we continue to offer competitors, and adversaries an outstretched hand, open to opportunities for cooperation but from a position of strength, and based on our national interests. Should cooperation fail, we will be ready to defend the American people, our values, and interests. The willingness of rivals to abandon aggression will depend on their perception of U.S. strength, and the vitality of our alliances, and partnerships.

Build a More Lethal Force

The surest way to prevent war is to be prepared to win one. Doing so requires a competitive approach to force development, and a consistent, multiyear investment to restore warfighting readiness, and field a lethal force. The size of our force matters. The Nation must field sufficient, capable forces to defeat enemies, and achieve sustainable outcomes that protect the American people, and our vital interests. Our aim is a Joint Force that possesses decisive advantages for any likely conflict, while remaining proficient across the entire spectrum of conflict.

Modernize key capabilities.

We cannot expect success fighting tomorrow's conflicts with yesterday's weapons or equipment. To address the scope, and pace of our competitors', and adversaries' ambitions, and capabilities, we must invest in modernization of key capabilities through sustained, predictable budgets. Our backlog of deferred readiness, procurement, and modernization requirements has grown in the last decade, and a half, and can no longer be ignored. We will make targeted, disciplined increases in personnel, and platforms to meet key capability, and capacity needs. The 2018 National Defense Strategy underpins our planned fiscal year 2019-2023 budgets, accelerating our modernization programs, and devoting additional resources in a sustained effort to solidify our competitive advantage.

Nuclear forces.

The Department will modernize the nuclear triad—including nuclear command, control, and communications, and supporting infrastructure. Modernization of the nuclear force includes developing options to counter competitors' coercive strategies, predicated on the threatened use of nuclear or strategic non-nuclear attacks.

Space, and cyberspace as warfighting domains.
The Department will prioritize investments in resilience, reconstitution, and operations to assure our space capabilities. We will also invest in cyber defense, resilience, and the continued integration of cyber capabilities into the full spectrum of military operations.

Command, control, communications, computers, and Intelligence, surveillance, and reconnaissance (C4ISR).
Investments will prioritize developing resilient, survivable, federated networks, and information ecosystems from the tactical level up to strategic planning. Investments will also prioritize capabilities to gain, and exploit information, deny competitors those same advantages, and enable us to provide attribution while defending against, and holding accountable state or non-state actors during cyberattacks"

Missile defense.
Investments will focus on layered missile defenses, and disruptive capabilities for both theater missile threats, and North Korean ballistic missile threats.

Cyber Warfare
Cyberwarfare is the 5th battle field in future wars, integrated throughout all military services in Army, Navy, Air force, Intelligence, DOD, perpetually practiced by intrusion exercises by/for Superpower cyber defense barriers. Penetration and bombing are commonly practiced by Superpowers to penetrate each other's cyber defenses 24/7, daily, exerting pressure on many nations. The country needs many more cyber warriors to interdict, fend off, and retaliate intrusions and hackings. Intrusion perpetuate each other's infrastructures such as Air Transport, Chemical, Construction, Data Processing, Electronics, Finance, Information, Internet, Manufacturing, Medical, Nuclear Plants, Power, Rail, Shipping, Social, Trade, Transit, Transportation, Utilities, and others.

Where the public, on all fronts of current superpower forces may not be aware of an ever-present, political tensions, governments have a completely different perspective on international tensions. Whether it is the lack of media coverage, or other reasons, such as diplomacy of good faiths, true sentiments, and differences in policies between cultures cannot be overstated. Cultural differences reach back to antiquity, when borders were created to protect individual customs, and cultures. Where the general public may not necessarily be aware, governments certainly are. It is this reasoning why the topic of Full Disclosure is so sensitive to governments, especially the western world. It is here where trends are initiated, and promoted, for the sole purpose to gain an edge on technology, and maintain leadership.

To successfully achieve it, confusion, and misperception is used wherever possible. It is confusion that ultimately clouds clear thinking, in turn, propagate cloaking, and concealment even further, all necessary for an effective defense. In plain words, "Let the adversary keep guessing."

Though nations have made great attempts, in recent decades, engaging in international trade, and commerce, from the cultural perspective, and sentiment, borders will prevail to protect national resources, and wealth. It is human nature, that distrust between ethnicity will prevail. But acts of distrust can be carried too far, especially when creating confusion among unsuspecting citizens. It is this distrust that I am trying to defuse with "Full Disclosure."

I have no other motives in mind. I am not seeking fame, nor do I desire fortune. I live by the seal of trust bestowed on me since birth, reinforced by responsibilities granted by the Department of Defense. However, as long as the United States of America maintains its technological lead, we don't have much to fear. The rest of the superpowers, at times, are agitating the free world with threatening behavior, only to flex their muscles. They want to be part of the game being played out, "pioneering unexplored territory, minerals, and resources."

THE PRESENT

Another happy occasion came to an end today, seeing off both Tracy, and Danielle at the airport. The Castle was quiet once more. Pacing the floors, I realized how restless I had become. "What's wrong?" I muttered, analyzing the present. "Company!" I answered my own question. "Wonder what Buzz is up to?"

"Hey," he answered on the second ring. "Haven't heard from you. Been out of town?" He must have expected my call since he had picked up. Though miles apart, at times, we could read each other's mental states many a time. *Telepathy*, I made a mental note as something to research, and study. Among mankind's unexplained mysteries, it was a topic I had been always intrigued with.

"Had company for a couple of weeks. Daughters paid me a visit."

"How's it going?" Buzz said.

"Oh, just hanging out. Want to come over?"

"I could be there in thirty minutes."

"See you when you get here." Though Buzz was married, he was always apt for a get together even on short notice. Sometimes I felt guilty when calling on him. He was a dedicated father, and family man in his own right. Much like myself, a job, or project demanded much of our personal life, and family. Called off on a minute's notice took great understanding from wife, and children. But we both knew the score. We lived on borrowed time. Borrowed mostly from the family.

As stated, thirty minutes later he showed up at the door. "Glad you could come over," I said, inviting him in. "How's the family?"

"Had some visitors of my own," he announced. "Daughter, and her kids were staying for a while."

"Feel like talking? Drink?"

"Beer's fine."

We sat, and briefly chatted, catching up as usual. Presently not working on the same project created an interest for sharing information. A few minutes later I came right out, and to the point for my call.

"Buzz," I said. "How long have we known each other?"

I gathered from his facial expression that my direct approach was somewhat unusual. He sat quietly, and somewhat perplexed for a moment, then said, "What's going on?"

"In all the years working together we never talked about personal things." It was true. I could not recall one instant where we talked about private topics many people shared. Where I thought we knew each other after thirty years, the opposite was true. When the subjects touched on religion, and politics, I knew more about my casual acquaintances than my best buddy. It may have been the sensitivity of the nature in personal views, or just a common respect to maintain individual privacy. I could hold a conversation with almost anybody on any topic, but Buzz maintained a certain distance from getting involved too personally. I was of a different faith, but when it came to politics, I was clueless about his views, and attachment. Today, neither one of those topics I was interested in. Today, I was interested in only one subject, extraterrestrials.

"My youngest daughter paid me a visit."

"Really? I thought you were estranged." He had met her years ago when Annette, and I were still married, and living together.

"Apparently," I enlightened him, "she reached out to be closer. At first, I was surprised but after she got here, we had a great time, especially when Tracy showed up." Buzz was a polite person. He was not prone to interrupt as many people habitually did. He sat quietly to let me continue since I had asked him over. "The main reason for her visit was to get some answers nobody had been able to satisfy."

"Now, you've got my interest."

"Buzz," I opened the dialogue, "have you been following recent news on UFOs, and Aliens?"

I gave him some time to respond. I could see his mind churning with images. It must have been the first time anyone had ever approached him with this subject. I understood. Though we had both worked on sensitive projects touching on this very nature, it was never up for discussion. To satisfy my own curiosity I needed to find out his opinion for "why."

"What are you getting at?" He avoided my challenging stare. I realized he was using reverse psychology, my usual strategy, by putting the responsibility on the other person. It was all right with me.

"I would like your opinion on the subject, and the reasons we never talked about it."

After giving it some thought, he replied, "Everybody has their own opinion on the matter. You have yours. I have mine."

"That's not what I asked. I want to know your own personal disposition. Do you believe they exist, or don't you?" I realized that I put him on the spot, but did not care. Everybody in the know had an opinion on things. He played caution right to the end. It was a tactic we both knew only too well. Never talk about a sensitive nature that might cause you your job, or worse, put you in prison.

"What do you think?" Again, he put the burden on me. So be it.

"I don't think they exist," I boldly stated. There it was, out in the open. I did not think he would ever commit himself to comment. He was not to blame. As far as I remembered, there had never been an occasion anybody on the team, or on a project ever talked about it, or had an opinion. Whether it was a topic off-limits, or for other reasons I probably would never find out. I thought it was up to me to investigate.

"Why do you think that?"

"In all of our careers," I ventured. "There was never an occasion to think otherwise, or was there?" Using my usual strategy, I gracefully dumped the challenge back on him. He only shrugged his shoulders, and waited for me to go on. *Smart Turkey*, I thought, non-committing.

"Okay, buddy. Have it your way. It's up to me now. Right?"

"Right."

"Okay. First question. Have you ever seen, or encountered a UFO or Alien?"

"I've seen strange things, but never had an encounter," Buzz said. I could sense a reluctance for him talking about it. It was exactly what I wanted to find out.

"Have you followed the Alien agenda at all," I probed. "Have you ever wondered why so many people report sightings when you never did?"

"Not necessarily. I don't get much involved with mainstream media. I don't know what to believe anymore. Besides," he said, "they don't cover UFO issues people claim.

"Exactly my point," I agreed, prodding further. "Then, you have no interest?"

"I do, but I don't dwell on it."

"Have you ever wondered why none of us in the community ever talked about the subject?"

"I did," he admitted. "But it's too sensitive a subject to talk about. You should know it." Buzz was true with his assumption.

"Sensitive or not," I said. "Most people have an opinion."

"I don't voice my opinions freely, you know that."

"You have to understand," accepting his position, I explained. "We live in a different world. Our world is one of facts, and reality. But, to understand the public, there is more to it."

"You'll have to explain."

"Okay. I'll give you some facts first, then the reasons."

"What makes you so smart on the topic?"

"I've studied the phenomenon ever since it surfaced many decades ago. Believe me," I said. "I had my doubts until I learned the facts."

"How can you claim to know the facts when the whole world is only guessing?"

"Because of the work we did with Intel."

"I worked in Intel. I didn't see the same facts as you."

"There was a time in the initial days I had access to data you didn't. It was a year before you joined."

"You know," he said, a puzzled look shading his face. "I've been waiting for the day when somebody surfaced with that claim."

"Your waiting days of uncertainties are over," I proclaimed with a grin on my face. "I shall enlighten you in the mysteries of coverups."

"I'm dying to hear." It was the queue I had been waiting. He opened up the gate of silence we had sworn to many years ago. Since we had worked in the same classified environment, carried the same security clearances, with much having been declassified in recent years, we could freely talk among ourselves. After many years of conjectures, and guessing, I felt that I finally had an ally.

"I'll have to give you some background first, I informed him. "Public sentiments prior to the 70s, when asked about UFOs, and ETs, were afraid of extraterrestrials visiting Earth from other planets, and being potentially harmful to mankind. That changed after the 70s. When asked now, the same people are afraid that we might be alone in the universe. Also, with the sentiment change a progression of new unexplained sightings were experienced."

"What do you mean?"

"It was flying saucers in the 50s. UFOs in the 60s through 2000. With millennials, from then to the present, it is unexplained phenomena. You figure it out."

"Nothing makes much sense, does it?" Buzz was as confused as most believers.

"The rationale expressed on both sides of the culture, conspiracy, and of recent science," I offered, "is an unconceivable thought that we are the only species in the vastness of the universe."

"It makes sense," Buzz agreed. "But why the controversy?"

"What makes sense?" I questioned. "Sentiment or species?"

"Species. But why the change in sentiment? Do you know?"

"I sure do. I followed the process. You interested?"

"Sure."

"World populations became educated. Educated not only in science, and technology, but also in astrophysics. We did not have Hubble until the 80s to confirm the expanse of the universe. Besides, people were afraid of many things including demons, devils, the paranormal, supernatural, ghosts, and many more apparitions."

"What made them change?"

"The markets became flooded with books, and literature. Books on ghost hunting, Bigfoot chases, the Loch Ness Monster, Himalayan Yeti, Chupacabra, demons, vampires, werewolves, witches, and zombies inundated the public. The list goes on, and on."

"I was never aware."

"In contrast to some people," I said, "I read everything on bookshelves from biographies to documentaries. It's my nature. My interests span a broad knowledge spectrum."

"But," he protested, "it doesn't explain why all the secrecy."

"I can explain that too."

"I'm dying to hear it."

"How about another beer?" I offered.

"Yes. I think I've earned it just listening to you."

"I know. I get carried away at times, especially when I have someone's ears. But, you," I figured, "you'd understand. We both live in the same environment. One of silence."

"Sometimes I wonder if it's worth it."

"What?"

"A life in silence."

"We both know that it is. We worked national security for many years. Without us, the nation may have already lost its identity, and freedom."

"I just wish that everybody thought so. With all the problems we are facing lately we may have already lost the land. There's too much internal discontent, and unrest."

"I totally agree with you. But there was a reason for our alliance to the government even at the threat of capital punishment. It doesn't matter what the public thinks. We know different. We worked on the inside."

"I wasn't involved with software development." It was true. Buzz, and many others on the team came into the fold afterwards, but it was commonly understood that the UFO question was one mostly of fabrication. Software engineers, and organizational management were the ones who held the facts. Working Intel, and defense database admittances through ten levels of access security, not one mention of Aliens was ever recorded. It was not until Project Blue Book that the government became involved, and acquired custody.

"Remember," I recalled, "back in the early days reports created certain doubts. But in recent years when the topic of UFOs, and Aliens came up, government, and military communities snickered at the thought of unexplained sightings. We all knew that reported objects were of earthly technology invented, designed, and built by humans. It's the reason why there will never be disclosure."

"What about the whistle blowers?"

"Most whistle blowers don't know much. They just want to feel important. Along the same lines, reengineering ET technology, claimed by conspirators, is a slap in the face for every inventor, scientist, and engineer that has ever lived. No matter what is revealed in books, conspiracists will never believe the truth as much as I cannot take any of their so-called facts with credibility. It is much like their claims, 'We never went to the Moon' or 'The earth is flat' or 'Our advancements are reengineered from extraterrestrial technologies.'"

"So," Buzz hinted. "Nothing will ever change. Stories, and tales will prevail."

"It makes for good entertainment."

I have written several books on matters of national defense, and created an unwavering personal credibility. Regardless of my acquired knowledge, conspiracy will prevail, nevertheless, and rightly so. It will keep the uninformed citizen, as well as the unsuspected, conspiracist, prophet, and psychic speculating on an existence open to endless possibilities as to life elsewhere in the universe.

I have done my part. The truth had to be told if only for the benefit of the experts, scientists, inventors, and engineers who dedicate their lives to the cause for the advancement in mankind's quest for universal knowledge, without the benefit in personal gain. Many of the dedicated work double shifts, and overtime and, in the process, sacrifice personal leisure, and quality time with friends, and family for one purpose only, to put creative thoughts on paper for future generations to benefit from. The stated experts selflessly dedicate their time, and lives without expecting any accolades, awards, or compensation for their efforts.

Regardless of UFOs, Aliens, and periodic predictions and prophecies proclaimed by spiritually minded individuals claiming, "The End of the World" or "The Second Coming is Near," it is the selfless dedication of the sober-minded individual that guarantees the survival of mankind.

My final response on the UFO question:

"We can talk and discuss UFOs and ETs, but the topic is not up for debate. Book IV, 'Invisible Warrior / Full Discussion' is based on irrevocable facts:

- There still are one to two dozen individuals alive that can substantiate and validate the facts as illustrated in this book.
- Only a small irresponsible group of people contrive conspiracies to purposely confuse the innocent population for their own indulgence. They have managed not only to confuse the United States of America population about the UFO/Alien agenda, but the rest of the world as well.

My teams and my 30-year career with DOD are based on facts and reality only. There is no time or need for gossip, or to propagate further confusion. The facts are as stated:

- The UFO question never came up because there was no case to discuss
- Newspaper reports were sporadic and subject to conjecture and speculation only

- Individuals involved with the AUTODIN system, a survivable network against direct hit through nuclear blast, where highly intelligent and capable Software and Computer system architects, engineers, and developers
- Us, as well as the general citizens had a different mindset back then
- It was an era of integrity, decency and truth
- People respected each other, their supervisor, coworkers, the Uniform, and Government without question."

UFOs AND ALIENS DEFINED

The reporting, and recording of UFOs has been taking place for millennia, dating back to biblical times. While shapes, and profiles of the sightings may have changed over time, it is still a phenomenon of the unexplained. It was only in recent times that man has developed science to effectively research, and investigate the mysteries of creation not only earthbound, but in the vast spaces of the universe. Science, derived from the Latin, means knowledge. It is knowledge that man's quest is intrinsically linked with. It is a drive most philosophers have pursued through all ages, gaining an understanding in the many disciplines of science. Some quests ended in vain while many succeeded in triumph. Where triumph excelled was in the areas of sub-atomic structure, biological life and organisms, earth science, evolution of species, and mathematics. Every fabric in man's existence has been explored. Many have been answered, but many more questions still remain. Therefore, it is science that man can principally rely on to help in their quest for knowledge. It was true ten thousand years ago; it is still true today, which brings us to the era we live in.

For all practicality, and for the success of scientific research, technological innovation developed alongside science. It is this codependency that assures success. For subjects of the mystical, and unexplained, our tools are still limited to man's acquired knowledge and understanding as it stands today. What the impending future in exploration will hold, the possibilities are endless. For unexplained phenomena, even here we have the tools. Ever since breaking through Earth's confinement of gravity in the 60s, science and technology have kept pace with man's explorations. Satellites went into orbit, scientific probes were sent into deep space, Hubble, Earth's most advanced telescope, was deployed, while on Earth, technology kept pace in radio, laser, microwave, and more sophisticated achievements, all aiding in the quest for man's knowledge. One such sophisticated system is the Allen Telescope Array (ATA) with large number of small dishes designed, and configured to explore, and survey conventional radio astronomy projects under the name of SETI (Search for Extra Terrestrial Intelligence).

Specifically, the purpose for SETI is searching for carrier signals indicative of technology in remote locations. The carrier signal detections would not necessarily contain any of the information transmitted. As such, a detection of a carrier signal would only indicate the presence of technology, but little about the content of the transmission with future developments to explore more complex transmissions of cosmic origins. Current operation of the Allen Telescope Array includes transient, and variable source surveys, pulsar science, spectroscopy of new molecular species, mapping of galactic magnetic filaments and imaging of comets, and other solar system objects. In plain words, extensive research is underway to explore any, and all possibilities to find the existence of species evolved on a habitable planet other than Earth.

To this day, if one believes in science, no such signal has been detected.

"Then," Buzz said, exhibiting his natural curiosity, "how can you explain the supposed Alien visitations?"

"All earthly initiated, and earthbound." As was the case when I had no visitors at the Castle, to break boredom, I had called on my buddy. Today was one such day. We had been tossing ideas around not only on potential projects we could get involved in, but in trying to answer the recent increase in mystical reports on unexplained sightings.

"But," he objected, and rightly so, "not all can be imaginary fabrications?"

"I agree with you." It was up to me now to press on, or to end the conversation on the topic. Personally, while I had my own opinion on it, I could never be sure of the interest, or patience, others had digging into specifics. Since Buzz did not give an indication on leaving, I assumed he was willing to stay to discuss possibilities for a plausible answer. It was still morning, so I offered, "Coffee?"

"Fine."

"Any specifics you want to discuss?" I was glad to have a sounding board to bounce ideas off of. As I normally did, I let the others drive the topic of interest to stimulate their imagination rather than me imposing my own ideas, possibly boring the visitor. I did not mind listening quietly, with brief interjections to let the other know my mind was alert, to what others had to say. Whereas I had observed on many occasions boredom, and drowsiness setting in with individuals who only had a limited knowledge, or intolerance listening to worldly things. I had learned many years ago that people who had no, or little interest in exploring life's mysteries were intolerant in such ideas. In contrast, a worldly traveler such as myself had little interest in local events, whether relatives, or politically oriented. I concluded that the space one lived in also created the sphere of involvement.

"How about where we left off the other day?"

"UFOs?"

"Suits me. I may not have your knowledge on the subject, but I am willing to listen to any solution."

"UFOs it is. By the way, I've been meaning to ask you," I prodded. "You know about the differences in UFOs?"

"What do you mean by differences?"

"There are none. They all are object sightings invented, conceived, and developed by man."

"What about the unexplained?"

"Same, but different," I proclaimed with a hint of a grin on my face.

"Now you are confusing me," he said, shaking his head.

"Let me explain," I offered. "By 'same' I meant earthly initiated image. It could be a distant bird, newly designed stealth craft, research balloon, popular Chinese lantern, but most likely a drone toy, or just an amateur hoax."

"I get your gist." He, since we fully trusted each other, in contrast to others, was satisfied by my explanation. But there was more to the phenomena. "What about spheres, disappearing images, colorful discs, fiery streaks across skies?"

"Same here. It all can be explained, but not only to earthly things, more likely of cosmic origin. Some are meteors, meteoroids, comets, and others are stealth crafts, helicopters, and navigation lighting. The darkness of night hides many images."

"How do you explain colored spheres, apparitions, and visions?"

"Now you are getting into the mystical, and spiritual realms." I had a question for him. "Do you believe in God?"

"What does God have to do with it all?"

"Everything."

"You better explain." He stared at me with a puzzled look. It was a reaction challenge I had seen many times in people. I knew how the subject of religion could affect people. Most of us had deep convictions about beliefs. I found it wise to stay distant from it, but also invited controversies when challenged. While most believers were blindly following one or another faith, for whatever personal reasons, I was open to alternative possibilities based on historical accounts. My personal conviction was linked to documented proof, and scientific research, and not the limitation of man's imagination. That was not to say that man was limited in thinking capability, it was only a small percentage that had the time and means to explore the yet unexplored. It was the future that held most of man's quests for knowledge, and enlightenment. My explanation, though still open ended, satisfied Buzz for the time being.

"What about the abductions?" He touched on an item many had tried to answer, though unsuccessfully. When it came to the sphere of spiritual existence, nobody, not the most brilliant minds, had been able to prove its origin with satisfaction. I was not different. I had to rely on my acquired knowledge as well as intuitive imagination. What I did have was undeniable proof experienced with my own mind.

"All man conceived by an over imaginative mind, vivid dream, or drug, and medically induced."

"Are you sure?" he replied. "Not every involvement can be explained away so simply. Can it?"

"I am not saying that everybody has an imaginative mind. What I am saying is that every instance could be explained in one of the stated means whether it was produced in the individual's mind, or received through spiritual means."

"I think you should explain your idea of spiritual."

"Now you've touched on a subject dear to me." I had researched, and experimented with the secrets of the human mind for many years. Short of clinical experimentation, since my knowledge was mostly based on documented results from institutional research, I had my own spiritual experiences I could not explain.

"I'm interested to hear it."

There had been instances throughout my life where I had witnessed unexplainable events. The first time, I recalled, took place in Pleasanton, CA. My business partner Leon, and I were sitting in front of individual desktop computers on the third floor of an office building. I was facing the window while he faced the interior. All of a sudden, my view was distracted from the Word document I was processing. In the corner of my left eye, from the distance, an object came flying directly towards me from the size of a spot to that of a sizable bird. I watched its shape increase rapidly with closing distance. It entered through the panel window, which were shut tight, without shattering glass, flew across my vision, turned right along the wall, turned right again passing in front of my partner's vision, turned towards the closed window to exit, in the time frame of two second, leaving a trail of sulfuric smelling dust in its wake.

When the object entered, my body reacted by jumping back in my seat while I yelled out, "Watch out!"

I was startled more than stunned when my partner proclaimed, "I've seen it before."

"What do you mean," I practically yelled at him, inspecting the window to be shattered. But there was no indication, not even an impact point from the object.

When I pressed him to explain, all I got out of him was, "I grew up with spiritual entities. They follow me everywhere." Since it was close to lunchtime, we left the office for the courtyard below. As soon as we stepped in the elevator, I sensed the same sulfuric smell inside. "You smell it?" he said.

"I do. What's going on?"

He then explained, "My dad is a minister. It may have something to do with religious practices. We could never figure it out. I suspect its demons chasing me."

I was not used to such spiritual matters. It was beyond my understanding. Of course, I was familiar with Voodoo, Shamanism, and Exorcism, but never gave them much credibility. Since I had experienced it, and witnessed it with my own senses, there was only one explanation that made sense: it was an apparition in the true sense. Since I was fully awake at work, my mind assuredly did not fabricate it.

"What else?" Buzz wanted to know. I think my recount triggered an interest in him since he was a religious person.

Since we had never discussed such topics, I related to him my experiences with psychic predictions on my life years ago. Even though the five years that I had read on my future all came true, I still remained a skeptic, but the ghostly experience in Pleasanton made me a believer that a spiritual world did exist. My problem is, I have absolutely no idea on how to approach this world of mystic, and supernatural phenomena. It was an element, I promised myself, yet to explore.

Along the lines of the supernatural, I imagined, was the mystery of vivid dreams. Reading books on the subject, I certainly had had my share.

"Let me in on it," Buzz requested.

"You heard of Coast-to-Coast AM, haven't you?"

"Not that I recall," he said, reaching for the coffee cup. "What's that?"

I could not believe that anybody in the country hasn't heard about the country's most prolific radio station on the topics of UFOs, Aliens, Crop Circles, Bigfoot, and all the other paranormal experiences. "It's a station that broadcasts nightly."

"I sleep at night," Buzz stated. "Don't you?"

"I don't. It's where I get educated on things mainstream media won't touch."

"I don't blame them," he said, shaking his head. "Who wants to listen to fairytales?"

"People who can't sleep, and it's not only fairytales. The station handles the broad spectrum of daily news, international, and local, scientific and technological achievements, and many more topics."

"I did not know," he admitted. "I'll have to check it out."

"You'll get hooked on it. Your wife won't like you staying up all night. There are many more stations. Not only radio, but conferences, and workshops every month throughout the year on the topics. An entire industry in the paranormal has developed in recent years."

"You ever attend any?" Unsure of my response, whether to believe me or not, he eyed me with suspicion.

"Never have." I was adamant. From the paranormal perspective, I listened to programs offered strictly for entertainment. I knew better.

"Then," he speculated. "You don't believe in any of it?"

"Even if I did," I explained. "I wouldn't. Exhaustive research has been conducted into all Alien cases without coming up with one shred of evidence. I will not fall prey like many followers do. It would defeat my writing on "Full Disclosure.""

Though I never spoke of it I was willing to share. The dreams had begun at about the same time as the increase in Alien encounters. It was also a time when I took some prescribed pain-killer medication for prior accidental injuries. My life had not been a simple one. When I was not active in one of many gyms around the globe, wherever I resided at the time, I explored new sports, and other challenging trades, in the process getting hurt on several occasions. I injured legs, knees, back, shoulders, and the head more than once. On top of that, I was involved in several automobile accidents, and falls on motorbikes, and skis, in addition to assaults on my body.

The sightings occurred while I was taking prescribed medication, specifically Ambien. While the medication proved effective by alleviating pain, it put me into deep sleep for eight hours. It was during those periods that dreams became vivid. I am a rational enough person to realize what was happening which I cannot claim for others for spreading rumors of Alien experiences, and abductions. With the proliferation of opioids in recent years, I am certain that many of the sightings could be explained as drug-induced visions. That still left unanswered questions, such as:

Where did intuition originate?

How about psychic revelations?

Where did knowledge come from?

What came first, individual inspiration or knowledge?

How did one explain the spiritual energy presence across the universe?

My answer would be: ESP is a prerequisite sense to the paranormal, and all psychic phenomena and supernatural like ghosts, apparitions, and spirits. Some minds have the ability to tap into universal events about to happen. Some psychics perceive malicious actions when planned, and conceived by evil doers.

I have asked myself many times, "What about my own intuition?" There had been times in the early phase of my career when traveling abroad. Much of my work had to be conducted somewhere in-, or up-country, away from populated areas, forcing me to stay at second, and third rated hotels. On checking in, I would be aware of a strange feeling, the feel of intuition. It was something new, and unfamiliar to my logically-tuned senses. It took me some time before making the connection between intuition, and gut-feeling. Gut-feeling, I could understand. That had been with me for many years. Intuition, things about to happen, I still have to explore. It was not long after each check-in that I would read news articles about hotels I'd stayed in burning down. In one instance, I woke up in a smoke-filled room, unable to penetrate through the layers of smoke. I had to feel my way to the door, and follow what I perceived to be other guests groping along corridors, and stairways leading to fire exits. At the end, I was thankful to still be alive.

The problem I have is with psychic claims. I can see flaws from claims such as "the future can be changed," and "you chose a different direction." Claims like this do not sit well with this author, and certainly not with science. In my mind, such personal insistence on claims could easily be cured. My solution to such claims is, "send them to a war zone, and let them detect the millions of boobytraps buried to clear the areas." It would be one sure act to separate fake from real. It was these unsubstantiated claims keeping me confused. People are not sure about the reality of things, especially when it comes to sightings.

Sightings are experienced worldwide, and reported, with many linked to local culture and practices. What does that tell you? The visions, as experienced, are linked to the individual's imagination, and mindset. There is something that can be speculated about mass consciousness. At this time, we just do not know enough. While some can be branded imaginary, many visions can be explained.

Since Buzz kept prodding for explanations, I will try to clarify some of the sightings. It should also serve the public to set their minds somewhat at ease whether I am convincing enough or not to reach the reader.

I hear the following question all the time: "Are UFOs for real?"

One has to define UFO for a better understanding. There are two sides to it, and neither is telling the truth. One side are the whistleblowers, and on the other, the government. As already stated, the so-called expert witnesses on the subject were guessing much like the rest of the population. They just did not know. One may have been assigned to a super-secret installation somewhere in the desert, and may have seen some strange designs, or materials being fabricated for a classified project, and not knowing the final product, assumed they'd seen something resembling a flying saucer. There are many ideas on blueprints. Most are designed for military purposes with some for cyberspace defense, and a few for space exploration. It is where the government was not telling the truth. As I have stated before, "it is not so much as to hide something from the public as to keep a technology advantage over adversaries." An adversary could be any ideology, a hostile nation, or terrorist faction fighting for freedom, a squadron on the warpath to expand borders, or a faction vying for world dominance.

Mankind cannot be completely trusted no matter what the aim, honorable or ill intended. Much depends on the culture's leadership. Over time, ethics change, and so do religious practices, lifestyles, and beliefs. While there might have been good intentions at a given time, greed, and personal ambition seem to get in between success, and prosperity.

Let's consider some of the UFO reports. I won't go into the topics of ET and abductions since I already presented my knowledge on them. Unfortunately for the naive, and trusting, UFOs have been associated with extraterrestrial life since the beginning of time. But who could blame anybody? It was a natural assumption to make the connection since the knowledgeable would not come forward to explain the facts.

Since I have already addressed strange landings in previous chapters, I will cite a few of the more highly controversial cases. The following accounts, through analysis, may be boring to some readers, but are necessary to get my point across. Don't believe everything you hear on the news. Use your own judgement. The world is full of deception in the name of self-interest.

SAMPLE CASE ANALYSES

CASE #1 – UFO CRASH
Roswell Incident
July 2, 1947
Roswell, New Mexico

The Roswell Incident case, to this day, is the most prominent, and is still talked about. What made it so popular was the way the reporting was handled, with a cover-up story the following day carried around the world. It was first sighted, and reported by the news media as a weather balloon that quickly changed when the government stepped in, cloaking a highly-classified U.S. Army/Air Force project designated "Project Mogul."

Project Mogul was a top-secret project by the U.S. Armed Forces involving microphones flown on high-altitude balloons, whose primary purpose was long-distance detection of sound waves generated by Soviet atomic bomb tests. Lasting from 1947 until early 1949, the project was moderately successful but also very expensive, and quickly superseded by a network of airborne, seismic detectors, and air sampling for nuclear fallout, which were cheaper, more reliable, and easier to deploy, and operate.

Project Mogul was conceived by Maurice Ewing, who had earlier researched the deep sound channel in the oceans, and theorized that a similar sound channel existed in the upper atmosphere: a certain height where the air pressure, and temperature resulted in minimal speed of sound, so that sound waves would propagate, and stay within that layer due to refraction. The project involved arrays of balloons carrying disc microphones, and radio transmitters to relay the signals to the ground.

One of the requirements of the balloons was that they maintain a relatively constant altitude over a prolonged period of time. Thus, instrumentation had to be developed to maintain such constant altitudes, such as pressure sensors controlling the release of ballast.

The early Mogul balloons consisted of large clusters of rubber meteorological balloons; however, these were quickly replaced by enormous balloons made of polyethylene plastic. These were more durable, leaked less helium, and also were better at maintaining a constant altitude than the early rubber balloons. Consistent altitude control, and polyethylene balloons were the two major innovations of Project Mogul.

The event took place during the first week of July 1947, and involved the recovery of wreckage by the military from a remote ranch northwest of Roswell, New Mexico. To cloak the true reasons, there was now considerable testimony from former members of the military known to have been involved, including two brigadier generals, who stated that the recovered material was not of terrestrial origin. Admittedly, such a claim taxed the limits of credibility for discerning, and rational individuals. It also tended to evoke a response of immediate dismissal. The preponderance of evidence, however, indicated the event occurred.

A rancher named Mac Brazel discovered strange metal strewn across a wide area of range land he tended. Because of the material's unusual characteristics, Brazel took pieces of the debris to the authorities in Roswell, New Mexico. Intrigued by the debris, Colonel Blanchard, commanding officer at Roswell Army Air Field, ordered two Intelligence officers to investigate. Roswell Army Air Field was the home of the 509th Bomb Group, which was an elite outfit for the only atomic action group in the world. The two officers Col. Blanchard sent to the crash site were Major Jesse Marcel, and Captain Sheridan Cavitt. Upon their report, Colonel Blanchard quietly ordered that the ranch area be cordoned off. Soldiers removed the debris, sending it to Army headquarters in Fort Worth, Texas. Lt. Walter Haut was the Public Information Officer at Roswell AAF. Within hours something had happened, and the press release was retracted, and further press coverage restricted.

The late General Thomas DuBose was a colonel, and General Ramey's chief of staff at Eighth Air Force Headquarters in Fort Worth, Texas, in 1947. Before his death in 1992, General DuBose testified that he himself had taken the telephone call from General Clements McMullen at Andrews Army Air Field in Washington, D.C., ordering the cover-up. The instructions were for General Ramey to concoct a "cover story" to "get the press off our backs."

At a press conference in Fort Worth, the Army explained that the Intelligence officer, and others at Roswell had misidentified the debris, which was, in fact, the remains of a downed balloon with a metallic radar reflector attached, and not a flying saucer. When announced, public interest quickly faded, and the Roswell event became a part of UFO folklore, with most Ufologists accepting the official government version of the story.

It was not until the late 1970s, with Jesse Marcel's decision to comment publicly on the strange material, and other aspects of the Roswell event, that the UFO crash story was revived. Since that time, new evidence indicates the weather balloon explanation was part of an elaborate government cover-up, and, in fact, the original report of a recovered flying disk was probably true. Investigations into the UFO crash story continue to this day with the goal of pressuring the United States government to end the cover-up, and to reveal to the American public what actually crashed on the New Mexican desert that night in July 1947.

For instance, publicity reports that followed the revival did not help in clarifying the situation: Fran Ridge (Reporting) - July 2, 1947; Roswell, New Mexico:

"I have always held that something extremely unusual happened at Roswell, something that was recognized as such by people in the know in July of 1947. I cannot believe for one minute that this was a balloon or cluster of balloons. A five-year-old may have wondered what the alleged balloons were used for, but would not have mistaken the materials, all off-the-shelf items of the day. There is a lot more to the story than I can mention at present, but the NICAP site will provide the reader with all the material, and links that are worth mentioning, and possible to list at this time."

A detailed report for this section is available in Appendix D-1.

POST ANALYSIS

The Roswell Incident was the first UFO incident extensively publicized after the contemporary UFO phenomena started in 1938, at the onset of WWII, initially shocking the public to its very foundation. But the shock effect was short lived once Orson Wells, playwright for the 1938 radio scare "War of the Worlds," released a statement that it was only a radio play. However, it left many of the public doubtful, and confused about the subject of UFOs until the 70s when investigative reporters began to research the once dormant phenomena. It did not take long for writers, and novelists to pick up the mystery surrounding past UFO reports. It had been few isolated cases, but FOIA researchers brought the phenomena into new light, creating an entirely new culture of Ufologists.

CASE #2 – UFO SIGHTING AT MISSILE BASE
Disc Hovers 500' Over Missile Silos
March 5, 1967
Minot AFB, North Dakota

Richard Hall Reporting:
"On March 5, 1967, Air Defense Command radar tracked an unidentified target descending over the Minuteman missile silos of the 91st Strategic Missile Wing at Minot AFB, ND. Base security teams quickly converged on the area, and saw a metallic, disc-shaped craft ringed with bright, flashing lights moving slowly. The disc stopped, and hovered about 500 feet (150 meters) off the ground, as security police held their fire, and watched in awe. Suddenly the object began moving again, and circled directly over the launch control facility. F-106 fighter-interceptors were standing by on the flight line, waiting impatiently for an order from NORAD to scramble. When the order was not forthcoming, base operations decided on their own to scramble the interceptors. At that moment the UFO climbed straight up, and streaked away at incredible speed."

Ray Fowler Reporting:
"On March 5, 1967, just 15 days prior to the Malmstrom AFB incident, the 91st Strategic Missile Wing at a sister base also had an unwelcome visitor. Aerospace Defense Command radar tracked an unknown target descending over the Minuteman missile installations at Minot AFB, North Dakota. Strike teams were alerted, and sighted a metallic disc-shaped craft ringed with bright flashing lights moving slowly over the supersensitive area.

"A civilian employee at Malmstrom told me a bright, round, white object circled the missile site for prolonged periods on April 10, and 11, 1967. Apparently, its altitude was beyond the operational capabilities of Air Force interceptors. Personnel who had sighted the strange object were told that it was a highly secret government test vehicle, and not to be discussed. The local radio station was told to keep quiet about it."

"Driving from Minot, ND last evening turning onto the US 52 E we observed a light that had an erratic path. At first, I thought it was a plane but there were 4 light balls that came out of it. The minute they separated they vanished but reappeared as black objects floating. It was odd. I decided to record. It was difficult to record as the winds were strong, and moving didn't help. After about 10 min of it flying it had made it over to the far east, and disappeared.

"All of a sudden nothing. At that point we arrived to Velva, it was dark by then so camera was not able to record - you could see the black, and regular AF choppers in the air, and they were low. The black choppers had no lights on them on at all times but would flash intermittently."

ADC Radar Confirmation
Project Blue Book case dated October 24, 1968, when missile crews, control personnel, and maintenance personnel observed a UFO in the vicinity of the base. The following account is the tape between the air controllers, and the B-52 crew with call sign JAG Three One.

At 0330 hours: The controllers received the information that there was a UFO, 24 miles to the northwest. "A B-52 jet bomber (JAG 31) flying at 2000 feet was on a calibration check, and requests a clearance from radar personnel."

At 0334: "MIB (Minot) approach control does JAG 31 have clearance to WT fix at Flight Level 2000?"

JAG 31, "Roger climb out on a heading of 290 climb, and maintain 5000. Stand by for higher altitude. We're trying to get it from center now."

At 0335, the controller asked, "And JAG 31 on your way out to the WT fix request you look out toward your one o'clock positions for the next fifteen miles, and see if you see any orange glows out there?"

"Roger, roger glows 31. Someone is seeing UFOs again!"

"Roger, I see a..." (Rest of transmission garbled)

At 0352, the controller then radioed, "Three One, the UFO is being picked up by weather's radar also. Should be at our one o'clock position, three miles now."

The pilot said, "We have nothing on our airborne radar, and I'm in some pretty thick haze now, and unable to see out that way."

At 0358, the pilot then requested an instrument guided approach, and received instructions. The pilot called, and then the transmitter went dead, but they could hear instructions from the ground. The controller asked them to squawk ident, which meant to use the aircraft's transponder which would paint the controller's radar with a large, glowing blip with the aircraft's identification.

At 0400, the controller then radioed, "JAG 31 if you hear me squawk ident..."

"JAG 31 ident observed."

Cleared for the approach attempt. "Contact on frequency 271 decimal three, and you're cleared for the low approach." They continued to have radio problems for another couple of minutes. At 0402, they were able to communicate easily.

The pilot said, "Our UFO was off to our left side when we started penetration."

"Roger, understand you did see something on your left side."

"We had a radar return at about a mile, and a quarter, at nine o'clock position for about the time we left 200 to 14..."

They discussed the troubles with the transmission, and then the controller asked, "Affirmative. I was wondering how far out did you see that UFO?"

"He was about one, and a half mile off our left wing at 35 miles when we started in, and stayed with us 'til about 10."

"I wonder if that could have been your radio troubles?"

"I don't know..."

But that's exactly when they started. "At 0413, Jag 31 are you observing any more UFOs?"

"Negative on radar. We can't see anything visually."

"JAG 31, request you have someone report to base ops after you land." What we have, then, was a group of sightings made by men on the ground, at the missile sites scattered around the base. There were radar sightings from ground, and weather's radar. There were visual sightings from the crew of the B-52, and an airborne radar sighting where the target traveled at 3,000 miles per hour. Scope photographs were taken. There were sightings made by S.Sgt. Bond the FSC at November Flight, S.Sgt. Smith at Oscar Flight -1, Juliet, and Mike Flight Teams, and a number of men in widely scattered locations. The object landed at location AA-43, and the entire observation lasted for 45 minutes. Fourteen other people in separate locations also reported the UFO. Security alarms were activated for both the outer, and inner ring at the missile sites. When the guards arrived at the outer door it was open, and the combination lock on the inner door had been moved.

A detailed report for this section is available in Appendix D-2.

POST ANALYSIS

Case No. 2 was the first of numerous UFO sightings observed, and reported from various missile silo sites over the following decades. One needs to understand that silos, for the most part, were unattended, and remotely monitored by the underground launch facility responsible for a specific silo cluster (flight). Onsite maintenance schedules were conducted periodically to test, and inspect system readiness on a second's notice.

Many of the sightings were based on crew sightings traveling to, and from their dedicated duties at launch control centers reporting independent external silo activities periodically scheduled through helicopters hovering or observation craft overflights unknown to the crew. Most inspections were conducted during the cloak of darkness within the crafts' mounted spotlights. It was the lighting configurations creating unusual images unfamiliar to the observers. Where most of the image shadows were helicopter shaped, the configurations changed with the technological craft designs over time. More recent sightings reported took on the triangle-shaped newly designed stealth craft, flying nighttime missions for observational purposes, at this time still highly classified.

CASE #3 – MISSILE SILO INTRUSION
Malmstrom AFB UFO/Missile Incident
Date: March 16, 1967
Location: Malmstrom AFB - Near Great Falls, MT

In central Montana, Thursday morning March 16, 1967, Captain Eric Carlson, and First Lieutenant Walt Figel, the Echo Flight Missile Combat Crew, were below ground in the E Flight Launch Control Center, LCC, or capsule. The Echo Flight LCC was located between Winfred, and Hilger, about 15 miles north of Lewistown.

Missile maintenance crews, and security teams were camped out at two of the launch facilities (LFs), having performed some work during the previous day, and stayed there overnight. During the early morning hours, more than one report came in from the security patrols, and maintenance crews that they had seen UFOs. A UFO was reported directly above one of the E Flight LFs, or silos. It turned out that at least one security policeman was so affected by this encounter that he never again returned to missile security duty.

Around 8:30 a.m., Figel, the Deputy Crew Commander, DMCCC, was briefing Carlson, the Crew Commander, MCCC, on the flight status when the alarm horn sounded. One of the Minuteman missiles they supervised had gone off alert status, becoming inoperable. It was one of the two sites where maintenance crews had camped out on site. Upset, thinking that the maintenance personnel had failed to notify him as required by procedure when maintenance work was done on a missile, that the missile was going off alert, Figel immediately called the missile site.

When Figel spoke with the onsite security guard, he reported that they had not yet performed any maintenance that morning. He also stated that a UFO had been hovering over the site. Figel recalled thinking the guard must have been drinking something. However, now other missiles started to go off alert in rapid succession. Within seconds, the entire flight of ten ICBMs was down. All of their missiles reported a No-Go condition. One by one, across the board, each missile had become inoperable. When the checklist procedure had been completed for each missile site, it was discovered that each of the missiles had gone off alert status due to a guidance, and control (G&C) system fault. Power had not been lost to the sites; the missiles simply were not operational because, for some unexplainable reason, each of their guidance, and control systems had malfunctioned.

Two Security Alert Teams (SAT) strike teams were dispatched from Echo to those sites where the maintenance crews were present. Figel had not informed the strike teams that one of the onsite guards had reported a UFO. On arrival at the LFs, the SAT reported back that UFOs had been seen hovering over each of the two sites by all of the maintenance, and security personnel present at each site.

Captain Don Crawford's crew relieved the Echo Flight crew later that morning. Crawford recalled that both Carlson, and Figel were still visibly shaken by what had occurred. Crawford also recalled that the maintenance crews worked on the missiles the entire day, and late into the night during his shift to bring them all back on alert. Not only had missiles been lost to our forces, but had remained out of service for an entire day.

A detailed report for this section is available in Appendix D-3.

POST ANALYSIS

Case No. 3 was one of multiple sightings reported by silo crews from the Malmstrom missile launch facility. Similar in nature to Case 2, inspections conducted were internal to the silo, independent of local crew awareness. Many such independent inspections were conducted over a period of decades as a result of missile readiness policy changes to a preemptive strike possibility. Today, much of the policy changes are on record held as uncommon knowledge to the general public, meaning that mostly historical researchers had access to individually requested, and governmentally approved information released.

CASE #4 – UFO CRASH LANDING
Shag Harbour Crash
Date: October 4, 1967
Location: Newfoundland

On the night of October 4, 1967, numerous residents of Shag Harbour, a small fishing village on Nova Scotia's southeast coast, witnessed a multi-lighted craft which eventually appeared to 'crash' into the Sound. The Sound is the western entrance to Shag Harbour proper. The unidentified flying object was observed drifting with the current on the Sound by more than a dozen witnesses including 3 RCMP officers. All of the witnesses both in, and around Shag Harbour reported what they thought was an airplane crashing near Shag Harbour. The three Mounties contacted local boat captains, and the Rescue Coordination Center (RCC) in Halifax, NS. The Mounties initiated a recovery operation, fully expecting to find bodies, and wreckage out on the water. Initially two fishing boats loaded with volunteers went out on the water, and searched. They were eventually joined by others, and Coast Guard Cutter 101. What was impressive was the amount of documentation collected from armed forces teletypes, principally the RCAF's AIRDESK in the nation's capital, Ottawa.

The newspapers responded by carrying stories about the event in eastern Canada's largest, conservative newspaper, the Chronicle Herald. For a short time, the Shag Harbour UFO Incident became a worldwide story and, as Case #34, was left unsolved in the Condon Report. The incident was in two components, the documented case, and the subsequent anecdotal case supplied by retired military personnel from the Canadian Army, Air Force, and Navy. During the first two hours of the incident Coast Guard Cutter 101 joined the search but it also brought news from RCC, Halifax. No airplanes were reported missing. This left the searchers, and witnesses wondering what they had seen that evening in the sky, and floating on the waters off Shag Harbour, a mystery still unsolved to this day. The Royal Canadian Air Force designated it a UFO event.

A detailed report for this section is available in Appendix D-4.

POST ANALYSIS

The Shag Harbour crash/retrieval became Case #34 in the infamous Condon Committee Report which would serve as Project Blue Book's final effort. The case was brought to Dr. Condon's limited attention by the late Jim Lorenzen of the Aerial Phenomena Research Organization (APRO). Dr. Levine, the investigator assigned to the case, allocated the grand total of two long distance phone calls to this investigation. One call was to the watch officer at Maritime Command, and the other was to an RCMP spokesperson. Dr. Levine was assured that there was nothing to the case, and that further investigation was futile. Thus, interest in the Shag Harbour case withered away, but not without leaving legacy remnants in the form of a UFO Center containing souvenir paraphernalia for the inquisitive visitor venturing to Halifax, Nova Scotia.

CASE #5 – NUCLEAR REACTOR INTRUSION
Incident at Indian Point Reactor Complex
Date: 1984
Location: Manhattan

As quoted by *Philip Imbrogno, principle reporter for this incident,* "The threat of UFOs compromising reactor security, as if the nuclear industry didn't have enough to deal with already, became a very real concern in 1984. Although officials would not admit it, several researchers have information that New York's Indian Point Reactor complex endured such a UFO problem during the long siege of sightings that happened throughout the state's Hudson Valley area. The portrayal of the event in this article was based primarily on the disclosures of unnamed sources.

The summer of 1984 was a troublesome season for authorities at the Indian Point nuclear reactor complex in Buchanan, New York. Two UFO appearances, one of which was verified by Carl Patrick, director of nuclear information for the New York Power Authority (NYPA), and later documented by the press, and the 1987 book Night Siege, apparently put the normally tight security of the plant to a severe test.

The first event entailed the brief flyover of a huge craft, witnessed by three security policemen on June 14. That was followed ten days later by a UFO incident of unprecedented impact. It was one of hundreds of UFO sightings in the Hudson Valley, but one the nuclear workers won't soon forget. "Here comes that UFO again!" an Indian Point security guard was said to have yelled on the night of July 24, 1984, alerting other security personnel by way of the plant's internal communications system. A UFO, variously described as looking like "an ice cream cone", and "boomerang," had lazily drifted over to Reactor #3, the only active reactor at the time, lingering about 300 feet above the domed construction for some ten minutes, sending security officials into an uproar.

Now, six years later, the principal UFO researcher on the case admitted that many aspects of the event remain confusing, and undisclosed, and although he's still receiving information, Philip Imbrogno calls his own lengthy investigation "stagnant."

"Every time new information comes up or I get a lead on something, I get very reluctant to deal with it again," said Imbrogno, who headed off the science department at the Windward School in White Plains, New York. "The entire case has caused me quite a bit of pressure." The event would indicate that whatever appeared over there, our state-of-the-art technology in defense was unable to deal with it." He suggested that from what his sources have said, a military aspect came into play. The Indian Point UFO represented an intolerable security breach.

Imbrogno says that "it is precisely that aspect which has had a lasting effect, and which has generated repercussions that continue to this day." According to the New York Power Authority, which oversees the reactor complex, Indian Point itself had no direct military association. Reactor #3 primarily serviced local, and state facilities in New York City, and Westchester County, including local school districts, the New York City subway systems, and some of New York's trains.

A detailed report for this section is available in Appendix D-5.

POST ANALYSIS

As one can easily see from the case reports, at almost every sighting, there was great controversy. It seemed that both sides, witnesses, and official(s), had their conviction or reason for denial. At times, the reports became so prolific that Operation Blue Book reporting, compiling the flood of cases, became highly overburdened. This was clearly visible through the impatience, and intolerance many sightings were recorded. After terminating operation Blue Book, numerous public organizations were created to take over the responsibility to record, investigate, and archive each case, detailed, as much as possible, categorized by type of sighting:

Close Encounter of the First Kind, within 500 feet of witness.

Close Encounter of the Second Kind, with physical evidence.

Close Encounter of the Third Kind, Alien entities On or Near craft.

Close Encounter of the Fourth Kind, Abduction by Aliens with special categories of Nuclear, and other highly sensitive facility encounters at places like Los Alamos, Oakridge, Sandia, Lawrence Livermore, and White Sands laboratories.

Many books have been written from direct witness accounts with data obtained from databases with the resultant conclusion, insufficient evidence. Aside from the Roswell incident, where pieces of aluminum metal, and plastic-type materials were collected, no other evidence was available for analysis to satisfy the scientific community as empirical proof. One should wonder that, after seventy years observing, and encounters with the UFO phenomena, some non-earthly created objects would exist. But so far, nobody has come forward with proof that extraterrestrials are real, do exist, or have had a presence on earth.

Where the public might be overzealous in making hasty reports of unexplained sightings, aside from encounters in a dreamlike state of awareness, military personnel thought twice before filing a report. Implications to unsubstantiated facts might prove damaging to individual career, and personal wellbeing, especially when the reported incident could be explained by a higher authority whose hands might be tied.

Sightings in, and around highly sensitive installations such as missile silos, and underground launch centers could be primary targets to close inspections by aliens, if ETs existed. But so far, with the knowledge this author has acquired, we are safe from attacks from outer space. In contrast, this is not the case with earthly origin. We must keep a wary eye on potential attacks from within our own borders, as well as from hostile nations, and terrorist factions with ill-tempered leadership intending to bring harm to our peace-loving heritage.

Though unrealistic in the author's interest, subjects on UFO, and extraterrestrials stimulate the mind, and provide fuel for endless, and unexplained possibilities. After all, we are only a mere speck in the vast expanse of an expanding universe with many more possibilities to explore. While interested in subjects of the mystical, and unknown, my mind is grounded to earthly events, verified, and proven through scientific, and archeological research efforts. However, that does not preclude the possibility of spiritual, and supernatural events I, and many others have experienced through their lifetimes. My intentions are to explore the invisible possibilities in upcoming novels.

Regardless of resultant turnout of his exploring mission, whether factual or fictional, I will share any, and all findings with my readers. While anchored to earth's ground, there are unexplained personal events that supersede logical, and rational thinking. For example, where do novel thoughts, and innovative inventions originate? Are they conceived by the individual mind or is the information received from a yet undetected transmission spectrum? In addition, and much more complex, is the unexplored presence of a spiritual, and supernatural realm taking hold of the individual's mind, whether in sleep, conscious, or subconscious state, a reality?

There have been uncountable accounts recorded worldwide about personal events substantiating the possibility of such dominion, and higher states of existence above, and beyond logical thinking. It is this possibility that intrigues many of the earthly population. Our minds have not yet developed far enough to explain the higher states of being, with questions like:

- Do spiritual beings exist?
- Are other worlds populated?
- What omnipresent being created the universe, created us?
- What will be the endgame of mankind?
- Where is the domicile of the creator?

One can only ponder about the wonders of creation. Possibilities are endless. Until we develop a higher state of consciousness, our minds are limited to only our own imaginations.

CASE #6 – ANIMAL MUTILATION

History

The earliest known documented outbreak of unexplained livestock deaths occurred in early 1606 with "...about the city of London, and some of the shires adjoining. Whole slaughters of sheep have been made, in some places to number 100, in others less, where nothing is taken from the sheep but their tallow, and some inward parts, the whole carcasses, and fleece remaining still behind. Most agree that it 'tended towards some fireworks.'" The outbreak was noted in the official records of the Court of James I of England. Charles Fort collected many accounts of cattle mutilations that occurred in England in the late 19th, and early 20th centuries.

John Keel mentioned investigating animal mutilation cases in 1966, while with Ivan T. Sanderson, that were being reported in the Upper Ohio River Valley, around Gallipolis, OH. The phenomenon remained largely unknown outside cattle-raising communities until 1967, when the Pueblo Chieftain in Pueblo, Colorado published a story about a horse named Lady near Alamosa, Colorado that was mysteriously killed, and mutilated. The story was republished by the wider press, and distributed nationwide. This case was the first to feature speculation that extraterrestrial beings, and unidentified flying objects were associated with mutilation.

Later developments

Democratic senator Floyd K. Haskell contacted the FBI asking for help in 1975 due to public concern regarding the issue. He claimed there had been 130 mutilations in Colorado alone, and further reports across nine states. A 1979 FBI report indicated that, according to investigations by the New Mexico State Police, there had been an estimated 8,000 mutilations in Colorado, causing approximately $1,000,000 damage.

Physical characteristics

In most cases mutilation wounds appear to be clean, and carried out surgically. Mutilated animals were usually, though not always, reported to have been drained of blood, and have no sign of blood in the immediate area or around their wounds.

George E. Onet, a doctor of veterinary microbiology, and cattle mutilation investigator, claimed that mutilated cattle were avoided by large scavengers "such as coyotes, wolves, foxes, dogs, skunks, badgers, and bobcats" for several days after their death. Similarly, domestic animals were also reported to be "visibly agitated", and "fearful" of the carcass.

According to a survey taken by the National Institute for Discovery Science (NIDS), mutilation of the eye occurred in 59 percent of cases, mutilation of the tongue in 42 percent of cases, the genitals in 85 percent of cases, and the rectum in 76 percent of cases. According to Dr. Howard Burgess, nearly 90 percent of mutilated cattle were between four, and five years old.

Some mutilations were said to have occurred in very brief periods. A 2002 NIDS report related a 1997 case from Utah. Two ranchers tagged a specific calf, then continued tagging other animals in the same pasture. The ranchers were, at most, about 300 yards from the calf. Less than an hour later, the first calf was discovered completely eviscerated—most muscle, and all internal organs were missing. There was no blood, entrails, or apparent disturbance at the scene. Independent analysts both uncovered marks on the calf's remains consistent with two different types of tools: a large, machete-type blade, and smaller, more delicate scissors.

The absence of tracks or footprints around the site of the mutilated carcass was often considered a hallmark of cattle mutilation. However, in some cases, strange marks or imprints near the site have been found. In the famous "Snippy" case, there was an absolute absence of tracks in a 100 ft radius of the carcass (even the horse's own tracks disappeared within 100 ft of the body). But within this radius several small holes were found seemingly "punched" in the ground, and two bushes were absolutely flattened. In Rio Arriba County, New Mexico, June 1976, a "trail of suction cup-like impressions" was found leading from a mutilated three-year-old cow. The indentations were in a tripod form, 4 inches in diameter, 28 inches apart, and disappeared 500 feet from the dead cow. Similar incidents were reported in the area in 1978.

A detailed report for this section is available in Appendix D-6.

POST ANALYSIS

Laboratory reports carried out on some mutilated animals have shown unusually high or low levels of vitamins or minerals in tissue samples, and the presence of chemicals not normally found in animals. However, not all mutilated animals displayed these anomalies, and those that did had slightly different anomalies from one another. On account of the time between death, and necropsy, and a lack of background information on specific cattle, investigators have often found it impossible to determine if these variations were connected to the animals' deaths or not.

CASE #7 – CROP CIRCLE

A crop circle or crop formation is a pattern created by flattening a crop, usually a cereal. The term was first coined in the early 1980s by Colin Andrews. Crop circles have been described as all falling "within the range of the sort of thing done in hoaxes" by Taner Edis, professor of physics at Truman State University. Although obscure natural causes or alien origins of crop circles were suggested by fringe theorists, there is no scientific evidence for such explanations, and all crop circles have been consistent with human causation.

The number of crop circles substantially increased from the 1970s to current times. There has been little scientific study of them. Circles in the United Kingdom were not distributed randomly across the landscape but appear near roads, areas of medium to dense population, and cultural heritage monuments, such as Stonehenge or Avebury. In 1991, two hoaxers, Bower, and Chorley, took credit for having created many circles throughout England after one of their circles was described by a circle investigator as impossible to be made by human hand.

Formations were usually created overnight, although some were reported to have appeared during the day. In contrast to crop circles or crop formations, archaeological remains can cause cropmarks in the fields in the shapes of circles, and squares, but they do not appear overnight, and they are always in the same places every year.

History
The concept of "crop circles" began with the original late-1970s hoaxes by Doug Bower, and Dave Chorley (see Bower, and Chorley, below). They said that they were inspired by the Tully "saucer nest" case in Australia, where a farmer claimed to first have seen a UFO, then found a flattened circle of swamp reeds.

Before the 20th century
A 1678 news pamphlet *The Mowing-Devil: or, Strange News Out of Hartfordshire* is claimed by some cereologist (advocates of paranormal explanations of crop circles) to be the first depiction of a crop circle. Crop circle researcher Jim Schnabel does not consider it to be a historical precedent because it describes the stalks as being cut rather than bent.

In 1686, British naturalist Robert Plot reported on rings or arcs of mushrooms (see fairy rings) in *The Natural History of Stafford-Shire*, and proposed air flows from the sky as a cause. In 1991 meteorologist Terence Meaden linked this report with modern crop circles, a claim that had been compared with those made by Erich von Däniken.

An 1880 letter to the editor of *Nature* by amateur scientist John Rand Capron described how a recent storm had created several circles of flattened crops in a field.

20th century
In 1932, archaeologist E. C. Curwen observed four dark rings in a field at Stoughton Down near Chichester but could examine only one: "a circle in which the barley was 'lodged' or beaten down, while the interior area was very slightly mounded up."

In 1963 amateur astronomer Patrick Moore described a crater in a potato field in Wiltshire, which he considered was probably caused by an unknown meteoric body. In nearby wheat fields, there were several circular, and elliptical areas where the wheat had been flattened. There was evidence of "spiral flattening." He thought they could be caused by air currents from the impact, since they led towards the crater. Astronomer Hugh Ernest Butler observed similar craters, and said they were likely caused by lightning strikes.

Since the 1960s, there has been a surge of Ufologists in Wiltshire, and there were rumors of "saucer nests" appearing in the area, but they were never photographed. There are other pre-1970s reports of circular formations, especially in Australia, and Canada, but they were always simple circles, which could have been caused by whirlwinds. In *Fortean Times* David Wood reported that in 1940 he had already made crop circles near Gloucestershire using ropes. In 1997, the *Oxford English Dictionary* recorded the earliest usage of the term "crop circles" in a 1988 issue of *Journal of Meteorology*, referring to a BBC film. The coining of the term "crop circle" is attributed to Colin Andrews in the late 1970s or early 1980s.

The majority of reports of crop circles have appeared in, and spread since the late 1970s as many circles began appearing throughout the English countryside. This phenomenon became widely known in the late 1980s, after the media started to report crop circles in Hampshire, and Wiltshire. After Bower's, and Chorley's 1991 statement that they were responsible for many of them, circles started appearing all over the world. To date, approximately 10,000 crop circles have been reported internationally, from locations such as the former Soviet Union, the United Kingdom, Japan, the U.S., and Canada. Sceptics note a correlation between crop circles, recent media coverage, and the absence of fencing and/or anti-trespassing legislation.

Although farmers expressed concern at the damage caused to their crops, local response to the appearance of crop circles was often enthusiastic, with locals taking advantage of the increase of tourism, and visits from scientists, crop circle researchers, and individuals seeking spiritual experiences. The market for crop-circle interest consequently generated bus and helicopter tours of circle sites, walking tours, T-shirts, and book sales.

21st century
Since the start of the 21st century, crop formations have increased in size, and complexity, with some featuring as many as 2,000 different shapes, and some incorporating complex mathematical, and scientific characteristics.

The researcher Jeremy Northcote found that crop circles in the UK in 2002 were not spread randomly across the landscape. He found that they always appeared in areas that were easy to access. This suggested strongly that these crop circles were more likely to be caused by intentional human action than by paranormal activity. Another strong indication of that theory was that inhabitants of the zone with the most circles had a historical tendency for making large-scale formations, including stone circles such as Stonehenge, burial mounds such as Silbury Hill, long barrows such as West Kennet Long Barrow, and white horses in chalk hills.

A detailed report for this section is available in Appendix D-7.

POST ANALYSIS

While crop circles are a relatively new phenomena, they are still fiercely debated among Ufologists, not so much whether they were real, but more so for the means in which they were created. Despite numerous announcements by groups of British ranchers claiming that they were the makers of all of the crafty designs, primitive earlier, and highly sophisticated in recent years, for the crop circles, Ufologists keep ignoring the declarations. The motives given for the creation of crop circles is for commercial reasons to attract visitors to a part of Britain mostly isolated from mainstream tourism. Nearby Stonehenge, for example, used to be a point of attraction mostly for archaeologists, but today, it is a major attraction for world travelers.

CASE #8 – BIGFOOT

In North American folklore, Bigfoot, or Sasquatch, is a hairy, upright-walking, ape-like being who reportedly dwells in the wilderness, and leaves behind large footprints. Strongly associated with the Pacific Northwest (particularly Washington state, and British Columbia), individuals have claimed to see the creature across North America. Over the years, the creature has inspired numerous commercial ventures, and hoaxes.

Folklorists trace the figure of Bigfoot to a combination of factors, and sources, including folklore surrounding the European wild man figure, folk belief among Native Americans, and loggers, and a cultural increase in environmental concerns.

A majority of mainstream scientists have historically discounted the existence of Bigfoot, considering it to be a combination of folklore, misidentification, and hoax, rather than a living animal.

People have claimed to have seen Bigfoot, describing it as a large, hairy, muscular, bipedal ape-like creature, roughly 6–9 feet (1.8–2.7 m) tall, covered in hair described as black, dark brown, or dark reddish.

The enormous footprints for which the creature was named have been claimed to be as large as 24 inches (60 cm) long, and 8 inches (20 cm) wide. Some footprint casts have also contained claw marks, making it likely that they came from known animals such as bears, which have five toes, and claws.

History

According to David Daegling, the legends existed before there was a single name for the creature. They differed in their details both regionally, and between families in the same community. Similar accounts, and legends of wild men are found on every continent except Antarctica.

Ecologist Robert Pyle argued that most cultures had accounts of human-like giants in their folk history, expressing a need for "some larger-than-life creature." Each language had its own name for the creature featured in the local version of such legends. Many names meant something along the lines of "wild man" or "hairy man," although other names described common actions that it was said to perform, such as eating clams or shaking trees. Chief Mischelle of the Nlaka'pamux at Lytton, British Columbia told such a story to Charles Hill-Tout in 1898; he named the creature by a Salishan variant meaning "the benign-faced-one".

Less-menacing versions have also been recorded, such as one by Reverend Elkanah Walker from 1840. Walker was a Protestant missionary who recorded stories of giants among the Indians living near Spokane, Washington. The Indians said that these giants lived on, and around the peaks of nearby mountains, and stole salmon from the fishermen's nets.

In the 1920s, Indian Agent J. W. Burns compiled local stories, and published them in a series of Canadian newspaper articles. They were accounts told to him by the Sts'Ailes people of Chehalis, and others. The Sts'Ailes, and other regional tribes maintained that the Sasquatch were real. They were offended by people telling them that the figures were legendary. According to Sts'Ailes accounts, the Sasquatch preferred to avoid white men, and spoke the Lillooet language of the people at Port Douglas, British Columbia at the head of Harrison Lake. These accounts were published again in 1940. Burns borrowed the term Sasquatch from the Halkomelem *sásq'ets*, and used it in his articles to describe a hypothetical single type of creature portrayed in the local stories.

Distribution of reported Bigfoot sightings in the United States, and Canada

About one-third of all claims of Bigfoot sightings have been located in the Pacific Northwest, with the remaining reports spread throughout the rest of North America. Most reports are considered mistakes or hoaxes, even by those researchers who say that Bigfoot existed.

Bigfoot has become better known, and a phenomenon in popular culture, and sightings have spread throughout North America. Rural areas of the Great Lakes region, and the southeastern United States have been sources of numerous reports of Bigfoot sightings, in addition to the Pacific Northwest. The debate over the legitimacy of Bigfoot sightings reached a peak in the 1970s, and Bigfoot has been regarded as the first widely popularized example of pseudoscience in American culture.

A detailed report for this section is available in Appendix D-8.

POST ANALYSIS

Proposed explanations for sightings

Various explanations have been suggested for the sightings, and to offer conjecture on what type of creature Bigfoot might be. Scientists have typically attributed sightings either to hoaxes or to misidentification of known animals, and their tracks, particularly black bears.

Misidentification

In 2007, the Bigfoot Field Researchers Organization put forward some photos which they claimed showed a juvenile Bigfoot. The Pennsylvania Game Commission, however, said that the photos were of a bear with mange. Anthropologist Jeffrey Meldrum, on the other hand, said that the limb proportions of the creature were not bear-like, they were "more like a chimpanzee."

Hoaxes

Both Bigfoot believers, and non-believers agree that many of the reported sightings are hoaxes or misidentified animals. Author Jerome Clark argues that the Jacko Affair was a hoax, involving an 1884 newspaper report of an apelike creature captured in British Columbia. He cited research by John Green, who found that several contemporaneous British Columbia newspapers regarded the alleged capture as highly dubious, and notes that the *Mainland Guardian* of New Westminster, British Columbia wrote, "Absurdity is written on the face of it."

Tom Biscardi is a long-time Bigfoot enthusiast, and CEO of Searching for Bigfoot Inc. He appeared on the *Coast to Coast AM* paranormal radio show on July 14, 2005, and said that he was "98% sure that his group will be able to capture a Bigfoot which they had been tracking in the Happy Camp, California area."

As for the author's analysis, all sightings could be explained in simple terms, hoaxes, and mistaken identities. The answer is simple: proof lies with fossils discoveries, and archaeological evidence. Where are they?

SANITY CHECK

For the author's research, and Post Analysis study it was immaterial what research category or belief system one treaded in. Whether the individual was a scientist, researcher, conspiracy follower or other, the resultant data, and information describing the various paranormal event criteria was taken from a scientific majority consensus such as listed on the Wikipedia website, with links referenced in Appendix C. With the knowledge the author has on UFOs, and ETs, only one conclusion fits the millions of reports collected from the public on the subject matter: other than military in origin, most, if not all, could be explained as hoaxes. There is, especially in recent decades, such an increase in deceit for the cause of individual celebrity that it is impossible for the general citizen to distinguish facts from fiction.

Amid this confusion, the UFO culture was created, and rightly so. For the confused population, I felt it my duty to shed some light on the situation. In light of things, I may or may not have succeeded without creating more confusion. The problem is not so much the reports of sightings, already in the millions of cases; the problem is entirely based on credibility. Whoever can break through the barrier of doubt, and disbelief among world populations may be able to establish some sort of psychological order. Where I, like much of the population, are coolheaded, skeptical individuals by nature, regardless of the true purpose behind UFO, and ET issues, I have no personal agenda for his disclosure attempt other than to set the record straight. With the knowledge I have acquired, I could have easily become a debunker on the stated subjects. Debunking, however, does not solve the trust issue with people kept in the dark for decades, trying to understand the reasoning behind the world's greatest deception of all time.

What was originally conceived as a cover-up, with good intentions, protecting the United States from adverse hostilities within the escalation of a mindless cold war by military, and political decision makers, turned into a psychological quagmire none had ever envisioned. We may be stuck for a long time living with the consequences. While many of the sighting reports were meant in good faith by a safety aware public, they only added to the mystique. Because of the ambiguous nature, and personal unpreparedness of most sightings, due to their swift appearance, and disappearance, clear and precise captures within the mind, camera, and video equipment left much speculation as to a precise, and meaningful post analysis interpretation.

Added to an already ambiguous equation is the editorial and, most times, imprecise susceptibility for errors by a citizen who often questioned their own sightings, like, "I have seen something in the sky. *Could* you explain it?" This is where the confusion came into play rather than being able to precisely pinpoint, and describe the object as, "I saw something in the sky. It *was* a UFO." While the first case is vague, subject to guessing, the second definition is precise with information captured by the witness. Which leaves us with, where is the evidence?

Though most witnesses will reply, "I was not prepared to take a picture," few will claim to have proof. However, and most unfortunately, post analyses, and examinations of the object(s) have left much to individual interpretation for pranks, hoaxes, and swindles. Which brings us to the next mystery. Why are UFOs visible?

One often wonders that, if ETs wanted to keep their presence unknown, why not just switch the lighting off during their nighttime activities? There are many such questions to test the logical purposes from unexplained sightings. What are their motives for stealth, and secrecy? The answer has been there all along. Unfortunately, it is a compromising one. It would prove simplicity to some, but not without complications to others.

By *some* I mean the military. By *others* I mean the public. Thence, the issue reaches a full circle that could easily be broken, and solved. The question remains, solved by whom?

That, my valued readers, is up to the governments. Not only ours but other countries' as well. It should be noted that other governments, at times, were more notorious about concealing things from the public. It all factors down to one common denominator: stealth designs, and cyberspace planning, the two most important military issues. While wars in the past could only be fought on or near the ground, emerging technology has escalated our fighting ability into space. It is space where future battles will be fought.

As for the growing increase in recent sightings most, if not all, can be explained as military, and experimental craft sightings and, more recently, the passion of fun-loving individuals flying remotely-controlled drones. It is up to the individual to personally evaluate, and assess their sightings in a more responsible manner without first jumping to conclusions. From a sober, and rational perspective, the hundreds of sightings recorded weekly on the many paranormal, and supernatural websites mostly read as gibberish, and nonsensical. But, as already stated, it is up to the individual to tolerate personal ridicule, and criticism when discussing topics on the greatly debated, controversial nature. In support of the paranormal follower, the Ufologists, aside from military issues, I would suggest giving science, and archeological investigative efforts a chance. After all, they have been providing us with uncountable artifacts left for mankind to enjoy, study, and collect as our ancient heritage, in contrast to non-extraterrestrial proof.

Furthermore, every phenomenon reported has been researched by the science community in one form or other to get to the truth. Where one side, the paranormal, is biased towards the supernatural, the other, scientific studies, are based on factual results. In between the two factions are the recently emerging, multi-colored orbs. What premonition, and euphoria it may have been for the Ufologist observers, when the answer could be as simple as a vision check. In science there is no room for speculation, and conjecture. In case a finding was open ended, a mathematician goes to work to prove a factual solution. It is this check, and balance system used to provide the primer for science, and technology.

For the supernatural and paranormal communities, whether they would be open to reason, and logical explanations will most likely prove impossible since the majority are prone to inexhaustible speculations, prolific propagations, and wishful thinking about an advanced lifeform elsewhere. As for a logical explanation to all of the mysterious sightings of UFOs, spherical apparitions, close encounters, and human abductions, much can be rationally explained. The question is, "do people really want to know the facts."

The answer is two-fold: One faction believes in the mysteries of the imaginative mind, while the other relies only on proof as stated in science. Chronologically, sightings, and contacts prior to the 40s were related to mythology, folklore, and legends interpretations. Stories about those went back to when man created the art of writing, in ancient times.

More recently, UFO events recorded between the 50s, and 60s could be contributed to covered up atomic secrets between the superpowers out of fear from a potential, but very real, nuclear strike.

UFO encounters between the 70s, and 80s were the results of the Cold War escalation between the Soviet Union, and the United States. Then President Ronald Reagan greatly inspired the population, and Hollywood, further visualizing a world of Sci-Fi, technologically advancing a thousand years with his Star Wars initiative.

The years following, between the 90s, and 2000 brought us stealth technology in the form of invisible aircraft beyond our imaginations. Technology, misinterpreted by Ufologists as being reengineered from extraterrestrial origin, turned out to be the creative products of ingenuity, and innovative minds from a vast pool of earthly scientists, and engineers.

And finally, the ensuing years to the present can only be described as stealth technology developed, and tested in the cloak of darkness to attain a space advantage, at this time only bestowed on the United States. There is no other nation on Earth that can even come close to the technological achievements incepted, developed, and launched into orbit for mankind, and their exploratory needs for the population of an ever-expanding cosmos.

More interestingly, where much of mankind has followed millennia of factual living subjected to tyranny, hardship, and natural disasters, it is only in recent times that facts have turned into fiction. The majority of the human population is still linked to factual events, but fiction, and science fiction have become parts of everyday life in the form of entertainment, and, to a much greater extent, military conquest. It is not to say that fiction, in the distant future, may turn back into facts once more, if other lifeforms are discovered. Until such time, it will be us that not only created fiction; it will be us that will live within the world of fiction propagated throughout the cosmos. We may not be alone for very long in the vastness of the universe, after all. It will be us that will become the extraterrestrials to populate cosmic space.

In a world of endless possibilities, to harbor life in every shape, and form after billions of years of evolution, one still ponders why there was created only one highly intelligent form of life. The answer may lie with our foremost scientist, Albert Einstein, as well as a few other notables. It was they, that mathematically produced the answer: travel is limited to the speed of light. Life may exist in other galaxies, but in order to encounter it, it would take millions of years to travel there.

As far as time travel, and wormholes are concerned, those are sciences in blueprint, and still have to developed, and explored. For now, for the time being, only the science fiction we created to inspire our despairing demands to achieve a higher state of being, whether spiritual or factual, remain to be explored.

VOLUME THREE

REALITY TODAY

DARPA ENGINEERING

Mystery-man was swamped with emails like usually on Monday mornings. Action-oriented, regardless of being strapped behind a desk, he would rather be on the go just to get out of the office. It was his prerogative to prioritize his daily workload. He contemplated an escape from the chore of reading through the office correspondence by attending a strategy meeting. Checking the roster for this morning's topics he decided against going. The reason was obvious after glancing at the agenda. One item in particular caught his attention: "Resolving UFO issues with the press."

He would rather not get involved with this time sensitive issue. Of late, mainstream media had put on tremendous pressure on government authorities to come up with some plausible answers for all the reported sightings. "The public deserves to know the truth…" with many more demands from the private sector. "It's not up to me," he felt, when his name was tossed in the drawing hat. It was not him that had caused all of the problems they had to live with almost daily. Public pressure caused too much distraction for everybody in the defense sector. He, like everybody else in the Pentagon, stayed away as far as possible from getting involved with the increase in demands for "Full Disclosure."

It might have been easy to defer an event, and put blame on aliens fifty years ago, but in today's world, with everybody informed, it was almost an impossibility to pull wool over the public's eyes. "But," he contemplated, "somebody has to take the blame, and it better not be me." He knew quite well that the career of whoever drew the short straw for a disclosure statement would come to an immediate end. The revelation, any revelation, would shake the Pentagon to its very foundation. Trust the public had with the government could dissolve, and crumble. "They might as well close this complex down," he rationalized.

"I need to talk with somebody," he concluded, trying to focus on something rational, and down to earth. "I need to get out of here," he muttered, determined to change the direction this week would take. It then came to him. "Bauer." Whenever one of us felt the strong urge to talk, the other generally felt a psychic ping on the brain. "What was it called again?" He tried to remember. "Ah yes. Telepathy." *Strange,* he thought. *Nobody ever talks about it anymore.* What he did not contemplate was that with the passage of time labels changed. Telepathy was one of them; today, it was commonly known as ESP, and mind reading.

He was about to pick up the phone, but was preempted with an incoming call. "Bauer," the caller ID displayed, "I'll be damned," he said. "Alex?"

"Felt like giving you a call," I said. "You've got time?"

"You have my ears," he replied.

"We need to meet. Want to keep your promise?"

"What promise?" He seemed startled. He did not remember committing to any such thing.

"My offer still stands. Spend a few days here. I'll fire up the jacuzzi for you."

"I sure miss the special treat soaking in your tub. Why not?" he decided. "Give me a couple of days."

"Let me know when to pick you up. You flying military or commercial?"

"I'll text you when I'm in transit."

"See you when you get here." Cheerfully, I hung up, looking forward to my buddy's visit.

Two days later I was called to attention by the chirp of my iPhone. "Arrive at Pete Field - 2:00 p.m." Thirty minutes later I shook hands with Mystery-man. "Welcome back. Glad you could make it."

"Always good to see you," he said, with a pleasing smile. "We should do it more often. Have you got company, or are you alone these days?"

"Alone. Daughters are out in California."

"Visiting mom?"

"And kids," I affirmed.

"What's on your mind? Must be something big," he prodded.

"We'll see." Other than a few casual comments about the scene bestowed by my living at the foot of Pikes Peak, our talk remained casual. He seemed to enjoy the view of the Rocky Mountains, something he dearly missed back in D.C. There seemed to be more that he missed. "I envy you living in pristine air, distinct four seasons, skiing, and hiking. What am I doing confined within five walls all of my life?" he burst out, shaking his head, trying to get my attention.

"What?"

"The Pentagon. Nothing but walls, and halls. The mountains, the view, the space, why should you get it all?"

"You could move here," I offered. "Could even set up command at the Castle. I've got all the communication gear you'd need, and more."

"The Mountain?"

"Yeah. NORAD."

"Just another hole in the wall."

"Big hole," I corrected him as we drove into town. Rather than spending time cooking, I decided on a local restaurant. "Steakhouse?"

"Lead on." The next two hours were spent on casual conversation. Mystery-man did most of the talking, reporting on the political climate, and covert projects in the making. He knew how trustworthy I was, and had no reservations revealing inner secrets from the defense department. Sitting together within a relaxed atmosphere was a time we both could enjoy.

Two hours later, stuffed with the town's best steak, and ample trimmings, I suggested, "Ready for a soak?"

"Not soon enough. I need one of your cool imports."

"You're staying a couple of days, I hope?"

"Unless I have an emergency. Count on it."

Thirty minutes later, I offered, "Here," handing over a pair of trunks reserved for my special guest. "You can change in the guestroom. You know the floor."

"I do. Thanks."

I had a frozen mug of beer waiting when he stepped into the spacious six-person tub. "Ah," he marveled. "How much I miss this."

"Why don't you get one for yourself?"

"It's not that simple. Any extravagance is considered an unnecessary luxury with the government. It takes paperwork, approvals, and authorization."

"With your status?"

"Yes. Even with my status." Mystery-man may be considered an icon within his community, retired military, his current status was civilian.

"Don't think I could handle such restriction." I had always been free of demand limitations. While I was not prone to free spending, there had been times when I purchased items at the spur of the moment.

"You'll get used to it. Once you decide to join the military you pretty much follow orders. Everybody reports to somebody up the chain of command. It's the discipline necessary. Otherwise," he explained, "you could not get anybody to fight on the frontlines."

"I know," I admitted. "It's mostly the young soldier taking the bullets. Who else, but a marine would be so brave?"

"It'll get better in the future, I assure you."

"Drones doing the fighting?"

"And robot soldiers."

"So," I speculated. "There's no win-win situation?"

"Whoever has hardware left comes out the winner."

"Then," I said, "what's the point in fighting?"

"Exactly. But enough. Let's move on to why I'm here."

"You start. You brought it up." I suspected the purpose for his visit, but remained silent.

"Remember the last time we've talked."

"Why don't you refresh my mind." I did not want to jump to conclusions.

"You brought up the subject of UFOs. You practically cornered me into submission."

"I didn't bend your arm, did I?" My suspecting the purpose for his visit became clear, but there were still the underlying reasons of why.

"I need to know how you got the information." It was a bold request I did not expect. I thought that he would have firsthand knowledge himself.

"Why ask me? You should know with all of your contacts. Doesn't anybody in the Pentagon ever talk about it?"

"Never. The topic is taboo even in close circles."

"Then," I hinted, "it's only the CIA that knows the true facts."

"They hold all the data. That's the reason I wanted to talk with you. You were involved with AUTODIN."

"Right. But so were you."

"I don't know the true facts."

"What makes you say that?" I was curious about what he was getting at.

"You had to have access to their database," he said, eying me with suspicion. I did not blame him for being somewhat ignorant about Aliens. There had been nothing but confusion for the past seventy years. Though I believe that after several generations in office the government itself had lost track of who had started it, and when it all began, I may be mistaken. It may have all been a calculated plan.

"Okay," I said, relenting to the inevitable. Trusted buddies for over thirty years, I thought that he deserved the truth. "Here are the facts." Since he had seen, and experienced it all during his career, he usually held a reserved attitude on covert topics. Today, and now, he had my undivided attention. "There are UFOs," I stated. "But you know that already. What you claim you don't know is, that there are no extraterrestrials, or what's referred today as Aliens."

"You mean, ever?" he probed, staring at me.

"We have never been visited by beings from another world." I watched his reaction that followed.

"How can you be so sure?" His reaction was similar to others I had explained to: stunned, disbelieving, and not expecting my response.

"There is no data on visitation from outer space in all of the data banks."

"Then," he huffed, "what about the sightings, and abductions?"

"Mostly imaginary."

"What about the images, and videos on tapes?"

"Doctored up with Photoshop."

"How about CIA documents?"

"Cover-ups."

"You'd better explain," he demanded. I detected clear denial in his eyes thinking, "how dare him suggesting…"

"Redacted[69] documents," I cut in, offering an explanation. "It's in response to public, and researchers' demands. Most names, and location text are blacked out."

"You mean for FOIA?"

"Precisely. CIA doesn't care much about public opinion. They never have, as long as they achieve their objectives."

"Which is?"

"Cover up their operations, and others' objectives."

"Then," he hesitated. "There are no Aliens?"

"None ever. We have never been visited by life forms from another planet, or from outer space." I was adamant, and stated so. "All a cover up."

"Tell me," he said, somewhat speechless. "Can I quote you on it?"

"Quote me as much as you want. It's not only me that holds the facts. There were dozens of others on the program that could attest to it. Where some are still alive, others many have already passed away, but you know that already."

"I thought that I'd knew it all," he said, shaking his head in denial. "How could I have missed it?"

"You were not on the program when the operating software and systems were developed. We had access to databases."

"Intel could have denied you access."

"Not a chance. It took database architects to design, and connect mainframe computers, and databanks with the Pentagon, and embassies overseas, let alone military command and control.

---

[69] Redacted is the censoring or obscuring of a text for legal or security purposes. More precisely, the process of editing text for publication: *"what was left after the redaction would be virtually useless."*

"What about the so-called experts? The whistleblowers claiming eye witness accounts."

"Whistleblowers? Forget it. They just want to feel important banking on public ignorance."

"How can you be so sure?" Mystery-man did not sound convinced.

"Think about it. Have you ever heard an astronomer report receiving a cohesive signal, or visual sighting from outer space?"

"Come to think of it," he admitted. "Not that I know."

"Have you ever seen a UFO, or confronted an Alien?"

"UFOs yes. Numerous times, but identified the designs as ours. I'm not totally ignorant," he said scornfully.

"Then," I said. "You are fine with it? No further questions?"

"No further questions, but I'm not totally convinced."

"What can I do to persuade you?" I understood him well. His reaction was not different from others I had educated.

"Go public."

"You know me too well. I don't care about publicity."

"Then," he pondered, "what do you get out of it?"

"Personal satisfaction by my books being published. I just want to set the record straight for the ones who care. Look," I volunteered. "The majority of the population could care less. They are either too absorbed in their work, with family or career, and just don't have the time. The minority, the conspirators, Ufologists, and paranormal researchers won't believe one word. Their minds are made up about the whole affair whether it's crop circles, animal mutilations, human abductions, strange sightings, close encounters, and whatever else they can conjure up."

"Then," he contemplated, probably feeling somewhat disappointed himself, "it's all a hoax? We are alone in the universe?"

"As far as I know, yes, but there's always the possibility for life elsewhere."

"Then you admit that there is extraterrestrial life?"

"Not at this time." It pretty much ended the topic, and purpose for his visit.

"You're aware of what you have to do next, don't you?" he insisted.

I thought about his remark for a second, then it dawned on me. "Call the CIA?"

"You'll need their blessings."

"I don't think they will sanction my publishing."

"You've got no choice."

"I'll make the call. Guess I'll find out."

"Good luck on that one."

"I'll need it." Whether I would take his advice, or disregard it remains to be seen. I still have to finish the book. Besides, I clearly recall the sentiment prevalent in the business world, "It is easier to beg for forgiveness than to ask for permission."

We spent the remainder of his time walking trails, dining, and drinking with more reminiscing on good old times with a promise to visit more often. Next time, it would be me paying him a visit.

Because of my intricate knowledge on the internal workings with Intel agencies, where I had achieved my resolution on the UFO versus Alien phenomena many years ago, I had found inner peace with myself. However, there was one thing that still bothered me. It was the prolific, and irresponsible means conspirators use to propagate their self-serving initiatives on increased confusion with the UFOs and Alien issues.

During quiet times, for instance, while resting in bed, I let my mind wander into the vast expanse of cosmos, and universe, pondering about its possibilities. It took some time, but I eventually made peace with conspirators, and paranormal supporters. It was them that provided fuel, and incentives inspiring the human mind to explore worlds other than just one lonely life-containing planet, Earth.

And so, I dream on, thankful to the conspirators, which, by the way, are decent people just as much as you, and I. Perhaps, I could put the confusion about it all to rest.

OUR FUTURE

Months have gone by since my last visitors left. I have been with my own thoughts again, for how long it would be, I don't know. I'd have to deal with the passage of time on my own again. "What does the future hold in store for me, and the rest of the world?" I have asked myself many times on such quiet moments. It seems the older I get the more isolated my life has become. Realizing that, I am making a personal effort to get out among the people, whenever I have the energy, and urge. Buzz, my buddy, in contrast a family man with grandchildren, pays me visits, as brief as a couple of hours, whenever he feels like talking. We, among others, have had a rich career for many years. Unfortunately, it has been mostly lived out of town spread across the globe. We both realized that, the older one got the more difficult travel became, especially when alone fighting airport, and airline crowds. What may not be obvious to the young traveler is that comfort, and luxury have, for the most part, disappeared, unless one has the means to afford a seat in first class. Where unlimited services, and airline offerings used to be the norm, in keeping competitive, most of the amenities have been cut out in past decades. Today, it is nothing but moving people in crammed, noisy, and at times disruptive surroundings with passengers rushing to their destination.

What have we become?

A rushed society driven by technology with seemingly no time left for leisure. I clearly recall a time when people were friendly, welcoming a conversation with a fellow traveler apt to listen, no matter how brief. What I see today is individuals with faces buried in iPhone and iPad screens shutting out the world, in the process passing off the beauty of everyday life. A beauty found everywhere one turns, whether strolling along an alley absorbing trees in blossom; watching the people bumping into things rushing to catch the subway, getting a laugh as a result; trying to make sense out of graffiti plastered along an otherwise gray wall, in the eyes of the artist, beauty, nevertheless; enjoying an otherwise arduous day amid coworkers, and their office chatter; waiting out the rush-hour at some stylish café; or planning out how to end the day. Unfortunately, the days of leisure have been cut short by runaway technology everybody is striving to keep up with whether through peer pressure, or individual demand, never to be recovered. Though there is one consolation: retirement, which most of us are forced into sooner or later, if one has the means, and health to sustain. It is the chance one could recapture lost time, and get a second chance to enjoy the beauty of life.

Currently, I was in Buzz's company, once more reliving the past. Since we were not working together anymore, though living in the same town, there was not much conversation about the present. Both of us did not relish much about current news, announcing an increase in crime rates, school shootings, and political backstabbing presented in between ridiculous-sounding commercials. It appears that in today's fast-paced world anything was acceptable, no matter how insulting it was to one's intelligence.

"Yeah," Buzz replied. "Those were the good days."

"Ever think of doing some more contracting?"

"Not since I completely retired." It was apparent that he enjoyed his retirement status. "What about you?"

"I miss working with people. I miss the excitement we used to have. I should feel like I have lived life to its fullest within my capacity, and means. I reached a goal not many could claim," I explained, "that of a childhood dream."

"Come to think of it," Buzz replied. "You never talked about it."

"Not everybody is interested in somebody else's life." It had always been one of my concerns to not burden people with my personal achievements. I'd learned to mostly listen. Most people liked to talk about themselves without being willing to share another's interests. It was not to say that Buzz was in that category. Since we'd had similar experiences in the past, we could sit in the quiet just to enjoy each other's company, but that was not in my nature. From my perspective, there were so many topics to expound, and explore in the rapidly-declining time element of the individual life.

"I am," he boldly stated. "We have worked and, at times, lived, and travelled together to many places, but do I know you? Hardly."

"The feeling is mutual," I said, not knowing otherwise.

"Tell me about it."

"How could I refuse such an offer?" I grinned at him. "If you really want to listen to my past, get comfortable." I also encouraged him to interrupt whenever he felt like doing so. It would only be fair. I was sure he felt my frustration, at times, to patiently listen to another's stories. His encouragement was based on my fairness to keep up a dialogue rather than a single-sided monologue.

"Another beer?"

"Sure." Buzz was always up for one. Since both of us were introduced to exotic alcoholic beverages served around the globe, we'd had ample opportunities to sample many foreign brands. Though we both enjoyed the variety, we appreciated quality over quantity. Neither of us ever got inebriated or drunk. "Tell me about your dreams, and aspirations."

"Well," I started, getting comfortable in the recliner. "My dream was to explore the world."

"We sure did, that's for sure."

"But there is more to it, much more," I explained. "You may or may not know, but I was presented with opportunities not many had. Opportunities I explored, and challenges I delivered with results I even surprised myself with at times. As you know, I'm not a dreamer dwelling on rewards. I am a realist. A realist in pursuit of the truth that many of us seek, and can never find."

"Truth about what?"

"About the purpose of life. You ever think about it?"

"Many times," he said with a shrug of the shoulders. "But I've given up hope. Nobody seems to have the answer."

"Ever delved into history?"

"I read. But not as much as you. I live in the world of today, and besides," he said, "I have a family I enjoy that lives with me."

"I fully understand. Many don't have the luxury of leisure time that I have. So," I offered, "to explore the secrets of life, I had to dig as far back into historical archives when man began to write." It was a statement that would make everybody's ears perk up.

"Did you come up with the answer?"

"I did not find the answers I was looking for, but found enough knowledge to draw my own conclusions." I could not have been more explicit. I had his full attention.

"That I need to hear."

What better invitation? A prompt like that was all I needed to get going, and share my knowledge. "As far back as recorded in ancient archives, man has been trying to understand the purpose of life."

"How far back are we talking about?" Buzz asked.

"About six thousand years. Way before Noah, and the flood."

"You serious? I thought the flood wiped everything from the face of the earth."

"Not true. If we had paper records, perhaps. True, it may have tumbled structures, but individual relics survived the worst of floods, and there were many."

"Relics?"

"No. Floods. You must have an open mind when digging into history. You cannot rely on scriptures alone. Most factual sources come from archaeological excavations. They're evidence of times, places, and events that took place millennia ago."

"I understand that, but what about the religious aspects?"

"There will always be clashes. You know that. We could argue about it until we are blue in the face," I reminded him. "That's why we stay away from it. We have enough tension just thinking about politics." I had realized decades ago that whenever I would touch on the subject of faith, he seemed to feel uncomfortable. It was much later that I found out about his religious denomination. It was different from mine. I respected that, and would avoid any personal confrontation.[70]

"The Bible insists there was only one flood. How can you contest that?" It was a challenge I was prepared for. I addressed it on past occasions.

"You may not be familiar with scriptures outside of yours, but there are many different faiths in the world with as many religious practices. I'll name just the principle ones practiced by the world population: Christianity, Judaism, Islam, Hinduism, Buddhism, Taoism, and perhaps Shinto. You can see that this covers every populated continent on earth. Each carry their own story of a flood."

"You see," Buzz jumped in happily. "It affected the entire earth."

"I said 'a flood,' not 'the flood.'"

"What's the difference?"

"The difference is whether it took place in all places at once, or only at one specific place, and whether it was factual, or carried across the globe as a legendary tale."

"Now you've got me confused."

"Alright then. Let me un-confuse you. How long have we known each other?"

"Many years, but that's not the issue."

---

[70] A special section on religion can be found in PART SIX – Personal Views.

"But it is. What is the single most important aspect of our work?" I had to put him to the test.

"Logic?"

"Precisely. It is logic, as well as facts conceived, developed, and tested by science. Right?"

"Right. But what does the flood have to do with it?"

"Everything. There is only one place on Earth where the flood could be proven archaeologically, in the cradle of mankind. Ever heard of the paleolithic, Mesolithic, Neolithic, and bronze age times?"

"Sure have, but you are talking hundreds of thousands of years."

"How about two hundred thousand years?"

"What's your point?" He did not take much to lecturing, but who did? Only history buffs like myself appreciated ancient facts.

"My point is that mankind dates back that far, but it was not until the bronze age when civilization began to take root."

"What are we talking about? Six thousand years?"

"Almost. More like five thousand some years," I stated. "It was when writing in Sumer was invented. That triggered the beginning of recorded history."

"Sumer. Eh? Where exactly are we talking about?"

"The region between the Tigris, and Euphrates rivers."

"You mean," he said, with a startled look on his face, "that's where the flood took place?"

"That's not what I meant. It is where archaeological findings pinpoint evidence of the flood."

"No place else?" There was disappointment written on his face, and rightly so. I could attest to it, being brought up in a strict Catholic environment. It was easy to understand when one followed the Bible, but very confusing from an archaeological perspective.

"Not proven," I said, thinking he'd had enough of history discussions for one day, but this was not the case.

"What do the other religions say?"

"Some carry tales, others don't mention anything in their scriptures. Just imagine a flood that would reach the plateaus of China, Tibet, Mongolia, Siberia? Even with all of the oceans, and lakes on Earth combined, it's physically impossible."

"No mentions of the flood?" He was seemingly disappointed. Probably not so much from the revelation, as much as it infringed on his beliefs. Now, the reader will understand why I keep my distance from discussing such a sensitive topic. While some will be offended with talks like this, others stay away from getting drawn into a debate only leading to misery, and discomfort.

"No mentions, but you should ease your mind with the following conjectures. Philosophers, academics, prophets, theorists, thinkers, and the common inquisitive person have tried to find written proof, but all have failed for the same recognition: we are humans, and are not enlightened enough to have come up with the definitive answer yet."

"It means," Buzz speculated, yielding to the unavoidable, "we must rely on faith?"

"That's right. Faith creates the strong bonds needed to procreate children, grandchildren, and to carry on family heritage. Without a belief there is no structure. Without structure there is no foundation. Without a foundation the nation will crumble."

"Now you are judgmental."

"I have read enough of history to know that every empire has crumbled for the same reasons. Lack of belief in higher authority, and discipline to the laws provided us. Cultures have collapsed, and will keep on crashing unless there is unity among its population. We, in the United States, have lost this unity. It may be too late to save our country from collapse."

"You sound gloomy. You're saying that we have no future as a United States."

"No future. The trends are visible to the informed. It comes on gradually. First there are amendments to the constitution to accommodate everybody, and every whim mandated. Quick to follow is legalizing social demands of every kind. Next are liberation movements for every cause. People," I further explained, "if you let them, will keep pushing more, and more. Pretty soon, personal pleasure, and instant gratification will take over obligation, and responsibility. It will be alcohol, drugs, free sex, nasty entertaining, and dirty jokes, abusing what our forefathers intended as clean freedom of speech. Nothing else will matter anymore except cultural demoralization with devil worship inviting evil spirits, and malicious behavior. We already have too many demons living on Earth without inviting more. Borders will open to the masses trying to get their slice of the good times, in turn, clouding, and polluting the inherited culture. Pretty soon, cultures will merge, and soon there will be no distinction left between people, customs, and country."

"I can't imagine it is happening." Though reluctantly, Buzz was taking it all in at face value. He knew me enough to trust my judgements.

"Believe me. It is happening all over the globe. Soon, globalization will replace democracy, resulting in the inevitable, war! Then, the cycle will start over again. All one can do is prolong the established national identity through strong leadership, discipline, and respect for the law, and law enforcement. Regardless of future consequences, we can consider ourselves lucky that our nation lasted as long as it did, 250 years."

"Not a bad track record?" Buzz said.

"It's not something to brag about," I informed him. "The Greek empire lasted 650 years. The Roman empire 2,000 years. Egyptian empire 2,100 years. Chinese empire over 5,000. India, 7,500 years. Want to hear more?"

"No. I've heard enough. I didn't expect such bad news. Not for us."

"Why should we be different?"

"Because we are an innovative people with a strong pioneering spirit."

"Pioneering only lasts until the land is explored, and populated. Once borders are defined, land development begins. Once that is saturated with people, and structures, where do we go?"

"Into space?"

"Now you understand."

"I've gotta go," Buzz said, checking his wristwatch. "Wife wants me back for dinner."

"See you. Keep in touch," I said. "Don't be a stranger." Alone once more, I contemplated what to do next. I kept in touch with my contracting partner in DC. "Should give him a call," I decided. I was still in the running for contracting with the government, if by chance, there was a budget. Since I had closed my own business, I relied on my partner to check on RFI and RFP announcements to possibly apply my skills. Unfortunately, in recent years, there had not been much budget allocations for national defense.

Undecided at the moment, I had a new thought, "why not give Mystery-man a call?" It'd been a while since we last talked.

"DARPA Engineering," the distant voice responded after a few rings.

"Mystery-man?" I queried.

"Alex, how in heck are you?" Apparently, other than me, no one in his department referred to the label.

"Just checking up on you," I replied, hoping he had the time. "Can we talk?"

"Sure. What's up?" Based on the past, we both knew that there was always a reason for us to call. Today was no exception.

"I'll be in your neighborhood in a couple of days. You want to get together?"

"Certainly. I'll always take the time to see you. Don't I? Anything important?"

"Nothing pressing other than the usual."

"Usual?" he questioned. "There's nothing usual about you, my friend."

"Okay," I said, submitting to my call. "I am always interested in new technology." There it was, my admittance to the visit. He realized I was probing, but did not know the reason.

"You know I can't talk about it," he cautioned. "Anything specific?"

"Just looking for contracting possibilities."

"In that case," he stated. "Stop on by. You know the place."

"Thanks. I'll be there."

Two days later I showed up at his office in Reston, VA. "Come on in," he greeted me with a gesture at the empty chair. "Have a seat." Passing by his desk I could not help but exclaim, "What's this," after catching a glance at a picture seemingly tossed on top of a stack of photograph.

He hesitated for a second, then said, "Something we've been working on." I could sense a reluctance with his reply almost regretting for having me in his office. He inadvertently revealed a secret kept tightly cloaked for however many years. While he was still reacting, I formulated a response to put him at ease, while he covered up the photos.

"Don't worry." I said, assuring him of my dedication to the same cause. "I won't jeopardize your credentials. But I am curious. Is it the famous Dark Star, rumors have it?" I had a quick glance at the photo label, "RQ-170." It was not a completely unfamiliar object. I had seen them flying in the sky.

"How did you know," he exclaimed in wonder what else I might have known. "One of my projects."

"I thought so."

"Listen," he said, accompanied with a warning. "Nothing you see here gets out of this office. Understand?"

"Completely. But let me assure you," I offered. "This is not the only project development facility for the government. There is Sandia... White Sands... Oak Ridge... LLL..."

"All right," he cut me short, then, "I know, but what I don't understand is that you, a contractor knows so much."

"I am detail oriented and wasn't asleep when I worked in AUTODIN, and Missile Defense, and..."

"Very well. I believe you."

It was all to be said on the subjects of trust and dedication. From here on, after reminding Mystery-man of my access clearances, there was no more barrier between us. For the rest of my visiting his office, we spent most of our time productively on satellite, defense grid, cybersecurity, Cyberforce, and other technologies in the planning.

"One more thing," he said, prior to my departing. "I am thinking of retiring."

"Not you," I rejected his declaration. "People like you and me don't have the luxury."

"No, really," he insisted. "I want to dedicate my time to the wife and family."

"In case you do," I said, not yet coming to terms with what he just said. "Don't shut me out of your life. We have too much to share."

"Don't worry. You'll hear from me."

That was it. It would be my last visit with him before his retirement. I truly miss the man. As far as I was concerned, there was only one Mystery-man. Fortunately, he kept connected through frequent emails, our mode of communication, just to assure his friends that he was still around watching over us, until the day his emails stopped – 2013.

His voice went silent. Forever.

INTEL AND SPYING

Espionage (colloquially, spying) is the obtaining of secret or confidential information without the permission of the holder of the information. Spies help agencies uncover secret information. Any individual, or spy ring, a cooperating group of spies, in the service of a government, company or independent operation, can commit espionage. The practice is clandestine, as it is by definition unwelcome, and in many cases illegal, and punishable by law. Espionage is a subset of "Intelligence" gathering, which includes espionage as well as information gathering from public sources.

Espionage is often part of an institutional effort by a government or commercial concern. However, the term tends to associate with state spying on potential, or actual enemies for military purposes. Spying involving corporations is known as industrial espionage.

One of the most effective ways to gather data, and information about the enemy, or potential enemy is by infiltrating the enemy's ranks. This was the job of the spy, or espionage agent. Spies could return all sorts of information concerning the size, and strength of enemy forces. They could also find dissidents within the enemy's forces, and influence them to defect. In times of crisis, spies could also oblige to steal technology, and sabotage the enemy in various ways. Counterintelligence is the practice of various means of thwarting enemy espionage, and Intelligence-gathering. Almost all nations have strict laws concerning espionage, and the penalty for being caught is often severe. However, the benefits of espionage are often great enough that most governments, and many large corporations make use of it to varying degrees.

Today

Today, espionage agencies target the illegal drug trade, and terrorists as well as state actors. Since 2008, the United States has charged at least 57 defendants for attempting to spy for China.

Different Intelligence services value certain Intelligence collection techniques over others. The former Soviet Union, for example, preferred human sources over research in open sources, while the United States has tended to emphasize technological methods such as SIGINT, and IMINT. Both Soviet political (KGB), and military Intelligence (GRU) officers were judged by the number of agents they recruited.

Legal Implications

Espionage is a crime under the legal code of many nations. In the United States it is covered by the Espionage Act of 1917. The risks of espionage vary. A spy breaking the host country's laws may be deported, imprisoned, or even executed. A spy breaking their own country's laws could be imprisoned for espionage, and treason, which in the USA, and some other jurisdictions could only occur if they took up arms, or aided the enemy against their own country during wartime, or even executed, as the Rosenbergs were. Hugh Francis Redmond, a CIA officer in China, spent nineteen years in a Chinese prison for espionage, and died there as he was operating without diplomatic cover, and immunity.

In United States law, treason, espionage, and spying are separate crimes. Treason, and espionage have graduated punishment levels.

History of espionage laws
From ancient times, the penalty for espionage in many countries was execution. This was true right up until the era of World War II. In modern times, many people convicted of espionage have been given penal sentences rather than execution. For example, Aldrich Hazen Ames is an American CIA analyst turned KGB mole who was convicted of espionage in 1994. He is serving a life sentence without the possibility of parole in the high-security Allenwood U.S. Penitentiary.

Use against non-spies
In the early 21st century, the act was used to prosecute whistleblowers such as Thomas Andrews Drake, and Edward Snowden. As of 2012, India, and Pakistan were holding several hundred prisoners of each other's country for minor violations like trespassing or visa overstay, often with accusations of espionage attached. Some of these include cases where Pakistan, and India both denied citizenship to these people, leaving them stateless. Most of the problems were attributed to tensions caused by the Kashmir conflict.

Difference Between Intelligence, and Espionage
The difference is a matter of life, and death. Intelligence is information gathering. Espionage is illegal when you break the law to obtain information secrets. There is a definite grey area when it comes to illegal activities involving lying, cheating, stealing, and misrepresenting. Unethical or immoral behavior that risks lawsuits, and making enemies is espionage or borderline espionage. The Society for Competitive Intelligence has guidelines, and a code of conduct for this sort of thing. People protect secrets for reasons. Stealing secrets is espionage.

Military conflicts
In military conflicts, espionage is considered permissible as many nations recognize the inevitability of opposing sides seeking Intelligence each about the dispositions of the other. To make the mission easier, and successful, soldiers or agents wear disguises to conceal their true identity from the enemy while penetrating enemy lines for Intelligence gathering. However, if they were caught behind enemy lines in disguises, they were not entitled to prisoner-of-war status, and were subject to prosecution, and punishment, including execution. Soldiers who penetrated enemy lines in proper uniforms for the purpose of acquiring Intelligence were not considered spies but were lawful combatants entitled to be treated as prisoners of war upon capture by the enemy.

Excluded from being treated as spies while behind enemy lines were escaping prisoners of war, and downed airmen as international law distinguished between a disguised spy, and a disguised escaper. It is permissible for these groups to wear enemy uniforms or civilian clothes in order to facilitate their escape back to friendly lines so long as they did not attack enemy forces, collect military Intelligence, or engage in similar military operations while so disguised. Soldiers who are wearing enemy uniforms or civilian clothes simply for the sake of warmth along with other purposes rather than engaging in espionage or similar military operations while so attired are also excluded from being treated as unlawful combatants.

Saboteurs are treated as spies as they too wore disguises behind enemy lines for the purpose of waging destruction on enemy's vital targets in addition to Intelligence gathering. For example, during World War II, eight German agents entered the U.S. in June 1942 as part of Operation Pastorius, a sabotage mission against U.S. economic targets. Two weeks later, all were arrested in civilian clothes by the FBI. Under the Hague Convention of 1907, these Germans were classified as spies, and tried by a military tribunal in Washington D.C., found guilty, and sentenced to death.

The U.S. codification of enemy spies of the Uniform Code of Military Justice provides a mandatory death sentence if a person captured in the act is proven to be "lurking as a spy or acting as a spy in or about any place, vessel, or aircraft, within the control or jurisdiction of any of the armed forces, or in or about any shipyard, any manufacturing or industrial plant, or any other place or institution engaged in work in aid of the prosecution of the war by the United States, or elsewhere."

Agents in Espionage

In espionage jargon, an "agent" is the person who does the spying. Citizen of one country, they are recruited by a second country to spy on or work against their own country or a third country. In popular usage, this term is often erroneously applied to a member of an Intelligence service who recruits, and handles agents. In espionage such a person is referred to as Intelligence officer, Intelligence operative or case officer. There are several types of agent in use today:

- Double agents engage in clandestine activity for two Intelligence or security services or more in joint operations, who provide information about one or about each to the other, and who wittingly withheld significant information from one on the instructions of the other or was unwittingly manipulated by one so that significant facts are withheld from the adversary. Peddlers, fabricators, and others who work for themselves rather than a service are not double agents because they are not agents. The fact that double agents have an agent relationship with both sides distinguishes them from penetrations, who normally are placed with the target service in a staff or officer capacity.
- Redoubled agents are forced to mislead the foreign Intelligence service after being caught as a double agent, and used against the later country.
- Unwitting double agents are offered or forced to recruit as a double or redoubled agent and, in the process, are recruited by either a third-party Intelligence service or his own government without the knowledge of the intended target Intelligence service or the agent. This can be useful in capturing important information from an agent that is attempting to seek allegiance with another country. The double agent usually has knowledge of both Intelligence services, and can identify operational techniques of both, thus making third-party recruitment difficult or impossible. The knowledge of operational techniques can also affect the relationship between the operations officer or case officer, and the agent if the case is transferred by an operational targeting officer to a new operations officer, leaving the new officer vulnerable to attack. This type of transfer may occur when an officer has completed his term of service or when his cover is blown.
- Triple agents work for three Intelligence services.

- Intelligence agents provide access to sensitive information through the use of special privileges. If used in *corporate Intelligence* gathering, this may include gathering information of a corporate business venture or stock portfolio. In *economic Intelligence*, "Economic Analysts may use their specialized skills to analyze, and interpret economic trends, and developments, assess, and track foreign financial activities, and develop new econometric, and modeling methodologies."
- Access agents provide access to other potential agents by offering profiling information that can help lead to recruitment into an Intelligence service.
- Agents of influence provide political influence in an area of interest, possibly including publications needed to further an Intelligence service agenda. This includes the use of the media to print a story to mislead a foreign service into action, exposing their operations while under surveillance.
- Agent provocateurs instigate trouble or provide information to gather as many people as possible into one location for an arrest.
- Facilities agents provide access to buildings, such as garages or offices used for staging operations, resupply, etc.
- Principal agents function as a handler for an established network of agents, usually considered "blue chip."
- Confusion agents provide misleading information to an enemy Intelligence service or attempt to discredit the operations of the target in an operation.
- Sleeper agents are recruited to wake up, *and* perform a specific set of tasks or functions while living under cover in an area of interest. This type of agent is not the same as a deep cover operative, who continually contacts a case officer to file Intelligence reports. A sleeper agent is not in contact with anyone until activated.
- Illegal agents live in another country under false credentials, and do not report to a local station. A nonofficial cover operative can be dubbed an "illegal" when working in another country without diplomatic protection.

Agents in Spying

A spy is a person employed to seek out top secret information from a source. Within the United States Intelligence Community, "asset" is a more common usage. A case officer, who may have diplomatic status (i.e., official cover or non-official cover), supports, and directs the human collector. Cutouts are couriers who do not know the agent or case officer but transfer messages. A safe house is a refuge for spies. Spies often seek to obtain secret information from another source.

In larger networks the organization can be complex with many methods to avoid detection, including clandestine cell systems. Often the players have never met. Case officers are stationed in foreign countries to recruit, and to supervise Intelligence agents, who in turn spy on targets in their countries where they were assigned. A spy needs not be a citizen of the target country—hence they do not automatically commit treason when operating within it. While the more common practice is to recruit a person already trusted with access to sensitive information, sometimes a person with a well-prepared synthetic identity (cover background), called a *legend* in tradecraft, may attempt to infiltrate a target organization.

These agents could be moles (who were recruited before they got access to secrets), defectors (who were recruited after they got access to secrets, and leave their country) or defectors in place (who got access but did not leave).

A *legend* is also employed for an individual who is *not* an illegal agent but is an ordinary citizen who is "relocated," for example, a "protected witness." Nevertheless, such a non-agent very likely would also have a case officer who would act as controller. As in most, if not all, synthetic identity schemes, for whatever purpose (illegal or legal), the assistance of a controller is required.

Spies may also be used to spread disinformation in the organization in which they are planted, such as giving false reports about their country's military movements, or about a competing company's ability to bring a product to market. Spies may be given other roles that also require infiltration, such as sabotage.

Many governments routinely spy on their allies as well as their enemies, although they typically maintain a policy of not commenting on this. Governments also employ private companies to collect information on their behalf such as SCG International Risk, International Intelligence Limited, and others.

Many organizations, both national, and non-national, conduct espionage operations. It should not be assumed that espionage is always directed at the most secret operations of a target country. National terrorist organizations and other extremist groups are targets too. This is because governments want to retrieve information that they can use to be proactive in protecting their nation from potential terrorist attacks.

Communications are necessary to both espionage, and clandestine operations, and also are a great vulnerability when the adversary has sophisticated SIGINT detection, and interception capability. Agents must also transfer money securely.

Methods, and terminology
Although the news media may speak of "spy satellites", and the like, espionage is not a synonym for all Intelligence-gathering disciplines. It is a specific form of human source Intelligence (HUMINT). Codebreaking (cryptanalysis or COMINT), aircraft or satellite photography (IMINT), and research in open publications (OSINT) are all Intelligence gathering disciplines, but none of them are considered espionage. Many HUMINT activities, such as prisoner interrogation, reports from military reconnaissance patrols, and from diplomats, etc., are not considered espionage. Espionage is the disclosure of sensitive information (classified) to people who are not cleared for that information or access to that sensitive information.

Unlike other forms of Intelligence collection disciplines, espionage usually involves accessing the place where the desired information is stored, or accessing the people who know the information, and would divulge it through some kind of subterfuge. There are exceptions to physical meetings, such as the Oslo Report, or the insistence of Robert Hanssen in never meeting the people who bought his information.

The U.S. defines espionage towards itself as "The act of obtaining, delivering, transmitting, communicating, or receiving information about the national defense with an intent, or reason to believe, that the information may be used to the injury of the United States or to the advantage of any foreign nation."

Targets of espionage

Espionage agents are usually trained experts in a specific targeted field so they can differentiate mundane information from targets of intrinsic value to their own organizational development. Correct identification of the target at its execution is the sole purpose of the espionage operation.

Broad areas of espionage targeting expertise include:

- Natural resources: strategic production identification, and assessment (food, energy, materials). Agents are usually found among bureaucrats who administer these resources in their own countries.
- Popular sentiment towards domestic, and foreign policies (popular, middle class, elites). Agents often recruit from field journalistic crews, exchange postgraduate students, and sociology researchers.
- Strategic economic strengths (production, research, manufacture, infrastructure). Agents recruit from science, and technology academia, commercial enterprises, and, more rarely, from among military technologists.
- Military capability Intelligence (offensive, defensive, maneuver, naval, air, space). Agents are trained by special military espionage education facilities, and posted to an area of operation with covert identities to minimize prosecution.
- Counterintelligence operations specifically targeting opponents' Intelligence services themselves, such as breaching confidentiality of communications, and recruiting defectors or moles.

Purpose, and Reasons for Intelligence, and Spying
Spying is necessary; every country does it. In spying, everybody becomes an adversary regardless of alliance. There are only two reasons for spying. One, to assess the other country's capabilities. Two, to assess the country's intentions.

Intelligence cycle management
Intelligence cycle management refers to the overall activity of guiding the Intelligence cycle, which is a set of processes used to provide decision-useful information (Intelligence) to leaders. The cycle consists of several processes, including planning, and direction, collection, processing, and exploitation, analysis, and production, and dissemination, and integration. The related field of Counterintelligence is tasked with impeding the Intelligence efforts of others. Intelligence organizations are not infallible (Intelligence reports are often referred to as "estimates," and often include measures of confidence, and reliability) but, when properly managed, and tasked, can be among the most valuable tools of management, and government.

The principles of Intelligence have been discussed, and developed from the earliest writers on warfare to the most recent writers on technology. Despite the most powerful computers, the human mind remains at the core of Intelligence, discerning patterns, and extracting meaning from a flood of correct, incorrect, and sometimes deliberately misleading information (also known as disinformation).

One basic model of the Intelligence process is called the "Intelligence cycle." This model could be applied and, like all basic models, it does not reflect the fullness of real-world operations. Intelligence is processed information. The activities of the

Intelligence cycle obtain, and assemble information, convert it into Intelligence, and make it available to its users. The Intelligence cycle comprises five phases:

1. *Planning, and Direction:* Deciding what is to be monitored, and analyzed. In Intelligence usage, the determination of Intelligence requirements, development of appropriate Intelligence architecture, preparation of a collection plan, issuance of orders, and requests to information collection agencies.
2. *Collection:* Obtaining raw information using a variety of collection disciplines such as human Intelligence (HUMINT), geospatial Intelligence (GEOINT), and others.
3. *Processing:* Refining, and analyzing the information.
4. Analysis, and production: The data that had been processed is translated into a finished Intelligence product, which includes integrating, collating, evaluating, and analyzing all the data.
5. *Dissemination:* Providing the results of processing to consumers (including those in the Intelligence community), including the use of Intelligence information in net assessment, and strategic gaming.

A distinct Intelligence officer is often entrusted with managing each level of the process.

Intelligence, Surveillance, and Reconnaissance (ISR) describes an activity that synchronizes, and integrates the planning, and operation of sensors, assets, and processing, exploitation, and dissemination systems in direct support of current, and future operations. This is an integrated Intelligence, and operations function.

Sensors (people or systems) collect data from the operational environment during the collection phase, which is then converted into information during the processing, and exploitation phase. During the analysis, and production phase, the information is converted into Intelligence.

Planning, and direction overview
The planning, and direction phase of the Intelligence cycle includes four major steps:

1. Identification, and prioritization of Intelligence *requirements*;
2. Development of appropriate Intelligence *architecture*;
3. Preparation of a *collection plan*; and
4. Issuance of *orders, and requests* to information collection agencies.

Requirements
Leaders with specific objectives communicate their requirements for Intelligence inputs to applicable agencies or contacts. An Intelligence "consumer" might be an infantry officer who needs to know what is on the other side of the next hill, a head of government who wants to know the probability that a foreign leader will go to war over a certain point, a corporate executive who wants to know what his or her competitors are planning, or any person or organization (for example, a person who wants to know if his or her spouse is faithful).

National Strategy

Establishing the Intelligence requirements of the policy-makers... "is management of the entire Intelligence cycle, from identifying the need for data to delivering an Intelligence product to a consumer," according to a report by the U.S. Intelligence Board. It is the beginning, and the end of the cycle—the beginning because it involves drawing up specific collection requirements, and the end because finished Intelligence, which supports policy decisions, generates new requirements.

The whole process depends on guidance from public officials. Policy-makers, the president, his aides, the National Security Council, and other major departments, and agencies of government initiate requests for Intelligence. Issue coordinators interact with these public officials to establish their core concerns, and related information requirements. These needs are then used to guide collection strategies, and the production of appropriate Intelligence products.

As the reader can see from the above illustrated spying versus espionage activities, gaining access, and gathering information, and data is not a simple task. Rules, and regulations have been carefully devised to guide the clandestine individual through every step, and possibility to gain an advantage over the adversary. Despite the many rules, and regulations available, I doubt that the actual recruit has knowledge in all of its phases. It is probably the case why many espionage agents have paid the price with their lives. No sane person would subject his/her life to a possible death sentence for a few thousand dollars of services rendered.

VIEWS ON TERRORISM

Just recently, I went to a gun show in town, which, as many readers will have noticed, have been on the increase in recent years. Following daily news items, whether on mainstream media, or in the newspaper, one cannot help but be informed about the reasons for the heightened interest in weapons. Inside the hall, watching the patrons moving from table to table, I took the time to watch their behavior. Most visitors seemed to be old-timers at the show. You could easily spot them by the clothes they wore, and the demeanor they displayed as being seasoned hunters or shooters. Their steady pace followed the general stream of visitors flowing up one row of tables then down the next. What was different were their eyes scanning rapidly over the offered wares on display. Then, there were the young, and anxious potential buyers, too impatient to follow the lines. They were the ones darting in and out squeezing their bodies through the lines to get to a table. Their focus was aimed at a specific object on display. They were not interest in knifes, archery equipment, and other trinkets and souvenirs up for sale. Their mind, and eyes were only focused on one thing: automatic weapons. It was no wonder with recent announcements by the government, and political factions to get better control over the rapidly-firing killing ordnance.

"You planning to buy one?" Buzz said, pacing alongside. Even he had expressed a desire to check out an automatic, the reason he was by my side. A family man, and devout Christian, he had a different view for owning a weapon. As far as I knew he did not own one.

"Maybe?"

In contrast, I had bought several firearms in the 70s. Mostly collectors' items, they were hand guns for the most part. I did have a pump-action shotgun by the side of my bed, just in case. I did not like surprises, especially not while asleep, a most vulnerable state. My interest in the automatic was for different reasons than the recent public craze for rushing to get the weapon before Congress banned the fully automatic. I was trained in firing guns, and automatic weapons during my assignments in Vietnam. In the early days, not only soldiers, but everybody on contract owned a weapon. Whether one had a reason to own a gun or not, it was the thing to have. "Self-protection," was the general reply when asked. In a way it was true, especially when in a warzone. In case of a direct assault, it was better to be caught with a weapon than not. It could save your life, or at least give you a chance for a fair fight, if there was such a thing in warfare. The days of the Gentlemen Wars, fought mostly by the British, had long passed. It was all stealth, and strategy directed by state-of-the-art technology.

Presently, we approached what seemed to be a popular display table. People were anxiously pushing for a position up front. There was a waiting line to get the attention of a sales person. "What model?" the weapons expert said, his eyes darting around the table seeking out the next customer. Today, it was not "How can I help?" That question was irrelevant. Everybody under the roof of the convention hall was focused on one object, the AR-15. It was the weapon of choice for government issue, and public alike, but for different reasons. Opposite reasons, I should point out.

"I am looking for an M-16."

"Don't have one," the expert claimed. "Can't sell it. I only carry the AR-15." He turned to a shelf in back, and produced a package containing a brand new, stripped down, black-powder coated assault weapon. He handed it to me then served the next customer. I weighed it in my hands. It felt like it was specifically made for me. Probably the reason for its popularity.

"Here," I handed it to Buzz. "Knock yourself out."

Like most of the buyers present, it was his first experience handling an automatic. I watched him handling the weapon. Without exception, anyone touching it for the first time experienced a new feeling surge through their body. It was the feel of power. Whether consciously or subconsciously, it was the power people sought out. I felt it too the first time I had held the M-16, blasting a few rounds at a target.

Seemingly satisfied, Buzz handed the weapon back to me. "Feels right, doesn't it?"

"Wait until it's loaded. This is still stripped down."

"What do you mean?"

I took him by the arm to a different section on the table. "See all these gadgets?" I pointed out items specifically designed as attachments, necessary or not, optional for the buyer. "You customize your purchase."

"What will I need?"

"Depends on what you'll use it for."

"Give me an idea." Like most people handling this kind of weapon for the first time, he needed some advice.

"I'll tell you what," I offered. "I will buy one with all the trimmings, and you can decide then."

"Deal," he agreed.

I knew what parts I wanted, and said so when the sales expert attended to my wishes. "Full complement," I ordered.

"Type of scope?" The make, and model scope were an individual preference.

"Laser spotter," I demanded.

"Magazine?"

"30 Rounds."

"Cartridge?"

"Make it a box of 223 Remington."

"Here," he handed me a clipboard with the purchase application attached. "I'll have your order ready in fifteen minutes."

It took several minutes, with Buzz looking over my shoulder, to fill in data the authorities wanted, necessary to conclude the sale. As long as your police record was clean, there were no obstacles for getting a weapon over the legal counter. While many hunters, and sportsmen preferred an unregistered firearm, it was safer to obtain one that could be registered. The consequences if getting caught with an unregistered weapon could land you in jail, and I, for one, was not a proponent of forfeiting my freedom. Though owning an automatic inferred to the protection of your freedom, it still had to be on legal terms, for the honest citizen.

"Here," the expert handed me the sales bill, in exchange for my Visa card. The total charge, including tax, was $1,125.

"Not bad a price," I beamed. "Eh?"

"How come it's so cheap?" Buzz had expected a much higher cost for something very much in demand.

"Remember Obama's gun control law that was never approved by Congress?"

"Sure do," he admitted. "Caused quite an uproar with conservatives."

"It caused an avalanche in weapons manufacturing. Everybody wanted to take the opportunity to get a firearm before they were banned from sales. Manufacturers geared up production. The public went crazy with buying. After the bill was vetoed, though many weapons landed in the hands of citizens, an over-production of arms wound up in stores unable to be sold. Initially, the cost of all firearms went up drastically, but shortly after dropped dramatically."

"That explains the low cost," Buzz surmised, deciding to get his own unit. "I want one just like his," he placed his order with the expert, pointing at the firearm in my hands.

The final configuration of my just-purchased firearm was the AR-15 long stock, and barrel, cooling grill surrounding the barrel casing, high performance, extended range, laser scope, including a package of cartridges, and various-sized targets. While waiting for Buzz's purchase I explained the difference between an M-16, and the AR-15. First off, the former, a fully automatic weapon, was banned from public sale in 1984. Since then it was only authorized, and issued to the military, and police. If one could find an M-16 on the black market today the cost would range in the thousands of dollars. The AR-15, a semi-automatic, was created as a result, but was modified to only fire one shot at a time.

The differences between the two models, as far as I could identify, were multiple. The M16-A1, original version, was built for portability in deployment, durability at the terrain, and reliability when confronted by the enemy. The handle was built into the stock for easy of handling. The firing mechanism was simple, but effective. The weapon was light in weight, and reliable when fired. It was the soldier's most favored firearm after WWII. The difference, and why the AR-15 gained so much popularity is configuration. Though only semi-automatic, one shot at a time, an assortment of optional components was available. The weapon provided a variety of applications from target sports to game hunting.

"I'm ready," Buzz proudly declared after his purchase. "Let's get out of here."

We were the proud owners of a semi-automatic rifle ready to do damage, if we chose so. But that was not my reason for today's purchase. I wanted to know Buzz's reasons. "Why did you decide on buying?"

"Can't you feel it?"

"Be more specific." I wanted to hear it from him.

"Power."

"Right." I was not surprised. It was the same response I got from everybody that purchased this type of firearm. Aside from the power trip you felt surging through your body when picking it up, and taking sight, it was the anticipation of scoring a bullseye target. Where most owners liked to blast away as quickly as the trigger allowed, my use was different. I was not interested in quantity of slugs I could deliver. I was only interested in precision shooting, one shot at a time, but delivered with accuracy. It'd been the reason my purchase was a long barrel, and gunstock in addition to a long-range scope.

The popularity of the AR-15 was its configuration versatility. Depending on component parts, it could be configured for long-range target select or, what was most popular these days, close-range rapid fire. Because of its options for short stock, and barrel sizes, the weapon could easily be hidden under a coat.

"By the way," Buzz interrupted my thoughts, "why did you buy the firearm? From what I know you already own some."

"Same reason as you. Power." I felt like I needed to explain. My power trip was not geared to defend my domicile in case of a civil conflict. I could not imagine facing dozens of military units sweeping into the neighborhood trying to confiscate personal firearms. It would be as foolish as demonstrated by school shootings with mass killers. Their intentions were to achieve instant fame with suicidal tendencies generally fulfilled by the SWAT team. I like life too much to be taken out. My purpose for the purchase was for protection against the ill-intended criminal breaking into my home for whatever devious purpose. A show of weapon would be the lifesaving deterrent since most, if not all, break-ins were attempted with a handgun.

"What about killing somebody?" Buzz, like most civilized people, would probably think twice before pulling the trigger. I may be wrong, but historical accounts show otherwise. It was this hesitation that an assailant would take to his advantage, and most likely take your life.

"Killing is not an easy task," I explained. "Just ask any veteran. You have to be trained to kill. Most soldiers are trained before called into conflict or war."

"What about the sniper?"

"Training to become a killer is another matter. It takes a person with iron nerves, and special skills."

"When you were in Vietnam," he boldly asked, "did you ever kill somebody?" The question startled me. I'd never thought on those terms. Shooting, for me, was mostly for sport. Though I was trained to expertly handle the automatic, I'd never had to shoot at a person. It was mostly for protection while on the frontlines of a conflict.

"Never had to. I was escorted by a squad of special forces wherever I went."

"What are you going to do for the rest of the day?" Buzz said. "I'll head home."

"Why don't you stop by tomorrow? We could go to the shooting range."

"Sounds great. See you then."

I got up early the next morning as I usually did after a few hours of sleep. Getting older, I found myself with less, and less sleep. I did not know how others at my age fared. I understood that some fortunate ones slept up to seven hours regularly, and did so without any sleep aid. I have tried over-the counter supplements such as melatonin, and similar products advertised as "guaranteed to fall asleep," but no such luck for me. Nothing short of actual prescribed sleeping pills by a physician would get me more rest. Though I had sampled some products over the years, I refrained from taking anything because all caused damaging side effects without exceptions. Warning labels were very clear: "Do not take if you have…" followed by a list of ailments, including impaired breathing, vital to life.

"Hey," I greeted Buzz when the doorbell rang. "Come right in. Just making coffee. Want some?"

"Sure. What have you been doing?"

"Writing, as I usually do."

"How's it coming?" He was referring to my current work.

"Making progress." He was always anxious to get the first printed copy, authored, and signed. After all, he deserved it. He was my buddy.

"Won't be long now," was my usual response. "What's with the sneakers? I thought we were going to the range."

"I forgot to buy bullets."

"You can use mine."

"I didn't bring the weapon. We could take a hike. It's nice outside."

"Hike it is. We can talk on the trail."

"Fine with me."

I put on my hiking gear to match his. Ten minutes later we were off on the trail. Trails in the foothills were abundant, but hilly as well. For the new visitor, as we had both experienced at one time, it could leave you gasping for air on the uphill slope. It usually took three weeks for the blood to thin out for the body to adjust to the altitude. But since we were acclimated already, striding along the path was a pleasure in the wooded area with frequent views into the snowcapped mountain peaks.

"You see the news last night?" Buzz said, a few hundred yards into the trail.

"You mean ISIS battling for territory?"

"Yes. Causing more destruction in Mosul."

"You know what irks me the most," I said, grimacing with disgust. I did not wait for his reply. "They are eradicating man's oldest cities along with thousands of years history, and priceless treasures."

"I know. It' a crime, but I don't know who to persecute. First, it's us trying to fight them off, then the Russians, and now the Arabs are getting involved. What's going on? When will the killing stop?"

"Never." My answer was clear. "They have been fighting for their cause for fourteen hundred years with a proclamation to 'destroy every tomb, historical site, and structure of the infidels until nothing remains.'"[71]

"What exactly is it they are fighting for? You know?"

"World dominance for Islam. Much like the Catholic Church a thousand years ago."

"What made them stop?"

"The Crusaders. They helped stop Islam advances."

"I didn't know."

"Most people don't. You have to be interested in history."

"How about a history lesson?"

"Now?"

"Why not. I don't get free time like you."

"I understand." I had taken a few minutes to contemplate what information to share when I had a thought. *Why not discuss the context of my recent research from what I'd learned?*

---

[71] ISIS leader on the destruction of one of man's oldest city, Mosul, with their proclamation to "destroy every tomb, historical site, and structure of the infidels until nothing remains," 28 April 2018, Russia Today (RT), network documentary, (Tony Cheng, Bangkok, Thailand broadcast segment).

"You sure you feel up to listening? It may take some time to clearly understand the issues."

He briefly checked his watch, and said, "Go ahead. I promise to be tolerant." It was good enough for me. It was not every day that somebody welcomed a history lesson, a dear subject of mine. I should warn the reader that the information may sound radical at times, but it is my true assessment based on researching its history, which, by the way, contrary to popular belief, was not so long ago. Here we go:

"Islam is currently passing through one of its most dynamic times since its rise fourteen hundred years ago. A dynamic period that started long before 9/11 as a fierce struggle, mainly against the West, culminating into a policy against any nation or group that dared to stand in its way. Most Muslims took this resurgence phase very seriously, and considered it as a decisive battle between Islam, and the non-Islam, which Mohammed told, and promised them they would win. Even though the West, currently, was largely in denial about it made no difference to the significance of this conflict exerted on the free world.

"Virtually unchallenged, Islam has survived, and expanded during the last fourteen centuries. The only time Islam has ever faced any challenges was in the first few years, when Mohammed's claims of being a prophet were questioned by the Mecca Arabs, and then by the Jews. During that period, which spanned over thirteen years, Mohammed failed to win any intellectual debate to prove his claims. The results reflected on Mohammed's failure to attract genuine followers. The dozens who joined him were mainly friends, and beneficiaries. Once Mohammed established his stronghold named Medina, which had flourished until few years before his arrival, after years of unsuccessful debating, became meaningless, and virtually non-existent. Since then, the only challenges Islam have had were military ones, with opposing forces more interested in military conquests than in propagating Islam's ideology.

"Islam has guarded its ideology by employing a thorough indoctrination program, and a systematic, and extensive brainwashing process of its adherents. The process is so incapacitating that it is incomprehensible to Muslims to contemplate their existence outside their religion.

"Over the past fourteen centuries, Islam was never openly challenged or critiqued, because those who knew about its myths also knew what it meant to disclose them. Those Muslims who did their own critical appraisal of their religion kept their results to themselves since they knew if they did not, they risked losing their heads by the authorities, or even by family members or friends who would be happy to do it for the sake of Allah.

"Even during the last few centuries, when the whole world started to open up to a new age of enlightenment, Islamic authorities managed to seal the minds of Muslims towards any outside views about Islam. The tight seal on the Muslims' minds continues even during our time. Unwanted materials, whether printed or televised, are simply filtered out. For fourteen centuries, Muslims never had a chance to see their religion from any perspective other than their own. Islam survived because it always had a suitable environment of darkness, and one-way coaching with no tolerance to different views.

"Since the introduction of the Internet all that has changed. Thanks to the power of the Internet, the world is now open to almost everyone, and Muslims can have access to the alternative views about Islam, something considered impossible in the past. The Internet was the first true challenge to Islam because it broke through all the Islamic security systems. The Internet did not recognize Islam's demands of submission, and total surrender of the mind. Everything about Islam was now subjected to critical scrutiny; people now ask logical questions, and demand logical answers. There was one factor that escalated the recent rise of Islam as Western cultural indicators identified. It was a decline of the Western civilization.

"The decline of the West is mainly an inherited problem that neither Islam nor any other external factors could be blamed for. But it was a disturbing observation that the West appears to be doomed with or without Islam, although Islam is taking advantage of the process, and is working hard to speed it up. The Islamic predators looked at the West as helpless prey, and were closing in waiting for the right moment to make a kill. They were hopeful to inherit the West without even having to fight for it, and they did not make a secret of it. A few years ago, the since then passed Colonel Ghaddafi said that 'Muslims could not take Europe by force in the past, but now they will take it without force.' If you did not believe the Libyan leader's remarks, you only needed to visit a classroom in a British primary school to see how the rest of the world would look like in the future.

"Nations behave like individuals because they are made up of individuals. An individual's performance was at its best, in times of stress, like preparing for exam or entering competition. Nations too, perform best in times of stress like wars or other struggles of conflict. During the last war, the West was at its peak. People took no chances; they went through some rough times, suffered hardship, fought wars, and lost lives to secure a good future for their children, and grandchildren. Unfortunately, today's Westerners enjoy a freedom, and democracy that they never earned, and seemed to be reluctant to defend.

"The West has had some very painful experiences because of Islam, like the attacks of 9/11, and the bombings in Madrid, London, and New York to mention only few. We all hate painful experiences, but it seems that pain is essential to the survival of individuals as well as nations. Pain is a warning system that alarms people about the more serious underlying problems that need attention.

"The bombing of Western targets all over the world during the last few decades should have been enough to motivate the West to take action about the root of the problem, which we all knew to be Islam. Instead, the West has opted to take painkillers in the form of politically correct justifications prescribed to them by the politically correct groups, a recipe for disaster.

"The weakness in the West played well in the hands of the Islamists, and hindered our campaign to enlighten Muslims, and defeat their cult. Western converts to Islam were used by the Islamists' propaganda engine to boost the Muslims' confidence in their religion. It was a common observation that when Muslims ran out of answers to defend the Islamic myths, they produced the most bizarre reasons for staying with Islam, stating, *'All those Westerners would not convert unless Islam is right.'*

"The West had been a safe haven to the radical Islamic organizations that were banned in their own Islamic countries. The Western social, and political systems facilitated some of the most notorious Islamic organizations, to survive, thrive, and terrorize innocents around the world. The remarks made by the head of the Anglican

Church about introducing Sharia law was just another reminder that the problem was largely a self-inflicted one. The response of the people to their problems were disappointing, to say the least. Those who recognized the problem left, and emigrated, while the rest turned a blind eye, and lived in denial.

"The largest denomination in Islam was Sunni Islam, which makes up 75 to 90% of all Muslims. The Koran, and the Sunnah (the example of Muhammad's life) as recorded in Hadith (Reports) are the primary foundations of Sunni doctrine. According to Sunni Islam, the normative example of Muhammad's life was called the Sunnah (literally 'trodden path'). This example was preserved in traditions known as Hadith, which recount his words, his actions, and his personal characteristics. The Sunnah is seen as crucial to guiding interpretation of the Koran. Sunnis believed that the first four caliphs were the rightful successors to Muhammad. Since God did not specify any particular leaders to succeed him, those leaders had to be elected. Sunnis believe that a caliph should be chosen by the entire community.

"After Sunni, Shia constitutes 10 to 20% of Islam, and is its second largest branch. They believe in the political, and religious leadership of Imams from the offspring of a certain Ali ibn Abi Talib, his righteous name, who Shias believed was the true successor after Muhammad. They believed that Ali ibn Abi Talib was the first Imam leader, rejecting the legitimacy of the previous Muslim caliphs. To most Shias, the Imam rules by right of divine appointment, and holds absolute spiritual authority among Muslims, having final say in matters of doctrine, and revelation. Shias regard Ali as the prophet's true successor, and believe that a caliph is appointed by divine will. Although the Shias share many core practices with the Sunni, the two branches disagree over validity of specific collections of Hadith.

"Sufism, the third major Islamic brand, on the other hand, is a mystical-ascetic approach to Islam that seeks to find divine love, and knowledge through direct personal experience of God. By focusing on the more spiritual aspects of its religion, Sufis strive to obtain direct experience of God by making use of intuitive, and emotional faculties that one must be trained to use. However, Sufism has been criticized for what they see as an unjustified religious innovation. Many Sufi orders could be classified as either Sunni or Shia, but others classify themselves simply as Sufi. The parallel can be drawn with Christianity, and its many religious beliefs such as Catholicism, Protestantism, Baptism, Seventh Day Adventism, Later Day Saints, and many others.

"That's it in a nutshell," I concluded, ready to face Buzz's response.

"Too big a shell to digest in one day. How about a break?"

We had arrived at the halfway point on the trail. We both took a seat on a nearby bench to cool off with bottles of Gatorade, his berry flavor, mine lemon-lime. "Where do you get all this stuff? Koran?"

"In part, yes. But mostly from scholastic researchers trained in Islamic scriptures, and laws."

"I envy your knowledge," he said with admiration.

"It's my passion to educate myself on historical accounts. Especially when our future is at stake."

"You think it's this serious?"

"Without a doubt. If not in our generation, surely within the next fifty years, the Western world will be dominated by Islam unless we make a combined effort to resist their takeover."

"What's the worst we can expect?"

"Be subjected to Sharia, and its dark-aged brutality. You make one mistake against their law, and you'll lose a hand or a foot or, worse yet, you'll be executed by having your head chopped off."

"Seriously?"

"Take my word." There was nothing more to be said on the Islamic cause. I illustrated the facts, as brutal as they were. If this reading does not shake the West out of its complacency, nothing else will. But then, I am only one voice.

"What about the people? They can't all be bad."

"Let me clarify one important fact," I offered. "Muslims, as a population, are people much like you and I. They are decent, hardworking individuals striving for a better life. While freedom is a major contributor to the wellbeing of a nation, the very essence has escaped Muslim ideology since the inception, and forced implementation of the Sharia Law. In contrast to the Western world, what has kept Muslims from achieving success was the brutal oppression enforced by Islam. I don't want to delve into specifics, but challenge you to study the history of Muslims' religious leader, and savior, Prophet Muhammad."

"I might just do it," Buzz conceded.

"Do it. Your, and your children's future freedom may depend on it. Freedom is what life is all about. If anyone does not appreciate the liberty we have in our country, they should pack up, and move."

"That's pretty radical, don't you think?"

"To live in this country, we have to honor the constitution, and respect the flag for what this land is built on."

SCIENTIFIC VIEWS

Another day, another morning session. "Here we go again," Buzz said, accompanied by a suppressed grunt. It almost sounded like a complaint to me, and I stated so. We were at it again, tossing ideas back and forth, with statements thrown mostly his way. But, after all the years working together, he knew me well enough to tolerate my persistence. As I had told him on many occasions, "To get a thorough understanding of things one has to talk through them." This motto had always been my philosophy. In general, I was not prone to dominate a conversation, despite the appearance of it. I would rather listen to others talk about their lives, and accomplishments. But, somehow, the burden to explain mostly landed in my lap. Was it my knowledge of things? Was it a determination to gain more knowledge? Whatever the reasons, I never complained when encouraged to deliberate. Today, I felt like sharing information I had acquired on science. I could boldly state that "science was a proof of concept to all things considered, but I will not."

"Why not?" Buzz jumped in, demanding an explanation. It may have sounded conceited to him.

"Because," I explained. "Science is fluid, and reliant on new discoveries. Discoveries we do not know to exist at this time. For all practical purposes our scientific achievements are in their infancies. We've only identified mathematical fundamentals, and learned how to use them." Whether applied to simple arithmetic or complex nuclear mathematics, what we learned was to test, and verify discoveries, inventions, explorations, and their essential mechanics.

"So," Buzz stipulated, "we don't know much."

"We know enough to get us through life, but at the end, we don't know how to prevent death, and what comes after."

"Too gloomy a topic," he complained. It was his way of saying, "I don't want to talk about it." I understood, and picked something we knew through scientific achievements.

"You will like this."

"What?" It seemingly piqued his interests.

"Creation of the universe."

"Now you are talking. It's been a mystery nobody has been able to solve. Have they? Have you?"

"Well," I said. "Let's take a look, and consider the conventional view on creation as we were taught by the great minds, we all know."

"Einstein?"

"Yes, among other contemporaries' views on matter, and energy, two major principles involved. But first, let me pass by you my own views on the fundamentals of creation, matter and energy."

Matter, and Energy – Popular concepts

- There are no parallel universes. Added universes would create the same issues as having only one universe when considering space, and total celestial body weight.

- The universe has always been in existence, created through a never-ending cyclic process. We, and everything else, live, and perish within its sphere.
- The universe is created out of nothingness. Since nothingness could not sustain itself, matter, and anti-matter were created. Matter creates anti-matter to balance mass-weight constant, and could be converted back to energy through energized forces. It does not matter what came first since it is an endless cycle of creation, and annihilation. Matter is created from energy, and energy causes its destruction. On collapse, new matter is created.
- The Creator, if there is one, is a consequential cause much like mankind is the cause that we consider natural evolution, only on an earlier cycle. The created energy contains all that is possible including information, and infinite knowledge that man is trying to attain.

That's my take until proven different. To get to this point in time we live in, consider yourself fortunate having been born to cast your seed, amidst millions of competing sperms struggling for life. You were born into this world from the best of breeds to propagate your seed through the universe. The message here is: strive to make life better for yourself and everybody else's future. It's a big world out there to explore. And explore we will. It is our destiny for survival. If restrained, we, as humans, will revert back to animal behavior.

As for Einstein's theory, "There were four fundamental interactions known to exist: the gravitational, and electromagnetic interactions, which produce significant long-range forces whose effects could be seen directly in everyday life, and the strong, and weak interactions, which produce forces at minuscule, subatomic levels, and govern nuclear interactions.

"Each of the known fundamental interactions could be described mathematically as a *field*. The gravitational force is attributed to the curvature of spacetime, described by Einstein's general theory of relativity. The other three forces are discrete quantum fields, and their interactions are mediated by elementary particles described by the *Standard Model* of particle physics.

"Within the *Standard Model,* the strong interaction is carried by a particle called the gluon, and is responsible for the binding of quarks together to form hadrons, such as protons, and neutrons. As a residual effect, it creates the nuclear force that binds the latter particles to form atomic nuclei. The weak interaction is carried by particles called W, and Z bosons, and also acts on the nucleus of atoms, mediating radioactive decay. The electromagnetic force, carried by the photon, creates electric, and magnetic fields, which are responsible for chemical bonding, and electromagnetic waves, including visible light, and forms the basis for electrical technology. Although the electromagnetic force is far stronger than gravity, it tends to cancel itself out within large objects, so over the largest distances (on the scale of planets, and galaxies), gravity tends to be the dominant force.

"All four fundamental forces are believed to be related, and to unite into a single force at high energies on a minuscule scale, the Planck scale, but particle accelerators cannot produce the enormous energies required to experimentally probe this. Efforts to devise a common theoretical framework that would explain the relation between the forces are perhaps the greatest goal of theoretical physicists today. The weak, and electromagnetic forces have already been unified with the electroweak theory of Sheldon Glashow, Abdus Salam, and Steven Weinberg, for which they received the 1979 Nobel Prize in physics. Progress is currently being made in uniting the electroweak, and strong fields within a *Grand Unified Theory*.

"A bigger challenge is to find a way to quantize the gravitational field, resulting in a theory of quantum gravity which would unite gravity in a common theoretical framework with the other three forces. Some theories, notably string theory, seek to quantize both the gravitation, and grand unified theory within one framework, unifying all four fundamental interactions along with mass generation within a *Theory of Everything*.

"It's pretty clear, if you ask me," Buzz stated, with an approving nod of his head. "Everything is proven through science for matter, and energy." Much like myself, he could visualize the fundamental concept because it grew from logical, and mathematical experimentations, and reasoning, basis for our lifelong career.

"It's not that simple," I said. "There are forces beyond our understanding."

"Name one."

"Consciousness." It was consciousness that had science, and physicists puzzled. The next section presents alternative views still fiercely under deliberation among science communities. None of it has been proven to exist. At this time, all is subject to conjectures, and speculations, much like science fiction. However, it does not preclude that someday, some, or perhaps all theories will be resolved. We don't know what consciousness is but sciences are working on trying to solve the mysteries of the brain. When solved, it will open up new horizons into the mystical and spiritual realms of the universe.

Then there are the Brain and the Mind, we believe contain the state of consciousness, that functions much like a computer. Following is my definition for equating the human brain with the computer:

a.　Short term memory is equal to the Cache memory. Much like an Index Server, it stores reference information such as visual, audio, and sensory inputs received by the brain while passing it on to long-term memory for permanent storage.

b.　Long-term memory is stored for life and for permanent retrieval unless the brain is damaged or deceased.

c.　There are five input sensory perceptions routed to the brain: sight, hearing, smell, taste and touch, each directed to a specific mental lobe.

d.　Metal lopes are: Frontal, Occipital, Temporal, Parietal, Cerebellum.

While the stated rendering describes only the very fundamental structure of the brain, the human design for it will take years to study and comprehend.

I would like to point out one important fact. Though as knowledgeable as I am in the various topics on views presented in the next sections, I am not an all-knowing omnipresence. I am only human with a limited brain capacity bestowed at birth. It is for this reason, while one could argue a number of alternatives on any given subject, I present two alternatives on topics under discussion. While there were many ideas, notions, concepts, and conclusions documented in national archives on any given scientific research, and experiment, I extracted information as brief as possible with enough data for the interested reader to understand the various concepts.

FALSE ASSUMPTIONS OF MODERN DAY SCIENCE

Quoted from Mike Adams, Natural News, Aug 22, 2013
The message of one of the most important books of our time was illustrated with the book *Science Set Free* by Rupert Sheldrake. The book outlined ten new pathways to discovery that promise to allow human civilization to leap forward into a new era of understanding, achievement, and the harnessing of the power of nature, and the cosmos. Rupert Sheldrake may be to the twenty-first century what Charles Darwin was to the nineteenth: someone who sent science spinning in wonderfully new, and fertile directions. – Larry Dossey, M.D., author of *Reinventing Medicine*

The ten false assumptions of modern-day science:
Both Mike Adams, and Rupert Sheldrake were very much "pro science," disturbed by how scientific advancement had become trapped in a cultural tar pit of delusional beliefs, and false assumptions. These false assumptions, listed below, held science back, and prevented human civilization from progressing toward a more profound understanding of nature, ourselves, and our universe.

1) The universe is mechanical

Modern science believes the entire universe is made of up material, and nothing else. There is no consciousness, no spirit, no mind, and nothing other than mechanical, and chemical substance.

This explains modern science's obsession with finding smaller, and smaller particles at CERN. Many scientists actually believe that if the smallest bits, and pieces of a mechanical universe are finally identified then the entire cosmos would finally be understood, and the delusion of God, creator, and architect could finally be dismissed forever. Their goal, by the pessimist, is to destroy any belief in a higher Intelligence, and to doom humans to living pointless lives that end in their total destruction at the moment of death.

2) All matter is unconscious

The most astonishing delusion in modern science is the fact that most modern scientists do not believe they are, themselves, conscious beings. Modern science assumes that humans are nothing more than biological robots, and that animals are not conscious either. They literally believe that consciousness is an illusory artifact of the chemical brain. Not surprisingly, they also do not believe that plants, and other living systems are conscious. Even further, the idea that inanimate objects such as minerals or crystals might have some sort of consciousness is considered heresy by most modern scientists.

3) The total amount of matter, and energy is always a constant

This assumption of modern science is especially suspicious, given that even conventional cosmologists readily admit that 96% of the universe has yet to be detected at all. That is the dark matter, and dark energy portion of the universe, and neither dark matter nor dark energy have ever been directly measured or seen by human scientists. Except for the theoretical Big Bang, there is no phenomenon by which modern scientists believe the totality of matter, and energy could come into existence or exit our universe.

4) The laws of nature are fixed

This, too, is an assumption that appears to have already been unraveled, thanks to the efforts of a few modern-day scientists. As a simple example, multiple physics experiments are now being conducted worldwide, and widely replicated, which show "faster than light" teleportation of information via quantum entanglement. In theory, instantaneous quantum teleportation could take place over a billion miles. The distance makes no difference. Quantum teleportation ignores the apparent laws of physics, including the "cosmological speed limit" known as the speed of light. According to classic laws of nature, such quantum teleportation is impossible. In fact, all quantum computing should be impossible, and, come to think of it, transistors should not function either. But they do, and they do it by breaking the classic laws of physics.

5) Nature is purposeless, with no goal or direction

The Darwinian framework of biological science assumes that nature achieves highly complex biological structures, social structures, mechanical engineering, and behavioral cultures simply through the process of natural selection. While natural selection is constantly taking place throughout nature, it alone is not sufficient to explain the ability of plants, animals, humans, and possibly even universes to achieve remarkable end goals purely through chance, and inheritance. There appears to be a "driving creative force" behind much of what we observe in nature, including in animals, and humans. This driving creative force appears to have a connection with spirit, a non-physical "mind" which gives consciousness to physical beings of all kinds.

What we see in the natural world, in ecosystems, plants, animals, and even humans, is not explainable through natural selection alone. There exists intention, consciousness, and a seeming desire to achieve complex goals by taking fantastic evolutionary leaps which modern science cannot explain. As a simple example of this, consider the fact that, although many thousands of humanoid-like fossils have been unearthed in the last two centuries, there are still no fossils that record the theoretical "missing link" which is supposed to link humans to primates. Why have no such fossils been found? Almost certainly because they do not exist.

6) All biological inheritance is material, carried in DNA

The idea that your DNA controls your body, and your life is now an ancient myth. Only in the materialistic circles of old school "science" do people still think DNA alone controls your health, your behavior, and all your inherited attributes. Today we know that there are epigenetic factors beyond DNA which strongly influence the development of biological beings. We also know that environmental factors (i.e. exposure to chemicals, heavy metals, nutrients, etc.) strongly influence either the suppression or the hyper-activation of genes. Vitamin D, for example, is one of the most powerful gene activators in human biology, turning on "healing genes" microscopic light switches.

7) There is no such thing as a "mind" other than an artifact of brain function

It is bewildering that most modern-day scientists still do not dare acknowledge the existence of the "mind," a non-material awareness, presence, and consciousness that coexists with the brain but is not derived from the mechanics, and chemistry of the brain. To date, there is no scientific proof whatsoever that supports the odd notion that consciousness does not exist or that the mind is not present in a conscious being. "Science" cannot disprove these things because the tools of modern-day science are materialistic by definition, and therefore incapable of proving or disproving non-material phenomena.

8) Memories are stored chemically in the brain, and disappear at death

In summary, modern scientists believe that memories are stored chemically, using the brain as some sort of biological hard drive, and that if they could only find the location of the brain in which these chemicals were stored, they could literally "read your mind" like copying files from a thumb drive. This assumption is wildly off the mark. There is evidence that memories are holographically stored across not only brain matter itself, but also in a non-material spirit matrix of some sort which interacts with the physical brain.

This could be why the physical location of memories in the brain has never been located by scientists. This is also why some people are shockingly found to be fully functional in our world even though they have virtually no brain matter whatsoever. For example, there was a story in "New Scientist" about a man who had almost no brain matter whatsoever but still possessed average IQ, and was a normal part of society, and yes, the man had memories. Therefore, if memories are "stored" somewhere in the brain, as modern-day scientists believe, then how could this man have memories if he had virtually no physical brain to begin with? How could he function at all?

9) Unexplained phenomena such as telepathy are illusory

Modern-day "skeptics" go to great lengths to try to disprove anything that even smacks of 'mentalism' or telepathy. But they cannot rationally refute the scientific work of people like Dean Radin, author of *The Conscious Universe: The Scientific Truth of Psychic Phenomena*. Radin has, over, and over again, scientifically shown strongly convincing evidence for low-level telepathy, and other phenomena such as premonition. Explanations for such phenomena are entirely consistent with quantum *non-locality*, and quantum entanglement.

The most likely explanation for all this is that the human brain, being a holographic, hybrid physical, non-physical computational, and awareness engine of sorts, is also "entangled" with all matter in the universe at a quantum level. The brain seems to be both a transmitter, and receiver of quantum information that is continually, and instantly rippling across the cosmos.

10) Mechanistic medicine is the only kind that really works

On this point, much of the Natural News website is dedicated to explaining why mechanistic medicine is a failed system of medicine. Understand this: most modern-day scientists do not believe that any vitamin, any mineral or any food has any biological effect whatsoever on the human body other than providing calories, sugars, proteins, fiber, and fat. This wildly delusional belief is enshrined in the FDA's regulatory framework, and is practiced throughout hospitals, and health clinics across the planet.

The physical part of the human being obviously requires physical building blocks. Those building blocks are nutrients, plant-based chemicals, minerals, proteins, and water. They are not statin drugs, blood pressure meds, chemotherapy, and radiation. The mechanistic model of medicine is an utter failure for human civilization. It has been a huge success in generating profits for drug companies, and hospitals, however, which is exactly why this failed system has been so desperately defended by those who profit from it.

"It is truly amazing what experiments take place, and what scientists have discovered in obscure laboratories," Buzz admitted. "I had no idea how far science has progressed."

"Most people don't. Laboratory experiments continuously detect new elements, but only major breakthroughs are announced to the public. It's that time that the public is made aware of physical science without really knowing how much effort went into the research."

"I guess," Buzz stated, "most people have no clue, or interest in what we are all about."

"I agree. But," I suggested, "let's take an alternative view on physics. You'll like this one as well, I'm sure."

"There is more?"

"Don't be coy. We haven't even touched on how new research is looking at the time element."

HIGGS BOSON AND GOD PARTICLE

Mike Adams, Natural News, Thursday, July 5, 2012
If it were not for great minds like Newton's formulations of the laws of gravity, Kepler's laws of motion, Bohr's modeling of the atom, Maxwell's equations on electromagnetic behavior, Einstein's theory of Special Relativity, and then General Relativity discoveries, we would still live in the dark ages. Our understanding of physics accelerated throughout the 20th century with theories on the Big Bang, inflation, and the inflation field, string theory, M-theory, super symmetry, quantum mechanics, parallel worlds, bubble universes, and much more. It was truly fascinating to observe all this as a conscious being sitting within the very universe we were all trying to figure out.

Particles, and Consciousness
Why would anyone want to spend billions of dollars smashing atoms together, and analyzing the results on the plotter? It is to find out what atoms are made of. But, more importantly, to find out what the universe is made of. It is what CERN was all about.

There is a huge gap in all this, unfortunately, and that gap has its origins in the thinking that atoms are made entirely of particles. The wildly misnamed "God particle," known as Higgs Boson, has been the single most sought-after particle by physicists in their quest to find physical evidence to back up their mathematical equations of the Standard Model of the universe.

Physicists, and especially cosmologists have spent an enormous amount of time working in the abstract realm of mathematics. The purpose of the mathematics is to attempt to model physical reality, which is engineered into the fabric of the universe with the language of mathematics.

What is often lacking in this scientific quest is physical experimental evidence that backs up the mathematics. Consequently, it only makes sense to attempt to conduct real-world experiments to either prove or disprove what the theory predicted. Now that the Higgs boson particle has been convincingly demonstrated to exist, this helps to explain many answers, thereby leading to a deeper exploration of other questions, each of which grants a measure of understanding to human civilization.

Ultimately, physicists are attempting to understand the origins of the universe, which have turned out to be a challenging quest for many reasons, some of which are almost impossible to imagine. In addition to the parallel worlds, and multiverse theories that have joined the complexities, there was also "brane theory" to deal with. It is a theory that says multiple universes coexist, intertwined with each other but not interacting. You could not touch another brane world even though it might exist right alongside our own brane world.

What is important to realize in all this is that even the so-called "Standard Model" of explaining everything is currently an unsatisfactory patchwork of equations, and mathematical transformations that do not play well together when it comes to different physical context such as really small things or really large, massive things. Virtually all present-day reality modeling equations break down at singularity events such as black holes.

There is little doubt that the Standard Model is only a temporary quick fix in the bigger picture. It is not "wrong" in the sense of being incorrect; it is most likely just incomplete. Ultimately, physicists hope to find a "unified theory" that explains everything with a single set of mathematical understandings, and equations that apply to all observable phenomena in the universe: electromagnetism, gravity, mass, light, and so on. Einstein spent a considerable portion of his life in search of the unification of these fundamental forces but was unable to achieve it. This is a goal of understanding that may yet take lifetimes to achieve. If it is achieved, it would represent one of the most profound achievements in the history of humankind.

"When did all this take place? CERN, Hicks Boson, God particle," Buzz cut in.

"It's been around for decades."

"I didn't hear much from mainstream media."

"You have to understand that physics research, for the most part, is boring to the general public. If there's no dramatic achievement, newscasts won't carry it."

"What is CERN working on? Do you know?"

"It took decades just to detect, and verify the God particle. Wait until you hear their current experiments."

"What?"

"Trying to fit consciousness into the mathematical equation."

"That I'll have to hear."

CONSCIOUS COSMOLOGY

Yet, there is still something missing from all this: consciousness. Without consciousness, the universe cannot be fully explained, as consciousness is increasingly emerging as a fundamental force impacting the very fabric of reality. This is really frustrating for many scientists because the majority of scientists do not believe in the existence of consciousness. Stephen Hawking was famous for his rather short-sighted remarks that people were mindless, soulless beings—biological robots—and that religion spirituality was a realm for people who were afraid of the dark.

This is frustrating for physicists because, to date, there are no equations that describe the behavior or properties of consciousness. Although consciousness could be experienced first-hand by conscious beings, it so far has defied measurement, and experimental validation. How could anyone prove consciousness existed? Other than the fact that it is self-evident to those who possess it.

This may ultimately prove impossible because of possible errors in the quest. To get a better understanding for this elusive element, an explanation is necessary. An "independent" measurement, in classical physics, describes a measurement being conducted by a mechanism that has no ties to any conscious observer. Yet in order to become aware of the measurements, a conscious being must, one way or another, interact with the results of the experiment. This interaction, as quantum theorists realized, is itself part of the experiment, and may alter its outcomes even after the fact. Thus, the Observer cannot be isolated from the events observed.

Gaining a deep understanding of this may be exceedingly difficult for human beings to achieve. It may be beyond the capabilities of biological beings with limited neurological capacity. Nevertheless, since science understands about the Higgs boson, quantum theory, particle physics, and cosmology, the closer science may be to initiating a scientific study of consciousness.

Consciousness, parallel worlds, and more

Consciousness is not made of particles. Thus, you cannot smash consciousness in a particle accelerator, and hope to see the tiny bits of what it is made of. Yet there is increasingly compelling evidence that consciousness interacts with the physical world, and may even create parallel physical worlds when it is exercised. Hints of this are emerging from the study of quantum physics, which immediately led to the possibility of "multiple worlds", and parallel realities.

The search for Higgs boson was an important one, but the approach was incomplete if our civilization sought to uncover the fundamental forces that unified our observable universe. Those forces do not exist in a vacuum absent the minds of the conscious inhabitants of the universe. Where there was life, there appeared to be consciousness, and if there was one thing most physicists, and cosmologists agreed on, it was that life was abundant across the cosmos. Not in terms of units of life per square meter, since most of the universe is just empty space. The average density of the known universe (approximately 28 billion light years across) had been estimated at 6 hydrogen atoms per cubic meter. That is a lot of empty space, but it is filled with literally trillions of stars, many of which could harbor life, and therefore consciousness.

Who or what created our reality?
There is the elusive question of the Architect of this reality. Even if humankind manages to decode the fundamental laws which govern the physical universe, there is not only the question of "Who or what created the universe in the first place" but the even more difficult question, "Who or what created the laws of physics that govern the universe?"

Because on that question, even a particle accelerator the size of the entire planet would not shed light on the question. The consensus view in physics circles today, which is dominated by people who do not believe in consciousness or free will, is that our universe created itself out of nothing, without any intelligent intervention. This is a strange argument of "effect without a cause," and it simply does not add up.

The far more believable argument is that our universe was created by a Great Intelligence, an Architect or Creator. Several prominent physicists are suggesting that our universe is a simulation, a physics experiment created by a vastly superior race of beings who inhabit a higher dimension. On the more spiritual side, the explanation quickly centered on a single consciousness known as God. There are seemingly endless additional theories, and thoughts on this subject involving a vast array of philosophical, and religious beliefs, but they all have in common one idea which should be obvious to even a brilliant physicist: the reason there is something rather than nothing is because someone (or something) had to put it there, which means there was an Intelligence, a consciousness that existed above, and beyond our known universe, something with the power that created our known universe.

These are divine concepts that underpin the deepest inner workings of our universe, far beyond Higgs boson or any theory of particle physics. This gets us to the Creator behind the very laws of physics. "How was the framework of quantum mechanics created in the first place? Who selected, and fine-tuned the cosmological constants to support the formation of stars? How was the framework of dark matter, and dark energy engineered?"

For the record, Mike Adams was trained in the sciences, and has long been a student of many fields of knowledge, including physics, philosophy, cosmology, anthropology, neurology, and spirituality. His strength is in understanding complex concepts, and explaining them in simple, everyday terms, usually in a way that is interesting to read. He intends to bring that skill to the forefront with focus on conscious cosmology which necessarily encompasses philosophy, spirituality, quantum theory, physics, and more.

"Wow," Buzz exhaled. "I am bewildered."

"You are not the only one." It was extremely difficult to understand just the fundamental theories in consciousness, and creation. To even think, and understand parallel universes was an entire new concept. Even more difficult to grasp was the thought of a Great Intelligence creating our cosmos.

That left us with the ultimate question, "Who created them?" The two alternatives presented above, physical being versus consciousness, were questions posed on concepts from experimentations from Old physical science versus New theoretical science.

"What's your understanding in all of it?" He said, challenging me for my opinion.

"Buzz." I wanted him to understand that I am only gifted with a human brain evolved over many thousands of years. I am nobody special. I don't have a super brain. I felt that each of us human beings have similar intellectual capabilities. All one has to do is exercise the various brain functions. "Here is my take," I said after a brief pause. "Awareness is an individual perception acquired early on in life just by being alive. Whereas knowledge is the sum of all thing's mankind has learned over a lifetime, combined into one universal element not yet identified: trying to understand the purpose for creation. Someday, we will have enough knowledge to make sense of it all."

"Where do you dream it all up?" Buzz, as others I encounter, have their own sphere of interests, not necessarily shared with the world, as easily as I do.

"Maybe the next segment will explain it," I said, hinting on more to come.

TIME TRAVEL AND ITS PARADOX

Some theories, most notably special, and general relativity, suggest that suitable geometries of spacetime or specific types of motion in space might allow time travel into the past, and future if these geometries or motions are possible. In technical papers, physicists discussed the possibility of closed time like curves, which are world lines that formed closed loops in spacetime, allowing objects to return to their own past. There are known to be solutions to the equations of general relativity that describe spacetimes which contain closed time like curves, such as Gödel spacetime, but the physical plausibility of these solutions is uncertain.

Many in the scientific community believe that backward time travel is highly unlikely. Any theory that would allow time travel would introduce potential problems of causality. The classic example of a problem involving causality is the "grandfather paradox." What if one were to go back in time, and kill one's own grandfather before one's father was conceived?

Some physicists, such as Novikov, and Deutsch, suggested that these sorts of temporal paradoxes could be avoided through the Novikov self-consistency principle or a variation of the many-worlds interpretation with interacting worlds.

General relativity
Time travel to the past is theoretically possible in certain general relativity spacetime geometries that permit traveling faster than the speed of light, such as cosmic strings, transversal wormholes, and Alcubierre drive. The theory of general relativity does suggest a scientific basis for the possibility of backward time travel in certain unusual scenarios, although arguments from semiclassical gravity suggest that when quantum effects are incorporated into general relativity, these loopholes may be closed. These semiclassical arguments led Hawking to formulate the chronology protection conjecture, suggesting that the fundamental laws of nature prevented time travel, but physicists could not come to a definite judgment on the issue without a theory of quantum gravity to join quantum mechanics, and general relativity into a completely unified theory.

Different spacetime geometries
The theory of general relativity describes the universe under a system of field equations that determine the metric, or distance function, of spacetime. There exist exact solutions to these equations that include closed time-like curves, which are world lines that intersect themselves; some point in the causal future of the world line is also in its causal past, a situation which is akin to time travel. Such a solution was first proposed by Kurt Gödel, a solution known as the Gödel metric, but his (and others') solution required the universe to have physical characteristics that it does not appear to have, such as rotation, and lack of Hubble expansion. Whether general relativity forbids closed time-like curves for all realistic conditions is still being researched.

Wormholes
Wormholes are a hypothetical warped spacetime which are permitted by the Einstein field equations of general relativity. A proposed time-travel machine using a traversable wormhole would hypothetically work in the following way: one end of the wormhole is accelerated to some significant fraction of the speed of light, perhaps with

some advanced propulsion system, and then brought back to the point of origin. Alternatively, another way is to take one entrance of the wormhole, and move it to within the gravitational field of an object that has higher gravity than the other entrance, and then return it to a position near the other entrance. For both of these methods, time dilation causes the end of the wormhole that has been moved to have aged less, or become younger, than the stationary end as seen by an external observer; however, time connects differently *through* the wormhole than *outside* it, so that synchronized clocks at either end of the wormhole would always remain synchronized as seen by an observer passing through the wormhole, no matter how the two ends move around.

This means that an observer entering the younger end would exit the older end at a time when it was the same age as the younger end, effectively going back in time as seen by an observer from the outside. One significant limitation of such a time machine is that it is only possible to go as far back in time as the initial creation of the machine; in essence, it is more of a path through time than it is a device that itself moves through time, and it would not allow the technology itself to be moved backward in time.

Quantum physics (No-communication theorem)
When a signal is sent from one location, and received at another location, then as long as the signal is moving at the speed of light or slower, the mathematics of simultaneity in the theory of relativity showed that all reference frames agreed that the transmission-event happened before the reception-event. When the signal travels faster than light, it is received *before* it was sent, in all reference frames. The signal could be said to have moved backward in time. This hypothetical scenario is sometimes referred to as a tachyonic antitelephone.

Quantum-mechanical phenomena such as quantum teleportation, the Einstein–Podolsky–Rosen (EPR) paradox, or quantum entanglement might appear to create a mechanism that allows for faster-than-light (FTL) communication or time travel, and in fact some interpretations of quantum mechanics such as the Bohm interpretation presumes that some information is being exchanged between particles instantaneously in order to maintain correlations between particles.

Nevertheless, the fact that causality is preserved in quantum mechanics is a rigorous result in modern quantum field theories, and therefore modern theories do not allow for time travel or FTL communication. In any specific instance where FTL has been claimed, more detailed analysis has proven that to get a signal, some form of classical communication must also be used. The no-communication theorem also gives a general proof that quantum entanglement could not be used to transmit information faster than classical signals.

Interacting many-worlds interpretation
A variation of Everett's many-worlds interpretation (MWI) of quantum mechanics provides a resolution to the grandfather paradox that involves the time traveler arriving in a different universe than the one they came from; it has been argued that since the traveler arrived in a different universe's history, and not their own history, this is not genuine time travel. The accepted many-worlds interpretation suggests that all possible quantum events could occur in mutually exclusive histories. However, some variations allow different universes to interact. This concept is most often used in

science fiction, but some physicists such as David Deutsch have suggested that a time traveler should end up in a different history than the one, he started from. On the other hand, Stephen Hawking argued that even if the MWI was correct, we should expect each time traveler to experience a single self-consistent history, so that time travelers remain within their own world rather than traveling to a different one.

Absence of time travelers from the future
The absence of time travelers from the future is a variation of the Fermi paradox. As the absence of extraterrestrial visitors does not prove they do not exist, so does the absence of time travelers not prove time travel is physically impossible; it might be that time travel is physically possible but was never developed or was cautiously used. Carl Sagan once suggested the possibility that time travelers could be here but were disguising their existence or were not recognized as time travelers. Some versions of general relativity suggest that time travel might only be possible in a region of spacetime that is warped a certain way, and hence time travelers would not be able to travel back to earlier regions in spacetime, before this region existed. Stephen Hawking stated that this would explain why the world had not already been overrun by "tourists from the future."

Forward time travel in physics (Time dilation)
There is a great deal of observable evidence for time dilation in special relativity, and gravitational time dilation in general relativity, for example in the famous, and easy-to-replicate observation of atmospheric muon decay. The theory of relativity states that the speed of light is invariant for all observers in any frame of reference; that is, it is always the same. Time dilation is a direct consequence of the invariance of the speed of light. Time dilation may be regarded in a limited sense as "time travel into the future": a person may use time dilation so that a small amount of proper time passes for them, while a large amount of proper time passes elsewhere. This could be achieved by traveling at relativistic speeds or through the effects of gravity.

For two identical clocks moving relative to each other without accelerating, each clock measures the other to be ticking slower. This is possible due to the relativity of simultaneity. However, the symmetry is broken if one clock accelerated, allowing for less proper time to pass for one clock than the other. The twin paradox describes this: one twin remained on Earth, while the other underwent acceleration to relativistic speed as they traveled into space, turned around, and traveled back to Earth; the traveling twin aged less than the twin who stayed on Earth, because of the time dilation experienced during their acceleration. General relativity treats the effects of acceleration, and the effects of gravity as equivalent, and shows that time dilation also occurs in gravity wells, with a clock deeper in the well ticking more slowly; this effect is taken into account when calibrating the clocks on the satellites of the Global Positioning System, and it could lead to significant differences in rates of aging for observers at different distances from a large gravity well such as a black hole.

"I have to say," Buzz said, trying to suppress a yawn. "Scientific research is demanding."

"I imagine it takes infinite patience, not to mention clinical discipline."

"I need something to perk me up."

"How about if I make us a pot of coffee?"

"I'd appreciate it." Whether writing or listening, coffee had always been an inspiration. Five minutes later, Buzz was ready for the next discussion.

"You'll like what's next," I said with renewed vigor.

"Is time explained in simpler terms we both can understand?"

"I'll let you be the judge," I said, not wanting him discouraged.

TIME ELEMENT

Time is the indefinite continued progress of existence, and events that occur in an apparently irreversible succession from the past through the present to the future. Time is a component quantity of various measurements used to sequence events, to compare the duration of events or the intervals between them, and to quantify rates of change of quantities in material reality or in the conscious experience. Time is often referred to as the fourth dimension, along with three spatial dimensions.

Time has long been an important subject of study in religion, philosophy, and science, but defining it in a manner applicable to all fields without circularity has consistently eluded scholars. Nevertheless, diverse fields such as business, industry, sports, the sciences, and the performing arts all incorporate some notion of time into their respective measuring systems.

Two contrasting viewpoints on time divide prominent philosophers. One view is that time is part of the fundamental structure of the universe—a dimension independent of events, in which events occur in sequence. Isaac Newton subscribed to this realist view, and hence it is sometimes referred to as Newtonian time. The opposing view is that *time* did not refer to any kind of "container" that events, and objects "move through", nor to any entity that "flowed", but that it is instead part of a fundamental intellectual structure (together with space, and number) within, in which humans' sequence, and compare events. This second view, in the tradition of Gottfried Leibniz, and Immanuel Kant, holds that *time* is neither an event nor a thing, and thus is not itself measurable nor could it be travelled.

Time in physics is unambiguously operationally defined as "what a clock reads." Time is one of the seven fundamental physical quantities in both the International System of Units, and International System of Quantities. Time is used to define other quantities, such as velocity, so defining time in terms of such quantities would result in a circularity of definition. An operational definition of time, wherein one says that observing a certain number of repetitions of one or another standard cyclical event (such as the passage of a free-swinging pendulum) constitutes one standard unit such as the second, is highly useful in the conduct of both advanced experiments, and everyday affairs of life. The operational definition left aside, the question is whether there is something called time, apart from the counting activity just mentioned, that flows, and that can be measured. Investigations of a single continuum called spacetime brings questions about space into questions about time, questions that have their roots in the works of early students of natural philosophy.

Temporal measurement has occupied scientists, and technologists, and is a prime motivation in navigation, and astronomy. Periodic events, and periodic motion have long served as standards for units of time. Examples include the apparent motion of the sun across the sky, the phases of the moon, the swing of a pendulum, and the beat of a heart. Currently, the international unit of time, the second, is defined by measuring the electronic transition frequency of cesium atoms. Time is also of significant social importance, having economic value ("time is money") as well as personal value, due to an awareness of the limited time in each day, and in human life spans.

Time is something we deal with every day, and something that everyone thinks they understand. However, a compact, and robust definition of time has proved to be remarkably tricky, and elusive.

Short Definitions
Among the many short, snappy definitions of time that have been put forward are:
- what clocks measure (physicists Albert Einstein, Donald Ivey, and others)
- what prevents everything from happening at once (physicist John Wheeler, and others)
- a linear continuum of instants (philosopher Adolf Grünbaum)
- a certain period during which something is done (Medical Dictionary)
- a continuum that lacks spatial dimensions (Encyclopedia Britannica)

Although each of these definitions is fine as far as it goes, none of them feel wholly satisfactory.

Dictionary Definitions
Various dictionaries have defined time as follows:
- the indefinite continued progress of existence, and events in the past, present, and future regarded as a whole (Oxford Dictionary)
- the measured or measurable period during which an action, process or condition exists or continues (Webster's Collegiate Dictionary)
- the continuous passage of existence in which events pass from a state of potentiality in the future, through the present, to a state of finality in the past (World English Dictionary)
- a continuous, measurable quantity in which events occur in a sequence proceeding from the past through the present to the future (Science Dictionary)
- the measured or measurable period during which an action, process or condition exists or continues (Merriam-Webster Dictionary)
- the dimension of the physical universe that orders the sequence of events at a given place (McGraw-Hill Encyclopedia of Science, and Technology)
- a non-spatial system in which events appear to happen in irreversible succession (Word-Smyth Dictionary)
- the inevitable progression into the future with the passing of present events into the past (Wiktionary)
- the indefinite continued progress of existence, and events in the past, present, and future regarded as a whole (Google)
- Perhaps the best, and most comprehensive overall definition is that offered by Wikipedia:

a dimension in which events can be ordered from the past through the present into the future, and also the measure of durations of events, and the intervals between them.

Past, Present, and Future
Another way of looking at time is as the totality of three separate elements: the past, the present, and the future.

The past may be defined as those events which occurred before a given point in time, events which are usually considered to be fixed, and immutable. It can be accessed through memory or, since the advent of written language, recorded history. The study of the past, in particular as it relates to humans, is called history.

The present may be defined as the time associated with the events perceived directly, and for the first time, i.e. not as a recollection of the past or as a speculation of the future. It is equivalent to the word "now", and is the period of time located between the past, and the future. Just how long a period of time the present incorporates, however, depends on the context, and can vary from an infinitesimal or duration-less moment to a day to a whole era, depending on how it is being used.
The future is the indefinite time period after the present moment.

It is the portion of the projected time line that is anticipated to occur, and may be considered as potentially infinite in its extent, or as circumscribed, and finite, depending on the context. While some people may see the future as fixed, and predetermined, most see it as essentially unknown (and perhaps unknowable), and open to many different possibilities, and permutations. The study of postulating possible, probable, and preferable futures, and worldviews is called futurology.

ALTERNATE EXPLANATION FOR TIME

As quoted by Frederick Turner, internationally known poet, lecturer, and scholar, and Founders Professor of Arts, and Humanities at the University of Texas at Dallas.

The Need for Time

Time, goes the old joke, is nature's way of making sure that everything does not happen at once. Like many jokes, this one has a fairly large grain of truth. If two states of the same object were allowed by the universe, such as being red, and being green, or being in one place, and being in another, or if two objects, such as two fundamental particles of the same mass, spin, and charge, could occupy exactly the same state, and place, then major problems arise. Either, in the first case, the principle of identity is violated—is it one object or two—or in the second case, there is not room in space for both objects at once (in physics, this problem is known as the Pauli exclusion principle). In a universe of pure space, without time, the laws of science could not exist because identity, and location could not be reliably established.

Time gives the universe a way of connecting different states of the same object (first it was red, then it turned green; first it was in one place, then it was in another), and of spacing out events, and objects so that they do not get in each other's way (first one atom was there, then another). Further, if one of the states of an object has to exist if the other is to exist, time provides an order of events. The tree could not exist unless its seedling had earlier existed, nor the seedling without the seed; whereas the seedling could exist without the tree but not without the seed. Time is whatever space a logical scheduling problem requires for its solution.

We can actually study situations where time almost did not exist. In the tiny, and always minutely brief world of quantum mechanics there is so little time that identity, and location do indeed lose a good deal of their clarity, and indeed their distinction from one another: a particle could exist in a state of superposition, in which two different things are true of the same object, and it could exist very tenuously in two places at once. But for objects with more solidity, and persistence, time is necessary, not just tautologically for them to exist "in" but also as a way of resolving paradoxes of being, and location. Another place where time almost does not exist is in black holes, where it is only their slow leakage, and eventual unlocking that prevents paradoxes such as that information could be destroyed (a contradiction of identity), and that two things could be in the same place (black holes could be almost infinitely dense with matter).

The Problem

The Enlightenment description of time, which is familiar to us all, and which, even after ninety years, has not been replaced in our intuitive imagination by relativity theory, let alone other modifications of it, sounds like the simplest way of providing the "spacing-out", and scheduling function that is so important to the universe. What it says is that time is very like a spatial dimension, say, length, extending out in a straight line, and that everything in the universe at any given moment is at the same point on that line; what is on one side of us is the past, what is on the other is the future, and where we all are is the present.

But wait: all is not well here. When it comes to the "passing" of time, the familiar model begins to get complicated. The present moment moves along the line in a futureward direction, providing each point in it with an infinitesimal moment of reality or, in the opinion of some physicists, and philosophers, the whole line is always already real, and our consciousness moves along the line, like a spotlight, giving us the illusion of encountering a new future, and leaving behind a dead past. But the space analogy has already begun to break down. Our experience of space does not necessarily include a "passing of space"; there is no necessary point of maximal existence along a line, or maximal human attention to it, and there is no place on a line that all of the universe is at, and if either reality or our awareness moves along the line, in what time is it moving? How fast? How many miles per what? Could it accelerate? How could we tell the difference between slow, and fast and, if we could not, how could we tell if it had or had not stopped altogether? What does "move" mean if there is no discernible distinction? Is there a second time in which reality or awareness moves along the line of the first time? Then why not a third time in which the reality of the reality or the awareness of the awareness moves along the second?

If the whole timeline is already there, moreover, then the future is merely awaiting its actualization or our attention to it, and could not be changed. So, we are bound to the rails of fate, and such fundamental values as morality, freedom, responsibility, and creativity are illusions. This reflection might be bearable for a philosopher who prefers truth to moralistic wishful thinking, if it does not also imply that the philosopher's own cogitations are part of the same clockwork, and the feeling that something must be logically true is too, so truth is also an illusion, and there is no way of checking whether such an automaton is correctly calibrated, so as to verify that the illusion of truth coincides with its reality.

Equally problematic is the direction of time. Space does not have a preferred direction. In space one could get from London to Paris, and from Paris to London, but whereas one could get from A. D. 1980 to A. D. 2001 in time, one could not, as one could with space, get a return ticket. Nineteenth-century thermodynamics showed that thermal, and energetic events in the universe always went one way: toward the increase of entropy. You could burn a log but not unburn it, you could let perfume diffuse out of an open bottle, but not suck it back in again, you could turn work into heat, and heat into work but only if you pay a tax or interest of work energy on the exchange each time. But then the study of biological metabolism, and evolution seemed to show that living systems could feed upon the flow of the increase of entropy, like paddle-wheels in a torrent. Without violating the Second Law of thermodynamics, a tree could turn ash (soil), and smoke (atmospheric CO_2), and heat (sunlight) back into a log, and a rose could suck chemicals out of air, and soil, and make perfume. So not only can time possess at least two directions, different kinds of organisms can take different directions.

In the twentieth century, relativity theory showed that the universe was not all at the same point in the line; a present moment is not something simply given to the universe, but rather something rather fuzzily earned by two-way communication among objects, and events that put them in synch with one another. An "in-synch" region is called an inertial frame. Some parts of the universe are in different inertial frames from others, and our present knowledge of them is necessarily of their past, while other parts of the universe are over our event horizon, and we could never know them, and if we could not know them, the proposition that they existed, and shared our present moment is a purely metaphysical, and unscientific notion–unless we improve our model of time.

More recently still, quantum theory showed that the state of knowledge that exists about a particle partly determines its nature, and identity; disturbing enough, but more so if we reflect that one could only know about something after it had happened, since even the fastest messenger, light, has a finite speed. This means that knowledge must somehow retroactively affect what it is knowledge of. Therefore, the present-point on the line can be neither the spotlight of awareness (we are aware only of past events), nor the place where reality momentarily condense (since it is busily condensing previous realities).

So, the Enlightenment time-line description ends up being not so simple after all, and worse still, it is full of contradictions. It is contradictions, after all, that we need time in order to resolve, and if our account of time just introduce more of them, we are worse off than we were before. (If it struck the reader that sliding back, and forth between the universe's need for ordered time in order to exist coherently, and our need for ordered time to explain the universe with, that slide was intentional: for after all we are part of the universe, and any problem of ours is thus a problem of the universe's as well.)

Evidently no simple description of time will do. It looks as if we may have to settle for a description that is at least not contradictory, and let the complications fall as they may. Certainly, we would have to abandon the timeline concept; which means that we will have to be very skeptical about clocks (analog ones which wind the timeline onto a dial, or digital ones which map it onto the line of natural numbers), and calendars (which winch it onto the larger pawls of months, and years).

The reader will recognize that much of these last chapters were clearly speculative, and poetic. But the model of time we have possessed for over two hundred years will clearly not hold up any more. The relationship between the past, and the future can no longer be seen as like a line, but more like a solid, a sort of expanding sphere whose innards are the past, whose surface is the present, and whose outside is all the possible futures.

"I'm burned out just from listening," Buzz protested. "What are you doing to me?"
"What?"
"I used to have a sound handle on time. You managed to completely confuse the issue."
"Sorry. Didn't mean to. Just thought you might be interested."
"Interested, yes. But simple. Like everybody else I lived in the past, and present, looking to the future. Now, I'm not sure anymore. We've spent the last hours discussing time elements but what have we learned?"
"That time is not a constant anymore. Time is scalable."
"Who cares?"
"Your children might," I pacified him. "If they migrate out into space."
"That will be the day."

POLITICAL VIEWS

I do not want to dwell on politics, and political issues. If I have learned nothing else in life, I learned that there are two topics to stay away from, religion, and politics. Either one could cause a negative response, and at times met with fierce reaction. If one is drawn into a conversation on the topics, or has to comment on either, the safest way is to politely agree, even though it may cause one personal distress. The lesson is, stay away from that individual in the future. I feel for the people caught up in a relationship, or worse yet, being married to a religious, and political rival, apt for a troublesome life. Keeping my distance from both factions turned out to be an impossibility, nevertheless. On the economic condition as a whole, arriving in the country as a young man at the age of twenty-one, there is one thing I must admit: the society seemed more structured, and better organized. Perhaps not through the entire population, but certainly true with the middle-class workforce.

Taking on my first job, I was practically told what political party I belonged to. Right from the start, it became obvious that workers signed up with two organizations, the workers' union, and the Republican party. Since I was indoctrinated on both, either one was fine with me since everybody in the company belonged to them. Little did I know that two weeks later I would be out of work. Shortly before my employment, local union members had planned to go on strike.

Back in the 60s, there was practically only one issue for the strike, higher wages. Again, I had no objections since the base bargaining was for an increase from $1.50 per hour, my starting pay, to $1.80. Since I had not been indoctrinated, or signed up into the union yet, I was given a choice, report to work the following Monday, or stay home, and face termination from a just-started job. Showing up on that morning I realized right away that it was impossible to get through the strikers' zone, the strikers carrying not only the signs, but baseball bats as well. The signs were clear: "Do Not Cross Lines."

I was caught in a quandary along with several other non-union members standing on the sidewalk some distance from the strikers, unable to get to our workplace. Undecided on how to proceed, minutes later, several vehicles drove up, dislodging a dozen club-carrying goons. Our problem to cross the striker lines was solved by the club-swinging thugs headed up by the Philadelphia Local 123rd Labor Union organizers. From that day, for the next three weeks, we were escorted into the building until the strike was settled. I was paid the new wage, but refused to join the union. Though, back then, I could not get a clear understanding for my refusing to join the union. My objection was personal. Years before, in Germany, I had refused union memberships on a couple occasions for the same reason: it was forced onto me. It brought back unpleasant memories from a time when Hitler was forcing his dictatorial power on the population. I did not want any such restraints placed on my freedom.

My assessment on the subject of unionization would become clear over the next several years when I realized how much it stifled industrial progress. Where, at one time, the Union may have been instrumental for elevating the workforce from a slaving position into prospering middle class, over time, many union members lost their zest to work. It became obvious that the mentality had changed from a dedicated worker to "Why should I bust my butt if I can get paid without it?" Such mentality seriously affected eastern seacoast cities whose industrial decline became obvious at the onset of the seventies. It was the very reason union-free Silicon Valley was created from relocated defunct eastern companies. During that migration period in the mid-seventies, working for Ford Aerospace at the time, was the reason for my moving to California's newly developed industrial region, in turn solving the union issue.

As far as my political affiliation was concerned, I joined the Republican party, and voted on most of their issues. I would learn soon enough what contrasting issues the parties held. There seemed a clear distinction between the two major parties, the liberals, and conservatives, with the majority of us respecting the differences to live, and work side-by-side. Such is not the case today in a world where political differences have become a battle ground. There was one enlightening moment. I thought it was a profound statement when my eldest daughter confronted me with the question, "Why can't both parties get together, and work things out peacefully without all of the accusations, and fighting?"

"It used to be that way," I explained. "But that was before you were born."

There is a simple solution, but a not so simple answer. We need to learn to respect each other again. Consider the lost values this nation used to abide by, honesty, morality, respect, and trust. There remains much work to be done. They were honored values one had to be taught from childhood on. They do not come naturally in today's world driven by disrespect, deceit, and dishonesty, trades carried by many of the population. Lying, and cheating, it seems, have become the norm in our everyday living. Where lying, at one time, was reason for punishment, today, for the most part, it is accepted without consequences.

There is no doubt that the democratic system devised by our forefathers, with its amendments that we practiced in this country, worked as intended, but that was over two hundred years ago. It may not be enough anymore in today's world to effectively rule the country. Regardless, rules, and policies have to be observed. In my opinion, there are too many amendments incorporated into the constitution trying to accommodate every citizen's demand. With the influx of illegal aliens, undesirable elements entering the country with forged documents, radical Islam, and many more exploit seekers, it can only get worse unless tighter control is exerted, but whose job is it?

The Government's!

As part of protecting the country's assets, and its citizens' safety, it is one of the government's responsibilities. It works as long as organizations are doing their jobs as delineated in the constitution. It is not my intention to bash the government, and corporate America for their acquired powers, and greed and, in the process ignoring the workforce that built, and sustained this nation. It may be one reason why the people have lost their respect for authorities. Sure, living in a free world provides ample liberties other countries do not enjoy, but there is a price to be paid, for freedom does not come cheap. One only has to consider the tax burden on the individual, in addition to driving the nation deeper into deficit with each year. Once the limit for irresponsible spending is reached, the consequence will be severe. The country will collapse with the middle class bearing the largest burden. The rich will maintain most of their wealth with the poor remaining poor.

Fortunately, there are alternatives to the inevitable. One, for example, as we currently experienced, is the present administration. Though, poorly politically oriented without strong sense of diplomacy, and mostly business driven to achieve results, the Senate, House, and the American people should support our leader's choices, and decisions, nevertheless. But what do they do?

Nothing but infighting and bickering without lending much support to policymakers. Political elections have always been difficult. What used to be mere mudslinging, today, looked more like character assassination. We have lost much of the admiration, and respect the world had for us, and the country at one time. Against all of the resistance, and nonsupport the current administration receives from liberal members, the president is working hard to solve the country's economic demise on top of international pressures we are facing. He should obtain the support of every citizen to get the country back to the powerful nation it once was. We may still claim to be number one, but in the eyes of many other nations, we had lost our leadership status decades ago.

As stated, our president is doing his best, and more each day than any other previous leader had accomplished. It does not mean that his accomplishments are in proportion to the endless hours spent on pending issues. It would be much easier for all parties to work together to achieve his goals. But to do so, there must be complete trust, cooperation, and alliances among party members.

We all want the same things in life. We want freedom, we want the chance for prosperity, we want as few people suffering as possible, we want healthy children, we want to have crime-free streets. The argument is in how to achieve them. The following table contains a brief, and general description of conservative, and liberal values from my political perspective. While we want the same things from the government, it would be difficult to merge every article as delineated by the parties. It becomes even more difficult when considering all registered parties representing the American citizens.

Conservatives believe in personal responsibility, limited government, free markets, individual liberty, traditional American values, and a strong national defense. They believe the role of government should be to provide people the freedom necessary to pursue their own goals. Conservative policies generally emphasize empowerment of the individual to solve problems.	*Liberals* believe in government action to achieve equal opportunity, and equality for all. It is the duty of the government to alleviate social ills, and to protect civil liberties, and individual, and human rights. They believe the role of the government should be to guarantee that no one is in need. Liberal policies generally emphasize the need for the government to solve problems.

The following table contains conservative, and liberal values from a religious perspective. The differences become even more challenging when considering the many religions practiced by man. It is here where individual values turn into conflicts incapable to reconcile. Many wars have been fought over beliefs far back into ancient history. Unless man can work out the differences, and unify belief, and faith, chances for peace, and lasting prosperity can never be reached.

Conservative	Liberal
The Bible is to be taken literally whenever possible.	Much of the Bible should be taken figuratively.
The Bible provides us with a completely accurate, representative account of Jesus, his life, and his divinity.	We could only guess at what the real Jesus was like, since the early Church fathers may have changed the accounts of Jesus' life to suit their purposes.
Jesus was fully God, and fully man.	Jesus was a great prophet, and teacher, but he was not divine.
Jesus was crucified, died, and rose from the dead.	Jesus was crucified, and died, but he did not rise from the dead.
Salvation is by faith in Christ, not good works. Good works followed as a natural byproduct of faith.	Although faith is involved in salvation, it must be proven by good works, and compassion.
Jesus judges each person on the basis of their extent, and quality of their faith in Him as their savior.	God judges each person in terms of their works. If the good works outweigh the bad, their fate in the afterlife would be favorably affected.
Emphasis is on correct doctrine, and spreading the Gospel. Other religions are viewed as being incorrect.	Emphasis is on compassion, social action, and tolerance. God is far more interested in the sincerity of a person's beliefs than in their correctness.

There are many more differences one could draw from the various party systems, too many to list, and perhaps too controversial for discussion since most were written with bias from their respective party perspectives. In itself, they would cause great controversy, disputes, and clashes among its devout.

As one can easily envision from the comparison tables, the differences in opinion, and policies are not too opposed, and different. They could easily be merged into a national effort to achieve a common goal of prosperity. The only thing missing is the common objective supported by the political parties. Where not every issue would satisfy each individual making up the body of the country's citizenship, because we all have our own free views, the opportunities would be enough to achieve a coexistence with one goal in view, that of a sound, and united nation.

The next chapter addresses functional issues with principle party guidelines compiled by "StudentNewsDaily.com" for conservatives, and liberals everybody should be familiar with. It provides the foundation for voting political candidates into office. The issues, explored for each of the primary political parties, are of utmost importance, and considered vital to the country, and its citizens.

CONSERVATIVE VS. LIBERAL BELIEFS

PRINCIPLE ISSUES:

ABORTION

Liberal
A woman has the right to decide what happens with her body. A fetus is not a human life, so it does not have separate individual rights. The government should provide taxpayer funded abortions for women who cannot afford them. The decision to have an abortion is a personal choice of a woman regarding her own body, and the government must protect this right. Women have the right to affordable, safe, and legal abortions, including partial birth abortion.

Conservative
Human life begins at conception. Abortion is the murder of a human being. An unborn baby, as a living human being, has separate rights from those of the mother. Oppose taxpayer-funded abortion. Taxpayer dollars should not be used for the government to provide abortions. Support legislation to prohibit partial birth abortions, called the "Partial Birth Abortion Ban."

AFFIRMATIVE ACTION

Liberal
Due to prevalent racism in the past, minorities were deprived of the same education, and employment opportunities as whites. The government must work to make up for that. America is still a racist society; therefore, a federal affirmative action law is necessary. Due to unequal opportunity, minorities still lag behind whites in all statistical measurements of success.

Conservative
Individuals should be admitted to schools, and hired for jobs based on their ability. It is unfair to use race as a factor in the selection process. Reverse-discrimination is not a solution for racism. Some individuals in society are racist, but American society as a whole is not. Preferential treatment of certain races through affirmative action is wrong.

DEATH PENALTY

Liberal
The death penalty should be abolished. It is inhumane, and is 'cruel, and unusual' punishment. Imprisonment is the appropriate punishment for murder. Every execution risk killing an innocent person.

Conservative
The death penalty is a punishment that fits the crime of murder; it is neither 'cruel' nor 'unusual.' Executing a murderer is the appropriate punishment for taking an innocent life.

ECONOMY

Liberal

A market system in which government regulates the economy was best. Government must protect citizens from the greed of big business. Unlike the private sector, the government is motivated by public interest. Government regulation in all areas of the economy is needed to level the playing field.

Conservative

The free market system, competitive capitalism, and private enterprise creates the greatest opportunity, and the highest standard of living for all. Free markets produce more economic growth, more jobs, and higher standards of living than those systems burdened by excessive government regulation.

EDUCATION – *VOUCHERS & CHARTER SCHOOLS*

Liberal

Public schools are the best way to educate students. Vouchers take money away from public schools. Government should focus additional funds on existing public schools, raising teacher salaries, and reducing class size.

Conservative

School vouchers create competition, and therefore encourage schools to improve performance. Vouchers would give all parents the right to choose good schools for their children, not just those who could afford private schools.

EMBRYONIC STEM CELL RESEARCH

Liberal

Support the use of embryonic stem cells for research. It is necessary (and ethical) for the government to fund embryonic stem cell research, which would assist scientists in finding treatments, and cures for diseases. An embryo is not a human. The tiny blastocyst (embryos used in embryonic stem cell research) has no human features. Experimenting on embryos/embryonic stem cells is not murder. Embryonic stem cells have the potential to cure chronic, and degenerative diseases which current medicine has been unable to effectively treat. Embryonic stem cells have been shown to be effective in treating heart damage in mice.

Conservative

Support the use of adult, and umbilical cord stem cells only for research. It is morally, and ethically wrong for the government to fund embryonic stem cell research. Human life begins at conception. The extraction of stem cells from an embryo requires its destruction. In other words, it requires that a human life be killed. Adult stem cells have already been used to treat spinal cord injuries, Leukemia, and even Parkinson's disease. Adult stem cells are derived from umbilical cords, placentas, amniotic fluid, various tissues, and organ systems like skin, and the liver, and even fat obtained from liposuction. Embryonic stem cells have not been successfully used to help cure disease.

ENERGY

Liberal

Oil is a depleting resource. Other sources of energy must be explored. The government must produce a national plan for all energy resources, and subsidize (partially pay for) alternative energy research, and production. Support increased exploration of alternative energy sources such as wind, and solar power. Support government control of gas, and electric industries.

Conservative

Oil, gas, and coal are all good sources of energy, and are abundant in the U.S. Oil drilling should be increased both on land, and at sea. Increased domestic production creates lower prices, and less dependence on other countries for oil. Support increased production of nuclear energy. Wind, and solar sources would never provide plentiful, affordable sources of power. Support private ownership of gas, and electric industries.

EUTHANASIA & PHYSICIAN-ASSISTED SUICIDE

Liberal

Euthanasia should be legalized. A person has a right to die with dignity, by his own choice. A terminally ill person should have the right to choose to end pain, and suffering. It is wrong for the government to take away the means for a terminally ill person to hasten his death. It is wrong to force a person to go through so much pain, and suffering. Legalizing euthanasia would not lead to doctor-assisted suicides of non-critical patients. Permitting euthanasia would reduce health care costs, which would then make funds available for those who could truly benefit from medical care.

Conservative

Neither euthanasia nor physician-assisted suicide should be legalized. It is immoral, and unethical to deliberately end the life of a terminally ill person (euthanasia), or enable another person to end their own life (assisted suicide). The goal should be compassionate care, and easing the suffering of terminally ill people. Legalizing euthanasia could lead to doctor-assisted suicides of non-critical patients. If euthanasia were legalized, insurance companies could pressure doctors to withhold life-saving treatment for dying patients. Many religions prohibit suicide, and euthanasia. These practices devalue human life.

GLOBAL WARMING/CLIMATE CHANGE

Liberal

Global warming is caused by an increased production of carbon dioxide through the burning of fossil fuels (coal, oil, and natural gas). The U.S. is a major contributor to global warming because it produces 25% of the world's carbon dioxide. Proposed laws to reduce carbon emissions in the U.S. are urgently needed, and should be enacted immediately to save the planet. Many reputable scientists support this theory.

Conservative

Change in global temperature is natural over long periods of time. Science has not shown that humans can affect permanent change to the earth's temperature. Proposed laws to reduce carbon emissions will do nothing to help the environment, and would cause significant price increases for all. Many reputable scientists support this theory.

GUN CONTROL

Liberal
The Second Amendment does not give citizens the right to keep, and bear arms, but only allows for the state to keep a militia (National Guard). Individuals do not need guns for protection; it is the role of local, and federal government to protect the people through law enforcement agencies, and the military. Additional gun control laws are necessary to stop gun violence, and limit the ability of criminals to obtain guns. More guns mean more violence.

Conservative
The Second Amendment gives citizens the right to keep, and bear arms. Individuals have the right to defend themselves. There are too many gun control laws – additional laws would not lower gun crime rates. What is needed is enforcement of current laws. Gun control laws do not prevent criminals from obtaining guns. More guns in the hands of law-abiding citizens mean less crime.

Full text of the Second Amendment to the U.S. Constitution: "A well-regulated Militia, being necessary to the security of a free State, the right of the people to keep, and bear Arms, shall not be infringed."

HEALTHCARE

Liberal
Support free or low-cost government-controlled health care. There are millions of Americans who cannot afford health care, and are deprived of this basic right. Every American has a right to affordable health care. The government should provide equal health care benefits for all, regardless of their ability to pay.

Conservative
Support competitive, free market health care system. All Americans have access to health care. The debate is about who should pay for it. Free, and low-cost government-run programs (socialized medicine) result in higher costs, and everyone receiving the same poor-quality health care. Health care should remain privatized. The problem of uninsured individuals should be addressed, and solved within the free market healthcare system – the government should not control healthcare.

HOMELAND SECURITY

Liberal
Airport security – Passenger profiling is wrong, period. Selection of passengers for extra security screening should be random. Using other criteria (such as ethnicity) is discriminatory, and offensive to Arabs, and Muslims, who are generally innocent, and law-abiding. Terrorists do not fit a profile.

"...Arabs, Muslims, and South Asians are no more likely than whites to be terrorists." (American Civil Liberties Union ACLU). Asked on 60 Minutes if a 70-

year-old white woman from Vero Beach should receive the same level of scrutiny as a Muslim from Jersey City, President Obama's Transportation Secretary Norman Mineta said, "Basically, I would hope so."

Conservative
Airport security – Choosing passengers randomly for extra security searches is not effective. Rather, profiling, and Intelligence data should be used to single out passengers for extra screening. Those who do not meet the criteria for suspicion should not be subjected to intense screening. The terrorists currently posing a threat to the U.S. are primarily Islamic/Muslim men between the ages of 18, and 38. Our resources should be focused on this group. Profiling is good logical police work.

"If people are offended (by profiling), that's unfortunate, but I don't think we can afford to take the risk that terrorism brings to us. They've wasted masses of resources on far too many people doing things that really don't have a big payoff in terms of security." – Northwestern University Aviation Expert, A. Gellman.

IMMIGRATION

Liberal
Support legal immigration. Support amnesty for those who enter the U.S. illegally (undocumented immigrants). Also believe that undocumented immigrants have a right to: all educational, and health benefits that citizens receive (financial aid, welfare, social security, and Medicaid), regardless of legal status—the same rights as American citizens. It is unfair to arrest millions of undocumented immigrants.

Conservative
Support legal immigration only. Oppose amnesty for those who enter the U.S. illegally (illegal immigrants). Those who break the law by entering the U.S. illegally do not have the same rights as those who obey the law, and enter legally. The borders should be secured before addressing the problem of the illegal immigrants currently in the country. The Federal Government should secure the borders, and enforce current immigration law.

PRIVATE PROPERTY

Liberal
Government has the right to use eminent domain (seizure of private property by the government with compensation to the owner) to accomplish a public end.

Conservative
Respect ownership, and private property rights. Eminent domain (seizure of private property by the government with compensation to the owner) in most cases is wrong. Eminent domain should not be used for private development.

RELIGION & GOVERNMENT

Liberal
Support the separation of church, and state. The Bill of Rights implies a separation of church, and state. Religious expression has no place in government. The two should

be completely separated. Government should not support religious expression in any way. All reference to God in public, and government spaces should be removed (e.g., the Ten Commandments should not be displayed in federal buildings). Religious expression has no place in government.

Conservative
The phrase *"separation of church, and state"* is not in the Constitution. The First Amendment to the Constitution states *"Congress shall make no law respecting an establishment of religion, or prohibiting the free exercise thereof..."* This prevents the government from establishing a national church/denomination. However, it does not prohibit God from being acknowledged in schools, and government buildings. Symbols of Christian heritage should not be removed from public, and government spaces (e.g., the Ten Commandments should continue to be displayed in federal buildings). Government should not interfere with religion, and religious freedom.

SAME-SEX MARRIAGE

Liberal
Marriage is the union of people who love each other. It should be legal for gay, lesbian, bisexual, and transgender individuals, to ensure equal rights for all. Support same-sex marriage. Opposed to the creation of a constitutional amendment establishing marriage as the union of one man, and one woman. All individuals, regardless of their sexual orientation, have the right to marry. Prohibiting same-sex citizens from marrying denies them their civil rights. [Opinions vary on whether this issue is equal to civil rights for African Americans.]

Conservative
Marriage is the union of one man, and one woman. Oppose same-sex marriage. Supported Defense of Marriage Act (DOMA), passed in 1996, which affirmed the right of states not to recognize same-sex marriages licensed in other states. Requiring citizens to sanction same-sex relationships violates moral, and religious beliefs of millions of Christians, Jews, Muslims, and others, who believe marriage is the union of one man, and one woman.

SOCIAL SECURITY

Liberal
The Social Security system should be protected at all costs. Reduction in future benefits is not a reasonable option. [Opinions vary on the extent of the current system's financial stability.] Social Security provides a safety net for the nation's poor, and needy. Changing the system would cause a reduction in benefits, and many people would suffer as a result.

Conservative
The Social Security system is in serious financial trouble. Major changes to the current system are urgently needed. In its current state, the Social Security system is not financially sustainable. It will collapse if nothing is done to address the problems. Many would suffer as a result. Social Security must be made more efficient through privatization and/or allowing individuals to manage their own savings.

TAXES

Liberal

Higher taxes (primarily for the wealthy), and a larger government are necessary to address inequity/injustice in society (government should help the poor, and needy using tax dollars from the rich). Support a large government to provide for the needs of the people, and to create equality. Taxes enable the government to create jobs, and provide welfare programs for those in need. Government programs are a caring way to provide for the poor, and needy in society.

Conservative

Lower taxes, and a smaller government with limited power would improve the standard of living for all. Support lower taxes, and a smaller government. Lower taxes create more incentive for people to work, save, invest, and engage in entrepreneurial endeavors. Money is best spent by those who earned it, not the government. Government programs encourage people to become dependent, and lazy, rather than encouraging work, and independence.

UNITED NATIONS (UN)

Liberal

The UN promotes peace, and human rights. The United States has a moral, and a legal obligation to support the United Nations (UN). The U.S. should not act as a sovereign nation, but as one member of a world community. The U.S. should submit its national interests to the greater good of the global community (as defined by the UN). The U.S. should defer to the UN in military/peacekeeping matters. The United Nations Charter gives the United Nations Security Council the power, and responsibility to take collective action to maintain international peace, and security. U.S. troops should submit to UN command.

Conservative

The UN has repeatedly failed in its essential mission to promote world peace, and human rights. The wars, genocide, and human rights abuses taking place in many Human Rights Council member states (and the UN's failure to stop them) proves this point. History showed that the United States, not the UN, has been the global force for spreading freedom, prosperity, tolerance, and peace. The U.S. should never subvert its national interests to those of the UN. The U.S. should never place troops under UN control. U.S. military should always wear the U.S. military uniform, not that of UN peacekeepers. [Opinions vary on whether the U.S. should withdraw from the UN.]

WAR ON TERROR/TERRORISM

Liberal

Global warming, not terrorism, poses the greatest threat to the U.S., according to Democrats in Congress. Terrorism is a result of arrogant U.S. foreign policy. Good diplomacy is the best way to deal with terrorism. Relying on military force to defeat terrorism creates hatred that leads to more terrorism. Captured terrorists should be handled by law enforcement, and tried in civilian courts.

Conservative

Terrorism poses one of the greatest threats to the U.S. The world toward which the militant Islamists strive cannot peacefully co-exist with the Western world. In the last decade, militant Islamists have repeatedly attacked Americans, and American interests here, and abroad. Terrorists must be stopped, and destroyed. The use of Intelligence-gathering, and military force are the best ways to defeat terrorism around the world. Captured terrorists should be treated as enemy combatants, and tried in military courts.

WELFARE

Liberal

Support welfare, including long-term welfare. Welfare is a safety net which provides for the needs of the poor. Welfare is necessary to bring fairness to American economic life. It is a device for protecting the poor.

Conservative

Oppose long-term welfare. Opportunities should be provided to make it possible for those in need to become self-reliant. It is far more compassionate, and effective to encourage people to become self-reliant, rather than allowing them to remain dependent on the government for provisions.

VOTING

On ending this section, since it applies to both liberals, and conservatives, I will leave the reader with a quote expressed by one of the world's most notorious leaders, Joseph Stalin:

> "It is not the people who vote that count. It is the people who count the votes."

ON FOREIGN POLICIES

The foreign policy of the United States is its interactions with foreign nations, and how it sets standards of interaction for its organizations, corporations, and system citizens of the United States.

The officially stated goals of the foreign policy of the United States, including all the bureaus, and offices in the United States Department of State, as mentioned in the *Foreign Policy Agenda* of the Department of State, are "to build, and sustain a more democratic, secure, and prosperous world for the benefit of the American people, and the international community." In addition, the United States House Committee on Foreign Affairs stated as some of its jurisdictional goals: "export controls, including nonproliferation of nuclear technology, and nuclear hardware; measured to foster commercial interaction with foreign nations, and to safeguard American business abroad; international commodity agreements; international education;, and protection of American citizens abroad, and expatriation." U.S. foreign policy, and foreign aid have been the subject of much debate, praise, and criticism, both domestically, and abroad.

Historical overview
The main trend regarding the history of U.S. foreign policy since the American Revolution has been the shift from non-interventionism before, and after World War I, to its growth as a world power, and global hegemony during, and since World War II, and the end of the Cold War in the 20th century. Since the 19th century, U.S. foreign policy also has been characterized by a shift from the realist school to the idealistic or Wilsonian school of international relations.

Foreign policy themes were expressed considerably in George Washington's farewell address; these included, among other things, observing good faith, and justice towards all nations, and cultivating peace, and harmony with all, excluding both inveterate antipathies against particular nations, and passionate attachments for others, steering clear of permanent alliances with any portion of the foreign world, and advocating trade with all nations. These policies became the basis of the Federalist Party in the 1790s. But the rival Jeffersonians feared Britain, and favored France in the 1790s, declaring the War of 1812 on Britain. After the 1778 alliance with France, the U.S. did not sign another permanent treaty until the North Atlantic Treaty in 1949. Over time, other themes, key goals, attitudes, or stances have been variously expressed by presidential doctrines, named for them. Initially these were uncommon events, but since WWII, these have been made by most presidents.

Jeffersonians vigorously opposed a large standing army, and any navy until attacks against American shipping by Barbary corsairs spurred the country into developing a naval force projection capability, resulting in the First Barbary War in 1801.

Despite two wars with European Powers, the War of 1812, and the 1898 Spanish-American War, American foreign policy is peaceful, and was marked by steady expansion of its foreign trade during the 19th century. The 1803 Louisiana Purchase doubled the nation's geographical area; Spain ceded the territory of Florida in 1819; annexation brought in the independent Texas Republic in 1845, and a war with Mexico in 1848 added California, Arizona, Utah, Nevada, and New Mexico. The U.S. bought

Alaska from the Russian Empire in 1867, and it annexed the independent Republic of Hawaii in 1898. Victory over Spain in 1898 brought the Philippines, and Puerto Rico, as well as oversight of Cuba. The short experiment in imperialism ended by 1908, as the U.S. turned its attention to the Panama Canal, and the stabilization of regions to its south, including Mexico.

21st century
In the 21st century, U.S. influence remains strong but, in relative terms, is declining in terms of economic output compared to rising nations such as China, India, Russia, and the newly consolidated European Union. Substantial problems remain, such as climate change, nuclear proliferation, and the specter of nuclear terrorism.

In 2017 diplomats from other countries developed new tactics to deal with President Donald Trump. The *New York Times* reported on the eve of his first foreign trip as president:
> "For foreign leaders trying to figure out the best way to approach an American president unlike any they have known, it is a time of experimentation. Embassies in Washington trade tips, and ambassadors send cables to presidents, and ministers back home suggesting how to handle a mercurial, strong-willed leader with no real experience on the world stage, a preference for personal diplomacy, and a taste for glitz."

Certain rules have emerged: "Keep it short—no 30-minute monologue for a 30-second attention span. Do not assume he knows the history of the country or its major points of contention. Compliment him on his Electoral College victory. Contrast him favorably with President Barack Obama. Do not get hung up on whatever was said during the campaign. Stay in regular touch. Do not go in with a shopping list but bring some sort of deal he can call a victory."

Trump had numerous aides giving advice on foreign policy, with chief diplomat, Secretary of State Rex Tillerson. His major foreign policy positions, which sometimes were at odds with Trump, include:
> "Urging the United States to stay in the Trans-Pacific Partnership, and the Paris climate accord, taking a hard line on Russia, advocating negotiations, and dialogue to defuse the mounting crisis with North Korea, advocating for continued U.S. adherence to the Iran nuclear deal, taking a neutral position in the dispute between Qatar, and Saudi Arabia, and reassuring jittery allies, from South Korea, and Japan to our NATO partners, that America still has their back."

Law
In the United States, there are three types of treaty-related law:

Treaties are formal written agreements specified by the Treaty Clause of the Constitution. The president makes a treaty with foreign powers, but then the proposed treaty must be ratified by a two-thirds vote in the Senate. For example, President Wilson proposed the Treaty of Versailles after World War I after consulting with allied powers, but this treaty was rejected by the Senate; as a result, the U.S. subsequently made separate agreements with different nations. While most international law has a broader interpretation of the term treaty, the U.S. sense of the term is more restricted.

Executive agreements are made by the president—in the exercise of his constitutional executive powers—alone.

Congressional-executive agreements are made by the president, and Congress. A majority of both houses make it binding, much like regular legislation, after it is signed by the president. The Constitution does not expressly state that these agreements are allowed.

In contrast to most other nations, the United States considers the three types of agreements as distinct. Further, the United States incorporates treaty law into the body of U.S. federal law. As a result, Congress can modify or repeal treaties afterward. It can overrule an agreed-upon treaty obligation even if this is seen as a violation of the treaty under international law.

Federal Level

At the federal level, there exist both federal police, who possess full federal authority as given to them under United States Code (U.S.C.), and federal law enforcement agencies, who are authorized to enforce various laws at the federal level. Both police, and law enforcement agencies operate at the highest level, and are endowed with police roles; each may maintain a small component of the other (for example, the FBI Police). The agencies have nationwide jurisdiction for enforcement of federal law. Most federal agencies are limited by the U.S. Code to investigating only matters that are explicitly within the power of the federal government. However, federal investigative powers have become very broad in practice, especially since the passage of the USA PATRIOT Act. There are also federal law enforcement agencies, such as the United States Park Police, that are granted state arrest authority off primary federal jurisdiction.

The Department of Justice (DOJ) is responsible for most law enforcement duties at the federal level. It includes the Federal Bureau of Investigation (FBI), the Drug Enforcement Administration (DEA), the Bureau of Alcohol, Tobacco, Firearms, and Explosives (ATF), the United States Marshals Service, the Federal Bureau of Prisons (BOP), and others.

The Department of Homeland Security (DHS) is another branch with numerous federal law enforcement agencies reporting to it. U.S. Customs, and Border Protection (CBP), U.S. Immigration, and Customs Enforcement (ICE), Federal Air Marshal Service (FAMS), United States Secret Service (USSS), United States Coast Guard (USCG), Homeland Security Investigations (HSI), and the Transportation Security Administration (TSA) are some of the agencies that report to DHS. It should be noted that the United States Coast Guard is assigned to the United States Department of Defense in the event of war.

At a crime or disaster scene affecting large numbers of people, multiple jurisdictions, or broad geographic areas, many police agencies may be involved by mutual aid agreements; for example, the United States Federal Protective Service responded to the Hurricane Katrina natural disaster. Command in such situations remains a complex, and flexible issue.

In accordance with the federal, as opposed to unitary or confederal, structure of the United States government, the national (federal) government is not authorized to execute general police powers by the Constitution of the United States of America. Each of the United States' 50 federated states (referred to simply as 'states' in the

United States despite their lack of full sovereignty) retain their own police, military, and domestic law-making powers. The U.S. Constitution gives the federal government the power to deal with foreign affairs, and interstate affairs (affairs between the states). For policing, this means that if a non-federal crime is committed in a U.S. state, and the fugitive does not flee the state, the federal government has no jurisdiction. However, once the fugitive crosses a state line, he violates the federal law of interstate flight, and is subject to federal jurisdiction, at which time federal law enforcement agencies may become involved.

State Level
On the state level, the United States District Courts or Courts of Appeals are the intermediate appellate courts of the federal court system, but not without geographically defined boundaries for the twelve circuits, starting with First Circuit Court in Boston, Maine, progressing west through California to Circuit Court Nine. Colorado, and surrounding states make up Circuit Court 10, Florida, and its surrounding states make up Circuit Court 11, and ending with twelfth Circuit Court in Washington DC.

INTERNATIONAL AGREEMENTS

Exporting Democracy
In United States history, critics have charged that presidents have used democracy to justify military intervention abroad. Critics have also charged that the U.S. helped local militaries overthrow democratically elected governments in Iran, Guatemala, and in other instances. Studies have been devoted to the historical success rate of the U.S. in *exporting* democracy abroad. Some studies of American intervention have been pessimistic about the overall effectiveness of U.S. efforts to encourage democracy in foreign nations.

Covert Actions
United States foreign policy also includes covert actions to topple foreign governments that have been opposed to the United States. According to J. Dana Stuster, writing in *Foreign Policy*, there are seven confirmed cases where the U.S.—acting principally through the Central Intelligence Agency (CIA), but sometimes with the support of other parts of the U.S. government, including the Navy, and State Department— covertly assisted in the overthrow of a foreign government:

> "Iran in 1953, Guatemala in 1954, Congo in 1960, the Dominican Republic in 1961, and numerous failed assassination attempt directed against Cuba's Fidel Castro, South Vietnam in 1963, Brazil in 1964, and Chile in 1973."

Missile Defense
The Strategic Defense Initiative (SDI) was a proposal by U.S. President Ronald Reagan on March 23, 1983 to use ground, and space-based systems to protect the United States from attack by strategic nuclear ballistic missiles, later dubbed *Star Wars*. The initiative focused on strategic defense rather than the prior strategic offense doctrine of mutual assured destruction (MAD). Though it was never fully developed or deployed, the research, and technologies of SDI paved the way for some anti- ballistic missile systems of today.

In February 2007, the U.S. started formal negotiations with Poland, and Czech Republic concerning construction of missile shield installations in those countries for a ground-based midcourse defense system.

Russia threatened to place short-range nuclear missiles on the Russia's border with NATO if the United States refused to abandon plans to deploy 10 interceptor missiles, and a radar in Poland, and the Czech Republic. In April 2007, Putin warned of a new Cold War if the Americans deployed the shield in Central Europe. Putin also said that Russia was prepared to abandon its obligations under an Intermediate-Range Nuclear Forces Treaty of 1987 with the United States.

On August 14, 2008, the United States, and Poland announced a deal to implement the missile defense system in Polish territory, with a tracking system placed in the Czech Republic. The fact that this was signed in a period of very difficult crisis in the relations between Russia, and the United States over the situation in Georgia showed that the missile defense system would be deployed not against Iran but against the strategic potential of Russia.

The Foreign Affairs advisors argued that U.S. missile defenses were designed to secure Washington's nuclear primacy, and were chiefly directed at potential rivals, such as Russia, and China. If the United States launched a nuclear attack against Russia (or China), the targeted country would be left with only a tiny surviving arsenal, if any at all. At that point, even a relatively modest or inefficient missile defense system might well be enough to protect against any retaliatory strikes.

This analysis was corroborated by the Pentagon's 1992 Defense Planning Guidance (DPG), prepared by then Secretary of Defense Richard Cheney, and his deputies. The DPG declared that the United States should use its power to "prevent the reemergence of a new rival" either on former Soviet territory or elsewhere. The authors of the DPG determined that the United States had to "Field a missile defense system as a shield against accidental missile launches or limited missile strikes by 'international outlaws'", and also must "Find ways to integrate the 'new democracies' of the former Soviet bloc into the U.S.-led system." The National Archive noted that Document 10 of the DPG included wording about "disarming capabilities to destroy" which was followed by several blacked-out words. "This suggests that some of the heavily excised pages in the still-classified DPG drafts may include some discussion of preventive action against threatening nuclear, and other WMD programs."

Global opinion on the United States
A global survey performed by *Pew Global* indicated that (as of 2014) at least 33 surveyed countries had a positive view (50% or above) of the United States. The top ten most positive countries were the Philippines (92%), Israel (84%), South Korea (82%), Kenya (80%), El Salvador (80%), Italy (78%), Ghana (77%), Vietnam (76%), Bangladesh (76%), and Tanzania (75%). 10 surveyed countries had the most negative view (Below 50%) of the United States, with those countries being Egypt (10%), Jordan (12%), Pakistan (14%), Turkey (19%), Russia (23%), Palestinian Territories (30%), Greece (34%), Argentina (36%), Lebanon (41%), and Tunisia (42%). Americans' own view of the United States was viewed at 84%.

TODAY AND FUTURE

We must be diligently wary of China, and Russia, and to a certain extent North Korea, Iran, Pakistan, and other potentially hostile, and rogue nations striving for world supremacy. It is not to say that they do not deserve equal status in world trade, economics, and technology, it is meant to control such ambitious countries from taking over other nations, acquiring territory belonging to another country, or destroying the free world. In today's world with boundaries defining each country, there is no free territory left for the taking. Each country's ruling power must accept, and honor the United Nations Security Council ruling body. While U.N. enforcing policies, in recent years, for African nations have been proven effective, to some extent, for the rest of the world, their law enforcing body still has to be evaluated, and demonstrated, especcially for major countries such as Russia, China, and the United States, which are not easy to submit to foreign rules, and regulations.

Supporting world nations by the primary supporter, the United States, must stop, or at least be curbed to a reasonable monetary amount appropriate with current economic limits within the States. Taxpayers have already been excessively burdened with social programs that have grown out of proportion. With countless agendas taking advantage of America's "good Samaritan citizens," always willing to help, it is no wonder that our own social security, the country's most dependent social system, as was predicted, is on the brink of financial collapse within the next couple of decades. We must learn, as a nation, to take care of our own disadvantaged, and deprived people first, regardless of international sentiments exerted on our world-renowned humanitarian notions.

People get used to free handouts, and keep asking for more, and more. Such monetary support is always welcome as long as it comes without reparation attachments. Aside from placing a great burden on our own citizens, for the disadvantaged dependent on handouts, it is not an incentive to seek work, and steady employment. Such compassionate practices lead to exploitation, and corruption of the entire system followed with eventual collapse of the society. Helping out in emergencies or national calamities is expected, as long as it is appreciated by the needy. Unfortunately, as demonstrated in many cases, much support is mismanaged, winding up in the wrong hands.

Along the same lines of support is fighting other country's wars without any compensation, a democratic practice unacceptable for our nation's wellbeing. The United States is a posterchild for such liberal practices. Foreign occupation in a country, in times of national turmoil, may be necessary to establish law, and order, hopefully leading to a peaceful settlement. In the long term, however, it has been proven over, and over that troubled countries do not appreciate foreign occupation to reestablish law, and order. If unsuccessful, and found necessary, there should be a time limit; otherwise, the helpful nation, as has been demonstrated throughout history, will eventually get kicked out of the country by force. War is not always the case of a "lesson learned." In many instances, the outgoing ruling power is merely replaced with another ambitious ruler taking the initiative. For such a country, changes to its government structure will not come easy, and naturally. The mindset of the entire nation will have to change, and that could only come from an external source.

It is this condition, an opportunity presented, for the Western world to step up, and help through successfully demonstrating democratic practices in changing the direction of a troubled nation's future. Democracy may not be the ultimate form of governing a country, but after centuries of peaceful intentions with proven success rates, it is still the popular form of government for the good of the country, and wellbeing of its people.

There is no place anymore for a dictatorship in today's world. Neither is there a place for infringing on another nation's borders, and properties. At one time a common practice, especially during the dark ages, and ancient times, where regions were structured in similar manner, people only knew of two principle forms of citizenships: the ruling class comprised mostly of one family heritage, and slaves making up its majority population. There were minor exceptions though: successful land barons in charge of the farming community, and the artisans with their crafty cultures. In either case, everybody outside of the ruling family was manipulated, and oppressed.

It is this heritage that old countries, linked to strong religious heritage, and practices their powerful ruling classes, are clinging to so desperately. It is only a matter of time before their citizens demand changes to alleviate some of the tax burdens. From a ruling class's perspective, it would take a compassionate successor to lessen the burden on the people. From the citizen's perspective, it was mostly a dream that never came true. Consequently, little ever changed until the Greek introduced philosophy to a struggling world with the Romans leading the way to a more educated life the people readily embraced. Though progress was made, slow but gradual, it took thousands more years for democracy to take roots. "Are we better off?" one might ask.

There is only one answer: "Definitely." Everybody is given the same opportunity to a free life with equal prospects, if one is willing to strive, and work for it. Where it was much easier for a new nation, such as the United States, to adapt to changes, old established countries will not easily adopt to new ways regardless of externally exerted political pressures. Complaints for a nonalignment of countries to modernize are usually one-sided sentiments, that of a modernized world. It should be them, the ones adapted to the new world, to have an understanding for old countries not willing to break away from ancient inherited practices. It is this tradition that provides us with the ancient treasures separating cultural practices, and long-standing customs for everybody to enjoy.

Imagine a world where culture, and customs are identical. Imagine a world without England, France, Japan, and China preserved by borders, and ancient heritage. Every one of us should protect this heritage, and fight against what seems to be inevitable, the undermining beast of globalization. It should not mean that globalization is a bad thing altogether. It should be restricted to trade, and commerce, but refused for political, and governing purposes, as desired by the world's powermongers. It should be everybody's desire to protect our heritage whether they inherited Egyptian, Roman, Nordic, Middle Eastern, European, Asian, African, and Australian cultures, regardless of color, belief, and creed.

However, there will come a time when the inherited values do not matter much anymore. It will be the time when nations, and people unite to build a common world.

It will be a world of endless possibilities in an infinite space. There is only one place left for mankind to such expansion, our planetary system first, followed with star systems, other galaxies with an eventual goal, the universe. It may not be everybody's goal, and desire, but for mankind with its inherited pioneering spirit, for the need of individual space to survive, it will be a necessity. We will become the missionaries of its time.

ECONOMIC STATE

Composition in Brief

The United States is the world's second-largest manufacturer, with a 2013 industrial output of U.S. $2.4 trillion. Its manufacturing output is greater than of Germany, France, India, and Brazil combined. Its main industries include petroleum, steel, automobiles, construction machinery, aerospace, agricultural machinery, telecommunications, chemicals, electronics, food processing, consumer goods, lumber, and mining.

The U.S. leads the world in airplane manufacturing, which represents a large portion of U.S. industrial output. American companies such as Boeing, Cessna, Lockheed Martin, and General Dynamics produce a majority of the world's civilian, and military aircraft in factories across the United States.

The manufacturing sector of the U.S. economy has experienced substantial job losses over the past several years. In January 2004, the number of such jobs stood at 14.3 million, down by 3.0 million jobs, or 17.5 percent, since July 2000, and about 5.2 million since the historical peak in 1979. Employment in manufacturing was its lowest since July 1950. The number of steel workers fell from 500,000 in 1980 to 224,000 in 2000.

The United States is estimated to have a population of 327,996,618 as of June 25, 2018, making it the third most populous country in the world. It is very urbanized, with 81% residing in cities, and suburbs as of 2014 (the worldwide urban rate is 54%). California, and Texas are the most populous states, as the mean center of U.S. population has consistently shifted westward, and southward. New York City is the most populous city in the United States.

The total fertility rate in the United States estimated for 2016 was 1.82 children per woman, which was below the replacement fertility rate of approximately 2.1, to sustain our nation. The United States Census Bureau showed a population increase of 0.75% for the twelve-month period ending in July 2012. Though high by industrialized country standards, this was below the world average annual rate of 1.1%.

There were about 125.9 million adult women in the United States in 2014. The number of men was 119.4 million. At age 85, and older, there were almost twice as many women as men (4 million vs. 2.1 million). People under 21 years of age made up over a quarter of the U.S. population (27.1%), and people age 65, and over made up one-seventh (14.5%). The national median age was 37.8 years in 2015.

Population

The United States Census Bureau defines white people as those "having origins in any of the original peoples of Europe, the Middle East, or North Africa." It includes people who reported 'White' or wrote in entries such as Irish, German, Italian, Lebanese, Near Easterner, Arab, or Polish. Whites constitute the majority of the U.S. population, with a total of about 245,532,000 or 77.7% of the population as of 2013. Non-Hispanic whites made up 62.6% of the country's population, despite changes due to immigration since the 1960s, and the lower birth-rates among whites.

The American population almost quadrupled during the 20th century—at a growth rate of about 1.3% a year—from about 76 million in 1900 to 281 million in 2000. It is estimated to have reached the 200 million-mark in 1967, and the 300 million-mark on October 17, 2006. Population growth was fastest among minorities as a whole, and according to the Census Bureau's estimation for 2012, 50.4% of American children under the age of 1 belonged to racial, and ethnic minority groups.

The non-Hispanic white population of the US is expected to fall below 50% by 2045. It has also been hypothesized in the Huffington Post that the Hispanic population of the United States citizenry would become the majority ethnic group by 2060. According to a Pew Research Center study released in 2018, by 2040, Islam would surpass Judaism to become the second largest religion in the U.S. due to higher immigration, and birth rates.

Hispanic, and Latino Americans accounted for 48% of the national population growth of 2.9 million between July 1, 2005, and July 1, 2006. Immigrants, and their U.S.-born descendants are expected to provide most of the U.S. population gains in the decades ahead.

The Census Bureau projects a U.S. population of 417 million in 2060, a 38% increase from 2007 (301.3 million), and the United Nations estimates the U.S. population would be 402 million in 2050, an increase of 32% from 2007. In an official census report, it was reported that 54.4% (2,150,926 out of 3,953,593) of births in 2010 were non-Hispanic white. This represented an increase of 0.3% compared to the previous year, which was 54.1%.

Ethnicity
The United States Census Bureau collects racial data in accordance with guidelines provided by the U.S. Office of Management, and Budget (OMB), and these data are based on self-identification. The Census Bureau uses five racial classifications that are defined as indicated below. State classifications of race may differ from federal classifications.

- *White*: A person having origins in any of the original peoples of Europe, the Middle East (i.e. West/Southwest Asia including Arabs, Assyrians, Jews, Kurds, Persians, and Turks), Central Asia (i.e. Uzbekistan, Turkmenistan, Tajikistan, Kazakhstan, and Kyrgyzstan), and North Africa (i.e. Morocco, Algeria, Tunisia, Libya, and Egypt).

- *Black*: A person having origins in any of the peoples of sub-Saharan Africa, including the aboriginal Austronesian peoples of Madagascar.

- *American Indian/Alaska Native*: A person having indigenous origins in any of the Amerindian peoples of the Americas or the Eskimo-Aleut peoples of Arctic North America.

- *Asian*: A person having origins in any of the original peoples of the East Asia, Southeast Asia, or South Asia - including the Austronesian aboriginal peoples of Taiwan, the Philippines, Malaysia, Singapore, Brunei, East Timor, and Indonesia.

- *Pacific Islander*: A person having origins in any of the original peoples of Australasia, Polynesia, Melanesia or Micronesia.

- Data about race, and ethnicity are self-reported to the Census Bureau. Since the 2000 census, Congress has authorized people to identify themselves according to more than one racial classification by selecting more than one category.

Birth, growth, and death rates

The growth rate was 0.76% as estimated from 2014–2010 by the U.S. Census Bureau. The birth rate was 12.5 births/1,000 population, estimated as of 2013. This is the lowest since records began. There were 3,957,577 births in 2013.

In 2009, *Time Magazine* reported that 40% of births were to unmarried women. The following is a breakdown by race for unwed births: 17% Asian, 29% White, 53% Hispanics, 66% Native Americans, and 72% Black American. The drop in the birth rate from 2007 to 2009 was believed to be associated with the late-2000s recession.

Per U.S. federal government data released in March 2011, births fell 4% from 2007 to 2009, the largest drop in the U.S. for any two-year period since the 1970s. Births had declined for three consecutive years, and were now 7% below the peak in 2007. This drop had continued through 2010, according to data released by the U.S. National Center for Health Statistics in June 2011. Numerous experts had suggested that this decline was largely a reflection of unfavorable economic conditions. This connection between birth rates, and economic downturns partly stemmed from the fact that American birth rates had now fallen to levels that were comparable to the Great Depression of the 1930s. Teen birth rates in the U.S. were at the lowest level in U.S. history. Despite these years of decrease, U.S. teen birth rates were still higher than in other developed nations. Racial differences prevailed with teen birth, and pregnancy rates as well. The American Indian/Alaska Native, Hispanic, and non-Hispanic black teen pregnancy rates were more than double the non-Hispanic white teen birth rate.

Immigration, and emigration

13% of the population was foreign-born in 2009, including 11.2 million illegal immigrants – a rise of 350% since 1970 when foreign-born people accounted for 3.7% of the population, 80% of whom came from Latin America. Latin America was the largest region-of-birth group, accounting for over half (53%) of all foreign-born population in US, and thus was also the largest source of both legal, and illegal immigration to U.S. In 2011, there were 18.1 million naturalized citizens in the United States, accounting for 45% of the foreign-born population (40.4 million), and 6% of the total U.S. population at the time, and around 680,000 legal immigrants were naturalized annually.

I thought it important to include a brief description of the economic state in the U.S. At times, numbers, and figures are over or understated, depending on sector bias by one or another census group. With the last national census taken in 2010, today's figures may have somewhat scaled upwards or downwards. What is important is presenting a general idea of where the individual citizen may fit in with the general economic state. Aside from the population growth, the U.S. economy, to a large extent, is not pegged against world's leading nations. It is not easy to track economic states between the rapid changes from emerging countries jostling for global positions.

What becomes obvious, though, is the speed with which China is gaining economic leadership amidst the Western world. It was only a few decades ago when China was an isolated nation clinging to inherited cultural values. While we may still have an edge on world leadership, unless we change our social behavior, we are guaranteed to lose such an edge to China. As has been historically proven over, and over, every empire will last only so long before it will be superseded by the next power striving for world dominance. The trends are obviously visible for the concerned. The individual may be fully aware of such a change, but it may be insignificant when gauged to the population as a whole.

What is important is the preservation of the country's cultural values that we may have, for the most part, already lost due to prolifically promoted, adversarial social liberties without much direction, and guidance from the authorities. It may be too late to save our country from collapse into a third-world nation. The best we can do is preserve what we have left from further deterioration, but that would take strong leadership from a visionary government. The only consolation we have is that China will follow the same path every other empire has taken since antiquity. Or will it? There is an old saying that may befit the predestined cycle for world power.

"Ignorance is Bliss," a phrase coined by Thomas Gray in his 'Ode on a Distant Prospect of Eton College.' There is much truth to Mr. Gray's expression, synonymous to a nation's future. Unfortunately, it is not an individual preamble to life's journey.

The next few chapters are important ones. They may be the most controversial topics for any man to confront, and understand. Since the beginning of mankind there has been reasons from personal affronting, though on a small scale, to human termination short of annihilating the entire human race. Because the issue may never be solved, we have to find the means to live with it in a civilized manner honoring individual striving. Where in the past many religious differences were settled through conflicts, and wars, in today's world, it would be better achieved through education, and understanding, but only if both worlds (scientific, and religious) are willing to compromise egotistical selfish behavior.

CREATION OF MAN

Human Prehistory – Scientific Perspective

Human prehistory is the period between the use of the first stone tools c. 3.3 million years ago, and the invention of writing systems. The earliest writing systems appeared c. 5,300 years ago, but writing was not used in some human cultures until the 19th century, or even later. The end of prehistory therefore came at very different dates in different places, and the term is less often used in discussing societies where prehistory ended relatively recently.

Sumer in Mesopotamia, the Indus valley civilization in India, and ancient Egypt were the first civilizations to develop their own scripts. This had already taken place by the early Bronze Age. Neighboring civilizations were the first to follow. Most other civilizations reached the end of prehistory during the Iron Age. The three-age system of division of prehistory into the Stone Age, followed by the Bronze Age, and Iron Age, remains in use for much of Eurasia, and North Africa, but is not generally used in those parts of the world where the working of hard metals arrived abruptly with contact from Eurasian cultures, such as the Americas, Oceania, Australasia, and much of Sub-Saharan Africa. These areas also, with some exceptions in Pre-Columbian civilizations in the Americas, did not develop complex writing systems before the arrival of Eurasians, and their prehistory reaches into relatively recent periods.

The period when a culture was written about by others, but had not developed its own writing was often known as the protohistory of the culture. By definition, there are no written records from human prehistory, so dating of prehistoric materials is crucial. Clear techniques for dating were not well-developed until the 19th century.

Beginning

The term "prehistory" can refer to the vast span of time since the beginning of the universe, or the Earth, but more often it refers to the period since life appeared on Earth or, even more specifically, to the time since human-like beings appeared.

End Times

The date marking the end of prehistory in a particular culture or region, that is, the date when relevant written historical records become a useful academic resource, varies enormously from region to region. For example, in Egypt it is generally accepted that prehistory ended around 3200 BC, whereas in New Guinea the end of the prehistoric era is set much more recently, at around 1900 AD. In Europe the relatively well-documented classical cultures of Ancient Greece, and Ancient Rome had neighboring cultures, including the Celts, and to a lesser extent the Etruscans, with little, or no writing, and historians must decide how much weight to give to the often highly prejudiced accounts of these "prehistoric" cultures in Greek, and Roman literature.

Time periods

In dividing up human prehistory in Eurasia, historians typically use the three-age system, whereas scholars of pre-human time periods typically use the well-defined geologic record, and its internationally defined stratum base within the geologic time scale. The three-age system is the periodization of human prehistory into three consecutive time periods, named for their respective predominant tool-making technologies: Stone Age, Bronze Age, and Iron Age.

Stone Age

The concept of a "Stone Age" is found useful in the archaeology of most of the world, though in the archaeology of the Americas it is called by different names, and began with a lithic stage, or sometimes Paleo-Indian. The sub-divisions described below are used for Eurasia, and not consistently across the whole area.

Paleolithic

Paleolithic means "Old Stone Age", and began with the first use of stone tools. The Paleolithic is the earliest period of the Stone Age.

The early part of the Paleolithic is called the Lower Paleolithic, which predated *Homo sapiens*, beginning with *Homo habilis* (and related species), and with the earliest stone tools, dated to around 2.5 million years ago. Evidence of control of fire by early humans during the Lower Paleolithic Era is uncertain, and has at best limited scholarly support. The most widely accepted claim is that *Homo erectus* or *Homo ergaster* made fires between 790,000, and 690,000 B.P. (before the present period). The use of fire enabled early humans to cook food, provide warmth, and have a light source at night.

Early *Homo sapiens* originated some 200,000 years ago, ushering in the Middle Paleolithic. Anatomic changes indicating modern language capacity also arose during the Middle Paleolithic. Sites in Zambia have charred bone, and wood that has been dated to 61,000 B.P. The systematic burial of the dead, creation of music, early art, and the use of increasingly sophisticated multi-part tools were highlights of the Middle Paleolithic.

Throughout the Paleolithic, humans generally lived as nomadic hunter-gatherers. Hunter-gatherer societies tended to be very small, and egalitarian, though hunter-gatherer societies with abundant resources or advanced food-storage techniques sometimes developed sedentary lifestyles with complex social structures such as chiefdoms, and social stratification. Long-distance contacts may have been established, as in the case of Indigenous Australian "highways" known as song lines.

Mesolithic

The Mesolithic, or "Middle Stone Age," was a period in the development of human technology between the Paleolithic, and Neolithic periods of the Stone Age.

The Mesolithic period began at the end of the Pleistocene epoch, some 10,000 B.P., and ended with the introduction of agriculture, the date of which varies by geographic region. In some areas, such as the Near East, agriculture was already underway by the end of the Pleistocene, and there the Mesolithic was short, and poorly defined.

Regions that experienced greater environmental effects as the last ice age ended had a much more evident Mesolithic era, lasting millennia. In Northern Europe, societies were able to live well on rich food supplies from the marshlands fostered by the warmer climate.

The Mesolithic is characterized in most areas by small composite flint tools. Fishing tackle, stone axes, and wooden objects, e.g. canoes, and bows, have been found at some sites in Africa, and cultures of the Levant.

Neolithic

Neolithic means "New Stone Age." Although there were several species of human beings during the Paleolithic, by the Neolithic only *Homo sapiens* remained. This was a period of primitive technological, and social development. It began about 10,200 BC in some parts of the Middle East, and later in other parts of the world, and ended between 4,500, and 2,000 BC. The Neolithic was a progression of behavioral, and cultural characteristics, and changes, including the use of wild, and domestic crops, and of domesticated animals.

Early Neolithic farming was limited to a narrow range of plants, both wild, and domesticated, which included einkorn wheat, millet, and spelt, and the keeping of dogs, sheep, and goats. By about 6,900–6,400 BC, it included domesticated cattle, and pigs, the establishment of permanently or seasonally inhabited settlements, and the use of pottery. The Neolithic period saw the development of early villages, agriculture, animal domestication, tools, and the onset of the earliest recorded incidents of warfare. The Neolithic era commenced with the beginning of farming, which produced the "Neolithic Revolution." It ended when metal tools became widespread (in the Copper Age or Bronze Age, or, in some geographical regions, in the Iron Age).

Settlements became more permanent with some having circular houses with single rooms made of mudbrick. Settlements might have a surrounding stone wall to keep domesticated animals in, and protect the inhabitants from other tribes. Later settlements had rectangular mud-brick houses where the family lived together in single, or multiple rooms. Burial findings suggest an ancestor cult where people preserved skulls of the dead. Most clothing appears to have been made of animal skins, as indicated by finds of large numbers of bone, and antler pins which were ideal for fastening leather. Wool cloth, and linen might have become available during the later Neolithic, as suggested by finds of perforated stones that may have served as spindle whorls or loom weights.

Religious Beginning

Six thousand years ago, in contrast to religious beliefs, farming had already been well established in the two great river valleys of ancient China, the Yellow River, and Mekong River, and had already spread to neighboring lands in South Asia, India, and the Middle East. While much of early history, such as the transition from *Homo Sapiens* to *Homo Erectus*, may have been lost to history because written language did not appear until some 5,300 years ago, much of the early accounts have been verified through archaeological excavations.

PREHISTORIC MAN VERSUS THE BIBLE

Human History – Religious Perspective
The following article was taken from the website source:
http://www.creationmoments.com/content/where-does-prehistoric-man-fit-bibles-history.

The Bible says that God created man in His own image. Where did "Prehistoric Man" enter the picture? Did this kind of person roam the Earth before God created Adam, and Eve?

The idea that there were "prehistoric men" before Adam, and Eve comes from those who do not understand the nature of the evidence. These creatures were often creations of men, and not of God.

Fortunately, many Christian teachers have been instructed by creationists who were better trained than they in this kind of evidence. Few Bible-believing teachers offer this explanation anymore. That there was an earlier race of creatures is mainly held by theistic evolutionists today. They often teach that it was out of this population of hominids that God chose two to be the first humans.

The conclusion that such a race existed is unsatisfactory, as far as the Bible goes. It is also scientifically unacceptable. Scripture teaches that sin came into the world by Adam, and that it was sin that resulted in death. St. Paul made clear that this state of affairs extended to the entire creation. To say that there was an earlier race of hominids living, and dying before Adam's creation attacks the redemptive work of the Second Adam. This is because Scripture tied the First, and the Second Adams together.

If an earlier race existed, so did death, and so did sin. If Scripture is wrong on the source of sin, and its result in death, how do we know it was right in the other things it says about our salvation?

Genesis, taken as literal history, is the perfect basis for St. Paul's words about the First, and Second Adam. Genesis mentions neither an earlier race, nor an earlier world. This silence offers no comfort for the "Christian evolutionist." Genesis clearly says that six days after the universe appeared, creatures that were completely, and fully human walked the Earth.

Further, Genesis rules out the claim that man was formed from earlier species of animals. Genesis says that man was created from the dust of the earth.

Scriptures' history, and message of salvation from sin, and its consequences leave no room for an earlier race of hominids. So, what about the "scientific evidence"?

There are no scientific facts that compel us to accept the existence of "prehistoric man." Were all the "hominids" that populate the various textbooks, and popular science magazines real creatures? Some of them were made by God, and some were made up by men.

One of the biggest frauds is "Lucy." The scientific literature says she was about three or so feet tall with a head about the size of a baseball. Yet she has been depicted in some popular modern science magazines as being similar in height to a modern woman. Likewise, she has been pictured as appearing nearly human, with a head perhaps only slightly smaller than ours. These fraudulent depictions were successful in convincing people that man evolved from something ape-like. Lucy was "reconstructed" from bones found at two different sites in the Hadar/Afar region of Africa. One site was called 162, the other was site 333. The sites, from which one "individual" had been built, were not even at the same geological level! Even evolutionists noted in their comments that the bones at site 333 were much like modern humans while the bones from site 162 were not. Other literature showed that the bones of Lucy's skeleton from site 162 were nearly identical to the pygmy chimp.

What would you find if, in a thousand years, you dug up a couple of cemeteries in the ruins of one of our cities? You'd be likely to run into human skeletons as well as the skeletons of animals we live with.

Other creatures, like Neanderthal, had been reclassified as Homo sapiens. Creationists have long said that Neanderthals fell into the presently known genetic range of human beings. Many evolutionists now admit that this was true. They have even conducted studies showing that very normal human beings had bone structures identical to Neanderthal.

The problem, admit evolutionists, lies in the fact that since Neanderthal was supposed to be primitive, he was "reconstructed" with "primitive" features. It was the reconstruction that created the image! We added that the same was true of "Lucy", and the full pantheon of the "hominids", and "primitive humans." Almost none of the "reconstructions" found in the popular magazines, and textbooks correspond to the creatures in the scientific literature.

These "evolutionary hominids" were really only dead apes, or tinker-toy-like constructions. If they were real, we would expect to find the famed evolutionary progression from more ape-like characteristics to human-like characteristics. Evolutionists claim this progression is there. Just as most used car salesmen would not tell you everything, neither do most evolutionists. They carefully select characteristics that seem to show evolutionary progression. The problem is, they have no objective way of telling whether a characteristic is "modern" or "primitive."

Worse, less-dogmatic evolutionists offered their conclusion that there was a lack of progression. For example, a comparison of the talus (foot) bones of man, and apes showed that creatures like *Homo Habilis*, and the Olduvai finds had little in common with humans. They were more like orangutans than humans.

A study of the cranial capacities also revealed a vast, unfilled gap. Brain complexity seems to serve relative to size. This means that evolutionists are claiming that 60-65 percent of man's 115 brain connections developed in only a few million years! Such a conclusion is too incredible to be accepted.

By every measure there is a gap between humans, and hominids, and none between apes, and hominids. Only one measure has been suggested which claimed a close relationship between apes, and man. According to Dr. John Gribbin, and Dr. Jeremy Cherfas in their book *The Monkey Puzzle,* there is a 99 percent similarity between humans, and apes. However, this work has not been without criticism. Saying that man was 99 percent gorilla was also to say that gorillas were 99 percent man! Even most hard-core evolutionists had trouble with that claim. They would have preferred that Gribbin, and Cherfas would have found that there was only a 50-60 percent similarity. That would have fit better with evolutionary theory.

There is absolutely no compelling scientific reason to believe that man was related to any ape-like creature. Many of the claims to the contrary were scientifically unsupported. Even worse, the theology of imagining that man had come from such creatures was disastrous for Christianity.

After having presented several alternative views on science, and religion, it should be clear to the reader that both views are burdened with controversy that may never be resolved. It becomes obvious that neither side, whether Evolutionist or Christian, would ever relinquish, or secede from their beliefs. To draw your own conclusion, it will be up to the reader to decide on what emerged first, *Homo Erectus*, *Homo Sapiens*, or Man as created by God. No matter who, what, and how we were created, we are here to stay. Regardless of design, in order to survive, man's mission is to proliferate, propagate, and explore the cosmos. Whatever we may discover in the process, in time, may enlighten us to the question we all harbor: "Who created the universe, and why are we here?"

And thus, man's arguments in the quest for creation continue. Where an army of archaeologists have unearthed ample proof for an existence of man dating back thousands of years prior to the emergence of the Sumerian era, science still has its hands full in trying to prove its side of man's creation with spirited enthusiasts not far behind. It all boils down to one common denominator: we don't have enough proof to come to a definite conclusion. Life's creation is still up to speculation.

RELIGIOUS VIEW

I was brought up in a southern part of Germany with a strong Italian secular influence. Much like in the U.S., religious practices were spread through many denominations with Lutheran, and Evangelism strong contenders to the Roman Catholic faith. At the age of five, the beginning of my first schoolyear, the weekly church ceremony on Sunday high-mass with a monthly visit to the confession booth became a standard practice. Raised in a sheltered environment in post-war Germany, I was not allowed to freely mix with neighborhood youngsters. Aside from my parents, there were only two people of importance in my life, my grade school teacher, and priest, both disciplinarians. I felt the bamboo stick on my back, and butt many times, for miniscule reasons in today's world of child education, including by forgetting some of the curriculum being taught.

Being born at the year's end, November, I had not turned six at the beginning of the schoolyear. In retrospect, I was not quite mature enough to compete with the other classmates. Through most of grammar school I always felt like the underdog, bullied, and mistreated. Aside from lagging behind in mental maturity, I was also the smallest kid in the class. It would stay this way through high school, after which I put on a few pounds to cover my bony body, adding inches to my height, the result from a starvation-like diet as a consequence from the war. For most of the population, a shortage on food was the norm. I remember the first time I would eat a full course meal was not until many years later at my sponsor's home, after arriving in the States at age twenty-two.

Back in Germany, my break into adulthood came with the offer of a scholarship from an aircraft company. Trained to become industrial engineer, like most of the students, I was paid a monthly stipend. Curriculums such as geography, advanced mathematics, aerodynamics design, and blueprint drafting were taught in the morning with hands-on work on industrial machines, and metal processing in afternoons. Making friends with likeminded students, aside from industrial training, I had the greatest time of my life learning the art of fencing, sculling, and even being on the scholastic soccer team. The four years went by in a rush before adult responsibilities set in.

I was hired fulltime by my company sponsor, Dornier GMBH, the only aircraft company remaining after the war. Companies like Heinkel, Focke-Wulf, and Messerschmitt were eliminated by the Allies, due to supporting Hitler's war efforts killing millions of citizens. Even to this day, Germany is not authorized to build aircraft out of fear of returning to old practices. With much of the German workforce being immigrants from surrounding countries, whether justified or not, the ruling class is still dominated by an established Prussian heritage.

In German postwar education, WWII history was not taught in schools. It was a taboo subject. Because of that I was completely ignorant of what lead to, transpired, and caused the rise and fall of the Third Reich, and everything in between, other than tons of bombs dropped daily on the land just after blaring air sirens went off. The results were families spending hours in cellars or local air raid shelters. Even the fear of death, a way of life, faded with years of bombings. One thing I clearly remember while huddled in shelters was people telling stories of how beautiful life could be without war. Being born into war I could not relate to what beauty or peace were. Without reading materials, since all literature was confiscated, and destroyed by Hitler's henchmen, a torn-apart environment was the only thing my mind could embrace. People owned nothing outside of tattered clothes, chipped cooking ware, and worn furniture to sit on with saggy mattresses to sleep on.

It was not until much later, after I arrived in the States, that war related documentaries began to surface on TV. I was stunned at the revelation of how Jewish people were treated, detained in concentration camps, and eliminated by the SS, by the millions. Unbelievable as it seemed, documented film footage served as proof to my ignorance. I could only describe my resultant feelings as riddled with guilt, a feeling that would remain with me for many years in the form of remorse. I overcame the personal complex only years later when discussing the subject one day with a dear friend Ed. "Every country in the world has a dark history," he stated. "Be proud of your heritage." It was a profound statement, but also a true one. I was thankful for his honest advice since I considered him, in view of his young age, a wise man.

It was also the time I began to wonder about the hardship mankind has had to endure over the ages. It triggered the thought that would hound me to this day: where was God during the uncountable persecutions, prosecutions, and exterminations of innocent people throughout the ages? Where was God to protect innocent children?

The next question is of even greater importance: is there a God? To find the answer became an important part in my life that I still research to this day. For this reason, when not writing novels, I read historical documents. I have much of the world's most renowned writers', and greatest philosophers' works on my iPad. Not only one important work, but their complete works, dating back to Aristotle, Plato, and Homer.

I did not postulate what I considered the world's most important question about creation. Every free thinker, philosopher, academic, scholar, astronomers, astrologers, and millions of others, I am certain, have contemplated the same thoughts that I harbor, but not one has come up with proof of God's existence. It does not mean that there was not a creator, or intelligent designer that created the universe, and us which, by the way, would be a foolish assumption. But, to get to the truth has yet to be established. Which ultimately led me to the question of religions: who invented them, and who devised them?

According to historical accounts, it was the Jewish that gave us God. One only has to read the Old Testament to verify the account. Aside from being one of the most controversial topics, the information dating back to the origin of man as handed down by Abraham. Consequently, every recorded scripture, whether hewn into clay, written on papyrus, codex or Bible, was religiously oriented. It may be good enough as proof of God for many people, but it was not good enough for me. There are many contrasts, and contradictions between each of the compiled works, beginning with Genesis, six thousand years ago.

Being an analyst, troubleshooter, and problem solver by profession, I work on the basis of science, and archaeological discoveries. By now, most of the world population has witnessed the unearthing of countless fossils throughout the globe. This fact alone cannot be ignored since much of the human remains date back tens of thousands of years farther than Genesis, and biblical accounts. My opinion is that ancient philosophers had been searching, and recoding signs of life for the creation of mankind for a long time. But the question still remains: where did the word of God come from? Who compiled most of the biblical accounts?

We only know the answer from reading the Bible, Torah, and Koran. Again, there were time constraints to the scriptures not verifiable by science. No matter how thoroughly one analyzes ancient writings, it was man itself that created the myth of God. Which brings us to the next question: should we question our creator, or should we just accept him at blind faith?

Blind faith is what most religious leaders command, and demand from their peers, and followers. The facts still stand that nobody has been able to figure out the secrets of life, why we were created, and ultimate purpose for our existence. As for my efforts in the quest, if I succeed in finding an answer on whether there was a God, or not, it does not matter much to me as long as I have found the answer. It would satisfy my quest to put my own mind at ease.

As for now, I thought ancient scriptures would hold the answers; I was much wiser about ancient history, and had obtained a thorough picture in the diversity of religions, but the myth still remained. Is there a God?

The problem I have is with religion itself. Who conceived it, and for what purpose? What will happen to innovative thinking by following blind faith? What makes the distinction between individuals? When it comes to personal beliefs and religion, people follow their internal instinct. The decent follow the righteous, and God's path, while the misguided follow evil and Satan's path. We may be able to sleep better, and die peacefully while the questions still remain. The quest I set out on was to discover the truth through studying, and researching historical accounts.

As indicated at the beginning of this chapter, "Religious Views" are entirely my own. It is not my intention to confuse the reader with religious aspects by injecting my own beliefs on the public, or even suggesting that there was no God. I merely stated the facts as I found ancient scriptures to contain. By no means did I interpret any of the great works already compiled, and published by great scholars, and researchers on man's history. I tried to get factual accounts as stored, and contained in the many databanks made available to the public, and interested parties. There is one thing I believe everyone agrees on: The Internet, and Google are marvelous things.

Who would have thought of the immense explosion of the Internet, and social media back in the 60s when we created it for the government? I did not, and neither did anybody else on the program.

As for *Social Media?* It is still subject to severe growing pains. Pains that still have to be solved. Where its inventors had good and honorable intentions to connect people, friends, and families, in a social means, criminal elements and conspirators jumped in and took procession, with only one thought in mind: manipulate, dominate, and confuse the innocent. However, there is one solution to prevent further mass delusion. Enforce tight membership for social media services.

As for the *Internet Development?* Throughout past decades, prolific speculations sprouted up among the U.S. population, "who created the Internet," and "when was it developed," and "who developed it."

As is the case with most secrets, there are many rumors attached. This Book will set the record straight and hopefully squelch all of the rumors. The core design was simple: store, forward, and process messages and information. While it was a complex system, it carrying the nation's entire secrets on its backbone.

In today's world of secrecies, AUTODIN, as a system, at the end of the 20th century, had been replaced with a much more sophisticated system, or systems, limited only to one's individual imagination.

CONTEMPORARY VIEW

Faith, and religious participation are a personal objective either inherited through established family practices or adapted through collective association with one, or another faith. If it takes a strong personal conviction to follow a dedicated belief system through a complete journey cycle in life, I have failed. Raised by devout Roman Catholic parents from both sides of the family tree, I was expected to follow my inherited faith, but destiny had another path in mind for my future. "Was it by design or was it my own choice?" I have asked myself many times. Being analytical by nature I concluded that, "I made the decision." It was past puberty, I recall, when I established my own religious grounds. It came on gradually following several events I had observed, but more importantly, reading historical accounts shaped the final decision.

My passion was studying history, ancient history, pre-biblical history, trying to get to the truth of creation. As of today, I am way past the point of religious origin. I am digging back further past antediluvian (pre-flood) times which science believes to have existed before the Great Flood of Noah. If human fossil records indeed survived the biblical flood as described in the Bible, then it shows evidence of antediluvian civilizations existence.

Whether factual, or not, there are several alternative views on how man came about. One such alternative, assumed by some evolutionists, is that humans reached advanced stages of technological developments before the flood. Such presuppositions were usually based on the Biblical genealogy, which states that ancient people lived to approximately ten times our current lifespan. Also, it was frequently mentioned that Adam, and Eve likely possessed higher than normal Intelligence since they were created as adults, with knowledge that subsequent humans obtained from their parents. Another theory stated that another antediluvian race existed called the Nephilim, which was superior to humans in every aspect.

Most accounts of the Great Flood from civilizations around the world indicate that there were civilizations before the flood. However, as a result of the destruction during the flood, and the passage of time, the remaining evidence is sparse. As a result of the flood, some stated, the earth was covered in hundreds of feet of sediment, and very little of the antediluvian horizon has been exposed. It is also problematic that the scientific community is quick to dismiss any artifacts that dispute their presupposed interpretation of the fossil record. Yet, any truly advanced civilization would have left durable traces, or construction that would have likely surfaced during excavations or revealed by erosion. Relatively insightful accounts can be drawn from the Bible, and ancient Babylonian, and Greek accounts of antediluvian civilizations.

Let us examine whether it is really logical to expect monuments such as the pyramids, sphinx, and other civilizations could have survived the flood. Following is a list of established populations by the time of the flood:

- East Asia – China, Manchuria, Korea: Established farming
- South East Asia – Indonesia, Malaysia: Established farming
- South Asia – India, Bangladesh, Myanmar, Thailand, Vietnam, Cambodia, Laos: Foundation established for great civilizations

- Middle East – Afghanistan, Pakistan, Iran, Iraq, Syria, Turkey: First civilization in history
- Europe – Germany, France, Poland, Austria, Hungary: Stone Age farming in villages
- Africa – Egypt, Ethiopia, Sudan: Emerging civilization in Egypt, and hunter-gatherers otherwise
- Australia – New Guinea, Solomon Islands: Island native villages around coastal, and river regions
- North America – Most all regions: Hunter-gatherers
- South America – Coastal, and river areas: Permanent villages along coastal, and river regions.

This section is an account suggested by Chris W. Ashcraft, New Creation: *http://www.newcreation.net/*

To get more specific, in the ancient city of Nippur, a tablet was excavated, which recounted the Sumerian version of the Great Deluge. This tablet contained a total of six columns of writing composed around the time of Hammurabi[72], relying upon material which was considerably older. In the first two columns of the tablet, there was a brief account of the founding of five cities, which they claimed to have been also prediluvian cities, including Shurippak, which, according to the Sumerians, was the city in which Utnapishtim (Noah) dwelt. This Shurippak, presently known as Shuruppak, was one of the oldest cities of the ancient people of southern Babylonia, some eighteen miles northwest of Uruk.

In this tablet, there was an actual account of cities, which were in existence when the world was one landmass, prior the Great Flood. All the inhabitants of the world were one race, and all spoke the same language. These were the ancestors of all the different nations, which comprised our present world. But they were not the ignorant cavemen, which evolutionists would have us believe. These were highly sophisticated men with elaborate cities, and advanced engineering knowledge in the art of building. These early Sumerians that inhabited the southern alluvial plain, which was created by the Tigris, and Euphrates Rivers, were probably the first postdiluvian settlers to arrive in the area, and dated as far back as the fourth Millennium BC.

Also included in the tablets was the Sumerian King List, an ancient list of Mesopotamian rulers, their names, their seat of power, and the length of their reigns. The list is of special interest to the biblical archaeological community, particularly because of its antediluvian portion. The list of pre-flood kings is interesting for two reasons. First, because it mentioned an antediluvian civilization, and a cataclysmic deluge, and second, because the pre-flood kings had really long life-spans (as was evidenced by their really long reigns). After the flood, the life-spans dropped dramatically, but remained inordinately long for a time. The length of monarchial reigns gradually decreased until they reflect ordinary life-spans. This parallels the

---

[72] Hammurabi, the sixth king of the Amorite First Dynasty of Babylon, reigned from 1792 to 1750 BCE, assumed the throne from his father, Sin-Muballit, and expanded the kingdom to conquer all of ancient Mesopotamia.

biblical account somewhat, except that the life-spans represented in the Sumerian King List were much longer than those in the biblical account. The average reign of the antediluvian king in the Sumerian King List was 30,150 years. The average life-span of the biblical antediluvian patriarch recorded in Genesis was 858 years.

It is believed that the information contained in the antediluvian portion of the Sumerian King List may have originated with the Semitic "Noah's Flood" tradition, and thus supported the Genesis account. Also believed is that the gross discrepancies in the ages could be accounted for quite simply by a major difference between the Semitic numbering system, and the Sumerians', and the fact that both civilizations used the same symbols to express numbers. Our technological development has only occurred as a result of an ability to store, and access large quantities of preexisting data. The knowledge possessed by any one person or even a hundred is insignificant in comparison to the libraries of previous learning that had now been obtained, and without which advancement to our level would not have happened. These libraries of knowledge did not begin to develop until the written word was invented, and no archaeological evidence of even the most primitive forms of writing have been discovered earlier than ancient Babylon, which followed the tower of Babel.

Even several hundred years later, during the time of the Egyptians, only hieroglyphics were in use. The Babel event suggested that the tower was the first major monument that mankind had ever built. Its purpose was to be a monument to human achievement, and to protect mankind from another flood disaster. The tower was not a particularly important technological development. It was built out of bricks, and was therefore incomparable to even the limestone pyramids. In comparison to our modern buildings, it was hardly more than a mud mound.

The development of symbolic language seemingly coincided with the decline in human longevity. Perhaps it was the shortened human lifespan that caused people to feel the need to write down their experiences, or what had been learned. There had become a sense of urgency to preserve one's essence in some permanent form. It may have been this reduction in life expectancy more than anything else that induced the formation of the written word, and ultimately the technological achievements we have made. Back when people lived to be 1000 years of age, there was little need to archive knowledge. God's original intention for man did not involve reading, and writing. Ancient texts reveal it only came about because of the sin at the tree of knowledge.

We cannot dispute the existence of atypical knowledge possessed by Adam, and Eve; however, we should also consider the Tower of Babel path as it related to human accomplishments to that date. Monumental constructions are a great source of pride for humans, but we cannot simply ignore their advanced knowledge. It seemed the tower had the ability to alter the world.

MODERN VIEW

It was stated that all religions are legends grown out of mythology, and folklore either through visions, vivid dreams, or drug-induced methods. Drugs, in ancient history, were an important part of man contacting spirits, and keeping connected with their ancestors. It was the Jewish that brought God to man. The Jews introduced one God to the living. Before that, it was idols, and idolatry practices, representing many gods. The reason it caught on so strong with Christianity was that it provided a guaranteed afterlife in the human form. It provided hope within the human misery, plagued by wars, oppression, slavery, and disease. Otherwise, mankind might have already perished.

God brought hope, salvation, and faith to all mankind. Before God, there was chaos, turmoil, killings, and wars. It was the reason why Jews were hated most, and have been persecuted, prosecuted, and expelled from most lands until accepted into the United States with the American Council for Judaism (ACJ), an organization of American Jews committed to the proposition that Jews were not a national, but a religious group, adhering to the original stated principles of Reform Judaism, as articulated in the 1885 Pittsburgh Platform.

It was here where Western ideology accepted the Jewish lifestyle into modern society. It was here where the educated man realized the rich, and ancient values with which the Jewish had been burdened on their own for millennia. It did not matter what belief system, or what religion one believed in, or was strongly connected with through family heritage, or other inspiration. What was important was that there was a belief. As far as biblical hell, and other ungodly places were concerned, they did not exist outside unearthly conditions, and places on our own earth. Some people, especially ones with ill intentions, and perhaps conspiracist inclinations, like to make up stories either to feel important in their otherwise troubled lives, or more significantly, to cause harm to the innocent, and unsuspecting targets of their misdeeds.

Personally, Jewish people are dear to me with their lifestyle, and inherited customary values. They are an educated, and dedicated branch of people among man. They take life seriously, respecting the virtues Earth provides us. I have lived among the Jewish, worked with the Jewish, and even worshiped with them at Bar/Bat Mitzvahs (son/daughter of the commandments.) They are the most revered, respected, and honored amid their society. Where in the past, as historically recounted in many countries, they had been persecuted, it was not so much for their lifestyle, but for the skills, and expertise they brought with them for managing money, craft, writing, and many other business opportunities not suitable to others. It was their successes that were persecuted by the ignorance of the unskilled. It was professional jealousy, and inadequateness from trade, and political sectors causing all their grief throughout the ages.

Much of my writing on historical accounts recorded, and archived in ancient libraries was verified, and complemented, dating back to the creation of man. I have read many of the renowned philosophers' great works, from Kant to Nietzsche, Descartes, Spinoza, Dostoyevsky, Ouspenski, Hegel, Schopenhauer, Aristotle, Plato, and Homer. Every one of these geniuses followed the same quest into history, trying to find the answers to man's ultimate quest: "Where did we come from," and "Who was the creator?" Nothing else rated of more importance to the learned. Material things were mostly designed, and fashioned for the common man not interested in the meaning of life.

I even own the complete works of Mark Twain, and Brothers Grimm, totaling over 500 short stories that I read to relax. Also, fun reading is Rudyard Kipling's tales from his life in India. I have studied many years, extending my readings into the Old Testament, past Genesis, and further back into history. My conclusion, aside from folk lore, predictions, and prophecies, indicates that religions were conceived by man. God is a creation of individual aspiration. Every human being, over the ages, including man's most brilliant minds, has posed the same questions: why we are here, who created us, is there life after death?

The answers are always the same: "We don't know!" There is, however, one element that makes most of us a believer. It is an omnipresence of a much higher power than man could ever achieve. A child could not be expected to know its spiritual, or embodiment implications for the life's journey ahead. That decision had to be made by the parent, or caretaker, but with the suggestion of leaving open personal alternatives. As an adult, religion, and faith are a matter of personal preference. Individual choice should be a conscious one to come from the heart.

It is hope that inspires our minds to move forward into the unknown. It is hope that has gotten us past wars, natural catastrophes, and manmade disasters, and it is hope that will get us over the uncertainty after a terminal point.

To satisfy this hope, over the ages, many means, and factions were conceived to suit every belief man was capable of. There are an estimated 4,200 different religions in the world, and these can be categorized into five mainstream religions. These include Christianity, Islam, Hinduism, Buddhism, and Judaism. There are many smaller, yet still prevalent religions, such as the Baha'i faith, and others. When including Roman Catholicism, Christianity is the world's largest religion. Christianity also includes Protestantism, and its many denominations, such as Lutherans, United Methodists, Southern Baptists, and the Assemblies of God. In addition, there are many non-denominational registered Christians.

From a global perspective, statistically, there are about 21 major world religions. About 1 billion people do not profess belief in any religion. Major religions are charted as: 1) Christianity, 2.1 billion. 2) Islam, 1.3 billion. 3) Secular/Irreligious/Agnostic/Atheist, 1.1 billion.[73]

With the majority of the world population believing in some kind of faith, it would not be prudent for me to suggest that God does not exist. My intentions are not to disprove the existence of an omnipresence. My quest is solely intended to satisfy my own curiosity on the secrets of the creation, and life which, by the way, I have not been able to attain yet. Therefore, the quest will continue until my passing, but not without an important message to the reader:

---

[73] Detailed data link for all world religions:

https://en.wikipedia.org/wiki/List_of_religions_and_spiritual_traditions.

"It is far better to believe in God, or a divinity than to turn into an agnostic, or atheist. Without a belief, for the sake of self-preservation, man is lost. I must also emphasize that without a belief, man will turn to the dark side of civility."

While I do not subscribe to the notions of Hell, and demons, from a practical perspective, they were created by man, reliant on one's intended exploit, devious, or desperate minds. One only has to follow the dramatic increase in recent years in devil worship, and consequential exorcisms, though grossly overstated at times, to learn of their ill-intended practices. To make life work, and livable in a world at times overwhelmed by turmoil, we all have to make the attempt to work towards a decent, and honest lifestyle everybody can live with.

One last thought on the subject of demons. Most were created through the use of drugs. With as many colleagues as I have worked with, and the thousands of people I have come in contact with, locally, and across the globe, being a lifelong student of human behavior, I could easily spot someone on drugs, or alcohol. I had to deal with my share of the addicted, and could spot the trends. While I fully understand the individual needs for a relaxing substance, especially in today's fast-paced world, and the ready access to drugs, I do not appreciate the stated habits. My observations are wholly gauged on individual performance on the job.

Many would demonstrate responsible intentions during their job performance, but they could never quite accomplish what they were hired for. Consequently, the burden to finish the job would fall on me, who had been overburdened with work, and responsibilities in the first place. I am not complaining about the liabilities displayed by some because at the end, after I realized shortfalls, and gains, I came out ahead with knowledge, and skills way past my own expectations.

RATIONAL THINKING

If I could choose my career over again, one of my choices would be researching ancient history. With as much time as I have spent in recent years researching the subject of creation, I feel that I have only touched a small percentage of the available information stored in the many archives around the world. To get a better understanding, I would have to camp out at places such as the Vatican, Library of Alexandria, and libraries that archived cultural texts, and artifacts in ancient Buddhist, Chinese, European, Egyptian, Greek, Hebrew, Hindu, Pre-Columbian, Mesopotamian, and Sumerian history.

In retrospect, from the scientific perspective, I would probably not be much wiser on the fundamental question of God, and his creation, since much would be religious, and faith oriented. In my mind, I have already established that all religions were a creation out of myths within their respective cultures. Christianity is one of few that provides an alternative choice to the end of the world, and death. It is probably the reason for its popularity. Before biblical accounts were put on paper in AD in the ancient world, many gods had been created by the Greek, Romans, and much earlier cultures in the forms of celestial bodies, cosmic origins, with eventual spiritual images taking shape in human form inherited from traits of love, jealousy, anger, and an ever-present fighting spirit.

It was no wonder that the people of the world grew up confused. It is not an easy task choosing one's belief based on the New Testament with much of the text borrowed from the Old Testament. In terms of real time, the transition took many thousands of years while the printed accounts transpired in only a short period. As for content, much is based on folklore, and conjecture stimulated by drug-induced visions. It is no secret that drug use was prolific in ancient times, much like in modern times with people confusing reality with myth, and self-imposed imageries. To understand the meaning, I will cite some present-day examples from people's claims:

- Flat Earth theory
- Hollow Earth
- Never visited the Moon
- Bermuda Triangle Mysteries
- Alien Technology transfer
- End-of-the-World fears

That the "earth is flat" is a repulsive insult to the intelligence of modern man. It may have been befitting for the ancient world without the telescope, but in today's world, one only has to take a round-the-world flight to see the beauty of Earth, shaped into its global splendor. My intentions are not to persecute the eccentric, but I do mind the idiocy spread among gullible individuals who are not taking their time to research, and learn the true facts using common sense.

The Hollow Earth claim, much like Flat Earth falls into the same category of ignorance. If conspirator mongers would take the time to apply their minds constructively, rather than wasting everybody else's, it would be a first step in the direction to sort out some of the confusion they had caused among mankind. While such claims were few and far between prior to the Internet, because most publishers would not subject themselves to such nonsense, in today's world of social media, every notion and idea seems to be acceptable.

The same misdirected mentality can be applied to the "never visited the Moon" claim. It is gross injustice to the astronauts and cosmonauts supported by an army of designers, engineers, manufacturers, and launch personnel who worked for decades to support the monumental effort of getting mankind off the surface of the Earth, and into space. I personally worked on the Mercury and Gemini programs, and can attest to the fact that we did indeed land on the Moon. Many of us alive during that period, watching the many space launch successes and failures, have experienced the thrill, following rocket flights from launch to landing. It would be gross injustice attributed to the surviving families, and loved ones, with astronauts and crews perished in the process.

The "Bermuda Triangle" myth is another such claim. Aircraft, and ships have sunk around the globe since their inception. We have proven that at some places the climate is more turbulent than others on top of prolific air, and sea travels causing unexplained disappearances. To state that the Triangle contains space portals is the creation of over imaginative minds, since I have already stated that there has never been alien visits, portals, wormholes, and other means of Sci-Fi travel across the vast spaces of galaxies.

"Alien technology transfer" is probably the most irrational claim. But nobody is to blame for it since rational citizens are grossly manipulated by some authorities. Alien visits started as a lie, and continue to be proliferated through lies. The guilty, though inherited with the untruth, will have to live with it unless someone has enough guts to come forward to reveal the biggest deception of all time. Until such time, the alien phenomenon will continue to be employed to suit government, and industry for their respective gains. Proliferating the alien UFO, and ET myths may be insulting to the general public, but may have deemed necessary at one time during the height of the cold war.

That the "end of the world" is near is another myth propagated by fearmongers, and religious fanatics. As stated earlier, with the confusion spread by religious believers through the many cultures, it is no wonder that people susceptible to an unsteady mind could be confused by finding salvation in an afterlife that may, or may not exist. Learned scholars interpreting the Bible for people of all walks of life to understand is one thing, but trying to decode Revelation, where there was no code, is downright irresponsible. I had a brother-in-law who was a Jesuit priest who, unfortunately, has already passed away. He, and I had many talks about biblical events. If anybody knew ancient records, it was him, since by trade, he had access to histories' secret writings stored away in Vatican archives. I clearly recall his reply when I asked him about the last chapter in the New Testament. "What about Revelation? How factual is it?"

"It should have never been in the Bible," he proclaimed with an unwavering face. "They are prophetic visions translated into imaginary fiction by crafty scribes."

I was not there when the accounts were written, but had a notion for what they were. The ensuing interpretations throughout the ages did not help the believers through difficult times, such as the medieval period, and the many wars fought over religious motivated origins. Christians claim that the Bible has hundreds of fulfilled prophecies, and is proof of its divine inspiration. In actuality, these so-called fulfilled prophecies failed, were false, or weren't prophecies at all. Many of these prophecies are so vague, they could, and have been attributed to many different events. It appears that almost every generation created the Messiah's return for the end-of-days. I will cite some examples for failed predictions of recent times.

Jim Jones of Jonestown massacre of November 1978. James Warren Jones was an American religious cult leader who initiated, and was responsible for a mass suicide, and mass murder in Jonestown, Guyana. He considered Jesus Christ as following an overarching belief in socialism as the correct social order. Jones was ordained as a Disciples of Christ pastor, and he achieved notoriety as the founder, and leader of the Peoples Temple cult. At the end, 918 innocent people followed him to his death.

In early 1993, a compound owned by the Branch Davidians, an extremist religious sect, was raided by the ATF, and the FBI. For 51 days, negotiations, demands, and compromises would go back, and forth between David Koresh, the leader of the Davidians, and hostage negotiators desperately trying in vain to reach a peaceful resolution to the conflict. The FBI, and ATF knew that there were many innocent women, and children trapped inside the compound whose lives were in danger. Koresh was communicating with negotiators the entire time via telephone, and by releasing homemade videotapes.

The Branch Davidians were considered to be a danger to themselves, and the local community as it was believed that they were stockpiling weapons, high-powered ammunition, and explosives. In what was known as the Waco Siege, the violence would culminate in the compound being set ablaze. 76 people perished in the fiery inferno, many of whom were children. Who was to blame, and what went wrong has been the subject of controversy since the tragedy occurred?

Heaven's Gate suicide massacre, March 1997. Hale-Bopp was a comet that was perhaps the most widely observed of the 20th century, and one of the brightest seen for many decades. Hale-Bopp was discovered on July 23, 1995 separately by Alan Hale, and Thomas Bopp prior to it becoming visible on Earth. Although predicting the maximum apparent brightness of new comets with any degree of certainty is difficult, Hale-Bopp met, or exceeded most predictions when it passed perihelion on April 1, 1997. It was visible for 18 months, and dubbed the Great Comet of 1997.

March 26, 1997 brought about the grisly discovery that 39 members of the Heaven's Gate cult had committed mass suicide, believing their souls would be transported to a spaceship trailing the Hale-Bopp comet. All 39 members of the Heaven's Gate cult who committed suicide were wearing the same shoes, and outfit. Each was draped in a purple cloth.

Marshall Applewhite was the 65-year-old leader of the Heaven's Gate group. As his mental health deteriorated, he led his followers down a deadly path. However, it was Heaven's Gate, a group led by a man who called himself 'Do', and believed he was a descendant of Jesus Christ, that brought the bizarre, delusional world of UFO-related cults to the attention of the outside world. The founder of the cult, Marshall Applewhite, told his followers that the world was due to be 'wiped clean' by the alien founders, and that they needed to leave the Earth.

Judgement Day of 2011. American Christian radio host Harold Camping stated that the Rapture, and Judgment Day would take place on May 21, 2011, and that the end of the world would take place five months later on October 21, 2011.

Camping, who was then president of the Family Radio Christian network, claimed the Bible as his source, and said May 21 would be the date of the Rapture, and the day of judgment "beyond the shadow of a doubt." Camping suggested that it would occur at 6:00 p.m. local time, with the Rapture sweeping the globe time zone by time zone, while some of his supporters claimed that around 200 million people (approximately 3% of the world's population) would be 'raptured,' in spite of his previous failed claim that the Rapture would occur in September 1994.

Following the failure of the predictions, media attention shifted to the response from Camping, and his followers. On May 23, Camping stated that May 21 had been a "spiritual" day of judgment, and that the physical Rapture would occur on October 21, 2011, simultaneously with the destruction of the universe by God. However, on October 16, Camping admitted to an interviewer that he did not know when the end would come, and made no public comment after October 21 passed without his predicted apocalypse.

There have been many more prophecies like this over the ages with most contributed to the second coming of Christ, arrival of the Antichrist, identified as number 666 to world leaders, with many more relatively minor, but greatly impacting world populations, in turn causing conflicts, and wars. No matter how many times one such event may be proven as a hoax, fearmongers will always be with us. It is their calling to disrupt life. There are already new biblical predictions in the working, linking ISIS, and Islamic extremists to the "end-of-days" trends.

"God created man," the Bible states. It is that simple. No questions asked. Undisputable fact. People get up each morning after a night's rest facing another productive day, eat, drink, and be happy with expected results to be repeated the next day, months, and years. I wish it were that simple for me. But there is more, much more, to sustain life. Even in its simplest form, after creating the universe, and to survive, man is presented with two choices, *Immortality*, and *Reproduction*.

Immortality, as much as we would desire it, is impractical. It is impractical for several reasons. The world may have been built with mathematical precision, but in reality, it was created out of disorder. Boiling from within, it caused unimaginable turmoil beneath Earth's surface, still visible today. Aside from internal upheaval, there are natural disasters through asteroid impact, diseases, and climatic extremes, all potential probabilities for annihilating mankind. Then, to survive, it is killing or be killed. That is true for all lifeforms, not only for humans, unless man was built in the form of robots without the need for eating, and breathing. But it would have created other problems such as the need for energy to power the mechanism, storage for sustaining the power, and access to it.

Reproduction is a better choice. It would assure the preservation of the human species. The process would propagate, duplicate, and multiply, preserving humans to eventually migrate to other planets while animal, and plant life would remain for eventual extinction. Fortunately, humankind has developed into intelligent beings capable of recognizing the present dangers posed on Earth, and planning ahead for eventual escape. The two choices hold true no matter who or what created us.

But in the greater themes of things is the universe. Its formation came much earlier, and still puzzles science about how it was created. It is up to us humans to generate the means, and tools to find the answers. Was it the Big Bang? Was it an infinite expansion, and contraction cycle? Was it through sub-atomic physics? Regardless of how it was created, there are three possibilities. The possibilities are either through divine intervention, by intelligent design, or by natural evolution processes.

There are no definitive secrets on record that we can draw on, and this may remain a secret forever. From the scientific perspective, all we know is that life exists in a universe still developing, and expanding. Who, what, and what circumstances existed to sprout life is unknown, and will be such until we discover proof, or some entity, divine or other, to enlighten us? The answers are with the creator, or conditions that initiated the cause and purpose of the universe, and subsequent creation of beings.

The possibility for intelligent design is too uncertain since we have not yet discovered a higher species of creation. But that may change with man's exploration into the far reaches of the galaxies. While astronomers are till probing the depths of space, we are preparing to travel to such places that possibly contain, or sustain life. Exploring the infinite dimensions of space, what we may find may be miraculous, or if unsuccessful, great disappointment. But to achieve that, it may take thousands of years to discover life elsewhere. In the meantime, all we can do is cling to the hope that there is a meaning to the creation, and life that nature provides.

Closer to home, Earth, religious followers, and believers in faiths have different issues to ponder. With the prolific dissemination through literature, and books written on alternative views of beliefs by overactive minds, new worlds of spiritual realms are sure to be created. One such example is reincarnation. One question comes immediately to mind: what is its purpose?

Again, there is no simple answer since no exhibited proof exists. One has to take the participant's words for it at blind faith since there is no mention of reincarnation in the Bible. A good reason is that the scriptures testify only to the truth, and there is no truth in reincarnation. On the contrary, the scriptures do describe the archenemy of mankind as a deceiver who blinds people from receiving the true message. Furthermore, reincarnation is the philosophical, or religious concept that the soul, or spirit, after biological death, can begin a new life in a new body. This doctrine is a central tenant of the Hindu religion. The Buddhist concept of rebirth is also often referred to as reincarnation, and is a belief that was held by such historic figures as Pythagoras, Plato, and Socrates.

There are even detailed processes for how reincarnation works. Natural life is cyclical. Day fades into night, and turns back into day as the sun rises. One season gradually gives way to the next. Over the passage of time, new generations are born, and old ones die. The continuous succession of birth, death, and rebirth permeates nature even though our own lives seem linear. So, it is no surprise that some ancient observers looked at the seeming linearity of human existence, and decided that life, like the natural world, might actually be more cyclical than linear. Multiple religions, philosophies, and movements adopted this belief in cyclic life, or reincarnation.

Specifically, reincarnation, also called transmigration, or metempsychosis, is the concept that the soul, or some aspect of the soul, is reborn into new lives. Depending on the religion, or philosophy, the soul could appear incarnate in humans, animals, or plants as it worked its way toward an eventual escape from the cycle of birth, death, and rebirth. Most religions that believe in reincarnation consider it the path to purity, and salvation.

Reincarnation is widely accepted by the major Eastern religions, most prominently Hinduism, and Buddhism. It also has a history in ancient Greek philosophy. However, for people more familiar with the major monotheistic religions, Christianity, Judaism, and Islam, the idea of reincarnation seems foreign, and strange. That is because Christianity, in contrast to Judaism, and Islam, conceives time as linear. Life is simply a short step that determines the quality of an afterlife. For those who believe in only one life followed by an eternal afterlife, reincarnation is like an unwieldy marathon run by relay instead of a short, concise sprint.

RELIGIOUS VIEWS ON HEAVENLY BELIEFS

In the following paragraphs, the reader can assess the origins of Heaven, and Hell for the world's principle religions as devised by leaders of their respective faiths. As indicated, religious beliefs developed from various sources, for the specific regions, based on spiritual concepts by the head of the tribe, sanctioned by an elder council. While there are variances between the beliefs, sometimes only slight variations for heaven, hell, and the afterlife, they are not earthshakingly different abodes.

I have cited only a minor fraction of belief systems commonly known to most people, namely Mesopotamian, Egyptian, Bahá'í (Persian), Buddhism, Chinese, Christianity, Hinduism, and Islam. It will be up to the reader to decide for what, and how much credence to credit to each faith. While Christianity is the world's most practiced faith, most other religions have their own dedicated scriptures (bibles) directing their lives, and laws, as well. For the devout follower, it is easy to demonstrate why there can arise conflicts between the different faiths, as history could attest. The best we could do, as an individual, and a culture, is to understand the differences, and accept, and respect the inherited beliefs. While Christians may be the world majority, we learned to not have the superior right to dominate the rest of the world's beliefs. It can only be hoped that Islam extremists will recognize their adapted dominance as well for the survival of their own faith.

Mesopotamia

The ancient Mesopotamians regarded the sky as a series of domes (usually three, but sometimes seven) covering the flat earth. Each dome was made of a different kind of precious stone. The lowest dome of heaven was made of jasper, and was the home of the stars. The middle dome of heaven was made of *saggilmut* stone, and was the abode of the Igigi. The highest, and outermost dome of heaven was made of *luludānītu* stone, and was personified as An, the god of the sky. The celestial bodies were equated with specific deities as well. The planet Venus was believed to be Inanna, the goddess of love, sex, and war. The sun was her brother Utu, the god of justice, and the moon was their father Nanna.

Ordinary mortals could not go to heaven because it was the abode of the gods alone. Instead, after a person died, his or her soul went to Kur, a dark shadowy underworld, located deep below the surface of the earth. All souls went to the same afterlife, and a person's actions during life had no impact on how he would be treated in the world to come. Nonetheless, funerary evidence indicates that some people believed that Inanna had the power to bestow special favors upon her devotees in the afterlife.

Egypt

Heaven was a physical place far above the Earth in a "dark area" of space where there were no stars, basically beyond the universe. According to the *Book of the Dead*, departed souls would undergo a literal journey to reach Heaven, along the way to which there could exist hazards, and other entities attempting to deny the reaching of Heaven. Their heart would finally be weighed against the feather of truth, and if the sins weighed it down their heart was devoured.

Bahá'í Faith

The Baha'i faith originated in 19th century Persia, present day Iran. The Bahá'í faith regards the conventional description of Heaven, and Hell, as a specific place as symbolic. The Bahá'í writings describe Heaven as a "spiritual condition" where closeness to God is defined as Heaven; conversely Hell was seen as a state of remoteness from God. Bahá'u'lláh, the founder of the Bahá'í faith, stated that the nature of the life of the soul in the afterlife was beyond comprehension in the physical plane, but that the soul would retain its consciousness, and individuality, and remember its physical life. The soul would be able to recognize other souls, and communicate with them.

For Bahá'ís, entry into the next life has the potential to bring great joy. Bahá'u'lláh likened death to the process of birth. He explained: "The world beyond is as different from this world as this world is different from that of the child while still in the womb of its mother." The analogy to the womb in many ways summarizes the Bahá'í view of earthly existence: just as the womb constituted an important place for a person's initial physical development, the physical world provides for the development of the individual soul. Accordingly, Bahá'ís view life as a preparatory stage, where one can develop, and perfect those qualities which would be needed in the next life. The key to spiritual progress is to follow the path outlined by the current Manifestation of God, which Bahá'ís believed was currently Bahá'u'lláh. Bahá'u'lláh wrote, "Know thou, of a truth, that if the soul of man hath walked in the ways of God, it will, assuredly return, and be gathered to the glory of the Beloved."

The Bahá'í teachings state that there exists a hierarchy of souls in the afterlife, where the merits of each soul determine their place in the hierarchy, and that souls lower in the hierarchy cannot completely understand the station of those above. Each soul could continue to progress in the afterlife, but the soul's development was not entirely dependent on its own conscious efforts, the nature of which we were not aware, but also augmented by the grace of God, the prayers of others, and good deeds performed by others on Earth in the name of that person.

Buddhism

In Buddhism there are several Heavens, all of which are still part of *samsara* (illusionary reality). Those who accumulate good karma may be reborn in one of them. However, their stay in Heaven is not eternal—eventually they would use up their good karma, and would undergo rebirth into another realm, as a human, animal or other being. Because Heaven is temporary, and part of *samsara*, Buddhists focus more on escaping the cycle of rebirth, and reaching enlightenment (*nirvana*). Nirvana is not a heaven but a mental state.

According to Buddhist cosmology the universe is impermanent, and beings transmigrate through a number of existential "planes" in which this human world is only one "realm" or "path." These are traditionally envisioned as a vertical continuum with the Heavens existing above the human realm, and the realms of the animals, hungry ghosts, and hell beings existing beneath it. One important Buddhist Heaven is the *Trāyastriṃśa*, which resembles Olympus of Greek mythology.

In the Mahayana world view, there are also pure lands which lie outside this continuum, and which were created by the Buddhas upon attaining enlightenment. Rebirth in the pure land of Amitabha is seen as an assurance of Buddhahood, for once reborn there, beings do not fall back into cyclical existence unless they choose to do so to save other beings, the goal of Buddhism being the obtainment of enlightenment, and freeing oneself, and others from the birth-death cycle.

Chinese faiths

In the native Chinese Confucian traditions, Heaven was a concept, where the ancestors resided, and from which emperors drew their mandate to rule in their dynastic propaganda. For example, as quoted from: https://en.wikipedia.org/wiki/Heaven.

Heaven is a key concept in Chinese mythology, philosophies, and religions, and was on one end of the spectrum a synonym of *Shangdi* (Supreme Deity), and on the other naturalistic end, a synonym for nature, and the sky. After their conquest of the Shang Dynasty in 1122 BC, the Zhou people considered their supreme deity *Tian* (Chinese character for "Heaven" or "sky)" to be identical with the Shang supreme deity *Shangdi*. The Zhou people attributed Heaven with anthropomorphic attributes, evidenced in the etymology of the Chinese character for Heaven or sky, which originally depicted a person with a large cranium. Heaven was said to see, hear, and watch over all men. Heaven was affected by man's doings, and having personality, was happy or angry with them. Heaven blessed those who pleased it, and sent calamities upon those who offended it. Heaven was also believed to transcend all other spirits, and gods, with Confucius asserting, "He who offends against Heaven has none to whom he can pray."

Other philosophers born around the time of Confucius such as Mozi took an even more theistic view of Heaven, believing that Heaven was the divine ruler, just as the Son of Heaven (the King of Zhou) was the earthly ruler. Mozi believed that spirits, and minor gods existed, but their function was merely to carry out the will of Heaven, watching for evil-doers, and punishing them. Thus, they function as angels of Heaven, and did not detract from its monotheistic government of the world. With such a high monotheism, it was not surprising that Mohism, "ancient Chinese philosophy of logic, rational thought, and science developed by the academic scholars who studied under the ancient Chinese philosopher Mozi, and embodied in an eponymous book: the Mozi," championed a concept called "universal love," which taught that Heaven loved all people equally, and that each person should similarly love all human beings without distinguishing between his own relatives, and those of others.

In Mozi's *Will of Heaven*, he writes: "I know Heaven loves men dearly not without reason. Heaven ordered the sun, the moon, and the stars to enlighten, and guide them. Heaven ordained the four seasons, Spring, Autumn, Winter, and Summer, to regulate them. Heaven sent down snow, frost, rain, and dew to grow the five grains, and flax, and silk that so the people could use, and enjoy them. Heaven established the hills, and rivers, ravines, and valleys, and arranged many things to minister to man's good or bring him evil. He appointed the dukes, and lords to reward the virtuous, and punish the wicked, and to gather metal, and wood, birds, and beasts, and to engage in cultivating the five grains, and flax, and silk to provide for the people's food, and clothing. This has been so from antiquity to the present."

Hinduism

Attaining heaven is not the final pursuit in Hinduism as heaven itself is ephemeral, and related to the physical body. Only being tied by the heaven could not be perfect either, and is just another name for a pleasurable, and mundane material life.

According to Hindu cosmology, above the earthly plane are several other planes. Since heavenly abodes are also tied to the cycle of birth, and death, any dweller of Heaven or Hell would again be recycled to a different plane, and in a different form per the karma, and the illusion of Samsara. This cycle is broken only by self-realization.

In the Vaishnava traditions the highest Heaven is Vaikuntha, which exists above the six heavenly lokas, and outside of the mahat-tattva or mundane world. It is where eternally liberated souls who have attained moksha reside in eternal sublime beauty with Lakshmi, and Narayana (a manifestation of Vishnu).

Islam

The Quran contains many references to an afterlife in Eden for those who do good deeds. Regarding the concept of Heaven (Jannah) in the Quran, verse 35 of Surah Al-Ra'd says, "The parable of the Garden which the righteous are promised! Beneath it flow rivers. Perpetual is the fruits thereof, and the shade therein. Such is the End of the Righteous;, and the end of the unbelievers is the Fire." Islam rejects the concept of original sin, and Muslims believe that all human beings are born pure. Children automatically go to Heaven when they die, regardless of the religion of their parents.

The concept of Heaven in Islam differs in many respects to the concept in Judaism, and Christianity. Heaven is described primarily in physical terms as a place where every wish is immediately fulfilled when asked. Islamic texts describe immortal life in Heaven as happy, without negative emotions. Those who dwell in Heaven are said to wear costly apparel, partake in exquisite banquets, and recline on couches inlaid with gold or precious stones. Inhabitants would rejoice in the company of their parents, spouses, and children. In Islam if one's good deeds outweigh one's sins then one may gain entrance to Heaven. Conversely, if one's sins outweigh their good deeds, they are sent to Hell. The more good deeds one has performed, the higher the level of Heaven one is directed to. It has been said that the lowest level of Heaven, the first one, is already over one-hundred times better than the greatest life on Earth. The highest level is the seventh Heaven. Houses are built by angels for the occupants using solid gold.

Christianity

Traditionally, Christianity has taught that Heaven is the location of the throne of God as well as the holy angels, although this is, in varying degrees, considered metaphorical. In traditional Christianity, it was considered a state or condition of existence (rather than a particular place somewhere in the cosmos) of the supreme fulfillment of theosis in the beatific vision of the Godhead. In most forms of Christianity, heaven is also understood as the abode for the redeemed dead in the afterlife, usually a temporary stage before the resurrection of the dead, and the saints' return to the New Earth.

The resurrected Jesus was said to have ascended to heaven where he now sits at the right hand of God, and will return to Earth in the Second Coming. Various people have been said to have entered heaven while still alive, including Enoch, Elijah, and Jesus himself, after his resurrection. According to Roman Catholic teaching, Mary, mother of Jesus, was also said to have been assumed into heaven, and was titled the Queen of Heaven.

The Gospel of Matthew frequently uses the phrase "Kingdom of Heaven," where the other Synoptic Gospels speak of the "Kingdom of God," one of the key elements of the teachings of Jesus in the New Testament. Revelation 12:7-9 speaks of a war in Heaven between Michael the Archangel, and his angels against Satan, and his angels, after which Satan, and his angels were "thrown down to the earth."

While the word used in all these writings, in particular the New Testament Greek, applies primarily to the sky, it was also used metaphorically as the dwelling place of God, and the blessed. Similarly, though the English word "heaven" still keeps its original physical meaning when used, for instance, in allusions to the stars as "lights shining through from Heaven," and in phrases such as heavenly body to mean an astronomical object, the Heaven or happiness that Christianity looks forward to what, according to Pope John Paul II, "neither an abstraction nor a physical place in the clouds, but a living, personal relationship with the Holy Trinity. It is our meeting with the Father which takes place in the risen Christ through the communion of the Holy Spirit."

Some religions may read as fairytales rather than rational thinking, but one has to understand the time, and environment that they were created in. While many of us have adapted to a modern world motivated by scientific achievements, and archaeology findings, the majority of ancient beliefs still cling to their ancient traditions. It proves my point that we apply to our fellow beings means, and methods that are best suited for the cultural environment, but questions still remain unanswered such as:

Where is harmony, and everlasting peace? One has to believe in a Heaven. Without it, an afterlife does not exist. Each individual existence would end with death, forever. While striving to create the best of a future for ourselves, our children, and their descendants, for most of us it is not a welcoming thought.

How can we cope in heaven after having adapted to modern life? While some of us, the devout followers of faith, may live an orderly life respecting one's religious belief within obeisance of inherited cultural values, others are not so dependent on values. One only has to follow Hollywood trend setting to get the idea. I will cite one example:

What about Liz Tailor, and Eva Gabor, who had been married seven, and eight times in their lives, respectively? Who would they spend eternal time with in Heaven? Their first husbands, their last, or all? Divorce, while readily practiced in life, is not an easy solution after we pass on into the afterlife, unless God allows the same practices in Heaven that we have created on Earth.

What about the rest of the world population? Who, and how will they live their eternal lives? How about people I had met through my career, and my relationships? What about theirs?

As one can see, there are many unanswered questions. Did God allow us free will and, if so, would he honor the choices we made to satisfy our needs, and desires? No matter how one turns, and twists our conscious, and unconscious decisions, one has to have faith. Without it, one only lives for the moment. Life is given to you with the first breath you take, and it will end with the last breath. Every moment in between should be treasured to its fullest.

CREATION MYTHS

Many accounts have been written about the creation of man, mostly originating either from biblical accounts or other inspiring sources. There is one exception that differed that I would like to present. It was written by Charles H. Long[74] on the general meaning of religion in history, and culture, and specifically about African religion in the Atlantic world, from a unique perspective. He participated in establishing the first curriculum for the study of religion at the University of Chicago.

Creation myth, also called cosmogonic myth, is the philosophical, and theological elaboration of the primal myth of creation within a religious community. The term myth here refers to the imaginative expression in narrative form of what was experienced or understood as basic reality. The term creation refers to the beginning of things, whether by the will, and act of a transcendent being, by emanation from some ultimate source, or in any other way.

Nature, and its Significance

The myth of creation is the symbolic narrative of the beginning of the world as understood by a particular community. The later doctrines of creation were interpretations of this myth in light of the subsequent history, and needs of the community. Thus, for example, all theology, and speculation concerning creation in the Christian community are based on the myth of creation in the biblical book of Genesis, and of the new creation in Jesus Christ. Doctrines of creation are based on the myth of creation, which expressed, and embodied all of the fertile possibilities for thinking about this subject within a particular religious community.

Myths are narratives that express the basic valuations of a religious community. Myths of creation refer to the process through which the world was centered, and given a definite form within the whole of reality. They also serve as a basis for the orientation of human beings within the world. This centering, and orientation specifies humanity's place in the universe, and the regard that humans must have for other humans, nature, and the entire nonhuman world; they set the stylistic tone that tends to determine all other gestures, actions, and structures in the culture. The cosmogonic (origin of the world) myth is the myth par excellence. In this sense, the myth is akin to philosophy, but, unlike philosophy, it is constituted by a system of symbols;, and because it is the basis for any subsequent cultural thought, it contains rational, and nonrational forms. There is an order, and structure to the myth, but this order, and structure is not to be confused with rational, philosophical order, and structure. The myth possesses its own distinctive kind of order.

Myths of creation have another distinctive character in that they provide both the model for nonmythic expression in the culture, and the model for other cultural myths.

---

[74] Charles H. Long – Cosmogonic Myth. According to Charles Long, the nature of religion, mythic, and scientific modes of thinking, and the general character of creation myths interprets five major types of such myths: creation from nothing, emergence myths, world-parent myths, creation from Chaos, and from the cosmic egg, and earth-diver myths. Original texts of creation myths can be extracted from a wide range of cultures that offer insights into the authentic ways of mythic thinking, and expression. Weblink: https://www.britannica.com/topic/creation-myth.

In this sense, one must distinguish between cosmogonic myths, and myths of the origin of cultural techniques, and artifacts. Insofar as the cosmogonic myth tells the story of the creation of the world, other myths that narrate the story of a specific technique or the discovery of a particular area of cultural life take their models from the stylistic structure of the cosmogonic myth. These latter myths may be etiological (i.e., explaining origins), but the cosmogonic myth is never simply etiological, for it deals with the ultimate origin of all things.

The cosmogonic myth thus has a pervasive structure; its expression in the form of philosophical, and theological thought is only one dimension of its function as a model for cultural life. Though the cosmogonic myth does not necessarily lead to ritual expression, ritual is often the dramatic presentation of the myth. Such dramatization is performed to emphasize the permanence, and efficacy of the central themes of the myth, which integrate, and undergird the structure of meaning, and value in the culture. The ritual dramatization of the myth is the beginning of liturgy, for the religious community in its central liturgy attempts to re-create the time of the beginning.

From this ritual dramatization the notion of time is established within the religious community. To be sure, in most communities there was the notion of a sacred, and a profane time. The prestige of the cosmogonic myth established sacred or real time. It was this time that was most efficacious for the life of the community. Dramatization of sacred time enabled the community to participate in a time that had a different quality than ordinary time, which tended to be neutral. All significant temporal events were spoken of in the language of the cosmogonic myth, for only by referring them to this primordial model would they have significance.

In like manner, artistic expression in archaic or "primitive" societies, often related to ritual presentation, was modelled on the structure of the cosmogonic myth. The masks, dances, and gestures were, in one way or another, aspects of the structure of the cosmogonic myth. This meaning may also extend to the tools that people used in the making of artistic designs, and to the precise technique they employed in the craft.

Mention has been made above of the fact that the cosmogonic myth situates humankind in a place, in space. This centering is at once symbolic, and empirical: symbolic because through symbols it defined the spatiality of human beings in ontological terms (of being), and empirical because it oriented them in a definite landscape. Indeed, the names given to the flora, and fauna, and to the topography are a part of the orientation of humans in a space. The subsequent development of language within a human community was an extension of the language of the cosmogonic myth.

The initial ordering of the world through the cosmogonic myth serves as the primordial structure of culture, and the articulation of the embryonic forms, and styles of cultural life out of which various, and differing forms of culture emerge. The recollection, and celebration of the myth enables the religious community to think of, and participate in the fundamentally real time, space, and mode of orientation that enables them to define their cultural life in a specific manner.

Types of Cosmogonic Myths
The world as a structure of meaning, and value has not appeared in the same manner to all human civilizations. There are, therefore, almost as many cosmogonic myths as there are human cultures. Until quite recently, the classification of these myths on an

evolutionary scale, from the most archaic cultures to contemporary Western cultures (i.e., from the assumedly simplest to the most complex), was the most dominant mode of ordering these myths. Recent 20th-century scholars, however, have begun to look at the various types of myths in terms of the structures that they reveal rather than considering them on an evolutionary scale that extends from the so-called simple to the complex, for, in a sense, there are no simple myths regarding the beginning of the world. The beginning of the world was simultaneously the beginning of the human condition, and it is impossible to speak of this beginning as if it were simple.

Creation by a Supreme Being
The 19th-century scholars who took an evolutionary survey of human culture, and religion (e.g., Sir James George Frazer, and Sir Edward Burnett Tylor) held that the notion of the creation of the world by a supreme being occurred only in the highest stage of cultural development.

Andrew Lang, a Scottish folklorist, challenged this conception of the development of religious ideas, for he found in the writings of anthropologists, ethnologists, and travelers' evidence of a belief in a supreme being or high god among cultures that had been classified as the most primitive. This position was taken up, and elaborated by an Austrian priest-anthropologist, Wilhelm Matthäus Schmidt, who reversed the evolutionary theory, holding that there was a primordial notion of a supreme being, a kind of original intellectual, and religious conception of a single creator god, that degenerated in subsequent cultural stages.

Though Schmidt's theories of cultural historical stages, and diffusion, and an original primordial revelation had for the most part been discredited, and abandoned, the existence of a belief in a supreme being among primitive peoples (a notion discovered by Andrew Lang) has been proven, and attested to over, and over again by investigators of numerous cultures. This belief has been found among the cultures of Africa, the Ainu of the northern Japanese islands, Amerindians, south central Australians, the Fuegians of South America, and in almost all parts of the globe.

Though the precise nature, and characteristics of the supreme creator deity may differ from culture to culture, a specific, and pervasive structure of this type of deity can be discerned. The following characteristics tend to be common: (1) They was all wise, and all powerful. The world came into being because of his wisdom, and he was able to actualize the world because of his power. (2) The deity existed alone prior to the creation of the world. There was no being or thing prior to his existence. No explanation could therefore be given of his existence, before which one confronted the ultimate mystery. (3) The mode of creation was conscious, deliberate, and orderly. This again was an aspect of the creator's wisdom, and power. The creation came about because the deity seemed to have a definite plan in mind, and did not create on a trial-and-error basis. In Genesis, for example, particular parts of the world were created seriatim; in an Egyptian myth, Kheper, the creator deity, said, "I planned in my heart," and in a Maori myth the creator deity proceeded from inactivity to increasing stages of activity. (4) The creation of the world was simultaneously an expression of the freedom, and purpose of the deity. His mode of creation defined the pattern, and purpose of all aspects of the creation, though the deity was not bound by his creation. His relationship to the created order after the creation was again an aspect of his freedom. (5) In several creation myths of this type, the creator deity removed himself from the world after it had been created. After the creation the deity went away, and only appeared again when a catastrophe threatened the created order. (6) The supreme creator deity was often a sky god, and the deity in this form was an instance of the religious valuation of the symbolism of the sky.

In creation myths of the above type, the creation itself or the intent of the creator deity was to create a perfect world, paradise. Before the end of the creative act or sometime soon after the end of creation, the created order or the intent of the creator deity was thwarted by some fault of one of the creatures. There was thus a rupture in the creation myth. In some myths this rupture was the cause of the departure of the deity from creation.

An African myth from the Dogon peoples of West Africa illustrates this point. In this myth the creator deity first creates an egg. Within the egg were two pairs of twins, each pair consisting of one male, and one female. These twins were supposed to mature within the egg, becoming at maturation androgynous (both male, and female) beings, the perfect creatures to inhabit the earth. One of the twins broke from the egg before maturation because he wished to dominate creation. In so doing he carried a part of the egg with him, and from this he created an imperfect world. The creator deity, seeing what he had done, sacrificed the other twin to establish a balance in the world. The creation was sustained by this sacrifice, and it was now ambiguous, instead of the perfect world intended by the god.

This myth not only shows how a rupture took place within the myth itself but also points out the fact that the characteristics of the supreme creator deity noted above seldom exist apart from other mythological contexts. The widespread symbols of dualism (the divine twins), the cosmic egg, and sacrifice are basic themes in the structure of this African creation myth. In myths of this kind, however, prominence must always be given to the might of a powerful creator sky deity under whose aegis the created order came into being.

Creation through Emergence
In contrast to the creation by a supreme sky deity, there is another type of creation myth in which the creation seemed to emerge through its own inner power from under the earth. In this genre of myth, the created order emerged gradually in continuous stages. It is similar to a birth or metamorphosis of the world from its embryonic state to maturity. The symbolism of the earth or a part of the earth as a repository of all potential form is prominent in this type of myth. In some myths of this type (e.g., the Navajo myth of emergence), the movement from a lower stage to a higher one was initiated by some fault of the people who lived under the earth, but these faults were only the parallels of an automatic upper movement in the earth itself.

Just as the supreme-creator-deity myth forms a homology to the sky, the emergence myth forms a homology to the earth, and to the childbearing woman. In many cases the emergence of the created order is analogous to the growth of a child in the womb, and its emission at birth. The underworlds prior to the created order appear chaotic; the beings inhabiting these places seem without form or stability, or they committed immoral acts. The seeming chaos was moving toward a definite form of order, however, an order latent in the very forms themselves rather than from an imposition of order from the outside.

From another perspective the emergence myth is homologous to the seed. When the homologue of the seed is referred to, the meaning of fertility, and death are at once introduced. The seed must die before it can be reborn, and actualize its potentiality. This symbolism is dramatically presented in a wide range of funerary rites: one was buried in the earth in hope of a renewal from the earth, or the earth was the repository of the ancestors from whom the new generation emerged. In every case, emergence myths demonstrate the latent potency immanent in the earth as a repository of all life forms.

Creation by World Parents
Closely related to the above type of myth is the myth that states that the world was created as the progeny of a primordial mother, and father. The mother, and father were symbols of earth, and sky, respectively. In myths of this kind, the world parents generally appear at a late stage of the creation process; chaos in some way exists before the coming into being of the world parents. In the Babylonian myth *Enuma elish*, it is stated:

> When on high the heaven had not been named,
> Firm ground below had not been called by name,
> Naught but primordial Apsu, their begetter,
> (And) Mummu-Tiamat, she who bore them all,
> Their waters comingling as a single body.

The Maori made the same point when they stated that the world parents emerged out of *po. Po* for the Maori meant the basic matter, and the method by which creation came about. There was thus some form of reality before the appearance of the world parents.

Even though the world parents are depicted, and described as in sexual embrace, no activity was taking place. They appear as quiescent, and inert. The chthonic (underworld) structure of the earth as latent potentiality tends to dominate the union. The parents were often unaware that they have offspring, and thus a kind of indifference regarding the union was expressed. The union of male, and female in sexual embrace is another symbol of completeness, and totality. As in the African myth from the Dogon referred to above, sexual union was a sign of androgyny (being both male, and female), and androgyny, in turn, a sign of perfection. The indifference of the world parents was thus not simply a sign of ignorance but equally of the silence of perfection. The world parents in the Babylonian, and Maori myths did not wish to be disturbed by their offspring. Unlike the parents, the offspring were signs of actuality, fragmentation, specificity; they define concrete realities.

The separation of the world parents is, again, a rupture within the myth. This separation was caused by offspring who wished either to have more space or to have light, for they were situated between the bodies of the parents. In some myths the separation is caused by a woman who lifted her pestle so high in grinding grain that it struck the sky, causing the sky to recede into the background, thus providing room for human activities. In both cases an antagonistic motive must be attributed to the agents of separation. In the Babylonian, and Maori versions of this myth, actual warfare took place as a result of the separation.

Against the primordial union of the world parents, there is the desire for knowledge, and a different orientation in space. After the separation, lesser deities related to solar symbolism take precedence in the creation. The sun, and light must be seen in these myths as representing the desire for a humanizing, and cultural knowledge against the passive, and inert forms of the union of the parent deities. From the point of separation, the mythic narrative of the world-parent myths states how different forms of cultural knowledge were brought to human beings by the offspring, the agents of separation. The separation of the world parents was the sign of a new cosmic order, an order dedicated to the techniques, crafts, and knowledge of culture.

Creation from the Cosmic Egg

In the Dogon myth referred to above, the creation deity began the act of creation by placing two embryonic sets of twins in an egg. In each set of twins was a male, and female; during the maturation process they were together, thus forming androgynous beings. In a Tahitian myth, the creator deity himself lived alone in a shell. After breaking out of the shell, he created his counterpart, and together they undertook the work of creation.

A Japanese creation narrative likened the primordial chaos to an egg containing the germs of creation. In the Hindu tradition the creation of the world was symbolized in the Chandogya Upanishad by the breaking of an egg, and the universe was referred to as an egg in other sources. The Buddhists speak of the transcending of ordinary existence, the realization of a new mode of being, as breaking the shell of the egg. Similar references to creation through the symbol of the egg are found in the Orphic texts of the Greeks, and in Chinese myths.

The egg is a symbol of the totality from which all creation comes. It was like a womb containing the seeds of creation. Within the egg were the possibilities of a perfect creation (i.e., the creation of androgynous beings). The egg, in addition to being the beginning of life, was equally a symbol of procreation, rebirth, and new life. In a version of the Dogon, one of the twins returned to the egg in order to resuscitate the other.

Creation by Earth Divers

Two elements are important in myths of this type. There is, first, the theme of the cosmogonic water representing the undifferentiated waters that were present before the earth had been created. Second, there is an animal who plunged into the water to secure a portion of earth. The importance of the animal is that the creature agent was a prehumen species. This version of the myth is probably the oldest version of this genre. This basic structure of the earth-diver myth has been modified in central Europe in myths that relate the story of the primordial waters, God, and the devil. In these versions of the earth-diver myth, the devil appears as God's companion in the creation of the world. The devil becomes the diver sent by God to bring earth from the bottom of the waters. In most versions of this myth, God does not appear to be omniscient or omnipotent, often depending on the knowledge of the devil for certain details regarding the creative act—details that he learns through tricks he plays upon the devil.

In still different versions of this myth, the relationship between God, and the devil moves from companionship to antagonism; they became adversaries, though they remain as co-creators of the world. The fact that the devil has a part in the creation of the world is one way of explaining the origin, and persistence of evil in the world.

Mircea Eliade, a noted 20th-century historian of religions, pointed to another theme in certain Romanian versions of this myth. After God has instructed the devil to dive to the bottom of the waters, and bring up the earth, the devil obeys, diving several times before he is able to bring up, and hold on to a small portion of earth. After the creation of the world from this small portion of earth, God sinks into a profound sleep. This sleep was a sign of mental exhaustion, for only the devil, and a bee knew the solution to certain details of the creation, and God must, with the help of the bee, trick the devil into giving him this vital information. God's sleep, according to Eliade, was a sign of his passivity, and disinterest in the world after it had been created, and it harks back to certain archaic myths in which the supreme deity retired from the world after its creation, becoming disinterested, and passive in the relationship with his work.

SCIENTIFIC VIEW ON CREATION

Where did Man come from?
"It would be very difficult to explain why the universe should have begun in just this way, except as the act of a God who intended to create beings like us."

- Stephen Hawking

What is Creation Science?
Creation science is the study of origins with respect to the Bible's account of God's creative acts. Creation science, to a degree, is also amenable to the presuppositions of assorted theists outside of Bible-based Christianity. Creation science is based in part on the following observations, and arguments:

- The universe (which is space, time, and matter) had a beginning, thus it had to have been affected by a pre-existing cause
- The cause (which had to pre-exist space, time, and matter) must have been independent of the space, time, and matter it preceded: i.e., was independent of space (limitless), independent of time (eternal), and independent of matter (immaterial)
- The more than 150 "coincidences" of extremely fine margins, and interrelated relationships by which the properties of the earth, and universe provide habitable conditions
- Discoveries indicating earth's primordial conditions were likely similar to today's conditions
- The impossibility of living cells to arise by chance (as even attested to by the discoverers of DNA)
- The virtual impossibility of mutations to favorably add to the genetic code
- The incapability of natural selection to advance, and improve pre-biological systems into biological ones
- Multiple, and complex life forms, and all the animal phyla appearing abruptly in the fossil record (the Cambrian explosion)
- The fossil record displaying zero species-to-species transitional forms (as attested by scientists from Darwin himself to modern day paleontologists)
- The reduction in the number, and type of animal species rather than the increase as evolutionary models predict
- The irreducible complexity of numerous biological systems (which Darwin stated would refute his theory if existent)
- Information-intensive structures such as DNA requiring an intelligent design agent
- Planetary geology more or less according to the geologic model of catastrophism
- The history of erroneous, and falsified findings by evolutionists, and the ongoing maintenance of those falsifications
- The absence of evidence for any material, extraterrestrial ancestors
- The presence of parallel accounts between the Bible, and scientific observations concerning the origin of the universe

- The presence of parallel accounts between the Bible, and scientific observations concerning the earth
- The presence of parallel accounts between the Bible, and scientific observations concerning humanity
- Belief in Scripture to be the Word of God.

How important is Scripture to Creation Science?

The belief in Scripture to be the Word of God is foundational to creation science; it is the starting point. Creation science began with the belief that God was our progenitor, and from there applied the natural sciences to confirm that belief.

Intelligent design theory, by contrast, neither employs Scripture nor invokes any presupposed being as part of its worldview. IDT evaluates the physical universe on the basis of whether or not it bears any evidence or characteristics of having been intentionally designed.

Generally speaking, creationists affirm nearly every aspect of intelligent design theory. The only substantial difference is that creationists began with Scripture-based reasoning which declares God was our designer, and are certain of it as they saw it confirmed in the evidence of the natural sciences.

The last word on Evolution vs. Creation

Darwin was concerned about the lack of evidence for his conjectures, and hoped confirming evidence would eventually be found. After well over a century of searching for the first of what was expected to be billions, and billions of transitional specimens, not one has been found. This did not send evolutionists running to the Bible, but it did cause them to abandon Darwinism for punctuated equilibria, and later punctuated equilibria for directed panspermia.

Now with the latest progress of science, and study by Hoyle, Behe, Denton, Crick, and others, the very foundation of all non-theistic theories of life's origin has been shaken with the conclusion that life could not have arisen by chance.

Evolutionists' writing increasingly attributes life, and the cosmos' origination to "god." Not god in the sense of the God of the Bible, but god in the sense of an indescribable cause which had affected the universe, and all life contained therein, a cause some concluded could not be physically or scientifically ascertained.

This unknown god is one that non-theists could comfortably reference because, for them, it is simply a place-card until such time a preferred answer came along. Their unknowable, unidentified god is one they called upon to fill in the gaps in their evolutionary worldview as did medieval scientists who invoked a god for their own shortcomings. Such a god makes no demands of them, does not care how they live, and can be as influential or comfortably non-existent as they want.

All premises are matters of faith. The premise taken in believing the Bible (that there is a God) has been shown to result in a reasonable explanation of the universe, the planet, and life around us. The reasonableness of this belief is the goal of these sections.

Meanwhile, the premise of no-God has been shown to result in a conclusion that approaches irrationality. The no-God worldview is such that it still requires invoking a god to bridge gaps of logic, and evidence. Of course, it is to be expected that some version of a no-God origin will always be believed.

Owen Chadwick writes of Darwin's time: "The public accepted the doctrine of evolution for a bigger reason than the simple probability established by Darwin, namely that, if they did not, their mental picture of the origins suddenly became an intolerable blank."

In other words, evolution was the crutch of atheism. For lack of amenable evidence, a committed atheist had nothing else on which to lean but the leading evolutionary belief of the day. Today's evolutionary belief appears to prefer the logical error of either infinite regression (or spontaneous generation) to the sound conclusion of believing that life was created by the God of the Bible; the same God who has evidenced himself in history, in Scripture, and in person.

Once again, the frustrated surrender to illogic by George Wald, the 1971 Nobel prize winner for biology: "I will not accept creation philosophically because I do not want to believe in God. Therefore, I choose to believe in that which I know is scientifically impossible – spontaneous generation arising to evolution."

Is not the evidence that *does* exist—evidence which points to creation—a better foundation for belief than blind, and unevidenced faith in erroneous logic? It is, for those who believe in evidence, and have the courage to accept the conclusion regardless of their presuppositions.

CREATION COMPARED

Belief Systems about the Origin of Life, and the Development of Species
Christian creation, evolution, and science beliefs, in brief. Debates on the Internet, within religious groups, and in the media about the origins, and development of species of plant, and animal life on Earth are often presented as a life, and death struggle between two competing beliefs: naturalistic evolution, and creation science.

This is not a particularly accurate description. There are, in reality, three main belief systems being promoted by individuals, and organizations in North America. Within these three main systems there are many variations.

The Three Main Belief Systems:
Hundreds of religions around the world teach creation stories which account for the diversity of life on Earth. The theory of evolution is also a popular belief, particularly among scientists, secularists, and religious liberals.

In North America, beliefs regarding the origins of the origins of species of plant, and animal life mostly fall into three general categories. Starting with the most popular:

- Creation science: God created the universe during 6 consecutive, 24-hour days less than 10,000 years ago, precisely as one of the literal interpretations of the Biblical book of Genesis would indicate. All of the various "kinds" of plants, and animals that currently exist (and that once existed but are now extinct) on Earth are descendants of the original life forms that God created during the single week of creation. However, within these original kinds of animals, microevolution has resulted in similar species developing. For example, God created a deer "kind" which developed into a variety of deer. This is the most popular belief system among the general public. It is the least popular among earth, and biological scientists. Over 99% of such scientists believe that a literal translation of Genesis does not represent reality, and thus that creation science is false.

- Theistic evolution view: The universe is about 14 billion years old. The Earth's crust developed about 4.5 billion years ago. Some believers in this option suggest that God created the first cell; others suggest that the first cell happened as a result of natural processes through abiogenesis. Subsequently, God used evolution as a tool to guide the development of each new species. By steering evolution over time, God eventually produced human beings.

- Scientific view: Evolution is driven by blind, unguided natural forces without a goal. Darwin's belief that naturally occurring differences among offspring lead to evolution of the species through natural selection is the main—or perhaps the only—driving principle behind evolution. If God existed, he played no part in the processes. If all life were to be wiped off of the face of the Earth—not that remote a possibility with the Earth's current levels of religious hatred, and supply of nuclear weapons—and life were to start over, there is absolutely no certainty that intelligent beings would evolve again. If they did, there is no certainty that they would look much like homo sapiens.

Those who believe in the inerrancy of the Bible attempt to follow eternal Biblical truths. However, they seem to have great difficulty in settling on a single understanding of the origins, and development of plant, and animal species. They have ended up with many different conflicting theories which cannot be harmonized. Meanwhile, the scientific community has arrived at an almost complete consensus in the theory of evolution. As new evidence is found, some details of the evolution of species are occasionally modified. Yet supporters of naturalistic evolution long ago reached a consensus on the overall evolutionary process.

"What is the end result?" one might ask, "and where do we go from here?"

Without principle proof for the ultimate process of creation, there may never be an end result to satisfy all of mankind. We are culturally too diversified to believe in one belief system.

Making matters worse, we have been confused, and will remain so until enlightened otherwise by a superior being, or we discover certifiable evidence for the origin of the universe. Regardless of the outcome, the best we can do is to lend our support in the evolution of mankind to benefit all, and to seek solace in the Biblical religion through blind faith, suitable to each individual's needs, and desires.

There will be many more discoveries science will uncover in the future. Regardless of future achievements, there are two important essentials a human being should never forget or change. One is faith. Faith is a good thing, no matter what religion or belief one follows, as long as it will stand up against time. There is one exception, however, and that is Islam. Unless Islam adapts their antiquated, and outdated brutalized Sharia Law while living in the Western world, it should be treated as a direct threat to our freedom, and living. As long as they choose to be contained within their own environment, a Muslim state, other nations should respect their belief as long as the Muslim population could tolerate their practices. For those who seek freedom from Islam oppression, they know where to migrate as long as they conform, and respect other nations' constitutions, religions, and laws.

For nonconformists, I suggest, remain where you feel most comfortable. With borders defined for two hundred individual countries, and cultures, there is absolutely no justifiable cause in today's world for border clashes, and border wars. It's why the world needs an effective internationally-sanctioned law-enforcing branch. By effective I mean holding lawbreakers responsible for their self-serving misdeeds without the endless stalling tactics through fruitless deliberations, and debates.

We can only hope that some power, or nation will emerge with enough courage befitting the bill before it is too late to save the dignity of mankind. The MAD doctrine from nuclear war should serve the world as a reminder that annihilation is not far from being triggered by a radical nation such as North Korea, Pakistan, or Iran.

The preceding sections PART TWO, "Personal Views," and PART THREE, "Global Outlook," are an important part of my life. Though not entirely my own views, since I present alternative views, and principles written by authorities within their personal perspectives, and disciplines, they more or less, represent history with its colorful past. Depending on its importance, most people, when asked, have an opinion on a subject. I have mine. While I am not subject to emotional outbursts, there are times when I suppress my inner feelings from screaming out loud. My reasons are multiple.

First, since I am mostly logically oriented, when I read, or hear something to the contrary, it feels like my intelligence is tested. I am not alone in this. There are many likeminded.

Second, being highly analytical, and at times critical in nature, my mind does not readily accept things that are of a mystical nature. By that I mean imaginary things such as paranormal, supernatural, and folklore.

Third, like many law-abiding citizens, I get frustrated when I see injustice committed on humanity, or lack of legal discipline instilled on criminals. While our legal system generally works, there is way too much crime going unpunished, or being insufficiently punished. Examples have to be set to reduce crime. The question remains, "what example would be fair to fit a crime?"

As the recent wave of social killings demonstrate, capital punishment does not seem to be sufficient anymore with the instigators frequently, remorseless, and suicidal to begin with. "What are the alternatives," one might ask. It all depends on the society we live in. Giving the diversity in legal practices exercised throughout the world, it is governments that need to lead, and set examples. Governments are only as strong as their practices, and governments are made up of people. The same people that need to be judged. If the judicial system is weakened, so are ethics, and morals.

That brings up the question, "where do we stand as a nation?"

Even though the majority rules, the answer is not simple. If the nation suffers, who is to blame? It means we all suffer together, and are blamed together as reward. It does not seem fair. Changes have to be made, and must come from either above, the government, or from below, the people otherwise a civil war is inevitable. This shall serve as a warning. History has never been wrong.

PERSONAL VIEWS ON THE WORLD TODAY

"Why don't you come on over?" I pleaded with Buzz after he picked up my call. Several weeks had passed since our last get together. "I need a good griping session."

He drove up thirty minutes later. "Up for coffee?" I offered.

"German brand?"

"If you prefer." He was not the only one that appreciated my brew. It took a little more effort to steam up a couple of espressos than just mixing instant. For years, I was able to purchase a special blend of coffee beans imported from Germany, but stores stopped carrying it some time ago. After a bit of a Google search, I learned the secrets of European blended beans, "Columbian Light." Ever since, I just walk into any local grocery store to grind up a one-pound package ready for takeout. Though the secret is out, I won't share it with just anybody. It was better to keep the myth preserved, and let my guests savor the special treat.

"What have you been up to?" I said, not expecting much of an adventure. In contrast to our earlier lives, his life today was pretty much regulated by family events.

"Just got back from visiting the kids." Both he, and his wife were grandparents with their children living out east. Or was it south? I never knew how to geographically place North Carolina from the direction of Colorado. You started out east, and eventually turned south. In any case, being a grandparent, one had the luxury of calling offspring "kids," no matter how much they had grown up.

"Son says hello."

"Thanks. How is he?" His son was an expert auto mechanic, and of recent, aircraft and helicopter specialist since he joined the army, serving on the team with the Golden Knights. He had worked on my muscle car several times to get more power from the engine. Yes, I am one of those guys who cling to the past, even though spare parts are hard to find. It is especially true for the '74 AMC Javelin I own, the only luxury I treasured. Initially, it came with a 304-size engine. It generated enough power for the Bay Area, where I had purchased it. After moving to Colorado Springs, the vehicle's power was not enough for the altitude. Buzz's son helped me replace the engine with a 401 one. We did not stop there. He reworked the engine bore, shaving down the block, turning it into a 450 with enough power to leave road competitors, and the police in its wake, while I rebuilt whatever else was under the hood. The result was a souped-up racing car, black-cherry red in color, envied every time I take it to the road, and auto shows.

My rationale for time, and effort spent was, "Everybody needs at least one toy, or hobby."

"What do you want to talk about?" Buzz said, urging me to the present. He knew how much I dwelled in the past. I was not the only one. He, too, was apt to relish the glorious times we'd had traveling the world during our rich, and colorful careers.

"Nothing in particular. I just needed some company before going stir crazy. But first," I said, "what's your view on Religion?"

"Don't want to talk about it," he said. I accepted his reply. I did not expect anything else since I knew his position on the subject. I brought it up since I had spent the past weeks analyzing mine, as well as expert scholarly views.

"What about creation, and the universe?" I pressed on.

"I don't…"

"I know," I cut him short. "You don't want to talk about it. What about world views? Are you happy with things?"

"Don't get me started," he said, eyeing me with suspicion.

"World events it is," I insisted. I knew well the position people carried on the way things had turned out in recent years. No matter who I queried, it seemed, everybody was unhappy about one or more issues, to say the least. When pressing on, a once balanced mood would generally change to frustration. Whenever given the opportunity, it was my intention to get to the core of people's displeasure. It was not only the individual displeased with the world today, but the trends could be seen everywhere, the Internet, social media, mainstream media, radio talk, and TV hosts in the nation.

I remember a time where people enjoyed every day to its fullest. No matter what the issues were, people would talk them over with sensible means, respecting each other's spaces, and opinions. I did not see it much these days. "Whatever happened to personality traits?" It was my opening question.

"You've noticed," he said with a concerned look on his face. "When we started our careers, we never had road rage, did we?"

"What about the cop killings? The school shootings? The suicides," I cut in.

"I know. How do you explain it?"

"Drugs," I boldly stated. Whether right or wrong, it was my opinion at the moment.

"You think so?"

"Think about it. Who is committing most of the crimes? It's the young generation. Ever talk to them?"

"I talk to my children. They don't have a problem."

"Yeah," I agreed. "But they grew up in a sound family environment. I think it's the cultural conditions that have changed. I think family values are part of the past."

"Not for everyone. From what I see, the young are still clinging to their parents."

"For different reasons. Where you, and I were kicked out of the home when we reached adulthood, today, they are forced to stay with their parents. The young can't afford their own place, let alone creating a future. The incentives are gone."

"I agree. I believe it's what causes all of the frustration, and rage. Stability, and constancy are gone."

"Not to mention honor, and respect." We'd both identified the fundamental problem for our topic. It was not isolated to only the United States. Other countries seemed to face similar issues, perhaps even worse, especially war-ravaged places in the Middle East. From a relatively peaceful perspective, as the United States had been for over a century without facing a direct internal war, one could hardly imagine life without water, and electricity with shortages of food, and supplies all around.

"It's probably the reason," Buzz agreed, "why we don't see much foreign news."

Years ago, I had learned that U.S. citizens, in general, did not have much interest in other cultures. We both understood that, one had to tune in on Russian, and Chinese broadcasts to keep current on international events. It left two important questions: "Who are we? What have we become?"

I felt like voicing my generally curtailed opinions when in the company of others. Sure, I cussed out situations at times when alone. I had the luxury of living alone for much of the time. Like many people, I imagined, there was a time when frustration reached a breaking point where the only means to let go was by shouting. "What do you do to release your frustrations?" I said, wondering how collected Buzz generally was.

"I have a beer," he said with a grin.

"Just one? With today's problems? I think you need many."

"The wife is not happy when I drink."

"I understand," I said. But in reality, I did not. Much was left unanswered, and I stated so. "What is happening to our society?

"What do you mean?" He was noncommittal.

"You have no questions? You are happy with the way things are?"

"What things?"

"Society."

"I try not to get involved in other people's issues. You can't help everybody."

"You don't worry about your children, and their children?"

"They will work things out. We did." It was a true statement, but somewhat flawed.

"We started our careers in a structured society. The mindset was different. People cared about each other. They cared about the country. Remember John F. Kennedy's declaration, 'My fellow Americans, ask not what your country can do for you, ask what you can do for your country.'"

"I remember well. It was a profound statement affecting the entire nation."

"So," I challenged him, "what can we do to save the country?"

"I don't think we need help. We are still the leaders in the world."

"From a technology perspective? Yes. But the society perspective? No," I stated.

"Maybe they don't want a change. They seem happy to me with their smart phones, and iPads."

"That's exactly what I mean. Gadgets are taking over people's lives. There's no time for anything else. What ever happened to undivided leisure time? I see everybody reaching for their mobiles day, and night, dictating their lives."

"Not much you can do. When your daughters come to visit you," he reminded me, "do you take away their phones?"

"Of course not. It'd probably cause a fight. There's too much of that in the world already."

"Then," he said with a challenging grin, "deal with it." I realized then and there that Buzz was a wise man, not readily visible because of his reserved personality. Contrary to my personal behavior, he kept his wisdom curtailed within his own mind.

"I can't give in. What will happen to my computers, modems, routers, hubs, and switches?"

"Technology is changing. Of all people," he reminded me, "you should know that."

"I guess so." But it left many questions unanswered. I had to put him to a test. "What do you know about cryptocurrency? Blockchain?"

"Nothing much other than it's already in use."

"Do you know that in a few years it will replace all world currencies, including the dollar?"

"Don't think it'll happen."

"Do you know that most countries already have cryptocurrencies?"

"I did not know that."

"Did you know that most banks are getting geared up to trade in it?"

"You can't be serious." He looked dumbfounded. It was a clear reflection of what was to come. "Who in their right minds could expect to deal with it? Everybody would have to turn banker, trader, merchant. There's no way to expect that from the public. It would be impossible to become an expert in all phases of trade, and commerce."

"Now we're talking," I said, beaming. We had a specific topic to discuss.

I had been studying bitcoin, cryptocurrency, and blockchain technologies for the past couple of years. It was not that difficult to understand if one knew about software development, and computer technologies. But it did not stop there.

"What do you know about it?" I asked. Buzz had always been part of technological developments, and understood what I was getting at. But unlike me, I knew that he had not studied cryptocurrency, and blockchain. Why should he? Most people in the world knew nothing about it.

"I'm not completely ignorant. I've heard of bitcoin, and blockchain."

"Sorry. I didn't mean to imply anything."

"I know. No offense taken. Since you think it's going to be part of our lives, tell me what I should know."

"I'll give you the highlights. I don't want to bore you, but remember," I cautioned him, "you asked for it."

"Don't be so dramatic."

"Okay then. There are about eight segments to it."

"Let's hear them."

"There is the cryptocurrency, blockchain technology, linked bank account, the wallet, a vault, trading site, trading tools, and crypto mining."

"That's it?" I nodded in agreement. "So, what do I do with it?"

"You'll have to become an expert in all segments."

"You know," he said, shaking his head. "You are crazy. The whole idea sounds crazy. No way in the world will people understand the concept, let alone the specifics."

"You, and everybody else in the world can shut your eyes, but believe me, it's coming, and coming soon."

"What about understanding banking ledgers, linking accounts, handling merchant transactions, creating wallets, and vaults, trading currency, buying, and selling, placing margins, and mining? No way!"

"It's what one needs to know." I realized that it was on, and above most people's understanding, let alone sphere of interests.

"Do you know all the parts?" he asked.

"I should. I traded in it."

It must have been a revelation to him. It showed with his response. "What?"

"I created all the parts, and bought currency."

"How come I didn't know?"

"Didn't want to discourage you. But," I enlightened him to ease his concerns, "there is help on the way."

"Explain."

"It's going to be automated. Completely. Banks and currency institutions will see to it. There will be no interaction between people and blockchain technology."

"Then," he challenged with a visible sigh, "I don't have to learn it?"

"That's right. It'll be an autonomous function to achieve one major function."

"I'm dying to hear."

"Complete security."

"What security?"

"Crime, hacking, theft protection."

"That'll be the day."

In my defense, banking and money institutions were already gearing up their internal accounting systems, currently awaiting government regulations and policies.

CHALLENGES BEYOND

As recollected throughout the earlier sections, *Volumes One*, and *Two*, whether brought on by myself or unforeseen events, my life has been filled with challenges. I should state that I thrive on challenges, otherwise, it would be a dull life for me. Where I was in control over my wellbeing for much of my life, aside from several health issues I had to struggle through, there had been times when life could have been cut short. Though I consider my life's journey in foreign lands colorful, and more rewarding as I had never anticipated at the onset, I would never allow letting my guard down, avoiding potential threats. Things had a way of happening at the most inappropriate times, and places. While much of my escapades were planned, and scheduled, mostly by the contracting office prior to departure, it was not always smooth sailing. I will cite several unexpected incidents that occurred out of my control.

During the height of the Vietnam War while supporting two Army Intel sites, onc up north near the DMZ with the other down south in the Mekong Delta, I flew in, and out of Vietnam on numerous occasions. The means of travel, and flight routes, usually on short notice, could be unpredictable. It could be a commercial airliner, or military transport delivering supplies for the war effort, mail to the troops, shuttle soldiers to their military assignments, or CIA agents to the frontlines. Where the main thrust of the war was directed to keep Chinese communists from taking over the south, the underlying war effort turned into a prolific drug trade, and weapons smuggling to fund other conflicts, such as the covert Iran-Contra affair.[75]

While one activity was clearly visible through the prolific use of drugs in Vietnam, the other, arms smuggling, was not because it took place within a different theater, the Middle East, with the Army transporting the illegal goods under management of the CIA. The drug of choice, opium at the time, though grown within the Golden Triangle, was mostly produced in Cambodia. It was usually the intermediate stopover for most flights in, and out of Vietnam. Landings were brief to load up cargo, but the takeoffs were always burdened by being overloaded. The first time I heard the sound on takeoff was jolting. Due to the short lengths of runways in such places, the pilots pulled the craft into a steep climb just short of the end of the runway. The resultant action was the tail of the craft dragging on runway asphalt, creating sparks, and smoke amid a metallic scraping sound alarming the passengers. But, with frequent flights, and over time, one got used to the unsettling occurrence, leaving one questioning the safety of the next flight, nevertheless.

The year was 1973. Buzz, and I were recalled from Europe for an assignment somewhere in Asia. To take advantage of our current location, Italy, since we had always wanted to visit the cradle of Christianity, Jerusalem, we decided to take a personal side trip to Israel to spend a few days strolling around historical sites. The flight was short, and uneventful until after we touched down in Tel Aviv one early morning. Expecting to head for the passenger terminal, instead we were shuttled to a

---

[75] Iran-Contra affair, in U.S. history, was a secret arrangement in the 1980s to provide funds to the Nicaraguan Contra rebels from profits gained by selling arms to Iran. The Iran-Contra affair was the product of two separate initiatives during the administration of President Ronald Reagan.

holding zone at the end of the runway. Before the pilot had a chance to announce the change in landing, the shooting began. It was here that we realized we had landed in the midst of a battle, later to be known as Yom Kippur War.[76]

While the battle may have been in the secret planning for the past months, we still found ourselves trapped at the airport for God only knew how long it would last. "See anything?" Buzz said, craning towards the window. Just after the craft landed, we were instructed by the pilot, enforced by the flight crew, to close all window shades. While I thought it was a customary practice, since Israel was prone to military conflicts, it turned out an alert situation beyond our knowledge.

Before our departure from the Army Intel site in Italy, I had noticed an increase in communication traffic on the site's monitoring screens, usually an indication, or forewarning of a potential military conflict. On the other hand, it could also be an annual wargame scheduled for the region. Depending on information sensitivity, the channel traffic could be in plain text, but was mostly encrypted to maintain government secrecy. In this case it was encrypted, thus preventing a forewarning of the developing events in which we had been trapped. I could have checked for current information with the crypto room, but since I was in a hurry to catch the flight, I did not.

Gradually, I nudged the window shade up a couple of inches to take a peek outside. I saw smoke amid the explosions we could hear from mortars going off nearby. The airport was under attack. Sweating it out in the airplane for the next eight hours, we were completely kept in the dark. It was the dark that finally came to our rescue. Since we were not permitted to exit into a battle situation, the airport authorities decided to let the flight depart in the darkness of night. It would be the end of our brief exposure to the Yom Kippur War. A brief account of the surprise attack on Israel can be found in Appendix I.

I was not a novice when it came to wars, and conflicts. There were numerous encounters I had come in contact with, and participated in. As a matter of fact, most of my activities were centered on conflicts, and emergency actions. While in the following years wars, for the most part, would slowly diminish, a new threat emerged on the modern world, the threat from Islamic extremists. The next decade would launch an unprecedented number of attacks on the Western world.

The date was 20 June, 1985, Frankfurt, Germany. I had arrived days earlier from England, reporting with RAF Intel, Upper Hayford, the first routine stops on my European service schedule. As specified by agreement, a five-year contracting obligation, the agenda was to lend my expertise, and technology skills to Intelligence centers in Europe, Asia, and the Pacific Rim. The second stop, my present European location, was to report in with the Army Intel center located forty-five miles southeast

---

[76] The Yom Kippur War, Ramadan War, or October War, also known as the 1973 Arab–Israeli War, was a war fought from October 6 to 25, 1973, by a coalition of Arab states led by Egypt, and Syria against Israel. The war mostly took place in Sinai, and the Golan—territories that had been occupied by Israel since the end of the 1967 Six-Day War—with some fighting in African Egypt, and northern Israel. Egyptian President Anwar Sadat's objectives were "to recover all Arab territory occupied by Israel following the 1967 war, and to achieve a just, peaceful solution to the Arab-Israeli conflict."

of the Frankfurt airport near the French border. Since it was a Friday, I took off early from the site location to meet my wife, who was scheduled to arrive from the U.S. I had made plans to meet her flight for her first time visit with my German family.

What I did not anticipate was the heavy morning traffic on the freeway streaming towards Frankfurt. Because of it, I fell behind schedule, but could not do anything about it. She would have to wait for me to get there. Anxiously, finally arriving at the airport, I parked my vehicle, jumped the shuttle, and headed directly for the Pan American arrival gate. The terminal was surprisingly quiet, but my mind sensed that something was not right when I heard distant emergency sirens from multiple sources headed for the arrival ports.

Hurried, and short on breath, I arrived at the Pan Am passenger arrival section then suddenly stopped short. I spotted a huge hole gaping in the floor, apparently ripped open by what appeared to be an explosion. It was not the only thing I spotted. People were strewn across the floor, covered in blood amid torn clothes, some wailing while others were silent. I had just walked in on the aftermath of a terrorist-initiated attack. What had saved my life was my late arrival after being delayed by commuter traffic.

I could not get any information from Pan Am staff other than an explosion had occurred just minutes before my arrival, and I was told that police, and emergency services had been alerted. "What about arrival flights?" I asked.

"Air traffic is put on hold," I was informed. I could breathe easier knowing that my wife was safe. About the same time, the place turned from hushed silence to chaotic pandemonium within seconds. Uniforms rushed in from every entrance, seeking out injured, and possible terrorist suspects. It took some time for the place to calm, and get organized. My wife's flight touched down an hour later before I met up with her. "What's going on?" she said, concerned about the delayed arrival, uninformed about the events.

"Terrorist attack," I said, watching her face turn ashen. "You could have been killed, if your flight had arrived on time."

"What about you?"

"We both could be laying here dead." I conveyed to her the situation I saw on my arriving here. "BOMB AT FRANKFURT AIRPORT KILLS 3, and WOUNDS 42," the headlines read hours later in a special report with the New York Times, and Frankfurt Times newspapers. "A powerful bomb ripped through an international departure lounge of the Frankfurt Airport, killing three people, and wounding 42, according to the police. There was no immediate claim of responsibility. The bombing came as world attention has been centered on the hijacking drama that started last Friday when Lebanese Shiite gunmen seized a T.W.A. airliner after takeoff from Athens. But various police spokesmen declined to link the two events. The explosive device, which the police said appeared to have been placed among seated passengers waiting for their flights, shattered glass windows, and tore a three-foot hole in the cement floor in the airport terminal, one of the world's busiest."

My next encounter with terrorist activities was a few months later, 27 December, 1985. It was early in the morning. I had just arrived at Rome's Da Vinci airport via a local commuter flight from Pisa, during my scheduled visit working with U.S. Army Intel,

Italy. With my checked-in luggage in transit back to the U.S., the only burden I carried was my briefcase. Impatiently waiting at the end of the line at the TWA[77] departure gate, I noticed the departure desk vacant with the ramp entrance locked up.

"Where's the ground crew?" I asked one passenger in the line waiting anxiously to depart. The flight was already thirty minutes behind departure schedule without any indication for cause or reason.

"Crew locked the gate, and left minutes ago."

"Strange," I muttered, contemplating what to do. I was not going to wait in line amid four hundred passengers getting restless without being informed about the strange departure delay. I decided on acting, and headed from the end of the line directly for the departure desk. It was then when the ramp door opened, and a ticket agent entered from the departure ramp. I watched her rush to the desk to fetch her valise. I yelled at her, "What's going on?"

"Flight is cancelled," she yelled back, promptly reentering the departure ramp, shutting the gate after her. I sensed something was seriously wrong. It forced me into caution. I slammed my briefcase on the counter, leaped across the desk, grabbed my case, and rushed for the departure ramp. A few strides later I was desperately knocking at the locked gate. To my surprise, the agent, who identified herself as departure control, opened up with a surprised look on her face, demanding, "Who are you?"

"Government," I replied, flashing my DOD credentials in front of her face.

"Come," she said, locking the exit gate once more, and rushed me down the ramp towards the airliner's entrance. I could hear the engines revving up preparing for an immediate departure. The ramp was still attached to the craft with us rushing up, banging at the entrance door. Seconds late, a flight attendant opened it, and peeked through the doorframe, insisting, "The flight is closed." Ready to close the door again, I shoved my body in the frame, and demanded, "I've got to be on the flight."

She hesitated a second then waved me in. "Take a seat." The gate was shut tight, the ramp retracted with the pilot accelerating the craft headed for the runway. Minutes later we were airborne. Aside from the crew, I was the only passenger in the B-747 jumbo jet. As soon as the craft reached cruising altitude, the alert lights went off. I headed for the purser, the crew's supervisor. "Where're we going?"

"Cannes, France."

"What about the passengers?"

"You are it," I was informed.

"I want some information," I demanded. Here, I spotted another passenger seated up front in first class.

"Talk to him," I was advised.

Somewhat dumbfounded, I headed in that direction. I had to find out.

"Hi," I said, then introduced myself.

The passenger, a distinguished-looking gentleman, well groomed, graying temples, ready to take a sip from a Martini he'd just been served, extended his hand, and said, "Ed Acker, CEO, Pan Am.[78] Have a seat. Who are you?"

---

[77] Trans World Airline, the second largest airline back then.

[78] Charles Edward Acker (born April 7, 1929) was an American businessman who served as CEO of Braniff Airways, Air Florida, and was appointed in 1982 to serve as CEO for Pan American World Airways.

It may have seemed rather unusual for a CEO to fly a competitive airliner unless one was familiar with world travel. In the early days of international air travel there were two airline companies, Pan Am, and TWA, both offering around the world flights. Though both captured world routes, each started out in the opposite directions, with one departing from San Francisco, and the other from New York City. If a passenger booked a flight to Europe, it was through TWA. If it was a Pacific flight, it was with Pan Am. I had taken the flights many times, and could make the call which airliner to book a flight with, while the home office arranged the final itinerary. My decision was one of convenience, or travel time.

"Civilian DOD contractor," I said, explaining my unexpected presence. "I've got to get back to DC." Surprisingly, probably due to the unusual circumstances, he understood, then explained the abrupt departure from Rome.

"My office received an anonymous call this morning that Da Vinci was about to get hit by terrorists."

"Wow," I responded, somewhat speechless.

"I happened to be at the airport when I was informed. There was no time for passenger boarding. I was instructed to depart immediately."

"You know," I informed him, "you left four hundred passengers stranded."

"It couldn't be helped. I was directed to leave. I am head of the company."

"How real do you think the call was, and why Cannes?"

"The closest airport outside Italy. We'll land there to await instructions."

While an inconvenience to my regular schedule following the European Intel tour, I did not mind the stopover. I had been to France's renowned vacation resort before, and could easily book a flight back to the States from there. Discussing current international events with him we arrived approximately one hour later at the destination. Whether the cockpit crew was informed while in flight, or not of the attack, the monitor headlines on our arrival read:

"Seven Arab terrorists attacked two airports in Rome, Italy, and Vienna, Austria with assault rifles, and hand grenades. Nineteen civilians were killed, and over a hundred others were injured before four of the terrorists were killed by El Al Security personnel, and local police, who captured the remaining three."

"Those poor people," Acker muttered, grieving. His hands shook while wiping his eyes dry with a napkin. He may have been a hardened executive with one of the country's major corporations, but like many people when in tragedies, he still became emotional.

"Don't blame yourself," I consoled him. "Terrorists are unpredictable." We were seated at the airport lounge waiting our return flight bookings. The TWA flight was on hold, waiting for instructions about when to return to Rome. In the meantime, we, and the crew were having drinks at the lounge, speculating what could have taken place at the Da Vinci airport. Shortly after, the headlines carried on the TV monitor presented the details:

"At 08:15 GMT, four Arab gunmen walked to the shared ticket counter for Israel's El Al Airlines, and Trans World Airlines at Leonardo da Vinci-Fiumicino Airport outside Rome, Italy, fired assault rifles, and threw grenades, killing 16, and wounding 99, including American diplomat Wes Wessels. Three of the attackers were killed by El Al security, while the remaining one, Mohammed Sharam, was wounded, and captured by the Italian police. The dead include General Donato Miranda Acosta, Mexican military attaché, and his secretary, Genoveva Jaime Cisneros.

"Minutes later, at Schwechat Airport (Vienna International Airport), Austria, three terrorists carried out a similar attack. Hand grenades were thrown into crowds of passengers queuing to check in for a flight to Tel Aviv, killing two people instantly, and wounding 39 others. First response came from several Austrian police officers, which opened fire on the terrorists. They were supported by two El Al security guards who helped to repel the attackers. Over 200 bullets were fired during the fight. The terrorists fled by car, and Austrian police, and El Al security guards gave chase. They killed one terrorist, and captured the other two."

"In all," the reporter concluded, "the two strikes killed 19, including a child, and wounded 140 others." It also claimed the gunmen intended to hijack jets at the airports, and blow them up over Tel Aviv.

"Oh God," Acker wailed out again. "I'm to blame for the dead."

"No, you're not," I insisted. "You may have saved many lives. Imagine if they had gotten their hands on the flights. We would have all been doomed. I should thank you for saving my life." I reached out, and shook his hand in gratitude as we watched the aftermath at the very airport terminal, we had left behind just minutes before the attack.

A flight attendant stepped up to hand us our tickets for flights back to the States, his to New York, mine to DC.

"Look me up if you're ever in the city," he offered, shaking my hand. "Anytime."

"I will," I promised, but we never crossed path again. Terrorist activities, though started in 1972, with the Munich massacre, had been on the increase in the years to follow. In addition, with the arrival of the Airbus, flying had taken a turn from predominantly business, and luxury flights to moving people, crammed into economy seating, squeezing more, and more profits from a booming air travel business.

INSPIRATIONS

When I set out as a young person in my life's journey I was filled with expectations. There was not a master plan I had developed. It was not even an orderly schedule. Like most of us, I tackled life's challenges one step at a time. One had to experience the decisions we made, and live with the consequences, the good, and the bad. It is the only means to learn about life, joys, and tragedies. It is said that one has to experience tragedy in order to learn, and not repeat mistakes. It held true with the job, as well as life's situations, which brings me to an element I have heard many times, "coincidence."

"There are no coincidences," some insisted. It puzzled me why one would claim this specific element had no merit.

"Coincidence," as described in Miriam Webster's Dictionary. "The occurrence of events that happen at the same time by accident, but seem to have some connection."

On close inspection, one has to believe in it. I will present two examples for why there is coincidence.

1. Imagine Mary living in Dallas wanting to visit her sister who lives in Denver. Halfway there, another driver sped through a red light, causing an accident. While Mary was injured, the other driver was killed. The question is, "Did Mary plan to kill the other driver, or was it a coincidence?"

2. An airliner takes off from New York Kennedy airport headed for Rome, Italy. It was summertime, and the flight was packed with 450 vacationers all originating from different places, but planning to spent time in Rome. Several hours into the flight total engine failure occurred. The pilot could not recover the flight, with a resultant crash into the ocean. Everybody perished. The question is, "Did God mean to seek out, and target each, and every passenger to be killed, or was it purely based on coincidence?"

I will let the reader decide. Back to my life's journey. There are still unanswered questions: Who am I? What is my personality? What does life mean to me? What were the critical moments, and important events that have impacted my life? What is my future outlook like? Not only did it take many years of living, and learning to form the person I presently am, every moment was recorded, processed, and stored in the brain.

"Who am I?"

I am not much different from everybody else. I wake up in the morning, head for the bathroom, shower, shave, brush teeth, groom hair, put on shirt, slip into pants one leg at a time, pull on socks, slippers and off I go into a world filled with possibilities. Where I slightly differ from others is in personality, habits, and activities. Depending on one's age, and status, whether attached to an active workforce, or retired, a day's activity has a wide range. Much like with politics, from the extreme right to extreme left, or somewhere in between.

My outlook was somewhere in the middle. It was a safe position. It left a margin in my expectations, open to explore, providing there were personal opportunities with an open mindset for adventure. I like to use adventure to start with. It may not turn out that way for everybody starting out. For some it may be an escapade. For others an exploit, quest, venture, or journey. It's where personality, and ambition came into play.

Setting out on my quest, I had no idea how it would turn out other than the desire to explore the world, my childhood dream. To equate, I recall a quote from the world of business where the question frequently surfaced: "I was lucky to get the job," or "how lucky could one get?"

Luck, in this matter, had nothing to do with it. The answer was plain, and simple, "Luck is when opportunity meets preparation." But for the sake of this writing I shall refer to it as luck.

Whether it was a result of God, a fluke, windfall, blessing, or a break, would be a matter of circumstances one could also call karma. But karma did not come into play at the start of life. Karma has to be earned. Regardless of my calling, I had been presented with all of the results stated above. I had been presented with every break one could attain whether it was a plain job, career opportunity, or prospecting lifestyle.

Right from the onset of my career I could just as well have become an industrial slave, the prevalent environmental conditions at the time. But instead, I was groomed to become a leader to rebuild the German industry after its total collapse following the second World War. It was a promise any sane person would have jumped at, but it was not good enough for me. I had a different goal in mind. My target was the world, a world of unlimited opportunities I sought out, and was headed for.

Arriving in the new world, the United States of America, luck followed me throughout my career. I was given first choice whenever there was an advancement for promotion. I never had to ask for a pay raise. I never had to report through the chain of command. I was always directly attached to either a military commander, or corporate executive. In either case it was a connection to the decision makers. Right from the start, management realized the criticality of my position. I did not have the luxury to waste time reporting through various levels of management for a decision. My direct connection was to the top. In case of deciding an issue, from a technical perspective, I could not expect any answers from anyone. The solution originated with me. There was nobody I could ask, or consult with unless it was a strategic decision for timeline, and scheduling. Delays happen with most projects, but my team, and I were never the source. It was always external forces beyond our control.

"What is my personality?"
I consider myself well balanced. I have never had any mental, or psychological issues unless caused by a severe health condition. There, I had my share of setbacks. Probably due to the environment I operated in, foreign countries, jungles, cultures susceptible to unhealthy living conditions, I contacted several of the strangest diseases one could encounter that I will list in the next volume section titled, "Personal Issues."

No matter where, or what my intentions were, I preferred a quiet environment. To demonstrate, I attended one concert in my life. It was Pink Floyd's "Millenia" tour I caught in Denver. While totally enjoying the five hours of being entertained by one for the world's renown bands, I could not get involved with the masses standing on chairs waving, and shouting from the top of their lungs. I figured out what my problem was afterwards; I did not have any prior alcohol, or drugs to get involved. It was a lesson learned for the next concert that, unfortunately, never materialized.

But not all was lost. Fortunately for man's technical advancements, multimedia entertainment was born. On most Saturday evenings, if I stayed home, I could catch a major concert televised either on MTV or AXS. It was the reason I had three sound systems interconnected with the channel source. When activating sense surround with the push of the button, a second later my home rocked to the waves of the sound. Fortunately, where I live, I had ample space not to interfere with my neighbors. I live in a residential area mostly populated by Air Force retirees in a wooded area interspersed with trees, and bushes. What I like most about it is wildlife such as deer with occasional bears and bobcats crossing properties. As a matter of fact, the first three years after I moved in, a family of bear took to hibernating beneath the dense hedges surrounding the house. I realized it was not the safest condition, and eventually trimmed the wall of hedges. Three weeks later, I had groomed them all into bonsai trees. Bears still showed up in the fall, but stride on, searching for a more secluded spot to hibernate through winters.

As far as my personality was concerned, except for Saturday evenings, I am a quiet person. In recent years, I have distanced myself from crowded places, malls, and commuter traffic. I do not want any part of road rage, and potential stampedes people are susceptible to in case of an unexpected calamity. With shootings, and killings being part of our current lifestyle, I try to schedule my activities in the safest manner by keeping distant. The reason is not out of fear, it is common sense. Where I could easily hold my own in case of a firing exchange, the consequences are too great for getting involved with the law. Most people don't think on those terms in the heat of an argument. One must ask oneself, "Is it worth going to jail because of somebody else's insanity?"

My life was not always as organized, and planned. For many years my activities took place at the frontlines of conflicts. Though not actively involved directly in a battle, I lent mission support through upkeep in vital, and classified communication, not far off, but always protected by a squadron of special forces. In a case, where soldiers would take the direct hits from the enemy, I watched the battle scenes from the distance, at times ducking, and dodging incoming rounds exploding nearby. I am mostly referring to my times in Vietnam. As for the Gulf War, and other conflicts, my position was in the safety at the Homefront, supporting the development of battle gear, and computer systems destined to the fronts.

But for the most part, my position was at one of a number of Intel sites located through Europe, Asia, and the Pacific Rim managed either by Naval, Air Force, Army, or DOD Intelligence forces.

From a personal point of view, I consider myself a peaceful individual unless provoked. If provoked, or backed into a corner for any reason, I come out fighting. I do not know from what recesses my internal rage originates, but it had to lurk somewhere within my usually well controlled, and well managed being.

"What does life mean to me?"

Life to me is the most precious commodity nature has to offer. I live it daily to its fullest within my health, and strength capacities. Filled with boundless energy during my younger years, whether on the job, or personal time, I applied myself to any given challenge life, and leisure threw at me. I treated everybody with equal quality of respect. I cannot recall one instance where I disrespected anybody, or abused somebody. In my eyes, everybody, whether rich or poor, privileged or deprived, weak or strong, deserved equal treatment. I, in return, expected the same. However, I was not a Samaritan that could be taken advantage of. I recognized dishonorable intentions in an ill-intentioned individual immediately, and maintained my distance. I knew my capabilities for retaliation if harm was directed at me. There were two potential causes for my retaliation, the taking of personal belongings, and accusations of wrongdoing.

I had experienced both on a few occasions. In each case, I confronted the evildoer with dire consequences dished out at him. It was a win-win either way for me. An apology, or fight, I would come out ahead. For much of my career, due to rigorous martial arts training, I was at the peak of strength, and agility, awarded with a win when confronted by an opponent.

Not bad a record, coming out unscathed every time.

It seemed that I could manage my human equal to my advantage, if called on. It was not the case with the invisible threat from microorganisms, and viruses. I had my bouts, but lost the fight each time, enduring with dire consequences.

The motto I lived by is: "Equal opportunity, and justice for all." In the modern world, my world, they are two important values assured by birthright. Everybody should be given the same right. After all, we did not live in tumultuous ancient days, medieval times, and imperialistic suppressed ages anymore. People living in the Western world today are educated enough not to fall prey to any such dominating power.

Those are the conditions I expect from anybody whether disciplined by the individual, a ruling class, or the government. Unfortunately, they are not always values being honored. As a matter of fact, misuse of these two prized values has rather became the norm today. I feel it my duty to work towards helping to restore these values. I am not the only one harboring such strong conviction. There are many activists on the frontlines of protests demanding equality. There is no doubt that at the end, justice will prevail.

"What were the critical moments, and important events that had impacted my life?"
Right from birth my life was impacted by being born into a world of hardship, and turmoil. I was not singled out. Everybody in the war-torn country was affected. However, it greatly impacted my way of thinking, and consequential actions with lasting personality traits, some good, others not. In retrospect on analyzing my life, it did not matter much. I came out ahead.

The second critical moment came when my mother died. She was my mentor, tutor, and protector through my early years of existence. I directly inherited her decency, and morality. She came from the aristocratic backdrop region of Prussia, the city of Leipzig, specifically. To distance themselves from the ravages of WWI, her family moved to Zurich, Switzerland, an independent sovereign nation. It was there where she met my father. Having been bestowed with dual citizenship she wound up living in southern Germany, where Dad was employed as an industrial engineer building dirigible airship during the pre-war years. Her decision would prove fatal for her. Like many citizens during the time she became a war casualty.

Heartbroken, and confused, I grew up with relatives for the most part thereafter. My life did not solidify until I was offered a scholarship with the one remaining aircraft company, Dornier, where my dad also worked. It was there where my life took on shape for an unimaginable future.

Other critical moments were many, as already illustrated through the many chapters in this book, and either shaped my future, or guided me through a rich, and colorful life. Provided ample career choices, whether through government, or privately related contracting opportunities only few individuals would attain, I felt my life guided by a higher force. The reason I felt this way was through my foreign accent restraints, susceptible to national security scrutiny. Notwithstanding many unexpected events, this flaw in inflection, inherited by birth, and growing up in German, did not greatly impact my career, and life.

Since I am of sound mind, and character, I should emphasize once more that the accounts described in this book are as factual as I could recall with individuals I interacted depicted throughout the book, equally factual.

"What does my future look like?"
Where many, after only one successful career, would disregard this question as part of their personal history, I still consider future career possibilities. It would not be in an active engineering or managing capacity. It would most likely be in an advisory, or consulting position. I have had my share of on-call emergencies, extended working hours, and commuter traffic to last the rest of my life. What I do miss is team spirit, and travel. I miss leading teams into the frontlines of actions directed through an unequaled social bond while away from home. I miss the individual adventure spirit that came with each trip when setting foot on foreign soil. I miss interacting with the diversity of foreign customs, and cultures, their peoples, and places. I have been to the world's most unusual and, in many cases, most beautiful places on Earth, providing exhilarating experiences.

In a way, I could invoke such a life at my own choosing. Since listing my resume, and career accomplishments on the business community, LinkedIn, I receive constant offers for contracting opportunities. The reason I am holding off on any commitment is the need for a right fit. To satisfy my needs, whether in my personal life or career, I need challenges. Perhaps with the promised budget allocation by the government for a cyberspace force, I can explore the possibility for my next business venture.

For the time being, my space is occupied with completing the current, as well as writing future novels, as my enthusiastic, and dedicated reader audience commands. I strongly feel that maintaining an active, and healthy state is through exercising mind, and body. I do my share for the mind through writing and, depending on the season, either ride my bicycle on the trail, or visit the fitness center for a workout.

POLITICAL ASSESSMENT

Rather than getting bogged down with political issues, I will briefly describe the conditions that shape governments, and politics. There is no comfortable means to discuss either faction without getting into personal arguments since everybody has either an inherited, or acquired, strongly-devoted opinion on both. From my own experience, it takes an earthshaking event to make one change their personal stand. It is this reasoning why most people maintain their distance from conferring on this most sensitive topic even with their spouse, family, and friends unless subscribing to the same political party. The same sentiments are prevalent with religion, and faith.

"Hey," Buzz greeted when I led him in. "What's happening?" He was as pleasant as ever seeing me as I was seeing him. He was such a welcomed incentive for my mind.

"Glad you could come over. It's been a while."

"Any news with the Cyberforce?" I had shared my business desires with him on several occasion, and offered him participation on such future possibilities, but he'd declined with, "I am done working. I enjoy my retirement."

Regardless of his present response, I hoped that he would change his mind with an appropriate compensation offer, once the time came. For today, since there were no pressing issues, it was going to be just another verbal session. Government, and politics presented ample opportunities for it.

"Tell me," Buzz prodded. "What could you do better in forming the government if you had the chance?"

"Wow," I groaned, surprised at his choice. "That's quite a bag full." What bag, and what filler substance I did not explain. What I did was present the elements for the needs of a government.

"We need a government to protect us from foreign invasions, meaning to provide for the common defense. We need the government to manage the exchange of money, goods, and trade with other countries, meaning to promote the general welfare. The purpose of a government is to provide for the safety, and protection of the citizens, and maintaining social order, policing streets to ensure people obey the laws of society." Those were the four basic reasons.

"You mean to say," he objected, "it was a preconceived plan through the ages?"

"Not at all. It came on gradually with the needs of society." I had my own ideas. It was human nature to gather into groups. People got together for security. As a result, families formed. Then settlements developed with towns soon followed by cities. It did not take long to divide into districts, neighborhoods, and corporate parks. "That's basically the public process."

"What about the government?"

"Similar process, but more focused."

"Explain," Buzz demanded. He knew very well what it took to manage people. But he wanted to hear my part.

"Every culture, every group, every distinction, to become effective, needs to be managed." The first step was seeking growth. The government was no exception. First, organizations are created, followed by specific agencies. Everything, everybody desires to grow. Soon, the inevitable developed in wealth, followed by greed, and eventually culminated into power, the ultimate goal. Once power was achieved, money was not of much importance. It became a biproduct of individual greed. "That's my take on the subject."

Whether one adapted to the concepts readily depended solely on which side of the front one entered the system. Governments were a vital necessity for any community. They created a sound authority to balance individual control for power, manage people's demands, and to maintain social order. The problem was to effectively manage not only the citizens, but the government body itself as well.

It angers me each time I think of, or have to watch the government either making excuses or accusing each other for the lack of initiative, finding more reasons not to implement an order rather than solving a problem. For eighteen years already we had been involved in conflicts, and wars nobody wanted, and nobody seemed to win. Effort of wars were shifted from nation to nation much like in business where responsibilities were handed off to another department when the budget dwindled. It appeared that Russia, and other superpowers, much like the United States, had taxation issues when budgets ran dry. What made it worse was ineffective government administration.

On the national scale, people were afraid of losing their jobs, or being unable to find one for similar reasons. While the Treasury took in record amounts of money from the working people, it kept outspending its income. It was no wonder that anger could be spotted through all civilian ranks. The only worry-free faces seemed to be the political, and government employed.

Our anger should be directed less at politicians, though justifiable, but more at ourselves for expecting more from the government than it could deliver. When the Founders pursued liberty, their intention was not only liberation from an oppressive English monarchy, but liberty for themselves, and their posterity. With liberty came responsibility.

We have not made efficient use of it while blaming the wrong people. The politicians care mostly about their careers. They will increasingly provide public benefits in exchange for votes. Republicans, much like their opposition, promised to end the insane spending, or at least slow it, but have done little to reduce the deficit, consequently directing anger at Republicans.

Democrats have not reduced poverty, or elevated the middle class, despite record amounts of spending on anti-poverty programs, and empty promises to support those who languish between wealth, and poverty. In contrast, both factions managed to almost eradicate the production force of the nation, the middle class.

No matter how many promises are made, and how many good intentions there are from politicians, we seem to elect the wrong candidates. Perhaps there are no righteous ones left in the nation. Everybody may be absorbed into the prevailing system without being given an opportunity to make things right again for the citizens.

The Constitution was written to put boundaries on government, and provide the maximum amount of liberty under the law to its citizens. Government has become dysfunctional because it has exceeded its constitutional boundaries. That is why liberals, and conservatives are discontent, though for different reasons. The left wants more of what was not working, and the right wants less, but are unable to obtain it because it requires self-examination. Where is the Budget Amendment Task Force?

Franklin Roosevelt, who, more than any other U.S. president, expanded the power, and cost of government, stated in 1938: "Let us never forget that government is ourselves, and not an alien power over us. The ultimate rulers of our democracy are not a president, and senators, and congressmen, and government officials, but the voters of this country."

"So," I said, facing my buddy. "What's your take on it?"

"I couldn't agree more." Buzz, while a resourceful individual, was a man of few words. As long as he was not protesting, everything I said made sense. With all of the sound advice people had, and people voiced, much of it fell on deaf ears. "But," he clarified, "it still leaves the issue of unresponsive management. What would it take to finally solve the problem?"

I, as usual, had the solution. "War."

"More wars?"

"Yes, more wars. But not to get involved with a foreign country. To shake up our own complacency."

"What do you mean by *our own*?" he challenged. "I would support any movement that was in favor of straightening out our leadership."

"We are just as much at fault as our honored policymakers."

"You better explain." It was not often that I saw Buzz's anger well up. He took offensive when his integrity was questioned. He was as balanced as I was.

"We let liberals take over for making decisions for both government and conservatives. It was their reasons for creating a bigger government, allowing as many social services as taxpayers would tolerate."

"It's too late now. They would never give up their power base." Buzz had hit the nail on the head.

"It's never too late," I countered. "Remember," I reminded him. "Luck is when opportunity meets preparation."

PERSONAL HEALTH ISSUES

On Psychic Views

Have you ever wondered about the success rate of the many psychics walking among us with overinflated claims? No matter what media one watches, or what city block one strolls, psychics, with their propositions, seem to be on the increase. What I could not understand is that people fall prey to their prolific claims. When questioning their predictions, the answer was an unwavering, "But many of my predictions have come through."

My response would be, "What do you mean by many? If you are a true psychic all of your predictions must come true; otherwise, you are just another opportunist."

To further their defense follow-up excuses would be, "the future can change" or "you made a different choice."

Regardless of excuses, neither are acceptable to this author. A true psychic foretells the future no matter what the world has in store for you. It always irks me when I heard such nonsense. That left the question, "What is a psychic, and what are their responsibilities?"

Can you trust a Psychic?

I recently came across an article, rather a definition, for a psychic's self-analysis, and could not agree more. I thought it important to share it with the reader. It may prevent future scamming of the innocent. We all need help and guidance along life's path. Depending on your situation, some may ask friends, colleagues, or professionals for assistance. Asking help is not a bad thing and consulting a psychic might be an enlightening experience. Still it is never a good idea to just blindly trust others. Nobody is perfect. We all have problems and sometimes we do not have an answer.

Some things to keep in mind if you want to consult a psychic.

1) Do they have the answer?

Even in modern days of science and technology there are urgent questions about life we do not have a common agreement on. So, making mistakes is human. Psychics are human too. Never forget that. Most are nice people with the right intentions, but do not consider them above yourself.

2) Selecting a psychic.

Wherever there is advertising space you will find a medium that offers to help you with all your problems. First thing one should know is the rule that quality needs no advertising. It is not because a psychic has a bigger add that she/he is better. It only indicates that she/he has a larger budget to spend. This brings us to the charges. How much are you willing to pay? A higher price might not guarantee a better reading. There are many frauds in the business from people who think they can make easy money.

Not everybody with a sixth sense has the capacities to use it to help others. Some may only believe they have the blessings for a reading, but would be better off when consulting, or provide psychological assistance. Then, there are the fraudulent who know they are not gifted, but are in business to make easy money. Be aware of many who offer a free reading, or minimal charge, but ask too much information up front.

3) Checking a psychic's reputation.
You may want to seek testimonials from other clients to judge if a psychic is right for you. The Internet and blogs are a good source, but beware of the psychic's websites. Read what others write, or say about a psychic. It is better to look elsewhere, such as reference books and trusted literatures for a reliable source. Also, trust your individual instinct.

Be aware of personal, bloated announcements when reading blogs and websites. It may be a fraudulent indication. Some psychics have no scruples, and are only in business to take an unsuspecting client's money. It may say nothing about the quality, or character of a medium. Anybody with the right paperwork to start a business can be an official psychic or medium.

4) How to recognize a good psychic.
The best practice for you is by listening to your own gut feeling. Good psychics do not have to sell their services. It comes natural through word of mouth, and client references. Be aware of those that guarantee too much and ask too much for their services. Check around for testimonials on who might be recommended. Good psychics might not always have the answers, but will be honest enough to let you know.

Keep in mind what you want to set out to know. Psychics have different talents. Those who are great communicators with access to spirits of the dead, might be able to help you contacting a dear beloved one on the other side, but may be unable to provide help and advice about choices that might affect your future.

Be specifically aware of fortune tellers. Nobody can efficiently predict the future. If so, all fortune tellers would be rich from winning lottery tickets. However, it will be up to the individual assessing the power of the human spirit. Never trust blindly whoever claims to know your future. But some talented psychics may give you sound advise on how to solve your problems using their personal skills. A tarot deck, for example, can give great insight in a person's life, as long as you can believe it.

Good astrologers and numerologist may give indications on future trends or events about to happen. It may be an indication for things to come, but does not provide a guarantee for your personal success, or positive outcome. What most individuals do not realize is that life depends on many factors, not only pertinent to the individual, or yourself.

To cite an example: a psychic may point out that you have great quality leadership, and may be well qualified for a more responsible, and better paid job. It may be an indication that you should apply for it, but the psychic might not be unable to read the mind of your present, or potential employer if she, or he is unwilling to give you the promotion.

5) What to keep in mind?
With advice you are willing to seek for events concerning your future, do not blindly trust just any adviser. Any genuine psychic will admit their limitations for their

inherited skills to possibly solve your problem. When claim differently, they might only be out to get your money. Keep in mind that only a fraud will guarantee their work, and will tell you whatever you want to hear.

A cautionary advice: If your visit is for a real health problem, do not seek out a psychic's advice without consulting a physician. In contrast, any reputable psychic will be able to boost your self-confidence and help you with problems by suggesting possible solutions. It is their calling and will charge you for it. But keep in mind that a caring psychic needs to make a living as well, but will most likely not charge more than a doctor's appointment and certainly not more than a life-saving surgery.

Also keep in mind that Psychics are only human, and are not miracle workers. Maintaining a sound combination between an open mind and a sceptic attitude will allow for a trusting relationship with anyone you may consult for your future.

As the reader can see there was no definitive answer to any question posed to a psychic. Where some advice made sense to me, it did not address or clarify my own paranormal experiences with psychics or mediums. I will briefly explain my dilemma, as I have already told in detail in the autobiography section of this work.

In brief, in 1972, I was living in Korea for a couple of years. Through a friend, I met a woman in her forties, at the time Korea's most renown psychic medium, and clairvoyant. She would give readings at the U.S. officer's club once a month. Because of her success rate, she gained fame with U.S. officers, and servicemen alike. I was more fortunate. My friend, and the psychic had been close friends for many years.

I should point out that fortune telling was a way of life in Korea. For example, a businessman, and store merchant would stop by a psychic in the morning before headed for the office for a daily reading. If, for instance, the reading for the day was favorable, the person would proceed to their place of business. If, on the other hand, the business prognosis was poor, the person would stay home, and not bother to show up to conduct business. This was how entrenched fortune telling was in the culture.

One evening, my friend arranged a private reading session for me. Because of her fame, I had expected it to be at a mansion, or affluent home. Instead, we arrived at a somewhat scanty dwelling in a poor neighborhood. She played host for about ten minutes, as was customary in Korea, and we were treated to tea, and rice cake. Shortly after, the woman began the first session by reading my palm. The next session was reading tea leaves, followed with a lengthy chanting. All in all, we spent four hours at her place. Our departure was accompanied by promises to see her soon again.

The basic session was a reading for the next five years, as I had requested. At the time, I placed no values on fortune telling, and palm reading. From my logical perspective, it was pure nonsense. It was mostly on my part from having been completely ignorant of the spiritual realm, which in my mind did not exist.

The resultant session revealed several predictions for the following five years. What was amazing was that all came true in due time, without exception. Each time, when I was confronted by the next event, I was reminded of the psychic reading. It was enough for me to become a believer. What still bothers me immensely was my inability to break through the curtain of the spiritual realm, something I may never achieve since my mind is constructed mostly to understand the logical world.

I went back to Korea twice afterwards to seek out the psychic. Unfortunately, she went into seclusion, and quit giving readings. The reason, I was told, was that she could not deal any longer with the hardship, and trauma destiny would place on her clients.

Again, in brief, my next experience came with a second psychic two years later. She happened to be the mother of my future wife, as predicted years earlier in Korea. Again, the prediction came true, but this time occurred in the Philippines, also predicted years earlier in Korea. Though a first-time visitor, I was welcomed, and treated without reservations. To show my gratitude to the host, I made the announcement, "I'll invite everybody to the beach tomorrow." A day on the beach was a special treat for the young. Amid the unexpected excitement all agreed except the mother, the matron of the home, the psychic, who proclaimed, "You don't want to go to the beach tomorrow."

Startled, I looked at her, and demanded, "Why not?"

"You will get sick." It was all I could get from her. Whether it was her limited skills with English or other reasons, she maintained her silence with me for the rest of the day. Around midnight I bade my goodbye, and turned in at a nearby hotel I was staying at. I showed up the next morning at the house. To my surprise, no children were present. "Where is everybody?" I asked the mother. I had decided the previous day to rent three jeepneys, a local mode of transportation, to accommodate the lot to the beach. The vehicles were there, but that was it. I retained one jeep for myself, my friend, and his lady friend. Twenty minutes later we arrived at the beach in utter surprise. There was nobody there. The city's most popular beach resort was completely vacant. I dispatched the driver to return early that afternoon to pick us up.

I had the entire beach for myself, and made use of it. I went for a swim. By then it was close to noon. Thirty minutes later I returned fully exhausted. I made it half way up the sandy slope, and collapsed. An immense desire for sleep overtook my will to stay awake. About two hours later, my friend's voice woke me from sleep. "What happened to you? You are all sunburnt."

My face, and body were blistering red, and painful to the touch. "We better get you to a doctor," he suggested. My condition worsened over the next several hours. In addition to the burn, I could not feel my toes, and soles anymore. Walking became difficult without the sense of balance. I decided to cut my visit short, and head back to Manila.

BACK IN COLORADO

Twelve years earlier, the year was 2007. The reasons I was forced to move back to Colorado Springs were two-fold. First, after closing the business in Silicon Valley, without an income, I needed a place I could make a living until the economy picked up again. With a cost of living at the highest in the nation, California was not the place. Second, because of career, and business demanding my full attention, initially through contracting followed by corporate commitments, over the decades, I had neglected my health. On the surface I may have displayed a sound body and mind, but beneath the surface, I was physically struggling to keep up the daily pace. My right knee was splintered, with leg damaged involved in an automobile accident from years earlier. I desperately needed a hernia operation in addition to some physical therapy on my back, and shoulder. Without health insurance coverage, and with medical cost overruns in California, one day, to the disappointment of my daughters, I packed up, and left for Colorado with a promise, "I'll be back."

As it'd turned out, I was able to find a home in the same neighborhood where I had lived years earlier. It was a community built for retired Air Force personnel that graduated from the Air Force Academy, and on retiring, returned to settle there. Even today, presenting ample greenery, and wildlife, it is a preferred region to live for anyone seeking a spacious home.

Though somewhat dated, the settlement having been built in late 70s, the home had potential once I renovated the interior. The structure was sound, but needed new carpeting, thermal windows, and interior and exterior paint in addition to new appliances from utility room to the kitchen. Landscaping, I would find out during the first winter, also became necessary. I'd found my new castle, but there was work to be done. With renovation on the mind, I unloaded the moving van into the garage for storage while putting up a temporary sleeping spot on the lower level. My plan was to start renovating the place from the top on down to the lowest floor of the 4-level split home.

Calling on contractors for estimates on carpeting, windows, interior, and exterior replacements prior to getting started, I was required to get an approval from the homeowner's association, and a construction permit issued by the county, when I came across a major obstacle. A title search on the property revealed a dilemma that would hound me for the next nine months. I had become victim of the current economic collapse, better known as sub-prime lending, or the housing collapse of 2008. The title could not be located, consequently forcing me into a quagmire. I became a squatter in my own home with an uncertain future. As luck had it, my real estate agent came to the rescue. I was able to sign a temporary lease with an option to buy. Though only temporary until the title could be located, it was a solution I could live with, but the problem was not solved. I could not do any improvements on the home until title was free, and clear.

With renovation plans on hold, I could focus on my physical neglect. I joined the 24-hour health, and fitness center. I spent forty minutes rotating between the universal machine, and treadmill, getting worked up, followed with a jump into the indoor pool to cool my body with a swim. I finished the day with the sauna. "Hey," a familiar voice sounded through the steam as soon as I walked in. "What are you doing here?" It was Buzz, face shiny with sweat.

"I just got back in town."

"For a visit?"

"No. I moved back for good."

"Wow. How come? I thought you'd stay in the Bay forever."

"You've probably heard. Business collapsed all around."

"Sure did. I still have a job."

"Consider yourself lucky. It's not easy to find employment."

"What about you?"

"Out of work."

"Where're you staying?"

"I bought a home, but it's not mine yet."

"I don't understand." He sounded concerned.

"Temporary setback. Got some title issues."

"Ah yes," he said, with a hint of empathy. "Everybody has, but I don't quite understand the problem."

"You would if you had to buy, or sell a home."

"Tell me more."

"It's complicated," I said.

"Try me."

We spent the next thirty minutes between wiping sweat from our faces, and discussing the economic dilemma. "It started with some Wall Street tycoon blowing the whistle. The next morning the market took a dive we had not seen in decades. The chain reaction that followed was felt around the globe. One by one exchanges collapsed, cascading through Asia, the Middle East, Europe, and every trading exchange on the globe. It took days to analyze the cause, and weeks, and months for banking, lending, and investment institutions to admit their faults. In the process, the world's most irresponsible gambling scheme was exposed. Unraveling it will have an economic ripple effect that would last ten years.

"In short, money institutions had traded national real estate assets, good, and bad property deeds lumped into bundles, offered through exchange trades to the rest of the world. Every country around the globe, especially China, and Russia, jumped into the opportunity to buy up U.S. real estate assets. The practice had already taken place for years when it came to an eventual collapse. As was the case with all pyramid schemes, all went well until there was a runup on banks, and lending institutions to sell. Regardless of the outcome, we, the U.S., gave up forty percent of our real estate assets to foreigner buyers, mostly Chinese. As a result, they own almost half of our county."

"What are you going to do?"

"I'll just have to wait until I get the title."

It took nine months to get a clear title on my home. The document was finally located with ownership to the Bank of China in Shanghai, and Bank of Hong Kong. Because of the collapse, banks were only too ready to unload their financial burdens from a failed investment scheme. I was able to secure the required loan to buy back the property at a rock-bottom price. At least I was able to start remodeling my home.

Over the following five years, starting from the top, I did just that. First thing was replacing the carpeting, followed with new windows all around, fifteen in all, including modernizing the bathrooms. The next step was a bigger challenge. Where it had been customary to have the principle living space divided into living room, dining room, and kitchen, separated by walls, I wanted one open living space. With the aid of a home modeling computer program I designed, and redesigned my vision until I came up with the perfect layout. I was happy, and so was my contractor.

The day finally came when we agreed on the work, timeline, and estimated cost. Three weeks later the result was astonishing. I had the home I'd envisioned. One great living space constructed from high-end quality cabinets, fixtures, and appliances weighed down with the best in granite tops decked out with the most durable imported bamboo wooden floor, projected in modern style fashion. There were still a number of things to improve on such as painting rooms, replacing utilities, and gutters I completed with help on and off over the following years.

The day finally came when all renovation projects were complete. "That's it."

"You finally got a life," Buzz said with a grin we both could appreciate.

As it'd turn out, it "wasn't it." Years of neglect of my health was about to cause a chain reaction I had never expected. Physically I felt in top shape, but health wise, not by a longshot. Finally getting around to having the hernia repaired, the second already, soon after I developed a condition known as Runaway Hives that would take three years to overcome. In the meantime, more health afflictions surfaced, one after the other. I was plagued with a persistent sinus infection carried back from California. Melanoma spots appeared on my back, shoulders, and forehead that had to be removed. Next, Olecranon bursitis, whatever that was, developed on one forearm, from what, I'll never know. Shortly after I developed a condition new to medicine, restless legs syndrome. In addition, I needed knee surgery to repair the damaged leg. Adding to all the misery, I suffered from stomach disorders, prostate infections, and whatever minor afflictions one could experience while my main problem, insomnia, still persisted. It felt like my body was falling apart. On top of that, I popped another hernia, my third, while moving the heavy pantry cabinet from the truck to the kitchen, causing another visit to the hospital.

"You sure have kept doctors, and surgery rooms busy," Buzz remarked, then, "I'm not familiar with most of your problems. Could you explain some?" Admitting my plight to a friend was difficult enough. I never thought it possible to succumb to so many health issues.

"I'll try with what I've learned. Runaway Hives is caused by chemical overload on the dermis, the skin. I am still not clear what conditions triggered mine, but I suspect it was my taste for spicy foods, tabasco, red pepper, and sun exposure all at the same time. It was the leisure time I had acquired lounging on the balcony in spring, and early summer waiting for the property title to clear. The same, I suspect, was the case with the sudden appearance of melanoma eating its way into my spine, and forehead that required surgery.

"The sinus infection was a carryover from the Asian flu, sweeping the country years before, and misdiagnosed by physicians as allergic reaction to dust mites. Since I finally took the time to research possible causes, I took matters into my own hands to cure the infection. I accomplished it with the aid of a Bik water spray, treating my sinuses with a daily rinse of salt and baking soda mix. It took many months of positive results for a final cure.

"As for the restless leg's syndrome, for those unfamiliar, sensations are frequently described as creeping or crawling, tingling, burning, aching or throbbing, creating a physical leg motion beyond conscious control. Though still in the dark as to the cause, research indicates that RLS is related to a dysfunction in the production of dopamine, a neurotransmitter that helps the brain control muscle movement. In my case, the best guess was lack of sleep. It eventually disappeared, under what circumstance I did not know.

"As for knee damage, stomach disorder, and prostate infections, I had knee surgery to remove bone splinters imbedded in my leg, began eating a balanced diet accompanied with daily supplement in probiotics, and scheduled a prostate biopsy to assure it was not cancerous. It turned out to be benign. I had to be sure because my brother died at an early age from the affliction. He was only fifty.

"There were, however, two serious conditions I acquired while living in Colorado. One was Runaway Hives and the other an undiagnosed condition causing a severely burnt throat, esophagus, stomach, and intestinal linings. The first was the most severe case in the family of hives. There was no precise diagnosis as to its cause other than by my personal physicians advising to stay away from possible agents such as spicy foods, and staying out of direct sunlight. What transpired in Runaway Hives was that a severe itchy patch appeared somewhere on my leg for ten to twenty minutes then mysteriously shifted to another spot with the same itchiness. Scratching did not help other than causing open sores followed by scarred tissue. The process of reddish tarnished skin traversing my body twenty-four hours a day and night lasted three years. At times it was unbearable, especially when trying to sleep. Three years later it mysteriously disappeared, as predicted by my physician.

"The second problem was severe, and lasted just as long. A friend I met at a weekend dance invited me home one evening after eating a pizza out. Dying of thirst, since the pizza was very salty, she poured each of us a glasses of water. Shortly after, since it was getting late in the evening I left to return to my home. The problem began as soon as I stretched out in bed. It started as a burning sensation in the pit of my stomach, rapidly traveled up into my throat, and down into my stomach, and quickly turned into a boiling condition. Getting out of bed to catch my breath did not help much. I could hardly keep the liquid down by continuously swallowing air. Minutes later I sat by the toilet, throwing up repeatedly for the next hour. The condition worsened through the night until it slowly burned out by morning.

"Analyzing the cause, I decided it was something I ate in the pizza causing an allergic reaction. Several days later, she invited me over to her place for spaghetti dinner. It was delicious, but this time, the same attack repeated while I was still at her place. Trying to get to the cause of it, I had noticed in the kitchen some water purifying contraption she had used to fill the glasses. If I was sick previously, this time the condition worsened with every hour, again through the night. Worse yet, the attack resulted in a burnt throat, esophagus, stomach, and intestinal linings that would plague me for months.

"Again, I had to educate myself on water purifiers, and their process. I learned that I had a severe allergy for ionized water, probably related to the hive attacks. My organs eventually healed, but not without many choking effects when drinking, and eating. The end result? Severe weight loss. It took close to two years to completely heal the burnt organs.

"There was one more health issue I had to overcome, arthritis of the knees. It is an affliction many will experience with age. It is something that comes on gradual, unless caused by a leg injury at any age, it comes on mostly with those over 50, or later age. Though extensive research has been conducted, regardless of what one reads in health journals and magazines, medical doctors are not quite sure what causes it. Based on my personal lifestyle, my analysis: causes could be many. As for my own experience, I am pretty sure that it was the cause of at least three factors.

First factor, I injured my right knee in a motorcycle accident in 1970 while on Guam. At the time I did not give it much thought other than, "grin and bear it," until it healed. That's what I did. The same knee I injured again in a vehicle crash in 1989 in the Bay Area. This time, the pain remained for many months before subsiding once more.

Second factor, after thirty years of intense martial arts practices, the results, damages to knee cartilage from abnormal wear and tear, crept in slowly over a period of years. Touching my right knee, predominant kicking leg, when moving back and fore, I could clearly feel the grinding of bone against bone. Pain gets worse over time to a point where one favors one leg over the other, causing a slight limping or hobbling, after hours on tired feet.

Third factor, and in my opinion the most common one for many. It's caused by side effects of living. By that I mean, eating and drinking some substances in excess. In my case I contributed it to alcohol and citrus liquids contained in oranges, lemons, and whatever else contains acidity. My research indicates that taking in excessive amounts of citric acid, for instance a quart of Orange juice a day, which I did on many occasions, the acid is too much for the kidneys to process, consequently leaking into legs and knees.

I should point out that my experimenting with health issues took some time to analysis and diagnose, by changing personal habits, and over time, I came up with a workable solution. In the case of knees, I tried several products on the market place, and found one that works. Again researching, I learned that many athletes take the same product available at Amazon at a very reasonable cost at one, two, or multiple 1 lbs. cannisters.

The product is Collagen Hydrolysate, produced by Great Lakes, ideal for rebuilding joint cartilage. I should caution though, it is not an overnight miracle cure. One has to stay with it until the arthritis is cured, or for the elders, for the rest of one's life. Once the daily routine is established, it is not a burden to your daily schedule. Easily soluble, I take one measure as recommended in the morning with coffee, tea, hot chocolate, or whatever your preferred drink may be. The product works.

"Today, I am completely recovered from all afflictions, and am enjoying a new lease on life, though I have grown cautious about eating spicy foods, and drinking alcoholic beverages. Both still cause problems to the affected internal digestive organs."

TRAUMATIC HEALTH EVENTS

I thought about whether to write this section, and share it with the readers. The question I posed to myself was, "Who would be interested in someone else's afflictions?" Getting hurt, attacked by viruses, incurred injuries, and contracted diseases, we all had our share. No matter how one minimizes, or waves off a sickness, it is always accompanied by misery and, many times, pain. As an afterthought, I thought it important, changed my mind, and included the miseries I had endured. The reasons were two-fold. First, I felt it important to identify a sickness in case one should come down with a similar condition. Second, I want to share possible cures that had worked for me. Unfortunately, as I have learned, there are diseases in the world without a possible cure, or medical solution. The reasons for that are simple, as told by AMA, and WHO: for rare diseases there is no funding allocated to research, and finding a solution.

To start with, I must include a disclaimer. In no way am I a doctor, physician, or healer. I can only present suggestions, not from a clinical, and professional perspective, but from my own experience, and remedies I devised. It was commonsense wisdom, after thorough, and diligent research, that allows me to sit in front of my computer today to enjoy writing my biography including life's virtues, and demises.

During the early part of my life, the growing up part, I was susceptible to childhood diseases most children experience. Perhaps more so since I grew up amidst a war with its shortages on water, food, and medicine. In addition, most able physicians had been drafted into the war from the onset, leaving the land, and its citizens to fend for themselves. Soldiers had priority for medical attention and support all around, and rightly so. It did not mean that wars should be condoned. Wars should be condemned, but if unavoidable, supported by the nation's people. After all, everybody's livelihood, and safety were at stake.

My opinion on conflicts, and wars?
Whoever intended to start a war should be prosecuted, and executed, if appropriate, through an internationally sanctioned organization. A message must be delivered to the adversary even if only for reasons of human rights, which we all have. To begin with, if anybody does not understand birthrights, every seed born into the world must be given a chance to live. It is unimaginable for anybody to take this right without just cause. War is no justification in this day, and age. Nation's leaders have to be reminded every so often that a right to live is the basis for creation. The same is true for every criminal element infringing on this right. For anyone who commits the atrocity of killing, or taking a life, punishment must be harsh. It is, "Your life for taking another's." Otherwise, man will not learn to take the law of human rights seriously.

It may be harsh judgement, but a deserving one, since history has proven that every national confrontation ends with deadly penalties always paid by the innocent, where in many cases the instigators got off free. Many wars have been started on a whimsical act only to justify personal ambition. Yes, we hear about fighting around the globe carried by mainstream media almost on a daily basis. But sitting in front of the TV screen, watching an unfolding battle, does not justify the drama that the affected population has to endure. One has to be in the midst of turmoil to experience what the ravages of war can do to the individual. One could only hope we, living in the free world, never have to endure the treachery of war again. But that is only wishful thinking. There is always the ill-intended forcing their evil intentions on others, mostly for egotistical reasons. If the cause is not for the money, it is for power. Agreed, there may be justifiable reasons for getting involved in a conflict or war, but it should only be reserved for defending your country, fellow citizens, and inherited natural resources. There is already too much negative pressure exerted on humankind from bacteria, microbes, and viruses without the devastating effects from war.

Setting out on my life's journey, as a young person, I had no idea what diseases were lurking in the world, especially from third-world countries, but I would learn quickly once my journey began. An important part for preparing a trip overseas is immunization. Depending on the destination, most of the times I was injected with twelve different antigens ranging from typhoid to malaria, and every possible harmful pathogen in between. To a lesser degree, susceptible places for bacterial infections, fungus, and parasites were Indochina, Vietnam, the Philippines, Thailand, India, and the Pacific, my regular route. I have battled bouts with almost every bug one could catch whether from the jungles of Indonesia, or the waters in the Pacific.

One of my first sickness bout was with amebic dysentery caught in Vietnam that would plague me for many weeks, landing me in the hospital back home. Next was something similar in Thailand. After a day's work I would head directly for the local market place. If one enjoyed fruit and vegetables as I did, it was the place to shop. Aside from the familiar tropical fruits such as bananas, pineapples, and melons, there was an entirely new assortment of fruits, and vegetables unknown to the Western world. I learned to cherish new tastes, and smells for jackfruit, durian, papaya, mango, star apple, coconut, guava, pomelo, and passion fruit. Ah yes, the passion fruit with its deserving name. With my insatiable cravings for fruit, it felt like paradise—until the following day. The first time there, for six weeks, every day, I was sick to my stomach. Because of the pain, and discomfort, I quit eating customary meals, but could not abstain from fruit. It was not until the second visit months later that I was educated by a local girl I had met. Soon after my arrival, dragging her to the market place, I had selected my favorites when she said, "You can't eat it."

I was startled because I was not the only person buying fruit. "Why not?"

"You foreigners get sick."

It was an unexpected declaration, but would explain my earlier visit with the miserable times I had. I came to learn that foreign visitors lacked the intestinal flora to safely digest many locally grown fruits because they were planted in the swamplands of Thailand. Most of the southern regions were saturated by klongs (canals) fed by three rivers traversing the land. Deliciously tasty, all fruits grown in the swampy grounds were affected by microbes. I had to make some adjustments in my eating preference, and decided on tree grown fruits, jackfruit, and durian. I was happy once more, but not for long. Since hotel rooms had no refrigerators, with the specific fruits giving off offensive odors, they smelled up not only the room, but hallways, and floors as well. Sure enough, the following day, after returning from the job I was boldly ordered by hotel management to get rid of the fruits or move out. They were two fruits banned from hotels.

There were other times, and places I would contact various strains of infections, but fortunately these were treatable with antibiotics. Health related issues, for the most part in my career, became a way of life. Some I was able to cure immediately, others stayed with me for years. While the time in Asia had caused most of my illnesses, I was not immune to them back home. There was one such event important enough to share with you.

The year was 1993. I had just arrived in California taking on a contracting position with Microsoft. While working daytime hours I'd decided to enroll in evening, and weekend training classes to earn the MCSE certification, necessary to represent Microsoft as a business solution provider, a highly sought after, and paid engineering, and business proposition. My territory assigned by Microsoft was Fortune-500 companies headquartered in San Francisco's prime Market District. To be successful entailed complete familiarity with Microsoft platform, and business applications. To attain these new technology skills, I bought a cluster of the latest model computer servers on the market, one for each business function, to host essential Windows applications for logging on to accounts server, web hosting, SQL database, exchange, commerce, streaming video, development, and staging servers necessary for effective customer presentations.

Once set up, I spent most of my time on the phone with my customers solving software, application, and technology issues. The compacted, but still sizable cell phone had just come on the market. It provided mobility, and flexibility to perform the job. The problem was, I could only spend fifteen minutes at a time with the phone pressed against my ear before the unit became too hot to handle. Keeping conversations as brief as possible, I had to make use of it, nevertheless. Analyzing the flaw, I contributed it to initial design features inherent to the phone. It was not until months later that I noticed graying hair discolorations appear on both sides of my head just above the ears. While I contributed it as early effects of aging, the spots grew larger over time.

It was not until years later when the top of my ears began to crack open, turning painful at first, quickly followed by crispy, and flakey skin. A subsequently physical examination revealed severe radiation burns. I had been aware of a controversial health issue, debated for years, about the damaging effects on the brain from early cell phones, but everybody—mainstream media, medical institutions, and physicians— waived patient complaints off as imaginary, and a psychological notion. The pain got worse over time to where I could not sleep on my sides anymore.

"We need to operate on your ears," the otolaryngologist (Ear, Nose & Throat) specialists proclaimed the day following a thorough medical examination. Also, a plastic surgeon had to reconstruct my ears, after slicing off an upper portion at both sides of the ears; the result was remarkable. Unless I point out the damaged sections to someone, it is hardly noticeable. The surgeon did a superb job by removing, and covering up the damaged skin, and cartilage sections.

As already illustrated in details in previous chapters, my first encounter plagued with the Guillain-Barre syndrome, I had overcome the potentially deadly virus only by sheer determination. After I fully recovered two years later, I contacted AMA[79] to report the incident. I did not want anybody else to experience what I had to endure, or at least present the circumstances. My aim was to provide specifics as to location, environment, and conditions causing the effects in the first place. Since neither I nor the doctors in the Philippines were aware of the syndrome I wanted to alert AMA. While I had not been singled out by the Guillain-Barre sickness, since the syndrome occurred in about three identified cases worldwide annually, until that time, doctors had treated the afflicted individuals unsuccessfully. Back then there was no treatment, or cure available. The reason it was labelled a syndrome, though it was suspected to be virus induced, is that the causes had not yet been identified, and categorized.

While I endured the horrifying cause to make a full recovery over several years, identifying the source took forty more. I clearly recall the incident just like it was yesterday. I jumped into the ocean for a swim. Thirty minutes later I returned to the beach. On exiting the water, I felt an itching in back of my right knee. To my astonishment there were three bugs clinging to my skin sucking out blood. I pulled them off one by one, and tossed them onto the hot sandy beach. Minutes later, I felt extreme exhaustion, dropped on to the sand, and succumbed to sleep. Hours later I was awakened by my friends alerting me of severe sunburn. But that was many years before, the early 70s.

The ensuing drama, and eventual promise for a renewed life was bestowed on me by the one person to whom I am still greatly deeply indebted, the neurosurgeon who identified the ailment I suffered from for years. Though there was no cure, the doctor's encouraging words were enough to give me renewed hope, "You have what is known as Guillain-Barre syndrome."

"I have good news, and bad ones," he said. "What do you want to hear first?"

"Good news."

"Since you are still alive after keeping yourself awake all this time, you will live. Let me explain. The common expression for your ailment is better known as a combination meningitis– encephalitis. It could be a viral or bacterial infection in the brain as well as the spinal cord. What made my case worse was that it was caused through bacterial infection. If identified as such, an appropriate antibiotic medicine becomes necessary. Where the virus caused symptom dies out weeks later after being attacked by the body's own defense system, bacterial caused symptom did not.

"What about the bad news?"

"There is no cure for the disease."

I was devastated. "Nothing you can do? Am I going to stay paralyzed?" That was the condition I was in. Paralyzed from head to toe without being able to move one limb.

"Let me explain. Since you survived this far, your survival is assured. Most people die from asphyxiation, as you have experienced. I should commend you on that. As far as I know nobody has ever survived without a life-support system. You are the first."

"What can I expect?"

---

[79] American Medical Association, the primary institution for reporting medical related issues.

Again, I was reminded of facing electric shock treatments. They were horrifying.

When recalling the event, I wondered about the bugs which, I thought, were the cause of the traumatic illness. It was only last year, when researching the Internet for a similar illness, that I came across a picture of bugs identified as isopod. What looked like a miniature armadillo, about one to two inches large, sure enough, the picture was accompanied by a medical description for the illness the creature caused. It was none other than Guillain-Barre infection. Further searching revealed pretty much the same limited information described forty years earlier, resulting in a "no cure." At least I had identified the source. As far as a cure, it may be many more years off, since the syndrome is shelved in the low priority categories.

I can only offer my own experience, advising, "Endure the illness. It's only a temporary setback until the virus destroys itself by the body's immune system or eliminated with antibiotics." As for recovery, it would take weeks, and months to even consider rebuilding your physical strength again. For that to occur, despite the pain while allowing your body tissue, and muscles to regenerate, you'd have to pull all of your strengths, and energy together. Years later, you will still watch, and feel muscle strands across your body jump, and quiver as they are being triggered by the brain during exercise.

In spite of all the medical advice I had received, such as, "You'll never regain a hundred percent of your muscle strength again," I had fully recovered, but the rebuilding process took close to five years. Though I should forewarn the reader, there is still no cure for Guillain-Barre, a precursor to Encephalitis. In many cases, both prove to be a deadly disease, not so much from a terminal virus, but more so for their ensuing consequences through the dysfunction of internal organs. The virus, by design, eats away the protective cover of your brain matter, as well as the protective insulation of the nerve system.

It was not the only time I had contacted such a destructive decease. Only recently, after moving back to Colorado, there was a second time I was afflicted, but this time by a close relative of encephalitis, the meningitis virus.

Three years ago, I decided to have some dental work performed. To preserve my teeth for the duration of my life, I had my lower molars capped. While the roots were still in order, on the dentist's advice, I had several metal fillings replaced with porcelain prior to being capped. The first visit went well. Though stressful, four molars in one session cramped up my jaw during the three-hour session. It took several months to get over the pain, and sensitivity to hot, and cold, and that was enough, aside from a couple cleaning visits, not to schedule the next session to do the other side for another year. Once fully recovered, I went back to face the dental office one more.

All went pretty much as the year before with one exception: I developed extreme sensitivity, and pain that just would not heal. As a matter of fact, I had to stop taking daily aspirin because with each day the pain increased in intensity. To get the full picture, I will describe the progression that took place over the next two years.

Following the dental visit, due to persistent pain, I was unable to get any sleep for days on end. I endured the condition sitting up at night with my mind in a constant state of daze. The only thing on my mind was how to get rid of pain, and get sleep.

Restlessly, I would stride up, and down my home most days, and nights, trying to seek some comfort. It went on for weeks until I finally decided to ask my physician's advice. He determined that, on top of all the misery, I had developed conditions he identified as trigeminal neuralgia, and toxic tinnitus. He even showed me on his laptop display the nerve strands connecting the lower jaw to the brain, and on to the spinal cord, and nerve strands.

As inquisitive, and patient as I was he endured with me, and explaining the cause, and eventual prognosis that, "There's no cure. You'll have to live with it for the rest of your life."

It was something no patient would want to hear. "But," I protested, "I can't go on like this. I am dying from the lack of sleep." The pain, and drowsiness took away all of my desire to eat or do anything else. I had lost twenty pounds.

"I can give you some medication," he offered. "It'll let you sleep."

I was grateful to him as never before, thanked him, and took the prescription to the nearby Walmart pharmacy window. "Gabapentin," the label indicated when I picked up the capsule container. It was a thirty-day supply authorizing two refills. Right from the first day, taking one tablet per day before bedtime, I was able to sleep soundly for five to six hours. I could not be happier until I discovered adverse side effects attached to the medication. I stayed with the medication for three full months as I gradually realized what was happening to me. Because of the dazed condition I faced daily, my body rapidly began to deteriorate. I was losing muscle tissue as never before. I made several attempts at exercises, and working out, but had to give in to a weakened body. I did not have the strength to even handle ten-pound dumbbells. But that was not the worst of it.

I had to decide: have a new prescription issued by my doctor, or quit taking the medication altogether. It was not an easy choice with my condition. Not only had my body deteriorated, but I was losing my mind. To test my mental capacity, after making numerous attempts to operate my computer to check emails, I finally gave up. I did not remember. Analyzing the cause, I suspected the medication, and paid my doctor a visit. As always, he displayed infinite patience, but also informed me of my predicament. "Your loss of memory is the side effect from medication."

"That's just great," I blurted out. "How am I going to go on without it?"

"Patients have managed to live many years taking Gabapentin. It's medication designed for nerve dysfunction. But since you are dissatisfied, let's try something else," he suggested while writing out a new prescription.

Hopeful, and optimistic I took another trip to Walmart. I don't remember the name of the next medicine I was handed because I tossed it a week later after my condition failed to improve. I had decided to try my chances without.

In pain, but somewhat encouraged by renewed vigor, I tackled my computer once more. Rifling through the many files to become familiar again, I came across a master directory containing books I'd formatted for publication. Puzzled, I opened the first file, and saw my name listed as the author. At first, I did not understand, but reading along I suddenly realized that I had actually wrote the books. It then dawned on me; I had lost all short-term memory, at least five years of it. From a health aspect, I again suffered pain, and sleeplessness, but decided to try, and live with it as long as my mind would function enough to see me through the day.

I had to find my mental bearing again. Since I had forgotten much, I took to prolific reading. I acquired the works of the time's great philosophers, and novelists, reading away day, and night. While distracting me from pain it helped reacquire lost memories. I became well enough to initiate Google searches on every health aspect of my sicknesses. First, I became familiar with both encephalitis, and meningitis conditions, followed by brain, and neve dysfunction.

Then, based on the symptoms I had experienced, I was able to acquire more knowledge, but no solution while my condition worsened over the months that followed. Though there were a number of nerve disorders people contracted, and endured, many contributed to the aging process, it appeared that I had caught the worst of them. Over the following weeks, and months, Google became my faithful companion. Day, and night I spent on the computer, becoming more, and more familiar with the body's vital functions. Unless one has studied the complexity of the human nerve system, and brain functions, one cannot fathom the miraculous design of the human body.

The following is an account, aside from not getting much sleep, of what I endured over the past year. It started right after the second dental session. I developed intense pain beginning with the left lower jaw, traversing along my cheek into the inner ear, causing a condition called trigeminal neuralgia. From there, the meningitis virus was eating its way into my brain, and down the vertebra through the body's nerve strands into arms, legs, and feet.

The damage the virus caused was eating away the nerve insulation, the myelin sheath,[80] exposing the bare nerve to the surrounding muscle tissue. What I'd learned, but did not read anywhere in medical journals, was the ensuing condition I'd already endured for many months. Following was the process, and resultant condition for the viral attack on my nerve insulations.

Every second, the brain shoots out an electric pulse that travels through the nerve strands. It provides body functions to allow muscle motion whenever you decide to take a step, move your arms, reach for an item, stoop down, and every other motion the body is capable of. It is an autonomous function triggered by the brain without being conscious of the motion. The electrical impulse, carried by the nerve, is to instruct the muscles to execute the next motion.

With the protective insulation eaten away, with nerves exposed, the current conducted directly into the surrounding body tissue. I could feel the perfectly clocked pulses shoot through my body with every second, making my legs, feet, and arms quiver. Also, a byproduct was heating up foot soles, numbing, and cramping toes day, and night. It became impossible to get any rest. Help came in the form of recently-created designer drugs. It was Gabapentin, and similar medications that prevented the electric current from jumping synapses to reach nerves traversing through the body, but not without severe side effects.

Either way, the electric current, or the loss of memory was a condition I would not be able to tolerate for very long. I had to find a remedy, or perish.

---

[80] Myelin is the fatty white substance that surrounds the axon of nerve cells, forming an electrically insulating layer around the nerves, essential for the proper functioning of the nervous system.

No matter how much I researched, the search results were always the same. Medical science had no solution. I had to take a different approach. I put my analytical skills to work. From a logical perspective I'd asked, "What is destroying my body?"

"The demolition of myelin."

I researched, and queried further, "What is the substance of myelin, and brain matter?"

"Cholesterol."

"How does the body derive cholesterol?"

"Mostly from eggs, and dairy products."

Reading on, I had an enlightening moment. "It couldn't be this simple?"

But, after many months of desperation, I had to give it a try. I started eating eggs.[81] What they provided was pure cholesterol from the egg yolk, and protein from the egg white. Each morning, I would either prepare a milkshake containing six raw eggs, or soft-boil eggs. Six eggs were about my limit before a gagging feeling set in. Subsequently, weeks later, I reduced my eggs intake to four soft-boiled, eaten frequently or whenever I felt the need. By need, I am referring to an unexpeted benefit the soft-boiled or poached eggs provided. It promotes prolific sperm production, proportionately in the amount taken in, you, your wife or lady friend will enjoy. One thing to remember, the egg yoke can be heated but still has to be in liquid form.

After only a few days I could feel the effects on my body. The electrical shocks slowly faded. Muscles began to function once more. The tinnitus faded to an ambient sound level. Facial, and muscle pain gradually diminished. And, best of all, my mind became clear again. Weeks later my brain regained its normal function. As for my nerve predicament, I was on the way to recovery.

There was still the problem with the original infection. As luck had it, it finally surfaced in the form of green colored, festering pockets along each affected molar. I finally had the proof I had sought for years. Another trip to my doctor, after providing proof, and I was prescribed a heavy dosage of the antibiotic Clindamycin. Ten days later my jaw, ears, and teeth were pain free.

I could not believe it. I had found a cure. I was euphoric. I could start life over again. There was a future after all, and here I sit, in front of my computer once more, writing a fourth book, but this time my biography.

I should add one more solution I had come across, the problem with toxic tinnitus. As it'd turned out, it was caused by my prolonged (daily) use of aspirin to kill the pain, and infection associated with the meningitis virus. In the preceding years of usage, unbeknownst to me, the over-the-counter aspirin dosage had changed from a general 250 mg to 320 mg. There was one more change I found when inspecting the package labels. Each product, from aspirin to acetaminophen, and on to NSAID, Advil, Aleve, Ibuprofen, and the rest of the lot, contains caffeine. The combination of the higher dosage of aspirin combined with caffeine was the apparent cause for toxic tinnitus.

Overdosing in pain pills came as complete surprise. The most I ever took was one 320 mg Aspirin pill per day. What surprised me even more was that Aspirin had severe

---

[81] Eggs are a nutrient goldmine! One large egg has varying amounts of 13 essential vitamins, and minerals, high-quality protein, all at only 70 calories. While egg whites contain some of the eggs' high-quality protein, riboflavin, and selenium, the majority of an egg is cholesterol packed in the yolk.

side effects. Aside from destroying liver, causing bladder inflammation, and damages to other life sustaining organs, in my case, caused an inflammation in my spinal cord resulting in severe pain to neck and shoulder muscles, the reason for my taking a pain killer daily. The result was a vicious cycle repeated with no end in sight to eliminate pain. When I finally broke the cycle, identified as toxic tinnitus by my physician, my body went into severe withdrawal symptoms as experienced by many drug users. For those inadvertently overdosing on aspirin, there is one caffeine free pain relief left in the marketplace, the "Bayer–Low Dose" aspirin, 81 mg. After quitting the damaging dosage, and enduring days of severe withdrawal symptoms, I found it worked effectively. I take it occasionally to eliminate shoulder, and neck pain whenever plagued from overwork, or exercise.

Already weeks into convalescence, after all the research, and trials, I felt like I had earned my doctorate. I am only kidding. Except for a healthy body, and mind once more, I am still the same person who set out on my life's quest. As time went on I also felt my sense of humor return which I had lost years ago because of my physical setbacks. As many individuals could attest, especially the elderly, living a life plagued by pain and agony has devastating effects on the human psyche, and wellbeing.

My personal advice: "Consider alternative means when modern medicine fails."

In retrospect, I felt like destiny permitted me several leases on life after overcoming severe afflictions that only a strong will, and determination could effectively cope with. I will apply the same determination from here onward no matter what the future has in store because I love the life, creation has provided us. The only aspiration I have is for mankind to be understanding enough to respect the beauty in nature we so many times take for granted. It is high time to clean up Earth from the mess we created, and will continue to create for years to come.

My personal respect, and gratitude to the functionaries that so diligently apply their time, and energy to the cause of achieving a cleaner world, and safer future for our children, and their descendants, even though it may hamper our inherited demand for leisure, entertainment, and personal gratification that we all are striving for in a world of endless opportunities.

I have recovered from afflictions others may never experience. Each time I came out stronger in body and mind. That does, however, not prevent the aging process. Aging, at this time cannot be curbed. It can be covered up with facial and body creams, which many do to face another day, meet up with a friend, go shopping, or just enjoy the day on your own. As many will experience, "sun and fun" may not be the ultimate of pleasures anymore. There I a price to pay. It comes on slowly but surely with age. I am talking about skin damages from dermatitis on the less severe, and on to melanoma (skin cancer), a common affliction in this day and age. Perhaps the future will hold a cure.

For now, for everybody, nature prepares every one of us for the End through bodily decay. Close to the End facing death, there is no fear.

NEW LEASE ON LIFE

I had just woken up after three hours of fitful sleep dreaming in black, and white. The colorless space was a rocky, slippery cliff line swarming with hostile enemy fighters pressing ashore. The absence of colors may have had some meaning in the world of dreams, but the scene was not segmented in short fractions as I usually experienced. It was a continuous scene of strike, and striking back, being stalked, and getting chased a time while taking aggressive actions the next. It felt like I had been fighting for hours warding off the aggressors. To make things worse, I could not locate a suitable weapon, and wound up grabbing at everything within reach. Finally, I was able to take hold of a stick, striking, and warding off the onrush of opponents advancing at an ever-increasing rate. Though rage inspired me to keep on fighting, I could feel my strength rapidly waning. Being overwhelmed a hundredfold, I could sense that death was not far off. It was here when I woke up, drenched in sweat, breathing heavily. If I believed in demons, and the supernatural, I would not want to sleep again. Luckily, I was too much anchored to reality so I knew that the world of dreams was not real. In short, it was human fear emerging in our world of dreams. Thus, in times like these, I was battling my own fears of imaginary demons. It took quite some time before I realized the cause of vivid dreams. The account just described was a side effect from taking the sleep aid Zolpidem.

Today, other than catching my typical 1 ½ hour nap on the living room sofa, I had been unable to sleep for days. Whatever conditions prevented me from regulated sleep must be related to the lifestyle I had acquired during my thirty-year career. I must have a mental block for sound sleep in the quiet of a darkened room in my comfortable bed. It had been a pattern for many years but especially for the past three years since my bout with nerve disorders. The result is usually a personal condition too exhausted to take up the daily chores I had planned. Consequently, I wind up on the sofa, watching TV for hours, until rest becomes too irritable with neck, and shoulder pain. To be exact, it was not so much a painful feeling as it was a soreness of the muscles.

On better days, I could sleep sound from about midnight until three in the morning when my body decided it was time to get up. Slightly drowsy but awake, I would look out windows in the darkness of night, checking for moving shadows, and other dark images prone to nighttime. Being early spring, it had snowed for hours the previous evening with the ground iced over at freezing temperatures. It was not an unusual condition for late March here at the altitude in the foothills of the Rockies.

As usual, my breathing would be slightly laborious on waking, a condition after taking a sleeping pill such as Zolpidem. It was a pattern repeated about once a month after getting too run down from the lack of sleep. Already for years I had tried to find an alternative solution such as melatonin, and other herbal remedies without success. I would go days without so much as a wink of sleep before it would catch up with me in the form of a dazed waking state. Though not ideal, I learned to live with it until I succumbed to another pill.

It had been more than ten years since I was prescribed Zolpidem by a Californian physician to suppress physical pain after an operation. It was a time prior to today's controversial opioid epidemic. While I'm not sure if Zolpidem falls into the same category, it was one substance that worked for me in times of desperation. I say desperation because I immensely dislike taking medication or drugs, any medication, whether for health conditions, or for lack of sleep. Taking a drug, for me, aside from undesirable side effects, has always been a stigma rather than a beneficial relief solution. Hopefully, I will be able to maintain my aversive disposition to drugs for the rest of my life. I feel compelled to explain.

The year was 1968, during my first travels to Vietnam when I became aware of the drug problem. While some would categorize it as condition, I slated it as problem. Shortly after arriving in the war zone I came across secretly held statistics on the drug use by American soldiers. I could not believe the consensus figures; neither would the public, if revealed back home. The reports stated that over sixty percent of our forces in Vietnam were using drugs on a continual basis. I was dumbstruck. I had no idea how anyone could even obtain the quantities of drugs under any conditions until I learned that Vietnam was situated in the midst of the Golden Triangle.

How long drug use had been going on was analogous with the beginning of the war in 1955. It was not the only revelation I had. Not only were military personnel involved in the drug use, civilians back home benefitted as well. As a matter of fact, drug supply had turned into an import business into the U.S. unlike ever seen before. Every military cargo flight returning from Vietnam contained shipments of heroin and opium smuggled, and managed by specifically-trained ground crews. It may be hypocritical of me to criticize drugs, its users, and related business opportunities, but, in my defense, my entire career would have been compromised if I had succumbed to drugs, considered as a major offense by the government for compromising national security.

Learning about the prolific trade, my trust in the national defense system was broken. I realized that people took to illicit opportunities when presented for the sake of profits, and pleasures, whether right or wrong. I had lost my initial respect for the laws. Though as devastating as the personal revelation was, it would get worse.

Not only were the military troops involved, and affected by drug smuggling, government agents, and civilians were involved as well. It became so widespread that even Marine sentries, watching the most sensitive operations, and facilities, became drug users. Among all of the units involved, I sympathized with the Marine most, standing hours on end at a remote outpost bored to death. Regardless, it was no excuse for taking to drugs. I sincerely questioned the effectiveness of our defense policies, and the lack of enforcement.

I sometimes felt that the very condition in lack of discipline caused us to lose the war in Vietnam. Imagine soldiers fighting at the frontlines with me, and my team true to the national spirit demanded by the constitution. Though I am not sure whether drug usage was specifically stated when our forefathers created the country's most sacred foundation, only to be undermined by lawless entrepreneurs for gaining personal wealth at the cost of many lives.

There were other incidents that turned my judgment against drug use. First, I could never envision myself subjected to a substance dependency. For the same reason I had maintained my independence from being micromanaged. Taking it further, I would not fit into the general rule for following the chain of command. Right from the start of a project I would insist on maintaining my independence. It was the very reason I would directly report to the program office or command echelon.

Second, I had witnessed too many individuals getting enslaved into drug use. From my personal perspective, it would not matter much since I kept my distance from such individuals. The matter was different on the job, or work location. That was where dependency surfaced through the lack of performance. Where a drug user may have had good intentions to complete a delegated task, the resultant performance suffered quality, and timeliness. With the tight project schedules I was forced to work, there was no room for tardiness. The results from enforcing my own high standard work, and personal performance policies were always appreciated by the customer in the form of follow-on projects. A typical example was AUTODIN. What initially was a five-year contract turned into thirty years, a lifelong career for many of us.

Whether right or wrong, it has to be said. As for my present lifestyle, I am still as conservative as when I started my career. I have made it my mission to live within the monthly earning budget I allocated to myself no matter what direction my career took. For all practical purposes, my life turned out to be successful in spite of a somewhat restrained income. I have learned that, in contrast to unrestrained career opportunities in the civilian world, working government contracts is limited to a ten percent profit margin for the contracting office, with a further reduction in payout to the individual employee.

While work rewards would be gauged by the personal recognition one attained, earnings provided only for limited, but contented living conditions, nevertheless. Since retirement, for personal leisure, when not writing novels, I generally reserve some weekend time to catch a popular concert show on TV that I had missed during my career. I was unable to attend popular bands performing in the 70s, and 80s. In today's world of social media, and instant program delivery, any kind of entertainment is available twenty-four hours a day.

My favorite music genre, for the most part, is Blues with its progressive, but mellow delivery. Coming to mind are famous creators, and performers such as Eric Clapton, B.B. King, Joe Bonamassa, Doyle Braham, Robert Cray, Bo Dittley, Buddy Guy, John Mayer, Robert Randolph, Carlos Santana, Jimmie Hendriks, Jimmy Vaughan, Joe Walsh, and ZZ Top. I am always amazed at their ingenuities, and boundless energies; to make the cut of the greats, one has to be creative, and logical minded. Creativity came into play with individual licks, and tones while notes, scale, and mathematics were part of the logical function. It had been said that skills cannot be acquired; one has to be born with it.

Where some applied their skills to the performing arts, and music, I applied mine to be the best in analyzing, troubleshooting, and solving technologically-related problems. I have yet to learn how to effectively apply the creative part of my brain. That part gradually surfaced with the first novel I created after retiring from an active, and colorful career. I should say that it provided copious amounts of materials for the trilogy I set out to write. But it will not stop there. I have a number more titles in the planning.

AFTERWORD

Many decades have passed since I was a child growing up in postwar Germany. I thought WWII came to an eventual end in 1945, but ensuing events proved otherwise. First, there was the Berlin Airlift initiated by the U.S. to help starving citizens in a war-torn country. Not long after followed the breakup of former allies U.S., Britain, and France, with the Soviet Union causing a long drawn out cold war affecting many lives. In today's world, many have forgotten, or do not know what the Cold War was about. In short, it was a political struggle between two ideologically opposing factions, the fight for democracy over communism by us, and fight for communism over democracy for the Soviets. Where one aspired for individual freedom for its people, the other sought totalitarian control over its citizens, and shared wealth.

There are many different means to govern a nation, and its peoples, but few have been tried effectively, with others short lived, or never getting off the ground. Too numerous to list them all, there are three major forms prevalent among nations, namely democracy (rule of majority), oligarchy (rule of the few), and autocracy (single ruler), governed by citizens elect, inherited nobility, or dictatorship, respectively. Within each category one will find many subdivisions to suit an ever-growing world population, if conditions are right. For a better understanding of governing bodies, see Appendix H.

Aside from governing bodies, I thought it important, in brief, to present the ideology for the Russian Federation, our past adversary, the former Soviet Union (USSR)[82]. While Russia, at times, may make overtures to cooperate economically with the West, from a political, and ethical perspective, we will always be worlds apart. To get a better understanding, as well as the reasoning why Russia is different from the Western world, the following is a brief history of Russia:

The Russian Empire was an empire that existed across Eurasia, and North America from 1721, following the end of the Great Northern War, until the Republic was proclaimed by the Provisional Government that took power after the February Revolution of 1917.

Initially, the House of Romanov ruled the Russian Empire from 1721 until 1762, and its German-descended branch, the House of Holstein, ruled from 1762. At the beginning of the 19th century, the Russian Empire extended from the Arctic Ocean in the north to the Black Sea in the south, from the Baltic Sea on west to the Pacific Ocean, and until 1867, including Alaska in North America. With 125.6 million subjects registered by the 1897 census, it had the third-largest population in the world at the time, after China, and India. Like all empires, it included a large disparity in terms of economics, ethnicity, and religion. There were numerous dissident elements, who launched frequent rebellions, and assassination attempts, closely watched by the secret police, ending with thousands exiled to Siberia.

Economically, the empire had a predominantly agricultural base, with low productivity on large estates worked by serfs until they were freed in 1861. The economy slowly industrialized with the help of foreign investments in railways, and

---

[82] USSR – Union of Soviet Socialist Republics, geographically fashioned after the Unites States of America.

factories. The land was ruled by nobility from the 10th through the 17th centuries, and subsequently by an emperor. Tsar Ivan III (1462–1505) laid the groundwork for the empire that later emerged. He tripled the territory of his state, ended the dominance of the Golden Horde, renovated the Moscow Kremlin, and laid the foundations of the Russian state. Emperor Peter the Great (1682–1725) fought numerous wars, and expanded an already huge empire into a major European power. He moved the capital from Moscow to the new model city of St. Petersburg, and led a cultural revolution that replaced some of the traditionalist, and medieval social, and political values with a modern, scientific, Europe-oriented, and rationalist system.

Empress Catherine the Great (1762–1796) presided over a golden age. She expanded the state by conquest, colonization, and diplomacy, continuing Peter the Great's policy of modernization along Western European lines. Emperor Alexander II (1855–1881) promoted numerous reforms, most dramatically the emancipation of all 23 million serfs in 1861. His policy in Eastern Europe involved protecting the Orthodox Christians from oppression of the Ottoman Empire. That connection by 1914 led to Russia's entry into the First World War on the side of France, the United Kingdom, and Serbia, against the German, Austrian, and Ottoman empires.

The Russian Empire functioned as an absolute monarchy until the Revolution of 1905, and once more became a constitutional monarchy. The empire collapsed during the February Revolution of 1917, largely as a result of massive failures in its participation in the First World War.

What Alexander II did in 1861, freeing all slaves, was a marvelous thing. His generosity went even further by setting aside a huge portion of his vast land for the settlement of the freed serfs. Subsequently, Slavic[83] nations were born, better known as Yugoslavia, Slovenia, Slovakia, and Czechoslovakia. Unfortunately for the Western world, Russia subscribed to Karl Marx's communism, popular at the time. I should point out that, in principle, communism is a good thing during depression periods, and political upheavals with the population depending on each other by pooling common resources. The problem is, it only works for small communities, hence the meaning for communism.

It was communism that drove a deep wedge between Russia, and the West, creating a lasting distrust. It was this distrust that President Reagan tried to break. In context with the nuclear disarmament, what followed was his famous statement that would be written into history: "Trust but verify."

Where a world power may have reign over international trade, and commerce for decades, and even centuries, tensions initiated by a political adversary can develop, and escalate at any time. A typical case is the recent aggressions by the Chinese to take over the Pacific region as their sphere of dominance. Whether lasting, or short-lived, the way things are progressing, they are sure to take control.

Next in line to exert power could be India, Iran, or another ambitious nation planning to expand. All that is required are likeminded allies to support your ambitious efforts. Historical accounts are all too real. One only has to read. All indicators are in place for the once mighty nation, us, to relinquish our world dominance unless we can

---

[83] Serfs is synonymous with Slavic. Slavic is Russian for slaves. Russia's freedom for slaves was instituted as a result of the American emancipation.

reestablish the power we once wielded. Unfortunately, as long as our policy makers are only interested in squabbling over their own political agendas, who committed this, and who committed that of a moral infraction, the big picture will be us losing our international powerbase, forever. Adversary powers do not have the least interest for what moral inflictions transpired internal to a country. Considered misdemeanors, and such will only enhance their opportunities to leverage their antagonistic intentions.

For me, and my career colleagues, sacrificing much of their personal lives, dedicating their time, and energy defending our inherited birthright, freedom, it may have been in vain, but we sure tried to maintain peace in a world of uncertainties. One had to be close to the source of potential vulnerabilities, as we were, to recognize the continuously changing political trends. The Department of Defense was such an entity. Where it may seem, at times, that such a complex organization may be governed by self-serving interests, it certainly was not the case here. There was only one path for U.S. national defense: protect its borders, national wealth, and the safety of its citizens. An army of millions of diligently working, and dedicated individuals made sure that the unique constitution of our country was preserved, and protected against any external threats to our nation.

Peace, it seems, is an ever-elusive commodity. It is the absence of peace that propelled the invisible warriors into action whenever called upon, with conflicts fought by the next generation, and the next. Unless mankind is able to change their still primitive mindset, lasting peace will only be wishful thinking. I thought it important to remind the reader how quickly world situations can change. Where many brilliant minds are born within our own borders, within every generation, they are only effective when allowed to be heard. It is the government's responsibility to see to it.

As for the UFO and Alien agenda, UFO sightings are deliberately initiated by the government to keep the extraterrestrial spirit alive and to suite their own agenda, the advancement of black projects. My sincere advice is following:

You travelers keep visiting exotic places, adventurers keep on exploring the globe, archaeologists keep on digging up earth, explorers keep on pioneering the lands, inventors keep on discovering, spiritualists keep on dreaming of imaginary worlds, Ufologists keep on watching the skies, conspiracists keep on making things up so that Sci-Fi writers can keep on writing.

While the truth can be stretched like a rubber band, it may not necessarily be desirable by everyone. However, without your intuition, imagination, and determination, Earth would be a dull place. Every one of you is needed and so are the readers.

My mission on earth was to uncover and telling the facts no matter how upsetting it may be to some. The majority of the world population still appreciate bare facts over speculations, but also enjoy good fiction, and livid entertainment.

Thank you, Hollywood, with my special appreciation to fiction writers. Documentary and category writers are already recognized by the reader for their dedication and efforts for digging up facts in the name of science, knowledge, and progress.

APPENDIX A – DIRECTED-ENERGY WEAPON PROGRAMS

X-ray Laser

An early focus of the SDI effort was an X-ray laser powered by nuclear explosions. Nuclear explosions gave off a huge burst of X-rays, which the Excalibur concept intended to focus using a lasing medium consisting of metal rods. Many such rods would be placed around a warhead, each one aimed at a different ICBM, thus destroying numerous ICBMs in a single attack. It would cost much less for the U.S. to build another Excalibur than the Soviets would need to build enough new ICBMs for a counter strike. The idea was first based on satellites, but when it was pointed out that these could be attacked in space, the concept moved to a "pop-up" concept, rapidly launched from a submarine off the Soviet northern coast.

However, on March 26, 1983, the first test, known as the Cabra event, was performed in an underground shaft, and resulted in marginally positive readings that could be dismissed as being caused by a faulty detector. Since a nuclear explosion was used as the power source, the detector was destroyed during the experiment, and the results therefore could not be confirmed. Technical criticism based upon unclassified calculations suggested that the X-ray laser would be of at best marginal use for missile defense. Such critics often cite the X-ray laser system as being the primary focus of SDI, with its apparent failure being a main reason to oppose the program. However, the laser was never more than one of the many systems being researched for ballistic missile defense.

Despite the apparent failure of the Cabra test, the long-term legacy of the X-ray laser program was the knowledge gained while conducting the research. Parallel developmental program advanced laboratory X-ray lasers for biological imaging, and the creation of 3D holograms of living organisms.

Chemical Laser

Beginning in 1985, the Air Force tested an SDIO-funded deuterium fluoride laser known as Mid-Infrared Advanced Chemical Laser (MIRACL) at White Sands Missile Range. During a simulation, the laser successfully destroyed a Titan missile booster in 1985; however, the test setup had the booster shell pressurized, and under considerable compression loads. These test conditions were used to simulate the loads a booster would be under during launch. The system was later tested on target drones simulating cruise missiles for the U.S. Navy, with some success. After the SDIO closed, the MIRACL was tested on an old Air Force satellite for potential use as an anti-satellite weapon, with mixed results. The technology was also used to develop the Tactical High Energy Laser (THEL) which was being tested to shoot down artillery shells.

During the mid-to-late 1980s a number of panel discussions on lasers, and SDI took place at various laser conferences. Proceedings of these conferences included papers on the status of chemical, and other high-power lasers at the time. The Missile Defense Agency's Airborne Laser program used a chemical laser which had successfully intercepted a missile taking off, so an offshoot of SDI could be said to have successfully implemented one of the key goals of the program.

Neutral Particle Beam

In July 1989, the Beam Experiments Aboard a Rocket (BEAR) program launched a sounding rocket containing a neutral particle beam (NPB) accelerator. The experiment successfully demonstrated that a particle beam would operate, and propagate as predicted outside the atmosphere, and that there were no unexpected side-effects when firing the beam in space. After the rocket was recovered, the particle beam was still operational. According to the BMDO, the research on neutral particle beam accelerators, which was originally funded by the SDIO, could eventually be used to reduce the half-life of nuclear waste products using accelerator-driven transmutation technology.

Laser, and mirror experiments

The High Precision Tracking Experiment (HPTE), launched with the Space Shuttle Discovery on STS-51-G, was tested June 21, 1985 when a Hawaii-based low-power laser successfully tracked the experiment, and bounced the laser off of the HPTE mirror.

The Relay Mirror Experiment (RME), launched in February 1990, demonstrated critical technologies for space-based relay mirrors that would be used with an SDI directed-energy weapon system. The experiment validated stabilization, tracking, and pointing concepts, and proved that a laser could be relayed from the ground to a 60 cm mirror on an orbiting satellite, and back to another ground station with a high degree of accuracy, and for extended durations.

Hypervelocity Railgun

Research out of hypervelocity railgun technology was performed to build an information base about railguns so that SDI planners would know how to apply the technology to the proposed defense system. The SDI railgun investigation, called the Compact High Energy Capacitor Module Advanced Technology Experiment, had been able to fire two projectiles per day during the initiative. This represented a significant improvement over previous efforts, which were only able to achieve about one shot per month. Hypervelocity railguns were, at least conceptually, an attractive alternative to a space-based defense system because of their envisioned ability to quickly shoot at many targets. Also, since only the projectile left the gun, a railgun system could potentially fire many times before needing to be resupplied.

A hypervelocity railgun worked very much like a particle accelerator insofar as it converted electrical potential energy into kinetic energy imparted to the projectile. A conductive pellet (the projectile) was attracted down the rails by electric current flowing through a rail. Through the magnetic forces that this system achieved, a force was exerted on the projectile, moving it down the rail. Railguns could generate muzzle-velocities in excess of 2.4 kilometers per second.

Railguns faced a host of technical challenges before they would be ready for battlefield deployment. First, the rails guiding the projectile must carry very high power. Each firing of the railgun produced tremendous current flow (almost half a million amperes) through the rails, causing rapid erosion of the rails' surfaces. Early prototypes were essentially single-use weapons, requiring complete replacement of the rails after each firing. Another challenge with the railgun system was projectile survivability. The projectiles experienced acceleration force in excess of 100,000 g. In order to be effective, the fired projectile must first survive the mechanical stress of firing, and the thermal effects of a trip through the atmosphere at many times the speed of sound before its subsequent impact with the target.

APPENDIX B – ARTIFICIAL INTELLIGENCE (AI)

1943 – WWII Triggers fresh thinking
In Britain, mathematician Alan Turing, and neurologist Grey Walter were two minds who initially tackled the challenges of intelligent machines. They traded ideas in an influential dining society called the Ratio Club. Walter built some of the first ever robots. Turing went on to invent the so-called Turing Test, which set the bar for an intelligent machine.

1950 – Science Fiction steers the conversation
Asimov was one of several science fiction writers who picked up the idea of machine Intelligence, and imagined its future. His work was popular, thought-provoking, and visionary, helping to inspire a generation of roboticists, and scientists. He was best known for the Three Laws of Robotics,[84] designed to stop our creations turning on us. But he also imagined developments that seem remarkably prescient – such as a computer capable of storing all human knowledge that anyone can ask any question.

1956 – A Top-down Approach
Top scientists debated how to tackle AI. Some, like influential academic Marvin Minsky, favored a top-down approach: pre-programming a computer with the rules that govern human behavior. Others preferred a bottom-up approach, such as neural networks that simulated brain cells, and learned new behaviors. Over time, Minsky's views dominated, and together with McCarthy he won substantial funding from the U.S. government, who hoped AI might give them the upper hand in the Cold War.

1968 – 2001: A Space Odyssey – Imagining where AI could lead
During one scene, HAL was interviewed on the BBC talking about the mission, and said that he was "fool-proof, and incapable of error." When a mission scientist was interviewed he said he believed HAL may well have genuine emotions. The film mirrored some predictions made by AI researchers at the time, including Minsky, that machines were heading towards human level Intelligence very soon. It also brilliantly captured some of the public's fears, that artificial Intelligences could turn nasty.

1969 – Tough problems to crack
Shakey was the first general-purpose mobile robot able to make decisions about its own actions by reasoning about its surroundings. It built a spatial map of what it saw, before moving. But it was painfully slow, even in an area with few obstacles. Each time it nudged forward, Shakey would have to update its map. A moving object in its field of view could easily bewilder it, sometimes stopping it in its tracks for an hour while it planned its next move. Shakey was not the first robot in operation. There had

---

[84] The Laws of Robotics are a set of **three** rules written by science fiction author Isaac Asimov. They are as follows:

1. A robot may not injure a human being or, through inaction, allow a human being to come to harm.

2. A robot must obey the orders given to it by human beings, except where such orders would conflict with the First Law.

3. A robot must protect its own existence as long as such protection does not conflict with the First or Second Law.

been others already implemented into the industrial environment, like the program I had participated. One such pioneering application was the industrialization at the VW Automobile mobilization in 1958 in Wolfsburg, Germany, turning the cumbersome framework welding process, up to now performed by humans, over to robots, and into an automated welding street one quarter of a mile long. Thus, immobile robotics was born.

1973 – The AI Winter

Though promising at the onset, there were several setbacks in the development especially after strong criticism from the U.S. Congress on top of leading mathematician Professor Sir James Lighthill who, in 1973, gave a damning health report on the state of AI in the U.K. His view was that machines would only ever be capable of an "experienced amateur" level of chess. Common sense reasoning, and supposedly simple tasks like face recognition would always be beyond their capability. Funding for the industry was slashed, ushering in what became known as the AI winter. Such negative assessments by prominent persons became predominant, usually based on the current limited technological capabilities.

1981 – A Solution for big business

It was here where U.S. policy makers stepped in, and funded a five-year AI research program. Commercialized, the efforts were far less ambitious than early AI. Instead of trying to create a general Intelligence, these 'expert systems' focused on much narrower tasks. That meant they only needed to be programmed with the rules of a very particular problem. The first successful commercial expert system, known as the RI, began operation at the Digital Equipment Corporation, helping configure orders for new computer systems. By 1986 it was saving the company an estimated $40m a year, a new promise for reviving AI.

1990 – Great controversy

For the following decades, great controversy followed. For instance, researchers from the related field of robotics, such as Rodney Brooks, inspired by advances in neuroscience, rejected symbolic AI, and focused on the basic engineering problems that would allow robots to move, and survive. Vision, for example, needed different "modules" in the brain to work together to recognize patterns, without the needs for central control. He argued that the top-down approach of pre-programming a computer with the rules of intelligent behavior was wrong. He helped drive a revival of the bottom-up approach to AI, including the long unfashionable field of neural networks.

1997 – Man vs. Machine: Fight of the 20th Century

When IBM-built machine Deep Blue beat Garry Kasparov in chess, the machine was acting intelligently far superior to Kasparov—capable of evaluating up to 200 million positions a second. But could it think strategically? The answer was a resounding yes. The supercomputer won the contest, dubbed "the brain's last stand," with such flair that Kasparov believed a human being had to be behind the controls. Some hailed this as the moment that AI came of age. But for others, this simply showed brute force at work on a highly specialized problem with clear rules.

2002 – The first Robot for the Home

Cleaning the carpet was a far cry from the early AI pioneers' ambitions. But Roomba was a big achievement. Its few layers of behavior-generating systems were far simpler than Shakey the Robot's algorithms, and were more like Grey Walter's robots over half a century before. Despite relatively simple sensors, and minimal processing power, the device had enough Intelligence to reliably, and efficiently clean a home. Roomba ushered in a new era of autonomous robots, focused on specific tasks.

2005 – War Machines
Prolific investments in autonomous robots began. BigDog, made by Boston Dynamics, was one of the first. Built to serve as a robotic pack animal in terrain too rough for conventional vehicles, it had never actually seen active service. iRobot also became a big player in this field. Their bomb disposal robot, PackBot, married user control with intelligent capabilities such as explosives sniffing. Over 2000 PackBots have been deployed for explosive detections in Iraq, and Afghanistan.

2008 – Cracking the Big Picture
It seemed simple. But this heralded a major breakthrough. Despite speech recognition being one of AI's key goals, decades of investment had never lifted it above 80% accuracy. It was here that Google stepped in with big bucks, pioneering a new approach by utilizing thousands of powerful computers, running parallel neural networks, learning to spot patterns in the vast volumes of data streaming in from Google's many users. At first it was still fairly inaccurate but, after years of learning, and improvements, Google now claims close to 100% accurate.

2010 – Dance Bots
These new computers enabled humanoid robots, like the Nao robot, an autonomous, programmable humanoid robot developed by Aldebaran Robotics, a French robotics company, to do things predecessors like Shakey had found almost impossible. Nao robots used much of the technology pioneered over the previous decade, such as learning enabled by neural networks. At Shanghai's 2010 World Expo, some of the extraordinary capabilities of these robots went on display, as 20 of them danced in perfect harmony for many minutes.

2011 – Man vs. Machine: Fight of the 21st Century
There were far greater challenges ahead for the machine than playing chess, GO, and other games. According to CNN, a study by surgeons at the Children's National Medical Center in Washington successfully demonstrated surgery with an autonomous robot. The team supervised the robot while it performed soft-tissue surgery, stitching together a bowel during open surgery, and *doing so better than a human surgeon,* the team claimed. IBM had created its own artificial Intelligence computer, the IBM Watson, which had beaten human Intelligence. Watson had to answer riddles, and complex questions. Its makers used a myriad of AI techniques, including neural networks, and trained the machine for more than three years to recognize patterns in questions, and answers. Watson trounced its opposition, the two best performers of all time on the TV show *Jeopardy,* and was hailed as a triumph for AI. Watson not only won at the game show against former champions but was declared a hero after successfully diagnosing a woman who was suffering from leukemia.

2014 – Are Machines intelligent now?

It was other, and much more challenging developments in 2014, and the following years that really demonstrated how far AI had come in 70 years. From Google's billion-dollar investment in driverless cars, to Skype's launch of real-time voice translation, intelligent machines were now becoming an everyday reality that would change all of our lives.

2015 – Military Applications

Once AI became a viable tool, it would not take much for the government, and military to get involved. While commercial applications were subjected to limited investment budgets, the military had no such constraints. Worldwide annual military spending on robotics rose from 5.1 billion USD in 2010 to 7.5 billion USD in 2015. Military drones capable of autonomous action quickly came to be widely considered as useful assets. In 2017, Vladimir Putin stated that "Whoever becomes the leader in artificial Intelligence will become the ruler of the world." Many artificial Intelligence researchers, though trying to distance themselves from military applications of AI, would not be able to stem progress for destructive uses. While having good intentions, initially, destruction is the way of mankind.

Philosophy, and ethics:

There are three philosophical questions related to AI:
1. Is artificial general Intelligence possible? Could a machine solve any problem that a human being can solve using Intelligence? Or are there hard limits to what a machine could accomplish?

2. Are intelligent machines dangerous? How can we ensure that machines behave ethically, and that they are used ethically?

3. Could a machine have a mind, consciousness, and mental states in exactly the same sense that human beings do? Could a machine be sentient, and thus deserve certain rights? Could a machine intentionally cause harm?

The limits of artificial Intelligence: "Could a machine be intelligent, and could it think?"

Alan Turing's "Polite Convention"

"We need not decide if a machine can 'think.' We need only decide if a machine can act as intelligently as a human being." This approach to the philosophical problems associated with artificial Intelligence formed the basis of the Turing test.

The Dartmouth Proposal

Every aspect of learning or any other feature of Intelligence can be so precisely described that a machine can be made to simulate it." This conjecture was printed in the proposal for the Dartmouth Conference of 1956, and represents the position of most working AI researchers.

Newell, and Simon's physical symbol system hypothesis

A physical symbol system has the necessary, and sufficient means of general intelligent action." Newell, and Simon argued that Intelligence consists of formal operations on symbols. Hubert Dreyfus argued that, on the contrary, human expertise depends on unconscious instinct rather than conscious symbol manipulation, and on having a "feel" for the situation rather than explicit symbolic knowledge.

Gödelian Arguments

Gödel himself, John Lucas in 1961, and Roger Penrose, in a more detailed argument from 1989 onwards, made highly technical arguments that "human mathematicians can consistently see the truth of their own, and therefore have computational abilities beyond that of mechanical Turing machines." However, the modern consensus in the scientific, and mathematical community is that these "Gödelian arguments" were ultimately doomed to failure.

The Artificial Brain Argument

The brain can be simulated by machines, and because brains are intelligent, simulated brains must also be intelligent; thus, machines can be intelligent." Hans Moravec, Ray Kurzweil, and others have argued that it is technologically feasible to copy the brain directly into hardware, and software, and that such a simulation would be essentially identical to the original.

The AI Effects

Machines were *already* intelligent, but observers have failed to recognize it. When Deep Blue beat Garry Kasparov in chess, the machine was acting intelligently. However, onlookers commonly discounted the behavior of an artificial Intelligence program by arguing that it was not "real" Intelligence. Thus, "real" Intelligence was whatever intelligent behavior people were able to do that machines still could not, known as the AI Effect: "AI is whatever hasn't been done yet."

Potential Risks, and Moral Reasoning:

Widespread use of artificial Intelligence could have unintended consequences that are too dangerous or undesirable. Scientists from the Future of Life Institute, among others, described some short-term research goals to see how AI influenced the economy, the laws, and ethics that were involved with AI, and how to minimize AI security risks. In the long-term, the scientists had proposed to continue optimizing function while minimizing possible security risks that come along with new technologies.

Machines with Intelligence have the potential to use their Intelligence to make ethical decisions. Research in this area includes machine ethics, artificial moral agents, and the study of malevolent vs. friendly AI.

Existential Risk

The development of full artificial Intelligence could spell the end of the human race. Once humans develop true artificial Intelligence, it would take off on its own, and redesign itself at an ever-increasing rate. Humans, who are limited by slow biological evolution, couldn't compete, and would be superseded. *—Stephen Hawking.*

APPENDIX C1 THROUGH C3 – UFO SIGHTINGS AND REPORTS

APPENDIX C–1 NEW YORK TIMES UFO REPORT
"December 16, 2017, WASHINGTON D.C.s, $600 billion annual Defense Department budgets, the $22 million spent on the *Advanced Aerospace Threat Identification Program* was almost impossible to find. Which was how the Pentagon wanted it."

For years, the program investigated reports of unidentified flying objects, according to Defense Department officials, interviews with program participants, and records obtained by The New York Times. It was run by a military Intelligence official, Luis Elizondo, on the fifth floor of the Pentagon's C Ring, deep within the building's maze.

The Defense Department has never before acknowledged the existence of the program, which it says it shut down in 2012. But its backers say that, while the Pentagon ended funding for the effort at that time, the program remains in existence. For the past five years, they say, officials with the program have continued to investigate episodes brought to them by service members, while also carrying out their other Defense Department duties.

The shadowy program — parts of it remain classified — began in 2007, and initially it was largely funded at the request of Harry Reid, the Nevada Democrat who was the Senate majority leader at the time, and who has long had an interest in space phenomena. Most of the money went to an aerospace research company run by a billionaire entrepreneur, and longtime friend of Mr. Reid's, Robert Bigelow, who is currently working with NASA to produce expandable craft for humans to use in space.

On CBS's "60 Minutes" in May, Mr. Bigelow said he was "absolutely convinced" that aliens exist, and that U.F.O.s have visited Earth.

Working with Mr. Bigelow's Las Vegas-based company, the program produced documents that describe sightings of aircraft that seemed to move at very high velocities with no visible signs of propulsion, or that hovered with no apparent means of lift.

Officials with the program have also studied videos of encounters between unknown objects, and American military aircraft—including one released in August of a whitish oval object, about the size of a commercial plane, chased by two Navy F/A-18F fighter jets from the aircraft carrier Nimitz off the coast of San Diego in 2004.

Mr. Reid, who retired from Congress this year, said he was proud of the program. "I'm not embarrassed or ashamed or sorry I got this thing going," Mr. Reid said in a recent interview in Nevada. "I think it's one of the good things I did in my congressional service. I've done something that no one has done before."

Two other former senators, and top members of a defense spending subcommittee—Ted Stevens, an Alaska Republican, and Daniel K. Inouye, a Hawaii Democrat—also supported the program. Mr. Stevens died in 2010, and Mr. Inouye in 2012.

While not addressing the merits of the program, Sara Seager, an astrophysicist at M.I.T., cautioned that not knowing the origin of an object does not mean that it is from another planet or galaxy. "When people claim to observe truly unusual phenomena, sometimes it's worth investigating seriously," she said. But, she added, "what people sometimes don't get about science is that we often have phenomena that remain unexplained."

James E. Oberg, a former NASA space shuttle engineer, and the author of 10 books on spaceflight who often debunks U.F.O. sightings, was also doubtful. "There are plenty of prosaic events, and human perceptual traits that can account for these stories," Mr. Oberg said. "Lots of people are active in the air, and don't want others to know about it. They are happy to lurk unrecognized in the noise, or even to stir it up as camouflage."

Still, Mr. Oberg said he welcomed research. "There could well be a pearl there," he said. In response to questions from The Times, Pentagon officials this month acknowledged the existence of the program, which began as part of the Defense Intelligence Agency. Officials insisted that the effort had ended after five years, in 2012.

"It was determined that there were other, higher priority issues that merited funding, and it was in the best interest of the DoD to make a change," a Pentagon spokesman, Thomas Crosson, said in an email, referring to the Department of Defense.

But Mr. Elizondo said the only thing that had ended was the effort's government funding, which dried up in 2012. From then on, Mr. Elizondo said in an interview, he worked with officials from the Navy, and the C.I.A. He continued to work out of his Pentagon office until this past October, when he resigned to protest what he characterized as excessive secrecy, and internal opposition. "Why aren't we spending more time, and effort on this issue?" Mr. Elizondo wrote in a resignation letter to Defense Secretary Jim Mattis.

Pentagon officials say the program ended in 2012, five years after it was created, but the official who led it said that only the government funding had ended then. Credit Charles Dharapak, Associated Press.

Mr. Elizondo said that the effort continued, and that he had a successor, whom he declined to name.

U.F.O.s have been repeatedly investigated over the decades in the United States, including by the American military. In 1947, the Air Force began a series of studies that investigated more than 12,000 claimed U.F.O. sightings before it was officially ended in 1969. The project, which included a study code-named Project Blue Book, started in 1952, concluded that most sightings involved stars, clouds, conventional aircraft or spy planes, although 701 remained unexplained.

Robert C. Seamans Jr., the secretary of the Air Force at the time, said in a memorandum announcing the end of Project Blue Book that it "no longer can be justified either on the ground of national security or in the interest of science."

Mr. Reid said his interest in U.F.O.s came from Mr. Bigelow. In 2007, Mr. Reid said in the interview, Mr. Bigelow told him that an official with the Defense Intelligence Agency had approached him wanting to visit Mr. Bigelow's ranch in Utah, where he conducted research. Mr. Reid said he met with agency officials shortly after his meeting with Mr. Bigelow, and learned that they wanted to start a research program on U.F.O.s. Mr. Reid then summoned Mr. Stevens, and Mr. Inouye to a secure room in the Capitol.

"I had talked to John Glenn a number of years before," Mr. Reid said, referring to the astronaut, and former senator from Ohio, who died in 2016. Mr. Glenn, Mr. Reid said, had told him he thought that the federal government should be looking seriously into U.F.Os, and should be talking to military service members, particularly pilots, who had reported seeing aircraft they could not identify or explain.

Luis Elizondo, who led the Pentagon effort to investigate U.F.O.s until October. He resigned to protest what he characterized as excessive secrecy, and internal opposition to the program. Credit Justin T. Gellerson for The New York Times

The sightings were not often reported up the military's chain of command, Mr. Reid said, because service members were afraid they would be laughed at or stigmatized.

The meeting with Mr. Stevens, and Mr. Inouye, Mr. Reid said, "was one of the easiest meetings I ever had."

He added, "Ted Stevens said, 'I've been waiting to do this since I was in the Air Force.'" (The Alaska senator had been a pilot in the Army's air force, flying transport missions over China during World War II.)

During the meeting, Mr. Reid said, Mr. Stevens recounted being tailed by a strange aircraft with no known origin, which he said had followed his plane for miles.

None of the three senators wanted a public debate on the Senate floor about the funding for the program, Mr. Reid said. "This was so-called black money," he said. "Stevens knows about it, Inouye knows about it. But that was it, and that's how we wanted it." Mr. Reid was referring to the Pentagon budget for classified programs.

Robert Bigelow, a billionaire entrepreneur, and longtime friend of Mr. Reid, received most of the money allocated for the Pentagon program. On CBS's "60 Minutes" in May, Mr. Bigelow said he was "absolutely convinced" that aliens exist, and that U.F.O.s have visited Earth. Credit Isaac Brekken for The New York Times.

Contracts obtained by The Times show a congressional appropriation of just under $22 million beginning in late 2008 through 2011. The money was used for management of the program, research, and assessments of the threat posed by the objects. The funding went to Mr. Bigelow's company, Bigelow Aerospace, which hired subcontractors, and solicited research for the program.

Under Mr. Bigelow's direction, the company modified buildings in Las Vegas for the storage of metal alloys, and other materials that Mr. Elizondo, and program contractors said had been recovered from unidentified aerial phenomena. Researchers also studied people who said they had experienced physical effects from encounters with the objects, and examined them for any physiological changes. In addition, researchers spoke to military service members who had reported sightings of strange aircraft.

"We're sort of in the position of what would happen if you gave Leonardo da Vinci a garage-door opener," said Harold E. Puthoff, an engineer who has conducted research on extrasensory perception for the C.I.A., and later worked as a contractor for the program. "First of all, he'd try to figure out what is this plastic stuff. He wouldn't know anything about the electromagnetic signals involved or its function."

The program collected video, and audio recordings of reported U.F.O. incidents, including footage from a Navy F/A-18 Super Hornet showing an aircraft surrounded by some kind of glowing aura traveling at high speed, and rotating as it moves. The Navy pilots can be heard trying to understand what they are seeing. "There's a whole fleet of them," one exclaims. Defense officials declined to release the location, and date of the incident.

"Internationally, we are the most backward country in the world on this issue," Mr. Bigelow said in an interview. "Our scientists are scared of being ostracized, and our media is scared of the stigma. China, and Russia are much more open, and work on this with huge organizations within their countries. Smaller countries like Belgium, France, England, and South American countries like Chile are more open, too. They are proactive, and willing to discuss this topic, rather than being held back by a juvenile taboo."

By 2009, Mr. Reid decided that the program had made such extraordinary discoveries that he argued for heightened security to protect it. "Much progress has been made with the identification of several highly sensitive, unconventional aerospace-related findings," Mr. Reid said in a letter to William Lynn III, a deputy defense secretary at the time, requesting that it be designated a "restricted special access program" limited to a few listed officials.

A 2009 Pentagon briefing summary of the program prepared by its director at the time asserted that "what was considered science fiction is now science fact," and that the United States was incapable of defending itself against some of the technologies discovered. Mr. Reid's request for the special designation was denied.

Mr. Elizondo, in his resignation letter of Oct. 4, said there was a need for more serious attention to "the many accounts from the Navy, and other services of unusual aerial systems interfering with military weapon platforms, and displaying beyond-next-generation capabilities." He expressed his frustration with the limitations placed on the program, telling Mr. Mattis that "there remains a vital need to ascertain capability, and intent of these phenomena for the benefit of the armed forces, and the nation."

Mr. Elizondo has now joined Mr. Puthoff, and another former Defense Department official, Christopher K. Mellon, who was a deputy assistant secretary of defense for Intelligence, in a new commercial venture called To the Stars Academy of Arts, and Science. They are speaking publicly about their efforts as their venture aims to raise money for research into U.F.O.s.

In the interview, Mr. Elizondo said he, and his government colleagues had determined that the phenomena they had studied did not seem to originate from any country. "That fact is not something any government or institution should classify in order to keep secret from the people," he said.

For his part, Mr. Reid said he did not know where the objects had come from. "If anyone says they have the answers now, they're fooling themselves," he said. "We do not know."

But, he said, "we have to start someplace."

APPENDIX C–2 DO UFOs EXIST

On December 16, 2017, the *New York Times* published two stories that read almost like science fiction. For at least five years, the Defense Department housed a $22-million, clandestine program to investigate UFOs. Military pilots had sent in reports of objects they observed that moved in unfamiliar ways; the mission of the Advanced Aerospace Threat Identification Program, as it was called, was to investigate those claims to see if there was truly something otherworldly behind those sightings.

American culture is steeped in depictions of what would happen if sophisticated aliens visited Earth, from *E.T.* to *Arrival* to *Independence Day*. Some are more hackneyed than others; some are downright terrifying. But outside the clear genres of fiction, most conversations about UFOs happen online, and with varying degrees of vehemence. Let's face it—believing in the paranormal has become shorthand for crazy.

60 years of folklorization, and Hollywood production have, in the minds of the general public, definitely trivialized the subject. It has become a 'standard' consumer product," Jean-Christophe Doré, the technical manager for UFO-SCIENCE, the French association that aims to scientifically evaluate aspects of UFO phenomena, tells Futurism.

But to some, that association might be changing. Luis Elizondo, the military official formerly in charge of the Advanced Aerospace Threat Identification Program, told *The New York Times'* Daily podcast:

"I think we're entering an era of actual evidence. We've reached a moment of critical mass of credible witnesses, and these are witnesses that are in charge of multi-million-dollar weapon platforms with, in some cases, the highest level of security clearances, and in some cases, they're trained observers. When these individuals are trying to report something, 'Hey I saw this when I was flying,' that can be turned around, and people say 'hey look if you're crazy, there goes your flight status.' Or all of a sudden commander so-and-so in charge of this very elite fighter wing will no longer be taken seriously. In fact, people are going to start to judge whether or not maybe our friend here might not be a little crazy, or maybe some loose screws. That's always a threat to these people's career, and let's face it, these people have to pay their taxes, they have to pay their mortgages, they have families, they're putting their kids through school, and frankly, they're just really good patriots, and they want to do the right thing, and that stigma is pretty powerful. It stops a lot of people from reporting something maybe they would normally report."

Government officials are no longer hiding their belief that extraterrestrials might be out there. Could this be a turning point for once-fringe communities, and open doors for those looking to bring scientific rigor to the quest to understand UFOs?

Logical Fallacy
Most phenomena thought to be the doings of extraterrestrials are eventually explained. Take Project Blue Book, for example, the U.S. government's program to investigate unidentified flying objects that ran from 1947 until 1969. Of the more than 12,000 reported sightings, investigators found out the real (not paranormal) story for all but

700 or so. That's a pretty good percentage, says Joe Nickell, senior research fellow at the Committee for Skeptical Inquiry, and paranormal investigator—about as much as you'd expect from any other scientific discipline. "A lot of these cases are never going to be solved because I don't know what you think you saw 10 years ago. They're not investigatable," Nickell tells Futurism.

In other disciplines, a certain amount of uncertainty will mean that more studies are needed to definitely prove a link. But that's not what happens with UFOs. "We spend all these years, virtually our entire lives (it's what I'm doing with mine), and we're solving most cases. We're down to, say, 5 percent [that we can't explain], and we're arguing over the 5 percent," Nickell says. You give someone a level-headed, thorough, earthly explanation for a particular report, and they'll just respond, "But what about *this other* one?" This is, as Nickell points out, an argument from ignorance—in essence, X must be true because you can't prove that X is false. "Why don't we assume that, if we can explain 95 percent, that if we knew the answer, it would fall into the same category as the others?" Nickell says.

Belief in extraterrestrials is fueled by a *lack* of evidence, not its presence. For some people, that's enough.

The Psychology of Believers
More than half of Americans believe that aliens exist, according to a 2015 poll. Scientists have evaluated what distinguishes believers, and non-believers, and didn't find much, *the Conversation* notes. But people that believe they had an abduction experience, perhaps a more extreme form of belief, are more likely to have fantasy-prone personalities, have experienced childhood trauma, or be prone to hypnosis that can make them suggestible to false memories, studies have shown. That doesn't mean they're lying about their experiences—they often genuinely believe they happened— but those experiences were often not quite what the individuals thought they were.

What distinguishes people who believe in Big Foot, for example, from those who believe in UFOs? It's the suspicion of government involvement, Nickell says. More people believe in conspiracies than ever; if someone were looking to find a black-ops government program, and a conspiracy to keep it secret, they'd find the Advanced Aerospace Threat Identification Program.

"I think, for most people who believe in these UFO claims, it's tied up with conspiracy. If you want to believe that UFOs are visiting the planet, there kind of has to be a cover up," Rob Brotherton, a psychology professor at Barnard College, and the author of *Suspicious Minds: Why We Believe Conspiracy Theories*, tells Futurism, and because they're built on secrecy, it's really hard to disprove a conspiracy theory, Brotherton points out.

Conspiracy theories about UFOs, in particular, are pretty widespread, and they have a psychological appeal that goes against the stereotype of weirdos wearing tinfoil hats. Conspiracy theories rely on the same pattern-recognition techniques we use in our daily lives, and in science as well. "Conspiracy theories make for great stories, they're tantalizing, mysteries not yet fully solved. Your brain is like, 'What's up with that?' it's not satisfied until it knows if these things are related."

Most of the time, people who believe in them are psychologically normal. But the belief that the government or aliens are specifically pursuing you as an individual—

a *me, and* not an *us* focus—might indicate a psychiatric disorder like schizophrenia, though that would be one of a number of symptoms.

"It's not impossible [that extraterrestrials are visiting Earth]," Brotherton says. "Maybe they're technologically advanced, maybe they are able to make it here. That's not beyond the realms of possibility; it doesn't defy the laws of physics necessarily. It's worth keeping an eye out for this stuff."

Worthy of Pursuit

Science hinges on discovery, and the pursuit to understand the unknown. It's not out of the realm of possibility, then, that some of these UFO reports are worthy of rigorous investigation. They could reveal something new about atmospheric phenomena, or physics, or, yes, possibly even extraterrestrials.

It's not easy to separate the mysterious sightings, the ones that could yield something scientifically interesting, from the sightings that can quickly be resolved. "These are, almost by definition, unusual things to start with, something in the sky that we don't know what it is. We don't see them every night. So, we have no idea [at the beginning of an investigation] if they're going to be productive or not," Nickell says.

Despite these difficulties, some investigators are already bringing the rigor of science to examine UFO reports. Some, like Nickell, are hunting down witnesses, and testing theories; others, like Chase Kloetzke, the deputy director of investigations at MUFON, the world's oldest, and largest UFO investigation group, are retrieving physical evidence, and testing alloys of unknown metals with cutting-edge microscopes, and trained metallurgists. A number of organizations receive private funding, which sometimes means they have fewer resources than they would if they received governments grants, and the work is often thankless. "I'm trying, in the name of science, to do what most scientists don't have time to do, what they consider frivolous nonsense," Nickell says. "UFOs have been looked into now by the tens of thousands, even by official government studies, and what do we have to show? Not a lot. How many more will we have to look into? I would say we will never be done. I'm in it for the long haul."

To do these sorts of investigations, it's irrelevant whether or not they believe that extraterrestrials have really visited Earth. All people need is a rigorous scientific mind, perseverance to investigate doggedly, and a sensitive nose for falsehoods.

Now that information about the Advanced Aerospace Threat Identification Program has spilled out, it buoys those who hope that the government might have evidence that could more clearly indicate the presence of extraterrestrials, something that stands up to the rigor of scientific evaluation. "Do we have a smoking gun? We do, it's just locked up," Kloetzke, of MUFON, says referring to the "physical material [the government] has been holding, and analyzing." "We're pushing down the doors. We're trying to breach this information," she says.

Still, opinions vary on how much evidence is enough to prove the existence of extraterrestrials. "I think most people are going to need a craft to land in Central Park [to believe UFOs are real]," Kloetzke says.

APPENDIX C–3 DETAILED REPORTING

The Most Famous UFO Cases of All-Time

Whether your interest in UFO sightings is new, or you've long been interested in extraterrestrial incidents, or perhaps you yourself have witnessed some phenomenon that you cannot explain, I invite you to read more about the top 20 most famous UFO cases in recorded history, as listed below in *ACTIVE INTERNET LINKS* (Major Incident Reports). For each, MUFON has compiled casebooks on these incidents, sourcing as many accounts as possible, and presenting as many views as possible using scientific methodology wherever possible.

You will gain a better understanding of the events surrounding the 1947 Roswell UFO Crash retrieval. Or revisit an episode you watched on Sci-Fi or the History Channel about Betty, and Barney Hill's harrowing encounter in New England in 1961. Did you hear about the recent possible non-extraterrestrial explanation for the Kecksburg PA crash in 1965?

Everyone seems to have heard about the Abduction of Travis Walton in 1975, but do you know all the details of his encounter, and subsequent treatment upon his return? What do you make of the Cash-Landrum incident in Texas in 1980 where eyewitnesses to an alleged UFO craft landing experienced skin, and hair issues consistent with radiation poisoning?

Many non-believer's gripe that UFO sightings, and other unexplained incidents seem to always occur in very remote areas. That does not explain the incident of UFOs over the U.S. Capitol building in Washington, D.C. in 1952, nor the more recent Phoenix Lights UFO craft sightings in 1997. Hundreds of credible witnesses reported lights flying in formation at extraordinary speeds over the city one evening. There are numerous home video records of the event including footage taken by a well-known local TV news personality.

These incidents are by no means the sole sightings reported at that time. There are literally hundreds of UFO, and related sightings every month. If you have experienced a sighting, have personally viewed a structured sky craft, have witnessed light orbs of any size, seen actual living entities that do not appear to be of earthly origin, have been abducted by aliens, or have discovered animal mutilations, or even crop circles, google:

https://www.nuforc.org – National UFO reporting center
https://www.mufon.com – Mutual UFO Network

MUFON and NUFORC will catalogue your report, and appreciates any level of detail that you can provide. These include testimony, photographs, and videos. If you wish to remain anonymous, they will respect your wishes.

Regarding the twenty most famous UFO cases I have cited here, you'll see that the earliest reported sightings have been compiled from limited resources. These include microfiche from the newspapers of the day as few eyewitnesses, if any, were still living at the time of the respective investigation.

Perhaps the most exciting prospect is that as technology progresses, after all, 15 years ago cell phones did not have cameras, and today few of us are ever without them, there will likely be more, and better documented sightings to research, and consider.

They readily invite believers as well as skeptics to review MUFON's case histories of these famous UFO cases, and decide for themselves.

ACTIVE INTERNET LINKS (Major Incident Reports)
    Aurora TX Crash - 1897
    Maury Island Incident - 1947
    Roswell UFO Retrieval - 1947
    Mantell Case - 1948
    UFOs over Washington, DC - 1952
    Hill Abduction - 1961
    Billy Meier - 1964 to Present
    Incident at Exeter - 1965
    Kecksburg Crash - 1965
    Pascagoula Mississippi - 1973
    Piedmont Missouri Case - 1973
    Travis Walton Abduction - 1975
    Iranian UFO Intercept - 1976
    Valentich Disappearance - 1978
    Cash Landrum Case - 1980
    Rendlesham Forest - 1980
    Japanese Air Flight 1628 - 1986
    America West Air Case - 1995
    Phoenix Lights - 1997
    Chicago O'Hare UFO - 2006
    Stephenville, TX - 2008

WIKIPEDIA LIST OF REPORTED UFO SIGHTINGS
    https://en.wikipedia.org/wiki/List_of_reported_UFO_sightings

ROSWELL INCIDENCE LIST
    The Roswell Story - The Primary Witnesses
    More witnesses
    Reluctant_Roswell_Widows2.doc (Robert Hastings)
    Roswell List of Witnesses - Kevin Randle
    The press conference
    The Timeline

GAO REPORT (General Accounting Office)
    Found: The Archaeologists - Update, 12/1/98 (Randle)
    Col. Blanchard's Press Release (Miller)
    Kent Jeffrey & Roswell (Friedman)
    Mack Brazel, Reconsidered, IUR 24-4 (Carey & Schmitt)
    Roswell: Clashing Visions of the Possible, IUR 22-3 (Swords)
    The *Popular Mechanics* Roswell Hoax (Durant)
    Major Jesse Marcel's Postwar Service Evaluations (Rudiak)

THE CIC AGENTS
Cavitt to Rickett on Roswell: "We Both Know What Really Happened Out There!" - Carey/Schmitt "It Looks Like Something Landed Here." - Carey/Schmitt
Did Sheridan Cavitt Visit the Same Crash Site? (Maccabee)

THE ROSWELL INCIDENT (CUFOS)
The Roswell Case Summary, The Whole Story, Rebuttal to the Air Force's Roswell Report Case Closed, The Glue Explanation Just Won't Stick, An Engineer Looks at the Project Mogul Hypothesis, A Conversation with Jesse Marcel, Jr., SOM 1-01 Manual: Alleged MJ-12 Document, Roswell: 52 Years of Unanswered Questions.

OTHER ROSWELL WEB SITES:
The UFOLOGY Resource Center: Roswell (Sci-Fi Channel) - 14 Articles
(Ramey Memo) Computer Enhancements (Burleson)
(Ramey Memo) Roswell Proof: What Really Happened? (Rudiak)
Story about J. Bond Johnson - VJ Enterprises (Shapiro)
The Project 1947 Roswell Page
Truthseeker At Roswell (Balthaser)

REPORTING CATEGORIES
Early Sightings
Visual:
Aircraft, Ball Lightning, Blimp, Civilian, Chaff, Cloud Formation, Disc Shaped, Kite, Military, Radar, Satellite, Searchlight, Sputnik, Submerged, Vehicle Light, Aircraft, Animal Mutilations.
Astrological:
Aurora, Birds, Comets, Contrails, Debris Reflections, Glass Reflections, Moon, Meteors, Mirage, Missiles, Planets, Ship lights, Stars, Sun, Targeting, Tow Objects, Crop Circles.
Photoshop Fabrication

LATER CASE SIGHTING
2012 to present
Colors reported – Every color in the spectrum

MUFON Shapes
Ball, Cigar, Cone, Chevron, Circle, Cross, Cylindrical, Diamond, Disc, Dumbbell, Egg, Flying Disc, Fireball, Ground-based Disc, Hovering Disc, Lantern, Oval, Saturn (Rings), Saucer, Sphere, Square, Triangle, Tube.

NICAP Reporting
Animal Effects Cases, Aircraft. Airship, Brilliant Lights, Close encounters, Crashing, Sounds, Distant encounters, Electro-Magnetic, Engine Sound, Entities (ETs), Hideous, Beings, Humming Sounds, Luminous Clouds, No sound,

Physical Evidence, Psychological, Pulsating Lights, Radar, Radiation, Roaring sound, Spaceship, Strange, Beings, Sucking, Sound, Unknown Objects, Wheels, Wing-shaped.

MORE SAMPLE REPORTS

Billy Meier's Encounter, Switzerland, 1964

Meier claims his extraterrestrial encounters began in 1942, at the age of five, when he met an elderly Plejaren man named "Sfath." After Sfath's death in 1953, Meier said, he began communicating with an extraterrestrial woman (though not a Plejaren) called "Asket." All contacts ceased in 1964, he said, then resumed on January 28, 1975, when he met "Semjase." the granddaughter of Sfath, and shortly thereafter another Plejaren man called "Ptaah." Other Plejarens, including a woman named "Nera," have since allegedly joined the dialog as well. Meier's photographs, and films are claimed by him to show alien spacecraft floating above the Swiss countryside. He calls the alleged spaceships "beamships" from Plejaren. According to Meier, the Plejaren gave him permission to photograph, and film their beamships so that he could produce evidence of their extraterrestrial visitations. Some of Meier's photos are claimed by him to show prehistoric Earth scenes, extraterrestrials, and celestial objects from an alleged non-Earthly vantage point. Meier's claims are widely characterized as fraudulent by scientists, skeptics, and most Ufologists, who say that his photographs, and films are hoaxes. In 1997, Meier's ex-wife, Kalliope, told interviewers that his photos were of spaceship models he crafted with items like trash can lids, carpet tacks, and other household objects, and that the stories he told of his adventures with the aliens were similarly fictitious. She also said that photos of purported extraterrestrial women "Asket", and "Nera" were really photos of Michelle DellaFave, and Susan Lund, members of the singing, and dancing troupe The Gold diggers later confirmed.

Incident at Exeter, NH, 1965

The Exeter incident was a highly publicized UFO sighting that occurred on September 3, 1965, approximately 5 miles (8 km) south of Exeter, New Hampshire, in the neighboring town of Kensington. Although several separate sightings had been made by numerous witnesses in the weeks leading up to September 3, the specific incident, eventually to become by far the most famous, involved a local teenager, and two police officers. In 2011, Joe Nickell, a prominent skeptic, and James McGaha, Major, USAF retired, proposed a possible explanation for the incident in the *Skeptical Inquirer*. As a pilot, McGaha had been refueled in flight by KC-97 tanker aircraft like the ones stationed at Pease AFB near Exeter in 1965. In the article, he claimed to have recognized the flashing red light pattern reported by the witnesses Bertrand, and Muscarello: one, two, three, four, five, four, three, two, one. According to Nickell, and McGaha, before refueling, the underbelly of the KC-97 tankers flashed five very bright red lights in that same pattern. The refueling boom hung down at a 60-degree angle, and would flutter in the air currents when not being controlled by the boom operator: hence "floating like a leaf" per witness Muscarello.

Kecksburg Crash, PA, 1965

The Kecksburg UFO incident occurred on December 9, 1965, at Kecksburg, Pennsylvania, United States. A large, brilliant fireball was seen by thousands in at least six U.S. states, and Ontario, Canada. It streaked over the Detroit, Michigan – Windsor, Canada area, reportedly dropped hot metal debris over Michigan, and northern Ohio, starting some grass fires, and caused sonic booms in the Pittsburgh metropolitan area. It was generally assumed, and reported by the press to be a meteor after authorities discounted other proposed explanations such as a plane crash, errant missile test, or reentering satellite debris. However, eyewitnesses in the small village of Kecksburg, about 30 miles southeast of **Pittsburgh**, claimed something crashed in the woods. A boy said he saw the object land; his mother saw a wisp of blue smoke arising from the woods, and alerted authorities. Another reported feeling a vibration, and "a thump" about the time the object reportedly landed. Others from Kecksburg, including local volunteer fire department members, reported finding an object in the shape of an **acorn**, and about as large as a **Volkswagen Beetle**. Witnesses further reported that intense military presence, most notably the United States Army, secured the area, ordered civilians out, and then removed an object on a **flatbed truck**. The official explanation of the widely seen fireball was that it was a mid-sized meteor. However, speculation as to the identity of the Kecksburg object (if there was one—reports vary) range from alien craft to a most likely debris from **Kosmos 96**, a **Soviet** space probe intended for Venus but failed, and never left the Earth's atmosphere.

Pascagoula Abduction, MS, 1973

On the evening of October 11, 1973, co-workers 42-year-old Charles Hickson, and 19-year-old Calvin Parker told the **Jackson County, Mississippi** Sheriff's office they were **fishing** off a pier on the west bank of the **Pascagoula River** in **Mississippi** when they heard a whirring/whizzing sound, saw two flashing blue lights, and an oval shaped object 30–40 feet across, and 8–10 feet high. Parker, and Hickson claimed that they were "conscious but paralyzed" while three "creatures" took them aboard the object, and subjected them to an examination before releasing them. Hickson claimed additional encounters with aliens in 1974, alleging that the aliens told him they were "peaceful". Aviation journalist, and UFO skeptic **Philip J. Klass** found "discrepancies" in Hickson's story. When Hickson took a **polygraph** exam, the examiner determined that Hickson believed the abduction story, but Klass argued that the test was administered by an "inexperienced" operator, and that Hickson refused to take another by a more experienced police operator. Klass concluded the case was a hoax based on these, and other discrepancies. Skeptical investigator **Joe Nickell** wrote that Hickson's behavior was "questionable", and that he altered or embellished his story when later appearing on television shows. Nickell speculated that Hickson may have fantasized the encounter with aliens during a **hypnagogic** "waking dream state", adding that Parker's corroboration of the tale was likely due to suggestibility since he told police he had "passed out at the beginning of the incident, and failed to regain consciousness until it was over".

Piedmont Missouri Case, MO, 1973

High school basketball coach Bone was no believer in UFOs -- at least not before the night of February 21 when with two team managers, and three of his players he was returning home along U.S. Highway 60 near Ellsinore, Mo., about 20 miles south of Piedmont. They were in poor spirits after losing a crucial tournament game by seven points, and were rehashing their defeat. Suddenly Bone, who was driving, noticed a "bright shaft of light beaming down out of the sky." A few miles later as the car passed through the Brushy Creek area, player Randal Holmes noticed something else. "Look!" he shouted. "There's that thing we saw back on Highway 60!" Bone pulled over to the side of the road, and the six piled out. It looked like it was about 200 yards off the road hovering over an open field, Bone said later. (Investigators from the International UFO Bureau (IUFOB) of Oklahoma City later estimated the object probably was about 400 feet above the ground.) "It was impossible to determine the size or shape because of the darkness. Anyway, we saw four lights that looked like portholes: red, green, amber, and white. We figured they were about three or four feet apart, all in a row. We just stood there, and watched it for about 10 minutes," Cary Barks, another witness, added. "Then all of a sudden the lights went directly up in the air with absolutely no noise, and just disappeared over a hill."

Travis Walton Abduction, AZ, 1975

According to Walton, on November 5, 1975 he was working with a lumbering crew in the **Apache-Sitgreaves National Forest** near **Snowflake, Arizona**. While riding in a truck with six of his coworkers, they encountered a saucer-shaped object hovering over the ground approximately 110 feet away, making a high-pitched buzz. Walton claims that after he left the truck, and approached the object, a beam of light suddenly appeared from the craft, and knocked him unconscious. The other six men were frightened, and supposedly drove away. Walton claimed that he awoke in a hospital-like room, being observed by three **short, bald creatures**. He claimed that he fought with them until a human wearing a helmet led Walton to another room, where he blacked out as three other humans put a clear plastic mask over his face. Walton has claimed he remembers nothing else until he found himself walking along a highway, with the **flying saucer** departing above him.

Skeptics consider the case to be a **hoax**, describing it as "sensationalizing on the part of the media", and "a put-up job to make money." UFO researcher **Philip J. Klass** considered Walton's story to be a hoax perpetrated for financial gain, and discovered many "discrepancies" in the accounts of Walton, and his co-workers. After investigating the case, Klass reported that the polygraph tests were "poorly administered," that Walton used "polygraph countermeasures" such as holding his breath, and uncovered an earlier failed test administered by an examiner who concluded the case involved "gross deception."

UFO Intercept, Iran, 1976

The 1976 Tehran UFO Incident was a **radar**, and visual sighting of an **unidentified flying object** (UFO) over **Tehran**, the capital of **Iran**, during the early morning hours of 19 September 1976. During the incident, two **F-4 Phantom II** jet interceptors reported losing instrumentation, and communications as they approached the object. These were restored upon withdrawal. Regarding pilot reports of "bright objects" falling to the ground, and "leaving a bright trail", author **Brian Dunning** observes that September 19, the day of the incident, was the height of two annual meteorite showers, the Gamma Piscids, and the Southern Piscids, and the tail of the Eta Draconids shower, so observation of falling objects or odd lights would not have been unusual. At the site where the falling light supposedly crashed, a beeping **transponder** from a C-141 aircraft was found according to investigating Col. Mooy.

Valentich Disappearance, Australia, 1978

Frederick Valentich was an Australian pilot who disappeared while on a 125-mile (235 km) training flight in a Cessna 182L light aircraft over Bass Strait on the evening of Saturday, 21 October 1978. Described as a "flying saucer enthusiast", twenty-year-old Valentich informed Melbourne air traffic control he was being accompanied by an aircraft about 1,000 feet (300 m) above him, and that his engine had begun running roughly, before finally reporting, "It's not an aircraft." There were belated reports of a UFO sighting in Australia on the night of the disappearance; however, the Associated Press reported that the Department of Transport was skeptical a UFO was behind Valentich's disappearance, and that some of their officials speculated that "Valentich became disorientated, and saw his own lights reflected in the water, or lights from a nearby island, while flying upside down." It has been proposed that Valentich staged his own disappearance: even taking into account a trip of between 30, and 45 minutes to Cape Otway, the single-engine Cessna 182 still had enough fuel to fly 800 kilometers; despite ideal conditions, at no time was the aircraft plotted on radar, casting doubts as to whether it was ever near Cape Otway;, and Melbourne Police received reports of a light aircraft making a mysterious landing not far from Cape Otway at the same time as Valentich's disappearance.

Cash Landrum Case, TX, 1980
On the evening of December 29, 1980, Betty Cash, and Vickie, and Colby Landrum (Vickie's seven-year-old grandson) were driving home to Dayton, Texas in Cash's Oldsmobile Cutlass after dining out. At about 9:00 p.m., while driving on an isolated two-lane road in dense woods, the witnesses said they observed a light above some trees. They initially thought it was an airplane approaching Houston Intercontinental Airport (about 35 miles away), and gave it little notice. A few minutes later on the winding roads, the witnesses saw what they believed to be the same light as before, but it was now much closer, and very bright. They claimed that the light came from a huge diamond-shaped object, which hovered at about treetop level. Its base was expelling flame, and emitting significant heat. Landrum told Cash to stop the car, fearing they would be burned if they approached any closer. However, her opinion of the object quickly changed: a born-again Christian, she now interpreted the object as a sign of the second coming of Jesus Christ, telling Colby: "That's Jesus. He will not hurt us." In 1998, journalist, and UFO sceptic Philip J. Klass, found a few reasons to doubt the story by Cash, and Landrum: when Schuessler inspected Betty's car in early 1981, and used a Geiger counter to check for radioactivity, he found none. Presumably [sic] he also checked for radioactivity when he visited the site of the (alleged) incident, and found no abnormal radiation. Schuessler provides NO medical data on Betty's health PRIOR to the UFO incident. Nor does he provide any medical data on the prior health of Vicki or Colby. Other UFO researchers point out that high-energy ionizing radiation of the kind that can cause damage to human beings (e.g. gamma radiation) does not induce radioactivity in objects, and would not have left behind any residual radioactivity in the area.

Rendlesham Forest, England, 1980
In late December 1980, there were a series of reported sightings of unexplained lights near Rendlesham Forest, Suffolk, England, which have become linked with claims of UFO landings. The events occurred just outside RAF Woodbridge, which was used at the time by the U.S. Air Force. USAF personnel, including deputy base commander Lieutenant Colonel Charles I. Halt, claimed to see things they described as a UFO sighting. The occurrence is the most famous of claimed UFO events to have happened

in the United Kingdom, ranking among the best-known reported UFO events worldwide. It has been compared to the Roswell UFO incident in the United States, and is sometimes referred to as "Britain's Roswell". One proposed theory is that the incident was a hoax. The BBC reported that a former U.S. security policeman, Kevin Conde, claimed responsibility for creating strange lights in the forest by driving around in a police vehicle whose lights he had modified. However, there is no evidence that this prank took place on the nights in question. The most widely accepted explanation is that the sightings were due to a combination of three main factors. The initial sighting at 3 am on 26 December, when the airmen saw something apparently descending into the forest, coincided with the appearance of a bright fireball over southern England, and such fireballs are a common source of UFO reports. The supposed landing marks were identified by police, and foresters as rabbit diggings. No evidence has emerged to confirm that anything actually came down in the forest.

Japanese Air Flight 1628, Over Alaska, 1986
Japan Air Lines flight 1628 was a UFO incident that occurred on November 17, 1986 involving a Japanese Boeing 747 cargo aircraft. The aircraft was in route from Paris to Narita International Airport, near Tokyo, with a cargo of Beaujolais wine. On the Reykjavík to Anchorage section of the flight, at 17:11 over eastern Alaska, the crew first witnessed two unidentified objects to their left. These abruptly rose from below, and closed in to escort their aircraft. Each had two rectangular arrays of what appeared to be glowing nozzles or thrusters, though their bodies remained obscured by darkness. When closest, the aircraft's cabin was lit up, and the captain could feel their heat on his face. These two craft departed before a third, much larger disk-shaped object started trailing them, causing the pilots to request a change of course. Anchorage Air Traffic Control obliged, and requested an oncoming United Airlines flight to confirm the unidentified traffic, but when it, and a military craft sighted JAL 1628 at about 17:51, no other craft could be distinguished. The sighting received special attention from the media, as a supposed instance of the tracking of UFOs on both ground, and airborne radar, while being observed by experienced airline pilots, with subsequent confirmation by an FAA Division Chief. Each object had a square shape, consisting of two rectangular arrays of what appeared to be glowing nozzles or thrusters, separated by a dark central section. Captain Terauchi speculated in his drawings, that the objects would appear cylindrical if viewed from another angle, and that the observed movement of the nozzles could be ascribed to the cylinders' rotation. The objects left abruptly at about 17:23:13, moving to a point below the horizon to the east.

America West Air Case, TX, 1995
The plane was designated as America West Flight 564, and was at 39,000 feet near Bovina, Texas, when First Officer John J. Waller, and a flight attendant observed a row of white lights which flashed from left to right. The lights were below their flying altitude. Waller immediately made radio contact with the Albuquerque FAA Air Route Traffic Control Center during the observation. Nothing could be found that should be flying in that space at that time. The B-757 continued its course, and the lights began to fall behind it. A group of dark thunderclouds formed, and enabled the UFO to be seen as a cigar-shaped object as its lights illuminated the back drop of the thunderclouds. Waller, and his co-pilot estimated the object's length at 300-400 feet.

The object was not visible on FAA radar, but one of the controllers contacted the North American Air Defense Command, and was told they NORAD was tracking an unidentified object. But, this object later turned out to be a small plane with a non-functioning transponder. The next day, the controller made another check with NORAD, and he was told that they had indeed tracked another unknown target the night before that was at first stationary, but then accelerated, and stopped again very rapidly. These quick darts were estimated at somewhere between 1,000, and 1,400 mph. When reports of the incident began to be leaked, Webb began to investigate. In addition to interviewing the airliner's crew, he also obtained the tapes of the conversation between FAA air traffic controllers, and their contacts during the sighting. He was able to make drawings of the UFO.

Phoenix Lights, AZ, 1997
The Phoenix Lights were a mass UFO sighting which occurred in Phoenix, Arizona, USA, and Sonora, Mexico on Thursday, March 13, 1997. Lights of varying descriptions were reported by thousands of people between 19:30, and 22:30 MST, in a space of about 300 miles (480 km) from the Nevada state line, through Phoenix, to the edge of Tucson. There were allegedly two distinct events involved in the incident: a triangular formation of lights seen to pass over the state, and a series of stationary lights seen in the Phoenix area. The U.S. Air Force later identified the second group of lights as flares dropped by A-10 Warthog aircraft that were on training exercises at the Barry Goldwater Range in southwest Arizona. Witnesses claim to have observed a huge, coherently-moving **V-shaped UFO** that produced no sound, and contained five spherical lights or possibly light-emitting engines. **Fife Symington**, the **governor** of Arizona at the time, was one witness to this incident. As governor, he ridiculed the idea of alien origin, but several years later he described the lights he saw as "otherworldly" after admitting he saw a similar UFO. In the April 26, 2007 episode of the **Skeptoid podcast** titled "The Alien Invasion of Phoenix, Arizona", **scientific skeptic** author **Brian Dunning** evaluated the details of the Phoenix Lights. After a lengthy analysis of the reported sightings, photographic evidence, media coverage, and controversy, Dunning concluded: "The Phoenix Lights were flares. Deal with it."

Chicago O'Hare UFO, IL, 2006
At approximately 16:15 CST on Tuesday, November 7, 2006, federal authorities at Chicago O'Hare International Airport received a report that a group of twelve airport employees were witnessing a metallic, saucer-shaped craft hovering over Gate C-17. The object was first spotted by a ramp employee who was pushing back United Airlines Flight 446, which was departing Chicago for Charlotte, North Carolina. The employee apprised Flight 446's crew of the object above their aircraft. It is believed that both the pilot, and co-pilot also witnessed the object. Several independent witnesses outside of the airport also saw the object. One described a "blatant" disc-shaped craft hovering over the airport which was "obviously not clouds." According to this witness, nearby observers gasped as the object shot through the clouds at high velocity, leaving a clear blue hole in the cloud layer. The hole reportedly seemed to close itself shortly afterward. Both United Airlines, and the Federal Aviation Administration (FAA) first denied that they had any information on the O'Hare UFO sighting until the *Chicago Tribune*, which was investigating the report, filed a Freedom

of Information Act (FOIA) request. The FAA then ordered an internal review of air-traffic communications tapes to comply with the *Tribune* FOIA request which subsequently uncovered a call by the United supervisor to an FAA manager in the airport tower concerning the UFO sighting. The FAA stance concludes that the sighting was caused by a weather phenomenon, and that the agency would not be investigating the incident. UFO investigators have pointed out that this stance is a direct contradiction to the FAA's mandate to investigate possible security breaches at American airports such as in this case; an object witnessed by numerous airport employees, and officially reported by at least one of them, hovering in plain sight, over one of the busiest airports in the world.

Stephenville, TX, 2008
January 8th 2008 Steve Allen, Mike Odom, and Lance Jones, were experiencing a typical Texas sunset when they spotted something very unusual in the sky. A UFO! Allen said the craft wasn't really visible, but its lights stretched out about a mile long, and a half a mile wide. The lights went from corner to corner, and were completely silent. They moved directly above Highway 67 traveling towards Stephenville at an estimated speed of 3000 miles per hour. He also stated two military jets possibly F16's, were in hot pursuit. Allen has had over 30 year's pilot experience, and is quite familiar with known aeronautical craft. Mike Odom said, "The experience was unbelievable", and Lance Jones said, "I've never seen anything like it before but it didn't scare me," excerpts taken from Stephenville Empire-Tribune article January 2008. A MUFON report, entitled "Special Research Report Stephenville, Texas" was written by Glen Schulze, and Robert Powell. Shulze has radar experience from working at the White Sands Missile Range. Powell has a chemistry degree, and has extensive experience with semiconductors from working for Advanced Micro Devices. Shulze/Powell concluded that the radar data confirms the witness observations of an object, as well as the Air Force's statement that said ten aircraft were operating in the area. They say that it is too difficult to say what the witnesses saw, but that there was something there. Twice, they say, radar picked up an object travelling at nearly 2,000 mph, and at other times it showed a slow-moving object. The Stephenville incident on January 8, saw dozens of witnesses reporting a large object in the evening sky that hovered above the community before it took off at high speed. Steve Allen, a pilot, observed the object from the ground, and described it as being a half-mile with flashing strobe lights. He also said that it was pursued by two fighter jets, when it disappeared at a speed he estimated to be 3,000 mph.

APPENDIX D1 THROUGH D10 – SAMPLE CASE STUDIES

APPENDIX D–1 Detailed Report on UFO Crash

CASE STUDY #1
Roswell Incident
July 2, 1947
Roswell, New Mexico

Competing Accounts
The existence of so many differing accounts by 1994 led to a schism among Ufologists about the events at Roswell. The Center for UFO Studies (CUFOS), and the Mutual UFO Network (MUFON), two leading UFO societies, disagreed in their views of the various scenarios presented by Randle–Schmitt, and Friedman–Berliner; several conferences were held to try to resolve the differences. One issue under discussion was where Barnett was when he saw the alien craft he was said to have encountered. A 1992 UFO conference had attempted to achieve a consensus among the various scenarios portrayed in *Crash at Corona*, and *UFO Crash at Roswell*, however, the publication of *The Truth About the UFO Crash at Roswell* had "resolved" the Barnett problem by simply ignoring Barnett, and citing a new location for the alien craft recovery, including a new group of archaeologists not connected to the ones the Barnett story cited.

In mid-1947, a United States Army Air Forces balloon crashed at a ranch near Roswell, New Mexico. Following wide initial interest in the crashed "flying disc", the US military stated that it was merely a conventional weather balloon. Interest subsequently waned until the late 1970s, when Ufologists began promoting a variety of increasingly elaborate conspiracy theories, claiming that one or more alien spacecraft had crash-landed, and that the extraterrestrial occupants had been recovered by the military, who then engaged in a cover-up.

In the 1990s, the US military published two reports disclosing the true nature of the crashed object: a nuclear test surveillance balloon from Project Mogul. Nevertheless, the Roswell incident continued to be of interest in popular media, and conspiracy theories surrounding the event persist. Roswell has been described as "the world's most famous, most exhaustively investigated, and most thoroughly debunked UFO claim".

Problems with Witness Accounts
Hundreds of people were interviewed by the various researchers, but critics pointed out that only a few of these people claimed to have seen debris or aliens. Most witnesses were repeating the claims of others, and their testimony would be considered hearsay in an American court of law, and therefore inadmissible as evidence. Of the 90 people claimed to have been interviewed for *The Roswell Incident*, the testimony of only 25 appeared in the book, and only seven of these people saw the debris. Of these, five handled the debris. Pflock, in *Roswell: Inconvenient Facts, and the Will to Believe* (2001), made a similar point about Randle, and Schmitt's *UFO Crash at Roswell*. Approximately 271 people were listed in the book who were "contacted, and interviewed" for the book, and this number did not include those who chose to remain anonymous, meaning more than 300 witnesses were interviewed, a figure Pflock said

the authors frequently cited. Of these 300-plus individuals, only 41 could be "considered genuine first- or second-hand witnesses to the events in, and around Roswell or at the Fort Worth Army Air Field," and only 23 can be "reasonably thought to have seen physical evidence, debris recovered from the Foster Ranch."
Of these, only seven had asserted anything suggestive of otherworldly origins for the debris.

As for the accounts from those who claimed to have seen aliens, critics identified problems ranging from the reliability of second-hand accounts, to credibility problems with witnesses making demonstrably false claims, or multiple, contradictory accounts, to dubious death-bed confessions or accounts from elderly, and easily confused witnesses. Pflock noted that only four people with supposed firsthand knowledge of alien bodies were interviewed, and identified by Roswell authors: Frank Kaufmann; Jim Ragsdale; Lt. Col. Albert Lovejoy Duran; Gerald Anderson. Duran is mentioned in a brief footnote in *The Truth About the UFO Crash at Roswell*, and never again, while the other three all had serious credibility problems. A problem with all the accounts, charge critics, was they all came about a minimum of 31 years after the events in question, and in many cases were recounted more than 40 years after the fact. Not only were memories this old of dubious reliability, they were also subject to contamination from other accounts the interviewees may have been exposed to. The shifting claims of Jesse Marcel, whose suspicion that what he recovered in 1947 was "not of this world" sparked interest in the incident in the first place, cast serious doubt on the reliability of what he claimed to be true.

In *the Roswell Incident*, Marcel stated, "Actually, this material may have *looked* like tinfoil, and balsa wood, but the resemblance ended there. They took one picture of me on the floor holding up some of the less-interesting metallic debris. The stuff in that one photo was pieces of the actual stuff we found. It was not a staged photo." Timothy Printy pointed out that the material Marcel positively identified as being part of what he recovered was material that skeptics, and UFO advocates agreed was debris from a balloon device. After that fact was pointed out to him, Marcel changed his story to say that that material was not what he recovered. Skeptics like Robert Todd argued that Marcel had a history of embellishment, and exaggeration, such as claiming to have been a pilot, and having received five Air Medals for shooting down enemy planes, claimed that were all found to be false, and skeptics felt that his evolving Roswell story was simply another instance of this tendency to fabricate.

Air Force reports, 1994–1997
In response to these reports, and after United States congressional inquiries, the General Accounting Office launched an inquiry, and directed the Office of the United States Secretary of the Air Force to conduct an internal investigation. The result was summarized in two reports. The first, released in 1994, concluded that the material recovered in 1947 was likely debris from Project Mogul, a military surveillance program employing high-altitude balloons. The second report, released in 1997, concluded that reports of recovered alien bodies were likely a combination of innocently transformed memories of accidents involving military casualties with memories of the recovery of anthropomorphic dummies in military programs such as the 1950s Operation High Dive, mixed with hoaxes perpetrated by various witnesses,

and UFO proponents. The psychological effects of time compression, and confusion about when events occurred explained the discrepancy with the years in question.

The Air Force reports were dismissed by UFO proponents as being either disinformation or simply implausible, though skeptical researchers such as Philip J. Klass, and Robert Todd, who had been expressing doubts regarding accounts of aliens for several years, used the reports as the basis for skeptical responses to claims by UFO proponents. After the release of the Air Force reports, several books, such as Kal Korff's *The Roswell UFO Crash: What They Don't Want You to Know* (1997), built on the evidence presented in the reports to conclude "there is no credible evidence that the remains of an extraterrestrial spacecraft were involved." In the 1990s, skeptics, and even some social anthropologists saw the increasingly elaborate accounts of alien crash landings, and government cover ups as evidence of a myth being constructed.

Evidence

Although there was no evidence that a UFO crashed at Roswell, believers firmly hold to the belief that one did, and that the truth had been concealed as a result of a government conspiracy. B.D. Gildenberg has called the Roswell incident "the world's most famous, most exhaustively investigated, and most thoroughly debunked UFO claim".

Pflock stated, "The case for Roswell is a classic example of the triumph of quantity over quality. The advocates of the crashed-saucer tale simply shovel everything that seems to support their view into the box marked 'Evidence', and say, 'See? Look at all this stuff. We must be right.' Never mind the contradictions. Never mind the lack of independent supporting fact. Never mind the blatant absurdities." Korff suggested there were clear incentives for some people to promote the idea of aliens at Roswell, and that many researchers were not doing competent work: "The UFO field is comprised of people who are willing to take advantage of the gullibility of others, especially the paying public. Let's not pull any punches here: The Roswell UFO myth has been very good business for UFO groups, publishers, for Hollywood, the town of Roswell, the media, and Ufology. The number of researchers who employ science, and its disciplined methodology is appallingly small."

B.D. Gildenberg wrote there were as many as 11 reported alien recovery sites, and these recoveries bore only a marginal resemblance to the event as initially reported in 1947, or as recounted later by the initial witnesses. Some of these new accounts could have been confused accounts of the several known recoveries of injured, and dead servicemen from four military plane crashes that occurred in the area from 1948 to 1950. Other accounts could have been based on memories of recoveries of test dummies, as suggested by the Air Force in their reports. Charles Ziegler argued that the Roswell story has all the hallmarks of a traditional folk narrative. He identified six distinct narratives, and a process of transmission via storytellers with a core story that was created from various witness accounts, and was then shaped, and molded by those who carry on the UFO community's tradition. Other "witnesses" were then sought out to expand the core narrative, with those who gave accounts not in line with the core beliefs being repudiated or simply omitted by the "gatekeepers." Others then retold the narrative in its new form. This whole process would repeat over time.

In September 2017, UK newspaper *The Guardian* reported on Kodachrome slides which some had claimed showed a dead space alien. First presented at a "Be-Witness" event in Mexico, organized by Jaime Maussan, and attended by almost 7,000 people, days afterwards it was revealed that the slides were in fact of a mummified Native American child discovered in 1896, and which had been on display at the Chapin Mesa Archeological Museum in Mesa Verde, Colorado for many decades.

It was no wonder that the public became utterly confused from the many contradictory reports received, and recorded by the various government offices, eventually released through FOIA. Everybody had a different agenda for how to hoodwink the public. The Roswell case, as it stood today was not better off. Nothing had changed other than many more so-called expert witnesses testifying to an ever increasingly mystifying tale that took place many decades ago.

It was the Roswell incidence that kicked off a UFO craze still active, and prolifically investigated today. It proved the point that the conspiracy-minded public needed a constant stream of information fed through sightings, and reports that could easily be explained as earthly objects if the government would be willing to share innovative projects contrived, and developed through black budget programs.

APPENDIX D–2 Detailed Report on UFO Sighting at Missile Base

CASE STUDY #2
Disc Hovers 500' Over Missile Silos
March 5, 1967
Minot AFB, North Dakota

Editor's Note:
"The case in my estimation was never investigated properly. Project Blue Book personnel never sent a representative, and the case was essentially written off despite the interest of several Strategic Air Command generals including 15th Air Force's Major General Nichols."

The sighting was officially explained on November 13, by Lt. Col. Hector Quintanilla who wrote, "The following conclusions have been reached after a thorough study of the data submitted to Foreign Technology Division. The ground visual sightings appear to be of the star Sirius, and the B-52, which was flying in the area."

The B-52 radar contact, and the temporary loss of the UHF transmission could be attributed to a plasma similar to ball lightning. The air visual from the B-52 could be the star Vega, which was on the horizon at the time, or it could be a light on the ground, or possibly a plasma. No further investigation by the Foreign Technology Division is contemplated.

This is a classic Blue Book case where dozens of Air Force personnel who see B-52s, and stars nightly have their testimony doubted. They know when they've seen a UFO. In this case the scientists doing the Condon report agreed that this was a real UFO.

The apparent damage to the missile site, and disruption of B-52 radio transmissions was in my opinion a threat to primary nuclear offensive systems, and should not have been trivialized. The records speak for themselves. This article was taken from Scientific Ufology written by Captain Kevin D. Randle USAFR.

"I consider this his finest book, and recommend its reading. This case like thousands of others are explained away with any simple mundane explanation that can be found. Yet many cases involve the tampering of key government weapon systems.

It appears Quintanilla either did not care or had instructions to write off most of the sightings with any available excuse. I wonder why the reports were white washed, while the Air Force's scientific advisor Alan Hynek was coming to the opposite conclusion that, UFOs were real?"

APPENDIX D–3 Detailed Report at Malmstrom AFB UFO/Missile Incident

CASE STUDY #3
March 16, 1967
Malmstrom AFB
Near Great Falls, MT

Because of this unique incident, as an ex-Missileer describes it: All Hell broke loose. Among the many calls to, and from the E Flight LCC one was to the MCCC of Oscar Flight which links to the equally dramatic story of what happened in another LCC that same morning.

The Oscar Flight LCC was located a mile or two, south of the town of Roy, about 20 miles southeast of the Echo Flight LCC. The following is as told by Robert Salas who was the DMCCC in O Flight that morning:

My recollection is that I was on duty as a Deputy Missile Combat Crew Commander below ground in the LCC, during the morning hours of 16 March 1967.

Outside, above the subterranean LCC capsule, it was a typical clear, cold Montana night sky, there were a few inches of snow on the ground. Where we were, there were no city lights to detract from the spectacular array of stars, and it was not uncommon to see shooting stars. Montana isn't called Big Sky Country for no reason, and Airmen on duty topside probably spent some of their time outside looking up at the stars. It was one of those airmen who first saw what at first appeared to be a star begin to zig-zag across the sky. Then he saw another light do the same thing, and this time it was larger, and closer. He asked his Flight Security Controller, FSC, the Non-Commissioned Officer, NCO, in charge of Launch Control Center site security, to come, and take a look.

They both stood there watching the lights streak directly above them, stop, change directions at high speed, and return overhead. The NCO ran into the building, and phoned me at my station in the underground capsule. He reported to me that they had been seeing lights making strange maneuvers over the facility, and that they weren't aircraft.

I replied: "Great. You just keep watching them, and let me know if they get any closer." I did not take this report seriously, and directed him to report back if anything more significant happened. At the time, I believed this first call to be a joke. Still, that sort of behavior was definitely out of character for air security policemen whose communications with us were usually very professional. A few minutes later, the security NCO called again. This time he was clearly frightened, and was shouting his words:

"Sir, there's one hovering outside the front gate."

"One what?"

"A UFO. It's just sitting there. We're all just looking at it. What do you want us to do?"

"What? What does it look like?"

"I can't really describe it. It's glowing red. What are we supposed to do?"

"Make sure the site is secure, and I'll phone the Command Post."

"Sir, I have to go now, one of the guys just got injured."

Before I could ask about the injury, he was off the line. I immediately went over to my commander, Lt. Fred Meiwald, who was on a scheduled sleep period. I woke him, and began to brief him about the phone calls, and what was going on topside. In the middle of this conversation, we both heard the first alarm klaxon resound through the confined space of the capsule, and both immediately looked over at the panel of annunciator lights at the Commander's station.

A No-Go light, and two red security lights were lit indicating problems at one of our missile sites. Fred jumped up to query the system to determine the cause of the problem. Before he could do so, another alarm went off at another site, then another, and another simultaneously. Within the next few seconds, we had lost six to eight missiles to a No-Go, inoperable, condition.

After reporting this incident to the Command Post, I phoned my security guard. He said that the man who had approached the UFO had not been injured seriously but was being evacuated by helicopter to the base. Once topside, I spoke directly with the security guard about the UFOs. He added that the UFO had a red glow, and appeared to be saucer shaped. He repeated that it had been immediately outside the front gate, hovering silently.

We sent a security patrol to check our LFs after the shutdown, and they reported sighting another UFO during that patrol. They also lost radio contact with our site immediately after reporting the UFO. When we were relieved by our scheduled replacement crew later that morning. The missiles had still not been brought on line by on-site maintenance teams.

Again, UFOs had been sighted by security personnel at or about the time Minuteman Strategic missiles shutdown.

An in-depth post incident investigation of the E Flight incident was undertaken. Full scale on-site, and laboratory tests at the Boeing Company's Seattle plant were conducted. Declassified Strategic Missile Wing documents, and interviews with ex-Boeing engineers who conducted tests following the E Flight Incident investigation confirm that no cause for the missile shutdowns was ever found. Robert Kaminski was the Boeing Company engineering team leader for this investigation. Kaminski stated that after all tests were done: There were no significant failures, engineering data or findings that would explain how ten missiles were knocked off alert, and there was no technical explanation that could explain the event.

The most that could be done was to reproduce the effects by introducing a 10-volt pulse onto a data line. Another Boeing Company engineer on the team, Robert Rigert, came up with this pulse that repeated the shutdown effects 80% of the time, but only when directly injected at the logic coupler. No explanation could be found for a source of such a pulse or noise occurring in the field, and getting inside the shielded missile system equipment.

Others on the engineering team checked other possibilities. Lightning, and problems in the commercial power system were acquitted as the source of the problem. William Dutton, another Boeing Company engineer, checked commercial power interruptions, and transients, and stated: No anomalies were found in this area.

Several military activities, and other engineering firms participated in the investigation, but no positive cause for the shutdowns was ever found, despite extensive, and concentrated effort. One conclusion was that the only way a pulse or noise could be sent in from outside the shielded system was through an electromagnetic pulse, EMP, from an unknown source. The technology of the day made generating an EMP of sufficient magnitude to enter the shielded system a very difficult proposition, requiring large, heavy, bulky equipment. The source of the actual pulse that caused the missile shutdowns remains a mystery to this day.

According to articles from the Great Falls Tribune newspaper, on February 8, 1967 Louis DeLeon saw two strange objects in the sky which did not look like airplanes, and they glowed an orange, and red color while driving east of Chester, MT. Later, ten miles east of Chester, Jake Walkman was awakened by a bright light at his home. From his back yard he sighted a flying saucer shaped object.

The next evening, George Kawanishi, a foreman for the Great Northern Railroad, saw a bright ball of light in the sky directly above the Chester train depot. These are but a few of the sightings which preceded the missile shutdown incidents later in March.

It was during this same period, according to Col. Don Crawford, USAF ret., that a two-person SAT, assigned to Echo Flight, was performing a routine check of the missile launch facilities a few miles north of Lewistown, MT. As they approached one of the launch facilities, an astonishing sight caused the driver to slam on his brakes. Stunned in amazement, they watched as, about 300' ahead, a very large glowing object hovered silently directly over the launch facility. One of them picked up his VHF hand microphone, and called then Captain Don Crawford who was the DMCCC on duty that evening:

"Sir, you wouldn't believe what I'm looking at, he said." He described what they were seeing. Crawford didn't believe him at first but the young airman insisted he was telling the truth, his voice revealing his emotional state. Eventually Crawford took him seriously enough to call the Command Post to report it. The officer on duty at the Command Post refused to accept the report, and simply stated: We no longer record those kinds of reports, indicating he didn't want to hear about the UFO. Crawford unsure of what to tell his shaken security guard, decided to give the guard his permission to fire his weapon at the object if it seemed hostile.

"Thanks, sir, but I really don't think it would do any good."

Seconds later the object silently flew away. There were sightings in the area before, and after the missile shutdown incidents by military personnel, and civilians. During the events of that morning in 1967, UFOs were sighted by security personnel at the Oscar Flight LCC, and at one O Flight LF, and by other security, and maintenance personnel at Echo Flight LFs. These sightings were reported separately to the capsule crews at both LCCs at or about the same time Minuteman Strategic missiles shut down at both sites. USAF has confirmed that all of Echo flights' missiles shutdown within seconds of each other, and that no cause for this could be found.

For many years, the Air Force has maintained that no reported UFO incident has ever affected national security. It is established fact that a large number of Air Force personnel reported sighting UFOs at the time many of our strategic missiles became none launchable. The incidents described above clearly had national security implications. In one previously classified message, SAC Headquarters described the E Flight incident as: loss of strategic alert of all ten missiles within ten seconds of each other for no apparent reason, and a cause for grave concern to SAC headquarters.

POST ANALYSIS

Case No. 3 is one of multiple sightings reported by silo crews from the Malmstrom missile launch facility. Similar in nature to Case 2, inspections conducted were internal to the silo, independent of local crew awareness. Many such independent inspections were conducted over a period of decades as a result of missile readiness policy changes to a preemptive strike possibility. Today, much of the policy changes are on record held as uncommon knowledge to the general public, meaning that mostly historical researchers have access to individually requested, and governmentally approved information released.

While the mystery about the unexplained missile shut downs still lingers, the true reasons behind the failures can easily be explained. I was indirectly involved in the induced shut downs during my Minuteman and Peacekeeper redesign effort on the nation's missile defense system during the 80s. My design had to be tested on the system to withstand an EMP impact in case of a direct hit by Soviet-built nuclear mega-warheads on underground Launch Facilities (LF) and missile Silos.

APPENDIX D–4 Detailed Report on UFO Crash Landing

CASE STUDY #4
Shag Harbour Crash
October 4, 1967
Don Ledger:

Detailed Account

On the night of 04 October 1967, shortly after 11:00 p.m., an object some 60 foot in diameter was seen to hover over the water near the tiny fishing village of Shag Harbour, Nova Scotia. The UFO, which displayed four bright lights that flashed in sequence, tilted to a 45-degree angle, and descended rapidly towards the water's surface. Upon impact, there was a bright flash, and an explosive roar. Concerned witnesses began calling the nearby Barrington Passage RCMP detachment. None of those witnesses mentioned anything about a UFO. Most believed that a large aircraft had ditched into the harbor, and that there might be survivors.

Eventually, three RCMP officers arrived at the shore near the impact site. Corporal V. Werbicki, and Constable Ron O'Brien, dispatched from the Barrington Passage Detachment, were approaching from east of the site. Constable Ron Pond, who was on highway patrol on Highway #3, was heading towards Shag Harbour from a position west of the impact site, and his position allowed him to view the object while it was still in flight. The unusual lighting configuration, and flight characteristics tipped Constable Pond off to the unusual nature of the object long before he heard from Cpl. Werbicki, who received his information through the initial complaints to the detachment.

When all three officers met at the impact site they found that the object was still floating on the water about a half-mile from shore. It was glowing a pale yellow, and was leaving a trail of dense yellow foam as it drifted in the ebb tide. Neither the Rescue Co-ordination Centre in Halifax nor the nearby NORAD radar facility at Baccaro, Nova Scotia, had any knowledge of missing aircraft, either civilian or military. Constable Pond reported that the object had "changed" during its descent to the water's surface, i.e., it changed shape, and that it appeared to be "no known object." Later, other local witnesses described much the same details as those of Constable Pond. Also, a coast guard lifeboat from nearby Clark's Harbour, and several local fishing boats were summoned to investigate, but the object had submerged before they reached the site. The sulfurous-smelling yellow foam continued to well to the surface from the point where it sank, and a 120 by 300-foot slick developed. Search efforts continued until 3:00 a.m., and then resumed at first light the next day. Everybody involved was convinced that "something" – something real, and unidentified – had gone into the water.

The next morning a preliminary report was sent to Canadian Forces Headquarters in Ottawa. After communicating with NORAD, Maritime Command was asked to conduct an underwater search ASAP for the object responsible for the concern in Shag Harbour. Seven navy divers from the HMCS Granby searched throughout the daylight hours until sundown of 08 October 1967. On Monday, 09 October 1967, Maritime Command canceled the search effort claiming "nil results." Outside of the local area, media attention quickly faded.

APPENDIX D–5 Detailed Report on Nuclear Reactor Intrusion

CASE STUDY #5
Reactor Complex
Incident at Indian Point, N. Y.
July 24, 1984

Philip Imbrogno, Principle Reporter
It was NYPA whose officials apparently spent considerable human energy trying to dissuade Imbrogno from writing about the July 24 event, concerned he would release information vital to the plant's security. "I think other agencies were using (the NYPA) to harass me," he said, noting that he was constantly subjected to their repetitive phone calls, threatening that he would be forced to appear at a hearing on the incident.

The NYPA's Patrick denied that any such documentation exists, and dismissed the incident by claiming that all Hudson Valley UFO sightings were later identified as light aircraft. There was no videotape taken by on-site surveillance cameras, Patrick insists, or audio recording of oral communications, both pieces of evidence which Imbrogno strongly feels do exist, and are being retained somewhere.

According to Imbrogno's sources, a security shakeup ensued the very next day. "A number of agencies came in, including the NRC, and military personnel, and they supposedly cleaned out everything. You have to remember that with nuclear reactors, you're only going to get 10 percent of the real story. They're overly terrified of bad publicity, and are really afraid of the anti-nuclear groups, which can cause trouble. Anything that happens is immediately covered up, including UFO sightings."

Imbrogno further alleges that shortly after the UFO infringement, "a crack in the reactor's casing was discovered. The public didn't hear about such a situation until a year later." The NYPA's Patrick denied any "crack," although he did recall a time when Reactor #2 may have developed an "irregularity."

Imbrogno says, "Indian Point officials" made a public statement that operations were not affected, that everything was normal. But I've been told by several people that they lost power, the security system dropped, and the reactor controls went crazy. Apparently, it was caused by the UFO.

"Any implication that the sightings of these 'light aircraft' in any way affected Reactor #3 is false," Patrick said. Imbrogno's sources indicate otherwise. Supposedly, a mass of sophisticated, high-accuracy tracking equipment was installed at the complex, enabling security to quickly generate a computer image of whatever aircraft might be affecting the equipment. Apparently, such problems were still going on. Patrick would not comment on what kinds of security equipment protect Indian Point but stressed that nothing new had been installed since the incident.

Imbrogno was also suspicious that the armed security forces at the site may have had reason to attempt firing on the craft, again an allegation flatly refuted by the NYPA. "I know a number of helicopters with rocket launchers were sent up, and followed the craft for some distance," Imbrogno commented, citing his anonymous sources for the info. "When these helicopters went on their way, the object moved off, and started crossing the Hudson, and disappeared up north."

"Officials will not talk to Imbrogno, nor answer his letters," he says. UFO researchers spoke with Cliff Spieler, vice president at the New York Power Authority.

He, like Patrick, basically dismisses the entire affair. "Having looked into this thing, and living two miles from Indian Point, think the UFO reports are nonsense," he said. "All Hudson Valley UFO sightings are linked to small planes flying out of Duchess County."

At one time, officials speaking for Indian Point made their position quite clear to Imbrogno, "They said, 'you can cooperate with us, or you don't have to cooperate with us. If you don't cooperate with us, you have to face the consequences, because you are dealing in an area of national security. The incident that took place over there involved national security because it was a breach of security at a nuclear reactor.' But they weren't ready to say who was breaching security!"

In considering the "who," Imbrogno took in a number of hypotheses, including the possibility that the incident was an elaborate test flight of a secret military craft, such as the B-2 Stealth bomber, or a covertly-planned contingency test of the plant's security operations, carried out under the guise of a UFO overflight. "Nothing is impossible," he'll admit. But the most tenable answer, he felt, was that the UFO was an extraterrestrial craft. "I don't think our government could be so bold with a craft of the kind that appeared at Indian Point," he said.

Editor's Note: In a letter to UFO researchers shortly after this article was written, Imbrogno added to his remarks. "It is hard to believe that people like John Lear, and Bill Cooper are revealing 'top secret' information with little or no repercussions. I just poked my nose a little too deep into an area of national security, and got my ears pinned back for it. My next step is to approach this in a legal way by asking for an investigation (preferably by a member of Congress) to find out how, and why the security at this government reactor was violated, and why information is being withheld."

APPENDIX D–6 Detailed Report on Animal Mutilation

CASE STUDY #6
Dulce
New Mexico
March 24, 1978.

Gabriel L Veldez, New Mexico Police
In one case documented by New Mexico police, and the FBI, an 11-month-old cross Hereford-Charolais bull, belonging to a Mr. Manuel Gomez of New Mexico. It displayed "classic" mutilation signs, including the removal of the rectum, and sex organs with what appeared to be "a sharp, and precise instrument", and its internal organs were found to be inconsistent with a normal case of death followed by predation. "Both the liver, and the heart were white, and mushy. Both organs had the texture, and consistency of peanut butter".

The animal's heart as well as bone, and muscle samples were sent to the Los Alamos Scientific Laboratory for microscopic, and bacteriological studies, while samples from the animal's liver were sent to two separate private laboratories.

Los Alamos detected the presence of naturally occurring Clostridium bacteria in the heart but was unable to reach any conclusions because of the possibility that the bacteria represented postmortem contamination. They did not directly investigate the heart's unusual color or texture.

Samples from the animal's liver were found to be completely devoid of copper, and to contain 4 times the normal level of zinc, potassium, and phosphorus. The scientists performing the analysis were unable to explain these anomalies.

Blood samples taken at the scene were reported to be "light pink in color", and "did not clot after several days" while the animal's hide was found to be unusually brittle for a fresh death (the animal was estimated to have been dead for 5 hours), and the flesh underneath was found to be discolored. None of the laboratories were able to report any firm conclusions on the cause of the blood or tissue damage. At the time, it was suggested that a burst of radiation may have been used to kill the animal, blowing apart its red blood cells in the process. This hypothesis was later discarded as subsequent reports from the Los Alamos Scientific Laboratory later confirmed the presence of anti-coagulants in samples taken from other cows mutilated in the region.

Conventional explanations
As with most disputed phenomena, there were a number of potential explanations to cattle mutilations, ranging from death by natural causes to purposeful acts by unknown individuals. U.S. governmental explanation. After coming under increasing public pressure, Federal authorities launched a comprehensive investigation of the mutilation phenomenon. In May 1979, the case was passed on to the FBI, which granted jurisdiction under Title 18 (codes 1152, and 1153). The investigation was dubbed "Operation Animal Mutilation".

The investigation was funded by a US$44,170 grant from the Law Enforcement Assistance Administration, and was headed by FBI agent Kenneth Rommel. It had five key objectives:

To determine the reliability of the information on which the grant was based, which entailed gathering as much information as possible about the cases reported in

New Mexico prior to May 1979. To determine the cause of as many mutilations as possible, especially those reported in New Mexico. To determine if livestock mutilations as described constituted a major law enforcement problem. If these mutilations did constitute a major law enforcement problem, to determine the scope of the problem, and to offer recommendations on how to deal with it. If it was shown that the mutilation phenomenon was not a law enforcement problem, to recommend that no further law enforcement investigations be funded.

Rommel's final report was 297 pages long, and cost approximately US$45,000. It concluded that mutilations were predominantly the result of natural predation, but that some contained anomalies that could not be accounted for by conventional wisdom. The FBI was unable to identify any individuals responsible for the mutilations. Details of the investigation were now available under the Freedom of Information Act. The released material included correspondence from Rommel where he stated that "most credible sources had attributed this damage to normal predator, and scavenger activity".

Prior to the involvement of the FBI, the ATF launched their own investigation of the phenomenon. Both federal investigations were preceded (and followed, to some extent) by a state level investigation carried out by enforcement officials in New Mexico. This investigation reported finding evidence that some mutilated animals had been tranquilized, and treated with an anti-coagulant prior to their mutilation. It also contended that alleged surgical techniques performed during mutilations had become "more professional" over time. However, officers in charge were unable to determine responsibility or motive.

The ATF investigation was headed by ATF Agent Donald Flickinger. The New Mexico investigation was headed by Officer Gabriel L Veldez of the New Mexico Police, with the assistance of Cattle Inspector Jim Dyad, and Officer Howard Johnston of the New Mexico Department of Game, and Fish.

Natural causes

Blowflies have been implicated as possible scavengers involved in making livestock carcasses look "mutilated." While many unconventional explanations have been put forward to explain cattle mutilations, a variety of scientists, veterinary workers, and knowledgeable observers (including farmers, and other agricultural workers) have suggested more conventional ideas, most of which revolve around the hypothesis that "mutilated" animals died of natural causes, and were subjected to known terrestrial phenomena – including the action of predators, parasites, and scavengers.

Missing or mutilated mouth, lips, anus, and genitalia are explained as:

- Contraction of missing/damaged areas due to dehydration.
- The actions of small scavengers, and burrowing parasites seeking to enter or consume the body in areas where skin is at its thinnest.

Missing/mutilated eyes, and soft internal organs are explained as:

- The action of carrion feeding insects such as blowflies, and opportunistic or carrion birds such as vultures, which are known to direct themselves toward an animal's eyes, and to enter the body through the openings of the mouth, and anus in order to feed on soft internal organs.

Absence of blood is explained as:

- Blood pooling in the lowest points in the body where it will break down into its basic organic components.
- Blood that is external to the body, or in the area of a wound being consumed by insects or reduced by solar desiccation.

Surgical incisions in the skin are explained as:
- Tears in the skin created when it is stretched by postmortem bloat and/or as dehydration causes the animal's hide to shrink, and split, often in linear cuts.
- Incisions caused by scavengers or predators, possibly exacerbated by the above.

The hypothesis that natural phenomena accounted for most mutilation characteristics had been validated by a number of experiments, including one cited by long-time scientific skeptic Robert T. Carroll, conducted by Washington County (Arkansas) Sheriff's Department. In the experiment, the body of a recently deceased cow was left in a field, and observed for 48 hours. During the 48 hours, postmortem bloating was reported to have caused incision-like tears in the cow's skin that matched the "surgical" cuts reported on mutilated cows, while the action of blowflies, and maggots reportedly matched the soft tissue damage observed on mutilated cows. No explanation was made however, for the entire absence of any blood.

Experiments have also been conducted to compare the different reactions of surgically cut hide/flesh, and predated hide/flesh to natural exposure. They demonstrated pronounced differences between surgical cut, and non-surgical cuts over time. This article did not address tearing due to bloating.

Some ranchers have disputed the more scientifically mainstream "natural causes hypothesis" on the grounds that the mutilated animals often fall outside of the normal categories of natural deaths by predation or disease. One reason cited was that the animals were healthy, and showed no sign of disease prior to death, and were large, and strong enough not to be a likely target for a predator. In some cases, ranchers have reported that the mutilated cattle were among the healthiest, and strongest animals in their herd.

Other critics of the accepted position include investigators involved in paranormal, and UFO research organizations, such as National Institute for Discovery Science which report the discovery of anomalies in necropsies which, they claimed, could not be explained by natural processes.

Animal cruelty, and human activity
It was alternatively hypothesized that cattle mutilations were the result of two unrelated deviant phenomena. The bulk of mutilations were the result of predation, and other natural processes, and those with anomalies that could not be explained in this way were the work of humans who derived pleasure or sexual stimulation from mutilating animals.

Attacks against animals were a recognized phenomenon. There had been many recorded cases around the world, and many convictions. Typically, the victims of such attacks were cats, dogs, and other family pets, and the actions of humans were usually limited to acts of cruelty such as striking, burning, or beating animals. However, attacks had also been recorded against larger animals, including sheep, cows, and horses. Humans, particularly those with sociopathic disorders, have been found to have mutilated animals in elaborate ways using knives or surgical instruments.

On April 20, 1979, Dr. C Hibbs of the New Mexico State Veterinary diagnostics Laboratory spoke before a hearing chaired by Senator Harrison Schmitt. Dr. Hibbs testified that mutilation fell into three categories, one of which was animals mutilated by humans (page 25). FBI records did not record the percentage of mutilated animals that fell into this category. The standard criminal charge for mutilating an animal, including cattle, is animal cruelty.

Cults

Closely related to the deviant hypothesis was the hypothesis that cattle mutilations were the result of cult activity. However, contrary to the deviancy hypothesis, which held that cattle were mutilated at random by individual deviants, the cult hypothesis held that cattle mutilations were coordinated acts of ritual sacrifice carried out by organized groups. Beliefs held by proponents of the cult hypothesis vary, but may include:

- That the apparent absence of blood at mutilation sites may indicate cult member harvests
- That organs have been removed from cattle for use in rituals
- That unborn calves have been harvested from mutilated cattle
- The hypothesis that cults were responsible for cattle mutilation was developed in the U.S. during the 1970s, and 1980s, a time of growing national concern over cults (such as the Peoples Temple, and Jonestown), and ritual satanic abuse "Satanic panic".

In 1975, the US Treasury Department assigned Donald Flickinger to investigate the existence of connections between cults, and the mutilation of cattle. The operation came under the jurisdiction of the Bureau of Alcohol, Tobacco, and Firearms.

Flickinger recorded a number of "unusual" incidents, and circumstantial evidence but was unable to find sufficient evidence of cult involvement for the ATF to take further action. Media reports of the time reported his investigation was dropped when it was determined cattle deaths were not a prelude to a coordinated campaign against elected officials by cult members.

However, there were various reports during the time of menacing groups prowling around mutilation sites. In September 1975, a forestry service employee in Blaine County, Idaho, reported seeing a group of people in black hooded robes. Several cattle were found mutilated in the area the following day. On October 9, 1975, a motorist on U.S Highway 95 in northern Idaho, in an area of frequent cattle mutilation, reported to police that some 15 masked individuals formed a roadblock with linked arms, forcing him to turn around.

Public interest in the cult hypothesis waned during the 1980s, but interest was maintained by proponents such as the Colorado based television evangelist Bob Larson, who campaigned to raise public awareness of links between cattle mutilations, and cult activity through his ministry, and radio shows.

Another proponent of the cult hypothesis is Montana author Roberta Donovan. In her 1976 publication *Mystery Stalks the Prairie* she documented the experiences of

Deputy Sheriff Keith Wolverton of Great Falls, Cascade County, investigating cattle mutilations with suspected cult involvement. Since the beginning of the cult hypothesis, law enforcement agents in several states, and provinces, including Alberta, Idaho, Montana, and Iowa have reported evidence implicating cults in several instances of cattle mutilations.

During their investigations, the FBI, and the ATF were unable to find appropriate evidence, including signs of consistency between mutilations, to substantiate that the animals had been the victims of any form of ritual sacrifice or organized mutilation effort. They were also unable to determine how or why a cult would perform procedures that would result in the anomalies reported in some necropsies, or to verify that the anomalies were 1) connected to the mutilations themselves 2) the result of human intervention.

In most cases, mutilations were either ruled due to natural causes, or the cattle were too far decayed for any useful conclusions to be drawn. Some cases of cult hysteria were traced back to fabrication by individuals unrelated to the incident. In one case it was concluded that claims had been falsified by a convict seeking favorable terms on his sentence in exchange for information. In another case, claims were traced back to local high school students who had circulated rumors as a joke.

Government or military experimentation
In his 1997 article "Dead Cows I've Known", cattle mutilation researcher Charles T. Oliphant speculated cattle mutilation to be the result of covert research into emerging cattle diseases, and the possibility they could be transmitted to humans.

Oliphant posits the NIH, CDC, or other federally funded bodies, may be involved, and they were supported by the US military. Part of his hypothesis was based on allegations that human pharmaceuticals had been found in mutilated cattle, and on the necropsies that showed cattle mutilations commonly involved areas of the animal that relate to "input, output, and reproduction". To support his hypothesis, Oliphant cited the Reston ebolavirus case in which plain clothes military officers, traveling in unmarked vehicles, entered a research facility in Reston, Virginia, to secretly retrieve, and destroy animals that were contaminated with a highly infectious disease.

Additionally, a 2002 NIDS report related the eyewitness testimony of two Cache County, Utah, police officers. The area had seen many unusual cattle deaths, and ranchers had organized armed patrols to surveil the unmarked aircraft which they claimed were associated with the livestock deaths. The police witnesses claim to have encountered several men in an unmarked U.S. Army helicopter in 1976 at a small community airport in Cache County. The witnesses asserted that after this heated encounter, cattle mutilations in the region ceased for about five years.

Biochemist Colm Kelleher, who had investigated several purported mutilations first-hand, argued that the mutilations were most likely a clandestine U.S. Government effort to track the spread of Bovine spongiform encephalopathy "Mad Cow Disease", and related diseases, such as scrapie.

Theories of government involvement in cattle mutilation have been further fueled by "black helicopter" sightings near mutilation sites. On April 8, 1979, three police officers in Dulce, New Mexico, reported a mysterious aircraft which resembled a U.S. military helicopter hovering around a site following a wave of mutilation which claimed 16 cows. On July 15, 1974, two unregistered helicopters, a white helicopter, and a black twin-engine aircraft, opened fire on Robert Smith Jr. while he was driving his tractor on his farm in Honey Creek, Iowa. This attack followed a rash of mutilations in the area, and across the nearby border in Nebraska. The reports of "helicopter" involvement have been used to explain why some cattle appear to have been "dropped" from considerable heights.

Aliens, and UFOs
In 1974, a few months after the first spate of alleged mutilations in the US, multiple farmers in Nebraska claimed to witness UFOs on the nights their cattle were harmed. One claimed he saw an object which "looked as if it had a little bluish-green light on each side with a glow surrounding it." The sightings were hailed by UFO researchers as the first physical evidence of extraterrestrial life.

Government Interference
At the same time that UFO reports were being filed with law enforcement, and larger number of ranchers claimed to see black helicopters around their fields, coinciding with the cattle mutilations. Although some initially thought these were used by cattle rustlers, suspicion soon pointed toward a military operation running out of Fort Riley, Kansas. Reporter Dane Edwards spread the theory that the government was testing cattle parts to develop biological weapons to use in Vietnam, going so far as to write to Floyd K. Haskell during his investigation to accuse agents of threatening him into silence. Vigilante groups were formed.

APPENDIX D–7 Detailed Report on Crop Circle
CASE STUDY #7

Bower, and Chorley

In 1991, self-professed pranksters Doug Bower, and Dave Chorley made headlines claiming it was they who started the phenomenon in 1978 with the use of simple tools consisting of a plank of wood, rope, and a baseball cap fitted with a loop of wire to help them walk in a straight line. To prove their case, they made a circle in front of journalists; a "cereologist" Pat Delgado, examined the circle, and declared it authentic before it was revealed that it was a hoax. Inspired by Australian crop circle accounts from 1966, Bower, and Chorley claimed to be responsible for all circles made prior to 1987, and for more than 200 crop circles in 1978–1991 (with 1000 other circles not being made by them). After their announcement, the two men demonstrated making a crop circle. According to Professor Richard Taylor, "the pictographs they created inspired a second wave of crop artists. Far from fizzling out, crop circles have evolved into an international phenomenon, with hundreds of sophisticated pictographs now appearing annually around the globe."

Paranormal

Since becoming the focus of widespread media attention in the 1980s, crop circles have become the subject of speculation by various paranormal, ufologically, and anomalistic investigators ranging from proposals that they were created by bizarre meteorological phenomena to messages from extraterrestrial beings. There had also been speculation that crop circles had a relation to ley lines. Many New Age groups incorporate crop circles into their belief systems.

Some paranormal advocates thought that crop circles were caused by ball lighting, and that the patterns were so complex that they had to be controlled by some entity. Some proposed entities were: Gaia asking to stop global warming, and human pollution, God, supernatural beings (for example Indian devas), the collective minds of humanity through a proposed "quantum field", or extraterrestrial beings.

Responding to local beliefs that "extraterrestrial beings" in UFOs were responsible for crop circles appearing, the Indonesian National Institute of Aeronautics, and Space (LAPAN) described crop circles as "man-made". Thomas Djamaluddin, research professor of astronomy, and astrophysics at LAPAN stated, "We have come to agree that this "thing" cannot be scientifically proven." Among others, paranormal enthusiasts, Ufologists, and anomalistic investigators have offered hypothetical explanations that have been criticized as pseudoscientific by skeptical groups, and scientists, including the Committee for Skeptical Inquiry. No credible evidence of extraterrestrial origin has been presented.

Folklore

Researchers of crop circles had linked modern crop circles to old folkloric tales to support the claim that they were not artificially produced. Circle crops were culture-dependent: they appeared mostly in developed, and secularized Western countries where people were receptive to New Age beliefs, including Japan, but they did not appear at all in other zones, such as Muslim countries.

Fungi could cause circular areas of crop to die, probably the origin of tales of "fairy rings". Tales also mentioned balls of light many times but never in relation to crop circles.

A 17th-century English woodcut called the *Mowing-Devil* depicts the devil with a scythe mowing (cutting) a circular design in a field of oats. The pamphlet containing the image states that the farmer, disgusted at the wage his mower was demanding for his work, insisted that he would rather have "the devil himself" perform the task. Crop circle researcher Jim Schnabel did not consider this to be a historical precedent for crop circles because the stalks were cut down, not bent. The circular form indicated to the farmer that it had been caused by the devil.

APPENDIX D–8 Detailed Report on Bigfoot
CASE STUDY #8

Bigfoot

On July 9, 2008, Rick Dyer, and Matthew Whitton posted a video to YouTube, claiming that they had discovered the body of a dead Sasquatch in a forest in northern Georgia. Tom Biscardi was contacted to investigate. Dyer, and Whitton received $50,000 from Searching for Bigfoot, Inc. as a good faith gesture. The story was covered by many major news networks, including BBC, CNN, ABC News, and Fox News. Soon after a press conference, the alleged Bigfoot body was delivered in a block of ice in a freezer with the Searching for Bigfoot team. When the contents were thawed, observers found that the hair was not real, the head was hollow, and the feet were rubber. Dyer, and Whitton admitted that it was a hoax after being confronted by Steve Kulls, executive director of SquatchDetective.com.

In August 2012, a man in Montana was killed by a car while perpetrating a Bigfoot hoax using a ghillie suit.

In January 2014, Rick Dyer, perpetrator of a previous Bigfoot hoax, said that he had killed a Bigfoot creature in September 2012 outside San Antonio, Texas. He said that he had scientific tests performed on the body, "from DNA tests to 3D optical scans to body scans. It is the real deal. It's Bigfoot, and Bigfoot's here, and I shot it, and now I'm proving it to the world." He said that he had kept the body in a hidden location, and he intended to take it on tour across North America in 2014.

He released photos of the body, and a video showing a few individuals' reactions to seeing it, but never released any of the tests or scans. He refused to disclose the test results or to provide biological samples. He said that the DNA results were done by an undisclosed lab, and could not be matched to identify any known animal. Dyer said that he would reveal the body, and tests on February 9, 2014 at a news conference at Washington University, but he never made the test results available. After the Phoenix tour, the Bigfoot body was taken to Houston.

On March 28, 2014, Dyer admitted on his Facebook page that his "Bigfoot corpse" was another hoax. He had paid Chris Russel of Twisted Toy Box to manufacture the prop from latex, foam, and camel hair, which he nicknamed "Hank". Dyer earned approximately US$60,000 from the tour of this second fake Bigfoot corpse. He said that he did kill a Bigfoot but did not take the real body on tour for fear that it would be stolen.

Scientific view

The evidence that did exist supporting the survival of such a large, prehistoric ape-like creature has been attributed to hoaxes or delusion rather than to sightings of a genuine creature. In a 1996 *USA Today* article, Washington State zoologist John Crane said, "There is no such thing as Bigfoot. No data other than material that's clearly been fabricated has ever been presented." In addition, scientists cite the fact that Bigfoot is alleged to live in regions unusual for a large, nonhuman primate, i.e., temperate latitudes in the northern hemisphere; all recognized apes are found in the tropics of Africa, and Asia.

Mainstream scientists did not consider the subject of Bigfoot an area of credible science, and there had been a limited number of formal scientific studies of Bigfoot.

Evidence such as the 1967 Patterson–Gimlin film had provided "no supportive data of any scientific value".

As with other similar beings, climate, and food supply issues would make such a creature's survival in reported habitats unlikely. Great apes have not been found in the fossil record in the Americas, and no Bigfoot remains were known to have been found. Phillips Stevens, a cultural anthropologist at the University at Buffalo, summarized the scientific consensus as follows:

"It defies all logic that there is a population of these things sufficient to keep them going. What it takes to maintain any species, especially a long-lived species, is you got to have a breeding population. That requires a substantial number, spread out over a fairly wide area where they can find sufficient food, and shelter to keep hidden from all the investigators."

In the 1970s, when Bigfoot "experts" were frequently given high-profile media coverage, Mcleod writes that the scientific community generally avoided lending credence to the theories by debating them.

Formal studies

The first scientific study of available evidence was conducted by John Napier, and published in his book, *Bigfoot: The Yeti, and Sasquatch in Myth, and Reality,* in 1973. Napier wrote that if a conclusion is to be reached based on scant extant "hard" evidence," science must declare "Bigfoot does not exist." However, he found it difficult to entirely reject thousands of alleged tracks, "scattered over 125,000 square miles" or to dismiss all the many hundreds of eyewitness accounts. Napier concluded, "I am convinced that Sasquatch exists, but whether it is all it is cracked up to be is another matter altogether. There must be *something* in north-west America that needs explaining, and that something leaves man-like footprints."

In 1974, the National Wildlife Federation funded a field study seeking Bigfoot evidence. No formal federation members were involved, and the study made no notable discoveries.

Beginning in the late 1970s, physical anthropologist Grover Krantz published several articles, and four book-length treatments of Sasquatch. However, his work was found to contain multiple scientific failings including falling for hoaxes.

A study published in the *Journal of Biogeography* in 2009 by J.D. Lozier et al. used ecological niche modeling on reported sightings of Bigfoot, using their locations to infer Bigfoot's preferred ecological parameters. They found a very close match with the ecological parameters of the American black bear, *Ursus americanus.* They also noted that an upright bear looked much like Bigfoot's purported appearance, and considered it highly improbable that two species should had very similar ecological preferences, concluding that Bigfoot sightings were likely sightings of black bears.

In the first systematic genetic analysis of 30 hair samples that were suspected to be from bigfoot, yeti, sasquatch or other anomalous primates, only one was found to be primate in origin, and that was identified as human. A joint study by the University of Oxford, and Lausanne's Cantonal Museum of Zoology, and published in the *Proceedings of the Royal Society B* in 2014, the team used a previously published cleaning method to remove all surface contamination, and the ribosomal mitochondrial DNA 12S fragment of the sample was sequenced, and then compared to GenBank to identify the species origin. The samples submitted were from different parts of the world, including the United States, Russia, the Himalayas, and Sumatra. Other than one sample of human origin, all but two are from common animals. Black, and brown bear accounted for most of the samples, other animals include cow, horse, dog/wolf/coyote, sheep, goat, raccoon, porcupine, deer, and tapir. The last two samples were thought to match a fossilized genetic sample of a 40,000-year-old polar bear of the Pleistocene epoch; however, a later study disputes this finding. In the second paper, tests identified the hairs as being from a rare type of brown bear.

APPENDIX D–9 Detailed Report on Time Travel
CASE STUDY #9
From Wikipedia, the free encyclopedia

Brief Account on Wormholes

Wormholes were a hypothetical warped spacetime which were permitted by the Einstein field equations of general relativity. A proposed time-travel machine using a traversable wormhole would hypothetically work in the following way: One end of the wormhole was accelerated to some significant fraction of the speed of light, perhaps with some advanced propulsion system, and then brought back to the point of origin. Alternatively, another way was to take one entrance of the wormhole, and move it to within the gravitational field of an object that had higher gravity than the other entrance, and then return it to a position near the other entrance. For both of these methods, time dilation caused the end of the wormhole that has been moved to have aged less, or become "younger", than the stationary end as seen by an external observer; however, time connected differently *through* the wormhole than *outside* it, so that synchronized clocks at either end of the wormhole would always remain synchronized as seen by an observer passing through the wormhole, no matter how the two ends moved around. This meant that an observer entering the "younger" end would exit the "older" end at a time when it was the same age as the "younger" end, effectively going back in time as seen by an observer from the outside. One significant limitation of such a time machine was that it was only possible to go as far back in time as the initial creation of the machine; in essence, it was more of a path through time than it was a device that itself moved through time, and it would not allow the technology itself to be moved backward in time.

According to current theories on the nature of wormholes, construction of a traversable wormhole would require the existence of a substance with negative energy, often referred to as "exotic matter". More technically, the wormhole spacetime required a distribution of energy that violated various energy conditions, such as the null energy condition along with the weak, strong, and dominant energy conditions. However, it was known that quantum effects could lead to small measurable violations of the null energy condition, and many physicists believed that the required negative energy may actually be possible due to the Casimir effect in quantum physics. Although early calculations suggested a very large amount of negative energy would be required, later calculations showed that the amount of negative energy could be made arbitrarily small.

In 1993, Matt Visser argued that the two mouths of a wormhole with such an induced clock difference could not be brought together without inducing quantum field, and gravitational effects that would either make the wormhole collapse or the two mouths repel each other. Because of this, the two mouths could not be brought close enough for causality violation to take place. However, in a 1997 paper, Visser hypothesized that a complex "Roman ring" (named after Tom Roman) configuration of an N number of wormholes arranged in a symmetric polygon could still act as a time machine, although he concludes that this is more likely a flaw in classical quantum gravity theory rather than proof that causality violation is possible.

Quantum Physics No-communication Theorem

When a signal was sent from one location, and received at another location, then as long as the signal was moving at the speed of light or slower, the mathematics of simultaneity in the theory of relativity showed that all reference frames agreed that the transmission-event happened before the reception-event. When the signal travelled faster than light, it was received *before* it was sent, in all reference frames. The signal could be said to have moved backward in time. This hypothetical scenario was sometimes referred to as a tachyonic antitelephone.

Quantum-mechanical phenomena such as quantum teleportation, the EPR paradox, or quantum entanglement might appear to create a mechanism that allows for faster-than-light (FTL) communication or time travel, and in fact some interpretations of quantum mechanics such as the Bohm interpretation presume that some information was being exchanged between particles instantaneously in order to maintain correlations between particles. This effect was referred to as "spooky action at a distance" by Einstein.

Nevertheless, the fact that causality was preserved in quantum mechanics was a rigorous result in modern quantum field theories, and therefore modern theories did not allow for time travel or FTL communication. In any specific instance where FTL has been claimed, more detailed analysis had proven that to get a signal, some form of classical communication must also be used. The no-communication theorem also gives a general proof that quantum entanglement could not be used to transmit information faster than classical signals.

Interacting many-worlds interpretation
A variation of Everett's many-worlds interpretation (MWI) of quantum mechanics provided a resolution to the grandfather paradox that involved the time traveler arriving in a different universe than the one they came from; it had been argued that since the traveler arrived in a different universe's history, and not their own history, this was not "genuine" time travel. The accepted many-worlds interpretation suggested that all possible quantum events could occur in mutually exclusive histories. However, some variations allow different universes to interact. This concept was most often used in science-fiction, but some physicists such as David Deutsch had suggested that a time traveler should end up in a different history than the one he started from. On the other hand, Stephen Hawking had argued that even if the MWI was correct, we should expect each time traveler to experience a single self-consistent history, so that time travelers remained within their own world rather than traveling to a different one. The physicist Allen Everett argued that Deutsch's approach "involves modifying fundamental principles of quantum mechanics; it certainly goes beyond simply adopting the MWI". Everett also argued that even if Deutsch's approach was correct, it would imply that any macroscopic object composed of multiple particles would be split apart when traveling back in time through a wormhole, with different particles emerging in different worlds.

Daniel Greenberger, and Karl Svozil proposed that quantum theory gave a model for time travel without paradoxes. The quantum theory observation caused possible states to 'collapse' into one measured state; hence, the past observed from the present was deterministic (it had only one possible state), but the present observed from the past had many possible states until our actions caused it to collapse into one state. Our actions would then be seen to have been inevitable.

Experimental results

Certain experiments carried out gave the impression of reversed causality but failed to show it under closer examination.

The delayed choice quantum eraser experiment performed by Marlan Scully involved pairs of entangled photons that were divided into "signal photons", and "idler photons", with the signal photons emerging from one of two locations, and their position later measured as in the double-slit experiment. Depending on how the idler photon was measured, the experimenter could either learn which of the two locations the signal photon emerged from or "erase" that information. Even though the signal photons could be measured before the choice was made about the idler photons, the choice seemed to retroactively determine whether or not an interference pattern was observed when one correlates measurements of idler photons to the corresponding signal photons. However, since interference could only be observed after the idler photons were measured, and they were correlated with the signal photons, there was no way for experimenters to tell what choice would be made in advance just by looking at the signal photons, only by gathering classical information from the entire system; thus, causality was preserved.

The experiment of Lijun Wang might also show causality violation since it made it possible to send packages of waves through a bulb of cesium gas in such a way that the package appeared to exit the bulb 62 nanoseconds before its entry, but a wave package was not a single well-defined object but rather a sum of multiple waves of different frequencies (see Fourier analysis), and the package could appear to move faster than light or even backward in time even if none of the pure waves in the sum did so. This effect could not be used to send any matter, energy, or information faster than light, so this experiment was understood not to violate causality either.

Absence of time travelers from the future

The absence of time travelers from the future was a variation of the Fermi paradox, and like the absence of extraterrestrial visitors, the absence of time travelers did not prove time travel was physically impossible; it might be that time travel was physically possible but was never developed or was cautiously used. Carl Sagan once suggested the possibility that time travelers could be here but were disguising their existence or were not recognized as time travelers. Some versions of general relativity suggested that time travel might only be possible in a region of spacetime that was warped a certain way, and hence time travelers would not be able to travel back to earlier regions in spacetime, before this region existed. Stephen Hawking stated that this would explain why the world has not already been overrun by "tourists from the future."

Several experiments have been carried out to try to entice future humans, who might invent time travel technology, to come back, and demonstrate it to people of the present time. Events such as Perth's Destination Day (2005) or MIT's Time Traveler Convention heavily publicized permanent "advertisements" of a meeting time, and place for future time travelers to meet. Back in 1982, a group in Baltimore, Maryland, identifying itself as the Krononauts, hosted an event of this type welcoming visitors from the future. These experiments only stood the possibility of generating a positive result demonstrating the existence of time travel but have failed so far—no time travelers were known to have attended either event. Some versions of the many-worlds interpretation could be used to suggest that future humans have traveled back in time but have traveled back to the meeting time, and place in a parallel universe.

Time Dilation

There was a great deal of observable evidence for time dilation in special relativity, and gravitational time dilation in general relativity, for example in the famous, and easy-to-replicate observation of atmospheric muon decay. The theory of relativity stated that the speed of light was invariant for all observers in any frame of reference; that is, it was always the same. Time dilation was a direct consequence of the invariance of the speed of light. Time dilation may be regarded in a limited sense as "time travel into the future": a person may use time dilation so that a small amount of proper time passes for them, while a large amount of proper time passes elsewhere. This could be achieved by traveling at relativistic speeds or through the effects of gravity.

For two identical clocks moving relative to each other without accelerating, each clock measured the other to be ticking slower. This was possible due to the relativity of simultaneity. However, the symmetry was broken if one clock accelerated, allowing for less proper time to pass for one clock than the other. The twin paradox described this: one twin remains on Earth, while the other undergoes acceleration to relativistic speed as they travel into space, turn around, and travel back to Earth; the traveling twin ages less than the twin who stayed on Earth, because of the time dilation experienced during their acceleration. General relativity treated the effects of acceleration, and the effects of gravity as equivalent, and showed that time dilation also occurred in gravity wells, with a clock deeper in the well ticking more slowly; this effect was considered when calibrating the clocks on the satellites of the Global Positioning System, and it could lead to significant differences in rates of aging for observers at different distances from a large gravity well such as a black hole.

A time machine that utilized this principle might be, for instance, a spherical shell with a diameter of 5 meters, and the mass of Jupiter. A person at its center would travel forward in time at a rate four times that of distant observers. Squeezing the mass of a large planet into such a small structure was not expected to be within humanity's technological capabilities in the near future. With current technologies, it was only possible to cause a human traveler to age less than companions on Earth by a very small fraction of a second, the current record being about 20 milliseconds for the cosmonaut Sergei Avdeyev.

Philosophy

Philosophers have discussed the nature of time since at least the time of ancient Greece; for example, Parmenides presented the view that time is an illusion. Centuries later, Newton supported the idea of absolute time, while his contemporary Leibniz maintained that time was only a relation between events, and it could not be expressed independently. The latter approach eventually gave rise to the spacetime of relativity.

Presentism vs. Eternalism

Many philosophers have argued that relativity implied Eternalism, the idea that the past, and future existed in a real sense, not only as changes that occurred or will occur to the present. Philosopher of science Dean Rickles disagreed with some qualifications but notes that "the consensus among philosophers seems to be that special, and general relativity are incompatible with presentism." Some philosophers viewed time as a dimension equal to spatial dimensions, that future events were "already there" in the same sense different places existed, and that there was no objective flow of time; however, this view was disputed.

The bar, and ring paradox were an example of the relativity of simultaneity. Both ends of the bar passed through the ring simultaneously in the rest frame of the ring (left), but the ends of the bar passed one after the other in the rest frame of the bar (right).

Presentism was a school of philosophy that held that the future, and the past existed only as changes that occurred or will occur to the present, and they had no real existence of their own. In this view, time travel was impossible because there was no future or past to travel to. Keller, and Nelson have argued that even if past, and future objects did not exist, there could still be definite truths about past, and future events, and thus it was possible that a future truth about a time traveler deciding to travel back to the present date could explain the time traveler's actual appearance in the present; these views were contested by some authors.

The Grandfather Paradox

A common objection to the idea of traveling back in time was put forth in the grandfather paradox or the argument of auto-infanticide. If one were able to go back in time, inconsistencies, and contradictions would ensue if the time traveler were to change anything; there was a contradiction if the past became different from the way it *is*. The paradox was commonly described with a person who travelled to the past, and killed their own grandfather, preventing the existence of their father or mother, and therefore their own existence. Philosophers questioned whether these paradoxes made time travel impossible. Some philosophers answered the paradoxes by arguing that it might be the case that backward time travel could be possible but that it would be impossible to actually *change* the past in any way, an idea similar to the proposed Novikov self-consistency principle in physics.

Ontological paradox

According to the philosophical theory of composability, what *can* happen, for example in the context of time travel, must be weighed against the context of everything relating to the situation. If the past *is* a certain way, it's not possible for it to be any other way. What *can* happen when a time traveler visits the past was limited to what *did* happen, in order to prevent logical contradictions.

Self-consistency principle

The Novikov self-consistency principle, named after Igor Dmitrievich Novikov, stated that any actions taken by a time traveler or by an object that travels back in time were part of history all along, and therefore it was impossible for the time traveler to "change" history in any way. The time traveler's actions may be the *cause* of events in their own past though, which led to the potential for circular causation, sometimes called a predestination paradox, ontological paradox, or bootstrap paradox. The term bootstrap paradox was popularized by Robert A. Heinlein's story "By His Bootstraps". The Novikov self-consistency principle proposes that the local laws of physics in a region of spacetime containing time travelers could not be any different from the local laws of physics in any other region of spacetime.

The philosopher Kelley L. Ross argued in "Time Travel Paradoxes" that in a scenario involving a physical object whose world-line or history formed a closed loop in time there could be a violation of the second law of thermodynamics. Ross used "Somewhere in Time" as an example of such an ontological paradox, where a watch was given to a person, and 60 years later the same watch was brought back in time, and given to the same character. Ross stated that entropy of the watch would increase, and the watch carried back in time would be more worn with each repetition of its history. The second law of thermodynamics was understood by modern physicists to be a statistical law, so decreasing entropy or non-increasing entropy were not impossible, just improbable. Additionally, entropy statistically increased in systems which were isolated, so non-isolated systems, such as an object, that interact with the outside world, could become less worn, and decrease in entropy, and it was possible for an object whose world-line formed a closed loop to be always in the same condition in the same point of its history.

APPENDIX D–10 Detailed Report on Wormholes
CASE STUDY #10

Schwarzschild wormholes

The equations of the theory of general relativity had valid solutions that contained wormholes. The first type of wormhole solution discovered was the Schwarzschild wormhole, which would be present in the Schwarzschild metric describing an eternal black hole, but it was found that it would collapse too quickly for anything to cross from one end to the other. Wormholes that could be crossed in both directions, known as traversable wormholes, would only be possible if exotic matter with negative energy density could be used to stabilize them.

An artist's impression of a wormhole from an observer's perspective, crossing the event horizon of a Schwarzschild wormhole that bridged two different universes. The observer originated from the right, and another universe became visible in the center of the wormhole's shadow once the horizon was crossed, the observer seeing light that had fallen into the black hole interior region from the other universe; however, this other universe was unreachable in the case of a Schwarzschild wormhole, as the bridge always collapsed before the observer had time to cross it, and everything that had fallen through the event horizon of either universe was inevitably crushed in the singularity.

Schwarzschild wormholes, also known as Einstein–Rosen bridges (named after Albert Einstein, and Nathan Rosen), were connections between areas of space that could be modeled as vacuum solutions to the Einstein field equations, and that were now understood to be intrinsic parts of the maximally extended version of the Schwarzschild metric describing an eternal black hole with no charge, and no rotation. Here, "maximally extended" referred to the idea that the spacetime should not have any "edges": it should be possible to continue this path arbitrarily far into the particle's future or past for any possible trajectory of a free-falling particle (following a geodesic in the spacetime).

In order to satisfy this requirement, it turned out that in addition to the black hole interior region that particles enter when they fell through the event horizon from the outside, there must be a separate white hole interior region that allowed us to extrapolate the trajectories of particles that an outside observer saw rising up *away* from the event horizon, and just as there were two separate interior regions of the maximally extended spacetime, there were also two separate exterior regions, sometimes called two different "universes", with the second universe allowing us to extrapolate some possible particle trajectories in the two interior regions. This meant that the interior black hole region could contain a mix of particles that fell in from either universe (and thus an observer who fell in from one universe might be able to see light that fell in from the other one), and likewise particles from the interior white hole region could escape into either universe. All four regions could be seen in a spacetime diagram that used Kruskal–Szekeres coordinates.

In this spacetime, it was possible to come up with coordinate systems such that if a hypersurface of constant time (a set of points that all have the same time coordinate, such that every point on the surface has a space-like separation, giving what is called a 'space-like surface') was picked, and an "embedding diagram" drawn depicting the curvature of space at that time, the embedding diagram would look like a tube connecting the two exterior regions, known as an "Einstein–Rosen bridge". Note that the Schwarzschild metric described an idealized black hole that existed eternally from the perspective of external observers; a more realistic black hole that formed at some particular time from a collapsing star would require a different metric. When the infalling stellar matter was added to a diagram of a black hole's history, it removed the part of the diagram corresponding to the white hole interior region, along with the part of the diagram corresponding to the other universe.

The Einstein–Rosen bridge was discovered by Ludwig Flamm in 1916, a few months after Schwarzschild published his solution, and was rediscovered by Albert Einstein, and his colleague Nathan Rosen, who published their result in 1935. However, in 1962, John Archibald Wheeler, and Robert W. Fuller published a paper showing that this type of wormhole was unstable if it connected two parts of the same universe, and that it would pinch off too quickly for light (or any particle moving slower than light) that fell in from one exterior region to make it to the other exterior region.

According to general relativity, the gravitational collapse of a sufficiently compact mass formed a singular Schwarzschild black hole. In the Einstein–Cartan–Sciama–Kibble theory of gravity, however, it formed a regular Einstein–Rosen bridge. This theory extended general relativity by removing a constraint of the symmetry of the affine connection, and regarding its antisymmetric part, the torsion tensor, as a dynamical variable. Torsion naturally accounted for the quantum-mechanical, intrinsic angular momentum (spin) of matter. The minimal coupling between torsion, and Dirac spinors generated a repulsive spin–spin interaction that was significant in fermionic matter at extremely high densities. Such an interaction prevented the formation of a gravitational singularity. Instead, the collapsing matter reached an enormous but finite density, and rebounds, forming the other side of the bridge.

Although Schwarzschild wormholes were not traversable in both directions, their existence inspired Kip Thorne to imagine traversable wormholes created by holding the "throat" of a Schwarzschild wormhole open with exotic matter (material that has negative mass/energy).

Other non-traversable wormholes included Lorentzian wormholes (first proposed by John Archibald Wheeler in 1957), wormholes creating a spacetime foam in a general relativistic spacetime manifold depicted by a Lorentzian manifold, and Euclidean wormholes (named after Euclidean manifold, a structure of Riemannian manifold).

Traversable wormholes

This Casimir effect showed that quantum field theory allowed the energy density in certain regions of space to be negative relative to the ordinary matter vacuum energy, and it had been shown theoretically that quantum field theory allowed states where energy could be *arbitrarily* negative at a given point. Many physicists, such as Stephen Hawking, Kip Thorne, and others, therefore argued that such effects might make it possible to stabilize a traversable wormhole. Physicists had not found any natural process that would be predicted to form a wormhole naturally in the context of general relativity, although the quantum foam hypothesis was sometimes used to suggest that tiny wormholes might appear, and disappear spontaneously at the Planck scale, and stable versions of such wormholes had been suggested as dark matter candidates. It has also been proposed that, if a tiny wormhole held open by a negative mass cosmic string had appeared around the time of the Big Bang, it could have been inflated to macroscopic size by cosmic inflation.

Image of a simulated traversable wormhole that connected the square in front of the physical institutes of University of Tübingen with the sand dunes near Boulogne sur Mer in the north of France. The image was calculated with 4D raytracing in a Morris–Thorne wormhole metric, but the gravitational effects on the wavelength of light had not been simulated.

Lorentzian traversable wormholes would allow travel in both directions from one part of the universe to another part of that same universe very quickly or would allow travel from one universe to another. The possibility of traversable wormholes in general relativity was first demonstrated in a 1973 paper by Homer Ellis, and independently in a 1973 paper by K. A. Bronnikov. Ellis thoroughly analyzed the topology, and the geodesics of the Ellis drain hole, showing it to be geodesically complete, horizonless, singularity-free, and fully traversable in both directions. The drain hole was a solution manifold of Einstein's field equations for a vacuum space-time, modified by inclusion of a scalar field minimally coupled to the Ricci tensor with antiorthodox polarity (negative instead of positive). (Ellis specifically rejected referring to the scalar field as 'exotic' because of the antiorthodox coupling, finding arguments for doing so unpersuasive.)

The solution depended on two parameters: which fixes the strength of its gravitational field, and which determines the curvature of its spatial cross sections. When it was set equal to 0, the drain hole's gravitational field vanished. What was left was the Ellis wormhole, a nongravitating, purely geometric, traversable wormhole. Kip Thorne, and his graduate student Mike Morris, unaware of the 1973 papers by Ellis, and Bronnikov, manufactured, and in 1988 published, a duplicate of the Ellis wormhole for use as a tool for teaching general relativity. For this reason, the type of traversable wormhole they proposed, held open by a spherical shell of exotic matter, was from 1988 to 2015 exclusively referred to in the literature as a *Morris–Thorne wormhole*.

Later, other types of traversable wormholes were discovered as allowable solutions to the equations of general relativity, including a variety analyzed in a 1989 paper by Matt Visser, in which a path through the wormhole could be made where the traversing path did not pass through a region of exotic matter. However, in the pure Gauss–Bonnet gravity (a modification to general relativity involving extra spatial dimensions which was sometimes studied in the context of brane cosmology) exotic matter was not needed in order for wormholes to exist—they could exist even with no matter. A type held open by negative mass cosmic strings was put forth by Visser in collaboration with Cramer *et al*, in which it was proposed that such wormholes could have been naturally created in the early universe.

Wormholes connected two points in spacetime, which meant that they would in principle allow travel in time, as well as in space. In 1988, Morris, Thorne, and Yurtsever worked out explicitly how to convert a wormhole traversing space into one traversing time by accelerating one of its two mouths. However, according to general relativity, it would not be possible to use a wormhole to travel back to a time earlier than when the wormhole was first converted into a time 'machine'. On the other hand, until this time it could not have been noticed or have been used.

Raychaudhuri's theorem, and exotic matter
To see why exotic matter is required, consider an incoming light front traveling along geodesics, which then crosses the wormhole, and re-expands on the other side. The expansion goes from negative to positive. As the wormhole neck was of finite size, we would not expect caustics to develop, at least within the vicinity of the neck. According to the optical Raychaudhuri's theorem, this required a violation of the averaged null energy condition. Quantum effects such as the Casimir effect could not violate the averaged null energy condition in any neighborhood of space with zero curvature, but calculations in semiclassical gravity suggested that quantum effects may be able to violate this condition in curved spacetime. Although it was hoped recently that quantum effects could not violate an achronal version of the averaged null energy condition, violations had nevertheless been found, so it remained an open possibility that quantum effects might be used to support a wormhole.

Faster-than-light travel
The impossibility of faster-than-light relative speed only applied locally. Wormholes might allow effective superluminal (faster-than-light) travel by ensuring that the speed of light was not exceeded locally at any time. While traveling through a wormhole, subluminal (slower-than-light) speeds were used. If two points were connected by a wormhole whose length was shorter than the distance between them *outside* the wormhole, the time taken to traverse it could be less than the time it would take a light beam to make the journey if it took a path through the space *outside* the wormhole. However, a light beam traveling through the wormhole would of course beat the traveler.

Time travel
If traversable wormholes existed, they could allow time travel. A proposed time-travel machine using a traversable wormhole would hypothetically work in the following way: One end of the wormhole was accelerated to some significant fraction of the speed of light, perhaps with some advanced propulsion system, and then brought back to the point of origin. Alternatively, another way was to take one entrance of the wormhole, and move it to within the gravitational field of an object that had higher gravity than the other entrance, and then return it to a position near the other entrance.

For both of these methods, time dilation caused the end of the wormhole that had been moved to have aged less, or become "younger", than the stationary end as seen by an external observer; however, time connected differently *through* the wormhole than *outside* it, so that synchronized clocks at either end of the wormhole would always remain synchronized as seen by an observer passing through the wormhole, no matter how the two ends moved around. This meant that an observer entering the "younger" end would exit the "older" end at a time when it was the same age as the "younger" end, effectively going back in time as seen by an observer from the outside. One significant limitation of such a time machine was that it was only possible to go as far back in time as the initial creation of the machine. It was more of a path through time rather than it was a device that itself moved through time, and it would not allow the technology itself to be moved backward in time.

According to current theories on the nature of wormholes, construction of a traversable wormhole would require the existence of a substance with negative energy, often referred to as "exotic matter". More technically, the wormhole spacetime required a distribution of energy that violated various energy conditions, such as the null energy condition along with the weak, strong, and dominant energy conditions. However, it was known that quantum effects could lead to small measurable violations of the null energy condition, and many physicists believed that the required negative energy may actually be possible due to the Casimir effect in quantum physics. Although early calculations suggested a very large amount of negative energy would be required, later calculations showed that the amount of negative energy could be made arbitrarily small.

In 1993, Matt Visser argued that the two mouths of a wormhole with such an induced clock difference could not be brought together without inducing quantum field, and gravitational effects that would either make the wormhole collapse or the two mouths repel each other, or otherwise prevent information from passing through the wormhole. Because of this, the two mouths could not be brought close enough for causality violation to take place. However, in a 1997 paper, Visser hypothesized that a complex "Roman ring" (named after Tom Roman) configuration of an N number of wormholes arranged in a symmetric polygon could still act as a time machine, although he concludes that this was more likely a flaw in classical quantum gravity theory rather than proof that causality violation is possible.

Inter-universal travel

A possible resolution to the paradoxes resulting from wormhole-enabled time travel rested on the many-worlds interpretation of quantum mechanics.

In 1991 David Deutsch showed that quantum theory was fully consistent (in the sense that the so-called density matrix could be made free of discontinuities) in spacetimes with closed time like curves. However, later it was shown that such model of closed time like curve could have internal inconsistencies as it would lead to strange phenomena like distinguishing non-orthogonal quantum states, and distinguishing proper, and improper mixture. Accordingly, the destructive positive feedback loop of virtual particles circulating through a wormhole time machine, a result indicated by semi-classical calculations, was averted. A particle returning from the future did not return to its universe of origination but to a parallel universe. This suggested that a wormhole time machine with an exceedingly short time jump was a theoretical bridge between contemporaneous parallel universes.

Because a wormhole time-machine introduced a type of nonlinearity into quantum theory, this sort of communication between parallel universes was consistent with Joseph Polchinski's proposal of an Everett phone (named after Hugh Everett) in Steven Weinberg's formulation of nonlinear quantum mechanics. The possibility of communication between parallel universes had been dubbed inter-universal travel.

APPENDIX E – NICOLAI TESLA

The Early years

Tesla was the fourth of five children. He had three sisters, Milka, Angelina, and Marica, and an older brother named Dane, who was killed in a horse-riding accident when Tesla was aged five. In 1861, Tesla attended primary school in Smiljan where he studied German, arithmetic, and religion. In 1862, the Tesla family moved to the nearby Gospić, Lika where Tesla's father worked as parish priest. Nikola completed primary school, followed by middle school.

In 1870, Tesla moved far north to Karlovac to attend high school at the Higher Real Gymnasium. The classes were held in German, as it was a school within the Austro-Hungarian Military Frontier.

Tesla would later write that he became interested in demonstrations of electricity by his physics professor. Tesla noted that these demonstrations of this "mysterious phenomena" made him want "to know more of this wonderful force". Tesla was able to perform integral calculus in his head, which prompted his teachers to believe that he was cheating. He finished a four-year term in three years, graduating in 1873.

In 1873, Tesla returned to Smiljan. Shortly after he arrived, he contracted cholera, was bedridden for nine months, and was near death multiple times. Tesla's father, in a moment of despair, (who had originally wanted him to enter the priesthood) promised to send him to the best engineering school if he recovered from the illness.

In 1874, Tesla evaded conscription into the Austro-Hungarian Army in Smiljan by running away southeast of Lika to Tomingaj, near Gračac. There he explored the mountains wearing hunter's garb. Tesla said that this contact with nature made him stronger, both physically, and mentally. He read many books while in Tomingaj, and later said that Mark Twain's works had helped him to miraculously recover from his earlier illness.

In 1875, Tesla enrolled at Austrian Polytechnic in Graz, Austria, on a Military Frontier scholarship. During his first year, Tesla never missed a lecture, earned the highest grades possible, passed nine exams (nearly twice as many as required), started a Serb cultural club, and even received a letter of commendation from the dean of the technical faculty to his father, which stated, "Your son is a star of first rank." During his second year, Tesla came into conflict with Professor Poeschl over the Gramme dynamo, when Tesla suggested that commutators were not necessary.

Tesla claimed that he worked from 3:00 a.m. to 11:00 p.m., no Sundays or holidays excepted. He was "mortified when his father made light of those hard-won honors." After his father's death in 1879, Tesla found a package of letters from his professors to his father, warning that unless he were removed from the school, Tesla would die through overwork. At the end of his second year, Tesla lost his scholarship, and became addicted to gambling. During his third year, Tesla gambled away his allowance, and his tuition money, later gambling back his initial losses, and returning the balance to his family. Tesla said that he "conquered his passion then, and there," but later in the U.S. he was again known to play billiards. When examination time came, Tesla was unprepared, and asked for an extension to study but was denied. He did not receive grades for the last semester of the third year, and he never graduated from the university.

In December 1878, Tesla left Graz, and severed all relations with his family to hide the fact that he dropped out of school. His friends thought that he had drowned in the nearby Mur River. Tesla moved to Maribor, where he worked as a draftsman for 60 florins per month. He spent his spare time playing cards with local men on the streets.

Working at Budapest Telephone Exchange
In 1881, Tesla moved to Budapest, Hungary, to work under Tivadar Puskás at a telegraph company, the Budapest Telephone Exchange. Upon arrival, Tesla realized that the company, then under construction, was not functional, so he worked as a draftsman in the Central Telegraph Office instead. Within a few months, the Budapest Telephone Exchange became functional, and Tesla was allocated the chief electrician position. During his employment, Tesla made many improvements to the Central Station equipment, and claimed to have perfected a telephone repeater or amplifier, which was never patented nor publicly described.

Working at Edison
In 1882, Tivadar Puskás got Tesla another job in Paris with the Continental Edison Company. Tesla began working in what was then a brand-new industry, installing indoor incandescent lighting citywide in the form of an electric power utility. The company had several subdivisions, and Tesla worked at the Société Electrique Edison, the division in the Ivry-sur-Seine suburb of Paris in charge of installing the lighting system. There he gained a great deal of practical experience in electrical engineering. Management took notice of his advanced knowledge in engineering, and physics, and soon had him designing, and building improved versions of generating dynamos, and motors. They also sent him on to troubleshoot engineering problems at other Edison utilities being built around France, and in Germany.

In 1884, Edison manager Charles Batchelor, who had been overseeing the Paris installation, was brought back to the US to manage the Edison Machine Works, a manufacturing division situated in New York City, and asked that Tesla be brought to the US as well. In June 1884, Tesla emigrated to the United States. He began working almost immediately at the Machine Works on Manhattan's Lower East Side, an overcrowded shop with a workforce of several hundred machinists, laborers, managing staff, and 20 "field engineers" struggling with the task of building the large electric utility in that city. As in Paris, Tesla was working on troubleshooting installations, and improving generators.

Historian W. Bernard Carlson notes Tesla may have met company founder Thomas Alva Edison only a couple of times. One of those times was noted in Tesla's autobiography where, after staying up all night repairing the damaged dynamos on the ocean liner SS *Oregon*, he ran into Batchelor, and Edison, who made a quip about their "Parisian" being out all night. After Tesla told them he had been up all night fixing the *Oregon* Edison commented to Batchelor that "this is a damned good man." One of the projects given to Tesla was to develop an arc lamp-based street lighting system. Arc lighting was the most popular type of street lighting but it required high voltages, and was incompatible with the Edison low-voltage incandescent system, causing the company to lose contracts in cities that wanted street lighting as well. Tesla's designs were never put into production, possibly because of technical improvements in incandescent street lighting or because of an installation deal that Edison cut with an arc lighting company.

Tesla had been working at the Machine Works for a total of six months when he quit. What event precipitated his leaving is unclear? It may have been over a bonus he did not receive, either for redesigning generators or for the arc lighting system that was shelved. Tesla had previous run-ins with the Edison company over unpaid bonuses he believed he had earned. In his own biography, Tesla stated the manager of the Edison Machine Works offered a $50,000 bonus to design "twenty-four different types of standard machines" "but it turned out to be a practical joke". Later versions of this story have Thomas Edison himself offering, and then reneging on the deal, quipping "Tesla, you don't understand our American humor." The size of the bonus in either story has been noted as odd since Machine Works manager Batchelor was stingy with pay, and the company did not have that amount of cash (equivalent to $12 million today) on hand. Tesla's diary contains just one comment on what happened at the end of his employment, a note he scrawled across the two pages covering December 7, 1884, to January 4, 1885, saying "Good bye to the Edison Machine Works".

In late 1886, Tesla met Alfred S. Brown, a Western Union superintendent, and New York attorney Charles F. Peck. The two men were experienced in setting up companies, and promoting inventions, and patents for financial gain. Based on Tesla's new ideas for electrical equipment, including a thermo-magnetic motor idea, they agreed to back the inventor financially, and handle his patents. Together they formed the Tesla Electric Company in April 1887, with an agreement that profits from generated patents would go 1/3 to Tesla, 1/3 to Peck, and Brown, and 1/3 to fund development. They set up a laboratory for Tesla at 89 Liberty Street in Manhattan, where he worked on improving, and developing new types of electric motors, generators, and other devices.

In July 1888, Brown, and Peck negotiated a licensing deal with George Westinghouse for Tesla's polyphase induction motor, and transformer designs for $60,000 in cash, and stock, and a royalty of $2.50 per AC horsepower produced by each motor. Westinghouse also hired Tesla for one year for the large fee of $2,000 ($54,500 in today's dollars) per month to be a consultant at the Westinghouse Electric & Manufacturing Company's Pittsburgh labs.

In the summer of 1889, Tesla traveled to the 1889 Exposition Universelle in Paris, and learned of Heinrich Hertz' 1886–88 experiments that proved the existence of electromagnetic radiation, including radio waves. Tesla found this new discovery "refreshing", and decided to explore it more fully. In repeating, and then expanding on, these experiments, Tesla tried powering a Ruhmkorff coil with a high-speed alternator he had been developing as part of an improved arc lighting system but found that the high frequency current overheated the iron core, and melted the insulation between the primary, and secondary windings in the coil. To fix this problem Tesla came up with his Tesla coil with an air gap instead of insulating material between the primary, and secondary windings, and an iron core that could be moved to different positions in or out of the coil.

Citizenship
On 30 July 1891, aged 35, Tesla became a naturalized citizen of the United States.

Steam-powered oscillating generator
Trying to come up with a better way to generate alternating current, Tesla developed a steam powered reciprocating electricity generator. He patented it in 1893, and introduced it at the Chicago World's Columbian Exposition that year. Steam would be forced into the oscillator, and rush out through a series of ports, pushing a piston up, and down that was attached to an armature. The magnetic armature vibrated up, and down at high speed, producing an alternating magnetic field. This induced alternating electric current in the wire coils located adjacent. It did away with the complicated parts of a steam engine/generator, but never caught on as a feasible engineering solution to generate electricity.

Polyphase System, and the Columbian Exposition
At the beginning of 1893, Westinghouse engineer Benjamin Lamme had made great progress developing an efficient version of Tesla's induction motor, and Westinghouse Electric started branding their complete polyphase AC system as the "Tesla Polyphase System". They believed that Tesla's patents gave them patent priority over other AC systems.

Westinghouse Electric asked Tesla to participate in the 1893 World's Columbian Exposition in Chicago where the company had a large space in a building devoted to electrical exhibits. Westinghouse Electric won the bid to light the Exposition with alternating current, and it was a key event in the history of AC power, as the company demonstrated to the American public the safety, reliability, and efficiency of a fully integrated alternating current system. Tesla showed a series of electrical effects related to alternating current as well as his wireless lighting system, using a demonstration he had previously performed throughout America, and Europe; these included using high-voltage, high-frequency alternating current to light a wireless gas-discharge lamp.

An observer noted: Within the room were suspended two hard-rubber plates covered with tin foil. These were about fifteen feet apart, and served as terminals of the wires leading from the transformers. When the current was turned on, the lamps or tubes, which had no wires connected to them, but lay on a table between the suspended plates, or which might be held in the hand in almost any part of the room, were made luminous. These were the same experiments, and the same apparatus shown by Tesla in London about two years previous, "where they produced so much wonder, and astonishment".

Tesla also explained the principles of the rotating magnetic field in an induction motor by demonstrating how to make a copper egg stand on end, using a device that he constructed known as the *Egg of Columbus*, and introduced his new steam powered oscillator AC generator.

Consulting on Niagara
In 1893, Edward Dean Adams, who headed up the Niagara Falls Cataract Construction Company, sought Tesla's opinion on what system would be best to transmit power generated at the falls. Over several years, there had been a series of proposals, and open competitions on how best to use power generated by the falls. Among the systems proposed by several US, and European companies were two-phase, and three-phase AC, high-voltage DC, and compressed air. Adams pumped Tesla for information about the current state of all the competing systems. Tesla advised Adams that a two-phased

system would be the most reliable, and that there was a Westinghouse system to light incandescent bulbs using two-phase alternating current. The company awarded a contract to Westinghouse Electric for building a two-phase AC generating system at the Niagara Falls, based on Tesla's advice, and Westinghouse's demonstration at the Columbian Exposition that they could build a complete AC system. At the same time, a further contract was awarded to General Electric to build the AC distribution system.

The Nikola Tesla Company

In 1895, Edward Dean Adams, impressed with what he saw when he toured Tesla's lab, agreed to help found the Nikola Tesla Company, set up to fund, develop, and market a variety of previous Tesla patents, and inventions as well as new ones. Alfred Brown signed on, bringing along patents developed under Peck, and Brown. The board was filled out with William Birch Rankine, and Charles F. Coaney. It found few investors; the mid-1890s was a tough time financially, and the wireless lighting, and oscillators patents it was set up to market never panned out. The company would handle Tesla's patents for decades to come.

Lab fire

In the early morning hours of March 13, 1895, the South Fifth Avenue building that housed Tesla's lab caught fire. It started in the basement of the building, and was so intense Tesla's 4th floor lab burned, and collapsed into the second floor. The fire not only set back Tesla's ongoing projects, it destroyed a collection of early notes, and research material, models, and demonstration pieces, including many that had been exhibited at the 1893 Worlds Colombian Exposition. Tesla told *The New York Times* "I am in too much grief to talk. What can I say?" After the fire Tesla moved to 46 & 48 East Houston Street, and rebuilt his lab on the 6th, and 7th floors.

X-ray experimentation

Starting in 1894, Tesla began investigating what he referred to as radiant energy of "invisible" kinds after he had noticed damaged film in his laboratory in previous experiments (later identified as "*Roentgen rays*" or "X-Rays"). His early experiments were with Crookes tubes, a cold cathode electrical discharge tube. Tesla may have inadvertently captured an X-ray image—predating, by a few weeks, Wilhelm Röntgen's December 1895 announcement of the discovery of x-rays—when he tried to photograph Mark Twain illuminated by a Geissler tube, an earlier type of gas discharge tube. The only thing captured in the image was the metal locking screw on the camera lens.

In 1898, Tesla demonstrated a radio-controlled boat which he hoped to sell as a guided torpedo to navies around the world.

In March 1896, after hearing of Wilhelm Röntgen's discovery of X-ray, and X-ray imaging (radiography), Tesla proceeded to do his own experiments in X-ray imaging, developing a high energy single terminal vacuum tube of his own design that had no target electrode, and that worked from the output of the Tesla Coil (the modern term for the phenomenon produced by this device is *bremsstrahlung* or *braking radiation*). In his research, Tesla devised several experimental setups to produce X-rays. Tesla held that, with his circuits, the "instrument will enable one to generate Roentgen rays of much greater power than obtainable with ordinary apparatus."

Tesla noted the hazards of working with his circuit, and single-node X-ray-producing devices. In his many notes on the early investigation of this phenomenon, he attributed the skin damage to various causes. He believed early on that damage to the skin was not caused by the Roentgen rays, but by the ozone generated in contact with the skin, and to a lesser extent, by nitrous acid. Tesla incorrectly believed that X-rays were longitudinal waves, such as those produced in waves in plasmas. These plasma waves can occur in force-free magnetic fields.

On 11 July 1934, the *New York Herald Tribune* published an article on Tesla, in which he recalled an event that would occasionally take place while experimenting with his single-electrode vacuum tubes; a minute particle would break off the cathode, pass out of the tube, and physically strike him:

Tesla said he could feel a sharp stinging pain where it entered his body, and again at the place where it passed out. In comparing these particles with the bits of metal projected by his "electric gun," Tesla said, "The particles in the beam of force... will travel much faster than such particles..., and they will travel in concentrations."

Radio remote control

In 1898, Tesla demonstrated a boat that used a coherer-based radio control—which he dubbed "telautomaton"—to the public during an electrical exhibition at Madison Square Garden. The crowd that witnessed the demonstration made outrageous claims about the workings of the boat, such as magic, telepathy, and being piloted by a trained monkey hidden inside. Tesla tried to sell his idea to the U.S. military as a type of radio-controlled torpedo, but they showed little interest. Remote radio control remained a novelty until World War I, and afterward, when a number of countries used it in military programs. Tesla took the opportunity to further demonstrate "Teleautomatics" in an address to a meeting of the Commercial Club in Chicago, while he was travelling to Colorado Springs, on 13 May 1899.

Attempting to develop inventions he could patent, and market, Tesla conducted a range of experiments with mechanical oscillators/generators, electrical discharge tubes, and early X-ray imaging. He also built a wireless-controlled boat, one of the first ever exhibited. Tesla became well known as an inventor, and would demonstrate his achievements to celebrities, and wealthy patrons at his lab, and was noted for his showmanship at public lectures.

Throughout the 1890s, Tesla pursued his ideas for wireless lighting, and worldwide wireless electric power distribution in his high-voltage, high-frequency power experiments in New York, and Colorado Springs. In 1893, he made pronouncements on the possibility of wireless communication with his devices. Tesla tried to put these ideas to practical use in his unfinished Wardenclyffe Tower project, an intercontinental wireless communication, and power transmitter, but ran out of funding before he could complete it.

After Wardenclyffe, Tesla went on to try to develop a series of inventions in the 1910s, and 1920s with varying degrees of success. Having spent most of his money, he lived in a series of New York hotels, leaving behind unpaid bills. Tesla died in New York City in January 1943. His work fell into relative obscurity following his death, but in 1960, the General Conference on Weights, and Measures named the SI unit of magnetic flux density the tesla in his honor. There has been a resurgence in popular interest in Tesla since the 1990s. His intellectual achievements, and originality have made him named by many a genius.

Moving to the US

Tesla Electric Light & Manufacturing
Soon after leaving the Edison company, Tesla was working on patenting an arc lighting system, possibly the same one he had developed at Edison. In March 1885, he met with patent attorney Lemuel W. Serrell, the same attorney used by Edison, to obtain help with submitting the patents. Serrell introduced Tesla to two businessmen, Robert Lane, and Benjamin Vail, who agreed to finance an arc lighting manufacturing, and utility company in Tesla's name, the Tesla Electric Light & Manufacturing. Tesla worked for the rest of the year obtaining the patents that included an improved DC generator, the first patents issued to Tesla in the US, and building, and installing the system in Rahway, New Jersey Tesla's new system gained notice in the technical press, which commented on its advanced features.

The investors showed little interest in Tesla's ideas for new types of alternating current motors, and electrical transmission equipment. After the utility was up, and running in 1886, they decided that the manufacturing side of the business was too competitive, and opted to simply run an electric utility. They formed a new utility company, abandoning Tesla's company, and leaving the inventor penniless. Tesla even lost control of the patents he had generated, since he had assigned them to the company in exchange for stock. He had to work at various electrical repair jobs, and as a ditch digger for $2 per day. Later in life Tesla would recount that part of 1886 as a time of hardship, writing "My high education in various branches of science, mechanics, and literature seemed to me like a mockery".

AC, and the induction motor
In 1887, Tesla developed an induction motor that ran on alternating current (AC), a power system format that was rapidly expanding in Europe, and the United States because of its advantages in long-distance, high-voltage transmission. The motor used polyphase current, which generated a rotating magnetic field to turn the motor (a principle that Tesla claimed to have conceived in 1882). This innovative electric motor, patented in May 1888, was a simple self-starting design that did not need a commutator, thus avoiding sparking, and the high maintenance of constantly servicing, and replacing mechanical brushes.

Along with getting the motor patented, Peck, and Brown arranged to get the motor publicized, starting with independent testing to verify it was a functional improvement, followed by press releases sent to technical publications for articles to run concurrent with the issue of the patent. Physicist William Arnold Anthony (who tested the motor), and *Electrical World* magazine editor Thomas Commerford Martin arranged for Tesla to demonstrate his AC motor on 16 May 1888 at the American Institute of Electrical Engineers. Engineers working for the Westinghouse Electric & Manufacturing Company reported to George Westinghouse that Tesla had a viable AC motor, and related power system – something Westinghouse needed for the alternating current system he was already marketing. Westinghouse looked into getting a patent on a similar commutator-less, rotating magnetic field-based induction motor developed in

1885, and presented in a paper in March 1888 by Italian physicist Galileo Ferraris, but decided that Tesla's patent would probably control the market.

During that year, Tesla worked in Pittsburgh, helping to create an alternating current system to power the city's streetcars. He found it a frustrating period because of conflicts with the other Westinghouse engineers over how best to implement AC power. Between them, they settled on a 60-cycle AC system that Tesla proposed (to match the working frequency of Tesla's motor), but they soon found that it would not work for streetcars, since Tesla's induction motor could run only at a constant speed. They ended up using a DC traction motor instead.

Market Turmoil

Tesla's demonstration of his induction motor, and Westinghouse's subsequent licensing of the patent, both in 1888, came at the time of extreme competition between electric companies. The three big firms, Westinghouse, Edison, and Thompson-Houston, were trying to grow in a capital-intensive business while financially undercutting each other. There was even a "War of Currents" propaganda campaign going on with Edison Electric trying to claim their direct current system was better, and safer than the Westinghouse alternating current system. Competing in this market meant Westinghouse would not have the cash or engineering resources to develop Tesla's motor, and the related polyphase system right away.

Two years after signing the Tesla contract, Westinghouse Electric was in trouble. The near collapse of Barings Bank in London triggered the financial panic of 1890, causing investors to call in their loans to W.E. The sudden cash shortage forced the company to refinance its debts. The new lenders demanded that Westinghouse cut back on what looked like excessive spending on acquisition of other companies, research, and patents, including the per motor royalty in the Tesla contract. At that point, the Tesla induction motor had been unsuccessful, and was stuck in development. Westinghouse was paying a $15,000-a-year guaranteed royalty even though operating examples of the motor were rare, and polyphase power systems needed to run it were even rarer.

In early 1891, George Westinghouse explained his financial difficulties to Tesla in stark terms, saying that, if he did not meet the demands of his lenders, he would no longer be in control of Westinghouse Electric, and Tesla would have to "deal with the bankers" to try to collect future royalties. The advantages of having Westinghouse continue to champion the motor probably seemed obvious to Tesla, and he agreed to release the company from the royalty payment clause in the contract. Six years later Westinghouse would purchase Tesla's patent for a lump sum payment of $216,000 as part of a patent-sharing agreement signed with General Electric (a company created from the 1892 merger of Edison, and Thompson-Houston).

New York laboratories

The money Tesla made from licensing his AC patents made him independently wealthy, and gave him the time, and funds to pursue his own interests. In 1889, Tesla moved out of the Liberty Street shop Peck, and Brown had rented, and for the next dozen years would work out of a series of workshop/laboratory spaces in Manhattan. These included a lab at 175 Grand Street (1889–1892), the fourth floor of 33–35 South Fifth Avenue (1892–1895), and sixth, and seventh floors of 46 & 48 East Houston

Street (1895–1902). Tesla, and his hired staff would conduct some of his most significant work in these workshops.

Tesla coil

In the same year, he patented his Tesla coil. A Tesla coil was an electrical resonant transformer circuit designed by inventor Nikola Tesla in 1891. It was used to produce high-voltage, low-current, high frequency alternating-current electricity. Tesla experimented with a number of different configurations consisting of two, or sometimes three, coupled resonant electric circuits.

Tesla used these circuits to conduct innovative experiments in electrical lighting, phosphorescence, X-ray generation, high frequency alternating current phenomena, electrotherapy, and the transmission of electrical energy without wires. Tesla coil circuits were used commercially in spark gap radio transmitters for wireless telegraphy until the 1920s, and in medical equipment such as electrotherapy, and violet ray devices. Today their main use was for entertainment, and educational displays, although small coils were still used today as leak detectors for high vacuum systems.

Wireless lighting

After 1890, Tesla experimented with transmitting power by inductive, and capacitive coupling using high AC voltages generated with his Tesla coil. He attempted to develop a wireless lighting system based on near-field inductive, and capacitive coupling, and conducted a series of public demonstrations where he lit Geissler tubes, and even incandescent light bulbs from across a stage. He would spend most of the decade working on variations of this new form of lighting with the help of various investors but none of the ventures succeeded in making a commercial product out of his findings.

In 1893 at St. Louis, Missouri, the Franklin Institute in Philadelphia, Pennsylvania, and the National Electric Light Association, Tesla told onlookers that he was sure a system like his could eventually conduct "intelligible signals or perhaps even power to any distance without the use of wires" by conducting it through the Earth.

Tesla served as a vice-president of the American Institute of Electrical Engineers from 1892 to 1894, the forerunner of the modern-day IEEE (along with the Institute of Radio Engineers).

Wireless power

From the 1890s through 1906, Tesla spent a great deal of his time, and fortune on a series of projects trying to develop the transmission of electrical power without wires. It was an expansion of his idea of using coils to transmit power that he had been demonstrating in wireless lighting. He saw this as not only a way to transmit large amounts of power around the world but also, as he had pointed out in his earlier lectures, a way to transmit worldwide communications.

At the time Tesla was formulating his ideas, there was no feasible way to wirelessly transmit communication signals over long distances, let alone large amounts of power. Tesla had studied radio waves early on, and concluded that part of existing study on them, by Hertz, was incorrect. Also, this new form of radiation was widely considered at the time to be a short-distance phenomenon that seemed to die out in less than a mile. Tesla noted that, even if theories on radio waves were true, they were totally worthless for his intended purposes since this form of "invisible light" would diminish over distance just like any other radiation, and would travel in straight lines right out into space, becoming "hopelessly lost."

By the mid-1890s, Tesla was working on the idea that he might be able to conduct electricity long distance through the Earth or the atmosphere, and began working on experiments to test this idea including setting up a large resonance transformer magnifying transmitter in his East Houston Street lab. Seeming to borrow from a common idea at the time that the Earth's atmosphere was conductive, he proposed a system composed of balloons suspending, transmitting, and receiving, electrodes in the air above 30,000 feet in altitude, where he thought the lower pressure would allow him to send high voltages (millions of volts) long distances.

Colorado Springs

To further study the conductive nature of low pressure air, Tesla set up an experimental station at high altitude in Colorado Springs during 1899. There he could safely operate much larger coils than in the cramped confines of his New York lab, and an associate had arranged for the El Paso Power Company to supply alternating current free of charge. To fund his experiments, he convinced John Jacob Astor IV to invest $100,000 to become a majority shareholder in the Nikola Tesla Company. Astor thought he was primarily investing in the new wireless lighting system. Instead, Tesla used the money to fund his Colorado Springs experiments. Upon his arrival, he told reporters that he planned to conduct wireless telegraphy experiments, transmitting signals from Pikes Peak to Paris.

There he conducted experiments with a large coil operating in the megavolts range, producing artificial lightning (and thunder) consisting of millions of volts, and up to 135 feet (41 m) long discharges and, at one point, inadvertently burned out the generator in El Paso, causing a power outage. The observations he made of the electronic noise of lightning strikes, led him to (incorrectly) conclude that he could use the entire globe of the Earth to conduct electrical energy.

During his time at his laboratory, Tesla observed unusual signals from his receiver which he speculated to be communications from another planet. He mentioned them in a letter to a reporter in December 1899, and to the Red Cross Society in December 1900. Reporters treated it as a sensational story, and jumped to the conclusion Tesla was hearing signals from Mars. He expanded on the signals he heard in a 9 February 1901 *Collier's Weekly* article "Talking With Planets" where he said it had not been immediately apparent to him that he was hearing "intelligently controlled signals", and that the signals could come from Mars, Venus, or other planets. It has been hypothesized that he may have intercepted Guglielmo Marconi's European experiments in July 1899—Marconi may have transmitted the letter S (dot/dot/dot) in a naval demonstration, the same three impulses that Tesla hinted at hearing in Colorado—or signals from another experimenter in wireless transmission.

Tesla had an agreement with the editor of *The Century Magazine* to produce an article on his findings. The magazine sent a photographer to Colorado to photograph the work being done there. The article, titled "The Problem of Increasing Human Energy", appeared in the June 1900 edition of the magazine. He explained the superiority of the wireless system he envisioned but the article was more of a lengthy philosophical treatise than an understandable scientific description of his work, illustrated with what were to become iconic images of Tesla, and his Colorado Springs experiments.

Tesla made the rounds in New York trying to find investors for what he thought would be a viable system of wireless transmission, wining, and dining them at the Waldorf-Astoria's Palm Garden (the hotel where he was living at the time), The Players Club, and Delmonico's. In March 1901, he obtained $150,000 ($4,412,400 in today's dollars) from J. Pierpont Morgan in return for a 51% share of any generated wireless patents, and began planning the Wardenclyffe Tower facility to be built in Shoreham, New York, 100 miles (161 km) east of the city on the North Shore of Long Island.

By July 1901, Tesla had expanded his plans to build a more powerful transmitter to leap ahead of Marconi's radio-based system, which Tesla thought was a copy of his own system. He approached Morgan to ask for more money to build the larger system but Morgan refused to supply any further funds. In December 1901, Marconi successfully transmitted the letter S from England to Newfoundland, defeating Tesla in the race to be first to complete such a transmission. A month after Marconi's success, Tesla tried to get Morgan to back an even larger plan to transmit messages, and power by controlling "vibrations throughout the globe". Over the next five years, Tesla wrote more than 50 letters to Morgan, pleading for, and demanding additional funding to complete the construction of Wardenclyffe. Tesla continued the project for another nine months into 1902. The tower was erected to its full 187 feet (57 m). In June 1902, Tesla moved his lab operations from Houston Street to Wardenclyffe.

Investors on Wall Street were putting their money into Marconi's system, and some in the press began turning against Tesla's project, claiming it was a hoax. The project came to a halt in 1905, and in 1906, the financial problems, and other events may have led to what Tesla biographer Marc J. Seifer suspected was a nervous breakdown on Tesla's part. Tesla mortgaged the Wardenclyffe property to cover his debts at the Waldorf-Astoria, which eventually mounted to $20,000 ($488,600 in today's dollars). He lost the property in foreclosure in 1915, and in 1917 the Tower was demolished by the new owner to make the land a more viable real estate asset.

Later years

After Wardencyiffe closed, Tesla continued to write to Morgan; after "the great man" died, Tesla wrote to his son Jack Morgan, trying to get further funding for the project. In 1906, Tesla opened offices at 165 Broadway in Manhattan, trying to raise further funds by developing, and marketing his patents. He went on to have offices at the Metropolitan Life Tower from 1910 to 1914; rented for a few months at the Woolworth Building, moving out because he could not afford the rent;, and then to office space at 8 West 40th Street from 1915 to 1925. After moving to 8 West 40th Street, he was effectively bankrupt. Most of his patents had run out, and he was having trouble with the new inventions he was trying to develop.

Living circumstances

Since 1900, Tesla had been living at the Waldorf Astoria in New York running up a large bill. In 1922, he moved to St. Regis Hotel, and would follow a pattern from then on of moving to a new hotel every few years leaving behind unpaid bills.

Tesla would walk to the park every day to feed the pigeons. He took to feeding them at the window of his hotel room, and bringing the injured ones in to nurse back to health. He said that he had been visited by a specific injured white pigeon daily. Tesla spent over $2,000, including building a device that comfortably supported her so her bones could heal, to fix her broken wing, and leg. Tesla stated:

I have been feeding pigeons, thousands of them for years. But there was one, a beautiful bird, pure white with light grey tips on its wings; that one was different. It was a female. I had only to wish, and call her, and she would come flying to me. I loved that pigeon as a man loves a woman, and she loved me. As long as I had her, there was a purpose to my life.

Tesla's unpaid bills, and complaints about the mess from his pigeon-feeding, forced him to leave the St. Regis in 1923, the Hotel Pennsylvania in 1930, and the Hotel Governor Clinton in 1934. At one point, he also took rooms at the Hotel Marguery.

In 1934, Tesla moved to the Hotel New Yorker, and Westinghouse Electric & Manufacturing Company began paying him $125 per month as well as paying his rent, expenses the Company would pay for the rest of Tesla's life. Accounts of how this came about vary. Several sources say Westinghouse was worried (or warned) about potential bad publicity surrounding the impoverished conditions under which their former star inventor was living. The payment has been described as being couched as a "consulting fee" to get around Tesla's aversion to accept charity, or by one biographer Marc Seifer as a type of unspecified settlement.

Death

On 7 January 1943, at the age of 86, Tesla died alone in Room 3327 of the New Yorker Hotel. His body was later found by maid Alice Monaghan after she had entered Tesla's room, ignoring the "do not disturb" sign that Tesla had placed on his door two days earlier. Assistant medical examiner H.W. Wembley examined the body, and ruled that the cause of death had been coronary thrombosis.

Two days later the Federal Bureau of Investigation ordered the Alien Property Custodian to seize Tesla's belongings, even though Tesla was an American citizen. John G. Trump, a professor at M.I.T., and a well-known electrical engineer serving as a technical aide to the National Defense Research Committee, was called in to analyze the Tesla items, which were being held in custody. After a three-day investigation, Trump's report concluded that there was nothing which would constitute a hazard in unfriendly hands, stating:

Tesla's thoughts, and efforts during at least the past 15 years were primarily of a speculative, philosophical, and somewhat promotional character often concerned with the production, and wireless transmission of power; but did not include new, sound, workable principles or methods for realizing such results.

POST ANALYSIS

Nikola Tesla may have been one of the great minds of inventors, but from a business perspective, he had been taken advantage at almost every invention. Though many of his inventions went unrecognized, several gained him notoriety namely, AC Power (alternate current as opposed to direct current), the Tesla Coil (Wireless lightning), and Wireless Power. Unfortunately, it was the wireless power technology that could have made him great fortunes. Short on funding, disillusioned at business failures, penniless, and without family, and friends, he died alone at age 86 but not forgotten.

It was not until 2003 when Elon Musk, an independent automaker, named his electrical car company in honor of the famed physicist Nicola Tesla, who otherwise may have been forgotten to the world for his brilliant achievements.

APPENDIX F – ALBERT EINSTEIN

From Wikipedia, the free encyclopedia
Albert Einstein 14 March 1879 – 18 April 1955, was a German-born theoretical physicist who developed the theory of relativity, one of the two pillars of modern physics alongside quantum mechanics. His work was also known for its influence on the philosophy of science. He was best known by the general public for his mass–energy equivalence formula $E = mc^2$ which had been dubbed "the world's most famous equation". He received the 1921 Nobel Prize in Physics for his services to theoretical physics, and especially for his discovery of the law of the photoelectric effect, a pivotal step in the evolution of quantum theory.

Near the beginning of his career, Einstein thought that Newtonian mechanics was no longer enough to reconcile the laws of classical mechanics with the laws of the electromagnetic field. This led him to develop his special theory of relativity during his time at the Swiss Patent Office in Bern 1902–1909, Switzerland. However, he realized that the principle of relativity could also be extended to gravitational fields and—with his subsequent theory of gravitation in 1916—he published a paper on general relativity. He continued to deal with problems of statistical mechanics, and quantum theory, which led to his explanations of particle theory, and the motion of molecules. He also investigated the thermal properties of light which laid the foundation of the photon theory of light. In 1917, he applied the general theory of relativity to model the large-scale structure of the universe.

Einstein always excelled at math, and physics from a young age, reaching some mathematical level years ahead of his peers. The twelve-year-old Einstein taught himself algebra, and Euclidean geometry over a single summer. Einstein also independently discovered his own original proof of the Pythagorean theorem at age 12. A family tutor Max Talmud says that after he had given the 12-year-old Einstein a geometry textbook, after a short time "Einstein had worked through the whole book. He thereupon devoted himself to higher mathematics. Soon the flight of his mathematical genius was so high I could not follow." His passion for geometry, and algebra led the twelve-year-old to become convinced that nature could be understood as a "mathematical structure". Einstein started teaching himself calculus at 12, and as a 14-year-old he says he had "mastered integral, and differential calculus".

At age 13, Einstein was introduced to Kant's Critique of Pure Reason, and Kant became his favorite philosopher, his tutor stating: "At the time he was still a child, only thirteen years old, yet Kant's works, incomprehensible to ordinary mortals, seemed to be clear to him."

Scientific career
Throughout his life, Einstein published hundreds of books, and articles. He published more than 300 scientific papers, and 150 non-scientific ones. On 5 December 2014, universities, and archives announced the release of Einstein's papers, comprising more than 30,000 unique documents. Einstein's intellectual achievements, and originality have made the word "Einstein" synonymous with "genius". In addition to the work he did by himself he also collaborated with other scientists on additional projects including the Bose–Einstein statistics, the Einstein refrigerator, and others.

Special relativity (General principles) Theory of relativity, and $E = mc^2$

Einstein's *"Zur Elektrodynamik bewegter Körper"* (On the Electrodynamics of Moving Bodies) was received on 30 June 1905, and published 26 September of that same year. It reconciles Maxwell's equations for electricity, and magnetism with the laws of mechanics, by introducing major changes to mechanics close to the speed of light. This later became known as Einstein's special theory of relativity.

Consequences of this include the time–space frame of a moving body appearing to slow down, and contract in the direction of motion when measured in the frame of the observer. This paper also argued that the idea of a luminiferous ether—one of the leading theoretical entities in physics at the time—was superfluous.

In his paper on mass–energy equivalence, Einstein produced $E=mc^2$ from his special relativity equations. Einstein's 1905 work on relativity remained controversial for many years, but was accepted by leading physicists, starting with Max Planck.

General relativity (General relativity, and the equivalence principle)

General relativity was a theory of gravitation that was developed by Einstein between 1907, and 1915. According to general relativity, the observed gravitational attraction between masses results from the warping of space, and time by those masses. General relativity had developed into an essential tool in modern astrophysics. It provided the foundation for the current understanding of black holes, regions of space where gravitational attraction was so strong that not even light could escape.

As Einstein later said, the reason for the development of general relativity was that the preference of inertial motions within special relativity was unsatisfactory, while a theory which from the outset preferred no state of motion, even accelerated ones, should appear more satisfactory. Consequently, in 1907 he published an article on acceleration under special relativity. In that article titled "On the Relativity Principle, and the Conclusions Drawn from It", he argued that free fall was really inertial motion, and that for a free-falling observer the rules of special relativity must apply. This argument was called the equivalence principle. In the same article, Einstein also predicted the phenomena of gravitational time dilation, gravitational red shift, and deflection of light.

In 1911, Einstein published another article "On the Influence of Gravitation on the Propagation of Light" expanding on the 1907 article, in which he estimated the amount of deflection of light by massive bodies. Thus, the theoretical prediction of general relativity could for the first time be tested experimentally.

Gravitational waves
In 1916, Einstein predicted gravitational waves, ripples in the curvature of spacetime which propagate as waves, traveling outward from the source, transporting energy as gravitational radiation. The existence of gravitational waves was possible under general relativity due to its Lorentz invariance which brought the concept of a finite speed of propagation of the physical interactions of gravity with it. By contrast, gravitational waves could not exist in the Newtonian theory of gravitation, which postulated that the physical interactions of gravity propagate at infinite speed.

The first, indirect, detection of gravitational waves came in the 1970s through observation of a pair of closely orbiting neutron stars, PSR B1913+16. The explanation of the decay in their orbital period was that they were emitting gravitational waves. Einstein's prediction was confirmed on 11 February 2016, when researchers at LIGO published the first observation of gravitational waves, on Earth, exactly one hundred years after the prediction.

Physical cosmology

In 1917, Einstein applied the general theory of relativity to the structure of the universe as a whole. He discovered that the general field equations predicted a universe that was dynamic, either contracting or expanding. As observational evidence for a dynamic universe was not known at the time, Einstein introduced a new term, the cosmological constant, to the field equations, in order to allow the theory to predict a static universe. The modified field equations predicted a static universe of closed curvature, in accordance with Einstein's understanding of Mach's principle in these years. This model became known as the Einstein World or Einstein's static universe.

Following the discovery of the recession of the nebulae by Edwin Hubble in 1929, Einstein abandoned his static model of the universe, and proposed two dynamic models of the cosmos, The Friedmann-Einstein universe of 1931, and the Einstein–de Sitter universe of 1932. In each of these models, Einstein discarded the cosmological constant, claiming that it was "in any case theoretically unsatisfactory".

Wormholes

In 1935, Einstein collaborated with Nathan Rosen to produce a model of a wormhole, often called Einstein–Rosen bridges. His motivation was to model elementary particles with charge as a solution of gravitational field equations, in line with the program outlined in the paper "Do Gravitational Fields play an Important Role in the Constitution of the Elementary Particles?". These solutions cut, and pasted Schwarzschild black holes to make a bridge between two patches.

If one end of a wormhole was positively charged, the other end would be negatively charged. These properties led Einstein to believe that pairs of particles, and antiparticles could be described in this way.

Quantum mechanics

Einstein's objections to quantum mechanics

Einstein was displeased with modern quantum mechanics as it had evolved after 1925. Contrary to popular belief, his doubts were not due to a conviction that God "is not playing at dice." Indeed, it was Einstein himself, in his 1917 paper that proposed the possibility of stimulated emission, who first proposed the fundamental role of chance in explaining quantum processes. Rather, he objected to what quantum mechanics implies about the nature of reality. Einstein believed that a physical reality exists independent of our ability to observe it. In contrast, Bohr, and his followers maintained that all we can know are the results of measurements, and observations, and that it makes no sense to speculate about an ultimate reality that exists beyond our perceptions.

Bohr versus Einstein

The Bohr–Einstein debates were a series of public disputes about quantum mechanics between Einstein, and Niels Bohr who were two of its founders. Their debates were remembered because of their importance to the philosophy of science. Their debates would influence later interpretations of quantum mechanics.

Between 1895, and 1914, he lived in Switzerland except for one year in Prague, 1911–12, where he received his academic diploma from the Swiss Federal Polytechnic in Zürich later the Eidgenössische Technische Hochschule, ETH in 1900. He later taught at that institute as a professor of theoretical physics between 1912, and 1914 before he left for Berlin. In 1901, after being stateless for more than five years, he acquired Swiss citizenship, which he kept for the rest of his life. In 1905, he was awarded a PhD by the University of Zürich. The same year, his *annus mirabilis* (miracle year), he published four groundbreaking papers, which were to bring him to the notice of the academic world, at the age of 26.

He was visiting the United States when Adolf Hitler came to power in 1933 and— being Jewish—did not go back to Germany, where he had been a professor at the Berlin Academy of Sciences. He settled in the United States, becoming an American citizen in 1940. On the eve of World War II, he endorsed a letter to President Franklin D. Roosevelt alerting him to the potential development of "extremely powerful bombs of a new type", and recommending that the U.S. begin similar research. This eventually led to what would become the Manhattan Project. Einstein supported defending the Allied forces, but generally denounced the idea of using the newly discovered nuclear fission as a weapon. Later, with the British philosopher Bertrand Russell, he signed the Russell–Einstein Manifesto, which highlighted the danger of nuclear weapons. He was affiliated with the Institute for Advanced Study in Princeton, New Jersey, until his death in 1955.

Einstein published more than 300 scientific papers along with over 150 non-scientific works. His intellectual achievements, and originality have made the word "Einstein" synonymous with "genius". Eugene Wigner wrote of Einstein in comparison to his contemporaries that "Einstein's understanding was deeper even than Jansci von Neumann's. His mind was both more penetrating, and more original than von Neumann's, and that is a very remarkable statement."

Early life, and education

Einstein's matriculation certificate at the age of 17, showing his final grades from the Argovian cantonal school (Aargauische Kantonsschule, on a scale of 1–6, with 6 being the highest possible mark). He scored: German 5; French 3; Italian 5; History 6; Geography 4; Algebra 6; Geometry 6; Descriptive Geometry 6; Physics 6; Chemistry 5; Natural History 5; Art, and Technical Drawing 4.

Albert Einstein was born in Ulm, in the Kingdom of Württemberg in the German Empire, on 14 March 1879. His parents were Hermann Einstein, a salesman, and engineer, and Pauline Koch. In 1880, the family moved to Munich, where Einstein's father, and his uncle Jakob founded *Elektrotechnische Fabrik J. Einstein & Cie*, a company that manufactured electrical equipment based on direct current.

The Einsteins were non-observant Ashkenazi Jews, and Albert attended a Catholic elementary school in Munich, from the age of 5, for three years. At the age of 8, he was transferred to the Luitpold Gymnasium, now known as the Albert Einstein Gymnasium, where he received advanced primary, and secondary school education until he left the German Empire seven years later.

In 1894, Hermann, and Jakob's company lost a bid to supply the city of Munich with electrical lighting because they lacked the capital to convert their equipment from the direct current (DC) standard to the more efficient alternating current (AC) standard. The loss forced the sale of the Munich factory. In search of business, the Einstein family moved to Italy, first to Milan, and a few months later to Pavia. When the family moved to Pavia, Einstein, then 15, stayed in Munich to finish his studies at the Luitpold Gymnasium. His father intended for him to pursue electrical engineering, but Einstein clashed with authorities, and resented the school's regimen, and teaching method. He later wrote that the spirit of learning, and creative thought was lost in strict rote learning. At the end of December 1894, he travelled to Italy to join his family in Pavia, convincing the school to let him go by using a doctor's note. During his time in Italy he wrote a short essay with the title "On the Investigation of the State of the Ether in a Magnetic Field".

In 1895, at the age of 16, Einstein took the entrance examinations for the Swiss Federal Polytechnic in Zürich, later the Eidgenössische Technische Hochschule, ETH. He failed to reach the required standard in the general part of the examination but obtained exceptional grades in physics, and mathematics. On the advice of the principal of the Polytechnic, he attended the Argovian cantonal school (gymnasium) in Aarau, Switzerland, in 1895, and 1896 to complete his secondary schooling. While lodging with the family of professor Jost Winteler, he fell in love with Winteler's daughter, Marie. Albert's sister Maja later married Winteler's son Paul. In January 1896, with his father's approval, Einstein renounced his citizenship in the German Kingdom of Württemberg to avoid military service. In September 1896, he passed the Swiss Matura with mostly good grades, including a top grade of 6 in physics, and mathematical subjects, on a scale of 1–6. At 17, he enrolled in the four-year mathematics, and physics teaching diploma program at the Zürich Polytechnic. Marie Winteler, who was a year older, moved to Olsberg, Switzerland, for a teaching post.

Einstein's future wife, a 20-year old Serbian woman Mileva Marić, also enrolled at the Polytechnic that year. She was the only woman among the six students in the mathematics, and physics section of the teaching diploma course. Over the next few years, Einstein, and Marić's friendship developed into romance, and they read books together on extra-curricular physics in which Einstein was taking an increasing interest. In 1900, Einstein passed the exams in Maths, and Physics, and was awarded the Federal Polytechnic teaching diploma. There have been claims that Marić collaborated with Einstein on his 1905 papers, known as the *Annus Mirabilis* papers, but historians of physics who have studied the issue find no evidence that she made any substantive contributions.

Statistical mechanics

Thermodynamic fluctuations, and statistical physics
Einstein's first paper submitted in 1900 to *Annalen der Physik* was on capillary attraction. It was published in 1901 with the title "Folgerungen aus den Capillaritätserscheinungen", which translates as "Conclusions from the capillarity phenomena". Two papers he published in 1902–1903 thermodynamics attempted to interpret atomic phenomena from a statistical point of view. These papers were the foundation for the 1905 paper on Brownian motion, which showed that Brownian movement can be construed as firm evidence that molecules exist. His research in 1903, and 1904 was mainly concerned with the effect of finite atomic size on diffusion phenomena.

Theory of critical opalescence
Einstein returned to the problem of thermodynamic fluctuations, giving a treatment of the density variations in a fluid at its critical point. Ordinarily the density fluctuations are controlled by the second derivative of the free energy with respect to the density. At the critical point, this derivative is zero, leading to large fluctuations. The effect of density fluctuations is that light of all wavelengths is scattered, making the fluid look milky white. Einstein relates this to Rayleigh scattering, which is what happens when the fluctuation size is much smaller than the wavelength, hand which explains why the sky is blue. Einstein quantitatively derived critical opalescence from a treatment of density fluctuations, and demonstrated how both the effect, and Rayleigh scattering originate from the atomistic constitution of matter.

Hole argument, and Entwurf (Draft) theory
While developing general relativity, Einstein became confused about the gauge invariance in the theory. He formulated an argument that led him to conclude that a general relativistic field theory is impossible. He gave up looking for fully generally covariant tensor equations, and searched for equations that would be invariant under general linear transformations only.

In June 1913, the Entwurf theory was the result of these investigations. As its name suggests, it was a sketch of a theory, less elegant, and more difficult than general relativity, with the equations of motion supplemented by additional gauge fixing conditions. After more than two years of intensive work, Einstein realized that the hole argument was mistaken, and abandoned the theory in November 1915.

In many Einstein biographies, it is claimed that Einstein referred to the cosmological constant in later years as his "biggest blunder". The astrophysicist Mario Livio has recently cast doubt on this claim, suggesting that it may be exaggerated.

In late 2013, a team led by the Irish physicist Cormac O'Raifeartaigh discovered evidence that, shortly after learning of Hubble's observations of the recession of the nebulae, Einstein considered a steady-state model of the universe. In a hitherto overlooked manuscript, apparently written in early 1931, Einstein explored a model of the expanding universe in which the density of matter remains constant due to a continuous creation of matter, a process he associated with the cosmological constant. As he stated in the paper, "In what follows, I would like to draw attention to a solution in which the density is constant over time." If one considers a physically bounded volume, particles of matter will be continually leaving it. For the density to remain constant, new particles of matter must be continually formed in the volume from space.

It thus appears that Einstein considered a steady-state model of the expanding universe many years before Hoyle, Bondi, and Gold. However, Einstein's steady-state model contained a fundamental flaw, and he quickly abandoned the idea.

Energy momentum pseudo tensor
General relativity includes a dynamical spacetime, so it is difficult to see how to identify the conserved energy, and momentum. Noether's theorem allows these quantities to be determined from a Lagrangian with translation invariance, but general covariance makes translation invariance into something of a gauge symmetry. The energy, and momentum derived within general relativity by Noether's prescriptions do not make a real tensor for this reason.

Einstein argued that this is true for fundamental reasons, because the gravitational field could be made to vanish by a choice of coordinates. He maintained that the non-covariant energy momentum pseudo tensor was in fact the best description of the energy momentum distribution in a gravitational field. This approach has been echoed by Lev Landau, and Evgeny Lifshitz, and others, and has become standard.

The use of non-covariant objects like pseudo tensors was heavily criticized in 1917 by Erwin Schrödinger, and others.

Equations of motion
The theory of general relativity has a fundamental law—the Einstein equations which describe how space curves, the geodesic equation which describes how particles move may be derived from the Einstein equations.

Since the equations of general relativity are non-linear, a lump of energy made out of pure gravitational fields, like a black hole, would move on a trajectory which is determined by the Einstein equations themselves, not by a new law. So, Einstein proposed that the path of a singular solution, like a black hole, would be determined to be a geodesic from general relativity itself.

This was established by Einstein, Infeld, and Hoffmann for point like objects without angular momentum, and by Roy Kerr for spinning objects.

Old quantum theory
The photoelectric effect. Incoming photons on the left strike a metal plate (bottom), and eject electrons, depicted as flying off to the right.

In a 1905 paper, Einstein postulated that light itself consists of localized particles (*quanta*). Einstein's light quanta were nearly universally rejected by all physicists, including Max Planck, and Niels Bohr. This idea only became universally accepted in 1919, with Robert Millikan's detailed experiments on the photoelectric effect, and with the measurement of Compton scattering.

Einstein concluded that each wave of frequency f is associated with a collection of photons with energy hf each, where h is Planck's constant. He does not say much more, because he is not sure how the particles are related to the wave. But he does suggest that this idea would explain certain experimental results, notably the photoelectric effect.

Quantized atomic vibrations
In 1907, Einstein proposed a model of matter where each atom in a lattice structure is an independent harmonic oscillator. In the Einstein model, each atom oscillates independently—a series of equally spaced quantized states for each oscillator. Einstein was aware that getting the frequency of the actual oscillations would be difficult, but he nevertheless proposed this theory because it was a particularly clear demonstration that quantum mechanics could solve the specific heat problem in classical mechanics. Peter Debye refined this model.

Bose–Einstein statistics
In 1924, Einstein received a description of a statistical model from Indian physicist Satyendra Nath Bose, based on a counting method that assumed that light could be understood as a gas of indistinguishable particles. Einstein noted that Bose's statistics applied to some atoms as well as to the proposed light particles, and submitted his

translation of Bose's paper to the *Zeitschrift für Physik*. Einstein also published his own articles describing the model, and its implications, among them the Bose–Einstein condensate phenomenon that some particulates should appear at very low temperatures. It was not until 1995 that the first such condensate was produced experimentally by Eric Allin Cornell, and Carl Wieman using ultra-cooling equipment built at the NIST–JILA laboratory at the University of Colorado at Boulder. Bose–Einstein statistics are now used to describe the behaviors of any assembly of bosons. Einstein's sketches for this project may be seen in the Einstein Archive in the library of the Leiden University.

Zero-point energy

In a series of works completed from 1911 to 1913, Planck reformulated his 1900 quantum theory, and introduced the idea of zero-point energy in his "second quantum theory". Soon, this idea attracted the attention of Einstein, and his assistant Otto Stern. Assuming the energy of rotating diatomic molecules contains zero-point energy, they then compared the theoretical specific heat of hydrogen gas with the experimental data. The numbers matched nicely. However, after publishing the findings, they promptly withdrew their support, because they no longer had confidence in the correctness of the idea of zero-point energy.

Einstein–Podolsky–Rosen (EPR) paradox

In 1935, Einstein returned to the question of quantum mechanics in the EPR paper. In a thought experiment, he considered two particles which had interacted such that their properties were strongly correlated. No matter how far the two particles were separated, a precise position measurement on one particle would result in equally precise knowledge of the position of the other particle; likewise, a precise momentum measurement of one particle would result in equally precise knowledge of the momentum of the other particle, without needing to disturb the other particle in any way.

Given Einstein's concept of local realism, there were two possibilities: (1) either the other particle had these properties already determined, or (2) the process of measuring the first particle instantaneously affected the reality of the position, and momentum of the second particle. Einstein rejected this second possibility popularly called "spooky action at a distance".

This principle distilled the essence of Einstein's objection to quantum mechanics. As a physical principle, it was shown to be incorrect when the Aspect experiment of 1982 confirmed Bell's theorem, which J. S. Bell had delineated in 1964. The results of these, and subsequent experiments demonstrate that quantum physics cannot be represented by any version of the classical picture of physics.

Although Einstein was wrong, his clear prediction of the unusual properties of *entangled quantum states* has resulted in the EPR paper becoming among the top ten papers published in Physical Review. It is considered a centerpiece of the development of quantum information theory.

Unified Field Theory

Following his research on general relativity, Einstein entered into a series of attempts to generalize his geometric theory of gravitation to include electromagnetism as another aspect of a single entity. In 1950, he described his "unified field theory" in a

Scientific American article titled "On the Generalized Theory of Gravitation". Although he continued to be lauded for his work, Einstein became increasingly isolated in his research, and his efforts were ultimately unsuccessful. In his pursuit of a unification of the fundamental forces, Einstein ignored some mainstream developments in physics, most notably the strong, and weak nuclear forces, which were not well understood until many years after his death. Mainstream physics, in turn, largely ignored Einstein's approaches to unification. Einstein's dream of unifying other laws of physics with gravity motivates modern quests for a theory of everything, and in particular string theory, where geometrical fields emerge in a unified quantum-mechanical setting.

Albert Einstein, and Robert Oppenheimer on Extraterrestrials
Albert Einstein, and J. Robert Oppenheimer together wrote a TOP SECRET six-page document in June of 1947 entitled "Relationships with Inhabitants of Celestial Bodies". It said the presence of unidentified spacecraft was accepted as de facto by the military. It also dealt with the subjects that you would expect competent scientists to deal with - i.e., where did they come from, what did the law say about it, what should we do in the event of colonization and/or integration of peoples, and why are they here?

Finally, the document addressed the presence of celestial astroplanes in our atmosphere as a result of actions of military experiments with fission, and fusion devices of warfare.

It also appeared that our governments were not exactly forthcoming when it came to offering information about their own research on the matter. We only needed to look at the CIA's announcement in August 2013 that Area 51 did not exist, despite decades of denying it, and brandishing anyone who dared to suggest it as a mere conspiracy theorist. Fortunately, there did exist some scientifically-driven organizations, such as SETI, and MUFON, which took an objective approach to the study of UFOs.

This brings us to an unclassified Top-Secret document written by Robert Oppenheimer, an American theoretical physicist, and Albert Einstein, a German theoretical physicist, who wrote a joint report on the issue of "Relationship with Inhabitants of Celestial Bodies".

The six-page document was the first document to use the phrase 'Extra-terrestrial Biological Entities' (EBEs). It said the presence of unidentified spacecraft was accepted as 'de facto' by the military –, and this was dated June 1947.

The document dealt with issues such as: where extra-terrestrials may come from, what the law said about it, what we should do in the event of colonization and/or integration of peoples, and why they were here. The document suggested that in the event that EBE's desire to settle here on earth there will be "profound change in traditional concepts" of law, and the possible need for a new "Law Among Planetary Peoples."

This document was important for two reasons. The first reason was that it addressed the possibility of life on other planets in a very logical, and coherent way, and explored what such a realization would mean. It also raised the question as to why if respected scientists such as Oppenheimer, and Einstein were able to approach the subject in an academic way, "were we unable to engage in such sensible discussion today?"

The analysis presented by Oppenheimer, and Einstein indicated that 'disclosure' of extra-terrestrial existence could cause irreversible damage to society, raising the possibility that our governments today may already know of extra-terrestrial existence but have considered the same issues raised by Oppenheimer, and Einstein, and ruled against disclosure.

If the population was told that intelligent extra-terrestrial beings not only existed but had been visiting our planets for thousands of years, being confronting with such evidence could cause upheaval in the domains of religion, society, law, and finance which, if not addressed properly, could bring chaos to the planet.

There were many questions to be answered. The document suggested that EBEs could be more intelligent, and technologically advanced than us, and asked if this was the case, "why would they come to Earth? Would it be to conquer, and inhabit Earth, to peacefully cooperate with humans, or to study us in the same way that we study any new species that we encounter?"

The document considered, if their civilization was more advanced than ours, how could a co-occupation of Earth be feasible?

Imagine the situation in which advanced technology was given to our civilization – powerful defense systems, unlimited energy, cloaking devices, space travel to other solar systems, instant transportation devices, and so on. Now considering the current state of our civilization, and the people that govern it, what would such a release of technology mean? One word: Chaos.

It was not hard to understand that if UFOs were kept hidden from the public, it was for multiple reasons, which were logically addressed in this document. It was for these reasons, that we may never see a disclosure of extra-terrestrial existence in our lifetime.

In the meantime, it seemed that the most sensible approach was to keep an open-mind. It was usually the case that a debate raged between two opposite extremes – one side wanted to believe wholeheartedly that the cave art, and mythological accounts were all descriptions of alien encounters, while the other side was so prepared to disbelieve that anything existed beyond the scope of their reason that they will ignore even the most blatant rendition. If scientists could overcome the ridicule, and disparaging remarks that come with exploring the subject matter, perhaps one day we will find irrefutable evidence that UFOs, and extra-terrestrials did exist.

POST ANALYSIS

Much like Nicola Tesla, Einstein, and Oppenheimer conceived many original ideas on their own while reworking some previously established theories by other well-known physicists. Where physics may have been established millennia ago by Greek philosophers, it took much time to develop the tools, and instruments necessary to prove validity on the many theories. One such instrument was the Hubble space telescope. Without it, we would still search for many answers that Hubble provided for modern science. Where Einstein fell short was his Unified Field theory. While his Special, and General Relativity theories greatly impacted the understanding of the universe such as energy vs. mass effecting speed of light, unifying all cosmic principles such as gravitational waves, and space/time into one unified equation still eloped him.

His most famous expression, "Gott würfelt nicht" (God does not play dice), was an indication of Einstein, regardless of his lifelong scientific conviction, aside from being a devout religious person, believed in cosmic order. It shall prove the argument that faith, and science could work hand-in-hand in harmony. It was this conviction that still inspired the scientific community into finding the truth of creation as much as discovering our purpose for life.

It should be noted that at the time of the scientists' involvements with classified government project, they, much like the public, were not authorized "need-to-know" access to UFO, and ET issues. In contrast, due to their intricate involvements with the development of the atom bomb, they were granted Atomal (Atomic) access to continue working with nuclear science projects.

From the official positions Tesla, Einstein, Oppenheimer, and past philosophers held on the subjects of UFOs, and ETs, "They were not factual, and they did not exist other than in the recesses of the human mind," may be a bold statement but with the lack of physical evidence, there was no other conclusion a sober minded person could draw. It did not mean that many of us were confused, and disoriented, it meant that the human mind had an infinitely inspired creativity unequaled to the creation of life.

The stated scientists may not precisely fit into the UFO, and ET case studies, but were selected by the author for reasons by association. It was obvious that they had their own opinions on the subject matter limited to public knowledge. UFOs, and ETs, at the time, were highly sensitive topics for professionals to get involved without severe career implications. It was this sentiment that prevented many from getting involved one way or the other. Today, some seventy-five years later, the same sensitivity still prevailed, but to a lesser degree. The reason for the sensitivity was simple, the majority of the scientists were employed by the government. One personal indiscretion may be subject to immediate career termination.

Einstein's most famous accomplishment will have to be the equation familiar to everybody:

"$E = MC^2$" – applicable to our own earth, cosmos, as well as the far reaches of the universe. According to this general relativity theory, there was Energy and there was Mass, but they cannot be the only forces. My conclusion is that there has to be more to it. There is Knowledge and there is Spirit. The question remains, "What came first? Knowledge or spirit?

One could argue that Knowledge had to exist to recognize that something existed even if there was nothingness. Something had to exist for Knowledge to come into being. Could Knowledge be transposed into Spirit or a spiritual realm? Then there is Reality-based science contrasting with Belief-based paranormal, supernatural, and spiritual beings. The dilemma prevails that Belief had no place with science and Reality had no place with the paranormal realm.

APPENDIX G – ADAM AND EVE

From Wikipedia, the free encyclopedia - Last modified on 15 April 2017, at 00:41.
Adam, and Eve, according to the creation myth of the Abrahamic religions, were the first man, and woman, and the ancestors of all humans. The story of Adam, and Eve is central to the belief that God created human beings in a Garden of Eden, although they fell away from that state into the present world full of death, evil, pain, and suffering. It provides the basis for the belief that humanity is in essence a single family, with everyone descended from a single pair of original ancestors. It also provides much of the scriptural basis for the doctrines of the fall of man, and original sin that are important beliefs in Christianity, but which are not generally held in Judaism or Islam.

In the Book of Genesis of the Hebrew Bible, chapters one through five, there are two creation narratives with two distinct perspectives. In the first, Adam, and Eve are not mentioned (at least not mentioned by name). Instead, God created humankind in God's image, and instructed them to multiply, and to be stewards over everything else that God had made. In the second narrative, God fashions Adam from dust, and places him in the Garden of Eden.

Adam is told that he can till the ground, and eat freely of all the trees in the garden, except for a tree of the knowledge of good, and evil. Subsequently, Eve is created from one of Adam's ribs to be Adam's companion. They are innocent, and unashamed about their nakedness. However, a serpent deceives Eve into eating fruit from the forbidden tree, and she gives some of the fruit to Adam. These acts give them additional knowledge, but it gives them the ability to conjure negative, and destructive concepts such as shame, and evil. God later curses the serpent, and the ground. God prophetically tells the woman, and the man what, will be the consequences of their sin of disobeying God. Then he banishes them from the Garden of Eden.

The story underwent extensive elaboration in later Abrahamic traditions, and it has been extensively analyzed by modern biblical scholars. Interpretations, and beliefs regarding Adam, and Eve, and the story revolving around them vary across religions, and sects; for example, the Islamic version of the story holds that Adam, and Eve were *equally* responsible for their sins of hubris, instead of Eve being the first one to be unfaithful. The story of Adam, and Eve is often depicted in art, and it has had an important influence in literature, and poetry. The story of the fall of Adam is often understood to be an allegory.

There is no physical evidence that Adam, and Eve ever literally existed, and their literal existence is incompatible with human evolutionary genetics. However, there is in some countries a large discrepancy between the scientific consensus, and popular opinion; a 2014 poll reports that 56% of Americans believe that "Adam, and Eve were real people", and 44% believe so with strong or absolute certainty.

Genesis

Creation of man
In the Book of Genesis, the Genesis creation narrative tells of the creation of the first humans, humankind, in Genesis 1:26–30 as male, and female. According to the Documentary hypothesis of the Genesis creation narrative, there are two stories that derive from independent sources: A Priestly source (P) (sixth-fifth centuries BCE) in Genesis 1:1–2:4a, and in Genesis 5; and an older Jahwist (J) or Jahwist-Elohist (J-E)

(tenth-ninth centuries BCE) in Genesis 2:4b-25. Scholars recognize two separate accounts of the creation in the Old Testament. In the Priestly narrative (Genesis 1:1-2:4a), God creates the world in six days, culminating in the creation of humanity, then rests on the seventh day.

Here, in the Priestly narrative, the emphasis is on the entirety of the universe, and its creation. In an older Jahwist or Jahwist-Elohist sources (tenth-ninth centuries BCE) in Genesis 2:4b-25, also known as the "subordinating (of woman) account", Yahweh fashions a man (Heb. *adam*, "man" or "mankind", Genesis 2:4–7, from the dust (Heb. *adamah*), and blows the breath of life into his nostrils. Here, in the Jahwist narrative, the emphasis is on the Earth within the universe, and humankind's residence on the Earth. Contrast, for example, the order of terms in Genesis 1:1where it says that God made the "heavens, and the Earth" with Genesis 2:4 where it says "God made the Earth, and the heavens".

In the Jahwist version of the story, God places the man in a garden in Eden where he is permitted to till the land, and tend the garden, and animals, Genesis 2:8–15. God also places a tree in the garden, the tree of the knowledge of good, and evil, and God prohibits the man from eating the fruit of this tree, warning him that he would die if he ate the fruit Genesis 2:17. But none of the animals are found to be a suitable companion for the man, so God causes the man to sleep, and creates a woman from a part of his body (English-language tradition describes the part as a rib, but the Hebrew word *tsela*, from which this interpretation is derived, having multiple meanings, could also mean "side").

The woman is established as subordinate to the man, as the impetus for her creation is to serve the needs of the man by being his "helpmate", and to ensure that he not "be alone", Genesis 2:18. However, some argue for a translation of the Hebrew *ezer* as "companion," as used elsewhere in the Bible; under that reading, the hierarchical relationship is not manifest in the original text but rather a result of mistranslation.

The man describes the woman in Genesis 2:23 as "bone of my bones, flesh of my flesh", and he calls his new partner "woman" (Heb. *ishshah*), "for this one was taken from a man" (Heb. *ish*). The chapter ends by establishing the state of primeval innocence, noting that the man, and woman were "naked, and not ashamed", Genesis 2:25, and so provides the departure point for the subsequent narrative in which wisdom is gained through disobedience at severe cost.

The Fall, and expulsion from Eden
The Adam, and Eve story continues in Genesis 3 with the "expulsion from Eden" narrative. A form analysis of Genesis 3 reveals that this portion of the story can be characterized as a parable or "wisdom tale" in the wisdom tradition. The poetic addresses of the chapter belong to a speculative type of wisdom that questions the paradoxes, and harsh realities of life. This characterization is determined by the narrative's format, settings, and the plot. The form of Genesis 3 is also shaped by its vocabulary, making use of various puns, and double entendres. The chapter is said to date to around 900s BCE during the reigns of King David or Solomon. The documentary hypothesis for this narrative portion can be attributed to Yahwist (J), due to the use of the tetragrammaton.

The expulsion from Eden narrative begins with a dialogue between the woman, and a serpent, identified in Genesis 3:1 as an animal that was craftier than any other animal made by God, although Genesis does not identify the serpent with Satan. The woman is willing to talk to the serpent, and respond to the creature's cynicism by repeating God's prohibition against eating fruit from the tree of knowledge (Genesis 2:17). The woman is lured into dialogue on the serpent's terms which directly disputes God's command.

The serpent assures the woman that God will not let her die if she ate the fruit, and, furthermore, that if she ate the fruit, her "eyes would be opened", and she would "be like God, knowing good, and evil" (Genesis 3:5). The woman sees that the fruit of the tree of knowledge is a delight to the eye, and that it would be desirable to acquire wisdom by eating the fruit. The woman eats the fruit, and gives some to the man (Genesis 3:6). With this the man, and woman recognize their own nakedness, and they make loincloths of fig leaves (Genesis 3:7).

In the next narrative dialogue, God questions the man, and the woman (Genesis 3:8–13), and God initiates a dialogue by calling out to the man with a rhetorical question designed to consider his wrongdoing. The man explains that he hid in the garden out of fear because he realized his own nakedness (Genesis 3:10). This is followed by two more rhetorical questions designed to show awareness of a defiance of God's command. The man then points to the woman as the real offender, and he implies that God is responsible for the tragedy because the woman was given to him by God (Genesis 3:12). God challenges the woman to explain herself, whereby she shifts the blame to the serpent (Genesis 3:13).

Divine pronouncement of three judgments are then laid against all the culprits, Genesis 3:14–19. A judgement oracle, and the nature of the crime is first laid upon the serpent, then the woman, and, finally, the man. On the serpent, God places a divine curse. The woman receives penalties that impact her in two primary roles: she shall experience pangs during childbearing, pain during childbirth, and while she shall desire her husband, he will rule over her. The man's penalty results in God cursing the ground from which he came, and the man then receives a death oracle, although the man has not been described, in the text, as immortal. Abruptly, in the flow of text, in Genesis 3:20, the man names the woman "Eve", (Heb. *hawwah*) "because she was the mother of all living", and Adam receives his name "the man", changing from "eth-ha'adham", before the fall to "ha'Adham" (with article/command), to Adam after the fall (disobedience). God makes skin garments for Adam, and Eve (Genesis 3:20).

The chiasmus structure of the death oracle given to Adam in Genesis 3:19, is a link between man's creation from "dust" (Genesis 2:7) to the "return" of his beginnings:" you return, to the ground, since from it you were taken, for dust you are, and to dust, you will return."

The garden account ends with an intra-divine monologue, determining the couple's expulsion, and the execution of that deliberation (Genesis 3:22–24}. The reason given for the expulsion was to prevent the man from eating from the tree of life, and becoming immortal: "Behold, the man is become as one of us, to know good, and evil;, and now, lest he put forth his hand, and take also of the tree of life, and live forever" (Genesis 3:22). God exiles Adam, and Eve from the Garden, and installs cherubs (supernatural beings that provide protection), and the "ever-turning sword" to guard the entrance (Genesis 3:24).

Offspring
Genesis 4 tells of the birth of Cain, and Abel, Adam, and Eve's first children, while Genesis 5 gives Adam's genealogy past that. Adam, and Eve are listed as having three children, Cain, Abel, and Seth, then "other sons, and daughters", Genesis 5:4. According to the Book of Jubilees (which is usually not considered canonical), Cain married his sister Awan, a daughter of Adam, and Eve.

Non-religious views
Some modern scholars, such as James Barr, Moshe Greenberg, and Michael Fishbane, see the story of Adam, and Eve as a representation of a rise to moral agency, at least as much as, if not more than the story of a fall from grace. Carol Meyers, and Bruce Naidoff view the tale as an explanation of agricultural conditions in the highlands of Canaan.

Abrahamic traditions

Judaism
It was also recognized in ancient Judaism, that there are two distinct accounts for the creation of man. The first account says "male, and female [God] created them", implying simultaneous creation, whereas the second account states that God created Eve subsequent to the creation of Adam. The Midrash Rabbah – Genesis VIII:1 reconciled the two by stating that Genesis one, "male, and female He created them", indicates that God originally created Adam as a hermaphrodite, bodily, and spiritually both male, and female, before creating the separate beings of Adam, and Eve. Other rabbis suggested that Eve, and the woman of the first account were two separate individuals, the first being identified as Lilith, a figure elsewhere described as a night demon.

According to traditional Jewish belief, Adam, and Eve are buried in the Cave of Machpelah, in Hebron.

In Reform Judaism, Harry Orlinsky analyzes the Hebrew word *Nefesh* in Genesis 2:7 where "God breathes into the man's nostrils, and he becomes *Nefesh hayya.*" Orlinksy argues that the earlier translation of the phrase "living soul" is incorrect. He points out that "Nefesh" signifies something like the English word "being", in the sense of a corporeal body capable of life; the concept of a "soul" in the modern sense, did not exist in Hebrew thought until around the 2nd century B.C., when the idea of a bodily resurrection gained popularity.

Christianity
Some early fathers of the Christian church held Eve responsible for the Fall of man, and all subsequent women to be the first sinners because Eve tempted Adam to commit the taboo. "You are the devil's gateway" Tertullian told his female listeners in the early 2nd century, and went on to explain that they were responsible for the death of Christ: "On account of your desert [i.e., punishment for sin, that is, death], even the Son of God had to die." In 1486, the Dominicans Kramer, and Sprengler used similar tracts in *Malleus Maleficarum* ("Hammer of Witches") to justify the persecution of "witches".

Medieval Christian art often depicted the Edenic Serpent as a woman (often identified as Lilith), thus both emphasizing the Serpent's seductiveness as well as its relationship to Eve. Several early Church Fathers, including Clement of Alexandria, and Eusebius of Caesarea, interpreted the Hebrew "Heva" as not only the name of Eve, but in its aspirated form as "female serpent."

Based on the Christian doctrine of the Fall of man, came the doctrine of original sin. St Augustine of Hippo (354–430), working with a Latin translation of the Epistle to the Romans, interpreted the Apostle Paul as having said that Adam's sin was hereditary: "Death passed upon [i.e., spread to] all men because of Adam, [in whom] all sinned", Romans 5:12 Original sin became a concept that man is born into a condition of sinfulness, and must await redemption. This doctrine became a cornerstone of Western Christian theological tradition, however, not shared by Judaism or the Orthodox churches.

Over the centuries, a system of unique Christian beliefs had developed from these doctrines. Baptism became understood as a washing away of the stain of hereditary sin in many churches, although its original symbolism was apparently rebirth. Additionally, the serpent that tempted Eve was interpreted to have been Satan, or that Satan was using a serpent as a mouthpiece, although there is no mention of this identification in the Torah, and it is not held in Judaism.

Conservative Protestants typically interpret Genesis 3 as defining humanity's original parents as Adam, and Eve who disobeyed God's prime directive that they were not to eat "the fruit of the tree of the knowledge of good, and evil" (NIV). When they disobeyed, they committed a major transgression against God, and were immediately punished, which led to "the fall" of humanity. Thus, sin, and death entered the universe for the first time. Adam, and Eve were ejected from the Garden of Eden, never to return.

Islam

In Islam, Adam, whose role is being the father of humanity, is looked upon by Muslims with reverence. Eve is the "mother of humanity." The creation of Adam, and Eve is referred to in the Qur'an, although different Qur'anic interpreters give different views on the actual creation story (Qur'an, Surat al-Nisa', verse 1).

In al-Qummi's tafsir on the Garden of Eden, such place was not entirely earthly. According to the Qur'an, both Adam, and Eve ate the forbidden fruit in a *Heavenly* Eden (*See also* Jannah). As a result, they were both sent down to Earth as God's representatives. Each person was sent to a mountain peak: Adam on al-Safa, and Eve on al-Marwah. In this Islamic tradition, Adam wept 40 days until he repented, after which God sent down the Black Stone, teaching him the Hajj. According to a prophetic hadith, Adam, and Eve reunited in the plains of Arafat, nearMecca. They had two sons together, Qabil, and Habil. There is also a legend of a younger son, named Rocail, who created a palace, and sepulcher containing autonomous statues that lived out the lives of men so realistically they were mistaken for having souls.

The concept of "original sin" does not exist in Islam, because according to Islam Adam, and Eve were forgiven by God. When God orders the angels to bow to Adam, *Iblīs* questioned, "Why should I bow to man? I am made of pure fire, and he is made of soil." The liberal movements within Islam have viewed God's commanding the angels to bow before Adam as an exaltation of humanity, and as a means of supporting human rights; others view it as an act of showing Adam that the biggest enemy of humans on earth will be their ego.

Gnostic traditions
Gnostic Christianity discussed Adam, and Eve in two known surviving texts, namely the "Apocalypse of Adam" found in theNag Hammadi documents, and the "Testament of Adam". The creation of Adam as Proto-Anthropos, the original man, is the focal concept of these writings.

Another Gnostic tradition held that Adam, and Eve were created to help defeat Satan. The serpent, instead of being identified with Satan, is seen as a hero by the Ophites. Still other Gnostics believed that Satan's fall, however, came after the creation of humanity. As in Islamic tradition, this story says that Satan refused to bow to Adam due to pride. Satan said that Adam was inferior to him as he was made of fire, whereas Adam was made of clay. This refusal led to the fall of Satan recorded in works such as the Book of Enoch.

Bahá'í Faith
In the Bahá'í Faith, Adam is seen as a Manifestation of God. The Adam, and Eve narratives are seen as symbolic. In *Some Answered Questions*, 'Abdu'l-Bahá rejects a literal reading, and states that the story contains "divine mysteries, and universal meanings", and that one of these meanings is that Adam symbolizes the spirit of Adam, and Eve his own self. The tree of good, and evil symbolizes the human world, and the serpent worldly attachment. After the 'fall' of Adam, humanity has been conscious of good, and evil. Other meanings from the Bábí, and Bahá'í faiths can be found in the introduction of Tahirih's poem *Adam's Wish*.

Dating Adam, and Eve
The Hebrew Bible (the Christian Old Testament) contains an internal Anno Mundi chronology, meaning one which commences with the creation of the world. Adam, and Eve are created on the first day of the first year of creation, i.e., in AM 1. Many attempts have been made over many centuries to identify AM 1 with real history, but the authors of the Bible were describing a mythical past which ended with the rededication of the Temple in 164 BCE – history, according to the mythical scheme adopted, began an ideal four thousand years in the past.

PHYSICAL EVIDENCE

Scientific Incompatibility
The story of Adam, and Eve contradicts the scientific consensus that humans evolved from earlier species of hominids, and is incompatible with human evolutionary genetics; in particular, if all humans descended from two individuals that lived several thousand years ago, the observed variation would require an impossibly high mutation rate. This entails a lower bound on the size of the ancestral group, currently thought to be of the order of 10,000 individuals.

Y-chromosomal Adam, and Mitochondrial Eve

The names Adam, and Eve are used metaphorically in a scientific context to designate the patrilineal, and matrilineal most recent common ancestors, the Y-chromosomal Adam, and the Mitochondrial Eve. Those are not fixed individuals, nor is there any reason to assume that they lived at the same time, let alone that they met or formed a couple. A recent study on the subject estimates that the Y-chromosomal Adam lived in prehistory 120 to 156 thousand years ago, while the Mitochondrial Eve lived 99 to 148 thousand years ago. Another recent study places the Y-chromosomal Adam 180 to 200 thousand years ago.

Impact on religion
The evidence against Adam, and Eve existing has caused many Christians to move away from a literal interpretation, and belief in the Genesis creation narrative to an allegorical approach, while others continue to believe in what they see as fundamental doctrines of the Christian faith. In particular the evidence for their non-existence casts doubt on original sin, and the origin, and nature of evil.

Arts, and literature
Adam, and Eve were used by early Renaissance artists as a theme to represent female, and male nudes. Later, the nudity was objected to more modest elements, and fig leaves were added to the older pictures, and sculptures, covering their genitals. The choice of the fig was a result of Mediterranean traditions identifying the unnamed Tree of Knowledge as a fig tree, and since fig leaves were actually mentioned in Genesis as being used to cover Adam, and Eve's nudity.

Treating the concept of Adam, and Eve as the historical truth introduces some logical dilemmas. One such dilemma is whether they should be depicted with navels (the Omphalos theory). Since they did not develop in a uterus, they would not have been connected to an umbilical cord like all other humans. Paintings without navels looked unnatural, and some artists obscure that area of their bodies, sometimes by depicting them covering up that area of their body with their hand or some other intervening object.

John Milton's *Paradise Lost*, a famous 17th-century epic poem written in blank verse, explores, and elaborates upon the story of Adam, and Eve in great detail. As opposed to the Biblical Adam, Milton's Adam is given a glimpse of the future of mankind, by the archangel Michael, before he has to leave Paradise.

American painter Thomas Cole painted *The Garden of Eden* (1828), with lavish detail of the first couple living amid waterfalls, vivid plants, and attractive deer.

Mark Twain wrote humorous, and satirical diaries for Adam, and Eve in both Eve's Diary (1906), and *The Private Life of Adam, and Eve* (1931), posthumously published.

C. L. Moore's 1940 story *Fruit of Knowledge* is a re-telling of the Fall of Man as a love triangle between Lilith, Adam, and Eve – with Eve's eating the forbidden fruit being in this version the result of misguided manipulations by the jealous Lilith, who had hoped to get her rival discredited, and destroyed by God, and thus regain Adam's love.

In Stephen Schwartz's musical *Children of Eden*, "Father" (God) creates Adam, and Eve at the same time, and considers them His children. They even assist Him in naming the animals. When Eve is tempted by the serpent, and eats the forbidden fruit, Father makes Adam choose between Him, and Eden, or Eve. Adam chooses Eve, and eats the fruit, causing Father to banish them into the wilderness, and destroying the Tree of Knowledge, from which Adam carves a staff. Eve gives birth to Cain, and

Abel, and Adam forbids his children from going beyond the waterfall in hopes Father will forgive them, and bring them back to Eden.

When Cain, and Abel grow up, Cain breaks his promise, and goes beyond the waterfall, finding the giant stones made by other humans, which he brings the family to see, and Adam reveals his discovery from the past: during their infancy, he discovered these humans, but had kept it secret. He tries to forbid Cain from seeking them out, which causes Cain to become enraged, and he tries to attack Adam, but instead turns his rage to Abel when he tries to stop him, and kills him. Later, when an elderly Eve tries to speak to Father, she tells how Adam continually looked for Cain, and after many years, he dies, and is buried underneath the waterfall. Eve also gave birth to Seth, which expanded hers, and Adam's generations. Finally, Father speaks to her to bring her home. Before she dies, she gives her blessings to all her future generations, and passes Adam's staff to Seth. Father embraces Eve, and she also reunited with Adam, and Abel. Smaller casts of the American version usually have the actors cast as Adam, and Eve double as Noah, and Mama Noah.

In C.S. Lewis' Science Fiction novel "Perelandra", the story of Adam, and Eve is re-enacted on the Planet Venus - but with a different ending. A green-skinned pair, who are destined to be the ancestors of Venusian humanity, are living in naked innocence on wonderful floating islands which are the Venusian Eden; a demonically-possessed Earth scientist arrives in a spaceship, acting the part of the snake, and trying to tempt the Venusian Eve into disobeying God; but the protagonist, Cambridge scholar Ransom, succeeds in thwarting him - so that Venusian humanity will have a glorious future, free of Original Sin.

POST ANALYSIS

Though I immensely enjoy reading the Bible, especially the Old Testament, I always treat the Creation of Man as reading a novel, rather than a book for the beginning of Man. As stated in earlier chapters, I am too much of a realist, a man of logic. There are people that do not agree with my philosophy on life, or science-based facts, I am not in dispute with religions, beliefs, and legends. I learned to live alongside all beliefs from the primitive to the sophisticated, respecting each and every individual choice, as long as they stay within the parameters of law and humanity.

Regardless of my attachment to science, I carry an open mind to alternatives. After all, science has an open door to all possibilities of fiction, which, in due time may turn factual. This is especially true, since we are on the threshold of populating planets, cosmos, and eventually the universe. But that is still far into the future, if we survive our own destiny as humankind. What is more important to the present, trying to live together with a common goal, make life easier for all to enjoy. The future, with all of its beauty, belongs to mankind to enjoy. Therefore, I recommend setting blind convictions aside, and listen to alternative views, opinions, and thoughts. It makes for lively conversations, as long as we respect others giving everybody a chance to voice personal concerns. I have one warning: "There is no place for crime in future endeavors." Technology will prevail and guide us through tumultuous times.

APPENDIX H – GENEALOGY FROM ADAM TO JESUS CHRIST

From Arthur Custance's book, "The Seed of the Woman."

(Numbers in parentheses indicate sequential birth trough ancient time.)

ADAM (1)
The Son of God, and The First Adam

SETH (2)

ENOS (3)

CAINAN (4)

MAHALEEL (5)

JARED (6)

ENOCH (7)

METHUSALEH (8)

LAMECH (9)

NOAH (10)

SHEM (11)

ARPHAXAD (12)

CAINAN (13)

SALA (14)

EBER (15)

PELEG (16)

RAGAU (17)

SARUCH (18)

NAHOR (19)

TERAH (20)

(1) ABRAHAM (21)

(2) ISAAC (22)

(3) JACOB (23)

(4) JUDA (24)   ---> Zera
m. Tamar   (Matthew 1:3)

(5) PHAREZ (25)

(6) ESROM (26)

(7) ARAM (27)

(8) AMMINADAB (28)

(9) NAASON (29)

(10) SALMON (30)   (Sala:
m. Rachab   Luke 3:32)

(11) BOAZ (31)
m. Ruth

(12) OBED (32)

(13) JESSE (33)

(14) DAVID (34)
m. Bathsheba (Luke 3:31)

(1) SOLOMON		NATHAN (35)
Matthew 1:6		(2 Sam.5.14)
(2) REHOBOAM		
(3) ABIA		MATTATHA (36)
(4) ASA		MENAN (37)
(5) JOSOPHAT	OMRI	MELEA (38)
		ELIAKIM (39)
	AHAB m. Jezebel		JONAN (40)
(6) JORAM	m. Athaliah	JOSEPH (41)
		JUDAH (42)
	(Ahaziah)	SIMEON (43)
	(Joash) (Amaziah)	LEVI (44)
(7) OZIAS		MATTHAT (45)
(8) JOATHAM		JORIM (46)
(9) ACHAZ		ELIEZER (47)

(10) EZEKIAS	JOSE (48)
(11) MANASSES	ER (49)
(12) AMON	ELMOD AM (50)
(13) JOSIAS	COSAM (51)
	ADDI (52)
(14) JEHOIKIM (who had brothers, Matthew 1:11)	MELCHI (53)

(1) JECHONIAS (55) m. --- >	(2) SALATHIEL (56)	Wido wed daughter husband deceased wife m. PEDAIAH NERI (54) <------

(Evidently Salathiel died childless, and Pedaiah, his brother, married his widow according to Deut. 25,5,6)	(Quite legally according to the Mosaic law, Pedaiah's name does not appear as the father of Zerubbabel in either Matthew or Luke.)

(3) ZERUBBABEL (57)
(1 Chr. 3:19)

Daughter
SHELOMITH --> m RHESA (58)

(4) ABIUD	JOANNA (59)
(5) ELIAKIM	JUDA (60)
	JOSEPH (61)
(6) AZOR	SEMEI (62)
	MATTA THIAS (63)
(7) SADOC	MAATH (64)
	NAGGE (65)
(8) ACHIM	ESLI (66)
	NAHUM (67)
(9) ELIUD	AMOS (68)

MATTA
THIAS (69)

(10) ELEAZER   JOSEPH
(70)

JANNA
(71)

(11) MATTHAN   MELCHI
(72)

LEVI
(73)

MATTH
AT (74)

(12)   HELI
JACOB   (75)

(13) JOSEPH   m.   MAR
Y (76)

(14) JESUS (77)
The Son of God, and the Last Adam

The Line of Jesus through Joseph
The book of the genealogy of Jesus Christ, the son of David, the son of Abraham. Abraham was the father of Isaac, and Isaac the father of Jacob, and Jacob the father of Judah, and his brothers, and Judah the father of Perez, and Zerah by Tamar, and Perez the father of Hezron, and Hezron the father of Ram, and Ram the father of Amminadab, and Amminadab the father of Nahshon, and Nahshon the father of Salmon, and Salmon the father of Boaz by Rahab, and Boaz the father of Obed by Ruth, and Obed the father of Jesse, and Jesse the father of David the king, and David was the father of Solomon by the wife of Uriah, and Solomon the father of Rehoboam and Rehoboam the father of Abijah, and Abijah the father of Asa, and Asa the father of Jehoshaphat, and Jehoshaphat the father of Joram, and Joram the father of Uzziah, and Uzziah the father of Jotham, and Jotham the father of Ahaz, and Ahaz the father of Hezekiah, and Hezekiah the father of Manasseh, and Manasseh the father of Amos, and Amos the father of Josiah and Josiah the father of Jechoniah, and his brothers, at the time of the deportation to Babylon, and after the deportation to Babylon: Jechoniah was the father of Shealtiel, and Shealtiel the father of Zerubbabel, and Zerubbabel the father of Abiud, and Abiud the father of Eliakim, and Eliakim the father of Azor, and Azor the father of Zadok, and Zadok the father of Achim, and Achim the father of Eliud, and Eliud the father of Eleazar, and Eleazar the father of Matthan, and Matthan the father of Jacob, and Jacob the father of Joseph the husband of Mary, of whom Jesus was born, who is called Christ. So, all the generations from Abraham to David were fourteen generations, and from David to the deportation to Babylon fourteen generations, and from the deportation to Babylon to the Christ fourteen generations. (Matthew 1:1-17)

The Line of Jesus Through Mary
Jesus, when he began his ministry, was about thirty years of age, being the son (as was supposed) of Joseph, the son of Heli, the son of Matthat, the son of Levi, the son of Melchi, the son of Jannai, the son of Joseph, the son of Mattathias, the son of Amos, the son of Nahum, the son of Esli, the son of Naggai, the son of Maath, the son of Mattathias, the son of Semein, the son of Josech, the son of Joda, the son of Joanan, the son of Rhesa, the son of Zerubbabel, the son of Shealtiel, the son of Neri, the son of Melchi, the son of Addi, the son of Cosam, the son of Elmadam, the son of Er, the son of Joshua, the son of Eliezer, the son of Jorim, the son of Matthat, the son of Levi, the son of Simeon, the son of Judah, the son of Joseph, the son of Jonam, the son of Eliakim, the son of Melea, the son of Menna, the son of Mattatha, the son of Nathan, the son of David, the son of Jesse, the son of Obed, the son of Boaz, the son of Sala, the son of Nahshon, the son of Amminadab, the son of Admin, the son of Arni, the son of Hezron, the son of Perez, the son of Judah, the son of Jacob, the son of Isaac, the son of Abraham, the son of Terah, the son of Nahor, the son of Serug, the son of Reu, the son of Peleg, the son of Eber, the son of Shelah, the son of Cainan, the son of Arphaxad, the son of Shem, the son of Noah, the son of Lamech, the son of Methuselah, the son of Enoch, the son of Jared, the son of Mahalaleel, the son of Cainan, the son of Enos, the son of Seth, the son of Adam, the son of God. (Luke 3:23:38)

The Combined Genealogies of Matthew, and Luke (from The Seed of the Woman)

The study of an ancient genealogy can be quite fascinating but it takes a little getting into, and demands more than ordinary dedication.

The two genealogies of our Lord which together establish his absolute right to the throne of David, both by blood relationship through Mary, and by title through Mary's husband, bear close examination. For they show how the two lines were preserved at one particularly critical period when almost all family relationships in Israel were being disrupted. This was at the time of the Captivity in Babylon. It is shown in a standard genealogy chart as a kind of "wasp-waist" joining the head, and the body of the genealogy above, and below Zerubbabel.

The details of this gate are the subject of this Appendix. It seemed important to say something about the circumstances here because it is at this point in the line that the blood relationship between the Lord, and David comes nearest to being destroyed.

The numbers which appear against the names in the Tabulation represent the two different systems of accounting adopted by Matthew, on the left side, and Luke, on the right. In Matthew, David appears as the 14th name from Abraham: in Luke David is the 34th name from Adam. The *red* line represents the blood line connection: the *yellow* line represents the carrying of title to the throne of David.

David had two sons who figure as heads of the two branches of the family as indicated in Matthew, and Luke, namely, Solomon, and Nathan. In Matthew's genealogy Solomon becomes No. 1 in the second group of 14 names:, and in Luke's genealogy Nathan becomes No. 35 on the other branch line.

From Solomon we move down to Joram, No. 6. Joram married Athaliah, the wicked daughter of a wicked father, and mother (Ahab, and Jezebel). As a consequence of this evil man, and his wife, his seed was cursed for four generations in accordance with the reference made in Exodus 20:5. Thus Matthew, who probably follows the Temple records faithfully in his list, omits the next three names (Ahaziah, Joash, and Amaziah) from his genealogy. There is little doubt that these Temple records had, by divine providence, removed these three generations from the register, so that Ozias (No. 7) appears as though he were the son of Joram, No. 6, in the accounting of Matthew 1:8. We know from 1 Chronicles 3:11, and 12 that in the original court records, these three missing names were written down. In this court record, Ozias (No. 7) is given an alternative name Azariah (1 Chron. 3:12), and elsewhere he is also called Uzziah (Isa. 6:1). These are merely variants of the same name.

We pass on to No. 14, Jehoiakim. It is important to note that his name ends with an M, not an N, and he is not to be confused with his son whose name was Jehoiakin (or alternatively Jeconiah, Jechonias, Coniah, and Conias). This multivariant form of a name applied to a single individual is common in many of the older cultures. It seems to be particularly prevalent in Russia, even today.

Now, with Jehoiakim (No. 14) we begin to see the hand of God at work in a very special way separating the thread of continuity of blood relationship, and titular right to the throne in David's family. Jehoiakim was the last king of Israel to come to the throne as a free man. Unfortunately, he was both an evil man, and a foolish one. He began his reign just when the Fertile Crescent was in a state of political turmoil, Nebuchadnezzar in particular having very ambitious designs for empire building which were challenged by Egypt. In this see-saw contest for power that habitually characterized the relationship between Egypt, and Babylon, Palestine stood at the pivot point. But Jerusalem itself need not really have become involved, for the city actually stood off the main route between the two warring parties. Any king of Judah who kept out of the fray, and conciliated the antagonists as they marched their armies back, and forth to attack each other, could expect to be left more or less alone except for paying token tribute.

Jehoiakim was not humble enough or wise enough to realize this, and provoked Nebuchadnezzar to attack Jerusalem. This was the Lord's way of punishing a wicked man who had unwisely aligned himself with the king of Egypt. His immediate punishment was to have his city besieged, and overrun, and to be carried captive to Babylon (2 Chron. 36:5,6). But for some reason Nebuchadnezzar decided to return him to Jerusalem as a puppet king while he completed his unfinished business in Egypt. His long-range punishment was foretold by Jeremiah (36:30) that none of his seed should ever sit upon the throne of David. This was a severe blow to him because he was in the direct line, as Matthew's genealogy shows, and probably had every expectation of seeing this greatest of all honors accorded to his seed in due time.

Meanwhile Nebuchadnezzar, having completed his Egyptian campaign, soon discovered that Jehoiakim was a treacherous man who could not be trusted by friend or foe. Indeed, so treacherous was he that even the people of his own city, Jerusalem, turned against him, murdered him, threw his body over the walls, and left him unburied outside the city - exactly as predicted by Jeremiah (22:18,19). Nebuchadnezzar must surely have known what had happened, but he did not interfere when Jehoiakin (i.e., Jechonias, No. 55) succeeded his father.

But this young prince who was only eighteen years old when thus honored (2 Kings 24:8) proved to have no more good sense than his evil father. He provoked Nebuchadnezzar (after only three months, and ten days on the throne) to invest the city once more, and depose him (2 Chron. 36:9). Jechonias, and all his court were taken captive to Babylon while his uncle, Zedekiah, was left as regent. Unfortunately, Zedekiah behaved as the rest of his family had done, and eleven years later, Nebuchadnezzar seized Zedekiah, put all his sons to death before his eyes, and then deliberately blinded him. Zedekiah was taken to Babylon, and died there. Jerusalem meanwhile was utterly destroyed (2 Kings 24:17-25:16).

Now Jechonias, after being taken to Babylon, was put in prison where he remained for some thirty-seven years. It appears that either before he was taken captive or possibly during his captivity he was married to a woman of appropriate status who appears to have been a daughter of Neri (No. 54 in Nathan's branch of the family), and therefore of David's line. In order to account for the subsequent relationships shown in the two converging genealogies, we have to assume that this woman was a widow whose husband had probably been killed in one of the many sieges which Jerusalem had suffered. It seems as though the prophet Zechariah had this circumstance in mind (12:12). This widow already had a son by her deceased husband when Jechonias took her as a wife. This son's name was Pedaiah. His name is not numbered in the genealogy shown in the chart. It appears only in 1 Chronicles 3:18 where he is shown as a son of Jehoiakin (i.e., Jechonias). If his widowed mother was married to Jechonias, he would by Jewish custom become the son of Jechonias automatically.

But Jechonias appears to have had a son of his own by this widow of the royal line. This son's name was Salathiel (No. 2, and No. 56 in the two pedigree lines). By this marriage of a widow to Jechonias, these two boys - sons of the same mother - would become brothers by Jewish custom.

However, Salathiel appears to have died childless, though not until he had reached manhood, and married a wife. Jehoiakim's *blood* line thus came to an end in his grandson Salathiel - indicated by termination of the red line. But as it happens the actual *title* to the throne remained active. The curse of Jeremiah 36:30 was to be fulfilled not by the removal of the title itself from Jehoiakim's line but by the denial of that title to anyone who happened to be a blood relative in the line. With the death of Salathiel this blood line terminated.

But now, according to Jewish custom as set forth in the principle of the Levirate (Deut. 25:5,6), it became incumbent upon Pedaiah, the deceased Salathiel's (step) brother, to take his widow, and raise up seed through her who would not therefore be of Salathiel's blood line but would be constituted legally as Salathiel's son through whom the title would pass to his descendants. The son of this Levirate union was Zerubbabel. In Matthew 1:12, and Luke 3:27 Zerubbabel is listed legally as Salathiel's son: but in 1 Chronicles 3:19 he is listed as the son of Pedaiah by actual blood relationship.

In the terms of biblical reckoning these two statements are in no sense contradictory. We might wish to be more precise by substituting such extended terms of relationship as son-in-law, stepson, and so forth. But Scripture is not required to adopt our particular terminology. It is required only to be consistent with itself, and the facts of the case as recorded of those who were the actors in the drama are precisely as stated.

We thus have a remarkable chain of events. Jehoiakim has a son, Jechonias, who has a son, Salathiel, who by Levirate custom has a son named Zerubbabel. This son, Zerubbabel, has no blood line connection whatever with Jechonias, for he has no blood relationship with Salathiel. The blood relationship of Zerubbabel is with Pedaiah, and through Pedaiah with Pedaiah's mother, and through this mother with Neri. Thus, Neri begat a grandson, Salathiel, through his daughter;, and Salathiel "begets" a son, Zerubbabel, through Pedaiah.

The blood line thus passes through Zerubbabel: but so, does the title. The former passes via Pedaiah's mother, the latter passes through Salathiel's father, and though this mother, and this father were also man, and wife, the blood line stopped with Salathiel who literally died childless. It is necessary to emphasize this word *literally,* for it appears that it was *literally* true. Jeremiah 22:30 had predicted that Jechonias would also die "childless"-but we are reasonably sure that this was not *literally* the case, for he had a son Salathiel whom we cannot otherwise account for. But Jechonias' subsequent history tells us the sense in which childlessness was to be applied to him.

Jechonias seems to have matured, and softened during his thirty-seven years of imprisonment in Babylon, and Nebuchadnezzar's son, Evil-Merodach, evidently took a liking to him, and set him free, giving him a pension for the rest of his life (2 Kings 25:27-30: Jer. 52:31-34). He would by now be nearing sixty, and probably be counted a harmless old man.

Reading these two records of Scripture concerning this surprising act of clemency accorded to the last genuine king of Israel (until Messiah shall be crowned), one has a strange sense of the mercy of God, and the potential for gracious action that even pagan kings could display in those days. It is a touching swan-song to the old kingdom of David's line which will yet be renewed in glory. At any rate, when Jechonias died, he seems to have died alone without male descendants, "childless" in his old age, as Jeremiah had predicted he would.

As to Zerubbabel, he became a very prominent, and worthy man in the rebuilding of Israel's fortunes after the Captivity, under the benevolent authority of Cyrus. He stands as No. 3, and No. 57 in the dual pedigree. He appears to have had several sons, and one daughter (1 Chron. 3:19). We do not know why his sons were disqualified: we only know that their sister, Shelomith, inherited the title, and carried the blood line. Both of these she passed on to her eldest son, Abiud, and so to Joseph. But with Joseph, as with Salathiel, the blood line terminated once again in so far as the Lord Jesus received nothing from him by natural procreation. However, Mary drew her line, the blood line, through Heli from Joanna (No. 59), the second son of Shelomith.

And thus, the Lord Jesus received the two guarantees of right to the throne of David: the blood line through his mother directly, and the title through his adopting father, Joseph. With his death, and resurrection these two rights became locked for ever in his Person, and cannot be passed on to, or henceforth claimed by, any other man.

POST ANALYSIS

I included the Table on "GENEALOGY FROM ADAM TO JESUS CHRIST," with this book, because it is not every day, perhaps never, the majority of earth's population gets to read it. With the diversity in religions man has developed, there is too much to understand and grasp the reasoning behind it all. After many years reading and studying the diversities, I came to the conclusion that it is up to the individual to decide one's belief. Although, many of us are introduced to one specific faith, through parental heritance and geographic environments, many of us reach out to learn, and ultimately practice alternatives.

It is what makes us unique, choice and free will. We must respect these choices. I am no different. It's the reason I don't enforce my acquired knowledge on others. Where the dedicated a lifetime researching archives, and archaeologically digging for proof through the past, I can only relay to the reader what I have learned, mostly from reading documents and scriptures, on my journey through life.

While there is undisputed evidence for the existence of man's historic genealogy, and line of heredity, there are vast differences in age and timeline. Where the Bible recorded mankind's first appearance at approx., six thousand years ago, a recent study on the subject estimates, that the Y-chromosomal Adam lived in prehistory 120 to 156 thousand years ago, while the Mitochondrial Eve lived 99 to 148 thousand years ago. A more recent study places the Y-chromosomal Adam 180 to 200 thousand years ago.

One should not completely disregard either finding without giving it serious consideration. Where either side, science versus faith, may object the opposing views, the ultimate choice still remains with the individual, living in the free society. After all, science is learning new techniques and processes, just as we human beings do. Where Believe does not exist in the world of science, the entire philosophical concept of it drives the devout individual.

APPENDIX I – CHALLENGES BEYOND

Yom Kippur

The Yom Kippur War of 1973, so-called because it began on the Day of Atonement (Yom Kippur), the holiest day of prayer, and fasting in the Jewish calendar, became also known as the October War. At the time of Yom Kippur, Israel was led by Golda Meir, and Egypt by Anwar Sadat.

The war started with a surprise Arab attack on Israel on Saturday 6th October 1973. On this day, Egyptian, and Syrian military forces launched an attack knowing that the military of Israel would be participating in the religious celebrations associated with Yom Kippur. Therefore, their guard would temporarily be dropped.

The combined forces of Egypt, and Syria totaled the same number of men as NATO had in Western Europe. On the Golan Heights alone, 150 Israeli tanks faced 1,400 Syria tanks, and in the Suez region just 500 Israeli soldiers faced 80,000 Egyptian soldiers.

Other Arab nations aided the Egyptians, and Syrians. Iraq transferred a squadron of Hunter jet fighter planes to Egypt a few months before the war began. Iraqi Russian-built MIG fighters were used against the Israelis in the Golan Heights along with 18,000 Iraqi soldiers. Saudi Arabia, and Kuwait effectively financed the war from the Arabs side. Saudi troops – approximately 3,000 men – also fought in the war. Libya provided Egypt with French-built Mirage fighters, and in the years 1971 to 1973, Libya bankrolled Egypt's military modernization to the tune of $1 billion which was used to purchase modern Russian weapons. Other Arabic nations that helped the Egyptians, and Syrians included Tunisia, Sudan, and Morocco. Jordan also sent two armored brigades, and three artillery units to support the Syrians, but their participation in the war was not done with vast enthusiasm – probably because King Hussein of Jordan had not been kept informed of what Egypt, and Syria planned.

Facing such an attack, the Israeli forces were initially swiftly overwhelmed. Within two days, the Egyptians had crossed the Suez Canal, and moved up to 15 miles inland of the most advanced Israeli troops in the Sinai. Syrian troops advanced by the same distance into the strategic Golan Heights in north Israel. By the end of October 7th, the military signs were ominous for Israel.

However, on October 8th, Israeli forces, bolstered by called-up reserves, counter-attacked in the Sinai. They pushed back the Egyptian military, and crossed the Suez Canal south of Ismailia. Here, the Israelis used the Suez-Cairo road to advance towards the Egyptian capital, Cairo, and got to within 65 miles of it.

The Israelis experienced similar success in the Golan Heights where the Syrian forces were pushed back, and Israel re-captured lost land. Using the main road from Tiberias to Damascus, the Israelis got to within 35 miles of the Syrian capital. On October 24th, a cease-fire was organized by the United Nations.

APPENDIX J – FORMS OF GOVERNMENT BY IDEOLOGY

By socio-political attributes
Monarchy/Republic:
Types of monarchy
Absolute monarchy
Constitutional monarchy
Crowned republic

Types of republic
Constitutional Republic
Democratic republic
Federal republic
Islamic Republic
Parliamentary republic
People's republic
Presidential Republic

By socio-economic attributes
Anarchism
Capitalism
Colonialism
Communism
Despotism
Distributism
Feudalism
Monarchism
Republicanism
Socialism
Totalitarianism
Tribalism

By geo-cultural attributes
Commune
City-State
National government
Intergovernmental Organizations
World Government

Forms of government by other attributes
- Rule according to higher law (unwritten ethical principles) vs. written constitutionalism
- Separation of church, and state or free church vs. state religion
- Civilian control of the military vs. stratocracy
- Totalitarianism or authoritarianism vs. libertarianism
- Majority rule or parliamentary sovereignty vs. constitution or bill of rights with separation of powers, and supermajority rules to prevent tyranny of the majority, and protect minority rights

- Androcracy (patriarchy) or gynarchy (matriarchy) vs. gender quotas, gender equality provision, or silence on the matter.